凱信企管

用對的方法充實自己，
讓人生變得更美好！

凱信企管

用對的方法充實自己，
讓人生變得更美好！

格林法則

秒殺解字

單字記憶法

六大名師陪練大考英單力，全民英檢、
統測、學測、高考、普考等公職考試必備

對於很多學習英語的人來說，最難克服的門檻之一是辨識單字、累積單字量，以及運用單字。英國著名語言學家威爾金斯在《語言學與語言教學》一書中曾提到：「沒有文法幾乎無法表達，沒有字彙根本無法表達。(Without grammar very little can be conveyed, without vocabulary nothing can be conveyed.)」這也解釋了為何市面上充斥著各種單字書，因為單字是口語溝通和書面表達的基石，四個語言技能中聽說讀寫都必須具備。

美國全國閱讀研究小組（National Reading Panel, NRP）強調英語閱讀的五大核心教學，其中包含字彙教學（vocabulary instruction），證實了單字教學的必要性。然而，許多人在學習單字時仍感到困難，只是死記硬背而不求理解，背得慢忘得快。當閱讀文章時，會感到有些單字曾見過，卻又陌生，這反映出學習者在背單字的過程中所使用的方法並不正確。學習單字必須兼顧字音、字形和字義這三個基本要素，若在學習過程中忽略其中任何一個面向，可能會導致不會發音、不會拼寫、不懂意思的結果。

因此，打造英語詞彙形音義三合一的學習法是必要的。英語是一個表音系統的語言，見字能讀、聽字能寫（phonics）和音韻覺識（phonemic awareness）是非常重要的基本功。從正確的發音出發，把字音學好，藉由發音來學習語音表義（sound symbolism）和語音轉換（sound switching）這兩種單字學習方法。

什麼是「語音表義」呢？英語中有許多音和音群具有意義上的象徵性，會引起對某種事物的聯想，這種感受或聯想稱為「語音表義」。舉例來說：發 /b/ 時，雙唇緊閉，氣流受到阻擋無法逸出口腔，彷彿受到「阻礙」時，動彈不得，好像受到「束縛」、「綑綁」，很多以「b__nd」的單字都有「束縛」、「綑綁」的意思，例如：band（樂團；樂隊）、bundle（捆；大量）、bind（捆；綁）、bandage（繃帶）、bond（束縛）。

什麼是「語音轉換」呢？語音轉換法是根據發音部位相同或相近的音可以互換的特點，利用熟悉的單字來學習陌生的單字，從已知推導未知。學習者只要運用唇舌，開口唸音，就可以輕鬆學會陌生字根。例如，以 father（父親）學習 pater。/p/ 是雙唇音，/f/ 是唇齒音，發音部位相近，可以互換。/ð/ 是齒間音，/t/ 是齒齦音，發音部位也相近，可以互換。接著學習字根 pater 的衍生單字，如：paternal（父親的）、patriotic（愛國的）、patron（贊助者）等單字。

此外，本書也提倡學習構詞的要素—詞素（morpheme），即俗稱的「字根、字首、字尾」。詞素是給予單字記憶點的好方法。筆者曾在演講中提倡過單字「不怕長不怕難，就怕沒有字根」的概念，請看下面這個學生愛學習的長難字：

pneumonoultramicroscopicsilicovolcanoconiosis（火山矽肺病）。

這個字對大多數人來說沒有學習的必要，因為在日常生活中幾乎用不到。但用這個字來驗證詞素學習的效果是非常有價值的，將這個字拆解如下：pneumono（肺）、ultra（超過）、microscopic（小到要用顯微鏡才看得到的）、silico（矽）、volcano（火山）、coni（灰）、osis（疾病），讀者會發現裡面出現熟悉的單字或詞素，像是 volcano、microscopic 等，這樣記憶單字的時候，是不是覺得親切許多了呢？

為了幫助讀者更深入瞭解本書的編排理念並掌握使用方法，特別整理七個特色供讀者參考：

一、收錄獨家秒殺解字，考據字源詳實精準。

本書的作者都是專精單字記憶的研究者，對於字源考據非常重視。書中提供的單字記憶方法和眾多同源字將大幅提升單字學習的效率。觀察市面上的單字書籍，大多只是單純列出字表，中英對照呈現，讓許多讀者感到畏懼。為了彌補這一缺憾，本書融入字根首尾、格林法則、語音表義等單字記憶法，可謂集單字記憶法之大成。讀者若能善加利用，必定能牢記所有單字。對於想深入了解字根首

尾和格林法則的讀者，可參考作者的相關書籍，如《格林法則單字記憶法》、《我的第一本格林法則英文單字魔法書》、《音義聯想單字記憶法》等。

二、全書收錄高頻單字，由易到難循序漸進。

作者研究了英檢、統測、學測、高考、普考等歷屆考題，找出重點單字，並由易到難，將單字分為 60 個章節，每個章節收錄 20 組核心單字，並列舉其同源字、同反義字以及詞語搭配。本書收錄的單字至少有 3000 個，如果再加上例句所含的單字，數量更多。然而，本書的編排理念並不是以字數多為考量，而是專注於收錄必考的高頻核心單字。此外，本書的編排循序漸進，前 20 回是基礎單字，中間 20 回是中階單字，後面 20 回是進階單字。本書所收錄的英檢或高中字相對簡單，不特別標記，但為提供考公職者參考，公職考試考過的單字都有註明考試類型和年度。

三、單字例句仿真度高，看例句培養閱讀力。

本書的每個例句都融入各種議題，主題力求多元，且設計時刻意拉長句子的長度，增加句子結構的複雜程度，提高仿真度，貼近各種考試中可能出現的例句。雖然本書不是討論閱讀技巧的書籍，但由於句子的可讀性高，若讀者能認真閱讀並學習字詞用法，臨場考試時對於文章將不再感到恐懼。

四、提供詞搭同反義字，培養全方位學習力。

本書不僅提供眾多同源字，還收錄許多同反義字和詞語搭配。讀者透過語意網絡的拓展，很自然地可以記住同反義字。此外，學習詞語搭配是當今的顯學，是閱讀和溝通流暢的關鍵技巧。每個單字都是一個孤島，但藉由詞語搭配，單字可以有意義地串連在一起。舉例來說，當我們想到 accuse 時，很自然地會想到 of；想到 decide 時，很自然地會想到 to。學習詞語搭配讓字與字之間形成有意義的連結，協助讀者從單字記憶跨越到詞語用法。總而言之，學習詞語搭配是培養語感的有效方法。

五、收錄仿真單字試題，勤練習考試不怯場。

　　全書收錄了作者精心編寫的 450 道題目，每兩回共 15 道單字題目，供讀者測試學習成效。這 450 道題目的設計秉承測驗評量的原則，仿真度高。讀者使用本書時，務必要勤加練習這 450 道題目，藉此檢視學習成效。作者深信這些具有高信效度的試題，可以幫助讀者大幅降低參加各種考試時的緊張程度。若讀者僅死背單字而不加以練習，學習效果仍將打折扣。

六、排版工整凸顯重點，建立索引查詢便利。

　　本書版型層次分明，左邊是主軸單字，右邊則是例句和眾多補充資料，一目了然。本書字體大小適中，並採用雙色印刷，讀者若想看秒殺解字或主軸單字等重要要素，只需留意藍色字體，即可輕鬆找到所需內容。此外，本書還建立了核心單字索引，方便查詢。遇到生疏的單字，不知道如何記憶時，讀者可以通過索引找到該單字的秒殺解字，並從中獲得記憶方法。這樣的設計在眾多單字書中顯得獨具匠心，為讀者提供了全方位的學習體驗。

七、單字例句真人發音，雲端下載隨掃隨聽。

　　本書的單字和例句是由資深美籍人士錄製的，發音地道自然。建議讀者多聽這些發音，增加語音輸入的機會，加深對單字的印象。為了讓現代讀者方便透過手機、平板等設備聽單字發音和句子朗讀，本書特別設計了雲端下載功能，讀者可隨時隨地掃描相關 QRCode，即可隨時聆聽發音。這樣的設計提供了更便利的學習方式，讓學習者不受限於時間和地點，更容易掌握單字的發音。

　　最後，本書的完成得益於所有共同的作者們的不眠不休和全力投入，才能共同完成這本書。同時，也感謝凱信出版社的鼎力協助，讓本書得以順利出現在讀者面前。最重要的是，我們要將這本書獻給所有正在學習英語，參加英檢、統測、學測、高考、普考等各種考試的學生和考生們。我們都深切理解並能感受到你們的辛苦。有了這本書，相信讀者必能在英語學習的路上無往而不利，自信地在考場上表現出色。我們衷心希望這本書能成為你們的得力助手，讓英語學習之路更加順遂。祝福你們在學習英語的旅途中取得豐碩的成果！

目錄 Contents

格林法則魔法學校六大名師
祝你一考就上！

Level 1

Unit 01 – Unit 20 基礎單字

因各家手機系統不同，若無法直接掃描，
仍可以至以下電腦雲端連結下載收聽。
（https://reurl.cc/35WArV）

mammal
[`mæml]
n. 哺乳動物

The red fox is the most common carnivorous land mammal in the world.
赤狐是世界上最常見的肉食性陸生哺乳類動物。

警特 107

（秒殺解字）mamma+al → mamma 源自拉丁語，表示「乳房」（breast），更早表示「媽媽」（mom）。「哺乳類動物」（mammal）的意思源自於「喝媽媽的奶」。

詞搭 | a marine mammal 海生哺乳動物

---

workshop
[`wɝk ʃɑp]
n. 研討會；工作室

This workshop will increase all the participants' understanding about recent fluctuations of oil prices.
這次的工作坊將會讓所有參與者更了解最近油價的波動。

（秒殺解字）work+shop → 可以在裡面「工作」的「工廠」，引申為「工作室」。

詞搭 | a theater workshop 戲劇研討會；a workshop on modern poetry 現代詩研討會

同義字 | seminar

---

problematic
[ˌprɑblə`mætɪk]
adj. 有問題的；
疑難的

Some team members thought the plan proposed by Juanita was problematic because it was not workable at all.
有些隊員認為 Juanita 所提的計畫是有問題的，因為一點也不可行。

普 101

（秒殺解字）problem+atic → 有「問題」的。

---

offshore
[`ɔf ʃor]
adj. 近岸的、離岸的；
向海的
adv. 離岸；向海面

The plan for offshore oil exploitation will cost a lot of money but will also earn a lot of profits once it is operational.
離岸石油開採的計劃將會耗費大量金錢，但是一旦可行，也會很有賺頭。

（秒殺解字）off+shore → 「離開」「岸邊」。

詞搭 | offshore oil drilling 近海石油鑽勘；offshore bank 海外銀行

system

[ˋsɪstəm]

n. 系統；制度

The president, quoting from our legal system, stressed the importance of equality for both sexes and the access to education for children of the whole country.

總統引用我們的法律制度來強調兩性平等以及全國兒童受教權的重要性。

秒殺解字 sy(=syn=together)+stem(stand) →「站」在「一起」形成「系統」。相關同源字有 sy**stem**atic (adj. 有系統的)、sy**stem**atically (adv. 有系統地)。

詞搭 the education system 教育制度；the digestive system 消化系統

普 105
警特 107

---

company

[ˋkʌmpənɪ]

n. 公司；伴侶、朋友；陪伴

Many companies financed the government for the research and development of the vaccine against COVID-19 viruses.

很多公司資助政府來做對抗新冠肺炎疫苗的研發。

秒殺解字 com(together)+pan(food, bread)+y →「一起」吃「食物」、「麵包」的「朋友」。可用 **food** 當神隊友，**p/f**、**d/n** 轉音，**母音通轉**，來記憶 pan，皆表示「**食物**」。相關同源字有 accom**pan**y (v. 陪伴，陪同)。

詞搭 keep good/bad company 與好 / 壞人交往

同義字 business, firm

普 102
103
108

---

companion

[kəmˋpænjən]

n. 同伴；指南、手冊

Nancy is a good travelling companion, so we usually go abroad together.

Nancy 是一個很好的旅行伴侶，所以我們通常一起出國。

詞搭 a travelling/dinner/drinking companion 旅伴 / 飯友 / 酒友；a companion to... ⋯⋯手冊 / 指南

警特 107
108

---

provide

[prəˋvaɪd]

v. 提供

In order to provide suitable safety protection, all medical masks should be inspected by Taiwan Food and Drug Administration.

為了要提供適當的安全防護，所有的醫療級口罩都必須要經過台灣食藥署的檢驗。

秒殺解字 pro(forward)+vid(see)+e →往「前」「看」，表示看到未來需求，引申為「提供」。相關同源字有 **vid**eo (n. 錄影)、e**vid**ent (adj. 明顯的)、e**vid**ence (n. 證據)、pro**vis**ion (n. 準備；供應)。

詞搭 provide + sb. + with + sth. = provide + sth. + for + sb. 提供某人某物；provide against + sth. 防備

同義字 offer, supply

普 100
110
高 110
警特 105
106
108

provider
[prə`vaɪdɚ]
n. 維持家庭生計者；
供應者、提供者

Gavin's father died early, so his grandmother became the main provider of the whole family.
Gavin 的父親很早去世，因此他的祖母成為主要維持家庭生計的人。

瞥 99
107

---

program
[`progræm]
n. 節目；程式
v. 設計程式

Melissa is conducting a geological survey program on toxic waste in this neighborhood.
Melissa 正在進行這個區域有毒廢棄物地質測量的一項計畫。

瞥 107

（秒殺解字）pro(forward)+gram(write) →「事先」「寫」出來的一個表演流程。相關同源字有 **gram**mar（n. 文法）、dia**gram**（n. 圖表）。

詞搭 a TV/radio program 電視／廣播節目；a computer program 電腦程式

---

important
[ɪm`pɔrtn̩t]
adj. 重要的

To prevent misunderstanding, it is important to distinguish the meanings of a gesture in different countries.
為了避免誤解，區分不同國家對某一手勢的意義是很重要的。

瞥 99
102
103
106
108
高 108

（秒殺解字）im(in)+port(carry)+ant →「攜（帶）」「入」「進口」，以前會「帶」「入」港口海關的一定是「重要的」物品。相關同源字有 im**port**（v./n. 進口）、ex**port**（v./n. 出口）、sup**port**（v./n. 支持）、re**port**（v./n. 報告；報導）、trans**port**（v. 運輸）。

詞搭 It is important（for + sb.）+ to V… / that + S + V… ……很重要

同義字 crucial, critical, vital, significant

---

importance
[ɪm`pɔrtn̩s]
n. 重要性

The president of Olive Oil Council then highlighted the importance of olive oil in both the European and global markets.
橄欖油協會的主席在當時強調橄欖油在歐洲及全球市場的重要性。

瞥 102

詞搭 the importance of health / education / regular exercise 健康／教育／規律運動的重要性

---

importantly
[ɪm`pɔrtn̩tlɪ]
adv. 重要地

I know you are very excited about going to Paris, but most importantly, don't forget to avoid being the victim of pickpockets.
我知道你對於去巴黎感到非常興奮，但最重要的是，不要忘記避免成為扒手覬覦的對象。

continue
[kən`tɪnju]
v. 持續、繼續

Due to serious pollution problems, marine life will continue to face rigorous problems and challenges.
由於嚴重的汙染問題，海洋生物將會持續面臨到嚴峻的問題和挑戰。

秒殺解字 con(together)+tin(hold)+u+e →本義「握」住放在「一起」，使之「連續」不斷。相關同源字有continuity (n. 延續)、continual (adj. 持續的)、continually (adv. 不斷地)。

詞搭 continue + Ving = continue + to V = go on + Ving 繼續……；
to be continued 未完待續

continuous
[kən`tɪnjuəs]
adj. 連續不斷的

The air conditioner makes a continuous noise, which suggests that it should be fixed.
這台冷氣發出連續的噪音，這表示它應該要修理了。

同義字 ceaseless, consecutive

〔普〕106

society
[sə`saɪətɪ]
n. 社會；社團

People in a democratic society enjoy equality among different groups and freedom of speech and actions.
民主社會的人民享有不同族群間的平等以及言論與行為的自由。

詞搭 a modern / civilized / primitive society 現代／文明／原始社會；
the evolution of human society 人類社會的演進

〔普特〕105

societal
[sə`saɪətl]
adj. 社會的

More and more college students are paying much attention to societal issues and are attempting to bring changes for the better.
越來越多的大學生非常關心社會議題，並試圖改變得更好。

詞搭 societal values / attitude 社會價值觀／態度

sociable
[`soʃəbl]
adj. 擅交際的

Betty is not a sociable kind of person, so she rarely goes to social events.
Betty 不善於交際，所以她很少參加社交活動。

反義字 unsociable

social
[`soʃəl]
adj. 社會的；社交的、聯誼性的；群居的

Social media users are free to produce and upload their videos online without any limitations.
社群媒體用戶可以自由地在網路上製作和上傳影片，不受任何限制。

〔普〕102

sociologist

[ˌsoʃɪ`alədʒɪst]

n. 社會學家

Recently, a sociologist did research on the relationship between environmental contamination, consumer markets, and people's health.
最近，一位社會學家對環境污染、消費市場和人們健康狀況之間的關係進行了研究。

 秒殺解字 socio(society)+logy(study of)+ist → 研究「社會」「學問」的「人」。

---

expect

[ɪk`spɛkt]

v. 期待；等待；預料

In the food and beverage industry, shop owners expect to ensure their customers of the high-quality hygiene and clean environment.
餐飲業的老闆們期望能確保顧客最高品質的衛生與乾淨的環境。

 秒殺解字 ex(out)+spect(look) → 往「外」「看」，表示「期待」，可用喜出「望」「外」記憶。因為 ex 已經包含 /ks/ 兩個子音，因此省略後面字根 spect 開頭 s。相關同源字有 unexpectedly（adv. 意外地）、spectator（n. 看比賽觀眾）、aspect（n. 方面）、inspect（v. 檢查）、respect（v./n. 尊敬）、suspect（v. 懷疑）、perspective（n. 觀點）、prospect（n. 展望）。

詞搭 expect + sb. + to V 預期某人會……

---

expectation

[ˌɛkspɛk`teʃən]

n. 期望

Contrary to all expectations, Cindy was awarded a full scholarship to the university.
與所有人的期望相反的是，Cindy 獲得了該大學的全額獎學金。

警特 105

詞搭 in expectation 期待；meet / come up to + sb.'s expectations 符合期望

---

remain

[rɪ`men]

n. 殘餘物 (~s)；化石
v. 保持

Students remained silent when the teacher asked them a pretty tricky question.
當老師問學生一個相當難的問題時，他們保持沉默。

警 106
110
警特 106
107
108

秒殺解字 re(back)+main(=man=stay) →「停留在」「後面」，表示「保持」、「停留」、「剩下」、「遺留」。相關同源字有 remainder（n. 餘額，剩餘部分）、mansion（n. 大廈）、permanent（adj. 永久的）。

詞搭 remain a puzzle 仍一直是個謎；the remains of a meal 剩菜

同義字 stay

remaining
[rɪ`menɪŋ]
adj. 剩下的

After the event, the remaining money will be donated to a nearby orphanage.
活動過後，剩餘的錢將會捐給附近一家孤兒院。

舊 101

paycheck
[`pe͵tʃɛk]
n. 薪水；付薪水的支票
(paycheque [英])

Most people would rather work for a small paycheck than start a business because they don't like to take risks.
大部分的人寧可工作領固定的低薪也不願創業，因為他們不喜歡冒風險。

（秒殺解字）pay+check → 是雇主「付」給員工薪水的「支票」。

詞搭 a weekly paycheck 一張週薪支票；a nice fat paycheck 豐厚的工資

同義字 salary, wage

president
[`prɛzədənt]
n. 總統；校長；董事長、公司總裁

The president of this bank was selected as Fortune's annual Businessperson of the Year.
這家銀行的總裁被財富雜誌選為年度最佳商業人物。

高 110

（秒殺解字）pre(before)+sid(sit)+ent →「主持」活動、會議的「人」，都「坐」在「前面」，如「總統」、「校長」、「公司總裁」。可用 **sit** 當神隊友，**z/s**、**d/t** 轉音，母音通轉，來記憶 **sid**，皆表示「坐」。相關同源字有 pre**sid**e (v. 主持)、pre**sid**ential (adj. 總統的)、pre**sid**ency (n. 總統、公司總裁的職位)、dis**sid**ent (adj. 意見不同的)、re**sid**ent (n. 居民)。

facial
[`feʃəl]
n. 臉部按摩
adj. 臉的、面部的

It is difficult to judge from Teresa's facial expression whether she agrees with the project or not.
很難從 Teresa 的臉部表情判斷出她是否同意這項企劃。

舊 101
104
警特 106

（秒殺解字）face+ial →「臉部」「的」。

consider
[kən`sɪdɚ]
v. 認為；考慮；把……視為

The city government would consider a number of priorities regarding this issue in the coming months.
在未來幾個月，市政府會考慮有關這項議題的幾個優先事項。

舊 100
警特 107

（秒殺解字）con(together)+sider(star) → 原指觀察「星星」，後來變成「視為」、「考慮」。同源相關字有 considerate (adj. 體貼的)、consideration (n. 考慮)。

詞搭 consider + Ving 考慮……；consider A (to be) B 將 A 視為 B

同義字 think, contemplate, meditate, ponder, reckon

considerable
[kənˈsɪdərəbl]

adj. 相當多的；相當大的

Consumers, food producers, and government agencies should put considerable emphasis on the issue of pesticide residue in food.
消費者、食品製造者，以及政府機構都應該重視食物中殺蟲劑殘留的議題。

普 110

---

considerately
[kənˈsɪdərəblɪ]

adv. 相當大地；頗為

Taking care of a newborn baby will increase the workload of a mother considerably.
照顧新生嬰兒將大大地增加母親的工作量。

普 108

同義字	greatly
反義字	slightly

---

result
[rɪˈzʌlt]

n. 結果
v. 起因於；導致、造成

Failure to follow the directions of this project can result in faulty survey results and even being flunked.
如未能遵守這項報告的指示可能會導致錯誤的調查結果甚至被當。

普 110
高 110

🖋 **秒殺解字** re(back)+sult(jump, leap) → 之前的付出「跳」「回來」，就是「結果」。相關同源字有 in**sult**（v./n. 侮辱）、as**sault**（v./n. 攻擊）、**sal**mon（n. 鮭魚）。

詞搭	result from... 起因於……；result in... 導致、造成……；as a result of... = because of... 由於……
同義字	outcome, consequence

---

increase
[ˈɪnkris]

n. 增加

[ɪnˈkris]

v. 增加、增大

The company is increasing the ratio of women in management and promoting them to significant positions.
這家公司正在提升管理階層女性的比例，並且拔擢她們至重要職位。

普 107
警特 107
108
109

🖋 **秒殺解字** in(in)+creas(grow)+e →「內部」「成長」，表示「增加」。

詞搭	be on the increase = be increasing 增加中
反義字	decrease

---

increasingly
[ɪnˈkrisɪŋlɪ]

adv. 漸增地

Increasingly, young people distrust all forms of government although the world has become more and more prosperous day by day.
儘管世界日益繁榮興盛，年輕人越來越不信任各種形式的政府。

反義字	decreasingly

develop

[dɪ`vɛləp]

v. 使……發達；發展；發育

With the rebuilding of the train station, this small town has developed into a more prosperous place.
隨著火車站的重建，這個小城已發展成更繁榮的地方了。

秒殺解字 de(=dis=undo)+velop(wrap) → 本義「取消」「包裝」，即「打開」，引申為「發展」。相關同源字有 developed（adj. 發達的）；underdeveloped（adj. 不發達的）、envelop（v. 包住；覆蓋）、envelope（n. 信封）。

曾 99
103
110

---

developing

[dɪ`vɛləpɪŋ]

adj. 發展中的、開發中的

Many international enterprises are looking forward to investing in these developing countries with the improvement of their communication infrastructure.
隨著這些開發中國家的通訊基礎設備的改善，很多國際企業正期望能在這些國家投資。

詞搭 the developing countries / nations 開發中國家

---

development

[dɪ`vɛləpmənt]

n. 發展、開發

Since Spielberg has several projects under development you are interested in, we will keep you informed of their developments.
由於 Spielberg 有幾個在開發中的項目您感興趣，因此我們將隨時向您通報其最新動態。

詞搭 under / in development 開發中；research and development 研發

曾 110

Unit 02

🎧TRACK 002

---

effect
[ɪˋfɛkt]
n. 效果；影響；結果

Dizziness and an upset stomach are possible <u>side effects</u> of this medicine.
這個藥物的副作用包括了暈眩和胃部不適。

🖋 秒殺解字 ef(=ex=out)+fect(do, make) →「做」「出來」的「影響」、「效果」。相關同源字有 af**fect**（v. 影響）、de**fect**（n. 缺點）、per**fect**（adj. 完美的）、in**fect**（v. 傳染）。

普 110
高 99
101
103
105

詞搭 <u>bring / put</u>...into effect 實施；take effect 生效、見效；have an effect on... 對……有影響；side effects 副作用

同義字 influence, impact

字辨 affect [əˋfɛkt] v. 影響

---

effective
[ɪˋfɛktɪv]
adj. 有效的

Yoga and jogging are two very effective ways of relieving one's stress from work.
瑜珈和慢跑是兩個對於減輕工作壓力非常有效的方式。

🖋 秒殺解字 ef(=ex=out)+fect(do, make)+ive →「做」的「出」「效果」的。

普 101
高 106
108

同義字 ineffective

---

effectively
[ɪˋfɛktɪvlɪ]
adv. 有力地；有效地

The pills work more effectively if you take them before meals.
如果你在飯前服用，這些藥會更有效。

普 107
高 103

---

receive
[rɪˋsiv]
v. 收到；接待

Judy received a strange penalty ticket for illegal parking, but she has never visited that place before.
Judy 收到一張奇怪的違規停車罰單，因為她根本沒去過那個地方。

🖋 秒殺解字 re(back)+ceiv(take)+e → 本義是「拿」「回」。相關同源字有 re**ceiv**er（n. 話筒；收件者）。

高 100

---

reception
[rɪˋsɛpʃən]
n. 接收；接待

The director's first movie got a wonderful reception from the audience.
導演的第一部電影獲得了觀眾的好評。

🖋 秒殺解字 re(back)+cept(take)+ion → 本義是「拿」「回」。相關同源字有 re**cept**ionist（n. 接待員，櫃檯服務人員）。

普 99

詞搭 reception area 接待處；poor reception 收訊不佳

receptive [rɪ`sɛptɪv] **adj.** （對新的思想等） 善於接受的	Some elderly people <u>are</u> not <u>receptive</u> to new ideas and views and therefore, misunderstandings are generated. 有些年長者並不太能接納新的想法與觀點，因而產生了誤解。	高 106
receptor [rɪ`sɛptə] **n.** 受體；接受器	When odors or scents enter the nose, they interact with the cilia of olfactory receptor neurons. 當氣味或味道進入鼻腔時，它們會與嗅覺受體神經元的纖毛相互作用。	普 106
office [`ɔfɪs] **n.** 辦公室；公職	Alan works in an international enterprise with offices in Paris, London, New York, and Beijing. Alan 在一家設有辦公室於巴黎、倫敦、紐約，和北京的國際企業上班。 🪶 **秒殺解字** of(=opus=work)+fic(do, make)+e → 「做」「工作」的地方。	普 105 高 103 107
	詞搭 box office 售票處、票房；the Foreign Office 外交部；a branch office 分公司	
official [ə`fɪʃəl] **n.** （文官）官員； 主管 **adj.** 官方的；正式的； 公開的	The president's official visit confirms a more stable relationship between the two countries. 總統的正式訪問證實了兩國之間更穩定的關係。 🪶 **秒殺解字** of(=opus=work)+fic(do, make)+ial → 「工作」「的」，引申為「正式的」、「公開的」。相關同源字有 officially（adv. 官方地，正式地）、officer（n. 軍官，官員）。	普 101 103
	同義字 formal	
require [rɪ`kwaɪr] **v.** 要求；需要	Not allowed to stay alone according to the law, children under 6 require a parent or guardian to accompany them. 根據法律規定，六歲以下孩童不能獨自待在家，必須要有家長或監護人陪伴。 🪶 **秒殺解字** re(again)+quir(ask, seek)+e → 本義「再次」「詢問」，引申為「要求」。相關同源字有 requirement（n. 要求，必要條件）、acquire（v. 獲得）、inquire（v. 詢問）。	普 99 105 高 99 105 107
	同義字 demand	

experience
[ɪkˋspɪrɪəns]
n. 經驗
v. 體驗；經歷

Fighting in World War II was an experience that Josh would never forget in his lifetime.
參與第二次世界大戰是 Josh 一輩子也不會忘的經驗。

秒殺解字 ex(out)+per(try, risk)+i+ence → 到「外面」「嘗試」、「冒險」，表示「經驗」。可用表示「恐懼」的 **fear** 當神隊友，**p/f 轉音**，母音通轉，來記憶 **per**，表示「嘗試」、「冒險」，因為「嘗試」或「冒險」過程中，遇到未知事物，容易產生「恐懼」情緒。相關同源字有 ex**per**iment (n./v. 實驗)、ex**per**t (n. 專家)。

詞搭 experience problems / difficulties 經歷問題／困難

同義字 go through, undergo

曾 104
107
高 101
104
110

---

experienced
[ɪkˋspɪrɪənst]
adj. 有經驗的

Miss Zeng is an experienced Mandarin teacher looking for a native English-speaking partner for language exchange.
曾小姐是一位經驗豐富的中文老師，正在尋找以英語為母語的伙伴以進行語言交換。

詞搭 be experienced in... 在……方面有經驗

高 107

---

involve
[ɪnˋvɑlv]
v. 包含；使涉入

The final exam of Dr. Johnson's course involves three parts, including a paper, an exam, and an oral presentation.
Dr. Johnson 的課程期末考含三個部分，包括報告、考試，以及口頭報告。

秒殺解字 in(in)+volv(roll)+e → 「捲」入某事「內」。相關同源字有 e**volv**e (v. 進化)、e**volu**tion (n. 發展)、re**volv**e (v. 旋轉)、re**volu**tion (n. 革命；旋轉)。

詞搭 be involved in... = involve oneself in / with... 涉入……

同義字 contain, include；implicate, entangle

高 100
警特 106
109

---

involvement
[ɪnˋvɑlvmənt]
n. 牽涉；參與

Felix denied any direct involvement in the incident, because he had an alibi for that night.
Felix 否認直接參與了這次事件，因為那天晚上他有不在場證明。

同義字 participation

曾 105

local
[`lokl]
n. 當地人；本地人
adj. 當地的；本地的

Lion Tours offers an all-inclusive package including accommodation, local transportation, meals, field visits, and tickets for museums at the price of 20,000 NT.
獅子旅遊公司提供一個完善的套裝行程，只需 2 萬台幣即包含住宿、當地交通、三餐、當地行程，以及博物館票券

高 104

🖋 **秒殺解字** loc(place)+al → 屬於某「地方」的，引申為「當地的」。

同義字 regional, native

---

locally
[`loklɪ]
adv. 局部地；在本地

The Michelin chef insists on using the fresh ingredients grown locally to cook his dishes.
米其林廚師堅持使用當地種植的新鮮食材烹製菜餚。

高 104

---

localize
[`lokl͵aɪz]
v. 確定……的地點；使局部化

The engineers spent the whole night trying to localize the faulty machine that slowed down the assembly line.
工程師們花了整個晚上找出減慢生產線速度變慢的那台故障機器。

高 107

---

locate
[lo`ket/`loket]
v. 使位於；找出……的位置

The factory is located in a residential area, for fear of being investigated by the government.
該工廠位於住宅區，因為擔心遭到政府調查。

警 106
高 104

🖋 **秒殺解字** loc(place)+ate → 將……放置於某「地方」，引申為「使位於」。同源相關字 location (n. 地點)。

同義字 situate

---

locational
[lo`keʃənl]
adj. 位置上的

People from all over the world bring diverse locational and historical stories to this city.
來自世界各地的人們為這座城市帶來了各式各樣地理位置和歷史的故事。

高 107

---

situation
[͵sɪtʃʊ`eʃən]
n. 處境；情勢

Maggie's assessment of the situation was correct, so people followed her instructions and escaped from the fire successfully.
Maggie 對於情況的評估是正確的，所以人們聽從她的指示並且成功逃離火場。

警特 108

🖋 **秒殺解字** sit(place)+u+ate+ion → 核心語義是「地點」，表示「處境」、「情勢」。相關同源字有 site (n. 地點)、situate (v. 使位於)。

詞搭 the political / economic / financial situation 政治／經濟／財政情勢

同義字 state, condition, circumstance

determine
[dɪˋtɝmɪn]
v. 決定；確定

The number of food and beverages we can take from the store will be determined by how much money we're allowed to spend.
我們能從商店中拿取食物和飲料的數量取決於我們可以花多少錢。

秒殺解字 de(off)+termin(end, limit)+e → 劃「分」「界線」需「決心」。相關同源字有 **termin**al（adj. 末期）、ex**termin**ate（v. 滅絕）。

詞搭 determine + to V = resolve + to V = make up one's mind + to V 下定決心要

同義字 decide, resolve

---

determination
[dɪˏtɝməˋneʃən]
n. 決心

Eileen is a woman of great determination, for no one can dissuade her from doing what she has decided to do.
Eileen 是一位很有決心的女人，因為沒有人能勸阻她不要做她已決定的事。

同義字 decision, resolution

---

determined
[dɪˋtɝmɪnd]
adj. 有決心的；果斷的

Several companies rejected Gina's proposal, but that just made her all the more determined.
幾家公司拒絕了 Gina 的提議，但這使她更加堅定了。

詞搭 be determined + to V 決心要……

同義字 decisive, firm

---

condition
[kənˋdɪʃən]
n. 狀況；條件

The living conditions of some underdeveloped countries still have room for improvement.
有些未開發國家的生活狀況仍有改善的空間。

秒殺解字 con(together)+dit(=dict=say)+ion →「共同」「說」，表示「同意」，後指「同意」的「狀況」、「條件」。

詞搭 be in good / poor condition 情況良好／不佳；under favorable / difficult conditions 在順／逆境；on condition that... = if... 條件是／如果……

minute
[`mɪnɪt]
n. 分鐘；紀錄
[maɪ`njut]
adj. 微小的

We still have three more minutes to prepare for our final speech introducing our country to the world.
距離介紹我們國家給世界認識的演講還有最後三分鐘可以準備。

高 101

🖊 **秒殺解字** min(small)+ute → 表示「微小的」。

詞搭 in a minute 馬上；a minute amount 微量

同義字 slight, tiny, miniature

community
[kə`mjunətɪ]
n. 社區；界；共同利益團體

My mother is very well-known in this local community for her kindness and generosity.
我的母親因為善良與慷慨而在這個社區相當有名。

曾 107
高 108

🖊 **秒殺解字** commun(common)+ity →「共同的」生活空間。可用 **common** 當神隊友，**母音通轉**，來記憶 **commun**，皆表示「共同的」。相關同源字有 **commun**icate（v. 溝通）、**commun**ism（n. 共產主義）。

詞搭 community-acquired infection 社區感染；sense of community 社區歸屬感

indicate
[`ɪndə͵ket]
v. 顯示、指出；暗示

Various studies indicate that swearing helps improve work efficiency and relieve pressure.
很多研究指出，罵髒話有助於增進工作效率以及減輕壓力。

曾 106
高 102
108
警特 108

🖊 **秒殺解字** in(in)+dic(show)+ate →「顯露」出「裡面」的真相。相關同源字有 in**dic**ation（n. 顯示）、**dic**tionary（n. 字典）、pre**dic**t（v. 預測）、ad**dic**t（n. 成癮者）、de**dic**ate（v. 奉獻）、con**di**tion（n. 情況）。

同義字 point out, signify, suggest

indicator
[`ɪndə͵ketɚ]
n. 指示物；指標

Stable commodity prices can be a useful indicator of the country's economic health.
穩定的商品價格可以成為該國經濟健康狀況的實用指標。

高 106
108

詞搭 economic indicators 經濟指標

同義字 pointer, signal

information
[ˌɪnfɚ`meʃən]
n. 消息；資料
（簡寫 info）

We strongly suggest that you not send private information via e-mail since it is not a secure method of communication.
我們強烈建議你不要使用電子信件來寄送私人資訊，因為那不是一種安全的通訊方式。

秒殺解字 in(in)+form(form)+ation → 本義賦予「形體」，引申為「消息」。相關同源字有 in**form**（n. 通知，告知）、in**form**ed（adj. 消息靈通的，根據情報的）、uni**form**（n. 制服）、re**form**（n./v. 改革）、trans**form**（v. 使徹底改觀）、con**form**（v. 遵守）。

高 101 102 103 105 107 警特 106 108

informative
[ɪn`fɔrmətɪv]
adj. 有內容的；
　　　能增進知識的

Mr. Smith's speech was very interesting and informative, and I really enjoyed myself this afternoon.
Smith 先生的演講非常有趣且內容豐富，我真的很享受今天下午的時光。

普 103

method
[`mɛθəd]
n. 方法；條理

The Village Chief criticized the methods of crowd control used by the government.
村長批評政府所做的人群管控方式。

秒殺解字 meta(after, in pursuit of)+od(way) → 「追隨」之「路」。

同義字 | way, manner, approach

高 101

century
[`sɛntʃərɪ]
n. 世紀

In 1959, Japan's Crown Prince Akihito got married to a non-royal bride, breaking centuries of tradition.
在 1959 年時，日本的明仁天皇打破好幾世紀的傳統，迎娶了一位非皇室的新娘。

秒殺解字 cent(hundred)+ury →一世紀等於「一百」年。c 在拉丁文裡發 k 的音。可用 **hundred** 當神隊友，**k/h**、**d/t** 轉音，**母音通轉**，來記憶 cent，表示「百」，亦有「百分之一」的意思。

詞搭 | at the turn of this century 在本世紀之交時；by the end of the 21st century 到了 21 世紀末

字辨 | year 一年；decade 十年；half a century 半個世紀

普 102 103 高 99 101 警特 106

material

[mə`tɪrɪəl] [U]

n. 材料；原料；資料；題材

adj. 物質的；具體的

Anderson is collecting materials for a report on English literature of the Renaissance.

Anderson 正在收集文藝復興時代英國文學報告的資料。

普 110
高 108
警特 108
109

🪶 秒殺解字 mater(matter)+ial → 「物質」的。可用 **mother** 當神隊友，**t/ð** 轉音，**母音通轉**，來記憶 mater，皆表示「**母親**」。「**物質**」（**matter**）泛稱所有組成可觀測物體的基本成份，就像構成萬物的「**母親**」（**mother**）。相關同源字有 **mater**ialism(n. 唯物主義) 等。

詞搭 material comforts 物質享受；a material world 物質世界

同義字 spiritual

include

[ɪn`klud]

v. 包括、包含

Symptoms of the flu include a high temperature, a sore throat, a persistent cough and sometimes muscle aches.

流感的症狀包括發燒、喉嚨痛、持續的咳嗽以及伴有偶發性的肌肉痠痛。

普 110
高 102
警特 105
107

🪶 秒殺解字 in(in)+clud(close)+e → 放「進去」「關」起來，表示「包括」。可用 **close** 當神隊友，**d/z/s/ʒ** 轉音，**母音通轉**，來記憶 **clud**、**clus**，皆表示「**關閉**」。相關同源字有 in**clud**ing (prep. 包括)、in**clus**ive (adj. 包含的，包括的)、ex**clud**e (v. 拒絕接納)、 ex**clud**ing (prep. 除……之外)、ex**clus**ive (adj. 排外的)、con**clud**e (v. 下結論)、con**clus**ion (n. 結論)。

同義字 contain, involve, enclose

反義字 exclude

purpose

[`pɝpəs]

n. 目的

The purpose of setting up this sign is to remind the drivers of the poor road conditions.

設立這個標誌的目的就是在提醒駕駛者道路崎嶇不平。

高 104
警特 105
107
108

🪶 秒殺解字 pur(=pro=forward)+pos(put)+e → 把東西「放」在「前面」，表示「目的」。相關同源字有 pur**pos**ely (v. 故意地)。

詞搭 for / with the purpose of + Ving 為了……目的；on purpose 故意地；for practical purposes 實際上

policy
[ˈpɑləsɪ]

n. 政策；保險單

(policies [ˈpɑləsɪz] pl.)

詞搭

Taiwan has the best insurance policy in the world, which provides health care at a reasonable expense.

台灣擁有世界上最好的保險政策，只需負擔合理費用即可提供健康照護。

（秒殺解字） polic(=polis=city, citizen)+y → **polis**, **polit** 同源，**t/s** 轉音，母音通轉，皆表示「城市」、「市民」，並衍生出「政府」（**government**）、「管理」（**administration**）的意思。相關同源字有 **polit**ics(n. 政治)、**polit**ical (adj. 政治的)、**polit**ician (n. 政客)、**polic**e (n. 警察)。

the government's economic policies 政府的經濟政策；
an insurance policy 保險單

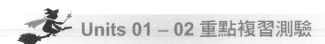
Units 01 – 02 重點複習測驗

01 ___ Although the brand-new vaccine for COVID-19 was revealed last week, it is still _____ and needs a lot of improvement.

(A) democratic (B) realistic
(C) dramatic (D) problematic

02 ___ Sunscreen lotion can have a great impact on _____ marine life, such as coral reefs or sea turtles. The chemical ingredients in the lotion will cause irreversible damage to these animals.

(A) offshore (B) official
(C) lush (D) migrant

03 ___ The Ministry of Education is trying to revolutionize the education _____. However, the outcome still leaves a lot to be desired.

(A) capitalism (B) development
(C) system (D) symptom

04 ___ Due to the emergency, the government offers emergency loans to _____ that are on the verge of bankruptcy. By doing so, the government hopes to prevent an economic depression in the country.

(A) contracts (B) societies
(C) companies (D) enemies

05 ___ Recently, a software developer has become a popular career choice. Especially, with the growing of gaming industry, people who are able to _____ become extermely valuable.

(A) program (B) produce
(C) provide (D) promote

06 ___ With the policy changes, the housing market is _____ to have a downturn next year, and property prices will also drop significantly because of the news.

(A) infected (B) expected
(C) detected (D) neglected

07 ___ Even after hundreds of years, the terrifying cases of Jack the Ripper still _____ as a mystery. No one knows what really happened at that time and we will never know who the real killer is.

(A) reports   (B) remains

(C) majors   (D) decides

08 ___ When a national crisis happens, the _____ of the country will take shelter in a fortified bunker to guarantee his or her safety.

(A) reviewer   (B) president

(C) physician   (D) consumer

09 ___ Last week, the New York Police Department raided a house and found a (an) _____ amount of drugs inside it.

(A) considerable   (B) reliable

(C) adaptable   (D) indispensable

10 ___ The new drug worked properly during animal testing, so now we are moving on to human experiments to see if the _____ of the medicine is working as intended.

(A) threat   (B) formula

(C) effect   (D) electricity

11 ___ The presidential candidate is _____ in a corruption scandal and is now under the investigation of FBI. This breaking news greatly damages the image of this candidate.

(A) involved   (B) derived

(C) thrived   (D) deprived

12 ___ The government official stated that the riot _____ is now under control. However, local residents still can see rioters all over their town.

(A) protection   (B) adoption

(C) exception   (D) situation

13 ___ The board members are heavily criticized for their _____ of running the company. Employees claim that the company never provides them with enough freedom to do their jobs.

(A) method   (B) estimate

(C) benefit   (D) impact

14 ___　_____ uncertainty influences our sales figures and thus creates a financial deficit in our company. As a result, we need to come up with a plan to fix the problem.

(A) Prison (B) Popularity
(C) Policy (D) Proposal

15 ___　Before you do anything, make sure you know your _____ so that you won't run around like a headless chicken. That way, you will feel confident in every challenge you come across.

(A) prescription (B) purchase
(C) population (D) purpose

process

[`prɑsɛs]

n. 過程

v. 處理

Aging is a continuous process that everyone has to experience throughout their lives.

老化現象是每個人一輩子都必須經歷的持續過程。

> **秒殺解字** pro(forward)+cess(go) →「往前」「走」，所以是「過程」。相關同源字有 pro**ceed**（v. 前進）、pro**cess**ing（n. 過程，處理）、pro**ced**ure（n. 程序）、pro**ceed**ings（n. 會議紀錄）、pro**ceed**s（n. 收益）。

警特 109

詞搭 | be in the process of + N / Ving 正在進行……中；process（ed）foods 加工食品

---

decide

[dɪ`saɪd]

v. 決定；選定

The committee decided to increase the budget for maintenance of this building because of inflation.

因為通膨關係，委員會決定要增加這棟大樓的維護修繕預算。

> **秒殺解字** de(off)+cid(cut)+e →「切割」「開」，做「決定」是要「當機立斷」的。相關同源字有 de**cide**（v. 決定）、de**cis**ive（adj. 決定性的）、sui**cide**（n. 自殺）、pesti**cid**e（n. 殺蟲劑）、insecti**cid**e（n. 殺蟲劑）。

普 100
高 110

詞搭 | decide + to V = make a decision + to V 決定要……；decide on... 選定……

同義字 | determine

---

decision

[dɪ`sɪʒən]

n. 決定

Audience makes the final decision by voting as to who should be eliminated from the competition.

觀眾透過投票最後決定誰應該從這項競賽中被淘汰。

高 108

詞搭 | make a decision = make up one's mind 做決定；come to / arrive at / reach a decision 達成決定

---

major

[`medʒɚ]

adj. 大部分的；主要的、重要的

v. 主修

n. 主修科目

Being popular with Taiwanese, Haruki Murakami's major works have all been translated into Chinese.

受到台灣人的喜愛，村上春樹的主要作品都已被翻譯成中文版。

> **秒殺解字** maj(great)+or → 原意是「較大的」（greater）。

警特 105

詞搭 | the major vote / opinion 多數票／意見；the major leagues 大聯盟；major in... = take...as sb's major 主修……

majority

[məˋdʒɔrɪtɪ]

n. 大部分、大多數

Anderson held a majority shareholding in his company; therefore, he sets salaries, benefits and bonuses, or he can decide to sell part or all of the company.

Anderson 持有其公司的多數股權；因此，他設定薪資、福利和獎金，或者他可以決定出售部分或全部公司。

普 99
106

---

available

[əˋveləbl]

adj. 可得到的；有空的

Owing to the shipping problem, the prototype of the latest sewing machine is not available right now.

由於運輸問題，目前是沒有最新縫紉機的樣品。

警特 105
106
107
109

秒殺解字 a(=ad=to)+vail(strong, worth)+able → 本義「值得的」，引申為「可使用的」。可用表示「價值」的 **value** 當神隊友，**母音通轉**，來記憶 **vail**，表示「強的」、「值得的」。

---

availability

[ə,velə`bɪlətɪ]

n. 可使用性；易得；可用

Adair was amazed at the availability of convenience stores in Taiwan, which is not the case back in US.

Adair 對台灣便利店的普及感到驚訝，而在美國卻不是這樣。

---

produce

[prəˋdjus]

v. 生產；出版

[ˋprɑdjus / ˋprɔdjus]

n. 農產品；乳製品

There are some mechanical problems that haven't been solved in producing the intricate watches.

製造這款精密的手錶仍有一些機械性問題尚未解決。

普 104
107
警特 107

秒殺解字 pro(forward)+duc(lead)+e →「往前」「領導」，才有辦法「生產」新產品。相關同源字有 edu**c**ate（v. 教育）、re**duc**e（v. 減少）、re**duc**tion（n. 減少）、intro**duc**e（v. 介紹；引進）、intro**duc**tion（n. 介紹；引進）、pro**duc**er（n. 生產者）、pro**duc**tivity（n. 生產力）。

同義字 | manufacture

---

product

[ˋprɑdəkt]

n. 產品；成果、結果

The products of this French winemaker were accused of being mixed with inferior wine to boost their profits.

這家法國製酒廠的產品被指控混入劣質酒來增加他們的獲利。

普 106
警特 106
107

詞搭 | natural products 天然產物；agricultural / dairy / software products 農業／乳酪／軟體產品

---

production

[prəˋdʌkʃən]

n. 生產

The new model cars will go into production next year.

新款車型將於明年投入生產。

普 106
107

詞搭 | production levels / targets 生產水準／目標；production line 生產線

productive
[prə`dʌktɪv]
adj. 多產的

According to the surveys, people tend to be more productive in the morning than in the afternoon.
根據調查，人們通常早上比下午更有生產力。

詞搭 a productive writer 多產作家；productive land 肥沃的土地

---

reproduce
[ˌriprə`djus]
v. 生殖、繁殖；複製；翻拍

People have in their nature both to reproduce and to care for their young.
人類具有繁殖和照顧幼小的天性。

秒殺解字 re(again)+produce →「再」「生產」，表示「繁殖」、「複製」。reproduction (n. 生殖；複製品)。

同義字 procreate, breed

---

reproductive
[ˌriprə`dʌktɪv]
adj. （生物）生殖的

The female reproductive organs include parts inside and outside the body.
女性生殖器官包括身體內部和外部的部分。

---

statement
[`stetmənt]
n. 聲明；陳述

The government is expected to issue a statement about the economic relief package to the press.
政府預計向媒體發佈有關經濟紓困計畫的聲明。

秒殺解字 sta(stand)+te+ment → sta 表示「站」，衍生出「使穩固」（make firm）、「穩固」（be firm）的意思。相官同源字有 state (n. 狀態)、statesman (n. 政治家)、overstate (v. 過於誇大)。

詞搭 make / give / issue a statement on / about... 發表……聲明；an official / public / formal statement 官方／公開／正式的聲明

---

modern
[`mɑdən]
adj. 現代的

Sydney Opera House is an example of modern architecture that mainly uses steel, glass and reinforced concrete.
雪梨歌劇院是一個主要使用鋼材、玻璃，和鋼筋混凝土的現代建築範例。

秒殺解字 mod(measure)+ern → 本指因應時宜，採取合適「措施」(measure)，引申為「最新的」、「當代的」。相關同源字有 modernize (v 使現代化)、modernization (n. 現代化)。

詞搭 modern art / dance / poetry / technology / architecture 現代藝術／舞蹈／詩／科技／建築

同義字 contemporary

反義字 old-fashioned, ancient

stage
[stedʒ]
n. 舞台；階段
v. 籌畫、發動；上演

Tokyo was scheduled to stage the Olympic Games in 2020, but faced the threat of a contagious disease.
東京預定在 2020 年舉辦奧運會，但卻面臨傳染性疾病的威脅。

 秒殺解字 sta(stand)+ge →「站」在「舞台」上。

詞搭 stage a strike / demonstration / sit-in 發動罷工／示威／靜坐；be on stage 在台上表演

---

attention
[ə`tɛnʃən]
n. 注意；立正

This YouTuber tries to catch everyone's attention by inviting many guests from a variety of fields.
這位 YouTuber 試著邀請來自不同領域的來賓以吸引大家的注意。

曾 100
高 108
警特 107
109

秒殺解字 at(=ad=to)+tent(thin, stretch)+ion → 本義「往……」「伸展」，特指「專注力」「偏向」某處，因此有「上學」、「出席」等衍生意思。相關同源字有 at**tend**（v. 注意；照料）、at**tent**ive（adj. 注意的）、at**tend**ance（n. 出席）、at**tend**ant（n. 隨從）。

詞搭 pay attention to... 注意……

---

economic
[ˌikə`nɑmɪk]
adj. 與經濟有關的

The surge in the price of stocks in the emerging markets marks the economic recovery.
新興市場的股價飆升表示經濟的復甦。

曾 100
高 108
110

詞搭 economic development / growth / contraction 經濟發展／成長／萎縮

---

economy
[ɪ`kɑnəmɪ]
n. 經濟；節儉

The global economy is seriously paralyzed as a consequence of the lockdown of many countries.
全球的經濟因為很多國家的封鎖而嚴重癱瘓了。

曾 100
高 108

秒殺解字 eco(house)+nom(manage, law)+y →「管理」「家」的「法則」，表示「經濟」、「節儉」。相關同源字有 **eco**nomical（adj. 節省的）、**eco**nomist（n. 經濟學家）。

詞搭 economy class / passengers 經濟艙／乘客；domestic economy 家庭經濟

同義字 frugality

---

economics
[ˌikə`nɑmɪks]
n. 經濟學

Keynes's theories have had a profound impact on modern economics.
凱恩斯的理論對現代經濟學產生了深遠的影響。

evidence

[ˋɛvədəns]

n. 證據
v. 證明

There is no relevant evidence to prove that the suspect is indeed linked to this murder case.
沒有相關的證據來證明那位嫌犯的確與這件謀殺案有關聯。

普 107 108

秒殺解字 e(=ex=out)+vid(see)+ence → 從「外」面很容易「看」到的東西，可當「證據」。相關同源字有 **vid**eo（n. 錄影）、pro**vid**e（v. 提供）、**evid**ent（adj. 明顯的）、**evid**ently（adv. 明顯地）。

詞搭 a piece of evidence 一項證據；verbal evidence 證詞

同義字 proof

---

apply

[əˋplaɪ]

v. 適用；應徵；申請；運用；塗抹（藥膏）

To lighten the economic burden, Shirley is planning to apply for a full scholarship to enter a college.
Shirley 計畫申請全額獎學金來就讀大學以減輕經濟負擔。

普 110 高 110 警特 105

秒殺解字 ap(=ad=to)+pl(fold)+y →「摺」過去是「應用」，也意味把自己放在合適的位置。相關同源字有 ap**pli**cable（adj. 適用的）。

詞搭 apply for... 申請／應徵……；apply to... 應用於……；apply A to B 把 A 運用到 B ／把 A 塗抹在 B 上

---

application

[͵æpləˋkeʃən]

n. 運用；申請

Please fill in this application form and wait here for further notice.
請填寫這份申請表格，並且在此等候更進一步通知。

普 106 警特 109

詞搭 an application form 申請表格；fill in（out）+ sb's application 填寫申請

---

applicant

[ˋæpləkənt]

n. 申請者

Many job applicants do not know how to write a compelling cover letter.
許多求職者不知道如何寫令人注目的求職信。

警特 106

詞搭 (un) successful applicants（未）錄取／用的申請人

---

describe

[dɪˋskraɪb]

v. 描述、形容

Viola insisted on describing the movie's plot to all of us, even if we haven't seen it yet.
即使我們都還沒看過這部電影，Viola 還是堅持要跟我們描述劇情。

秒殺解字 de(down)+scrib(write)+e →「寫」「下來」是「描寫」。相關同源字有 pre**scrib**e（v. 開藥方）、de**scrip**tive（adj. 描述的，描寫的）、pre**scrip**tion（n. 藥方）。

詞搭 describe + sb. / sth. + as... 把某人／某物描述成……

同義字 depict, portray

description
[dɪˋskrɪpʃən]
n. 描述、形容

This reference book provides a comprehensive description of each mathematical formula.
這本參考書提供了每個數學公式詳細通盤的講解。

詞搭 be beyond description 非筆墨所能形容

---

education
[ˏɛdʒəˋkeʃən]
n. 教育

The government should finance the education of children of migrant workers.
政府應該資助移工小孩的教育。

普 103
警特 107
108

詞搭 secondary / primary (elementary) / higher education 中等 (中學) ／基礎 (小學) ／高等教育；vocational education / training 在職教育／訓練；compulsory education 義務教育

---

educate
[ˋɛdʒəˏket]
v. 教育

Young people must be educated about the dangers and risks of drugs.
年輕人必須被教導有關毒品的危險與風險。

警特 106

秒殺解字 e(=ex=out)+duc(lead, tow)+ate → 「教育」的真諦是「引導」「出來」，旨在激發學生潛能。相關同源字有educational (adj. 教育的)、educator (n. 教育學家)、produce (v. 生產)、production (n. 生產)、reduce (v. 減少)、reduction (n. 減少)、introduce (v. 介紹；引進)、introduction (n. 介紹；引進)、induce (v. 唆使)。

---

property
[ˋprɑpə·tɪ]
n. 財產；特性

The company was accused of having infringed the intellectual property rights of its competitor.
這家公司被控告侵犯它的競爭對手的智慧財產權。

普 110
警特 105
109

秒殺解字 proper(own)+ty → 屬於「自己的」，表示「財產」。

詞搭 property developer 房地產開發商；property tax 財產稅；the property prices / market 房地產價格／市場

---

create
[krɪˋet]
v. 創造；造成

Fujimoto Hiroshi created the famous cartoon characters "Doraemon" and "Nobi Nobita."
藤本弘（藤子不二雄）創造了有名的卡通角色「多拉 A 夢」和「大雄」。

普 103

秒殺解字 cre(grow)+ate → 「創造」隱含「成長」、「增加」的意思。相關同源字有 creator (n. 創造者)、procreate (v. 繁殖)、recreation (n. 消遣)、recreational (adj. 娛樂的)、increase (v./n. 增加)、decrease (v./n. 減少)。

creative
[krɪ`etɪv]
adj. 有創造力的

This top-class international restaurant operated by Jamie Oliver is recruiting new cooks with <u>creative thinking</u>.
這家由 Jamie Oliver 所經營的頂級國際餐廳正在招募具有創意想法的廚師。

普 106 110
警特 108

---

creature
[`kritʃɚ]
n. 生物

It is reported that many people have witnessed the mysterious creature from outer space.
根據報導，許多人目睹了來自太空的神祕生物。

警特 107 109

詞搭 living creatures 生物

---

creativity
[ˌkrie`tɪvətɪ]
n. 創造力

Ludwig van Beethoven was <u>a man of creativity</u>, because his talent for music composition had left people awestruck and impressed.
貝多芬是一位富有創造力的人，因為他在音樂創作方面的才華使人們感到敬畏和印象深刻。

普 107

---

spatial
[`speʃəl]
adj. 空間的

An aesthetic house is subject to the designer's spatial arrangements and attitudes toward sustainability.
一個藝術美學的房子取決於其設計師的空間佈局和對永續性的態度。

秒殺解字 spat(space)+i+al →「空間」的。相關同源字有 space (n. 空間；太空)、spacious (adj. 寬敞的)。

詞搭 spatial <u>planning / concept / pattern / arrangement</u> 空間規劃／概念／格局／布置

---

private
[`praɪvɪt]
adj. 私人的、個人的；私立的

New mothers seldom have private time to relax and do things they like.
新手媽媽很少有個人時間可以放鬆和做她們喜愛的事。

普 100 110
警特 109

秒殺解字 priv(own)+ate →屬於「自己的」，表示「私人的」。priv, propr, proper，p/v 轉音，母音通轉，和字首 pre, pro 同源，核心語意皆表示「前」（before）。自己的事會擺在「前面」，因此衍生出「自己的」、「私人的」意思。相關同源字有 privilege (n. 特權)、proper (adj. 適合的)、property (n. 財產)、appropriate (adj. 適合的)。

詞搭 in private 私底下；private property 私人財產

反義字 public

privacy
[`praɪvəsɪ]
n. 隱私；私生活

The colleagues in my department like to enquire into others' privacy and enjoy spreading what they find out.
我部門的同事喜歡打聽他人隱私並且散播出去。

警特 105

| 詞搭 | an invasion of + sb's privacy 隱私權的侵犯 |

privately
[`praɪvɪtlɪ]
adv. 私下地

All my colleagues were discussing the matter privately, wondering what kind of decision I would make.
我所有的同事都在私下討論此事，想知道我會做出什麼樣的決定。

| 反義字 | publicly |

opportunity
[ˌɑpɚ`tjunətɪ]
n. 機會；良機

Jared is seizing the opportunity to cooperate with this international company.
Jared 抓住這次機會與這間國際企業合作。

普 100
103

🖋 **秒殺解字** op(=ob=before, toward)+port (=harbor)+un+ity → 船隻是否能順利進「港」，關鍵在於風，風決定了成功的「機會」高低。相關同源字有 im**port**（v./n. 進口）、ex**port**（v./n. 出口）、sup**port**（v./n. 支持）、re**port**（v./n. 報告；報導）、trans**port**（v. 運輸）。

| 詞搭 | a golden opportunity 千載難逢的良機；take / seize an opportunity 把握機會 |

| 同義字 | chance |

actually
[`æktʃʊəlɪ]
adv. 事實上、實際上

Actually, my mother is not my biological mother, but we do have a good relationship.
事實上，我的母親並非我的親生母親，但是我們關係良好。

🖋 **秒殺解字** act(do)+u+al+ly → 「做」、「行動」出來地，表示「事實上」。相關同源字有 **act**ual（adj. 真實的）、**act**（n. 行為；法案）、**act**ion（n. 行動）、**act**ive（adj. 積極的）、**act**ivity（n. 活動）、**act**or（n. 演員）、**act**ress（n. 女演員）、**act**ing（n. 表演）；re**act**（v. 反應）、re**act**ion（n. 反應）。

| 同義字 | really, in fact, in reality, as a matter of fact |

 **Unit 04**

---

recognize
[ˋrɛkəɡˏnaɪz]

v. 認出;承認;認可

The police are trained to recognize drugs which are being disguised.
警方受過訓練能辨識出偽裝的毒品。

普 99
高 108
警特 106
107
108

> 🖊 **秒殺解字** re(again)+co(together)+gn(know)+ize →「再一次」「全盤」「知道」,表示「辨識」、「認出」。

同義字｜ identify

---

recognition
[ˏrɛkəɡˋnɪʃən]

n. 認出;承認;認可

Our government intends to increase the educational budget <u>in recognition of</u> the advantages of early childhood education.
有鑑於幼兒教育的優點,我們政府打算增加教育預算。

普 107

詞搭｜ <u>beyond / out</u> of recognition 難以辨認

同義字｜ acknowledgement, identification

---

cognitive
[ˋkɑɡnətɪv]

adj. 認知的、認識能力的

According to some medical studies, cognitive impairment can appear suddenly or gradually while aging, and can be temporary or become worse day by day.
根據一些醫學研究,認知障礙可能在年紀增長時突然或逐漸出現,並且可能是暫時的或是日益惡化的。

詞搭｜ cognitive psychology 認知心理學

---

surface
[ˋsɝfɪs]

n. 表面

About 71 % of Earth's surface is covered with water and the rest is land, composed of continents and islands.
大約 71% 的地球表面是水,而其餘部分則是由大陸與島嶼所組成的陸地。

普 100
高 108
警特 107

> 🖊 **秒殺解字** sur(=super=over)+face(face) →「面」之「上方」,是「表面」。

詞搭｜ <u>on / beneath</u> the surface 表面上／下;come to the surface 浮出檯面

contain
[kənˋten]

v. 包含；裝有；容納

This product may contain some food allergens, so you should consider whether to buy it or not.
這項產品可能含有食物過敏原，所以你應該考慮是否購買。

🖋 **秒殺解字** con(together)+tain(hold) → 把東西「握」住「一起」是「包含」。相關同源字有 con**tain**er (n. 容器)、ob**tain** (v. 得到)、enter**tain** (v. 使歡樂)、main**tain** (v. 維持)、sus**tain** (v. 維持)。

同義字 | include

警特 105
107
109

---

report
[rɪˋpɔrt]

n. 報導；報告
v. 報導；報告

It's reported that a severe typhoon is coming toward Taiwan this weekend.
根據報導這周末有一個強烈颱風正朝向台灣前進。

🖋 **秒殺解字** re(back)+port(carry) → 把新聞「帶」「回」「報導」。相關同源字有 re**port**er (n. 記者)、im**port** (v./n. 進口)、ex**port** (v./n. 出口)、sup**port** (v./n. 支持)、trans**port** (v. 運輸)。

普 101
警特 109

---

organization
[ˌɔrgənaɪˋzeʃən]

n. 組織；籌辦

Many international aid organizations are NGOs which are not funded by the governments.
很多國際救援組織都是不由政府所資助的非政府組織。

🖋 **秒殺解字** org(work)+an+ize+ation → 表示「工作」的「組織」。**work** 當神隊友，**g/k** 轉音，母音通轉，來記憶 **org**，皆表示「作用」、「工作」。

詞搭 | a non-profit organization （NPO）非營利組織；illegal terrorist organizations 非法恐怖組織

同義字 | institution

普 105
高 108
警特 105

---

organic
[ɔrˋgænɪk]

adj. 有機的

This supermarket only sells organic produce and healthy food, which makes it simple for residents nearby to improve their diets.
這家超市只出售有機農產品和健康食品，這讓附近居民改善飲食習慣變得簡單。

詞搭 | organic matter / chemistry / fertilizer / food 有機物／化學／肥料／食物

普 102
高 108
警特 105

---

organize
[ˋɔrgəˌnaɪz]

v. 組織

The librarians organize the books on the shelves in alphabetical order.
圖書館員以字母順序來排列架上的書籍。

🖋 **秒殺解字** org(work)+an+ize → 表示「工作」的「組織」。相關同源字有 **org**anizer (n. 組織者；籌辦者)、**org**anized (adj. 有組織的)。

高 108

organism
[`ɔrgənɪzməm]
n. 有機體、生命

It's really amazing to know that the world's largest living organism is a fungus in Oregon, US.
知道世界上最大的生物是美國俄勒岡州的一種真菌，真是令人驚訝。

警特 109

詞搭｜ living organisms 生物體

---

industry
[`ɪndəstrɪ]
n. 工業；勤勉

There is a large population in the tourism industry influenced by the recent economic downturn.
有一大群旅遊業的人員受到最近經濟衰退的影響。

普 106 110　警特 106

秒殺解字｜ indu(=endo=en=in)+stry(build) → 本義在「內部」「建造」，衍生為「工業」的意思。

詞搭｜ the tourist / shipbuilding / textile industry 觀光／造船／紡織業

---

industrial
[ɪn`dʌstrɪəl]
adj. 工業的

The factory has followed a legal way of dealing with industrial waste.
這家工廠遵守合法的方式來處理工業廢棄物。

普 100　高 108

詞搭｜ the Industrial Revolution 工業革命；industrial park 工業園區；industrial relations 勞資關係

字辨｜ industrious [ɪn`dʌstrɪəs] adj. 勤奮的、勤勞的

---

establish
[ə`stæblɪʃ]
v. 建立、創立

The company was established in 1950 and since then, expanded its business worldwide.
這家公司在 1950 年創立，並且開始往全世界擴張其事業。

普 105　警特 108

秒殺解字｜ e+stabl(stable)+ish → 使「穩固」，表示「建立」。相關同源字有 established (adj. 確立的)、establishment (n. 建立)。

同義字｜ found, set up

---

defense
[dɪ`fɛns]
n. 防禦；辯護

The defense contractor stated that there were no buyers expressing their intentions of buying this new type of fighter.
這家國防承包商指出目前沒有買家表達對於這款新型戰鬥機的意願。

普 103

秒殺解字｜ de(away)+fens(strike)+e → 避「開」「攻擊」。fence 是用來阻擋「攻擊」的「柵欄」，可用 fence 當神隊友，d/s 轉音，來記憶 fend, fens，表示「打」、「攻擊」。相關同源字 defensible (adj. 可防禦的)、defensive (adj. 防禦性的)。

詞搭｜ in defense of... 以辯護……；legal defense 正當防衛；the Department of Defense 國防部；defense attorney 辯護律師

反義字｜ offense

defenseless

[dɪˋfɛnslɪs]

adj. 無防禦的、無保護的；不能自衛的

同義字　unarmed

We should all protect small defenseless children from being abused or neglected by anyone.
我們都應保護沒有防衛能力的兒童免於受到任何人的虐待或忽視。

---

defend

[dɪˋfɛnd]

v. 防禦；辯護

詞搭　defend... from... 保護……免於……

A lioness successfully defended her cubs against a ferocious enemy.
一隻母獅子面對兇猛的敵人成功地保護它的孩子。

曾 105
警特 109

---

defendant

[dɪˋfɛndənt]

n. 被告

同義字　the accused 被告

The defendant was accused of murdering his beloved wife and jeopardizing his children's lives.
被告被指控謀殺他心愛的妻子，並且試圖危害其子女的生命。

曾 101

---

principle

[ˋprɪnsəpl]

n. 原則；原理

秒殺解字　prin(first)+cip(take)+le →「第一」要「拿」的，表示最重要的，引申為「原則」。principal 是拼法接近的同源字，「第一」要「拿」的，表示「主要的」。

詞搭　in principle 原則上；a man of principle 有原則的人

字辨　principal [ˋprɪnsəpl] n.（中小學）校長 adj. 主要的、首要的

I refuse to compromise my principles by buying an overseas product.
我拒絕對我的原則讓步來購買海外的產品。

曾 100

---

operation

[ˌɑpəˋreʃən]

n. 操作；外科手術；作用；營運

秒殺解字　oper(work)+ate+ion →「工作」，表示「操作」、「外科手術」。

詞搭　come / go into operation 開始運轉；perform an operation on... 對……做手術；put... into / in operation 實施……中

同義字　surgery

A new metro line in Taichung will come into operation next year.
明年一條新的捷運路線將會在台中開始運行。

operate
[`ɑpəˌret]

v. 運轉；動手術；操作

Only Allen knows how to operate this machine because it's a top secret.
只有 Allen 知道如何操作這台機器，因為那是最高機密。

警特 107 108

---

operator
[`ɑpəˌretɚ]

n. 接線生；總機；操作人員

Angus is a computer operator in a large high-tech company.
Angus 是一家大型高科技公司的電腦操作員。

詞搭 | a computer / machine operator 電腦／機械操作員

---

operative
[`ɑpərətɪv]

adj. （計劃、法律等）實施中的；起作用的

Old insurance coverage is no longer operative, so you have to refer to new policies.
舊的保險範圍不再有效，因此您必須參考新的保單。

普 106

詞搭 | become operative 實施

---

source
[sɔrs]

n. 來源、出處

The police refused to reveal the sources of the evidence that cleared this man's charge of guilt.
警方拒絕透露讓這位男子有罪的證據來源。

高 110 警特 107 108

秒殺解字 source(=surge=rise) → 本義「上升」，引申為「來源」。相關同源字有 resource（ n. 資源）。

詞搭 | at source 在根源；a reliable source 可靠的來源
同義字 | origin

---

permit
[pɚ`mɪt]

v. 准許

[`pɝmɪt]

n. 許可證

Smoking is not permitted in public places as well as in some confined spaces.
在公共空間以及一些密閉空間中，抽菸是禁止的。

警特 105

秒殺解字 per(through)+mit(send) →「通過」錄取門檻，將人或物「送」入某個地點或機構。相關同源字有 permissive（ adj. 許可的）、permission（ n. 允許）、promise（ v./n. 答應）、admit（ v. 承認）、admission（ n. 准許）、submit（ v. 呈遞）、submission（ n. 呈遞）、omit（ v. 遺漏）、omission（ n. 遺漏）。

詞搭 | if circumstances permit 情況許可的話；if the weather permits = weather permitting 天氣許可的話；a parking / work permit 停車／工作許可證
同義字 | allow
反義字 | ban, prohibit

natural
[`nætʃərəl]
adj. 大自然的；不做作的；天然的

Examples of natural disasters happening recently are floods, hurricanes, volcanic eruptions, and earthquakes.
最近發生的自然災害的例子有洪水、颶風、火山爆發，以及地震。

普 110
警特 109

 秒殺解字 nat(birth, born)+ure+al → **nat**ural 是「天生的」，不假人工雕飾。相關同源字有 **nat**uralist (n. 自然主義者)、**nat**urally (adv. 天然地)。

詞搭 natural <u>gas / food</u> 天然氣／食品；natural enemies 天敵

反義字 unnatural, artificial, man-made

---

naturalistic
[ˌnætʃrə`lɪstɪk]
adj. 自然的；自然主義的

The English naturalistic painter Marianne North was notable for her plant and landscape paintings.
英國的自然主義畫家瑪麗安娜•諾斯是以植物和自然景觀的畫作聞名的。

高 108

---

volume
[`vɑljəm]
n. 量、容量；冊；音量

With this remote control, you can easily raise or lower the volume of microphones.
你可以輕易地用這個遙控器提高或降低麥克風的音量。

高 108

秒殺解字 volu(roll, turn)+me → 古羅馬時的書是寫在羊皮紙卷上，書籍似卷軸般「捲」起。隨著印刷機的發明，紙頁裝訂成冊的書開始取代卷軸式的書，語意衍生為「量」、「容量」。此外，音量最早是由一個可「轉動」的旋鈕來調控的，語意再衍生為「音量」。

詞搭 turn the volume <u>up / down</u> 把音量開大／關小

---

particular
[pə`tɪkjələ]
adj. 特別的；挑剔的

Maria is searching every store for a particular kind of succulent plant.
Maria 在每一家商店尋找某一特殊種類的多肉植物。

警特 106

秒殺解字 part(part)+i+cul(small, tiny)+ar →「微小的」「部分」也在意，表示「特別的」、「挑剔的」。

詞搭 in particular = particular 特別地、尤其地；be particular about... 對……很挑剔／講究

反義字 同義字：special, fussy, picky, choosy, selective

---

particularly
[pə`tɪkjələ˙lɪ]
adv. 特別地

Our CEO is particularly interested in collecting furniture from royal families.
我們執行長對收集皇室家族的家具特別感興趣。

普 106
警特 106
107

同義字 especially

charge
[tʃɑrdʒ]

n. 索費；控訴；負責
v. 索費；充電；控訴

The mayor dismissed the charge that he had misled the city government.
市長駁回對於他帶領市政府無方的指控。

警特 108

秒殺解字 char(=car=load)+ge → char 是 car 變形，本義是把貨物裝載到可以「跑」得很遠的馬車上，因此 char 亦產生「裝載」（load）的意思。相關同源字有 over**char**ge（v. 索價過高）、re**char**geable（adj. 可再充電的）；dis**char**ge（v. 允許離開；排放）。

詞搭 charge + sb. + for + 費用 向某人索取費用；charge + sb. + with... 指控某人犯了某項罪名；in charge 負責照料；take charge of... 負責管理……；be free of charge 免費

---

entire
[ɪnˋtaɪr]

adj. 整個的、全部的

He spent his entire life working in the hospital to save people's lives.
他花了一輩子的時間在醫院工作拯救人們的生命。

高 110
警特 107
109

秒殺解字 entire(intact, complete) → entire 和表示「整數」的 integer 同源，字面上的意思是「沒有」「接觸」過的，表示沒被汙染，仍是「完整的」。entire 的 **en 等於 in**，「沒有」「接觸」過的，表示「全部的」。

同義字 all , whole

---

entirely
[ɪnˋtaɪrlɪ]

adv. 完全地

Chester discovered the solution to this complicated riddle entirely by accident.
Chester 完全是意外地找到了解決這個複雜難題的方法。

同義字 completely

反義字 partly, partially

---

especially
[əˋspɛʃəlɪ]

adv. 特別地；專門地

I especially appreciate your patient guidance on my child and all the other students.
我尤其感激你耐心的指導我的小孩以及所有其他學生。

高 108

秒殺解字 e+spec(species, kind)+ial+ly → e 只是為了好發音而填補上去的字母，並非 ex 的省略。後期羅馬人發現把 e 加在 sp、sc、st 前面，會更好發音。special 本指獨特的「種類」，後指「特別的」，前面加了 e 並不影響單字的核心語意。相關同源字有 **spec**ial（adj. 特別的）、**spec**ific（adj. 特定的）、**spec**ialize（v. 專攻）、**spec**ialist（n. 專家）、**spec**ify（v. 具體指出）、**spec**ialty（n. 專長；名產）、**spec**iality（n. 專長；名產）。

詞搭 particularly

remove

[rɪˋmuv]

v. 移開；除去

Using boiling water is one of the good ways to remove a red wine stain on the tablecloth.
使用熱水是去除掉桌布上紅酒汙漬的其中一個好方法。

普 108
警特 106
109

（秒殺解字）re(back)+mov(move)+e → 「往後」「移動」開，表示「除去」、「移開」等。相關同源字有 re**mov**al (n. 移開)。

詞搭 remove A from B 將 A 從 B 中除去

同義字 get rid of... 除去⋯⋯

represent

[͵rɛprɪˋzɛnt]

v. 代表；象徵

Representing her husband, Clara attended the funeral of their best friend.
Clara 代表她的丈夫參加他們的好友的喪禮。

普 105

（秒殺解字）re(intensive prefix)+present → 本義「存在」，引申為「代表」。相關同源字有 re**present**ation (n. 代表；呈現)、re**present**ative (n. 代表者；adj. 代表性的)。

同義字 symbolize, stand for

01 ___ In the realm of business, people do not pay attention to how hard the _____ is. On the contrary, they only care about the outcome.

(A) process (B) excess
(C) access (D) success

02 ___ Marriage is an important _____ in life that is going to affect not only your family but also your partner's family. As a result, you need to think twice before making any decision.

(A) decision (B) recession
(C) transmission (D) aggression

03 ___ The meeting room in our company is not always _____. Thus, make sure you reserve one before our next conference.

(A) unexplainable (B) interchangeable
(C) available (D) reliable

04 ___ This bio-tech company mainly focuses on how to _____ genetically-engineered fruit with lower costs.

(A) introduce (B) reproduce
(C) seduce (D) reduce

05 ___ The official _____ of the police mentioned nothing about the reason behind the crime. As a result, people are furious and asking for a transparent investigation.

(A) involvement (B) development
(C) harassment (D) statement

06 ___ The terrorist group has _____ the attacks for years. The FBI is now tracing the source to find the man behind the scene.

(A) staged (B) qualified
(C) responded (D) defended

07 ____ There was no _____ to prove that the man is guilty of the
crime. After only a quick recess, the man was released without any
conditions.

(A) consequence (B) essence
(C) evidence (D) audience

08 ____ In the U.S., if you trespass or invade any _____ property, the
owner of the property has the right to shoot at you in self-defense.

(A) appropriate (B) private
(C) separate (D) ultimate

09 ____ In court, the judge _____ the suspect from middle school. The
two were classmates in middle school, but they followed two very
different paths. One became a judge, and the other became a criminal.
(A) authorized (B) recognized
(C) organized (D) localized

10 ____ On the _____, the case seemed simple and easy to solve.
However, after a deeper look, the detective found out that the case
was much more complicated than he had expected.

(A) prejudice (B) narration
(C) surface (D) abstraction

11 ____ The tourism _____ was devastated by the pandemic. With
every country shutting down the border, the profits from tourism were
reduced and it resulted in millions of people losing their jobs.

(A) dynasty (B) validity
(C) adversity (D) industry

12 ____ There are countless unsung heroes in the world. For example,
Alexander Hamilton _____ the foundation of America's economic
system, but few people knew about his contribution.

(A) punished (B) established
(C) banished (D) published

13 ___ The new regulation will come into _____ on the 16th of this month. As a result, be sure to pay attention to the date and details of the law.

(A) transaction   (B) destination
(C) operation   (D) extinction

14 ___ To keep the room clean and tidy, food and drinks are not _____in this room. As a result, anyone who brings food and drinks inside needs to take them out immediately.

(A) permitted   (B) transmitted
(C) committed   (D) admitted

15 ___ Emma Watson is a believer of sustainable fashion. She has used her visibility to promote brands that _____ her beliefs. She wears clothes that work with zero-waste factories and environmental-friendly materials.

(A) refuse   (B) repeat
(C) remove   (D) represent

attitude
[`ætə͵tjud]
n. 態度

Recycling can help students develop a <u>positive</u> <u>attitude</u> towards the use of resources on our planet.
回收可以幫助學生培養一個對於運用地球資源的正向態度。

曾 102

秒殺解字 att(=apt=fit)+i+tude → **apt**itude 和 **att**itude 是「雙飾詞」（**doublet**），簡言之就是同源字。attitude 本指畫像、雕像等藝術品的人物所擺出「合適的」動作或姿態，後指動作或姿態所呈現、反映出的「內心狀況」，引申為「態度」。

詞搭 an attitude <u>to / toward / towards</u> + sth. 對某事物的態度

字辨 aptitude [`æptə͵tjud] n. 性向；資質；
altitude [`æltə͵tjud] n. 高度、海拔

---

quality
[`kwɑlətɪ]
n. 品質；特質

Quality alone doesn't decide the prices of products, but mostly the supply and demand determines them.
單靠品質無法決定一個產品的價格，而是絕大多數由供需來決定。

詞搭 quality control 品管；quality products 優質產品

字辨 quantity [`kwɑntətɪ] n. 量

---

qualify
[`kwɑlə͵faɪ]
v. 使合格、使有資格；有資格

It takes seven years' training to qualify as a doctor.
獲得醫生資格需要七年的培訓。

曾 103
警特 106

秒殺解字 qual(of what kind)+i+fy(make, do) →「使」成為「某一類」的人或物，表示「使」其具有「資格」。相關同源字有 **qual**ity、**qual**ify、**quan**tity（n. 量）、**quo**te（v./n. 引用；報價）、**quot**ation（n. 引用；報價）、**quot**a（n. 配額），和 **what**（det. 什麼）、**how**（adv. 多少）同源，k/h 轉音，母音通轉；**qual**ity 和 **qual**ify 核心語意是「某一類」（of **what** kind）；**quan**tity 核心語意是「多少」（**how** much）；**quo**te 和 **quot**ation 核心語意是「多少」（**how** many）；**quot**a 核心語意是「多大一份」（**how** large a part）。

詞搭 qualify as + 職位 = be qualified as + 職位 有資格擔任某職位；
qualify for + sth. = be qualified for + sth. 有資格獲得某物

reduce
[rɪ`djus]

v. 使減少、降低；
減輕；使淪為

The company manufacturing instant noodles promised to reduce the amount of chemicals used in them.
製造泡麵的業者允諾會降低在泡麵裡化學物質的使用量。

普 110
高 110
警特 105
106

> 秒殺解字 re(back)+duc(lead, tow)+e →「拉」「回」，表示「減少」。相關同源字有 **educ**ate（v. 教育）、pro**duc**e（v. 生產）、pro**duc**tion（n. 生產）、intro**duc**e（v. 介紹；引進）、intro**duc**tion（n. 介紹；引進）、in**duc**e（v. 唆使）。

詞搭 reduce + sb. + to + Ving 使某人淪為⋯⋯

同義字 cut, decrease, lower

反義字 increase

---

dropping
[`drɑpɪŋ]

n. 落下；滴落物；
[軍] 空投；糞便 (~s)

It's really unbelievable that a consumer found rat droppings in his lunch box.
一位消費者在午餐盒中發現老鼠糞便，這真是難以置信。

---

drop
[drɑp]

n. 滴；下跌
v. 落下；降低、減少

The glut of pineapples caused a sharp drop in prices.
鳳梨的產量過剩導致價格的急遽下滑。

> 秒殺解字 dr 開頭的字大多是「跟水有關的動作或事物」，推測可能是發音會讓人想到「滴滴答答」的雨聲，**dr**op 表示「水滴」。相關單字有 **dr**ip（v. 滴下）、**dr**ink（v. 喝）、**dr**ift（v. 漂流）、**dr**ought（n. 旱災）。

---

religious
[rɪ`lɪdʒəs]

adj. 虔誠的；宗教的

Owing to different religious beliefs, the couple finally broke up and became friends again.
由於不同的宗教信仰，這對夫妻最終分開並再次成為朋友。

普 105

詞搭 different religious beliefs 不同的宗教信仰；a religious service 宗教儀式

---

religion
[rɪ`lɪdʒən]

n. 宗教

People should respect everyone's freedom of religion and political opinions.
人們應該尊重每個人的宗教和政治意見的自由。

> 秒殺解字 re(intensive prefix)+lig(tie, bind)+ion →「宗教」也透過教義、儀式將一群同溫層的人緊密「綁」在一起。可用 **lea**gue 當神隊友，**g/dʒ 轉音，母音通轉**，來記憶 **lig**，皆和「綁」、「束縛」有關。相關同源字有 **lea**gue（n. 聯盟）、re**lig**ion（n. 宗教）、ob**lig**e（v. 使負義務）。

factor

[ˋfæktɚ]

n. 因素

The main factor contributing to the difference is the reduction in the budget of training new employees.

導致差異的主要因素是因為降低了訓練新進員工的預算。 🔖 108

 秒殺解字 fact(do, make)+or ，「做」事情的「因素」。相關同源字有 **fact**（n. 事實）、**fact**or（n. 因素）、**fact**ory（n. 工廠）、manu**fact**ure（v. 製造）、arti**fact**（n. 手工藝品）。

詞搭 environmental factors 環境的因素

同義字 cause, reason, element

---

similarity

[͵sɪməˋlærətɪ]

n. 相似；相似之處

There were indeed some similarities between their exam papers, which aroused the teacher's suspicion.

在他們的考卷中的確有一些相似之處，因而引起老師的懷疑。 🔖 103

秒殺解字 simil(one, same, similar)+ar+ity → 「相似的」。可用 **same** 當神隊友，**母音通轉**，來記憶 **simil**，核心語意是「單一」（one），後來衍生出「相同的」、「相似的」、「像」等意思。

詞搭 bear similarity / a resemblance to... 與……相似；
striking similarity 異常相似之處

同義字 likeness, resemblance

反義字 difference

---

similarly

[ˋsɪmələˑlɪ]

adv. 相仿地；同樣地

Tracy and Pan usually dress similarly, so they are easily mistaken for each other.

Tracy 和 Pan 通常穿著相似的衣服，因此很容易被誤認為是對方。 🔖 103

反義字 differently

support

[sə`port]

n. 支持
v. 支持；供養

The members of the Legislative Yuan urge our government to support young people in all possible ways to start their businesses.

立法院的委員敦促政府用所有可能的方式支持年輕人創業。

秒殺解字 sup(=sub=up from under)+port(carry) → 「由下往上」「提」著，為「支持」、「支撐」。相關同源字有im**port**（v./n. 進口）、ex**port**（v./n. 出口）、re**port**（v./n. 報告；報導）、trans**port**（v. 運輸）。

詞搭 support + sb. + in + sth. 支持某人某事；in support 贊成；give support to... 給……支持

supporter

[sə`portə]

n. 支持者、擁護者

The President's supporters gathered in the square to show their passion for this country.

總統的支持者聚集在廣場上，以表達他們對這個國家的熱愛。

同義字 proponent

反義字 opponent

character

[`kærɪktə]

n. 品德；性格；人物；人格特質；文字

The main character Tom Sawyer in the novel *The Adventures of Tom Sawyer* is described as a naughty, troublesome, but intelligent boy.

《湯姆歷險記》裡的主角 Tom Sawyer 是被描述成是一個調皮、愛惹麻煩，但又聰明的男孩。

秒殺解字 最原始意思是「在……上雕刻（字或圖案）」（engrave），雕刻出來的符號或字母都有其象徵之意義，語意衍生產生「人格特質」、「性格」、「人物」等意思。

詞搭 a man of good / noble / great / sound character 有高尚品德的人

characteristic

[ˌkærəktə`rɪstɪk]

n. 特徵、特色；人格特質
adj. 有特色的；典型的

One of the wombat's characteristics is their cube-shaped poos.

袋熊的特徵之一是它們的立方體形的糞便。

詞搭 be characteristic of... 是……的特徵／寫照

同義字 feature, trait, attribute

trial

[`traɪəl]

n. 考驗；審判；試用、試驗

The letter that was read aloud during his trial turned 　📚 101
out to be a forgery.
在他審判過程中所唸出來的那封信結果是偽造品。

🖋 **秒殺解字** try+al → 試驗，衍生出「考驗」、「審判」的意思。

詞搭　be on trial for... 因……而受審；trial and error 嘗試錯誤

---

military

[`mɪləˌtɛrɪ]

n. 軍方
adj. 軍人的

Her husband serves in the military, so they can only 　📚 99
get together on weekends.
她的先生在軍中服役，所以他們成為假日夫妻。

🖋 **秒殺解字** milit(fight)+ary →「戰鬥」的，引申為「軍方的」。

詞搭　join the military 從軍；military service 服役

同義字　the forces

---

militia

[mɪ`lɪʃə]

n. 民兵部隊

The anarchists in this region started to form an anti-
government militia.
這區域的無政府主義者開始組成一支反政府的部隊。

詞搭　a left-wing militia group / leader 左翼民兵團體／領袖

---

militiaman

[mə`lɪʃəmən]

n. 民兵、國民兵

Many scenes of armed militiamen fighting in the
streets make the movie more appealing.
許多武裝民兵在街頭搏鬥的場景使這部電影更具吸引力。

---

maintain

[men`ten]

v. 保持；整理；維修保養；主張、堅持

The roads leading to the town were poorly maintained 　📚 102
after the election. 103
通往城裡的道路在選舉過後維護不善。 107
　📚特 105

🖋 **秒殺解字** main(hand)+tain(hold) →「維修」、「保養」一
開始是用「手」處理的。相關同源字有ob**tain**（v. 得到）、
enter**tain**（v. 使歡樂）、sus**tain**（v. 維持）。

---

various

[`vɛrɪəs]

adj. 各式各樣的

After the ceremony, cleaners tried to collect all the 　📚 101
garbage from various parts of the auditorium. 　📚特 109
典禮過後，清潔工試著收集禮堂裡各個部份的垃圾。

🖋 **秒殺解字** var(change)+i+ous → var 表示「變化」，有了變化
就是「不同的」。

詞搭　various kinds of... = a variety of... 各式各樣的……

同義字　diverse [daɪ`vɝs / dɪ`vɝs] adj. 多樣的

vary
[`vɛrɪ]

v. 變化;改變

曾 99

The symptoms of the disease <u>vary from person</u> to person and may fluctuate from time to time.
這個疾病的症狀因人而異,並且可能會不時的改變。

同義字 differ, change, diversify

---

variety
[vəˋraɪɪtɪ]

n. 變化(性);種類

曾 103
警特 106
107
109

There is a wide variety of red wines for customers to choose from in this winery.
這家釀酒廠有各式各樣的酒供顧客選擇。

---

equipment
[ɪˋkwɪpmənt]

n. 裝備

曾 105

My parents gave our camping equipment a final check before hitting the road.
在出發前,我的父母對於露營裝備做最後一次確認。

秒殺解字 equip(fit out a ship)+ment → equip 源自法語,表示將必要的用具、裝置裝備於「船」上,字源和 ship 有關;equipment 是「裝備」。

詞搭 <u>a piece(bit) / lot of</u> equipment 一件 / 很多裝備

---

opinion
[əˋpɪnjən]

n. 意見;觀點

Our principal is of the opinion that students are the most important assets to the school.
我們的校長認為學生是學校最重要的資產。

秒殺解字 opin(think)+ion → 表示「想法」、「觀點」。有字源學家推測,opinion 和 **opt**ion (n. 選擇)、ad**opt** (v. 採用) 同源。

詞搭 In + sb's opinion, … = In + sb's view, … 依某人之見,……;
public opinion 輿論

同義字 view, viewpoint, perspective, point of view

---

researcher
[ˋrisɝtʃɚ / rɪˋsɝtʃɚ]

n. 研究人員

曾 99
警特 109

The researchers found that 20% of the samples examined failed the inspection.
研究人員發現所檢查的樣本中有 20% 是不合格的。

秒殺解字 re(intensive prefix)+search+er → 表示「研究人員」。認真「找」是「研究」的重要精神。

image
[`ɪmɪdʒ]

n. 形象；意象；影像

The actor attempted to clean up his tarnished image after the scandal.
這名演員在誹聞過後企圖要端正他不良的形象。

> **秒殺解字** im(copy, imitate)·age → **im**age、**im**agine、**im**agination、**im**aginative、**im**itate [`ɪməˏtet] (v. 模仿)、**im**itation (n. 模仿) 同源，核心語意都是「**模仿**」。

詞搭　project the right image 樹立良好形象；a real / virtual image 實／虛像

📖 104
警特 105
106

---

imagine
[ɪ`mædʒɪn]

v. 想像；幻想

Please imagine you are the richest man in the world and what you are going to do with all the money.
請你想像你是世界上最富有的人，以及你將會如何使用這些錢。

詞搭　imagine (+ sb.) + Ving 想像……；imagine A as B 想像 A 成 B

📖 99

---

imagination
[ɪˏmædʒə`neʃən]

n. 想像力

The story caught children's imagination and therefore the author intended to write a sequel.
這個故事引起了孩子們的想像，因此作者打算寫續集。

詞搭　fire / stretch + sb's imagination 激發／發揮某人的想像力；capture / catch + sb's imagination 使某人出神入迷

📖 104
警特 105
107

---

imaginative
[ɪ`mædʒəˏnetɪv]

adj. 富有想像力的

Prof. Wei always welcomes imaginative answers to his questions, so don't be afraid to express your ideas.
對於魏教授提出的問題，他始終歡迎富有想像力的答案，因此不要害怕表達你的想法。

同義字　creative, innovative

📖 102
警特 107

---

sprinkle
[`sprɪŋkl]

v. 噴灑、撒

The pizza was sprinkled with some special herbs so that it was highly distinctive.
這個披薩上有撒了一些特殊香草，所以它才會如此獨特。

> **秒殺解字** spr 開頭的單字大多有「**噴灑**」、「**擴散**」的意思。相關單字有 **spr**ead (v./n. 擴散)、**spr**ay (v./n. 噴灑)、**spr**inkle (v./n. 噴灑)、**spr**ing (n. 彈簧；泉；春天；v. 彈起)、**spr**out (v./n. 發芽)、**spr**awl (v./n. 攤開四肢坐或躺；雜亂地擴展)。

詞搭　sprinkle a lawn 澆水於草坪

同義字　scatter

📖 101

express
[ɪk`sprɛs]

n. 快車；快遞
v. 表達
adj. 快速的；快遞的

The dancer expresses her emotions in her movements to the accompaniment of music.
有著音樂的陪伴，這位舞者透過動作表現她的情緒。

秒殺解字 ex(out)+press(press) → 將想法往「外」「壓」，意味著「表達」。相關同源字有 **press**（v. 壓 n. 新聞界；新聞輿論）、**press**ure（n. 壓力 v. 對……施加壓力）、im**press**（v. 使印象深刻）、de**press**（v. 使沮喪；使蕭條）、op**press**（v. 壓迫）、re**press**（v. 壓抑；鎮壓）、sup**press**（v. 鎮壓；壓抑）。

詞搭 express oneself 表達自己的意思；express delivery 快遞；an express lane 快車道

高 108

---

expression
[ɪk`sprɛʃən]

n. 表達；表情；用語

Sue always wears a poker face, so nobody can tell how she feels from her facial expression.
Sue 總是一張撲克臉，所以沒人能從臉部表情中看出她的感受。

詞搭 a facial expression 臉部表情；verbal expression 言詞表達

高 104
警特 106

---

expressive
[ɪk`sprɛsɪv]

adj. （善於）表達的；表示的

Giving 99 roses is expressive of a lifetime of love and commitment.
99 朵玫瑰表達了一生的愛和奉獻。

片語 be expressive of feeling / gratitude 表達感情／感激

普 101

---

prevent
[prɪ`vɛnt]

v. 阻止；預防；避免

This new legislation effectively prevents people from trafficking.
這項新的法令有效地防止人們進行非法交易。

秒殺解字 pre(before)+ven(come)+t → 本義「來」到「前面」阻擋，因此有「預防」的意思。相關同源字有 ad**ven**ture（n. 冒險）、in**ven**t（v. 發明）、e**ven**t（n. 事件）、e**ven**tual（adj. 最後的）、con**ven**ient（adj. 便利的）、con**ven**e（v. 集會）、con**ven**tion（n. 大型會議，習俗）、con**ven**tional（adj. 傳統的）、a**ven**ue（n. 大街）、re**ven**ue（n. 國家稅收）。

詞搭 prevent / stop / keep + sb. + from + Ving 阻止某人……，使某人無法……；prevent disease / progress 預防疾病／妨礙進步

同義字 stop

普 106
警特 109

---

prevention
[prɪ`vɛnʃən]

n. 預防；阻止；避免

There goes a saying that prevention is better than a cure.
有一句諺語是這麼說的：「預防勝於治療。」

詞搭 crime / disaster / accident prevention 犯罪／災難／事故預防

普 108
警特 106

medical
[`mɛdɪkl]

adj. 醫療的；內科的

The medical tests showed that he still needed more physical exams to find out the cause of the disease.
醫學檢測報告顯示他還需要更多的身體檢查來找出病因。

🔑 秒殺解字 med(heal)+ical → 「醫療」的。相關同源字有 **med**ication (n. 藥物)、re**med**y (n. 治療)。

詞搭 a medical school 醫學院；medical records 病歷表；a medical ward 內科病房

📚 104
105

---

medicine
[`mɛdəsn̩]

n. 藥（物）；醫學

Taking medicine has become a daily routine for him after he was diagnosed with diabetes.
在他被診斷出糖尿病之後，吃藥已經成為他每日例行公事了。

詞搭 clinical / preventive medicine 臨床／預防醫學；
practice medicine 行醫；prescribe a medicine 開藥方

📚 104
110

---

responsibility
[rɪˌspɑnsə`bɪlətɪ]

n. 責任

Sami people living in the Arctic bear the responsibility of protecting the natural environment and herding reindeer.
住在北極圈的薩米人承擔著保護自然環境以及放牧馴鹿的責任。

詞搭 a sense of responsibility 責任感；take responsibility for N / V-ing 對……承擔責任

📚 104
110
警特 109

---

response
[rɪ`spɑns]

n. 反應；回應、回答

To my surprise, the response to our new flavor of ice cream has been beyond our expectations.
令我驚訝的是，對於我們新的冰淇淋口味的反應是超乎預期的。

🔑 秒殺解字 re(back)+spons(promise) +e → 「保證」「回覆」就是會做出「反應」、「回答」。相關同源字有 re**spons**ible (adj. 負責任的)。

詞搭 in response to... 對……做出回應

同義字 reaction, reply

高 108
警特 105

respond
[rɪ`spɑnd]

v. 反應；回應、回答

The winning candidate <u>responded</u> <u>to</u> today's election results and thanked all who voted for him.
獲勝的候選人對今天的選舉結果做出了回應，並感謝所有投票支持他的人。

〔同義字〕 react, reply

學99
102
警特106

---

responsive
[rɪ`spɑnsɪv]

adj. 有反應的；敏感的

Johnson finally came out of the coma and was responsive in the hospital, but he was still in serious condition.
Johnson 終於在醫院脫離昏迷險境，並且有了反應，但情況仍然很嚴重。

---

authority
[ə`θɔrətɪ]

n. 權威；當局 (~s)；權威人士

The WHO should exercise its authority to direct international health work and help obtain the highest possible level of all people's health.
世界衛生組織應該行使它的權力來指導國際衛生工作，並且幫助所有人民獲得最佳健康程度。

〔秒殺解字〕 auth(increase)+or+ity → 「增加」。

〔詞搭〕 an authority on... 在……方面的權威人士；the authorities concerned 有關當局

警特105
106

---

authorization
[ˌɔθərə`zeʃən]

n. 授權；認可

Without the authorization of patients, medical records can't be revealed to others.
沒有病人的授權，醫療紀錄不能透露給其他人。

〔同義字〕 permission

---

authorize
[`ɔθəˌraɪz]

v. 授權；認可

Our accounting director queried who authorized this expenditure without his permission.
我們的會計主管詢問誰未經他的許可授權此項支出。

〔詞搭〕 詞搭：authorize + sb. + to V 授權某人去……

〔同義字〕 allow, permit

---

discover
[dɪs`kʌvə]

v. 發現

A lost leopard cat was discovered in a deserted house in this neighborhood.
在這附近的一間廢棄屋子裡發現了一隻迷路的石虎。

〔秒殺解字〕 dis(opposite)+cover(cover) → 「覆蓋」的「相反」動作，表示「揭開」，引申為「發現」。

〔同義字〕 uncover, find out

高110

discovery

[dɪs`kʌvərɪ]

n. 發現；被發現的事物

The discovery of Jack's being alive held great promise to his wife.
發現 Jack 有生命跡象帶給他的妻子很大的希望。

警特 107
109

| 詞搭 | make a discovery 有所發現；chance discovery 偶然的發現 |

---

undiscovered

[ˌʌndɪs`kʌvərd]

adj. 未被發現的

Archaeologists found that some undiscovered artifacts may worsen within a short time due to climate changes and pollution.
考古學家們發現，由於氣候變化和污染，一些未發現的文物可能會在短時間內惡化。

高 108

---

generally

[`dʒɛnərəlɪ]

adv. 一般地

Generally speaking, students' transcripts will be sent two weeks after the exams are taken.
一般來說，學生的成績單將會在考試結束兩周後寄出。

秒殺解字 gen(kind)+er+al+ly → 大家都是「同類」，表示「一般地」。相關同源字有 general (adj. 一般的，普遍的)、generalize (v. 概括論定；歸納)。

| 同義字 | usually, broadly, widely, normally |

---

generalization

[ˌdʒɛnərəlaɪ`zeʃən]

n. 歸納；概括；普遍化

The CDC makes several generalizations about the causes and symptoms of this uncommon disease.
疾管署對這種罕見疾病的原因和症狀進行了幾項歸納整理。

---

approach

[ə`protʃ]

n. 方法；通路；靠近
v. 接近

Kids are usually excited about the approach of trains when waiting in the station.
在車站等待時，小孩通常會對火車的進站感到興奮。

曾 105
高 108
警特 105

秒殺解字 ap(=ad=to)+proach(near) → 「往……」「靠近」。

| 詞搭 | an approach to + N / V-ing 做……的方法／管道 |

As Rita approached the woods, a rabbit ran out of the trees and surprised her.
Rita 靠近樹林時，一隻兔子從樹叢間跑了出來，使她驚訝不已。

| 詞搭 | be fast approaching = be near at hand = be coming soon = be around the corner 即將來臨 |

account

[əˋkaʊnt]

n. 帳戶；理由；報導；考慮

v. 說明、解釋

If you want to open a bank account, don't forget to bring at least two forms of identification.

如果您想開設銀行帳戶，不要忘記攜帶至少兩種形式的身份證明。

秒殺解字 ac(=ad=to)+count(count, compute) → 本義是「去」「計算」。相關同源字有 ac**count**able (adj. 應負責的)、ac**count**ant (n. 會計師)。

詞搭 on account of + N = as a result / consequence of + N = in consequence of + N = because of + N = owing to +N = due to + N = thanks to + N 因為、由於；take... into account = take...into consideration 考慮……

警特 105
106
109

---

distance

[ˋdɪstəns]

n. 距離

Being quite a good distance from the nearest town, the people here try to make themselves self-sufficient.

這裡離最近的城鎮有相當遠的距離，因此人們讓生活可以自給自足。

秒殺解字 dis(apart,off)+sta(stand)+ance →「站」「開」一點，表示「距離」。相關同源字有 di**st**ant (adj. 遙遠的)。

詞搭 in the distance 在遙遠的地方；keep + sb. + at a distance 疏遠某人；be within walking distance 走幾步路的範圍內

普 100
106
警特 107
108

---

technique

[tɛkˋnik]

n. 技巧；手法；技能

Our company has developed a new technique to help its employees to work from home.

我們公司開發了一種新技術來幫助其員工在家工作。

秒殺解字 techn(art, skill)+ique(study of) → 核心語意是「藝術」、「技巧」。

詞搭 techniques of / for + N / Ving ……的方法／技術

同義字 method, skill , approach

普 106
警特 106

---

language

[ˋlæŋgwɪdʒ]

n. 語言，措詞

Prof. Huang devoted his whole life to maintaining indigenous languages in Taiwan.

黃教授終其一生致力於維護台灣本土語言。

秒殺解字 langu(tongue)+age → 如果從轉音角度來觀察 tongue, language，會發現兩者是同源字，**t/l 轉音**，母音通**轉**。language 原意即是「舌」，從拉丁語 lingua 演變而來。有趣的是，漢語不少和說話有關的詞語也帶有一個「舌」，如「嚼舌根」、「三寸不爛之舌」、「舌戰」、「唇槍舌劍」、「油嘴滑舌」等等。

詞搭 mother tongue = native language / tongue = first language 母語；body / gesture language 肢體語言

普 103
109
高 110
警特 109

extend
[ɪk`stɛnd]

v. 延長；延期；擴大

The deadline for filing income taxes is being extended due to the coronavirus pandemic.
由於冠狀病毒流行疫情，所得稅的繳交期限得以延長。

🖋 **秒殺解字** ex(out)‖tend(thin, stretch)，「延展」「出去」。相關同源字有ex**ten**sion (n. 延期，延長)、ex**ten**t (n. 程度)、ex**ten**sive (adj. 廣泛的；大量的)。

詞搭 extend a invitation / congratulations to + sb. 向某人發請帖／賀詞

同義字 lengthen , prolong

🗒 110

respect
[rɪ`spɛkt]

n. 尊敬；方面
v. 尊敬；尊重

Teachers and students should develop an agreeable relationship based on mutual respect.
師生應在相互尊重的基礎上發展良好的關係。

🖋 **秒殺解字** re(back)+spec(look)+t → 「回」頭「看」，表示「尊敬」。相關同源字有 **spec**tator (n. 看比賽觀眾)、a**spec**t (n. 方面)、in**spec**t (v. 檢查)、su**spec**t (v. 懷疑)、per**spec**tive (n. 觀點)、pro**spec**t (n. 展望)。

詞搭 show respect for... 向……表敬意；hold + sb. + in high respect

同義字 admiration

🗒 101
108
🗒特 109

respectable
[rɪ`spɛktəbl̩]

adj. 值得尊敬的；相當不錯的

Harvard University is such an eminently respectable school that it attracts elite students from all over the world.
哈佛大學是一所非常受人尊敬的學校，因此它吸引了來自世界各地的精英學生。

🗒 103

obtain
[əb`ten]

v. 獲得

It is necessary to obtain the patients' permission if you would like to be in part of this project.
如果你想參與這項計畫，則必須獲得患者的許可。

🖋 **秒殺解字** ob(before)+tain(hold) → 「向前」「握」住東西是「獲得」。相關同源字有enter**tain** (v. 使歡樂)、main**tain** (v. 維持)、sus**tain** (v. 維持)。

同義字 get, acquire

🗒 103

immediately
[ɪˋmidɪɪtlɪ]

adv. 立刻、馬上

Details of the emergency meeting this afternoon are not immediately available.
今天下午緊急會議的細節尚未立即公佈。

🏆 105
108
110
👮特 109

> 🪶秒殺解字 im(not)+medi(middle)+ate+ly → 「沒有」「中間」間隔，表示必須「馬上」行動。

詞搭 immediately after ……之後沒多久

同義字 instantly, at once, right now / away / off, straight away / off, in no time, without delay, this minute

---

immediate
[ɪˋmidɪɪt]

adj. 立刻的、立即的

The government promised immediate action to help the unemployed.
政府承諾採取立即行動來幫助失業者。

🏆 101
105
107

詞搭 immediate response 第一反應；in the immediate / near future 在不久的將來

同義字 instant

---

observe
[əbˋzɝv]

v. 觀察；遵守

Dr. Smith has lived in the Amazon rainforest for a year to observe the local endangered species.
Smith 博士已經在亞馬遜熱帶雨林中生活了一年，以觀察當地瀕臨絕種的生物。

🏆 101
102
105
👮特 108

> 🪶秒殺解字 ob(before)+serv(watch, protect, keep)+e → 在「前面」「觀看」，表示「觀察」。為了「保護」法律、協議去「遵守」。

詞搭 observe + sb. + Ving 觀察到某人正在做……；under close observation 受到密集觀測

同義字 notice , obey

---

observation
[ˏɑbzɚˋveʃən]

n. 觀察

60 people were kept under observation in the hospital due to food poisoning.
由於食物中毒，有 60 人被留在醫院觀察。

🏆 105
107

詞搭 make an observation on / about… 觀測／評論……

---

international
[ˏɪntɚˋnæʃənḷ]

adj. 國際的

Colton is now employed as a financial advisor in an international company.
現在 Colton 在一家國際公司中擔任財務顧問。

👮特 105
109

> 🪶秒殺解字 inter(between)+nation+al → 在「國家」「之間」的。

詞搭 international relations 國際關係；international trade 國際貿易

internationally
[͵ɪntə`næʃənḷɪ]
adv. 國際上

This controversial movie will still be released internationally.
這部有爭議的電影仍將在全球發行。

智 107
108

詞搭 an internationally known / famous / recognized YouTuber 國際知名 YouTube 自媒體人

individual
[͵ɪndə`vɪdʒʊəl]
n. 個人、個體
adj. 個別的；個人的

Lola's philosophy is being aware of oneself as an independent individual.
Lola 的哲學是意識到每個人為一個獨立的個體。

警特 107
108

秒殺解字 in(not)+divid(divide)+u+al → 個體「無法」再「分」。

enemy
[`ɛnəmɪ]
n. 敵人

The Red King Crabs in Northern Norway have no natural enemies and can affect the local marine ecology.
紅帝王蟹在挪威北部沒有天敵，因此影響了當地的海洋生態。

警特 106

秒殺解字 en(=in=not)+em(=am=friend)+y → 「敵人」代表「不是」「朋友」。

詞搭 make an enemy of... 與……為敵

同義字 foe, adversary, opponent

反義字 friend

citizen
[`sɪtəzṇ]
n. 公民；市民

Senior citizens in Taiwan enjoy some discounts while taking a bus.
台灣的老年人在搭乘公車時可以享受一些折扣。

高 106
警特 108

字辨 resident, inhabitant, dweller

instance
[`ɪnstəns]
n. 例子；情況

This instance showed how important it is to check the safety devices before operating the machines.
這個例子顯示出在操作機器之前檢查安全裝置的重要性。

高 108
警特 106

秒殺解字 in(in, near)+sta(stand)+ance → 「站」在「附近」，表示近在咫尺，可以當「例子」。

詞搭 for instance / example 例如；take... for instance / example 舉……為例

同義字 example

01 ___ In this school, we not only teach you knowledge, but also cultivate your _____ in all aspects. We want our students become more than a test machine.

(A) altitude
(B) aptitude
(C) attitude
(D) attempt

02 ___ Due to the financial crisis, the company is planning a series of moves to _____ the cost. First, they will start by laying off unnecessary employees. Then, the budget of numerous projects will also be cut.

(A) introduce
(B) reproduce
(C) seduce
(D) reduce

03 ___ No matter your gender, race, _____, sexual orientation, age, ability or citizenship, all people should be equal and should be treated fairly.

(A) expression
(B) religion
(C) attention
(D) production

04 ___ During this hard time, everyone is in the same boat. As a result, the company is going to _____ every member of the team. We promise that no one will be laid off during the crisis.

(A) support
(B) discomfort
(C) comfort
(D) report

05 ___ When going to a job interview, make sure you show your positive _____ to the interviewers. Try to be passionate and open-minded. That way, you will have a higher chance of getting hired.

(A) characteristics
(B) errands
(C) glimpses
(D) specifications

06 ___ Disney is branching out into the online streaming business. They offer a 10-day free _____ on Disney Plus. People only need to register on their websites and they can enjoy thousands of free movies and TV shows for free for 10 straight days.

(A) arrival   (B) medal
(C) survival   (D) trial

07 ___ Under this chaotic situation, it is hard for the government to _____ order. As a result, the president ordered a curfew a few days ago to try to stop the riots.

(A) attain   (B) obtain
(C) maintain   (D) entertain

08 ___ As the saying goes, "_____ is better than cure." We need to think of a back-up plan before the typhoon hits the town.

(A) demonstration   (B) prevention
(C) designation   (D) transformation

09 ___ In traditional Chinese society, women have the _____ of all the household chores. However, people nowadays believe that everyone in the family needs to share the burden of household chores.

(A) simplicity   (B) penalty
(C) responsibility   (D) gravity

10 ___ He had neither the _____ nor the right to ignore the direct command from his commander. In his commander's eyes, he was no more than a piece of machinery.

(A) warranty   (B) feasibility
(C) unanimity   (D) authority

11 ___ The murderer tried all kinds of _____ to get near the target, but he failed every time because the security was airtight.

(A) approaches   (B) poisons
(C) monitors   (D) therapies

12 ___ The poor farmer begged the wealthy banker to _____ the due date of his payments. However, the banker didn't agree with his proposal and still took away the farmer's house.

(A) pretend
(B) offend
(C) extend
(D) comprehend

13 ___ The spy had _____ the enemy's camp for five straight days. She memorized every detail of the camp and drew it on a piece of cloth.

(A) preserved
(B) reserved
(C) observed
(D) deserved

14 ___ At the end of the semester, the coach will examine every _____ performance. Anyone who fails the test will be disqualified from the class immediately.

(A) merchant's
(B) tourist's
(C) passenger's
(D) individual's

15 ___ As a common _____, I have no way to fight against giant corporations. I need to gather all the help I can get and wait for a chance to organize a huge strike against them.

(A) citizen
(B) opponent
(C) specialist
(D) volunteer

obvious

[`ɑbvɪəs]

adj. 明顯的

It is quite <u>obvious that</u> the stock markets are influenced by the recent agreement between these countries.

很明顯的，股市受到這些國家最近的協議所影響。

📖 105

🪶 **秒殺解字** ob(before, against)+vi(=via=way)+ous → 在「路」「前」，因此容易被看見，表示「明顯的」。相關同源字有 **way**（n. 路）、**via**（prep. 經由）、pre**vi**ous（adj. 以前的）。

| 同義字 | evident, apparent, clear, conspicuous |

---

obviously

[`ɑbvɪəslɪ]

adv. 顯然地

Obviously, the students didn't receive any previous notice about today's speech.

很明顯的，學生們並沒有事先收到任何有關今天演講的通知。

| 同義字 | evidently, apparently, clearly, conspicuously |

---

population

[ˌpɑpjə`leʃən]

n. 人口；居民

The population of the white rhinos is approximately 18,000, but among them only two northern white rhinos are left.

白犀牛的數量大約是一萬八千頭，但是裡面只剩兩隻北白犀。

📖 107

🪶 **秒殺解字** popul(people)+ation → 表示居住的「人口」。

| 詞搭 | have a population of... 擁有……人口；a <u>large / small</u> population 人口眾多／稀少；areas of <u>dense / sparse</u> population 人口稠密／稀少的地區 |

---

populate

[`pɑpjəˌlet]

v. 使居住於

This area <u>is</u> heavily <u>populated by</u> foreign immigrants, so there are many exotic restaurants here.

很多外國移民居住於這個區域，因此這裡有很多異國情調的餐廳。

📖 108

| 詞搭 | a <u>densely (thickly)</u> / <u>sparsely (thinly)</u> populated 居住密度高／低的 |

treatment
['tritmənt]
n. 對待；治療

Our government provides special treatment to aboriginal tribes to assist them in preserving their culture and living environment.
我們政府提供特殊待遇給原住民族來協助他們保存其文化與生活環境。

 秒殺解字 treat(act toward, cure, heal)+ment → 「對待」、「治療」的名詞。

| 普 104 |
| 105 |
| 高 108 |
| 警特 109 |

詞搭 medical treatment 醫療；special / preferential treatment 特殊待遇／優待

同義字 cure, remedy

---

impatient
[ɪm'peʃənt]
adj. 不耐煩的

With so much that needs to be improved, the manager as well as all the colleagues is impatient for change .
有太多事情需要改善，經理迫不急待想要改變，而所有的同事也都是如此。

普 108

 秒殺解字 im(not)+pati(suffer)+ent → 「無法」「忍受苦難」的。

反義字 patient

---

audience
['ɔdɪəns]
n. 聽眾；觀眾

During this event, the audience was reminded that the key to fighting climate change in difficult times would involve cooperation and innovation.
在這個活動期間，觀眾被提醒在艱困時期對抗氣候改變的關鍵包括了合作與創新。

普 106

 秒殺解字 aud(hear)+i+ence → 「聽」眾，通常是看電影、戲劇或演唱會的觀眾。

詞搭 a large audience 一大群觀眾

同義字 viewer, spectator

---

deny
[dɪ'naɪ]
v. 否認；拒絕給予

The police denied Gene's claim that he was assaulted while he was in custody.
警方否認 Gene 宣稱自己在被拘留時受到攻擊。

普 100

秒殺解字 de(away)+neg(not)+y → 「不」允許某對象「離開」，引申為「否認」、「拒絕」。相關同源字有 **nec**essary (adj. 必要的)、**neg**ative (adj. 負面的)、**neg**lect (v. 忽視)。

詞搭 deny + N / Ving 否認從事……；deny + sb. + sth. 拒絕某人某物；
There is no denying that + S + V 不可否認，……；
deny oneself + sth. 克制某物

同義字 refute

反義字 admit, confess

shareholder

[`ʃɛr͵holdə]

n. 股東 [英]

The dividends of this company will be sent to its shareholders approximately at the end of this month.

這家公司大約在這個月底會發放股息給它的股東們。

🪶 **秒殺解字** share+holder →「股份」「持有者」，即「股東」。

警特 107

同義字	stockholder [美]

design

[dɪ`zaɪn]

n. 設計
v. 設計

All the public buildings should be designed from wheelchair users' points of view.

所有的公共建築都必須考量從輪椅使用者的觀點來設計。

🪶 **秒殺解字** de(out)+sign(mark) → 本義把「記號」畫「出來」，引申為「設計」、「指派」。相關同源字有 **sign** (n. 記號)、**sign**ature (n. 簽名)、**sign**al (n. 信號)、**sign**ify (v. 表示)、as**sign** (v. 分配)、re**sign** (v. 辭去)。

普 104

詞搭	by design 故意地；industrial design 工業設計

designer

[dɪ`zaɪnə]

n. 設計師

As a fashion designer, Olive is very sensitive to the material and texture of clothes as well as the cutting-edge trends.

身為一個時尚設計師，Olive 對於衣服的材質與質地以及最新的趨勢都很敏感。

警特 108

詞搭	a dress / fashion designer 服裝／時尚設計師

moral

[`mɔrəl]

n. 寓意；道德原則
adj. 道德的

Supporting the underdeveloped countries is a moral obligation of international communities.

支持未開發國家是國際社會的一項道德義務。

🪶 **秒殺解字** mor(manner, custom)+al →「風俗」的，風俗和道德相關，衍生出「道德的」的意思。

普 102

詞搭	a moral lesson 教訓
同義字	ethical
反義字	immoral, wicked

unlikely

[ʌn`laɪklɪ]

adj. 不大可能的
adv. 不太可能

It is considered unlikely that the committee will approve the cuts to the future budgets.

委員會將不太可能會同意減少今後預算的支出。

🪶 **秒殺解字** un(not)+like+ly →「不」太「可能」會發生的。

普 108

詞搭	be unlikely + to V 不太可能……
同義字	improbable
反義字	likely, probable

institute

[`ɪnstə͵tjut]

n. 機構；學院

v. 制定；展開

We have instituted some safety guidelines in this dormitory for students to follow.

我們制訂了一些這棟宿舍的安全守則讓學生遵循。

（秒殺解字）in(in)+stitut(stand)+e → 本義「立」於……之「內」，因此有「制定」、「展開」等衍生意思。

詞搭 institute / establish / set up a system 建立制度

The research institute confirms that an unidentified virus is the main cause of the syndrome.

研究院證實一種不明的病毒是這個症狀的主因。

institution

[͵ɪnstə`tjuʃən]

n. 機構

It would usually be suggested that people with dementia stay in a medical institution to receive more thorough care.

有失智症的人通常會被建議待在醫療機構接受更完善的照顧。

詞搭 an educational institution 教育機構

同義字 organization, institute

succeed

[sək`sid]

v. 成功；順利完成；繼承、繼位

If you want to succeed in business, you need to acquire a competitive spirit, critical thinking and discipline.

如果你想要事業有成，你需要養成具備競爭的精神、批判性思考和紀律。

（秒殺解字）suc(=sub=next to, after)+ceed(go) → 跟在「後面」「走」，因此有「繼任」、「連續」等意思。

反義字 fail

success

[sək`sɛs]

n. 成功；成功者／事

The foreign delegation visiting here hopes to emulate the success of our country's health insurance system.

來參訪的外國代表團希望能效法我們國家健保制度的成功。

詞搭 with great success 非常成功地

反義字 failure

successful
[sək`sɛsfəl]
adj. 成功的

To become successful, you have to try a little harder and make progress every day.
為了成功，你必須加倍努力並且每天進步。

普 99
高 110
警特 109

詞搭 be successful in + N / Ving 成功地……

反義字 unsuccessful

---

successfully
[sək`sɛsfəlɪ]
adv. 成功地

Many restaurant owners are forced to think about how to successfully pivot their business during difficult times.
許多餐廳老闆被迫思考如何在艱難時期成功地開展業務。

普 110

---

successor
[sək`sɛsɚ]
n. 繼承人、繼任者

The king did not have a son, so it was a difficult decision to choose a distant relative as a successor to the throne.
這國王沒有兒子，所以選擇一位遠親繼承王位是個艱難的決定。

普 108

反義字 predecessor

---

reflect
[rɪ`flɛkt]
v. 反射；反映；思考；反省

The investigation report clearly reflected the discussions made and the agreement achieved.
調查報告清楚地反映出所做的討論和達成的協議。

普 105
高 108

秒殺解字 re(back)+flec(bend)+t → 本義「彎」「回去」。

詞搭 reflect on + sth. / oneself 思考／反省……

---

settle
[`sɛtl̩]
v. 解決（糾紛）；定居；安頓

Many countries in the world are still trying hard to settle the problems of territorial disputes.
世界上很多國家仍然努力想要解決領土紛爭的問題。

秒殺解字 set(sit)+t+le → 「坐」落下來，就是「安頓」。可用 sit 當神隊友，母音通轉，來記憶 set，皆表示「坐」。

詞搭 settle down 安定下來；settle in 定局、遷入（新居）

---

settler
[`sɛtlɚ]
n. 開拓者；移民

The settlers block the main entry of this area because they found abundant deposits of rare earths.
這些定居者封鎖了該地區的主要入口，因為他們發現了大量的稀土礦。

同義字 colonizer, pioneer

structure

[`strʌktʃɚ]

n. 結構；建築物

The flimsy structure of this building can't even resist the impact of mild earthquakes.

這棟建築物脆弱的結構甚至無法抵抗輕微地震的衝擊。

(秒殺解字) struc(build)+t+ure →「建造」出來的成品，引申為「建築物」。

普 107
警特 109

同義字 | framework, architecture , building

---

project

[`prɑdʒɛkt] /

[prə`dʒɛkt]

n. 計畫

v. 企劃；預估；投射

They've started up a research project to investigate the impact of the electricity price system on households.

他們啟動一項研究計畫來調查電價制度對家庭的影響。

(秒殺解字) pro(forward)+jec(throw)+t →「往前」「丟」，表示「計畫」。相關同源字有 re**jec**t (v. 拒絕)、sub**jec**t (v. 使臣服)、ob**jec**t (v. 反對)、in**jec**t (v. 注射)、e**jec**t (v. 逐出)。

普 100
101
108
警特 108
109

詞搭 | project + sth.+ onto + sth. 把……投射到……

---

director

[də`rɛktɚ]

n. 導演；主管；指導者

Inspired by Steven Spielberg's films, Ives is determined to be a film director.

受到了 Steven Spielberg 的電影啟發，Ives 下定決心要成為一名電影導演。

(秒殺解字) di(=dis=apart)+rect(straight) → 設定一方向，「直」走離「開」的人，引申為「導演」、「指導者」。

普 110

詞搭 | a board of directors 董事會

---

staff

[stæf]

n. （全體）職員；幕僚

The sign reads "Staff Only", and therefore, we may not be able to go this way.

標牌上寫著「只供職員使用」，因此我們可能無法往這邊走。

(秒殺解字) 本指「木棍」，後指「警棍」、「軍棍」。以前跟隨指揮官的軍官常配戴「軍棍」，因此軍棍也用來代替一群「軍官」，後來語意改變，代指跟隨老闆的一群「職員」。

詞搭 | the teaching staff 全體教師

字辨 | faculty [`fækļtɪ] n. 教職員

progress

[`prɑgrɛs]

n. 進步；進展

[prə`grɛs]

v. 進行；進步

Scientific and technological progress has brought great convenience to people and enriched people's lives.
科學與科技上的進步已經帶給人們極大的便利並且豐富了人們的生活。

🖋 **秒殺解字** pro(forward)+gress(walk, go, step) → 往「前」「走」。相關同源字有ag**gress**ion（n. 攻擊）、con**gress**（n. 國會）。

📕104

詞搭 make progress 前進，進步；in progress 在進行中

同義字 development, advancement

---

progressive

[prə`grɛsɪv]

adj. 進步的；逐漸的

The implementation of a progressive taxation system is a challenge for the government, but it is good for the community.
累進稅率的實施對政府來說是一大挑戰，然而對社會來說是有助益的。

📕105

詞搭 a progressive change / decline 逐漸改變／下降

---

suffer

[`sʌfɚ]

v. 遭受；受苦

Derrick was fortunate to suffer no injury during the car accident while his friend was not so lucky.
Derrick 很幸運的在車禍中毫髮無傷，然而他的朋友就沒有如此幸運了。

🖋 **秒殺解字** suf(=sub=under)+fer(bear) → 在「下」方「承受」，表示「受苦」或「遭受」到不好的事情。相關同源字有dif**fer**（v. 不同）、in**fer**（v. 推論）、pre**fer**（v. 寧願）、、re**fer**（v. 提到）、trans**fer**（v. 轉移）、con**fer**ence（n. 正式會議）。

📕102
108
📙106
📘特106

詞搭 suffer from... 飽受（疾病）之苦，罹患（疾病）

---

sufferer

[`sʌfərɚ]

n. 受害者

Most cancer sufferers need psychological support and perseverance to go through courses of chemotherapy.
大部分的癌症患者都需要心理支持與毅力來經歷化療的過程。

📕99

---

suffering

[`sʌfərɪŋ]

n. 痛苦；痛苦的經歷

The drug did not relieve Vicky's suffering, so she was again brought to the hospital.
這種藥物不能減輕 Vicky 的痛苦，所以她再次被送往醫院。

同義字 pain, agony

feature
['fitʃɚ]

n. 特徵、特色
v. 以……為主要特色

The salient feature of this machine is its automatic judgment function drawing much international attention.
這部機器的顯著特徵是它吸引很多國際關注的自動判斷功能。

曾 99
104
警特 109

秒殺解字 feat(do, make)+ure →「做」出來的「特徵」。

Reading over the writer's novels and proses, you'll find that self-depreciation is featured often.
讀過這位作家的小說與散文後，你常會發現自我貶低是主要的特色。

詞搭 a significant feature of the age 該時代的一大特徵

同義字 characteristic, trait

circumstance
['sɚkəm͵stæns]

n. 情況；環境

Under this circumstance, we have to re-examine the impact that this new detergent may have on the environment.
在這種情況之下，我們必須重新檢查這個新的洗潔劑對環境的影響。

曾 102

秒殺解字 circum(around)+sta(stand)+ance → 一個人所「站」之處的「周遭」環境，引申為「情況」。

詞搭 Under no circumstances / By no means / In no way / On no account ＋ 倒裝句 絕不……

storehouse
['storhaʊs]

n. 倉庫；寶庫

Random Access Memory (RAM) is the short-lived storehouse for the data flowing to and from your computer's processor.
隨機存取記憶體（RAM）是資料匯入匯出你的電腦處理器的短暫存放區。

秒殺解字 store+house →「儲存」東西的「房子」，引申為「倉庫」。

同義字 warehouse

professional

[prə`fɛʃənl]

n. 專家；職業選手

adj. 專業的；職業的

Students with special educational needs can enjoy equal working opportunities and professional training.
特教生能夠享有平等的工作機會與專業的訓練。

普特 108

秒殺解字 pro(forward)+fess(speak)+ion+al → 對著「前方」「說」的，源自動詞 profess，原意是公開宣稱，後來衍生為「和需要接受較高階教育或訓練的職業相關的」。相關同源字有 pro**fess**ion (n. 職業)、pro**fess**or (n. 教授)、con**fess** (v. 承認)。

詞搭 go / turn professional 轉入職業；professional education / skill 專業教育／技能

反義字 amateur

---

professionali-sm

[prə`fɛʃənl͵ɪzəm]

n. 專業水準和操守

Safety, innovation, and professionalism are the key philosophy for our business.
安全、革新以及專業是我們事業的主要理念。

---

improve

[ɪm`pruv]

v. 改善、好轉；增進

Our company is trying to improve the working environment especially for those who are physically challenged.
我們公司試著改善工作環境，尤其是為那些身體不便的人。

普 100
107
普特 105
106
109

---

improvement

[ɪm`pruvmənt]

n. 改善

Continuous improvement in every possible way is what our boss expects.
在各方面持續不斷的改善進步是我們老闆所期望的。

普 101
普特 109

詞搭 (still have) room for improvement 仍有進步的空間

---

publish

[`pʌblɪʃ]

v. 出版；發表、公開

We have made special efforts to publish a compendium on issues about the reviving of the film industry.
我們已經做了特別的努力來出版一本有關復興電影業的手冊。

普 100
106
普特 106

秒殺解字 publ(people)+ish → 等同 make public，「出版」是讓「大眾」知道的。可用 **people** 當神隊友，**b/p 轉音**，母音**通轉**，來記憶 **publ**，皆表示「人」。相關同源字有 **publ**ic (adj. 公眾的 n. 公眾)、**publ**icity (n. 公眾的關注)、re**publ**ic (n. 共和政府)。

publication
[ˌpʌblɪˈkeʃən]
n. 刊物;發表、公布

The brochure on island vacations will be ready for publication by the end of this month.
海島度假的宣傳冊子將會在這個月底前準備好出版。

---

stylish
[ˈstaɪlɪʃ]
adj. 時髦的、流行的

This stylish Bluetooth stereo headset can serve as a remote control for your smartphone.
這個時尚的藍牙立體聲耳機可以當作是你智慧型手機的遠端搖控器。

普 103
警特 106

秒殺解字 style+ish → 「時髦」的。

詞搭 fashionable, trendy, hot, cool

反義字 unfashionable

---

complete
[kəmˈplit]
v. 完成
adj. 完全的;完整的; 完成的

This country should complete the reforms to help banks reduce the deficit and cope with the impact of the recent pandemic.
這個國家應該完成改革來幫助銀行減少赤字並且處理最近流行病疫情的影響。

普 100
警特 106
107

秒殺解字 com(intensive prefix)+pl(fill)+ete → 填「滿」,就是「完成」。可用 **fill** 當神隊友,**p/f 轉音**,母音通轉,來記憶 **plet**,皆表示「充滿」。

詞搭 complete + sb's college courses 完成大學學業

同義字 finish, total, whole

---

completely
[kəmˈplitlɪ]
adv. 十分地;完全地

This new model of car has completely changed the way we think, because its company has cooperated with another designer.
這款新車完全顛覆我們的想像,因為它的公司與另外一位設計師合作。

同義字 totally, absolutely

---

incomplete
[ˌɪnkəmˈplit]
adj. 不完全的、不完整的

Considering students "emotional feelings, schools should mark students" work "incomplete" instead of "failing".
考慮到學生的情緒感受,學校應該標記學生的作品為「未完成」而不是「失敗」。

高 108

同義字 partial

energy
[ˋɛnə·dʒɪ]
n. 能源；體力、精力

Wind energy technology with wind turbines makes the greatest contribution to this country's energy output.
這個國家發電量的最大貢獻是風力發電機的風能技術。

 秒殺解字 en(at)+erg(work)+y → 等同於 work at，表示「從事於」，引申為做事所需的「活力」。可用 **work** 當神隊友，**k/d** 轉音，母音通轉，來記憶 **erg**，皆表示「作用」、「工作」。相關同源字有 all**erg**y（n. 過敏症）、**org**an（n. 器官）、**surg**eon（n. 外科醫生）、**surg**ery（n. 手術）。

詞搭 energy crisis 能源危機；an energy-saving device 節約能源的裝置；energy drink 提神飲料；energy-intensive technology 高效能技術

衍生字 energetic [ˌɛnə·ˋdʒɛtɪk] adj. 活力充沛的（= active [ˋæktɪv] adj. 好動的；vigorous [ˋvɪgərəs] adj. 精力充沛的；dynamic [daɪˋnæmɪk] adj. 有活力的）

普 104
警特 105
109

workforce
[ˋwɝ·kfors]
n. 勞動力

An educated and highly-skilled workforce will be vital to help boost the world's post-pandemic recovery.
受過良好教育和高技能的勞動力對於幫助推動全球疫情後的恢復相當重要。

 秒殺解字 work+force → 表示「勞動」「力」。

詞搭 workforce diversity 工作多樣性

警特 105

compare
[kəmˋpɛr]
v. 比較；比喻；匹敵

Compared with the previous version, this new one is much more convenient and user-friendly.
與先前版本比較，新的版本更加便利並且方便用戶使用。

 秒殺解字 com(together)+par(equal)+e → 將兩樣有「相等」屬性的事物拿來做「比較」。相關同源字有 **par**（n. 相等）、**pair**（n. 一對、一雙、一副）、**peer**（n. 同儕）、um**pire**（n. 裁判），核心語意是「相等的」。

詞搭 compare A with B 比較 A 與 B；compare A to B 把 A 比喻為 B；compare with... 與……比較

高 100
普 108

comparable
[ˋkɑmpərəbl̩]
adj. 可匹敵的、可相比的

Our country now has comparable food prices to other advanced countries; however, our average wages don't seem to change.
我們國家的食物價格與其他先進國家相當，然而，我們的平均薪資似乎卻沒有改變。

詞搭 be comparable with / to... 可與……相比

普 105

comparative

[kəm`pærətɪv]

adj. 比較的；相對的

同義字 | relative

Fresh seafood and meat have become a comparative rarity in the remote area.
在偏遠地區，新鮮的海鮮和肉類已成為比較稀有的食物。

---

depend

[dɪ`pɛnd]

v. 依賴；視…而定

秒殺解字 de(down)+pend(hang) → 可在其「下」「懸掛」，表示可以「依靠」。相關同源字有 ex**pend** (v. 花費)、ex**pense** (n. 費用)、sus**pend** (v. 停止；懸掛)、sus**pense** (n. 懸念)、dis**pense** (v. 分配)、de**pend**ence (n. 依賴)、inde**pend**ence (n. 獨立)、de**pend**able (adj. 可靠的)。

詞搭 | depend on... = rely on... = count on... 依賴……

The values of fish depend on the quantities of the fish caught this season and their quality.
魚的價值視當季漁獲量和其品質而定。

---

dependent

[dɪ`pɛndənt]

adj. 依賴的

詞搭 | be dependent on... 依賴……，視……而定

反義字 | independent

警特 109

The wildfire season will be dependent on local weather patterns, duration of dry periods and wind directions.
野火季節將取決於當地的天氣型態、乾燥期的持續時間和風向。

---

dependably

[dɪ`pɛndəblɪ]

adv. 可靠地

Our company will provide 10 years of warranty protection dependably for all our products.
我們公司將為所有產品提供可靠的 10 年保修服務。

---

original

[ə`rɪdʒənl̩]

n. 原著、原文
adj. 原來的；原創的

詞搭 | an original edition 原版

普 103
106

The singer's original statement has been completely misrepresented by the media.
這位歌手的原始聲明已經完全被媒體所扭曲了。

秒殺解字 ori(rise)+gin+al → 從「源頭」衍生「開」，表示「原來的」。ori 表示「升起」，有「開始」、「誕生」、「源頭」等衍生意思。相關同源字有 ab**ori**gine (n. 原住民)、ab**ori**ginal (adj. 原住民的 n. 原住民)、**ori**ent (n. 東方)、**ori**ental (adj. 東方的)、**ori**ented (adj. 以……為導向的)、**ori**entation (n. 導向；傾向)。

originally
[ə`rɪdʒənlɪ]
adv. 原本；最初地

While this was originally done to protect minority students from being bullied, it turned out to label them.
原本這麼做是為了保護少數學生免受霸凌，可是結果卻把他們標籤化了。

同義字 | in the beginning, at first, initially

習 100
107

function
[`fʌŋkʃən]
n. 功能；職責
v. 運作、產生功能；擔任……的工作

With the success of its previous air fryers, this company has released a new version with an extra "keep warm" function.
由於之前氣炸鍋的成功，這家公司發行了有「保溫」功能的新型號。

詞搭 | function as... 充當……

習 101
106
108
警特 107

dysfunction
[dɪs`fʌŋkʃən]
n. 功能障礙／不良

Smell dysfunction is also a symptom of this contagious disease.
嗅覺功能障礙也是這種傳染性疾病的症狀。

秒殺解字 dys(bad)+function → 「壞的」「功能」。

習 99

additional
[ə`dɪʃənl]
adj. 額外的；另加的

Anyone who needs additional information regarding this event is encouraged to contact the office.
任何有需要有關這個活動其他資訊的人歡迎與辦公室聯繫。

秒殺解字 ad(to)+d(give)+it+ion+al → add 本義「給」，給了就會「增加」。additional 是形容詞。

詞搭 | an additional / extra + 數字額外若干……

同義字 | extra

manage
[`mænɪdʒ]
v. 經營；管理

Managing your time well means enjoying working efficiency and having more free time.
善於管理時間意味著享受工作效率並擁有更多的空閒時間。

詞搭 | manage + to V 設法並成功做到……

習 100

manager
[ˋmænɪdʒɚ]
n. 經理

As a good manager, you have to possess organizational ability and create innovative ways to connect people.
身為一名優秀的經理，你必須具備組織能力並創造嶄新的方式來連結人群。

108
警特 106

詞搭 general manager 總經理；assistant manager 副理

---

management
[ˋmænɪdʒmənt]
n. 經營；管理

The management of the local bikesharing service causes great trouble to both the city government and the company.
在地共享單車服務的管理，確實給當地政府和公司造成了很大麻煩。

詞搭 under + sb's management 在某人的管理下

---

advantage
[ədˋvæntɪdʒ]
n. 優勢；優點、益處

Some companies take advantage of the gray areas of their contracts, which lead to consumer losses.
一些公司利用其契約的灰色地帶，導致消費者的損失。

警特 107
109

秒殺解字 adv(av=ab=from)+ant(=ante=before)+age → 「從……」「前面」出來，表示占有先機、「優勢」。

詞搭 take advantage of 占便宜；利用

反義字 disadvantage

---

repeat
[rɪˋpit]
n. 重複
v. 重複

As the old saying goes, "History repeats itself."
如同一句諺語這麼說：「歷史會一直重演。」

高 108
警特 105

秒殺解字 re(again)+peat(=pet=go, seek) → 「一再」「去」「追」。相關同源字有 **pet**ition (v./n. 請願)、ap**pet**ite (n. 食慾)、com**pet**e (v. 競爭)、re**peat**ed (adj. 再三的)、re**pet**itive (adj. 反覆而無聊的)、re**pet**ition (n. 重複)。

同義字 reiterate

---

refuse
[rɪˋfjuz]
v. 拒絕

My brother working in a high-tech company <u>refuses to</u> divulge how much he earns.
我在一家高科技公司上班的弟弟拒絕透露他的收入

警特 109

秒殺解字 re(back)+fus(pour)+e → 「倒」「回去」，表示「拒絕」。相關同源字有 con**fus**e (v. 使困惑)、dif**fus**e (v. 使擴散；散布)、trans**fus**ion(n. 輸血)。

同義字 turn down, reject

motion

[`moʃən]

n. （物體的）運動；手勢

v. 向……打手勢；打手勢

Ben fears that the violent motion of the ship may upset his stomach.

Ben 擔心船的劇烈搖晃可能會使他的胃不舒服。

秒殺解字 mot(move)+ion → 「運動」。

|詞搭| in motion 運轉中；the motion of the planets 行星的運行

---

motive

[`motɪv]

n. 動機

詈 108

The police are investigating the motive of this bombing tragedy.

警方正在調查這次爆炸悲劇的動機。

|詞搭| a motive for murder 殺人的動機；of / from + sb's own motive 自動自發地

---

motivate

[`motə͵vet]

v. 促使、激發；給……動機

詈 100

The board of directors discusses the different methods that they can use to better motivate their employees and achieve improved results.

董事會討論了可以用來更加激勵員工並且提高業績的各種不同方法。

|詞搭| motivate + sb. + to V 激發某人從事……

|同義字| encourage, inspire, stimulate

---

motivation

[͵motə`veʃən]

n. 動機；幹勁；行動力

詈 107
警特 106

Students' learning motivation has plummeted due to the addiction to mobile games and lack of accomplishment.

由於手機遊戲成癮和缺乏成就感，學生的學習動機直線下降。

|同義字| motive

01 ___ Although the outcome of the game is _____, the losing team is still fighting hard to show their competitiveness. Everyone in the crowd is also touched by their spirit and starts to cheer for them.

(A) luxurious (B) mysterious
(C) nervous (D) obvious

02 ___ In Greek mythology, the Amazons were believed to have _____ Anatolia for hundreds of years. They were most famous for their military force, because their army consisted of only female warriors.

(A) legitimated (B) discriminated
(C) accelerated (D) populated

03 ___ After President Trump was diagnosed with corona virus, he was getting the best and latest _____. As a result, he recovered from the disease three days after he had been sent to the hospital.

(A) treatments (B) supplements
(C) compliments (D) advertisements

04 ___ After the extraordinary performance, the _____ gave the cast a standing ovation to show their appreciation and fulfillment.

(A) consequence (B) audience
(C) evidence (D) essence

05 ___ The lady took out her credit card to pay for her clothes, only to find that every credit card she got from her father was _____. It turned out that her father was bankrupt and the bank froze his accounts.

(A) supplied (B) applied
(C) accompanied (D) denied

06 ___ Warren Buffett told us that the only way to _____ is to work hard and be vigilant. He firmly believes in his motto, "Fearful when others are greedy, and greedy when others are fearful."

(A) exceed (B) dread
(C) succeed (D) breed

07 ___ Bill Gates goes on a one-week vacation every year to relax and _____ on himself. He will take the time to think about what he did wrong or what he could have done better.

(A) perfect   (B) infect
(C) reject   (D) reflect

08 ___ My grandfather was an immigrant from Taiwan. He came to America in the 1970s and _____down in New Jersey. At first, he could only find temporary jobs to make a living. However, through his hard work and determination, he finally started his own business of trading goods.

(A) sampled   (B) settled
(C) stamped   (D) whistled

09 ___ The new song of DJ Khaled and Drake _____ Justin Bieber as the main character of the music video. The combination of the three superstars certainly made a noise in the music industry.

(A) treasured   (B) featured
(C) postured   (D) gestured

10 ___ Considering the difficult _____ you are now facing, I will give you a payment extension. In other words, you will have an extra month to save and return the money to me.

(A) circumstance   (B) performance
(C) sustenance   (D) insurance

11 ___ After Lara Croft finds the final piece of the puzzle, the map will be _____. By then, we will know exactly where the treasure is.

(A) completed   (B) automated
(C) incorporated   (D) deleted

12 ___ The value of the goods _____ on the quality and quantities. I cannot tell you how much your goods are worth until I see them in person.

(A) concentrates   (B) requests
(C) depends   (D) insists

13 ___ The machine is not working properly. We need to send a mechanic down to the engine room to see which part is not _____ as intended.

(A) fashioning   (B) fabricating
(C) fastening   (D) functioning

14 ___ The first tip I can give you is that you need to show your _____ and hide you shortcomings. However, never lie to the interviewers. Because whenever you lie, you will need to come up with even more lies to make up for the first lie.

(A) percentages   (B) damages
(C) packages   (D) advantages

15 ___ Sherlock Holmes was trying to figure out the _____ of the suicide. He didn't understand why a happy person like him would commit suicide.

(A) moisture   (B) motive
(C) miracle   (D) motion

assure

[əˈʃʊr]

v. 使放心；向……保證

Measures should be taken to assure child safety and high standards of hygiene.

應採取措施確保兒童安全和高標準的衛生保健。

秒殺解字 as(=ad=to)+sure(sure) → 「去」「確認」。相關同源字有 **sure**（adj. 確定的）、reas**sure**（v. 使放心；使消除疑慮）、en**sure**（v. 擔保、確定）、in**sure**（v. 買保險；確定）、in**sur**ance（n. 保險）。

詞搭 assure + sb. + that + S + V 向某人保證……；assure + sb. + of + sth. 向某人保證某事

同義字 reassure, ensure, insure, make sure

avoid

[əˈvɔɪd]

v. 避免；躲開

Using VR to explore the city may be a good way to avoid crowds on weekends.

使用 VR 去探索城市可能是避開週末擁擠人群的好方法。

秒殺解字 a(=ex=out)+void(empty) → 本義「排」「空」。

詞搭 avoid + N / Ving 避免從事……；avoid...like the plague 避開……如瘟疫

同義字 prevent, escape, shun

select

[səˈlɛkt]

v. 選擇、挑選

Edward was selected as our class leader, beating the other three candidates.

Edward 擊敗了其他三名候選人，被選為我們班的班長。

普 105
警特 109

秒殺解字 se(apart)+lec(choose, gather)+t → 把「選擇」的東西「分開」來。相關同源字有 col**lec**t（v. 收集；聚集）、e**lec**t（v. 選舉）、neg**lec**t（v. 忽視、疏忽）、recol**lec**t（v. 回憶）、intel**lec**t（n. 智力）、**lec**ture（n./v. 講課；演講）。

同義字 choose, pick

selection

[səˈlɛkʃən]

n. 選擇

Director Wei will be hosting an open selection of emerging actors for the upcoming new movie.

魏導演將為即將上映的新電影舉辦新銳演員的公開選拔。

普 107

同義字 choice, option, alternative

selective
[sə`lɛktɪv]
adj. 精挑細選的

Our boss <u>is</u> very <u>selective</u> <u>about</u> who will be chosen to be on the team for this emergency case.
我們的上司對於應挑選誰加入這個緊急專案的團隊非常嚴格。

同義字 picky, particular, choosy, fussy

---

destroy
[dɪ`strɔɪ]
v. 毀壞、破壞

A man was reported to have destroyed the statue of a politician in the park and then was arrested for vandalism.
據報導，一名男子摧毀了公園裡一名政治人物的雕像，然後因破壞公物罪名而被捕。

秒殺解字 de(down)+stroy(=struc=build) →「建築」「倒下」，引申成「破壞」、「毀滅」。相關同源字有 **struc**ture (n. 結構；建築物)、con**struc**t (v. 建造、建設)、in**struc**t (v. 教導；命令)、in**stru**ment (n. 儀器；樂器)、ob**struc**t (v. 阻塞；阻止)。

同義字 ruin, spoil, devastate, wreck

反義字 build, construct

---

destructive
[dɪ`strʌktɪv]
adj. 有破壞力的

After the destructive typhoon, thousands of residents in the mountains still awaited the return of power.
強烈颱風過後，山上仍有數千名的居民在等待電力恢復。

普 106

詞搭 destructive force 破壞力

反義字 constructive

---

supply
[sə`plaɪ]
n. 補給品；供給
v. 供應

Threats from the global economic crisis are reordering supply chains.
全球經濟危機帶來的威脅正在重新調整供應鏈。

高 108
警特 105
　　 106
　　 108

秒殺解字 sup(=sub=up from under)+pl(=ple=fill)+y → 從「下」往上「填滿」，表示「供給」。

詞搭 supply + sb. + with + sth. = supply + sth. + to + sb. 供應某人某物；supply and demand 供需；supply <u>department / line</u> 採購部／補給線；supply for… 為……供應

同義字 provide, offer

contribute

[kən`trɪbjut]

v. 捐助；貢獻；促成；導致

Students from diverse societies <u>contribute</u> not only to educational excellence but also to acculturation.
來自不同社會的學生不僅為教育精進，而且也為文化的適應做出了貢獻。

（秒殺解字）con(together)+tribute(give, allot, pay) → 把東西「一起」「給」、「分配」、「付」出去。相關同源字有 **tribute**（n. 貢物；敬意）、dis**tribute**（v. 分發、分配）、at**tribute**（v. 歸咎於 n. 屬性）。

詞搭 contribute to... = bring about... = lead to... = result in... = give rise to... 導致……

指 102
高 108
警特 105
108

contribution

[ˌkɑntrə`bjuʃən]

n. 捐獻；貢獻

Doctor Lee was honored with a special contribution award for his lifetime devotion to the development of vaccines.
李醫生因一生致力於研發疫苗而獲得特別貢獻獎。

詞搭 make a contribution to... 對……貢獻

指 103

popular

[`pɑpjələ]

adj. 流行的、受歡迎的；大眾的

People are wondering what makes Zoe so popular in Taiwan.
人們想知道是什麼原因讓 Zoe 在台灣如此受歡迎。

（秒殺解字）popul(people)+ar(al) →表示有「人」氣的。

詞搭 be popular <u>with / among</u>... 受……歡迎

指 104
105
107
警特 109

popularity

[ˌpɑpjə`lærətɪ]

n. 流行；名望

The popularity of mobile devices causes serious conflicts between parents and children.
行動裝置的普及導致父母與孩子之間的嚴重衝突。

詞搭 <u>gain / lose</u> popularity 擄獲／失去人心

指 104
106
110

unpopular

[ʌn`pɑpjələ]

adj. 不受歡迎的

The comedian is becoming increasingly unpopular and is even suffering from depression.
這位喜劇演員變得越來越不受歡迎，甚至還罹患憂鬱症。

詞搭 be unpopular <u>with / among</u>... 不受……歡迎

temperature
[ˋtɛmp(ə)rətʃə]
n. 溫度；體溫

Our lab is testing the effect of temperature on the resilience of rubber.
我們的實驗室正在測試溫度對橡膠彈性的影響。

普 100
107
高 108

> **秒殺解字** temper(moderate, mix)+ature → temper 是「脾氣」，有好有壞，須持平「適度」宣洩，降低極端的情緒。temperature 本指「合適的」比例，1670 年才用以指「溫度」。

詞搭 take + sb's temperature 量某人的體溫；temperature control 控溫器

---

mission
[ˋmɪʃən]
n. 任務

Agnes flew to the earthquake zone to join an aid team on a mercy mission.
Agnes 飛到地震區，加入一個援助小組，執行救援任務。

警特 107

> **秒殺解字** miss(send)+ion → 被派「送」去出「任務」。相關同源字有 pro**mise**（v./n. 答應）、ad**mit**（v. 承認）、ad**miss**ion（n. 准許）、per**mit**（v. 允許）、per**miss**ion（n. 允許）、sub**mit**（v. 呈遞）、sub**miss**ion（n. 呈遞）、o**mit**（v. 遺漏）、o**miss**ion（n. 遺漏）。

詞搭 on a mission 執行任務；a trade / goodwill mission to Europe 派往歐洲的貿易／友好訪問團

---

reveal
[rɪˋvil]
v. 透露、揭露

The politician's autobiography revealed that he didn't take any bribes from anyone who asked for his help.
這位政治家的自傳透露，他沒有接受任何尋求他幫助的人的賄賂。

普 103
105
警特 108

> **秒殺解字** re(opposite, back)+veal(veil) → veal 等同 veil，「揭露」「面紗」，就是「洩露」、「揭露」不為人所知或藏起來的祕密。

詞搭 reveal a secret 洩密；reveal + sb's hand 攤牌

同義字 disclose

反義字 conceal, hide

---

revelation
[͵rɛvḷˋeʃən]
n. 披露、揭露

Elaine couldn't help crying after the revelation that her husband had cheated on her.
在 Elaine 的丈夫婚外情暴露之後，她忍不住哭了起來。

詞搭 revelations about / concerning + sth. 揭發某事的真相

090

measure

[ˋmɛʒɚ]

n. 度量單位;措施;手段

v. 測量;衡量;量起來有……

The newlywed couple is measuring the room for a new curtain.

這對新婚夫婦正在測量房間,準備新的窗簾。

普 99 / 100 / 110
警特 109

秒殺解字 meas(mens=measure)+ure → 「測量」。

詞搭 measure up to / ive up to / meet + sb's expectations 符合/達到某人的期望;precautionary / preventative measure 預防措施;take measures / action / steps 採取措施

insist

[ɪnˋsɪst]

v. 堅決、堅持

My grandmother insists on preparing every meal all by herself.

我的祖母堅持要自己準備每頓飯。

普 103 / 110
警特 105 / 109

秒殺解字 in(upon)+sist(stand) → 「站」在某處「上方」不移動,表示有所「堅持」。相關同源字有 consist (v. 包含)、exsist (v. 存在)、persist (v. 堅持)、resist (v. 抗拒)。

詞搭 insist that + S + 一般時態動詞 堅信……;insist that + S + (should) + 原形動詞 堅持要求……

admit

[ədˋmɪt]

v. 容許;准許入場/入學;承認

At the beginning, Allen denied that he stole the bike, but later he grudgingly admitted it.

一開始,Allen 否認他偷了自行車,但後來他勉強承認了。

警特 105 / 108

秒殺解字 ad(to)+mit(send) → 「往……」「送」,表示「承認」、「准許」。

同義字 confess, acknowledge

反義字 deny

tradition

[trəˋdɪʃən]

n. 傳統

It is a Taiwanese tradition to hold a ceremony in the 7th lunar month in order to comfort "good brothers."

在農曆七月舉行儀式來祭拜「好兄弟」是一種台灣傳統。

警特 105 / 109

秒殺解字 tra(=trans=over)+d(give)+it+ion → 「跨越」世代,傳承「給予」。

詞搭 by tradition 按傳統

同義字 convention, custom

traditional
[trə`dɪʃənḷ]
adj. 傳統的

A traditional British Sunday lunch, also called the Sunday roast, contains roast meat along with Yorkshire Pudding, gravy, and vegetables.
傳統的英國周日午餐，也稱為周日烤肉，包含烤肉、約克夏布丁、肉汁以及蔬菜。

普 107

詞搭 traditional industries 傳統產業

同義字 conventional

---

traditionally
[trə`dɪʃənḷɪ]
adv. 傳統上

Traditionally, Chinese people will give red envelopes to their families on Lunar New Year.
傳統上，中國人會在農曆新年時給家人紅包。

普 100

---

affect
[ə`fɛkt]
v. 影響；(疾病)侵襲；感動；假裝

It is this infectious disease that affects people's lives in every aspect.
正是這種傳染病在各個方面影響著人們的生活。

普 105
106
110

秒殺解字 af(=ad=to)+fec(do, make)+t → 「去」「做」，表示「影響」。相關同源字有 ef**fect**（n. 影響）、de**fect**（n. 缺點）、per**fect**（adj. 完美的）、in**fect**（v. 傳染）

---

affected
[ə`fɛktɪd]
adj. 做作的；受到影響的；受(疾病)侵襲的

Eric had brain damage from an accident, and he made an appointment at the hospital to scan the affected area of the brain.
Eric 因意外而腦部受損，於是他到醫院預約做受影響區域的掃描檢查。

---

agent
[`edʒənt]
n. 代理商；經紀人

The undercover agent confessed that he had revealed the secret rendezvous to others.
臥底供稱，他已將祕密聚會地點透露給其他人。

普 101
105
警特 107

秒殺解字 ag(do)+ent → 幫你「做」事者。可用 **act** 當神隊友，**k/d** 轉音，母音通轉，來記憶 **ag**，皆表示「做」、「行動」。相關同源字有 **ag**enda（n. 議程）。

詞搭 a sole agent 獨家代理商

---

agency
[`edʒənsɪ]
n. 代辦處；機關

People can expect that there will be a plunge in profits in travel agencies around the world this year.
人們可以預期，今年全球旅行社的利潤將暴跌。

警特 106

詞搭 a news agency 新聞通訊社；a(n) travel / advertising / detective agency 旅行／廣告／偵探社；a general agency 總代理店

division

[də`vɪʒən]

n. 分配；分裂；部門；除法

Tom has been transferred to the sales division, and Susan will take his position from now on.
Tom 已被調到銷售部門，Susan 將從現在開始接替他的職位。

🖊 **秒殺解字** di(apart)+vis(=vid=separate)+ion → division 源自動詞 divide，由「分開」（**di = apart**）和「分開」（**vid = separate**）所組成，「寡婦」（widow）是 divide 的同源字，**v/w** 對應，母音通轉，因為寡婦永遠與丈夫「分開」。

🔖 100

---

encourage

[ɪn`kɝɪdʒ]

v. 鼓勵；助長

The local council launched a campaign to encourage residents to use public transportation.
地方議會發起了一項運動，鼓勵居民使用公共交通工具。

🖊 **秒殺解字** en(make)+courage →「使」人有「勇氣」，表示「鼓勵」。

反義字 discourage

🔖 103
106
107

---

frequently

[`frikwəntlɪ]

adv. 經常地、頻繁地

Winston is organizing the frequently asked questions on how to use the software and is posting them online.
Winston 正在整理有關如何使用此軟體的常見問題並將它們發布在網路上。

🖊 **秒殺解字** frequent(crowded, full)+ly → 經常地。

詞搭 frequently asked questions 常見問題（FAQ）

🔖 103
104

---

frequency

[`frikwənsɪ]

n. 頻率

The frequency of extreme droughts and floods across the world is predicted to rise due to the greenhouse effect.
由於溫室效應，全球極端乾旱和洪水的頻率預計將會增加。

詞搭 frequency modulation 調頻廣播（FM）

connect
[kə`nɛkt]
v. 連結、關聯

The engineers in this department are responsible for ensuring that all the machines are connected to a stable power supply.
此部門的工程師負責確保所有機器都連接到穩定的電源。

 秒殺解字 con(together)+nect(tie) →「綁」在「一起」。

詞搭 | connect A with B 將 A 與 B 聯想在一起；connect A to B 使 A 與 B 有關聯

反義字 | disconnect

---

connection
[kə`nɛkʃən]
n. 關係、關聯

The connection between the stock markets and the public health is still being studied by a group of experts.　　　　警特 106
一群專家仍在研究股票市場與大眾健康之間的關係。

詞搭 | have a connection with... 和⋯⋯有關係

同義字 | association, relation, link

facility
[fə`sɪlətɪ]
n. 設備；設施

The government is upgrading public facilities for people to use them more conveniently.
政府正在升級公共設施，使人們使用起來更加便利。

普 103
警特 106
109

🔖(秒殺解字) fac(=easy, do)+ile+ity → 「讓人「做」事「容易」的「設施」。

詞搭 sports / educational / nuclear facilities 運動／教育／核子設施；give / accord / afford + sb. + full facilities for... 給予某人……的充分便利

demand
[dɪ`mænd]
v. **n.** 要求；需求

Some stock investors saw the overwhelming demand for cleaning supplies and sanitizers.
一些股票投資者看到了對於清潔用品和消毒劑的大量需求。

普 107

🔖(秒殺解字) de(completely)+mand(order) → 「命令」對方「全」照自己意思行事。相關同源字有 com**mand**（v./n. 命令、指揮）、de**mand**（v. 強烈要求）、**mand**atory（adj. 強制的、法定的）、recom**mend**（v. 建議；推薦）。

詞搭 meet / satisfy + sb's demands 達到某人的要求；be in demand 有需求；on demand 備索；supply and demand 供需

同義字 request

communicate
[kə`mjunə͵ket]
v. 傳達；溝通

Vibration is one of the means that animals use to communicate with each other, and jumping spiders are one such example that uses vibration.
振動是動物相互交流的溝通方式之一，而跳蛛（蠅虎）就是利用振動的其中一個例子。

普 102

🔖(秒殺解字) commun(common)+ic+ate → 有「共同的」的語言才能「溝通」、「傳達」。

詞搭 communicate with + sb. 與某人溝通

communica-tion
[kə͵mjunə`keʃən]

n. 聯絡；通訊；傳播（學）

After the devastating tsunami, all sorts of communications were broken and the city was a living hell.
毀滅性極大的海嘯過後，各種通訊中斷了，這座城市就像一個地獄。

| 曾 99 |
| 100 |
| 警特 106 |

詞搭 mass communication 大眾傳播（學）；be in mutual communication with... 與……互通訊息；a means of communication 交通工具

---

justice
[`dʒʌstɪs]

n. 公道；公平正義；司法審判

The man pleaded innocence and called for social justice, hoping that the case would be re-investigated.
那男子辯稱無罪，並且呼籲社會公正，希望此案能得到重新調查。

曾 100

秒殺解字 just(law, right)+ice → 本義「法律」、「正當的」，引申為「公平正義」。

詞搭 social justice 社會正義；a sense of justice 正義感；do + sb. / sth. + justice = do justice to + sb. / sth. 公平對待某人／某事；bring + sb. + to justice 使某人歸案受審

同義字 fairness

反義字 injustice

---

employee
[͵ɪmplɔɪ`i]

n. 員工、雇員

Jessica was elected as the Employee of the Month and was awarded 1000 dollars.
Jessica 當選本月最佳員工，並獲得 1000 美元獎金。

| 曾 100 |
| 103 |
| 104 |

秒殺解字 employ+ee → 「被」「雇」者，字尾 **ee** 源自法文，表示「被……者」，如：train**ee**、interview**ee**，和表示「動作的執行者」的字尾 **or**、**er**，形成對比。

詞搭 the elimination of surplus employees 裁減冗員

同義字 worker

---

employer
[ɪm`plɔɪɚ]

n. 雇主、老闆

Employers should reimburse a certain portion of costs from Internet to utilities while their employees work from home.
當員工在家工作時，從網路費到基本水電，雇主應補償部分費用給員工。

曾 102

experiment
[ɪk`spɛrəmənt]

n. 實驗;試驗
v. 實驗;試驗

Scientists are <u>conducting an experiment</u> on how the temperature would affect the existence of viruses.
科學家們正在進行有關溫度如何影響病毒存在的實驗。

🏛 106
警特 105

秒殺解字 ex(out)+per(try, risk)+i+ment ,到「外面」「嘗試」、「冒險」,表示「實驗」。可用表示「恐懼」的 **fear** 當神隊友,**p/f 轉音**,母音通轉,來記憶 **per**,表示「嘗試」、「冒險」,因為「嘗試」或「冒險」過程中,遇到未知事物,容易產生「**恐懼**」情緒。相關同源字有 ex**per**ience (n./v. 經驗)、ex**per**t (n. 專家)。

詞搭 | <u>conduct / do / perform / carry out / make</u> an experiment 做實驗;experiment <u>on / with</u> + sth. 對某物作實驗

attempt
[ə`tɛmpt]

n. 企圖;嘗試

It is reported that a prisoner attempted to escape from the jail while he took out the garbage.
報導指出,一名囚犯在倒垃圾時試圖逃獄。

🏛 99
警特 107

秒殺解字 at(=ad=to)+tempt(try) → 「去」「嘗試」。

詞搭 | make an attempt + to V = attempt + to V 企圖要……;in an attempt + to V;an attempt at murder 殺人未遂

aware
[ə`wɛr]

adj. 知道的;察覺的

More and more people are aware of the importance of environmental protection and pollution reduction.
越來越多的人意識到環境保護和降低污染的重要性。

警特 108

秒殺解字 a(intensive prefix)+ware(wary, careful) → 「小心」翼翼去「察覺」、「意識」。

詞搭 | be <u>aware / conscious</u> of... 知道……,察覺到……;be aware that + S+ V 知道…

同義字 | conscious

反義字 | unaware

crisis
[`kraɪsɪs]

n. 危機 (crises [`kraɪsiz] pl.)

The global financial crisis in 2008 brought about severe depression and the loss of confidence from all the investors.
2008 年的全球金融危機帶來了嚴重的蕭條,並使所有投資者失去了信心。

秒殺解字 cr(decide, judge)+is(it)+is → 「緊急關頭」需正確「判斷」,做正確「決定」。

詞搭 | oil crisis 石油危機;be in crisis 處於危機之中

memory
[`mɛmərɪ]
n. 記憶力；回憶

Studies show that dogs have short memories, and they tend to forget an event in two minutes.
研究顯示，狗的記憶力很短，往往會在兩分鐘內忘記一件事。

警特 106 109

🪶 秒殺解字 memor(remember)+y → 「記憶力」、「回憶」。

詞搭 in memory of... 以紀念……；if my memory serves me correctly / right 如果我沒記錯；to + sb's memory = to the memory of + sb. 紀念 (已故的) ……

memorable
[`mɛmərəbl]
adj. 難忘的；值得紀念的

David is trying to write a memorable obituary for his beloved grandfather.
David 正試圖為他心愛的祖父寫一篇令人難忘的訃聞。

普 107

同義字 unforgettable

memorize
[`mɛmə͵raɪz]
v. 背誦、記憶

In times of solitary living, memorizing poetry and listening to music can serve as a calming agent.
在獨居的生活中，背詩和聽音樂可以具有撫慰作用。

**普 99
警特 106**

memoir
[`mɛmwɑr]
n. 回憶錄；自傳

Amanda described how she faced the childhood tragedy in her memoirs.
Amanda 在回憶錄中描述了她如何面對童年的悲劇。

status
[`stetəs / `stætəs]
n. 地位；身分；情況

The social status of women in India hasn't improved over the past few years.
在過去的幾年中，印度女性的社會地位沒有改善。

普 105

🪶 秒殺解字 stat(stand)+ us → 所「站」的「狀態」，表示「身分」、「地位」。

詞搭 marital status 婚姻狀況；status symbol 地位的象徵

status quo
[͵stetəs`kwo / ͵stætəs`kwo]
n. 現狀

The two countries held peace talks and reached a consensus to maintain the status quo.
兩國舉行了和平談判，並達成共識維持現狀。

secure
[sɪ`kjʊr]

v. 獲得；弄牢
adj. 安全的

It's getting harder and harder to secure a place to live in big cities.
越來越難在大城市中謀求居住的地方了。

警指 105
106
108

🖋 **秒殺解字** se(free from)+cure(care) → 「不用」「擔心」，表示「安全的」、「穩固的」、「有信心的」。

詞搭 ┊ secure a contract 取得一份合約；secure a ladder with a rope 以繩索把梯子繫緊

同義字 ┊ confident

反義字 ┊ insecure

security
[sɪ`kjʊrətɪ]

n. 安全

A mother's arms are the most comfortable place for babies, because they provide a <u>sense of</u> security.
母親的手臂是嬰兒最舒適的地方，因為它們可以提供安全感。

普 102
警指 108
109

詞搭 ┊ sense of security 安全感；security guard 警衛

atmosphere
[`ætməs͵fɪr]

n. 大氣；空氣；氛圍

Factories are not allowed to release toxic gases into the atmosphere.
工廠不能夠排放有毒氣體至大氣當中。

高 108
警指 108

🖋 **秒殺解字** atmo(vapor, steam)+sphere(ball, globe) → 圍繞在「球體（地球）」的一層「氣層」。相關同源字有 **sphere**（ n. 球體；範圍 ）、hemi**sphere**（ n. 半球 ）、bio**sphere**（ n. 生物圈 ）、 eco**sphere**（ n. 生態圈 ）。

詞搭 ┊ a tense atmosphere 緊繃的氣氛；atmosphere person 製造氣氛的人

atmospheric
[͵ætməs`fɛrɪk]

adj. 大氣的；有藝術氛圍的

The atmospheric decor indeed makes the restaurant go viral among Internet celebrities.
獨特氛圍的裝飾確實讓這家餐廳在網紅中造成轟動。

高 108

詞搭 ┊ atmospheric <u>music / lighting</u> 氣氛音樂／照明；atmospheric pressure 大氣壓力

replace
[rɪ`ples]

v. 取代；替換

The employer <u>replaced</u> the permanent staff <u>with</u> part-time workers in order to cut down on costs.
雇主用兼職人員來取代長期職員，以降低成本。

🈂普 103

（秒殺解字）re(back, again)+place → 「再」「回到」「位置」上，表示「代替」、「更換」。

詞搭 A replace B = A take the place of B = A take B's place = A substitute for B　A 代替 B；replace B with A = substitute A for B　用 A 代替 B；replace a dead battery 更換沒電的電瓶

同義字 displace

---

device
[dɪ`vaɪs]

n. 裝置；設計；儀器；設備

Museums must install thermostatic devices for controlling temperature so as to protect the paintings and antiques.
博物館必須安裝可以控制溫度的恆溫裝置，以保護繪畫和古董。

警特 105
106

（秒殺解字）devise(=divis=divide) → devise 本義「劃分」，劃分需計畫和心思縝密，衍生出「設計」的意思。device 是名詞。

詞搭 an explosive device 爆炸裝置

同義字 gadget

---

agreement
[ə`grimənt]

n. 同意；一致；協定；契約

The man and woman have <u>reached an agreement</u> to simplify their wedding ceremony.
這對男女已達成協議要簡化他們的婚禮。

🈂普 107

（秒殺解字）a(=ad=to)+gree(pleasing)+ment → 本義「使」人「喜悅」。

反義字 disagreement

---

collect
[kə`lɛkt]

v. 收集、蒐集（郵票等）；聚集、集合

The opposition party is collecting signatures of voters to carry out a recall vote.
反對黨正在收集選民的簽名以進行罷免投票。

警特 106
107
108

（秒殺解字）col(together)+lec(gather)+t → 把東西給「聚集」在「一起」。相關同源字有 elect（v. 選舉）、select（v. 選擇）、neglect（v. 忽視、疏忽）、recollect（v. 回憶）、intellect（n. 智力）、lecture（n./v. 講課；演講）。

詞搭 collect <u>bills / taxes</u> 收帳／稅款

failure

[`feljɚ]

n. 失敗；失敗的事情；失敗者

The election campaign was a total failure, because the voter turnout was quite low.　🔊 102

選舉活動完全失敗，因為選民投票率很低。

🪶 **秒殺解字** fall(deceive, untrue)+ure → 核心語意是「欺騙」、「不正確的」。

詞搭 a heart failure 心臟衰竭；a power failure 停電；a failure of crops = a crop failure 歉收；a failure in health 健康衰退

反義字 success

equal

[`ikwəl]

n. 可與匹敵的人；同等

v. 等於；匹敵

adj. 平等的

Americans hold the belief that all men are created equal as stated in the Declaration of Independence.

美國人堅信在《獨立宣言》中所述，所有人都是平等的。

🪶 **秒殺解字** equ(=equi)+al → 「平等的」。

詞搭 be equal in... 在……方面相當；equal A in B 用 B 與 A 匹敵；equal a world record 平世界紀錄

衍生字 equivalent [ɪ`kwɪvələnt] adj. 相對等的；equality [ɪ`kwɑlətɪ] n. 平等，同等

同義字 match , rival

反義字 unequal

equation

[ɪ`kweʃən]

n. 方程式；等式；相等；平衡

The equation was so difficult to solve that Mandy spent the whole night working on it.　🔊 108

這個方程式如此地難解，以至於 Mandy 整夜都在研究它。

message

[`mɛsɪdʒ]

n. 訊息；信息

Animals sometimes send messages by leaving a scent in certain places.　🔊 99
　　　　100
　　　　104

動物有時會透過在某些地方留下氣味來傳遞訊息。

🪶 **秒殺解字** mess(=miss, mit=send)+age → 「發送」出去的文字、圖檔等是「訊息」。mess 等同 miss、mit，表示「送」（send）。

詞搭 leave a message with + sb. 留言給某人；take a message（幫某人）留言／傳話；an oral message 口信；the President's message to Congress 總統給國會的咨文

衍生字 messenger [`mɛsəndʒɚ] n. 使者；信差

字辨 massage [mə`sɑʒ] v. 按摩 n. 按摩

01 ___ A few weeks ago, the insurance agent _____ me that he would help me deal with all the insurance problems for my vehicle. However, I can't get in touch with him now and the phone is never answered.

(A) assured (B) provided
(C) performed (D) measured

02 ___ The process for choosing the representative athlete is very_____, measuring the running speed and arm strength.
(A) attractive (B) objective
(C) selective (D) effective

03 ___ The _____ earthquake shattered the old building, and ten people were killed in the tragedy. To prevent this kind of accident from happening again, the government is now passing a new law to ensure the safety of old buildings.

(A) decorative (B) informative
(C) destructive (D) positive

04 ___ We need to show our deepest appreciation to the war veterans for their _____ and sacrifice to the country. Because of their bravery, we can live in harmony and peace.

(A) ejection (B) alleviation
(C) argumentation (D) contribution

05 ___ Nowadays, a lot of Internet celebrities choose not to _____ their true faces to the public. In this way, they can live a rather normal life when they are not working.

(A) reveal (B) manage
(C) conceal (D) improve

06 ___ To slow down the enemy's progress, the general decided to use extreme _____. He ordered his troops to burn down everything when they were forced to retreat. He didn't want to leave anything for the enemy to collect.

(A) gestures   (B) measures
(C) treasures   (D) postures

07 ___ The general manager _____ that people followed her opinion and refused to listen to other people's advice. In the end, she did a terrible job on the presentation of the products and ruined a profitable business.

(A) concentrated   (B) insisted
(C) displayed   (D) resisted

08 ___ Although the prosecutor provided substantial evidence against the presidential candidate, he still refused to _____ to the accusation of corruption.

(A) permit   (B) transmit
(C) commit   (D) admit

09 ___ After two years of rest because of the injury, the famous NBA star returned in yesterday's game with an underwhelming performance. Some said that he is _____ by his injury and he is not the same superstar as he used to be.

(A) infected   (B) expected
(C) affected   (D) neglected

10 ___ As long as the _____ is still there, we can keep making our products. We are the only supplier of this product, so it is still profitable. You just need to find a way to sell the items.

(A) response   (B) burden
(C) demand   (D) amendment

11 ___ In the NBA dunk contest, every contestant has three _____ to finish their performances. However, most players try to show their best with the first try and save their strength for later rounds.

(A) loans   (B) cosmetics
(C) extracts   (D) attempts

12 ___ Because this year's financial _____ was caused by a pandemic, the government cannot replicate what they did in the 2007-2008 financial crisis to save the current situation. The scenarios are just different.

(A) crisis   (B) comment
(C) psychology   (D) behavior

13 ___ During WWII, Hitler broke the peace _____ between Germany and Soviet Union by invading Czechoslovakia. Most historians agreed that this was one of the biggest mistakes that Hitler made during his prime.

(A) treatment   (B) supplement
(C) agreement   (D) advertisement

14 ___ On July 4th, 1776, the American Congress signed the Declaration of Independence in Philadelphia claiming that all men are created _____.

(A) equal   (B) fatal
(C) fortunate   (D) guilty

15 ___ After his _____, the knight locked himself in the castle and refused to see anyone. He couldn't accept the fact that he lost to a farmer's son.

(A) tradition   (B) facility
(C) income   (D) failure

解答
1.(A) 2.(C) 3.(C) 4.(D) 5.(A) 6.(B) 7.(B) 8.(D) 9.(C) 10.(C) 11.(D) 12.(A) 13.(C) 14.(A) 15.(D)

standard

[`stændəd]

n. 標準；水準；模範

adj. 標準的

Oscar gets up early every day to set the standard for his children.

Oscar 每天早上早起，為孩子們樹立標準。

警 103
警特 108

🪶（秒殺解字）stand(stand)+ard(hard) → stand 和 hard 的混合字，源自古法語，字面上的意思是「堅固地站立」，引申為「軍隊集結地點」，因為在軍隊的集結地點上，會用竿子將旗幟固定在地上，15 世紀以後衍生出「標準」、「規格」等意思，有字源學家推測此字義可能跟軍隊所訂定的規範有關。但也有一派語言學家認為這是「通俗辭源」（folk etymology），並不正確，比較傾向 standard 和 extend 同源，字面上是「延展」（thin、stretch）「出去」（out）。

詞搭 a high / low living standard 高／低生活水準；below standards 在標準以下；safety standards 安全標準

同義字 criterion

---

standardized

[`stændədaɪzd]

adj. 標準化的

In the past, each school had its own set of exams for their students, but now tests are standardized throughout the nation.

以前每間學校都有自己的考試，但現在全國的考試都是標準化的。

---

declare

[dɪ`klɛr]

v. 宣布；宣稱；宣告

The president has declared that we are now in an emergency state to help control the outbreak of the virus.

總統宣布我們現在處於緊急狀態，以幫助控制病毒的爆發。

警特 106

🪶（秒殺解字）de(intensive prefix)+clar(clear)+e → 講「清楚」，表示「宣布」、「聲明」。可用 clear 當神隊友，母音通轉，來記憶 clar，皆表示「清楚的」、「清澈的」。相關同源字有 clarity（n. 清楚；清晰）、clarify（v. 澄清）、clarification（n. 澄清）。

詞搭 declare independence 宣布獨立；declare war on... 向……宣戰；declare + sb's position 表明某人的立場

同義字 announce, state

extent

[ɪk`stɛnt]

n. 程度；大小

Though I don't totally believe what he has just said, I do agree with him to some extent.

儘管我不完全相信他的話，但我在某種程度上同意他的看法。

秒殺解字 ex(out)+tent(thin, stretch) → 「延展」「出去」。

詞搭 to a / an... extent = to a / an... degree 到……的程度；in extent 大小

tension

[`tɛnʃən]

n. 緊張

The tension in the Middle East is getting unbearable, and a war seems inevitable.

中東的緊張局勢變得難以忍受，戰爭似乎不可避免。

秒殺解字 tens(thin, stretch)+ion → 本義「延展」、「變細」、「變薄」、「變緊」。

詞搭 under tension 在緊張下；relieve the tension of the muscles 舒解肌肉的緊張；surface tension 表面張力

學 103
學特 109

campaign

[kæm`pen]

n. （社會、宣傳）運動

v. 從事運動

Our school is launching an anti-bullying campaign in response to the recent bullying incident.

為了響應最近的霸凌事件，我們學校正在發起反霸凌運動。

秒殺解字 camp(filed)+aign → 和 campus 同源，核心意思皆是「野外」。以前的軍事活動大多發生在野外，因此 campaign 有「戰役」的意思，後來語意改變，引申為「社會宣傳運動」。

詞搭 a(n) election / sales campaign 競選／促銷活動；a campaign for women's rights / against smoking 女權／反菸運動

學 101

signal

[`sɪgnḷ]

n. 號誌；信號

v. 發出信號

Pedestrians should wait for the traffic signals, or they can get fined.

行人應等待交通號誌燈，否則將被罰款。

秒殺解字 sign(mark)+al → 本義「做記號」，引申為「信號」、「發信號」。

詞搭 a traffic signal 交通號誌；by signal 以信號；signal + sb. + to V 向某人打手勢，要某人……

同義字 beckon, gesture

divide
[dəˋvaɪd]
n. 一份
v. 劃分；除以

Perry divided his speech into three parts, and his first part was designed mainly to get the audience's attention.
Perry 將演講分為三個部分，而第一部分的設計主要是為了吸引觀眾。

普 101
警特 109

🖊 **秒殺解字** di(apart)+vid(separate)+e → 由「分開」（di=apart）和「分開」（**vid=separate**）所組成，「**寡婦**」（**wid**ow）是 di**vid**e 的同源字，**v/w** 對應，母音通轉，因為寡婦永遠與丈夫「分開」。

詞搭 | divide + sth.+ into... 把某物分成……；divide A by B A 除以 B

apartment
[əˋpɑrtmənt]
n. 公寓 [美]

When Leo went to college in Taipei, he rented a one-bedroom apartment.
當 Leo 在台北讀大學時，他租了一間單房的公寓。

普 104
107
警特 109

🖊 **秒殺解字** a(ad)+part(separate)+ment → 將房子劃分成好幾個小部分，引申為「公寓」。

詞搭 | a three-room apartment 三房的公寓；Apartments for Rent 公寓招租 [美]（= Flats to Let [英]）

同義字 | flat [英]

introduce
[ˌɪntrəˋdjus]
v. 介紹；引進；推出（產品等）

Recently, the company has introduced an identification system in order to distinguish employees from visitors.
最近，這家公司引入了身份識別系統，以區分員工和訪客。

普 103
104
高 108
警特 106
107
109

🖊 **秒殺解字** intro(into)+duc(lead)+e → 「引導」「進來」，就是「引進」、「介紹」。

詞搭 | introduce A to B 把 A 介紹給 B；introduce A to/into B 引進 A 到 B

introduction
[ˌɪntrəˋdʌkʃən]
n. 介紹；傳入、引進；（書）序、前言

Before the class began, the teacher made a brief self-introduction.
在上課之前，老師做了簡短的自我介紹。

高 108

詞搭 | a letter of introduction 介紹信

introductory
[ˌɪntrəˋdʌktərɪ]
adj. 介紹的

Mary has taken an introductory course on English literature this semester.
Mary 這學期選了英國文學入門課程。

高 108

詞搭 | an introductory speech 開場白；introductory remarks 序言

career
[kə`rɪr]
n. (終身)職業
adj. 職業的

After the scandal, the singer realized that his career was over.
在醜聞過後,這位歌手意識到自己的事業已經結束。

🖋 **秒殺解字** car(run)+eer →「跑」道,指人一生所經歷的「職涯」生活。

普 103
警特 105

詞搭 a career woman / soldier / diplomat 職業婦女／軍人／外交官;
make + sb's career 事業發跡獲得進展

同義字 vocation, occupation, profession

recommend
[ˌrɛkə`mɛnd]
v. 建議、推薦

I definitely recommend this director's films, because he is skilled in creating an elegant atmosphere.
我絕對推薦這位導演的電影,因為他善於營造幻想的氛圍。

🖋 **秒殺解字** re(intensive prefix)+com(intensive prefix)+mend(order, entrust) → 將某人「託付」給其他人的意味。相關同源字有com**mand**(v./n. 命令、指揮)、de**mand**(v. 強烈要求)、**mand**atory(adj. 強制的、法定的)。

普 100
101
警特 107
108

詞搭 recommend + Ving 建議……;recommend that + S + (should) + V 建議……

perform
[pə`fɔrm]
v. 執行;表演、表現

Adam's favorite singer is to perform in tonight's charity concert, so he will definitely be there.
Adam 最喜歡的歌手會在今晚的慈善音樂會上表演,所以他一定會在那裡。

🖋 **秒殺解字** per(thoroughly)+form(provide) →「完全地」「提供」,才能「執行」。

普 110
警特 106
109

詞搭 perform a task / job / duty 執行任務／工作／職責;perform an operation / investigation 進行手術／調查

同義字 carry out

performance
[pə`fɔrməns]
n. 表演、表現

The singer has established a fixed routine to prepare to give a live performance on New Year's Eve.
這位歌手依慣例在每年跨年夜進行現場表演。

普 106
警特 106

traitor

[`tretɚ]

n. 叛徒

These kids had a serious fight, and one of them was even called "a traitor" by all the others.

普 101

這些孩子在爭吵，而其中一個甚至被所有其他人稱為「叛徒」。

(秒殺解字) tra(=trans=over)+it(=dit=give)+or → 把東西「給」敵方的人。

詞搭 turn traitor to... 背叛……

字辨 trait [tret] n. 特點、特性

---

recall

[rɪ`kɔl]

v. 回想；記得；召回；回憶

The cars of this model are being recalled because there are some safety concerns about their automatic transmissions.

警特 108

目前這款汽車正在被召回，因其自動變速箱存在一些安全隱憂。

(秒殺解字) re(back, again)+call → 「再次」「叫」「回來」，表示「回憶」、「召回」。

詞搭 recall + N / Ving 記得……；beyond recall 不能憶起／撤銷

同義字 remember, recollect, think back, look back

---

previously

[`prɪvɪəslɪ]

adv. 先前地；以前

Some tasks previously done by human operators are now completed by intelligent robots.

普 106
警特 105
107

以前由人類操作員完成的某些任務現在由智能機器人完成。

(秒殺解字) pre(before)+vi(=via=way)+ous+ly → 「以前」走過的「道路」。相關同源字有 **way**（n. 路）、**via**（prep. 經由）、ob**vi**ous（adj. 明顯的）、pre**vi**ous（adj. 以前的）。

詞搭 two days previously 兩天以前

同義字 formerly

solution

[sə`luʃən]

n. 解決之道；解答；溶劑

The best solution that the dentist could come up with was to make a temporary filling.
牙醫可以想出的最佳解決方案是進行暫時填補。

🖋 秒殺解字 solu(=solv=loosen)+tion → 「鬆」開問題的結。solv、solu 同源，u/v 對應，皆表示「鬆開」、「使鬆開」。相關同源字有 **solv**e（v. 解決）、re**solv**e（v. 決定；解決）、re**solu**tion（n. 決心；決議）、re**solu**te（adj. 堅決的、斷然的）、dis**solv**e（v. 分解、使溶解；解散）、ab**solu**te（adj. 完全的；絕對的）。

詞搭 a solution to a problem 某問題的解決之道；a strong / weak solution 濃／稀溶液

警特 106

---

remark

[rɪ`mɑrk]

n. 評論

v. 說、談到；評論

Byron was not accepted for the job interview because he once made a radical remark online.
Byron 不被接受面試，因為他曾經在網上發表過激進言論。

🖋 秒殺解字 re(intensive prefix)+mark(mark) → 特別「標示」出來，以示區隔，1690 年代產生「評論」的語意，re**mark**able 表示「出色的」。

詞搭 make a remark 評論，批評；remark on... 評論有關……

同義字 comment

普 103

---

remarkable

[rɪ`mɑrkəbl]

adj. 了不起的、非凡的

Alex has made remarkable progress in math since he attended Mr. Smith's course.
自從參加 Smith 先生的課程以來，Alex 在數學上有顯著進步。

同義字 outstanding, exceptional, wonderful

普 99
警特 109

---

combination

[ˌkɑmbə`neʃən]

n. 結合；聯合

The combination of milk, avocados, and honey makes a wonderful drink.
牛奶，酪梨和蜂蜜的組合是一道絕佳的飲料。

🖋 秒殺解字 com(together)+bi(two)+n+ation → 把「兩」者放在「一起」。

詞搭 a combination lock 密碼鎖；in combination with 與……結合在一起

同義字 mixture

appearance
[ə`pɪrəns]

n. 出現；外表

Those who are not satisfied with their physical appearance may take risks in undergoing plastic surgery.

那些對自己的外表不滿意的人可能會冒風險接受整形手術。

📖 103
104
107

✒️ **秒殺解字** ap(=ad=to)+pear(=par=appear,visible)+ance → 「向前」移動，可讓人「看見」，表示「出現」、「外表」。相關同源字有 ap**pear**（ v. 出現 ）、ap**par**ent（ adj. 明顯的 ）、disap**pear**（ v. 消失 ）、disap**pear**ance（ n. 失蹤 ）、trans**par**ent（ adj. 透明的、能看穿的 ）。

詞搭 | judge by appearance 以貌取人； by all appearances 外表上看來

---

arise
[ə`raɪz]

v. 產生；形成

More problems will arise if one tells a lie in the first place.

如果一開始說謊，後面就會出現更多的問題。

📖 105

✒️ **秒殺解字** a(of)+rise(rise) → 「從……」「上升」，表示「發生」。a**rise**、**rise**（ v./n. 上升 ）、**raise** [rez]（ v. 舉起；提高；募捐；養育；種植 ）同源，**母音通轉**，核心語意都是「**上升**」（**rise**）。

時態 | arise, arose [ə`roz], arisen [ə`rɪzn̩]

詞搭 | arise from... = result from... 起因於……、由……引起、由於……

字辨 | arouse [ə`raʊz] v. 激發；喚醒

 **Unit 12**

---

backpacker

[ˋbæk͵pækɚ]

n. 背包客

Chris was encouraged to explore the world as a backpacker for a year after he graduated from senior high school.

Chris 從高中畢業後，被鼓勵以背包客的身份探索世界一年。

 秒殺解字 back+pack+er →背包客。

---

devote

[dɪˋvot]

v. 致力於；貢獻

After retirement, Edison devoted all of his time to farming in the countryside.

退休後，Edison 將所有時間都花在鄉下耕種上。

曾99

秒殺解字 de(away)+vot(vow)+e → 藉由「發誓」來表達自己願意犧牲付「出」。vote 原指「誓言」（vow）和對神的「承諾」（promise），後來衍生為「願望」（wish），1552 年再轉義，指藉由「投票」來表達自己的願望或意圖。vow 與 vote 本是同根生，是一組同源異形異義的「雙飾詞」（doublet）。

詞搭 devote / dedicate A to B 將 A 奉獻於 B；devote / dedicate oneself to + N / Ving 某人奉獻於……、某人致力於……

同義字 dedicate

---

devoted

[dɪˋvotɪd]

adj. 奉獻的；忠實的

Dr. Martin is devoted to improving chronic disease and helping patients get off medications.

Martin 醫生致力於改善慢性疾病並幫助患者擺脫藥物治療。

詞搭 be devoted / dedicated to + sth. 熱衷於某事；a devoted wife 忠實的妻子

同義字 dedicated

---

decade

[ˋdɛked]

n. 十年

This small fishing village has developed into an international trade center in the last couple of decades.

在過去的幾十年中，這個小漁村已發展成為國際貿易中心。

曾106

秒殺解字 deca(ten)+ade →「十」年。可用 ten 當神隊友，**d/t 轉音**，母音通轉，來記憶 deca、dec。deca 來自希臘文 deka，表示「十」，若後面加接母音，則縮減為 dec。

income

[`ɪn͵kʌm]

n. 收入

Average incomes of people in this country have risen by 2%, which is lower than that of neighboring countries.

該國人民的平均收入增長了 2%，低於鄰國。

🖋 秒殺解字 in+come → 「進」「來」，表示「收入」。

詞搭 | a high / low income 高／低所得；income tax 所得稅

字辨 | outcome [`aʊt͵kʌm] n. 結果

同義字 | earnings

反義字 | expenditure, expense

essential

[ɪ`sɛnʃəl]

n. 要素；要點

adj. 必要的、不可或缺的；本質的

Water and air are essential for humans to live on Earth.

水和空氣對於人類在地球上的生活至關重要。

警特 106 107

🖋 秒殺解字 ess(be)+ent+ial → 本義是「存在」，表示「必要不可缺的」、「基本的」。

詞搭 | be essential for / to... 對……是不可或缺的

同義字 | necessary, basic, fundamental, vital

essentially

[ɪ`sɛnʃəlɪ]

adv. 本質上、基本上

This house is essentially a museum with an exhibition of a variety of valuable antiques.

這房子本質上是一個博物館，裡面陳列著各種有價值的古董。

同義字 | basically, in essence

essence

[`ɛsəns]

n. 本質；要素；精髓；萃取物

The essence of Confucian thoughts is education without discrimination.

儒家思想的本質是有教無類。

警特 105

詞搭 | in essence 本質上；of the essence 最重要的；meat essence 肉精

primary

[`praɪˌmɛrɪ]

adj. 主要的、首要的；初級的

The primary concern of this enterprise is to provide its employees with a safe and comfortable working environment.

這家企業的主要關切的事是為員工提供安全舒適的工作環境。

普 102
警特 109

秒殺解字 prim(first)+ary → 「首要的」。可用 **first** 當神隊友，**p/f 轉音**，母音通轉，來記憶 **prim**、**prin**、**prem**，皆表示「第一的」。此外，**prim**、**prin**、**prem** 也和字首 **pre**、**pro** 同源，母音通轉，核心語意皆表示「前」（**before**），在「前」，就表示「第一的」。

詞搭 primary school 小學；primary education 初等教育；primary election 初選

同義字 main, chief, principal, major, core

---

fashion

[`fæʃən]

n. 流行；時裝；方式
v. 塑造

Bell-bottomed pants used to be the fashion in the 70s, but now they have come back again.

喇叭褲曾經是 70 年代的時尚，但現在又重新流行了。

警特 106
107
109

秒殺解字 fash (=fac=do, make)+ion → 「流行」是「塑造」或「做」出來的。

詞搭 be in fashion 流行；be / go out of fashion

字辨 fad [fæd] n. 一時的流行

---

relief

[rɪ`lif]

n. 舒解；解除；救濟；救濟物資

It is such a relief to know that the missing child has been found.

知道找到失蹤兒童真是令人欣慰的事。

警特 109

秒殺解字 re(intensive prefix)+lief(lift, light) → 「提起」使痛苦變「輕」。相關同源字有 re**lieve**（v. 減輕）、re**lev**ant（adj. 相關的）、**lev**er（n. 槓桿）、al**lev**iate（v. 緩和）、e**lev**ate（v. 提升）。

詞搭 To + sb's great relief = Much to + sb's relief 令某人感到欣慰；breathe a sigh of relief 鬆一口氣；a relief organization 救濟組織

democracy

[ˌdə`mɑkrəsɪ]

n. 民主；民主國家

The president has claimed that we are the most advanced democracy in the world.
總統宣稱我們是世界上最先進的民主國家。

（秒殺解字）dem(people)+o+crac(=crat=rule) +y →「人民」「統治」。

詞搭 direct democracy 直接民主

反義字 tyranny

---

democratic

[ˌdɛmə`krætɪk]

adj. 民主的

普 108
警特 109

The role of media is really significant in a democratic country, especially its power of oversight.
在民主國家，媒體的角色非常重要，尤其是監督的力量。

詞搭 a democratic country / government 民主國家／政府；the Democratic Party 民主黨 [美]

---

democratiza-tion

[dɪˌmɑkrətɪ`zeʃən]

n. 民主化

To boost democratization, it is crucial to allow a free and unrestricted society.
為了促進民主化，建立一個自由和不受限制的社會至關重要。

---

current

[`kɝ·ənt]

n. 水流；氣流
adj. 當前的

普 107
高 108
警特 107

Michelle is not satisfied with her current job because of the heavy workload and high-stress environment.
由於工作量大而且環境壓力也大，Michelle 對她目前的工作不滿意。

Learning things is like sailing a boat against the current; it either advances or retreats.
學如逆水行舟，不進則退。

---

currently

[`kɝ·əntlɪ]

adv. 當前、目前

Since online testing is currently becoming increasingly popular, secure online examination systems are in high demand.
由於線上測驗目前變得越來越流行，因此對安全的線上測驗系統的需求很高。

同義字 now, at the moment, presently, at present, at the present time, right now, at this time

deliver
[dɪ`lɪvɚ]

v. 遞送、傳送；生產；使解脫

Voters' pamphlets will be delivered to every family this week.
選民的選舉手冊本週將分發給每個家庭。

> **秒殺解字** de(away)+liver(free) → 本義賦予「自由」允許「離開」，因此有「遞送」、「接生」等意思。**liber**、**liver** 同源，**b/v 轉音**，皆表示「自由的」。相關同源字有 **liber**ty（ n. 自由 ）、**liber**al（ adj. 自由的 ）、**liber**ate（ v. 釋放 ）、**liber**ation（ n. 釋放 ）、**liber**ally（ adv. 任意地、大方地 ）。

詞搭 deliver a <u>speech / report</u> 發表演講／報告；deliver the goods 交貨

曾 110
警特 106

---

delivery
[dɪ`lɪvərɪ]

n. 遞送、傳送

This Italian restaurant offers free delivery on orders over 100 dollars.
這家義大利餐廳提供超過 100 美元的訂單免費外送服務。

詞搭 （cash）on delivery 貨到時（付款）；special delivery 限時專送

曾 99

---

ancestor
[`ænsɛstɚ]

n. 祖先；前身

On Tomb Sweeping Day, Taiwanese people show great respect to their ancestors by visiting their graves and preparing food.
在清明節，台灣人會前往祖先墳墓並準備食物，以表示對祖先的敬意。

> **秒殺解字** an(=ante=before)+ces(=cess=go)+t+or →「走」在「前」，表示「祖先」。

同義字 antecedent, forefather, forebear

反義字 descendant

曾 99
警特 107

---

ancestry
[`ænsɛstrɪ]

n. 家世、門第；祖譜

Michael's family can trace their ancestry back to the 19th century.
Michael 一家可以追溯其祖先到 19 世紀。

詞搭 Australians of Chinese ancestry 華裔澳洲人

曾 103

---

ancient
[`enʃənt]

adj. 古老的、古代的

The most exciting part of this journey is to visit the ancient historic site of Machu Picchu in Peru.
此旅程中最令人興奮的部分是參觀秘魯馬丘比丘的古老歷史遺跡。

> **秒殺解字** anci(=ante=before)+ent → 在「前」，表示「古代的」。

反義字 modern, new

emerge

[ɪˋmɝdʒ]

v. 顯現、出現、冒出

The sun <u>emerged from</u> behind the mountains, which excited all of us.
太陽從山後露臉，讓我們所有人都興奮。

秒殺解字 c(=ex=out)+merg(dive)+e → 往「外」「浮現」。

| 同義字 | appear, come out |

---

emergency

[ɪˋmɝdʒənsɪ]

n. 緊急狀況、緊急事件

In case of <u>emergency</u>, please press the red button on the wall and somebody will come to your rescue.
萬一發生緊急情況，請按牆壁上的紅色按鈕，然後會有人來救援。

普 106
警特 109

| 詞搭 | the emergency room 急診室（ER）；an emergency landing 緊急降落；emergeycy measures 緊急措施；the emergency exit 緊急出口 |

---

significant

[sɪgˋnɪfəkənt]

adj. 重要的；顯著的；有意義的

There has been a significant change in Tom, since he has lost his parents in a short time.
Tom 經歷了很大的變化，因為他在短時間內失去了父母。

普 106
107
警特 106
109

秒殺解字 sign(mark)+i+fic(make, do)+ant → 本義「做」「記號」，引申為「重要的」、顯著的」。相關同源字有 **sign**ify（v. 表示）、**sign**（n. 記號）、**sign**ature（n. 簽名）、**sign**al（n. 信號）、de**sign**（v. 設計）、as**sign**（v. 分配）、re**sign**（v. 辭去）。

| 同義字 | important |
| 反義字 | insignificant , trivial |

---

objective

[əbˋdʒɛktɪv]

n. 目標
adj. 客觀的

The department has succeeded in its major objective of cutting costs by laying off some part-timers.
此部門已透過裁減兼職員工而成功地實現了削減成本的主要目標。

普 102
110
警特 109

秒殺解字 ob(before, toward, against)+jec(throw)+t+ive → 「往」「前面」「丟」，表示「目標」。相關同源字有 ob**jec**t（v. 反對）、re**jec**t（v. 拒絕）、sub**jec**t（v. 使臣服）、in**jec**t（v. 注射）、e**jec**t（v. 逐出）。

詞搭	<u>achieve / attain / gain / win</u> an objective 達到目標
同義字	goal, purpose, aim, target, object
反義字	subjective

117

address
[`ædrɛs / ə`drɛs]

n. 地址；演說

[ə`drɛs]

v. 對……發表演說；寄信給……

Henry gave a false address to the salesman in case he wanted send advertising in the mail.
Henry 給推銷員一個假的地址，以防他寄送廣告信件。

警特 107 109

秒殺解字 ad(to)+dress(direct=straight) → 原意是「弄直」，後來變成「地址」、「演講」等意思。

詞搭 make / give / deliver an address 發表演說；address book 通訊錄；address oneself to... 向某人說話

---

financial
[faɪ`nænʃəl]

adj. 金融的；財務的

People who are doing recycling should be encouraged with financial incentives.
進行回收的人應該運用經濟激勵措施給予鼓勵。

普 102
高 110

秒殺解字 fin(end, limit)+ance+ial → 原指「結束」債務。

詞搭 a financial crisis 金融危機；a financial problem 財務問題

---

non-financial
[nʌnfaɪ`nænʃəl]

adj. 非金融的；非財務的

After the banking scandal, Ian decided to pursue his career in a non-financial company.
在發生銀行醜聞後，Ian 決定任職於一家非金融公司。

---

escape
[ə`skep]

n. 逃脫；逃避
v. 逃脫；逃避

Poisonous gas escaped from the chemical factory and led to serious air pollution in this neighborhood.
有毒氣體從化工廠中散發出來，導致附近嚴重空氣污染。

普 110
高 108
警特 105

秒殺解字 es(=ex=out)+cape(cape) → 字面意思是「離開」「斗篷」，意指留下斗篷「逃脫」，故佈疑陣，頗具金蟬脫殼意味。

同義字 avoid

---

examine
[ɪg`zæmɪn]

v. 檢查；檢驗；考試

Everyone should go to the hospital to have their health examined on a regular basis.
每個人都應該去醫院進行定期健康檢查。

秒殺解字 exam+ine → 考試、調查。

詞搭 examine + sb. + in / on + sth. 考某人某科／某事；examine oneself 自省

同義字 check, inspect

examination

[ɪgˌzæməˋneʃən]

n. 考試；檢查；檢驗；審問

The entrance examination for colleges will take place from July 1 to July 3.　🔊 102

大學入學考試將於 7 月 1 日至 7 月 3 日進行。

詞搭　a physical examination = a physical check-up 體檢；make an examination of… 檢查、審查；take an examination 應試

---

reexamine

[ˌriɪgˋzæmɪn]

v. 重考；再檢查

Our teacher asks us to reexamine our answers before we hand in the exam papers.

老師要求我們在交卷之前重新檢查答案。

01 ___ The new virus contains genes that have never been seen before. Consequently, the _____ treatments for similar viruses do not apply to this case.

(A) brand (B) standard
(C) restoration (D) dissatisfaction

02 ___ Only after the Japanese attacked Pearl Harbor did the Americans _____ war against the Axis. By the time they did that, the Germans had already taken over most parts of Europe.

(A) devoure (B) declare
(C) deposit (D) dedicate

03 ___ During the cold war, the _____ between the U.S. and the Soviet Union was so high that people were afraid of all-out nuclear warfare.

(A) tradition (B) foundation
(C) obsession (D) tension

04 ___ The new 5G technology has revolutionized the society. With its _____ transmitting faster and farther, the application of related technologies is beyond imagination.

(A) signal (B) odor
(C) animation (D) cuisine

05 ___ One of the most valuable merits is humbleness. If a person stays humble, he or she will more likely to become successful. For example, most Oscar winners will express their gratitude toward people who have helped them as the _____ of their acceptance speech.

(A) reception (B) introduction
(C) condition (D) speculation

06 ___ For this job, I highly _____ Peter to represent us. He is young, energetic, and polite. No one is more suitable for this job than he.

(A) interact (B) magnify
(C) recommend (D) offend

07 ___ In the past, when pirates discovered _____ on their ship, they would chain rocks to them and force them to jump off the ship.

(A) traitors   (B) legislators
(C) pioneers   (D) colleagues

08 ___ In this game, the player can design their character's _____, gender, and even personality at will. The choices and combinations are unlimited.

(A) resistance   (B) allowance
(C) dominance   (D) appearance

09 ___ Alexander Hamilton was one of the founding fathers of America. He, along with other founding fathers like George Washington, was _____ to building the foundation of a free world.

(A) anticipated   (B) devoted
(C) delivered   (D) liberated

10 ___ This area has been dominated by the mafia for _____. The police department of the city has tried many times to clear the area, but always ends up failing.

(A) accounts   (B) decades
(C) drops   (D) volumes

11 ___ One of the most _____ aspects of doing business is credit. If you promise someone about something, you have to try your best to fulfill the promise. Otherwise, no one will work with you in the future.

(A) spatial   (B) differential
(C) essential   (D) influential

12 ___ Former British prime minister Winston Churchill once said, "_____ is the worst form of government except all the others that have been tried." In other words, it is currently our only choice.

(A) literacy   (B) frequency
(C) democracy   (D) dynasty

13 ___ For the longest time, scientists and theologians have been arguing about whether human's _____ are monkeys or not.

(A) ancestors (B) employees

(C) agents (D) managers

14 ___ When the sun finally _____ from the horizon, the exhausted travelers felt relieved and smiled at each other.

(A) managed (B) charged

(C) imagined (D) emerged

15 ___ Scientists need to be as _____ as possible when doing research. Because they are finding the truth instead of personal opinions.

(A) creative (B) objective

(C) cognitive (D) productive

Unit 13

🎧TRACK 013

---

legal
[`lig!]
adj. 合法的;與法律
相關的

Same-sex marriage has become legal in many countries as well as in Taiwan.
同性婚姻在許多國家和台灣已經合法。

📖秒殺解字 leg(law)+al → 合乎「法律」規範的。相關同源字有 il**leg**al (adj. 違法的)、**leg**islate (v. 立法)、privi**leg**e (n. 特權)、**leg**acy (n. 遺產)、**leg**itimate (adj. 合法的)、al**leg**e (v. 宣稱、指控)。

詞搭 legal age 法定年齡;legal aid 免費法律服務

同義字 lawful

反義字 illegal, unlawful

---

legally
[`ligəlɪ]
adv. 合法地

Legally speaking, Tom and Amy are still a married couple, but they aren't in love with each other.
從法律上來講,Tom 和 Amy 仍然是已婚夫妻,但他們彼此沒有相愛。

普 108

反義字 illegally

---

resource
[rɪ`sɔrs / `risɔrs]
n. 資源

Canada is rich in <u>natural resources</u> and possesses vast territory.
加拿大擁有豐富的自然資源,和廣闊的領土。

普 107

📖秒殺解字 re(again)+source(=surge=rise) → 本義「再次」「上升」,填補匱乏或不足,引申為「資源」。

詞搭 <u>energy / human</u> resources 能源／人力資源

字辨 source [sɔrs] n. 來源

---

advance
[əd`væns]
n. 進步;預支
v. 促進;前進、行進

Dr. Myles had written a report about advances in medicine over the last few years.
Myles 醫生撰寫了一份有關過去幾年醫學進展的報告。

普 106
普特 106
109

📖秒殺解字 adv(=av=ab=from)+ance(=ante=before) → 「從……」「前面」出來,引申為「前進」、「升級」,這個字是源自於古法文的 avancir,可上溯到拉丁文的 abante,此處的 ab 進到古法文中轉音成 av,b/v 轉音,約 16 世紀時,當時的人誤以為單字開頭的 av 是源自 ad,故在 av 中加了 d 字母。此處的 adv 是 ab 的變體,但來源撲朔迷離,讀者不必細究。

詞搭 in advance = beforehand 事先、預先;in advance of 在……

123

contrast

[ˋkɑntræst]

n. 對比;差異

[kənˋtræst]

v. 比較

The contrast between these two colors makes the painting more vivid.

這兩種顏色之間的對比使得這幅畫更加生動。

普 110
警特 109

秒殺解字 contra(against)+st(stand) → 「站」在「相反」的一方。

詞搭 By contrast, ... 相對之下,……;in contrast to... 與……成對比;contrast A with B 將 A 與 B 做對照;the contrast between light and shade 光影的對比

---

accompany

[əˋkʌmpənɪ]

v. 陪同、陪伴

Children under 12 must be accompanied by an adult to see this movie.

12 歲以下的兒童必須有成人陪同才能觀看這部電影。

秒殺解字 ac(=ad=to)+com(together)+pan(food, bread)+y → 本義「一起」「去」「吃飯」,引申為「伴隨」。可用 **food** 當神隊友,**p/f**、**d/n 轉音**,母音通轉,來記憶 **pan**,皆表示「食物」。相關同源字有 com**pan**y (n. 公司;同伴、朋友)、com**pan**ion (n. 同伴、伴侶)。

詞搭 accompany + sb. = keep + sb. + company 陪伴某人

---

exception

[ɪkˋsɛpʃən]

n. 例外

There is always an exception to rules, so it's nearly impossible to make perfect rules.

規則總是有例外,因此制定完美的規則幾乎是不可能的。

高 108

秒殺解字 ex(out)+cept(take) +ion → 本義是「拿」「出去」,表示「排除」在「外」。

詞搭 without exception 沒有例外;with the exception of = except (for) 除了……以外;make an / no exception 把……除外/一視同仁

---

exceptionally

[ɪkˋsɛpʃənəlɪ]

adv. 異常地

Rafael Nadal is an exceptionally talented tennis player and is considered to be one of the greatest of all time.

Rafael Nadal 是一位非常有才華的網球員,而且被認為是有史以來最偉大的網球運動員之一。

普 104

詞搭 exceptionally beautiful 美得冒泡的;exceptionally cold 出奇地冷

同義字 outstandingly, extremely

assign

[əˋsaɪn]

v. 分配；指派

Sharon was assigned to investigate a murder case that happened last night. 警特 109
Sharon 被指派調查昨晚發生的一起謀殺案。

秒殺解字 as(=ad=to)+sign(mark) →「去」「做記號」，方便「分配」。相關同源字有 **sign**（n. 記號）、**sign**ature（n. 簽名）、**sign**al（n. 信號）、**sign**ify（v. 表示）、de**sign**（v. 設計）、re**sign**（v. 辭去）。

詞搭 assign + sb. + sth. = assign + sth. + to + sb. 分配某人某事；assign + sb. + to V 指派某人從事……

assignment

[əˋsaɪnmənt]

n. 指定作業；任命；派定的工作

I haven't come up with any ideas for my geography assignment, so can you give me some suggestions?
關於地理作業，我還沒有任何想法，你能給我一些建議嗎？

motorist

[ˋmotərɪst]

n. 開車的人、駕駛

Thirty thousand motorists are fined for speeding every year.
每年有三萬名駕駛因超速而被罰款。

秒殺解字 motor(motorcar)+ist → 開「車」的「人」。

同義字 driver

issue

[ˋɪʃʊ]

n. 重大議題；爭議；期刊
v. 發行

Stimulus vouchers were issued by the government to boost economic activities and consumer spending. 曾 102
108
110
高 110
警特 108
109
政府發行了振興券，以促進經濟活動和消費者支出。

秒殺解字 iss(=ex=out)+ue(=it=go) → 此字源自古法文，字根和字首變體差異較大。本義「走」「出去」，引申為「發行」。

詞搭 at issue 在爭論中；make an issue of... 把……當作重大議題

desire

[dɪˋzaɪr]

n. 慾望
v. 渴望、想要

Tara has a strong desire to win the contest, so she practices every day.
Tara 渴望贏得比賽，因此每天都要練習。

秒殺解字 de(down)+sire(=sider=star) → 在「下方」向「星星」許願，達成「渴望」。

詞搭 a desire + to V 想要…；a desire for... 對……的慾望；leave nothing to be desired 無懈可擊；leave much / a lot to be desired 尚待改進

同義字 wish, hope, longing

promise

[ˋprɑmɪs]

n. 諾言；可能性；潛能

v. 承諾

The chairman apologized and promised that appropriate action would be taken to solve the problem.

主席表示歉意，並承諾將採取適當行動解決這一問題。

圖 108

> **(秒殺解字)** pro(before)+mis(send)+e → 「往前」「送」，表示「答應」、「承諾」。相關同源字有 **miss**ion (n. 任務)、ad**mit** (v. 承認)、ad**miss**ion (n. 准許)、per**mit** (v. 允許)、per**miss**ion (n. 允許)、sub**mit** (v. 呈遞)、sub**miss**ion (n. 呈遞)、o**mit** (v. 遺漏)、o**miss**ion (n. 遺漏)。

詞搭 promise (+ sb.) + to V = make a promise + to V 承諾 (某人) 從事……；keep one's promise 守信；break one's promise 背信

---

ordinary

[ˋɔrdəˌnɛrɪ]

adj. 平常的、普通的、平凡的

This novel mainly deals with the happiness and worries of ordinary people in Paris.

這本小說主要探討巴黎平民百姓的幸福和煩惱。

108

> **(秒殺解字)** ord(order)+in+ary → 按一般「順序」，表示「普通的」、「平常的」。相關同源字有 **order** (n. 順序、次序)、extra**ordin**ary (adj. 異常的)、co**ordin**ate (v. 協調)、sub**ordin**ate (adj. 下級的 n. 下屬)。

詞搭 in the ordinary way = as normal 按往例

同義字 average, common, usual

反義字 extraordinary

---

excellent

[ˋɛksələnt]

adj. 絕佳的、出色的、極優秀的

Many studies show that the drug has been tested with excellent results, so it may come onto the market soon.

許多研究顯示，此藥物經測試具有絕佳的結果，因此可能很快就會上市。

106
107

> **(秒殺解字)** ex(out)+cell(rise)+ent → 在眾人中顯得特別「突出」，近似「脫穎而出」。c 在拉丁文裡發 k 的音。可用 **hill** 當神隊友，**k/h 轉音**，母音通轉，來記憶 **cel**、**cell**，皆和「山丘」、「突出的」有關。

詞搭 have an excellent command of... 有 (某語文) 很好的造詣

同義字 outstanding, brilliant, superb, amazing

excel [ɪk`sɛl] **v.** 表現優異；突出；善於	Pushing children to <u>excel</u> in school may give them a lot of stress and make them lose self-confidence. 逼迫孩子在學校裡表現出色可能會給他們很大的壓力，並使他們失去自信心。
時態	excel, excelled [ɪk`sɛld], excelled
詞搭	excel <u>in / at</u> + <u>N / Ving</u> 在……方面很突出、優異

capable [`kepəbl] **adj.** 有能力的	The sales team desperately needs a capable leader to organize all this mess. 銷售團隊迫切需要一個有能力的領導者來處理所有這些混亂。　　曾108 警特105 106
	秒殺解字 cap(grasp, take, have)+able →「有」能力的。
詞搭	be capable of + <u>N / Ving</u> = be able + to V 有能力……的、可以……的
同義字	able
反義字	incapable, unable

quarter [`kwɔrtɚ] **n.** 四分之一；兩毛五（25分錢）；一季（三個月） **v.** 分為四份	The company's profits rose in the first quarter of the year, which was the first increase within 5 years. 這家公司的營利在今年第一季上升，也是5年來的首次上升。　　曾110
	秒殺解字 quar(four)+t+er → 表示「四」分之一。

preserve [prɪ`zɝv] **n.** 果醬；蜜餞 **v.** 保存；維持；醃製	More and more experts suggest preserving the traditions and languages of Taiwanese aborigines. 越來越多的專家建議保留台灣原住民的傳統和語言。　　曾107 警特105
	秒殺解字 pre(before)+serv(protect, keep)+e → 本義在「前方」「保護」、「保持」。相關同源字有con**serv**e (v. 保存；節約)、ob**serv**e (v. 觀察；注意到；遵守)、re**serv**e (v. 保留；預定)。

protect [prə`tɛkt] **v.** 保護；防禦	A series of meetings were held to discuss how to protect endangered species. 一系列會議被舉辦來討論如何保護瀕臨絕種的生物。　　曾102 110 警特106
	秒殺解字 pro(before)+tec(cover)+t → 在「前方」「遮蔽」，就是「保護」。相關同源字有de**tec**t (v. 查出、發現)。
詞搭	protect + sb. + <u>from / against</u>... 保護某人免於……
同義字	guard, shield

protection

[prə`tɛkʃən]

n. 保護；保護物

The witness <u>is under</u> 24-hour police <u>protection,</u> because the criminal is still at large.
由於罪犯仍然逍遙法外，證人受到 24 小時警察保護。

| 詞搭 | be under the protection of... 在⋯⋯的保護下；protection money 保護費 |

---

protector

[prə`tɛktɚ]

n. 保護者

A plastic screen protector is necessary for you to prevent cracks in the screen.
塑膠螢幕保護貼對於防止螢幕的破裂是必要的。

---

satisfy

[`sætɪs͵faɪ]

v. 使滿足；符合 (要求、條件)

Though the environmental impact assessment has been passed, even this failed to satisfy environmentalists.
儘管已經通過了環境影響評估，但即使這樣也不能使環保主義者滿意。

秒殺解字 satis(enough)+fy(make, do) →「使」「滿足」。

| 詞搭 | satisfy + sb's <u>curiosity / needs</u> 滿足某人好奇心／需要 |

---

satisfied

[`sætɪs͵faɪd]

adj. 感到滿意的

The aim of this restaurant is to make every customer go home with <u>a satisfied smile</u>.
這家餐廳的目的是讓每位顧客帶著滿意的笑容回家。

| 詞搭 | be <u>satisfied / content</u> with... 對⋯⋯感到滿意；a satisfied <u>smile / customer</u> 滿意的笑容／顧客 |

| 同義字 | content |

---

distinguish

[dɪ`stɪŋgwɪʃ]

v. 分辨、區別；使揚名

Kids learn how to <u>distinguish</u> <u>between right and wrong</u> through proper education.
孩子們透過合宜的教育學習如何辨別是非。

醫 99
108
警特 108
109

秒殺解字 dis(apart)+sting(stick, prick)+u+ish → 用「刺」挑出來「分開」。相關同源字有 extinguish (v. 熄滅)、distinct (adj. 截然不同的)、instinct (n. 本能)。

| 詞搭 | <u>distinguish / tell</u> A from B 區別 A 與 B 的不同；distinguish oneself 使自己揚名 |

separate

[`sɛpə͵ret] / [`sɛpərɪt]

v. 使分開；區分、隔開；分手

adj. 分開的

A separate study found that 80% of students are spending more time on mobile games. 🎧 100
102

一項單獨研究發現，80%的學生將更多時間花在手機遊戲上。

（秒殺解字）se(apart)+par(prepare)+ate → 「準備」「分開」。
此外，several、separate 同源，**p/v** 轉音，母音通轉。
相關同源字有 pre**par**e (v. 準備)、**par**ade(n./v. 遊行)、ap**par**atus (n. 裝置、設備)、re**pair** (v./ n. 修理)。

詞搭 separate A from B = keep A and B apart 把 A 與 B 區分開；
separate / divide into… 分成……；separate maintenance 贍養費

同義字 divide

separately

[`sɛpərɪtlɪ]

adv. 分開地；各自地

It is weird that the couple arrived at the same time, but left separately. 🎧 103

很奇怪的是，這對夫婦是同時到達但各自離開。

同義字 together

positive
[`pɑzətɪv]

adj. 積極的；肯定的；
正面的；確定的

The authorities need to take positive steps to improve the situation and living environment of families in poverty.
當局需要採取積極步驟，改善貧困家庭的狀況和生活環境。

普 102
警特 109

🪶(秒殺解字) pos(put)+it+ive → 本義是「放」，在拉丁文中衍生出「正式制定」(formally laid down) 的意思，後來更衍生出「確信的」、「確定的」等意思，至於心理學上表示「正向的」、「積極的」等意思，於 20 世紀始見於紀錄。

同義字　sure, certain

反義字　negative, unsure

captain
[`kæptɪn]

n. 船長；機長；隊長

The captain and crew members welcomed all of the visitors as they came on board.
機長和船員們歡迎登上船的所有訪客。

普 100

🪶(秒殺解字) capt(head)+ain →「頭」子，表示「船長」、「機長」、「隊長」。

adoption
[ə`dɑpʃən]

n. 採用；收養

The charity provides psychological support and practical suggestions before and after adoption.
慈善機構在收養前後會提供心理支持和實用建議。

普 99

🪶(秒殺解字) ad(to)+opt(choose)+ion →「採用」、「收養」皆是經過「選擇」。

survive
[sə`vaɪv]

v. 生還；留存；生存

Doctors considered that Marcus would not survive with such severe complications.
醫生認為，Marcus 無法在如此嚴重的併發症中存活下來。

普 102
108
警特 109

🪶(秒殺解字) sur(=super=over)+viv(live)+e →「活」下來的時間「超過」預期，表示「倖存」、「生還」。相關同源字有 **viv**id (adj. 清楚的；鮮明的)、re**viv**e (v. 使復甦、復活)、**vit**al (adj. 極重要、不可缺的)、**vit**amin (n. 維他命)、**vi**able (adj. 可實施的)。

survival

[sə`vaɪvl]

n. 倖存；生存；存活

| 詞搭 | the survival of the fittest 適者生存

---

survivor

[sə`vaɪvɚ]

n. 生還者；獲救者

The doctor says his chances of survival from lung cancer are not good.
醫生說他從肺癌中存活下來的機會並不高。

Living as a breast cancer survivor, Marisa spends every day living to the fullest.
身為乳癌倖存者，Marisa 充實地度過她的每一天。

警特 105
108

| 詞搭 | survivor syndrome 生存者症候群

---

impact

[`ɪmpækt]

n. 影響；衝擊

The smartphone's impact on the way people communicate has been remarkable.
智慧型手機對人們溝通方式的影響非常顯著。

普 110
高 108
警特 105

（秒殺解字）im(in)+pac(fasten)+t → 把東西「固定」到某物之「內」，造成「影響」。

| 詞搭 | have an impact on / upon... 對……有影響／衝擊

| 同義字 | influence, effect, sway

---

investigate

[ɪn`vɛstə͵get]

v. 調查

The police are investigating a murder case in this apartment.
警方正在調查這間公寓中的一起謀殺案。

普 99

（秒殺解字）in(in)+vestig(track, trace, footprint)+ate → 深入「內部」，「追查」「足跡」。

| 同義字 | look into, make inquiries, probe

---

investigation

[ɪn͵vɛstə`geʃən]

n. 調查

The investigation into bribery has continued for nearly three months, and the result hasn't come out yet.
調查賄賂已經持續了近三個月，結果還沒有出來。

| 詞搭 | on / upon investigation 經調查；make investigation into... 對……加以調查

prefer

[prɪ`fɝ]

v. 較喜歡

This type of owl prefers a rainforest habitat and stays solitary.

這種類型的貓頭鷹喜歡雨林棲息地，並且保持獨居。

> 秒殺解字 pre(before)+fer(bear, carry) → 把較喜歡的東西，「拿」來「前方」。可用 bear 當神隊友，**b/f 轉音**，母音通轉，來記憶 **fer**，表示「攜帶」、「生育」、「承受」。相關同源字有 dif**fer**（ v. 不同 ）、in**fer**（ v. 推論 ）、suf**fer**（ v. 受苦 ）、re**fer**（ v. 提到 ）、trans**fer**（ v. 轉移 ）、con**fer**ence（ n. 正式會議 ）。

詞搭 prefer A to B 喜歡 A 甚於 B（ A 與 B 可為名詞、動名詞 ）

---

contract

[`kɑntrækt] /

[kən`trækt]

n. 合約、契約

v. 感染；收縮；簽契約

Boston officials have confirmed that they will sign a two-year contract with this multinational corporation.

Boston 官員已經確認，他們將與這家跨國公司簽署兩年的契約。

> 秒殺解字 con(together)+tract(drag, draw) →「拉」在「一起」是「收縮」、「簽契約」。可用 **drag** 當神隊友，**d/t**、**g/k 轉音**，來記憶 **tract**，皆表示「拉」。相關同源字有 at**tract**（ v. 吸引 ）、dis**tract**（ v. 使分心 ）、abs**tract**（ adj. 抽象的 ）、re**tract**（ v. 撤回 ）、sub**tract**（ v. 減去 ）、ex**tract**（ v. 提煉 ）。

詞搭 a breach of contract 違約；sign a contract 簽署契約書；a marriage contract 婚約

同義字 agreement

Dr. Fillmore is trying to find out how many people may have contracted the disease in this neighborhood.

Fillmore 醫生試圖找出附近有多少人感染了這個疾病。

詞搭 contract a marriage with... 與……訂婚；contract + sb's muscles / eyebrows / forehead 收縮／皺緊肌肉／眉頭／額頭

反義字 expand

convict

[.kən`vɪkt]

n. (被定罪或服刑中的)囚犯

[`kɑnvɪkt]

v. 使定罪

Nick has been convicted of shoplifting, but he was really starving at that time.

🔊 101

Nick 因到店裡行竊而被定罪,但那時他確實餓了。

> 🖋 **秒殺解字** con(intensive prefix)+vict(conquer) → 判決時被「說服」,「判定有罪」。可用 **Vict**or、**Vict**oria、**Vinc**ent、**Vinc**e 等流行名字當神隊友,**t/s/ʃ 轉音**,來記憶 **vict**、**vinc**,皆和「打敗」、「征服」有關。相關同源字有 **vict**or (n. 勝利者)、**vict**ory (n. 勝利)、con**vinc**e (v. 使相信)、pro**vinc**e (n. 省;州)。

詞搭	convict + sb. + of... 判某人有……的罪;a convicted murderer 被判有罪的謀殺犯;an escaped convict 逃犯
同義字	prisoner
反義字	acquit

conviction

[.kən`vɪkʃən]

n. 信念;定罪

The residents possess the conviction that public hygiene is the key to combating the viruses.

居民們堅信公共衛生是抵抗病毒的關鍵。

| 詞搭 | It is + sb's conviction / belief that + S + V 某人堅持……;a murder conviction 殺人罪判決;previous convictions 前科 |
| 同義字 | belief |

murder

[`mɝdɚ]

n. 謀殺(案)

v. 謀殺

Oswin was falsely accused of murder, but then committed suicide by taking poison.

Oswin 被錯誤地指控犯有謀殺罪,但隨後因服用毒藥而自殺了。

> 🖋 **秒殺解字** murder 和 mortal 同源, d/t 轉音,母音通轉,皆和「死亡」有關。

| 詞搭 | commit murder 犯謀殺罪;attempted murder 意圖謀殺;first-degree murder 一級謀殺 |

reasonable

[`riznəbl]

adj. 合理的;講理的

It is not reasonable to ask a three-year-old kid to behave well like an educated man.

🔊 105

要求一個三歲的孩子表現得像受過良好教育的人那樣是不合理的。

> 🖋 **秒殺解字** reason+able → 合理的。

詞搭	at a reasonable price 以公道的價格
同義字	rational, fair
反義字	unreasonable, irrational, unfair

customer
[ˋkʌstəmɚ]
n. (商店的) 顧客

Foodpanda has launched a big sales campaign in order to bring in new customers.
為了吸引新客戶，Foodpanda 發起了大規模的銷售活動。

普 106
警特 107

秒殺解字 custom+er → 「習慣」向某家商店、公司或餐廳購買商品或服務的「顧客」。

詞搭 a regular customer 老主顧

同義字 client

custom
[ˋkʌstəm]
n. 習俗
adj. 訂製的

It's the custom for the bride's mother to spill some water after the wedding car is driven away.
禮車開走後，新娘母親灑水是一種習俗。

警特 109

customary
[ˋkʌstəm͵ɛrɪ]
adj. 依慣例的；合乎習俗的

It is customary for my father to prepare meals for all of us in my family.
父親習慣為我們全家人做飯。

普 102

同義字 usual

benefit
[ˋbɛnəfɪt]
n. 利益
v. 有益於；獲益

The new MRT system will be <u>of great benefit</u> to our commuters.
新的捷運系統將為我們的通勤者帶來極大的好處。

高 **108**
警特 107
109

秒殺解字 bene(well)+fit(do, make) → do + sb. + good，就是給人帶來「好處」。

詞搭 of benefit to... 對……有裨益；for the benefit of... 為……的利益；unemployment benefit 失業津貼；benefit <u>from / by</u>... 從……中獲益

muscle
[ˋmʌsl̩]
n. 肌肉

Strengthening muscles is very important when people are getting older.
當人們變老時，強化肌肉非常重要。

普 102
警特 109

秒殺解字 mus(mouse)+cle → muscle, mouse 同源，母音通轉，核心語意是「老鼠」，因為鼓起的「肌肉」形如同「小老鼠」。

ignore

[ɪg`nɔr]

v 忽視、不理會

Ignoring the warning signs set up out there, many people are barbecuing near this beautiful beach.

許多人正在這個美麗的海灘附近烤肉而忽略了設置在那邊的警告標誌。

🪶(秒殺解字) i(=in=not)+gnor(know)+e → 本義「不」「知道」，但 ignore 卻表示視若無睹，故意「忽視」本來知道的事；ignorance 和 ignorant 仍然保有「無知」的意思。k 在現代英語不發音，但仍可用 **know** 當神隊友，**g/k 轉音**，母音通轉，來記憶 **gnor**，皆表示「知道」。

同義字 | neglect, disregard

---

ignorant

[`ɪgnərənt]

adj. 無知的；不知道的

I didn't want to appear ignorant, so I wouldn't raise any questions.

我不想顯得無知，所以我不會提出任何問題。

📖101

詞搭 | be ignorant of... 對……無知的

---

generate

[`dʒɛnə,ret]

v. 產生（光、電、熱）；引來（財富）

Wind power is a useful and clean technique for generating electricity.

風力發電是一種有用且乾淨的技術。

🪶(秒殺解字) gen(birth, produce)+er+ate →「產」「生」。

詞搭 | generate excitement / interest / support 引起興奮／興趣／支持；generate electricity / power / heat 發電／電力／熱

同義字 | create, produce, cause

---

generation

[,dʒɛnə`reʃən]

n. 世代

The recipe for this homemade apple pie has been passed down from generation to generation.

這種自製蘋果派的食譜世代相傳。

📖99
106
📖110
📖109

詞搭 | a generation gap 代溝

---

independent

[,ɪndɪ`pɛndənt]

adj. 獨立的

Many small independent bookshops are closing down and transforming into online bookstores.

許多小型獨立書店正在關閉，然後轉型為線上書店。

🪶(秒殺解字) in(not, opposite)+dependent →「不」「依靠的」，表示「獨立的」。

詞搭 | be independent of... 不依賴……、脫離……而獨立

同義字 | dependent

pleasure
[`plɛʒɚ]
n. 快樂、樂趣

It's a pleasure to watch an enjoyable ball game on Friday night.
在星期五晚上觀看一場愉快的球賽是一件樂事。

秒殺解字 please+ure → 能「取悅」人的事物。

詞搭 take pleasure in + <u>N / Ving</u> 樂於……、以……為樂；for pleasure 為消遣；with pleasure 高興地、非常樂意

同義字 enjoyment, delight

---

unpleasant
[ʌn`plɛzn̩t]
adj. 令人不愉快的

Jill and Bob argued the whole time, so it was a pretty unpleasant journey.
Jill 和 Bob 一直在爭論，所以那是一段非常不愉快的旅程。

詞搭 an unpleasant smell 難聞的氣味；unpleasant weather 討厭的天氣

同義字 nasty, disgusting

反義字 pleasant, nice

---

headquarters
[`hɛd͵kwɔrtɚz]
n. （公司的）總部
（單複同形）
（= HQ）

The motor company announced the move to its new headquarters in an effort to accommodate rapid personnel expansion.
這家汽車公司宣布遷至新總部，以容納快速增加的員工。

秒殺解字 head+quarters(military dwelling place) → 本指軍隊「指揮官」的「居住所」，引申為「總部」。

詞搭 at headquarters 在總部；general headquarters 總司令部

---

associate
[ə`soʃɪ͵et]
n. 合夥人
v. 使有關聯；交往；結交
adj. 副的

Most people associate high prices with good quality, but that's not always the case.
大多數人將高價格與高質量連結在一起，但事實並非總是如此。

曾 102

秒殺解字 as(=ad=to)+soci(join)+ate → 去「加入」某團體，指「結交」、「使有關連」。相關同源字有 **soci**ety (n. 社會)、**soci**al (adj. 社會的；社交的)、**soci**able (adj. 好社交的)、**soci**alize (v. 交際)。

詞搭 associate A with B 因 A 聯想 B；A be <u>connected / associated</u> with + B = A be related to B = A be linked <u>with / to</u> B = A <u>have / be</u> something to do with B = A be bound up with B = A go hand in hand with B = A and B go hand in hand A 與 B 有關聯

01 ___ In some states of America, carrying recreational marijuana is
_____. For example, California is one of them. However, in
Taiwan, carrying or owning marijuana will result in jail time.

(A) medical   (B) particular
(C) imaginative   (D) legal

02 ___ Natural _____ can bring wealth and fame to a country.
Nonetheless, sometimes it will also bring destruction upon your land.
Some speculated that the reason behind the 2003 invasion of Iraq lies
in the oil under their land.

(A) resources   (B) designs
(C) responses   (D) techniques

03 ___ The movie is not suitable for kids. Even if the kid is _____ by
his or her parents, the movie is still too violent and brutal for young
children.

(A) accompanied   (B) applied
(C) supplied   (D) denied

04 ___ To control the ongoing virus, there will be no _____ for anyone.
If you come back from abroad, you need to be quarantined for at least
14 days to make sure you are not infected.

(A) publication   (B) dysfunction
(C) exception   (D) institution

05 ___ He has a strong _____ to win. He will never be satisfied with just
a small victory, and will keep on fighting until there is no enemy left.

(A) vogue   (B) desire
(C) harassment   (D) addiction

06 ___ Due to the pandemic, the launch day of the game will be postponed indefinitely. However, rumor has it that the game is going to be released in the second _____ of 2021.

(A) visa   (B) brink
(C) utensil   (D) quarter

07 ___ The NBA final is always a drawn-out war. Both teams are tired after a long series, and it is the time to see which team is superior in _____ their energy for the last game.

(A) preserving   (B) reserving
(C) conserving   (D) observing

08 ___ It is sometimes really hard to _____ the twin brothers, Marcus and Mark, because they look alike and always dress the same.

(A) allocate   (B) manipulate
(C) retaliate   (D) distinguish

09 ___ The great war lasted for decades. Countless families and friends were forced to be _____ for a long time.

(A) distorted   (B) operated
(C) separated   (D) vibrated

10 ___ Before the _____ of your kitten, we have to assess your financial situation and also your personal background. By doing so, we hope to provide the kitten with the best home.

(A) combination   (B) connection
(C) adoption   (D) revelation

11 ___ The _____ of the airplane crash was miraculously unharmed physically. However, he was diagnosed with the so-called "survivor syndrome", which made him feel extremely guilty of his survival.

(A) survivor   (B) supporter
(C) ambassador   (D) predecessor

12 ___   The _____ of the car accident was so severe that he forgot
everything happening that night. The police are still trying to piece
together what really happened during the rainy night.

(A) myth   (B) impact
(C) excess   (D) anxiety

13 ___   Once you sign the _____, our work shall begin. Remember that if
you decide to do this, there is no turning back for you.

(A) contract   (B) ceremony
(C) designation   (D) monument

14 ___   Students love to go to this restaurant. The owner is friendly and the
price of the food is _____. It is so popular that if you don't get
there within 10 minutes after school, you will have no chance to taste
the food there.

(A) flexible   (B) vulnerable
(C) reasonable   (D) heritable

15 ___   When we see people getting bullied, we should never _____
them and move on. We must try our best to help the victims and teach
the bullies a lesson.

(A) recruit   (B) simplify
(C) disrupt   (D) ignore

解答
1.(D) 2.(A) 3.(A) 4.(C) 5.(B) 6.(D) 7.(A) 8.(D) 9.(C) 10.(C) 11.(A) 12.(B) 13.(A) 14.(C) 15.(D)

estimate

[ˈɛstəmɪt]

n. 估計

[ˈɛstəˌmet]

v. 估計

During the pandemic, the public deficit was estimated to be around USD 3 billion.
在流行病期間，公共赤字估計約為 30 億美金。

普 103
警特 106

🖋 **秒殺解字** estim(value)+ate → 表示「估價」，和 **esteem** 同源，母音通轉。

詞搭   be estimated to <u>be / have / cost</u> 估計；an estimated + 數字 估計有……；estimate at... 估計有……

---

practical

[ˈpræktɪkl]

adj. 實際上的；務實的；實用的

This book offers practical and effective methods for parents to help their kids in dealing with stress.
本書為父母提供了實用有效的方法來幫助孩子應對壓力。

普 106
107
高 108
警特 106

🖋 **秒殺解字** practice+al →「實」際上「的」。

詞搭   practical <u>difficulties / experience</u> 實際的困難／經驗；for practical purposes 實際上

同義字   realistic

反義字   impractical

---

interpret

[ɪnˈtɝprɪt]

v. 解釋、詮釋；翻譯；口譯；視為

Sigmund Freud attempted to interpret the meaning of dreams, and found out how these dreams could help people understand themselves.
Sigmund Freud 試圖解釋夢想的含義，並找出這些夢如何幫助人們了解自己。

警特 106

---

interpretation

[ɪnˌtɝprɪˈteʃən]

n. 解釋、詮釋；口譯

Ken's wrong interpretation of May's letter may be the main reason why they finally got divorced.
Ken 對 May 來信的錯誤解釋可能是他們最終離婚的主要原因。

詞搭   interpret A as B 將 A 解釋／詮釋為 B

disease
[dɪˋziz]

n. 疾病

Because of vaccines, measles and chickenpox are rare diseases these days, but they are quite contagious.

由於疫苗的緣故，麻疹和水痘是近來罕見的疾病，但它們具有很強的傳染性。

秒殺解字 dis(away)+ease(ease) →「離開」「舒適」的環境，常會造成「不舒服」、「不便利」，14 世紀末時出衍生出「疾病」的意思。

詞搭 a(n) incurable / hereditary disease 絕症／遺傳病；catch / contract a disease 染上疾病

普 104
105
警特 105

---

electric
[ɪˋlɛktrɪk]

adj. 電的；用電操作的；電動的

A big fire broke out last night in this house, and the investigators are wondering if the electric blanket was the major cause.

昨晚在這間房子裡發生了大火，調查人員想知道電熱毯是否是主要原因。

秒殺解字 electr(electric, electricity)+ic → **electr**、**electro** 表示「電的」或「電」，本義是「琥珀」（**amber**），源自希臘文。古希臘人發現琥珀摩擦時會產生靜電，會吸引羽毛、線頭等小東西，這種摩擦起電的現象被稱為 elektron，進入拉丁語後寫作 electrum。

普 102

---

electricity
[ɪˏlɛkˋtrɪsətɪ]

n. 電；電力

Due to the earthquake, the supply of electricity to many homes in this area has been cut off.

由於地震關係，此地區許多房屋的電力供應被切斷。

詞搭 by electricity 以電力；negative / positive electricity 陰／陽電

普 100
警特 109

---

electronic
[ɪˏlɛkˋtrɑnɪk]

adj. 電子的

Electronic banking may be convenient to most people, but there indeed are risks that exist.

電子銀行對於大多數人來說可能很方便，但是確實存在風險。

普 99
警特 108

---

electronics
[ɪˏlɛkˋtrɑnɪks]

n. 電子學

In the electronics industry, more than 500 job openings are available right now.

在電子業中，目前有 500 多個職位空缺。

詞搭 an electronics company 電子公司

普 104

trafficking

[ˋtræfɪkɪŋ]

n. 走私

The two men were arrested for drug trafficking in Thailand, and are to be sentenced to death.

這兩名男子在泰國因販毒被捕，將被判處死刑。

秒殺解字 tra(=trans=across)+ffic(=friction=rub)+ing → 「跨越」「磨擦」，毒品、槍枝等「走私」的非法交易，和交通一樣，都是從一方「跨越」到另一方，也容易產生衝突、「磨擦」。

詞搭 drug / baby trafficking 販毒／販嬰

---

consequence

[ˋkɑnsəˏkwəns]

n. 結果、後果；重要

Polar bears are going south in search of food as a consequence of global warming.

由於全球暖化影響，北極熊正往南尋找食物。

普 102
警特 105
107

秒殺解字 con(together)+sequ(follow)+ent → 本義「跟著」「一起」走，表示「尾隨」，有先後順序的意思，隱含「因果」概念。可用 second 當神隊友，母音通轉，來記憶 sequ，表示「跟隨」。second 是「跟隨」在第一名後面，所以是「第二的」，而 second 當動詞時，有「贊成」、「附議」的意思，意味著「跟隨」別人的意見。相關同源字有 sequel (n. 續集；隨之而來的事)、sequence (n. 順序；連續)、consequent (adj. 隨之而來的、由此引起的)、consequently (adv. 因此)、consecutive (adj. 連續的)、execute (v. 執行；處死)、subsequent (adj. 隨後的)。

詞搭 in consequence of... = as a consequence of... = as a result of... = because of... = on account of... 因為……；of no / little / some / great consequence / importance 不／不太／有些／非常重要

同義字 result

---

dramatic

[drəˋmætɪk]

adj. 戲劇的；戲劇性的；顯著的；強烈的

Schools in Taiwan have suffered a dramatic drop in student numbers as a result of the low birth rate.

由於出生率低，台灣的學校學生人數急劇下降。

秒殺解字 drama+t+ic → 「戲劇」性的。

conclude

[kən`klud]

v. 作結論；結束

The chairman cleared his throat and concluded that 曾 103
cooperation would be the only way for survival.
主席清清喉嚨並且做出合作將是生存的唯一途徑的結論。

秒殺解字 con(together)+clud(close)+e → 把所有東西「關」
在「一起」，表示「下結論」。可用 **close** 當神隊友，**d/z/**
s/ʒ 轉音，母音通轉，來記憶 **clud**、**clus**，皆表示「關閉」。
相關同源字有 ex**clud**e (v. 拒絕接納)、 ex**clud**ing (prep.
除……之外)。

詞搭 conclude that... 斷定／論定……；To conclude 總而言之

conclusive

[kən`klusɪv]

adj. 決定性的；確實
的

The police still have no conclusive evidence that 高 108
Morgan was at the scene of the crime.
警方仍然沒有確切的證據證明 Morgan 當時正在犯罪現
場。

反義字 inconclusive

illustrate

[`ɪləstret]

v. 為……畫插圖；説
明

Children's books are usually illustrated with pictures 警特 109
for better understanding.
為了更好理解，兒童讀物通常附有圖片。

秒殺解字 il(in)+lustr(light, clear, bright)+ate → 在「裡面」「照
光」，使意思更「清楚」，表示「舉例説明」。

illustration

[ˌɪlə`streʃən]

n. 圖解 ；插圖

Polly presented a full-page illustration in order to 曾 105
explain her project to her manager.
Polly 展示了整頁的圖示，以便向經理解釋她的計畫。

enable

[ɪn`ebl̩]

v. 使能夠

The social media apps enable people to
communicate in a modern way. 警特 105
社群媒體應用程式使人們能夠以現代方式進行溝通交流。

秒殺解字 en(make)+able →「使」「能夠」。

ultimate

[`ʌltəmɪt]

n. 極致

adj. 最後的；終極的

My boss will make the ultimate decision about who 高 108
will be transferred to the sales department. 警特 105
我的老闆將做最後決定誰將轉調至銷售部。

秒殺解字 ultim(=final)+ate → 到了「最後」階段。

詞搭 be the ultimate in... 是……方面的最高點； ultimate destination
最終目的地；the ultimate penalty 極刑

同義字 final

surround
[sə`raʊnd]
v. 環繞

The camping site <u>is surrounded by</u> mountains and forests, and the best part is a lake in the center of it.
這個露營地被群山和森林所環繞，且最好的是營地中心的湖泊。

 104

（秒殺解字）sur(=super=over)+r+ound(=und=water, wet, wave) → 「水」「超過」負荷，滿了出來，可想像淹水時房子都遭水「圍繞」著。17 世紀時，拼字受到 round 影響，添加了一個 r。坊間書籍和網路幾乎都會犯一個錯誤，把 surroud 和 round, around 歸類在一起，但事實上它們並不同源。

---

eliminate
[ɪ`lɪmə‚net]
v. 殲滅；剔除；（比賽中）淘汰

Sanitation workers are trying to eliminate the possibility of transferring any germs.
清潔人員正在努力消除細菌傳播的可能性。

普 100
警特 108

（秒殺解字）e(=ex=out)+limin(threshold)+ate → 排除在「門檻」之「外」，表示「消除」沒有必要的事物，或者經由選擇或競爭，「淘汰」較差的人或物。可用 limit 當神隊友，**t/n 轉音**，來記憶 limin，表示「界線」、「限制」、「門檻」。相關同源字有 **limit**（n./v. 限制）、pre**limin**ary（adj. 預備的、初步的 n. 預賽）、sub**lim**e（adj. 極好的 n 極好之物）。

詞搭 eliminate waste matter from the body 把廢物排出體外

同義字 get rid of, eradicate, root out

---

elimination
[ɪ‚lɪmə`neʃən]
n. 殲滅；淘汰

We were all disappointed by the elimination of our national team in the semi-finals.
我們都對於國家隊在準決賽中被淘汰感到失望。

---

emotion
[ɪ`moʃən]
n. 情緒；激動之情

After being separated for so many years, Rose faced her mother with mixed emotions.
分離多年後，Rose 面對母親充滿了複雜的情緒。

普 102
106
警特 107

（秒殺解字）e(=ex=out)+mot(move)+ion → 「移動」到「外」，示愛、恨、憤怒等等「情緒」。

詞搭 with emotion 激動地；a man of strong emotions 感情強烈的人

同義字 feeling

define
[dɪˋfaɪn]

v. 下定義；解釋

If you don't know how to define a word, just look it up in a dictionary.
如果你不知道如何定義某個字，只需查字典就可以了。

秒殺解字 de(completely)+fin(limit, bound)+e → 「完全地」立「界線」，引申為「下定義」。相關同源字有 **fin**ish (v. 完成)、**fin**al (adj. 最後的)、**fin**e (n./v. 罰款)、**fin**ance (n. 財政 v. 提供資金)、con**fin**e (v. 限制)、re**fin**e (v. 改進；提煉)。

詞搭 define A as B 將 A 定義為 B

definite
[ˋdɛfənɪt]

adj. 明確的；肯定的

The company hasn't released a definite answer to the question of when the amusement park will reopen.
該公司尚未就遊樂園何時重新開放問題發布確切答案。

普 103
108

同義字 clear

反義字 indefinite

definitely
[ˋdɛfənɪtlɪ]

adv. 絕對；非常

To explore the world of art, Chimei Museum is definitely worth a visit.
為了探索藝術世界，奇美博物館絕對值得一遊。

普 108

同義字 absolutely, certainly

afford
[əˋford]

v. 買得起、負擔得起

Our country can't afford to build another high-speed railway.
我們國家負擔不起修建另一條高速鐵路的費用。

普 100
警特 106
108

秒殺解字 af(=ad=to)+ford(=forth=forward=carry out) → 能「帶」「往前」，引申為「買得起」、「有時間做」。

詞搭 can afford + sth. 買得起某物；can afford + to V 有能力從事……

formula
[ˋfɔrmjələ]

n. 配方；公式；方程式

We think we might have hit on a successful formula to better manage our time.
我們認為我們可能已經找到了管理自己時間的成功方法。

普 105
警特 108

秒殺解字 form(form)+ule+a → 按既有「形式」來的，表示「公式」。

複數型 formulas / formulae [ˋfɔrmjəli]

formulate

[ˈfɔrmjəˌlet]

v. 判定；規劃；想出；制定配方

The association is trying to formulate the game plan to follow, in case the typhoon causes delays. 　📅 108

協會正試圖制定比賽計劃，以防颱風造成延賽。

---

apparent

[əˈpærənt]

adj. 明顯的；表面的

It is fairly apparent from recent studies that the drug has some troublesome side effects. 　📅 104

從最近的研究中可以很明顯地看出這種藥物具有一些麻煩的副作用。

（秒殺解字）ap(=ad=to)+par(appear, visible)+ent →「出現」可讓人「看見」，表示「明顯的」。可用 **appear** 當神隊友，**母音通轉**，來記憶 **par**、**pear**，表示「出現」或「可看見的」。相關同源字有 ap**pear**（v. 出現）、ap**pear**ance（n. 出現；外表）、disap**pear**（v. 消失）、disap**pear**ance（n. 失蹤）、trans**par**ent（adj. 透明的、能看穿的）。

詞搭 | It is apparent that + S + V...……是明顯的

同義字 | obvious, evident, clear

---

instruction

[ɪnˈstrʌkʃən]

n. 教導；指示；（機器）使用說明

Don't forget to read the instructions on the package before using it. 　📅 103 108 / 警特 108

使用前，請不要忘記閱讀包裝上的説明。

（秒殺解字）in(in)+struc(build) +t → 在人腦「內」「建構」知識。相關同源字有 **struc**ture（n. 結構；建築物）、con**struc**t（v. 建造、建設）、de**stroy**（v. 破壞）、in**stru**ment（n. 儀器；樂器）、ob**struc**t（v. 阻塞；阻止）。

詞搭 | give / receive instruction in... 給予／接受……方面的教導；
under + sb's instruction / guidance / direction 在某人的教導下

culture [`kʌltʃɚ] **n.** 文化	The TV program is devoted to rock music, fashion, popular food and other parts of youth culture. 高 100 107 這個電視節目專門播放搖滾音樂，時尚，流行食品和青年文化的其他部分。

秒殺解字 cult(cultivate)+ure → 「耕種」，表示「農業」。文化發軔大多和「耕種」有關。

詞搭 pop culture 流行文化；culture shock 文化衝擊

---

cultural [`kʌltʃərəl] **adj.** 文化的	Though America and the United Kingdom speak the same language, they do have many cultural differences. 高 107 警特 105 107 儘管美國和英國使用相同的語言，但它們確實有許多文化差異。

詞搭 cultural exchange / conflict / heritage 文化交流／衝突／遺產

---

eventually [ɪ`vɛntʃʊəlɪ] **adv.** 終究；最後	Thomas eventually had good luck, but it was actually a low-paid service job. 普 100 104 警特 105 107 109 Thomas 最終好運降臨，但實際上從事低薪服務工作。

秒殺解字 e(=ex=out)+ven(come)+t+u+al+ly → 本義「跑」「出來」，表示「最後」。相關同源字有 event (n. 事件)、eventual (adj. 最後的)、adventure (n. 冒險)、invent (v. 發明)、prevent (v. 阻止)、convenient (adj. 便利的)、convene (v. 集會)、convention (n. 大型會議，習俗)、conventional (adj. 傳統的)、avenue (n. 大街)、revenue (n. 國家稅收)。

同義字 finally, ultimately, in the end

---

preparation [ˌprɛpə`reʃən] **n.** 準備；預備	Months of preparation are needed to organize a grand music festival. 高 106 需要幾個月的準備來策畫盛大的音樂節。

秒殺解字 pre(before)+par(prepare)+ate+ion → 「先」「準備」。相關同源字有 prepare (v. 準備)、parade (n./v. 遊行)、apparatus (n. 裝置、設備)、separate (v. 隔開；分開 adj. 個別的)、several (adj. 幾個的；各自的)、repair (v./n. 修理)。

詞搭 in preparation for... 以準備……；make preparations for... 為……做準備

revolution

[ˌrɛvə`luʃən]

n. 革命；旋轉；（星球）運行；（天體的）公轉

The French people overthrew the monarchy and established a republic in the famous French Revolution.

在著名的法國大革命中，法國人民推翻了君主制，並建立了一個共和國。

🖋️ **秒殺解字** re(back)+volu(roll)+tion →「轉」「回去」。**volv**、**volu** 同源，**u/v** 對應，皆表示「**旋轉**」、「**滾動**」。**volv**、**volu** 普遍存在動詞和名詞間的對應，如 revolve、revolution，不妨用 **Volvo**（富豪汽車）當神隊友，來幫助記憶。相關同源字有 e**volv**e（v. 逐漸演變）、e**volu**tion（n. 發展）in**volv**e（v. 牽涉；參與；包含）、re**volv**e（v. 旋轉）re**volv**ing（adj. 旋轉的）、re**volt**（v./n. 反叛）、**volu**me（n. 音量；量）。

詞搭 a revolution in communications 通訊的大變革

revolutionary

[ˌrɛvə`luʃənˌɛrɪ]

n. 革命家
adj. 革命性的；創新的

Having good weather and enough rainfall, we have achieved revolutionary growth in our farm.

憑藉良好的天氣和充足的降雨，我們的農場達成了革命性的增長。

同義字 innovative

revolutionize

[ˌrɛvə`luʃənˌaɪz]

v. 徹底改革

5G technology is going to revolutionize everything we do and how we live in this modern world.

5G 技術將徹底改變我們所做的一切以及我們在這個現代世界中的生活方式。

詞搭 revolutionize the treatment of this disease 徹底改革這種病的治療方法

trend

[trɛnd]

n. 趨勢、潮流

A lot of youngsters don't have their own ideas, but they just follow the latest trends.

許多年輕人沒有自己的想法，而只是跟隨最新趨勢。

🖋️ **秒殺解字** 源自古英語「朝向」、「轉動」的意思，引申為「趨勢」。

詞搭 set / start a / the trend 創造流行；keep up with the trends 趕上潮流；follow the trends 跟著潮流走

attract

[ə`trækt]

v. 吸引;引起注意或興趣

Alice's recent post on Facebook has attracted a lot of criticism, but she chose to ignore it.

Alice 最近在 Facebook 上的貼文引起了很多批評,但她選擇不理會。

圖 107
警特 106

> 秒殺解字 at(=ad=to)+trac(drag, draw)+t → 「拉」住某人注意力。可用 **drag** 當神隊友,**d/t**,**g/k** 轉音,來記憶 **trac**t,皆表示「拉」。相關同源字有 dis**trac**t (v. 使分心)、abs**trac**t (adj. 抽象的)、con**trac**t (n. 契約)、re**trac**t (v. 撤回)、sub**trac**t (v. 減去)、ex**trac**t (v. 提煉)。

詞搭 be attracted to / by... 對⋯⋯著迷、被⋯⋯深深吸引;attract / draw attention from... 吸引⋯⋯的注意力

attractive

[ə`træktɪv]

adj. 有吸引力的;誘人的

The prospect of spending seven whole days in one room isn't very attractive.

想到在一個房間裡待上整整七天這並不是很誘人。

圖 104

同義字 charming, appealing, alluring, fascinating

proposal

[prə`pozl]

n. 提議;提案;求婚

Our management committee has rejected the latest proposal put forward by the residents to install a new elevator.

我們的管理委員會拒絕了住戶提出的安裝新電梯的最新建議。

圖 106
警特 106

> 秒殺解字 pro(forward)+pos(put)+al → 把東西「放」在「前面」,表示「建議」。

詞搭 approve / reject a proposal 贊成/反對某項提議; put forward proposals for increasing sales 提議增加銷路;proposal of marriage 求婚

proposed

[prə`pozd]

adj. 提議的

The city government released proposed regulations to battle drunk driving.

市政府發布了擬議的法規以打擊酒後駕車。

圖 104

expert

[ˋɛkspɚt]

n. 專家
adj. 熟練的

The gardening expert Johnson suggests not overwatering the plants during the heatwave, or they may die from too much "love."
園藝專家 Johnson 建議在熱浪中不要給植物澆水，否則它們可能會因過多的「愛」而死亡。

普 99 104 108 高 106 108 警特 107

> **秒殺解字** ex(out)+per(try, risk)+t → 到「外面」「嘗試」、「冒險」，表示「專家」。可用表示「恐懼」的 **fear** 當神隊友，**p/f 轉音，母音通轉**，來記憶 **per**，表示「**嘗試**」、「**冒險**」，因為「嘗試」或「冒險」過程中，遇到未知事物，容易產生「**恐懼**」情緒。相關同源字有 ex**per**ience (n./v. 經驗)、ex**per**iment (n./v. 實驗)。

同義字	specialist
反義字	layman, beginner, novice

candidate

[ˋkændəˌdet / ˋkændədɪt]

n. 候選人；應徵者

Eating too much fast food could make you a probable candidate for obesity.
吃太多速食可能會讓你成為肥胖的候選人。

普 110 高 100 106 警特 106

> **秒殺解字** cand(shine, white, bright)+id+ate → cand 的核心語意是「發光」，後來衍生出「白色的」、「明亮的」、「純潔的」等意思。古羅馬人以前選舉或求公職都要穿「白」袍。相關同源字有 **cand**le (n. 蠟燭)、**cand**id (adj. 坦白的)、**cand**or (n. 坦白)、**chand**ler (n. 做、賣蠟燭的人)。

詞搭	a presidential candidate = a candidate for <u>president / the presidency</u> 總統候選人；a Ph.D. candidate = a candidate for the Ph.D. 博士候選人

gradual

[ˋgrædʒʊəl]

adj. 逐漸的

After a half a year of rehabilitation, my grandfather had noticed a gradual improvement in his knees.
復健半年後，我的祖父注意到他的膝蓋逐漸好轉。

普 104

> **秒殺解字** grad(walk, go, step)+u+al → 本義「走」，表示「逐漸的」。

反義字	sudden

gradually

[ˋgrædʒʊəlɪ]

adv. 逐漸地

As the years passed, Sandy gradually accepted the death of her husband.
隨著歲月的流逝，Sandy 逐漸接受了丈夫的去世。

普 100 103

同義字	little by little, bit by bit, by degrees
反義字	suddenly

appropriate

[ə`propriɪt] /

[ə`propriˌet]

v. 撥（款）
adj. 適當的、合適的

It would not be appropriate for parents to have a fight in front of their children.

父母在孩子面前吵架是不合適的。

普 108

🖊 **秒殺解字** ap(=ad=to)+propr(own)+i+ate → 此字當動詞時，意思是挪為「己」用，形容詞是表示對「自己」「適合的」。**priv**、**propr**、**proper**，p/v 轉音，母音通轉，和字首 **pre**、**pro** 同源，核心語意皆表示「前」（**before**）。自己的事會擺在「前面」，因此衍生出「自己的」、「私人的」意思。相關同源字有 **priv**ate（adj. 私人的）、**priv**acy（n. 隱私）、**priv**ilege（n. 特權）、**prop**er（adj. 適合的）、**proper**ty（n. 財產）。

同義字 | suitable, proper, right

反義字 | inappropriate, unsuitable, improper, wrong

misguide

[mɪs`gaɪd]

v. 誤導

The plastic surgeries misguide the singer's fans in believing he is only 20 years old.

整形手術誤導了這位歌手的歌迷以為他只有 20 歲。

高 108

threat

[θrɛt]

n. 威脅、恐嚇；惡兆

Serious air pollution poses a threat not only to humans but also to animals and plants.

嚴重的空氣污染不僅對人類而且對動物都構成威脅。

普 107
110
警特 105

🖊 **秒殺解字** threat(thrust, push) → 本義是「戳」、「刺」、「用力推」，表示「威脅」。

詞搭 | death threat 死亡威脅；make / issue a threat against + sb. 恐嚇某人；pose a threat to... 對……構成威脅

同義字 | menace, intimidation

threaten

[`θrɛtn̩]

v. 威脅

According to some researchers, global warming has been threatening the survival of all creatures on earth.

一些研究人員認為，全球暖化已在威脅地球上所有生物的生存。

高 105

詞搭 | threaten + to V... 威脅要……；threaten + sb. + with + sth. 以某事威脅某人

同義字 | menace, intimidate

threatening
[`θrɛtnɪŋ]

adj. 脅迫的；險惡的

After Barbie received a threatening phone call, she immediately called the police for confirmation.
Barbie 接到恐嚇威脅電話後，立即致電警察進行確認。

普 105

詞搭 a threatening phone call / letter 恐嚇電話／信

---

absence
[`æbsn̩s]

n. 缺席、不在場；缺乏

If you need an immediate response, please contact my colleagues during my absence.
如果您需要立即的答覆，在我不在期間請與我的同事聯繫。

高 101
105

秒殺解字 ab(away, off)+s(=ess=be)+ence → 「離開」現場，不「存在」，表示「缺席」。

詞搭 in / during + sb's absence 在某人不在時；in the absence of... 缺乏……；absence of mind 心不在焉；absence without leave 不假外出

反義字 presence

---

unique
[ju`nik]

adj. 與眾不同的；獨有的

This hotel has unique appeal to international tourists, so it's not easy to make a reservation.
這家飯店對國際遊客具有獨特的吸引力，因此要預訂並不容易。

普 102
高 105
110

秒殺解字 uni(one)+que → 獨「一」無二的。

詞搭 be unique / native / indigenous to + 地方 為某地方所獨有

---

typical
[`tɪpɪkl]

adj. 典型的；特有的

We are now having the typical August heat with occasional thunderstorms in the afternoon.
我們現在正處於典型的八月高溫氣候，下午偶有雷陣雨。

高 104
警特 106

秒殺解字 type+ic+al → 屬於某一種「類型」的，引申為「典型的」。

詞搭 be typical of... 是……的典型，有代表性的

reject

[rɪ`dʒɛkt]

v. 拒絕、回絕

Modern women reject traditional notions that women should stay home and take care of children.
現代婦女拒絕了傳統觀念如婦女應留在家中並照顧孩子。

> **秒殺解字** re(back)+jec(throw) +t →「丟」「回去」，表示「拒絕」。相關同源字有 sub**jec**t（v. 使臣服）、ob**jec**t（v. 反對）、in**jec**t（v. 注射）、e**jec**t（v. 逐出）。

| 同義字 | refuse, turn down |
| 反義字 | accept |

高 108
警特 109

perfect

[pə`fɛkt] / [`pɝ-fɪkt]

v. 使完美
adj. 完美的；完全的

Bonnie perfected her cooking skills after she gave birth to a child.
Bonnie 生完孩子後，更加精進了烹飪技巧。

> **秒殺解字** per(thoroughly)+fec(do, make)+t →「完全地」「做」到好才是「完美」。

| 同義字 | ideal, faultless, flawless , impeccable |
| 反義字 | imperfect, flawed |

高 101

conflict

[`kɑnflɪkt] / [kən`flɪkt]

n. 衝突；爭執
v. 衝突

This controversial issue brought the government into conflict with those more conservative politicians.
這個有爭議的問題使政府與那些比較傳統的政客發生衝突。

> **秒殺解字** con(together)+flic(strike)+t →「一起」「打」，表示「衝突」。相關同源字有 in**flic**t（v. 施加）、af**flic**t（v. 使痛苦）。

| 詞搭 | in conflict 衝突的；come into conflict with… 與……衝突；an armed conflict 交戰 |

高 108
警特 106

participate

[pɑr`tɪsə͵pet]

v. 參加

Our employees are welcome to participate in any company trips.
我們歡迎員工參加任何的員工旅遊。

| 詞搭 | participate in... = take part in...= partake in 參加…… |
| 反義字 | partake, take part |

曾 103
107

01 ___ The housing market is _____ to have a downturn this winter. As a result, owners are trying their best to sell their properties before it is too late.

(A) abused   (B) estimated
(C) induced   (D) reinforced

02 ___ The theory of the teaching method sounds valid. However, it still needs more _____ experiments to prove its worth.

(A) local   (B) practical
(C) critical   (D) clinical

03 ___ Cancer is always the top killer of humanity. However, a new treatment introduced by a Japanese scientist might become the ultimate cure for the deadly _____.

(A) panic   (B) loop
(C) disease   (D) tornado

04 ___ The criminal group was guilty of baby _____ and was sentenced to jail for a long time. However, they showed no regret and still played around in court without realizing they were in trouble.

(A) transportation   (B) constitution
(C) insurance   (D) trafficking

05 ___ The criminal is trying to talk his way out. However, the evidence presented is clear and trustworthy. What he said has little _____ to the case.

(A) consequence   (B) violence
(C) absence   (D) experience

06 ___ The movie received mostly positive reviews. Moreover, people praised the director and the writer for their creativity of coming up such a _____ ending for the film.

(A) plastic   (B) unrealistic
(C) dramatic   (D) specific

07 ___ Exercising not only strengthens people's muscles and bones, but it also _____ their nerve system to become more responsive.

(A) responds (B) evaluates
(C) rebels (D) enables

08 ___ Steve Jobs _____ our way of life by driving the popularization of the smartphones. Now, almost no one can live without a smartphone in their pockets.

(A) circulated (B) revolutionized
(C) classified (D) evolved

09 ___ Being conventionally beautiful has numerous advantages. According to science, people who are perceived as _____ are more likely to get hired for jobs and seem trustworthy.

(A) objective (B) attractive
(C) selective (D) effective

10 ___ The debate between the two _____ turned out to be a total disaster. They were supposed to express their policies to the voters, but the whole event became a shouting match.

(A) traitors (B) protesters
(C) candidates (D) conductors

11 ___ We often encourage students to read newspapers or watch TV news. However, if one only receives messages without processing and digesting information by themselves, they will often be _____ and misinformed.

(A) summoned (B) nominated
(C) distorted (D) misguided

12 ___ The _____ symptoms of this disease include sneezing, coughing, and loss of taste. If you experience any kind of the symptoms mentioned above, please wear a mask and go to the nearest hospital as soon as possible.

(A) typical (B) vocal
(C) alarming (D) ethnic

13 ___ If one doesn't know when and how to _____ other people's requests, he or she may end up feeling frustrated and exhausted due to the heavy interpersonal pressure.

(A) reject (B) dominate
(C) undergo (D) ensure

14 ___ The religious _____ between Christians and Muslims has lasted for thousands of years. Even until today, people still hurt each other simply because of differences in religions.

(A) review (B) conflict
(C) reservation (D) decline

15 ___ Tens of thousands of people flooded the street to _____ in the protest against the government. People in this country have put up with the royalty for way too long, and now is the time to step up.

(A) enforce (B) melt
(C) differ (D) participate

pilot
[`paɪlət]
n. 飛行員；舵手；嚮
導
v. 駕駛（飛機）

The devastating crash was reported to be caused by a pilot error.
據報導，這次嚴重的墜機是由飛行員錯誤造成的。

🔖106

（秒殺解字）pil(=ped=foot)+o+t(one who) → 源自希臘文「方向槳」(steering oaf)，pilot 本義是「舵手」。pil 和表示「腳」的字根 ped 有關，**d/l 轉音，母音通轉**。「舵手」和「腳」兩者同源的具體原因不詳，推測是因為兩者皆可用以控制「**行進方向**」。

---

compete
[kəm`pit]
v. 競爭

Athletes from 25 universities competed in this national sports event held in Pingtung.
來自 25 所大學的運動員參加了在屏東舉行的這項全國性體育比賽。

🔖106
警特 106

（秒殺解字）com(together)+pet(go, seek)+e → 大家「一起」「去」「競逐」目標。可用表示「**羽毛**」的 **feather** 當神隊友，**p/f，t/ð 轉音，母音通轉**，來記憶 pet，後引申為「**翅膀**」（**wing**），核心語意是「飛」（**fly**）、「衝」（**rush**），更衍生出「去」（**go**）、「尋求」（**seek**）、「攻擊」（**attack**）、「往……目標前進」（**aim for**）、「掉落」（**fall**）等諸多語意。相關同源字有 **pet**ition (v./n. 請願)、ap**pet**ite (n. 食慾)、re**peat** (v./n. 重複)、re**peat**ed (adj. 再三的)、re**pet**itive (adj. 反覆而無聊的)、re**pet**ition (n. 重複)。

詞搭 compete <u>with / against</u> 與／為……競爭；compete <u>for</u> 爭奪……

---

competition
[ˌkɑmpə`tɪʃən]
n. 競爭 ；比賽

Adair is running a privately-owned grocery store in the downtown area, and it <u>was in</u> direct <u>competition with</u> other chain stores.
Adair 在市中心開了一家自營手作雜貨店，與其他連鎖店直接競爭。

🔖103
106

詞搭 be in competition with... 與……競爭；<u>fierce / stiff / intense</u> competition

同義字 contest, rivalry

competent

[`kɑmpətənt]

adj. 能幹的、有能力的；勝任的

A competent teacher should be able to deal with students' bullying behavior.
稱職的老師應該能夠處理學生的霸凌行為。

警特 107

| 詞搭 | be competent + to V 有能力從事……；be competent for 能勝任某事 |

incompetent

[ɪn`kɑmpətənt]

adj. 不能勝任的；無能力的

The government is described as corrupt and incompetent, because people are feeling annoyed by low salaries and rising prices.
政府被描述為腐敗無能，因為人們對低薪和物價上漲感到苦惱。

高 103 106

| 詞搭 | be incompetent + to V 不能勝任…… |

literary

[`lɪtə͵rɛrɪ]

adj. 文學的

This university set up a literary corner to display many writers' life stories.
這所大學設立了文學角落來展示許多作家的生平故事。

高 110

秒殺解字 liter(letter)+ary → 和「文字」有關的，表示「文學的」。可用 **letter** 當神隊友，**母音通轉**，來記憶 **liter**，皆和「文字」有關。相關同源字有 **letter**（n. 字母；文字；信）、**liter**al（adj. 字面的；逐字的）、**liter**ature（n. 文學；文學作品）。

| 詞搭 | literary criticism 文學批評 |

literate

[`lɪtərɪt]

n. 識字者
adj. 識字的

Being literate in reading and math is essential to every child in elementary school.
對於小學的每個孩子來説，能識字閲讀與數學方面的能力至關重要。

illiterate

[ɪ`lɪtərɪt]

n. 不識字的人
adj. 不識字的、文盲的

We can hardly find anyone illiterate in this modern society.
在這個現代社會中，我們幾乎找不到文盲。

高 110

秒殺解字 il(not)+liter(letter)+ate →「不」識「字」的人。

| 詞搭 | computer illiterate 電腦文盲的；technologically illiterate 科技文盲的 |

literacy
[ɪˋlɪtərəsɪ]
n. 識字；素養

同義字 illiteracy

Competition, adventure and joy are basic tenets of physical literacy.
競爭、冒險和歡樂是體育素養的基本宗旨。

---

factory
[ˋfæktərɪ]
n. 工廠

High standards for safety and occupational health at the factory are highly required by our management.
我們管理階層對工廠的安全標準和職業健康提出了很高的要求。

📖 103

秒殺解字 fac(do, make)+ory(place)+t → 「做」東西的「場所」。

---

adjust
[əˋdʒʌst]
v. 適應；調整；調節

Some of the students found it challenging to adjust to the changes in online learning technology.
一些學生覺得要適應線上學習技術的改變很具有挑戰性。

📖 107
110

秒殺解字 ad(to)+just(join, next) → 使「連結」「靠在一起」，引申為「調整」。

詞搭 adjust / adapt / accustom oneself to + N / Ving 使自己適應於；
adjust / adapt to + N / Ving = get used to + N / Ving =
get / become / grow accustomed to + N / Ving 適應於

同義字 adapt

---

adjustment
[əˋdʒʌstmənt]
n. 適應；調整；調節

Going to college in a big city has been a difficult adjustment for those from the countryside.
在大城市上大學，對於那些來自鄉下的人來說蠻難以適應的。

📖 105

同義字 adaptation

---

distribute
[dɪˋstrɪbjut]
v. 分發；分配；散發

The local church has started distributing food and blankets to villagers in the disaster area.
當地的教堂已經開始向災區的村民分發食物和毯子。

秒殺解字 dis(individually)+tribu(give, assign, pay)+t+e → 把東西「給」、「分配」、「付」每一個「個體」。相關同源字有 **tribu**te (n. 貢物；敬意)、con**tribu**te (v. 貢獻；造成；投稿)、at**tribu**te (v. 歸咎於 n. 屬性)。

同義字 give out

distribution

[ˌdɪstrəˈbjuʃən]

n. 分配;分佈;散發

It will be a tough nut to crack when it comes to vaccine distribution in pandemic times.
在疾病大流行時期,疫苗的分配變成是一個棘手的問題了。

普 100
高 108
警特 105
106

detailed

[ˈditeld / dɪˈteld]

adj. 詳細的

Liang's new book describes much detailed information about how he got along with his father.
Liang 的新書描述了有關他與父親相處方式相當多的細節。

秒殺解字 de(completely)+tail(cut)+ed →「完全地」「切開」,本義「切成一片片」,引申為「詳細的」。可用表示「裁縫師」的 **tail**or 當神隊友,來記憶 **tail**,表示「切」,「裁縫師」必須幫客戶「量身訂做」、「裁切」、「修改」衣服。相關同源字有 **tail**or (n. 裁縫師 v. 量身訂做)、de**tail** (n. 細節 v. 詳細列舉)、re**tail** (n./v./adv. 零售地)。

詞搭 a detailed <u>report / account</u> 詳細報告/說明

distinct

[dɪˈstɪŋkt]

adj. 清楚的;不同的、獨特的

She is playing football, which is distinct from rugby.
她正在踢的是足球,不是橄欖球。

秒殺解字 dis(apart)+stinc(stick, prick)+t → 用「刺」挑出來「分開」,表示「清楚的」、「不同的」。相關同源字有 di**sting**uish (v. 辨別)、ex**ting**uish (v. 熄滅)、ex**tinc**t (adj. 絕種的)、in**stinc**t (n. 本能)。

詞搭 be distinct from... 不同於……

普 103

distinction

[dɪˈstɪŋkʃən]

n. 差別、區別;卓越;特色

There is an obvious distinction between what parents want and what children need.
父母想要和孩子需要之間有明顯的區別。

同義字 difference

普 102
103
警特 105

distinctly

[dɪˈstɪŋktlɪ]

adv. 清楚地;無疑地

Mothers always distinctly remember the days they gave birth to their babies.
母親總是會清楚地記得她們生下嬰兒的那天。

distinctive

[dɪˈstɪŋktɪv]

adj. 特殊的

The most distinctive feature of this school is its open and free learning environment.
這所學校最鮮明的特點是其開放和自由的學習環境。

高 108

distinctively

[dɪ`stɪŋktɪvlɪ]

adv. 特殊地；區別地

According to a study, older people who can distinctively smell the differences between roses and lemons may not be likely to suffer from dementia.
一項研究顯示，能夠嗅出玫瑰和檸檬之間的差異的老年人，他們可能不太會罹患癡呆症。

普 108

---

necessity

[nə`sɛsə͵tɪ]

n. 需要；必要性；必需品

It's reported that free Wi-Fi has become more of a necessity than anything else in a café.
據報導，免費 Wi-Fi 已成為咖啡館中的必需品。

普 100
警特 108

秒殺解字 ne(no, not)+cess(go)+ity → 「無法」「走」，引申為「需要」。

詞搭 the basic / bare necessities 生活必需品；of necessity 必然地

---

faculty

[`fækḷtɪ]

n. 教職員；才能；官能

Clifford is over ninety but still is in possession of most of his faculties.
Clifford 已經超過九十歲了，但仍然擁有大多數身體機能。

警特 105

秒殺解字 fac(=easy, do)+ule+ty → 「擁有「輕易」完成該領域任務的「才能」。

詞搭 the faculty of hearing / speech / observation 聽力／語言／觀察能力

---

critical

[`krɪtɪkḷ]

adj. 危急的；批評的

Keeping high motivation and maintaining progress are absolutely critical for success.
保持高積極度與維持進步對成功至關重要。

警特 106
109

秒殺解字 cri(decide, judge)+t+ic+al → 「危急的」關頭需正確「判斷」，做正確「決定」。

詞搭 be in a critical condition 處於危急的情況；be critical of... 對……批評

同義字 crucial

---

identify

[aɪ`dɛntə͵faɪ]

v. 指認；認定；視為同一；對……感同身受

The corpse was difficult to identify, because he was hit by a high-speed truck.
由於受到高速卡車撞擊，因此屍體難以識別。

普 99
高 108
警特 105
106
108

秒殺解字 ident(same)+i+fy(make, do) → 本義「使」「相同」，「辨識」就是現實和記憶中情況比對，找出「相同」者。

詞搭 identify A as B 將 A 認定為 B；identify A with B 將 A 與 B 視為相等

commit

[kə`mɪt]

v. 犯（罪）；奉獻

普 99 102

Detectives are investigating the crime scene in which a man committed suicide at around 8:30 pm.
偵探正在調查犯罪現場，一名男子在晚上 8:30 左右自殺。

秒殺解字 com(together)+mit(send) → 本義「送」在「一起」，現表示「承諾去做」、「犯錯」等。相關同源字有 **miss**ion（ n. 任務 ）、pro**mis**e（ v./n. 答應 ）、ad**mit**（ v. 承認 ）、ad**miss**ion（ n. 准許 ）、per**mit**（ v. 允許 ）、per**miss**ion（ n. 允許 ）、sub**mit**（ v. 呈遞 ）、sub**miss**ion（ n. 呈遞 ）、o**mit**（ v. 遺漏 ）、o**miss**ion（ n. 遺漏 ）。

詞搭 commit an err 犯錯；commit suicide 自殺；commit a crime / murder 犯罪／殺人罪；commit robbery 犯搶劫罪；commit / devote / dedicate A to B 將 A 奉獻於 B；commit oneself to... 盡力於……

commitment

[kə`mɪtmənt]

n. 委託；承諾；奉獻

Thanks to Miranda's participation and commitment, the cultural festival was a huge success.
由於 Miranda 的參與和付出，這個文化節慶活動才能獲得了極大的成功。

詞搭 make a commitment to N / Ving / V 致力要……、對……做承諾；sb's commitment to + N / Ving = sb's dedication to + N / Ving 某人對……的奉獻；meet + sb's commitments 盡自己的義務

cattle

[`kætḷ]

n. 牛群 (pl.)

It is amazing to know that painting eyes on the buttocks can save cattle from being killed by predators.
令人驚訝的是，在臀部畫上眼睛圖案可以避免牛群被獵捕者殺死。

秒殺解字 cattle(capital=head) → 一個國家的「大腦」就是「首」都（ **capit**al ）。英文句子起「頭」的第一個字，都要「大寫」（ **capit**al ）。古代人沒有衍生性金融商品，就以 **cattle** 的數量，也就是用牲口有幾「頭」來決定資產的多寡，同源字 **capit**al 也表示「資本」，而 **dairy cattle** 是指「乳牛」，**beef cattle** 是指「肉牛」。

詞搭 a herd of cattle 一群牛；60 head of cattle 六十頭牛

derive

[dɪˋraɪv]

v. 取得;源自

Arisa <u>derives</u> great satisfaction from going inline skating. 📷 101

Arisa 從滑直排輪中獲得了極大的滿足感。

🪶(秒殺解字) de(from)+riv(stream)+e →「從」「溪流」源頭處流下,表示「得到」,又引申出義「源自」、「衍生於」的意思。值得一提的是,本書宗旨在仔細探討英文字彙的「起源」(derivation),幫助學習者突破單字記憶瓶頸,鍛鍊思維能力。de**riv**e、**riv**al (n. 競爭對手 v. 匹敵、比得上)、**Rh**ine (n. 萊茵河)、**run** (v. 跑)、**ran**dom (adj. 隨意的、任意的) 同源,**母音通轉**,核心語意是「跑」(**run**)、「流動」(**flow**),因為河流、溪流都會「跑」和「流動」。**riv**al 本指住在「小溪」對面的人,共同使用一條溪,為了爭水產生衝突,後來由鄰居變成「**競爭對手**」;相關同源字還有 **riv**alry (n. 較勁)、un**riv**alled (adj. 無可匹敵的)。

詞搭 | derive A from B 從 B 取得 A;<u>derive / stem / come</u> from... 源自……

steeply

[ˋstiplɪ]

adv. 急遽地

The exports of this international company dropped steeply, even though it tried hard to get into Asian markets.

儘管這家國際公司試圖進入亞洲市場,但其出口卻急遽下降。

🪶(秒殺解字) → steep 指「高」、「深」,高深的地形代表險峻,引申為「急遽的」,其副詞是 steeply。

approve

[əˋpruv]

v. 批准、核可;贊成

Donald will only buy the house if Sally's parents approves their daughter's marriage to him.

Donald 只有在 Sally 的父母同意女兒嫁給他的情況下才會買房。

🪶(秒殺解字) ap(=ad=to)+prov(prove, test)+e → 通過「試驗」、「證明」是好的事物,就同意放行,表示「贊成」、「批准」。

詞搭 | approve of... 贊同……

反義字 | disapprove

approval

[əˋpruvl̩]

n. 贊成、同意

Children need to have their parents' approval before they open a bank account.

孩子在開設銀行帳戶之前需要得到父母的批准。

詞搭 | with your approval 承蒙贊成

反義字 | disapproval

appoint
[əˈpɔɪnt]

v. 選定；約定；指派

To our surprise, our teacher didn't <u>appoint</u> Davis <u>as</u> the class leader.

令我們驚訝的是，我們的老師沒有任命 Davis 為班長。

普 104
警特 106

🖊️ **秒殺解字** ap(=ad=to)+point(point) → 將人派到某個「點」上。

詞搭 appoint + sb. + to V 指定某人從事……；appoint + sb. + as + 職位… 指定某人擔任……職位

---

liberal
[ˈlɪbərəl]

adj. 自由的；開明的

From the interview, we know the chairman holds a more liberal attitude toward the management.

從採訪中我們知道，董事長對管理階層抱持更為寬鬆的態度。

🖊️ **秒殺解字** liber(free)+al → 「自由的」。

詞搭 liberal education 通識教育

同義字 free, broad-minded, tolerant

反義字 conservative

---

liberate
[ˈlɪbəˌret]

v. 解放；使自由

The army helped liberate those who were captured by the enemy.

軍隊幫助解放了被敵人俘虜的人。

詞搭 liberate + sb. + from + sth. 將某人從某事中解放

同義字 free

---

liberty
[ˈlɪbətɪ]

n. 自由

A teacher is not at liberty to reveal a student's academic performance and personal information to others.

老師無權向他人透露學生的學習成績和個人資訊。

詞搭 liberty of <u>speech / the press</u> 言論／出版自由；the Statue of Liberty 自由女神像；<u>individual / religious</u> liberty 個人／信仰的自由

---

expose
[ɪkˈspoz]

v. 暴露；接觸

Rod threatened to expose my secret to others unless I do as what he asked me to do.

Rod 威脅要把我的祕密暴露給他人，除非我按照他的要求去做。

圖 108

🖊️ **秒殺解字** ex(out)+pos(put)+e → 「放」「外面」，表示「暴露」、「揭露」。

詞搭 expose A to B 使 A 暴露於 B、使 A 接觸 B；expose a(n) <u>plot / scandal / imposter</u> 揭發陰謀／醜聞／騙徒

confuse
[kən`fjuz]

v. 使困惑；混淆；弄錯

Facial masks can confuse people because they can't read others' facial expressions.
口罩會使人感到困惑，因為他們無法看到別人的臉部表情。

> 🖋 **秒殺解字** con(together)+fus(pour)+e → 把所有東西都「倒」在「一起」，使人「困惑」。con**found** 和 con**fus**e 是「雙飾詞」（**doublet**），**d/z 轉音**，母音通轉。相關同源字有 re**fus**e（v. 拒絕）、dif**fus**e（v. 使擴散；散布）、trans**fus**ion（n. 輸血）。

曾 101
警特 105

詞搭 confuse A with B 將 A 與 B 混淆

同義字 puzzle, perplex, bewilder, baffle

confusion
[kən`fjuʒən]

n. 混亂；混淆；困惑

To avoid confusion, this mother prepares clothes of different colors for her twins.
為避免混亂，這位母親為雙胞胎準備了不同顏色的衣服。

曾 103
110

possess
[pə`zɛs]

v. 擁有、持有

Ned possessed an unusual ability to quickly memorize details of what he has seen.
Ned 具有非凡的能力可以快速記住他所看到的細節。

> 🖋 **秒殺解字** poss(=pot=powerful)+sess(=sed=sit) → 行使「權力」佔位置「坐」，可用「坐擁」來聯想。

曾 105

intellectual
[ˌɪntḷ`ɛktʃʊəl]

n. 知識份子
adj. 智力的

Labor organizations say there is a manpower shortage of those caring for people with intellectual disabilities and the challenges have only just begun.
勞工組織說，照顧智能障礙人士的人手短缺，而挑戰才剛剛開始。

> 🖋 **秒殺解字** intel(=inter=between)+lec(choose)+t+u+al →「從中」「挑選」事物所需的區辨能力，後引申為「智力的」。相關同源字有 intel**lec**t（n. 智力）、intel**lig**ent（adj. 聰明的）、intel**lig**ence（n. 聰明才智；情報）、col**lec**t（v. 收集；聚集）、e**lec**t（v. 選舉）、se**lec**t（v. 選擇）、neg**lec**t（v. 忽視、疏忽）、recol**lec**t（v. 回憶）、**lec**ture（n./v. 講課；演講）。

詞搭 the intellectual faculties / powers 智能／力

衍生字 intellectually [ˌɪntḷ`ɛktʃʊəlɪ] adv. 智力上；intellect [`ɪntḷˌɛkt] n. 智力

同義字 intelligent [ɪn`tɛlədʒənt] adj. 聰明的（intelligence [ɪn`tɛlədʒəns] n. 聰明才智；情報）

construct

[kən`strʌkt]

v. 興建、建造

Sagrada Família was constructed more than 100 years ago, however, it is still not complete.
聖家堂建造於 100 多年前，但尚未完成。

普 105
警特 107

(秒殺解字) con(together)+struct(build) → 把所有建材放在「一起」「建造」起來。相關同源字有 **struct**ure (n. 結構；建築物)、de**stroy** (v. 破壞)、in**struct** (v. 教導；命令)、in**stru**ment (n. 儀器；樂器)、ob**struct** (v. 阻塞；阻止)。

| 同義字 | build |
| 反義字 | destroy |

prospect

[`prɑspɛkt]

n. 可能性；前途、前景

v. 勘探、勘察

Prospects for a peaceful settlement of their dispute are not very likely for the time being.
和平解決他們爭端的希望暫時是不太可能。

普 102
高 108

(秒殺解字) pro(forward)+spect(look) →「往前」「看」，表示「前景」。相關同源字有 **spect**ator (n. 看比賽觀眾)、a**spect** (n. 方面)、in**spect** (v. 檢查)、re**spect** (v./n. 尊敬)、su**spect** (v. 懷疑)、per**spect**ive (n. 觀點)。

| 詞搭 | in prospect 預期的 |
| 同義字 | outlook |

suspect

[`sʌspɛkt]

n. 嫌疑犯

[sə`spɛkt]

v. 懷疑；猜想

Duncan was suspected of revealing our company's confidential information to a competitor.
Duncan 涉嫌向一位競爭對手洩露我們公司的機密信息。

普 107
高 108
警特 105

(秒殺解字) sus(=sub=up from under)+spect(look) → 從「下」往上偷偷「看」別人，引申為「懷疑」。

詞搭 suspect + sb. + of + N / Ving 懷疑某人犯了……之罪；
suspect danger 查覺到危險

The suspect who defrauded an old lady is in custody and will soon be charged.
涉嫌詐騙老太太的嫌疑人已被拘留，並將很快被起訴。

resolve

[rɪˋzɑlv]

v. 解決;下決心

The principal called for a third meeting to resolve the problem of the shortage in special education services.

校長召開第三次會議,以解決特殊教育服務不足的問題。

秒殺解字 re(back)+solv(loosen)+e → 本義是「鬆開」,將事物「還原」成原本成分,自 1520 年代後才有「決定」、「決心」的意思。solv、solu 同源,u/v 對應,皆表示「鬆開」、「使鬆開」。相關同源字有 **solv**e (v. 解決)、**solu**tion (n. 解決方法)、re**solu**te (adj. 堅決的、斷然的)、dis**solv**e (v. 分解、使溶解;解散)、ab**solu**te (adj. 完全的;絕對的)。

詞搭 resolve / solve a problem 解決問題;resolve + to V= be resolved + to V 下定決心要……

習 102
104
警特 106

resolved

[rɪˋzɑlvd]

adj. 下定決心的;斷然的

Fitch is resolved to propose to his girlfriend with a perfect plan.

Fitch 下定決心用一個完美的計劃來向女友求婚。

resolution

[͵rɛzəˋluʃən]

n. 志願;期望;決心

The city council has passed a resolution that restaurants can expand their outdoor seats to parking lots in order to meet social distancing guidelines.

市議會已通過一項決議,要求餐館可以將其戶外座位擴展到停車場,以滿足社交距離的指引方針。

詞搭 make a resolution + to V 下定決心要……

習 100

comfort

[ˋkʌmfɚt]

n. 舒適

v. 安慰

Most people won't step out of their comfort zone to truly explore the world.

大多數人不會走出自己的舒適區來真正探索世界。

秒殺解字 com(intensive prefix)+fort(strong) → 使人「堅強」,表示「舒適」、「安慰」。可用 **force** 當神隊友,**t/s 轉音**,母音通轉,來記憶 **fort**,表示「強壯的」、「堅固的」、「力量」。相關同源字有 **force** (v. 強迫 n. 力量)、en**force** (v. 實施;強迫)、rein**force** (v. 強化;加強)、**fort** (n. 要塞、堡壘)、**fort**ify (v. 加強)、ef**fort** (n. 努力)。

詞搭 give / bring / provide / offer + sb. + comfort 安慰某人;find / take comfort in... 在……中尋找安慰

同義字 consolation, console

警特 106
108

167

comfortable
[ˈkʌmfɚtəbl]

adj. 舒適的；自在的

A lot of mothers have a problem finding comfortable positions for breastfeeding.
許多母親在尋找舒適的姿勢餵母乳時都會遇到問題。

曾 101
警特 107

---

discomfort
[dɪsˈkʌmfɚt]

n. 不舒服、不適
v. 使不舒服

If the medicine causes discomfort, stop taking it and consult a doctor immediately.
如果藥物引起不適，請停止服用並立即就醫。

曾 104

---

brilliant
[ˈbrɪlɪənt]

adj. 明亮的；出色的

Faith came up with a brilliant idea for saving the dying kangaroo.
Faith 提出了一個絕妙的主意來挽救垂死的袋鼠。

秒殺解字 brill(to shine)+i+ant → 閃閃發亮，表示「明亮的」、「出色的」。

詞搭 a brilliant performance 出色的表演

曾 104
高 108

---

disappear
[ˌdɪsəˈpɪr]

v. 消失

If humans continue to destroy our living environment, more and more animals will disappear in the near future.
如果人類繼續破壞我們的生活環境，在不久的將來會有越來越多的動物消失。

秒殺解字 dis(opposite)+appear →「出現」的「相反」動作就是「消失」。

詞搭 disappear from... 從……消失；disappear behind... 消失在……後
同義字 vanish, fade away / out, melt away
反義字 appear

---

accounting
[əˈkaʊntɪŋ]

n. 會計；會計學

Hedy majors in accounting, while her twin sister majors in physical education.
Hedy 主修會計，而她的雙胞胎姐姐則主修體育。

秒殺解字 ac(=ad=to)+count(count, compute)+ing → 本義是「去」「計算」。

---

accountancy
[əˈkaʊntənsɪ]

n. 會計工作；會計學

The workload in an accountancy firm is excessive especially before the tax season.
會計師事務所的工作量非常大，尤其是在報稅季前。

advise

[əd`vaɪz]

v. 建議；勸告、忠告

The psychology counselor advised teachers how to combat emotional fatigue during the upcoming school year.
心理諮商師建議教師們如何應對新學年的情緒疲勞。

🪶（秒殺解字）ad(to)+vis(see)+e → 依我之「見」、「看」法，表示「建議」、「忠告」。

詞搭 advise + sb. + to V 勸某人從事……；advise + sb. + against + N / Ving 建議某人不要去……

同義字 suggest, recommend, urge, propose

📖 101

emphasize

[`ɛmfə͵saɪz]

v. 強調

The report emphasizes the importance of regular exercise and healthy diet for children.
該報告強調定期運動和健康飲食對兒童的重要性。

🪶（秒殺解字）em(=en=in)+phas(=phan=show)+ize → 將「內部」的重點「顯現」出來。

同義字 stress, highlight, underline

foundation

[faʊn`deʃən]

n. 地基；基礎；建立；基金會

The earthquake last night seemed to have shaken the foundations of this house, because I noticed several cracks on the wall.
昨晚的地震似乎已經動搖了這座房屋的地基，因為我注意到牆上有幾處裂縫。

🪶（秒殺解字）found(bottom)+ation →「底」部，表示「地基」、「基礎」、「創辦」。可用 **bottom** 當神隊友，**b/f 轉音**，**t/n 轉音**，母音通轉，來記憶 **fund**、**found**，皆表示「底部」、「基礎」。**bottom**（n. 底部 adj. 底部的）、**fund**（n. 基金 v. 提供資金）、**fund**amental（adj. 基本的；重要必須的）、**found**（v. 建立；創辦）、pro**found**（adj. 深遠的；深奧的）、un**found**ed（adj. 無根據的）、well-**found**ed（adj. 有事實根據的）。

詞搭 lay a foundation for... 為……奠下基礎；a foundation for research 研究基金

同義字 basis, base, founding, establishment

founder

[`faʊndɚ]

n. 創立者

Salman Amin Khan is the founder of Khan Academy, which has provided various free online courses since 2006.
Salman Amin Khan 是可汗學院的創辦人，該學院自 2006 年以來提供各種免費的線上課程。

📖特 106

assembly
[ə`sɛmblɪ]

n. 集會；（機器的）
裝配

Due to the hot weather, our school replaced outdoor assemblies with classroom broadcasting.
由於天氣炎熱，我們學校用教室廣播代替了室外集會。

秒殺解字 as(=ad=to)+sembl(same, seem, similar)+y → 集合志「同」道合者，使成「一」起。

| 同義字 | gathering, meeting

---

substance
[`sʌbstəns]

n. 物質；本質

A firefighter may sometimes be exposed to unknown harmful chemical substances.
消防員有時可能會接觸未知的有害化學物質。

秒殺解字 sub(under)+sta(stand)+ance → 「立」於「下方」構成事物的「物質」。

| 詞搭 | in substance 實質上；harmful substances 有害物質

---

substantiate
[səb`stænʃɪˌet]

v. 證實；使實體化

To curb misleading ads, the authorities ask the company to substantiate the claims about the effects of their products.
為了遏制誤導性廣告，當局要求該公司證實有關其產品功效的主張。

普 105

---

encounter
[ɪn`kaʊntə]

v. n. 遭遇；與……
不期而遇

Many of the students encountered some difficulty in learning trigonometry.
許多學生在學習三角函數時遇到了一些困難。

普 108
警特 105

秒殺解字 en(in)+counter(against) → 從「相反的」方向進「入」，表示沒有經過事先安排，「遭遇」一些問題或反對，或者「不期而遇」，或者「初次見面」。

| 詞搭 | encounter problems / difficulties 遭遇到困難；encounter + sb. = run/bump into + sb. 與某人不期而遇

Ella still remembered her first encounter with Wilson back in 1990 when she was still an intern.
Ella 仍然記得 1990 年與 Wilson 第一次見面，當時她還是一名實習生。

phenomenon

[fə`namə‚nan]

n. 現象 (sg.)

The increasing phenomenon of the single parent family shouldn't be ignored by the authorities.
主管當局不應該忽視單親家庭日益增多的現象。

普 104
警特 109

🪶 秒殺解字 phen(phan=show)+omen+on → 「顯現」的是「現象」。

詞搭 a natural phenomenon 一種自然現象

---

phenomena

[fə`namənə]

n. 現象 (pl.)

To convey important messages about these geological phenomena, some retired geologists will present a webinar.
為了傳達有關這些地質現象的重要訊息，一些退休的地質學家將舉辦一場網路研討會。

警特 109

---

nose

[noz]

n. 鼻子

v. 嗅出；小心翼翼地向前移動；聞

Amelia carefully nosed the car forward through the narrow street, hoping to find her guesthouse soon.
Amelia 小心翼翼地將汽車駛過狹窄的街道，希望能很快找到她的旅館。

🪶 秒殺解字 n 是全世界所有語言中最不可或缺的鼻音，為鼻音之祖，很多和鼻子相關的單字都有 n，例如：nasal (adj. 鼻音的)、nostril (n. 鼻孔)、nuzzle (v. 用鼻子觸) 等。nose 當動詞使用時，表示去「嗅」、「聞」，引申出「搜尋」、「打探出」等意思，這些動作都是需謹慎、慢慢完成，因此又引申出「小心翼翼地向前移動」的意思。

---

promote

[prə`mot]

v. 促進；提倡；升遷

Haley goes from door to door to promote his newly-developed products.
Haley 挨家挨戶推廣他新開發的產品。

普 106
警特 106

🪶 秒殺解字 pro(forward)+mot(move)+e → 「往前」「動」，表示「升遷」、「促進」、「提倡」。

---

promotion

[prə`moʃən]

n. 促進；提倡；升遷

The United Nations suggests the promotion of energy conservation especially in developed countries.
聯合國建議特別是在已開發國家中提升節能效率。

警特 106

01 ___ The _____ was arrested on suspicion of being drunk before flight. He claimed that he was sober the whole time. However, the blood alcohol test shows otherwise.

(A) breeder (B) pilot
(C) racist (D) sceptic

02 ___ These two teams are not on the same level. In other words, if these two teams want to _____ with each other, one team is going to lose by a large margin.

(A) stimulate (B) strive
(C) compete (D) intervene

03 ___ Peter Parker is an outstanding young man. However, he is not suitable for this job. I'm not saying that he is _____, but he is just not the right person for this mission.

(A) current (B) incompetent
(C) ancient (D) primary

04 ___ It is hard for the elders to _____ to the ever-changing technologies. During the prime of their lives, things didn't change as fast as they do nowadays.

(A) recall (B) divide
(C) equal (D) adjust

05 ___ The emergency food rations should be _____ to everyone with care. We don't have that much food to waste. No one is allowed more than their ration of food.

(A) populated (B) contributed
(C) attributed (D) distributed

06 ___ Before Michael, Trevor, and Franklin executed one of the biggest heists in modern history, they had designed a _____ plan. It was really a sink or swim situation for them.

(A) enlightened (B) heightened
(C) detailed (D) destined

07 ___ The Internet has become a _____ for modern people. It is safe to say that almost no one can live without the Internet.

(A) majority　　　　　　　　(B) authority
(C) necessity　　　　　　　　(D) community

08 ___ With the two major forces on the verge of war, we should stand together as one to solve the issue. During this _____ time, there should be no bias between the two political parties.

(A) critical　　　　　　　　(B) fundamental
(C) mental　　　　　　　　(D) physical

09 ___ Two centuries ago, the case could not be solved due to the lack of evidence. However, modern technology allows us to _____ who the real killer was.

(A) satisfy　　　　　　　　(B) identify
(C) classify　　　　　　　　(D) qualify

10 ___ The serial killer _____ a series of murder cases. Moreover, he had no regret after he was captured. As a result, the cold-blooded monster will be sentenced to death.

(A) permitted　　　　　　　　(B) transmitted
(C) committed　　　　　　　　(D) admitted

11 ___ The sales number dropped _____ this month. Please arrange a meeting with the sales department. We have to come up with a plan to stop the loss.

(A) originally　　　　　　　　(B) traditionally
(C) dependably　　　　　　　　(D) steeply

12 ___ Dubai already owns the tallest building in the world. This year, they plan to _____ yet another building that is even taller than the current tallest building in the world.

(A) release　　　　　　　　(B) impose
(C) appreciate　　　　　　　　(D) construct

13 ___ Even though the boss kept _____ how important the project was, his employees still found a way to ruin the plan.

(A) emphasizing   (B) sympathizing
(C) memorizing   (D) specializing

14 ___ To build a solid _____ for your English ability, you have to immerse yourself in an all-English environment. In this way, you will learn the language easier and faster.

(A) consumption   (B) regulation
(C) anticipation   (D) foundation

15 ___ Although he works hard every day, he never gets a chance to be _____. Some said that it is because of his awful attitude toward his supervisors.

(A) promoted   (B) suspended
(C) recovered   (D) debated

abandon

[ə`bændən]

v. **n.** 放棄；丟棄

Many farmers in Africa abandoned their farmlands as a result of the attacks by the insurgents.
由於叛亂分子的襲擊，非洲許多農民放棄了耕地。

> **秒殺解字** a(=ad=to)+bandon(power, jurisdiction) → bandon 和表示「禁令」的 ban 有關，而 ban 本指領主在自己的土地上擁有管轄權，可要求或「禁止」人們做什麼。abandon 字面意思就是「使自己處於某人的力量或管轄之下」，形同「丟棄」自己的權利或義務。

| 同義字 | leave, give up, forsake

---

radiation

[ˌredɪ`eʃən]

n. 放射；散發

As people seek outdoor activities for excitement and relaxation, it is important to remember that bathing in the sunshine comes with the risks of the Sun's <u>ultraviolet radiation</u>.
當人們尋求戶外活動的刺激和放鬆時，重要的是要記住，日光浴會帶來太陽紫外線輻射的風險。

高 108

> **秒殺解字** radi(ray, radiate)+ate+ion → 可用 **ray** 當神隊友，來記憶 **radi**、**radio**，皆和「光線」、「放射」有關。radius 在拉丁文原指「光線」，英文表示「圓或球體的半徑」，意味著周圍以某點為圓心，「放射」出來的範圍。同源字 **radio**，原指「光線」，後有「無線電」、「收音機」的意思。

---

mistake

[mɪs`tek]

n. 錯誤

v. 誤認

A hunter mistook a pet cat for a rabbit and shot it dead.
一位獵人把寵物貓誤認為是兔子，並把它射殺了。

普 100
102
警特 105
106

> **秒殺解字** mis(badly, wrongly)+take →「壞地」、「錯地」「認為」，表示「誤認」。

| 時態 | mistake, mistook [mɪs`tʊk], mistaken [mɪs`tekən]

| 詞搭 | make a mistake 犯錯；by mistake ≠ deliberately, on purpose 錯誤地、意外地；mistake A for B 誤將 A 當成 B

| 同義字 | error

frightening

[ˈfraɪtnɪŋ]

adj. 令人害怕的、嚇
人的

Driving along a steep cliff can be a pretty frightening experience for many people.
對於許多人來說，沿著陡峭的懸崖行駛可能會是非常恐怖的經歷。

秒殺解字 fright(fear)+en+ing → 令人「害怕」的。

同義字 scary, terrifying, horrifying, horrific

---

request

[rɪˈkwɛst]

n. **v.** 請求；要求

普 101
108

Haiti's government made an urgent request for international aid because of the huge earthquake.
由於發生大地震，海地政府緊急要求提供國際援助。

秒殺解字 re(again)+quir(ask, seek)+e → 本義「再次」「詢問」，引申為「要求」。相關同源字有 **quest**（n. 探索；尋求）、**quest**ion（n. 問題 v. 詢問）、**quest**ionnaire（n. 問卷）、**quer**y（n./v. 疑問）、con**quer**（v. 征服）、con**quest**（n. 征服）、ac**quir**e（v. 獲得）、ac**quis**ition（n. 獲得；學到；收購）、in**quir**e（v. 詢問）、in**quir**y（n. 詢問）、in**quis**itive（adj. 好奇的、好問的）、re**quir**e（v. 需要；要求）、ex**quis**ite（adj. 精美的；高雅的）。

詞搭 at + sb's request 應某人的請求；on / upon request 備索；by request 依照請求

n. 同義字 demand

v. 同義字 ask, require, demand

---

valuable

[ˈvæljʊəbl̩]

adj. 有價值的、珍貴
的

警特 109

Mr. Wang keeps their most valuable belongings locked in a safe in the bank.
王先生將他們最有價值的物品鎖在銀行的保險箱中。

秒殺解字 value(worth)+able → 有「價值」的。

同義字 precious

反義字 valueless, worthless

---

mental

[ˈmɛntl̩]

adj. 心理的；精神的

高 108
警特 105
106

The charity provides assistance and funds for people suffering from mental illness.
這家慈善機構為患有精神疾病的人們提供幫助和資金。

秒殺解字 men(mind, think)+t+al → 是出自內「心」、大腦的「想」法。可用 **mind** 當神隊友，**d/t** 轉音，母音通轉，來記憶 **ment**，表示「心（智）」、「思考」。相關同源字有 **mind**（n. 心智；想法 v. 在意）、re**mind**（v. 提醒、使想起）、**ment**ality（n. 心態）、**ment**ion（v./n. 提到）、**ment**or（n. 導師、指導者）、com**ment**（v./n. 評論）、absent-**mind**ed（adj. 心不在焉的）、**man**ia（n. 瘋狂）、**man**iac（n. 瘋子）、**man**darin（n. 華語）、auto**mat**ic（adj. 自動的）。

反義字 physical

pursue
[pɚˋsu]

v. 追求

After being a volunteer in a local hospital during her senior year, Betty decided to pursue surgical technology.

Betty 在高三時去當地一家醫院擔任志工之後決定追求學習外科技術。

(秒殺解字) pur(=pro=forward)+sue(=secut=follow) →「往前」「跟隨」是「追求」、「追蹤」。

詞搭 pursue a goal / an aim / an objective 追求目標

警特 106 108

burden
[ˋbɝdn̩]

n. 負擔
v. 使……負擔

The burden of taxation has risen substantially, because James has been responsible for his father's medical bills.

繳稅負擔大大增加了，因為 James 一直負責父親的醫療費用。

(秒殺解字) 源自古英語「被搬運之物」(that which is borne)，burden 的 bur 即 bear (傳運)。

詞搭 shoulder / bear / carry the burden of... 負起……的重擔

curious
[ˋkjʊrɪəs]

adj. 好奇的；古怪的、不尋常的

Young children are curious about everything they see, hear, and feel, and adults should always try to satisfy their needs.

幼兒對他們看到、聽到和感覺到的一切感到好奇，大人應該努力滿足他們的需求。

(秒殺解字) cur(=cure=care)+i+ous → 因「好奇」而「小心」求知。相關同源字有 **cure** (v./n. 治療)、**cur**iosity (n. 好奇心)、**cur**io (n. 古董、珍品)、ac**cur**ate (adj. 精確的)、ac**cur**acy (n. 精確性)、se**cure** (adj. 安全的；穩固的 v. 獲得；使安全)、se**cur**ity (n. 安全防護措施；保障)。

同義字 inquisitive

victim
[ˋvɪktɪm]

n. 受害者；犧牲者

Actually, leaving an abuser is the most difficult part for victims of domestic abuse.

實際上，對於家庭暴力的受害者來說，離開施虐者是最困難的部分。

(秒殺解字) 源自拉丁文，表示「作犧牲的動物」。

詞搭 fall victim / prey to... 成為……的受害者／犧牲品；the victim of a swindler 被騙子騙的受害者

衍生字 victimize [ˋvɪktɪ͵maɪz] v. 使犧牲；使痛苦

曾 100 高 108

supreme
[sə`prim]

adj. 至高無上的；最大程度的

For most diabetics, dieting requires a supreme effort of willpower.
對於大多數糖尿病患者而言，節食需要極大的意志力。

 (秒殺解字) supre(=super=over)+me → 源自拉丁文 supremus，是 super 衍生形容詞 superus 的最高級，表示「最高的」、「最重要的」、「最大的」。

詞搭 the supreme court 最高法院；the supreme commander 最高統帥；make the supreme sacrifice 捐軀

---

supremacy
[sə`prɛməsɪ]

n. 至高無上；霸權

The supremacy of the current leading manufacturers in the field of dairy products has our company aiming to catch up with them.
我們公司的目標是趕上當前乳製品領域領先製造商的地位。

普 106

---

manufacturer
[ˌmænjə`fæktʃərə]

n. 廠商；製造商

Manufacturers of face masks are working (a)round the clock to fulfill the needs of the consumers.
口罩製造商日以繼夜地趕工以滿足消費者的需求。

(秒殺解字) man(hand)+u+fac(do, make)+t+ure+er →「做」東西的「人」製造商。工業革命前用「手」「做」東西。

同義字 maker, producer

---

sample
[`sæmpl̩]

n. 樣本
v. 抽樣檢查；試吃

The hotel provides an excellent package tour, from which visitors can sample the delights of white water rafting and river tracing.
這家飯店提供了一個極佳的套裝行程，遊客可以嘗試泛舟和溯溪的樂趣。

普 107
警特 108

(秒殺解字) s(=ex=out)+ampl(=empl=take)+e →「拿」「出來」做示範。sample 和 example 同源，s 是 ex 的縮減。

80% of the people in the sample said that they only want to pay \$1 for a mask, because it has become a daily necessity.
樣本中的 80％的人說，他們只想支付 1 美元購買口罩，因為它已成為日常必需品。

詞搭 a blood sample 血液樣品；free samples of shampoo / perfume 免費的洗髮精／香水樣品；random sampling 隨機抽樣

tragedy

[`trædʒədɪ]

n. 悲劇、慘劇

Researchers are still working on the development of the vaccines for this virus, which has caused the tragedy of millions of deaths.

研究人員仍在研發這種病毒的疫苗，這已造成數百萬人死亡的悲劇。

📖 100

🖋️**秒殺解字** trag(goat)+ed(sing)+y → 戲劇表演中「唱」「山羊之歌」等悲歌，據説可能是因為最初在宗教儀式中，要用羊作為「犧牲」，而在宰殺羊時所唱的歌很悲慘，由此而轉義為「悲劇」。tragic 和 tragedy 同源，但從拼字上已看不出字根 ed 的拼字樣貌。可用表示「頌詩」、「頌歌」的 **ode** 當神隊友，**母音通轉**，來記憶 **od, ed**，表示「唱」、「歌曲」。相關同源字有 **ode**（n. 頌詩、頌歌）、mel**ody**（n. 旋律）、com**edy**（n. 喜劇）、trag**edy**（n. 悲劇）。

詞搭 Tragedy struck... 悲劇降臨到……

反義字 comedy

conceive

[kən`siv]

v. 懷孕；構思；設想

Most people can't conceive of the extinction of the polar bears because of the melting ice sheets.

大多數人無法想像北極熊由於冰層融化而滅絕的時刻。

📖 100
110
🎧**特** 109

🖋️**秒殺解字** con(intensive prefix)+ceiv(take)+e → 去「拿取」，拿進身體內，表示「懷孕」；拿進腦袋中，表示「構想」、「想像」。

詞搭 conceive a child 懷了一個小孩；conceive of + N / Ving 想像／想到某事

衍生字 concept [`kɑnsɛpt] n. 觀念、概念、想法；conception [kən`sɛpʃən] n. 懷孕、看法、概念

numerous

[`njumərəs]

adj. 許的

Numerous movies have dealt with the issue of dissociative identity disorder.

許多電影都處理了解離性身份障礙症（多重人格障礙）的問題。

📖 103

🖋️**秒殺解字** numer(number)+ous →「數目」很大的，表示「許多的」。可用 **number** 當神隊友，**母音通轉**，來記憶 **numer**，皆表示「**數字**」。相關同源字有 number（n. 數字；數量）、out**number**（v. 數量上超過）、**numer**al（n. 數字）、**numer**ical（adj. 數字的）、in**numer**able（adj. 無數的）。

詞搭 too numerous to mention / list 不勝枚舉

同義字 many, countless, innumerable

prominent

[ˋprɑmənənt]

adj. 重要的；顯著的；突出的；著名的

Daphne played a prominent role in her sister's childhood, because their mother died young from a traffic accident.

Daphne 在妹妹的童年時期扮演著重要角色，因為她們的母親因交通意外而早逝。

（秒殺解字）pro(forward)+min(project, jut out, stand)+ent →「向前」「突出」，表示「顯著的」。

同義字 important

醫 106
107

---

fundamental

[ˌfʌndəˋmɛntl̩]

adj. 重要的；基本的；基礎的

To improve sales performance, we have to deal with the fundamental cause of the problems.

為了提高銷售業績，我們必須處理問題的根本原因。

（秒殺解字）fund(bottom)+a+ment+al → 可用 **bottom** 當神隊友，**b/f 轉音**，**t/n 轉音**，**d/t 轉音**，母音通轉，來記憶 **fund**，**found**，皆表示「底部」、「基礎」。**bottom**（n. 底部 adj. 底部的）、**fund**（n. 基金 v. 提供資金）、**found**（v. 建立；創辦）、**found**er（n. 創立者、創辦人）、**found**ation（n. 地基；基礎；創辦；基金會）、pro**found**（adj. 深遠的；深奧的）、un**found**ed（adj. 無根據的）、well-**found**ed（adj. 有事實根據的）。

詞搭 fundamental human rights 基本人權

同義字 basic, necessary, essential

醫 100

---

concentrate

[ˋkɑnsn̩ˌtret]

n. 濃縮物
v. 集中

Kyle was finding it difficult to concentrate on the textbooks.

Kyle 發現很難集中精力在教科書上。

（秒殺解字）con(together)+centr(center)+ate →「一起」往「中心」聚集，表示「集中」。相關同源字有 **center**（n. 中心 v. 集中）、**centr**al（adj. 中心的）、ec**centr**ic（adj. 古怪反常的 n. 古怪的人）。

詞搭 concentrate / center / focus on 集中精神於；concentrate A on B 將 A 集中在 B 上面

高 108
警特 105

---

concentration

[ˌkɑnsənˋtreʃən]

n. 專心、專注；集中

By taking physical education classes, students can improve their concentration on classroom lectures.

藉由上體育課，學生可以提高他們在課堂上的注意力。

詞搭 powers of concentration 專注力；a concentration camp 集中營

opposite
[`ɑpəzɪt]

n. 相反的情形
adj. 相反的；相對的
prep. 在……對面

I thought the soft music would make the baby sleep, but it has the opposite effect.
我以為輕柔的音樂會使嬰兒入睡，但效果相反。

曾 110

秒殺解字 op(=ob=before, against)+pos(put)+ite →「放」在「前面」「反對」，表示「相反的」。

詞搭 the opposite sex 異性；quite the opposite 正好相反；in the opposite direction 朝反方向；face / meet / be met with opposition 遭遇反對；the opposition party 反對黨 ≠ the ruling party

medium
[`midɪəm]

n. 中間；中等；媒體
adj. 中等的

Many small and medium-size businesses are beginning to feel optimistic about the future, because their businesses are gradually growing.
許多中小型企業開始對未來感到樂觀，因為他們的企業正在逐漸成長。

曾 105

秒殺解字 med(middle)+i+um →「中間」。可用 **middle** 當神隊友，**母音通轉**，來記憶 **med**，皆表示「中間」。相關同源字有 **mid**dle (adj. 中間的 n. 中間)、**mid**st (n. 中間)、a**mid** (prep. 在……之中)、a**mid**st (prep. 在……之中)、**med**ia (n. 媒體)、multi**med**ia (adj./n. 多媒體)、**med**iate (v. 調停解決、斡旋)、**med**ieval (adj. 古中時期的)、im**med**iate (adj. 立即的)、inter**med**iate (adj. 中間的)、**Med**iterranean (n. /adj. 地中海)。

詞搭 of medium height 中等身材；by / through the medium of… 透過……的媒介

複數型 mediums, media

display
[dɪ`sple]

n. 陳列、展覽；展覽品
v. 展示

Victor's collections of paintings were proudly displayed on the wall.
Victor 很驕傲他的畫作被展示在牆上。

曾 104

秒殺解字 dis(apart)+play(=plic=fold) → 等同 unfold，將「對摺」的東西攤「開」，表示「陳列」、「展示」等。

詞搭 be on display / show / exhibition 陳列展示，展出中

n. 同義字 show, exhibition, show

v. 同義字 show, exhibit, demonstrate

percentage
[pə`sɛntɪdʒ]
n. 百分比

A high percentage of the illegal drugs they produce are trafficked to the US.
他們生產的毒品中有很大一部分被販運到美國。

秒殺解字 per+cent(hundred)+age → 「每一」「百」，表示「百分比」。**c** 在拉丁文裡發 **k** 的音。可用 **hund**red 當神隊友，**k/h**，**d/t** 轉音，母音通轉，來記憶 **cent**、**centi**，表示「百」，亦有「百分之一」的意思。相關同源字有 **hund**red (n. 一百)、**cent** (n. 分)、**cent**ury (n. 世紀)、per**cent** (n. 百分比、百分之……)、**cent**imeter (n. 公分)、**cent**ipede (n. 蜈蚣)、**Cent**igrade (n. 攝氏)。

詞搭 a large percentage of... 相當大百分比的……；a small percentage of... 很小百分比的……、一小部分……

---

percent
[pə`sɛnt]
n. 百分之（幾）

A 2 percent handling fee will be charged on every banking activity.
每次銀行業務都將收取 2% 的手續費。

📖 110

---

interior
[ɪn`tɪrɪə]
n. 內部
adj. 內部的

A savvy interior decorator transformed a waste glass bottle into a stylish lamp.
一位能幹的室內設計師將一個廢玻璃瓶變成了時尚的檯燈。

📖 102

秒殺解字 inter(between)+ior → 在「內部」「之間」。**inter** 和表示「在……裡面」、「在……之上」的 **en**、**em**、**in**、**im** 系出同源，和表示「裡面」的 **intra**、**intro** 也同源。

詞搭 interior design / decoration 室內設計；the Department of the Interior 內政部長 [美]

反義字 exterior

---

extreme
[ɪk`strim]
n. 極端
adj. 極度的

The Central Weather Bureau calls upon road users to exercise extreme caution during typhoon Phoenix.
中央氣象局呼籲道路使用者在鳳凰颱風期間要格外小心。

秒殺解字 extr(=exter=outside)+eme → 「最外面」，表示「極度的」、「極端」。

詞搭 go to extremes 走極端；in the extreme 極度地；take / carry + sth. + to extremes 將某事做得過火

extremely
[ɪk`strimlɪ]

adv. 極端地；非常地

Eliminating toxins and checking up on medications are extremely important for pregnant mothers.
對於孕婦而言，消除有毒物質和檢查所吃藥物極為重要。

警特 106
108

同義字 | exceedingly, exceptionally, outstandingly, remarkably

---

sympathy
[`sɪmpəθɪ]

n. 同情、憐憫；同感

Teachers <u>have</u> absolutely no <u>sympathy for</u> students who get caught cheating on exams, because they are asking for trouble.
對於在考試中被發現作弊的學生，老師絕對不表示同情，因為他們是在自找麻煩。

警特 105

秒殺解字 sym(=syn=together)+path(feeling)+y → 能「同」「感」身受。相關同源字有 **path**etic (adj. 無用的；令人同情的、可憐的)、**path**os (n. 悲愁)、anti**path**y (n. 反感、憎惡)、anti**path**etic (adj. 引起反感的、敵對的)、a**path**etic (adj. 無感的)、em**path**y (n. 同理心)。

詞搭 | have sympathy for... = sympathize with... 對……感到同情

同義字 | pity, compassion

---

sympathize
[`sɪmpə,θaɪz]

v. 同情、憐憫

The iconic tower will turn off its lights for an hour to <u>sympathize with</u> the leopard cats which were killed by mistake.
這座標誌性的塔樓將關燈一個小時，以憐憫被誤殺的石虎。

同義字 | pity

---

absorb
[əb`sɔrb]

v. 吸收；理解

If travel companies are forced to absorb losses for another quarter, they could reach the point of going bankrupt.
如果旅行社被迫承擔另一個季度的虧損，它們可能會破產。

高 108
警特 108

秒殺解字 ab(away, off)+sorb(suck up) →「吸取」使之「離開」。

詞搭 | be absorbed in... 全神專注於……

plenty

[ˋplɛntɪ]

n. 大量

pron. 充分

Willie's got <u>plenty of</u> time before he needs to hand in his final paper.

Willie 在繳交他的期末報告截止日前還有很多時間。

🖊 **秒殺解字** plen(full,fill)+ty → 填「滿」，衍生出「充分」、「大量」。可用 **full**、**fill** 當神隊友，**p/f 轉音**，母音通轉，來記憶 **plen**，皆表示「充滿」、「充滿的」。

| 詞搭 | in plenty 富裕地；plenty more 還有很多；plenty of 很多的 |

---

scheme

[skim]

n. **v.** 計畫、方案；詭計、陰謀

Agatha's scheme for saving money is practicable and simple.

Agatha 省錢的方案既實用又簡單。

🖊 **秒殺解字** 源自希臘文，表示「形」，引申為形成「計畫」、「方案」、「陰謀」等。

| n. 同義字 | program, plot, conspiracy |
| v. 同義字 | plot, conspire |

---

deserve

[dɪˋzɝv]

v. 應得

The rescue team members really deserved people's praise, because they risked their lives to save others.

救援隊成員確實值得人們稱讚，因為他們冒著生命危險來拯救他人。

🖊 **秒殺解字** de(completely)+serve(serve) → 提供「全部」「服務」，即服務良好，表示「應得」。

| 詞搭 | deserve + N 應得、值得；deserve + to V 應得、值得；sb. + deserved it 某人應得 |

---

purchase

[ˋpɝtʃəs]

n. 購買

v. 購買

Teenagers under 18 are not permitted to purchase alcohol.

18 歲以下的青少年不允許購買酒。

🖊 **秒殺解字** pur(=pro=forward, intensive prefix)+chase(=catch= cap=take) → 「購買」是為了「追逐」、「取得」某東西。

| 詞搭 | make a purchase 購買 |

---

resist

[rɪˋzɪst]

v. 抗拒；抵抗

Studies show that the air purifier is able to resist most dust mites.

研究表明，空氣淨化器能夠阻擋大多數塵蟎。

| 詞搭 | resist + <u>N / Ving</u> 抗拒；cannot resist + <u>N / Ving</u> 無法抗拒⋯⋯ |

resistance
[rɪ`zɪstəns]
n. 抗拒;抵抗(力)

The residents mounted stiff resistance to the proposal of building up an incinerator in this neighborhood.
居民強烈反對在附近修建焚化爐的提議。

普 107

詞搭　the line / path of least resistance 最容易的方法; offer / put up resistance 做抵抗

irresistible
[ˏɪrɪ`zɪstəbl̩]
adj. 無法抗拒的

I'm still on the fence about which to pick, because the menu contains many types of irresistible chocolate desserts.
我仍然無法做任何選擇,因為菜單上包含了各種難以抗拒的巧克力甜點。

秒殺解字 ir(not)+resist+ible → 「不」「可」「抗拒」的。

衍生字　an irresistible force 不可抗拒的力量

irresistibly
[ɪrə`zɪstəblɪ]
adv. 無法抵抗地

The movie is irresistibly entertaining, and no wonder it succeeded at the box office.
這部電影的娛樂性令人難以抗拒,難怪它在票房上大獲成功。

persuade
[pɚ`swed]
v. 說服

After this event, it will be difficult for Sophie to persuade her parents that living alone in an apartment is safe.
事件發生後,Sophie 很難說服父母獨自一人住是安全的。

普 110
警 特 107
　　108

秒殺解字 per(thoroughly)+suad(sweet)+e → 用「甜」言蜜語,給人「甜」頭,「徹底」「說服」他人做事。可用 **sweet** 當神隊友,**u/w** 對應,**d/t/s/ʒ** 轉音,母音通轉,來記憶 **suad**、**suas**,皆表示「甜的」。

詞搭　persuade / convince + sb. + to V 說服某人去……; persuade + sb. + into Ving 說服某人去……; persuade / convince + sb. + of + sth. 使某人相信某事

同義字　convince

反義字　dissuade

persuasion

[pɚˋsweʒən]

n. 説服（力）；信念

| 反義字 | dissuasion |

It took a lot of persuasion to get our teacher to agree on having a class party.
我們很努力説服老師同意舉辦班級同樂會。

高 108

persuasive

[pɚˋswesɪv]

adj. 有説服力的

| 同義字 | convincing |

| 反義字 | dissuasive |

The advertisement was persuasive, but the sales depend on the product's effectiveness.
廣告具有説服力，但銷售取決於該產品的實際效果。

普 101

loan

[lon]

n. 貸款
v. 借給

Grace can't afford to buy a new car until she pays off her student loan.
在我還清她的學生貸款之前，Grace 買不起新車。

🖊**（秒殺解字）** loan(lend) → loan、lend 同源，母音通轉，核心語意是「借出」（lend）。

| 詞搭 | be on loan 已借出；<u>loan / lend</u> + sb. + sth. = <u>loan / lend</u> + sth. + to + sb. 把某物借給某人 |

accuse

[əˋkjuz]

v. 指控

The woman <u>was accused of</u> having slapped the four-year-old daughter of her boyfriend across the face.
這名女子被指控摑她男友的四歲女兒耳光。

普 101
110

🖊**（秒殺解字）** ac(=ad=to)+cus(cause)+e → 「指控」他人之前要先找到「原因」。可用 **cause** 當神隊友，**母音通轉**，來記憶 **cus**，皆表示「原因」、「動機」。相關同源字有 **cause**（v. 引起 n. 原因）、be**cause**（conj./prep. 因為）、ex**cus**e（v. 原諒）。

| 詞搭 | accuse + sb. + of... 指控某人……；sb. + be accused of... 某人被指控… |

| 衍生字 | accusation [͵ækjəˋzeʃən] n. 指控 |

consult

[kən`sʌlt]

v. 諮商；研討；查閱；請教

Before making any decisions, consult your family to find out which college is the most appropriate for you.

在做出任何決定之前，請諮詢你的家人，以找出最適合你的大學。

📻 101

🪶 **秒殺解字** con(together)+sul(=sel=take)+t → 「一起」「拿取」建議，表示「諮詢」、「查閱」、「商量」。

詞搭 consult + sb. + about + sth. 請教某人某事；consult with + sb. 與某人商量、討論；consut a dictionary 查字典；look up the word / number in the dictionary / phone book 查字典／電話簿內的某單字／號碼

衍生字 consultant [kən`sʌltənt] n. 顧問；consultation [͵kɑnsəl`teʃən] n. 請教、諮詢

release

[rɪ`lis]

n. 釋出、釋放；發行
v. 釋出、釋放；發行

Brad Pitt's new movie is due to be released in Taiwan very soon.

Brad Pitt 的新電影即將在台灣上映。

📻 107

詞搭 release A from B 釋放……；release on bail 保釋

同義字 free

confirm

[kən`fɝm]

v. 確認；證實

The finding of stone tools seems to confirm that people lived in China over 2 million years ago.

石器的發現似乎證實了 200 萬年前人們已經生活在中國。

📻 105

🪶 **秒殺解字** con(intensive prefix)+firm(firm) → 本義「穩固」。相關同源字有 firm（adj. 堅實的）、affirm（v. 斷言、堅稱、證實）。

衍生字 衍生字：confirmation [͵kɑnfɚ`meʃən] n. 證實、認可

同義字 affirm, verify

quantity

[`kwɑntətɪ]

n. 量

The police found a considerable quantity of chemical waste, which had been dumped in a remote wasteland.

警察發現大量化學廢物被傾倒在偏遠的荒原中。

秒殺解字 quant(how much)+ity → 核心語意是「多少」，表示「量」。**qual**ity（n. 品質）、**qual**ify（v. 使有資格）、**quant**ity（n. 量）、**quot**e（v./n. 引用；報價）、**quot**ation（n. 引用；報價）、**quot**a（n. 配額）、**what**（det. 什麼）、**how**（adv. 多少）同源，**k/h 轉音**，母音通轉；**qual**ity 和 **qual**ify 核心語意是「某一類」（of **what** kind）；quantity 核心語意是「多少」（**how** much）；**quot**e 和 **quot**ation 核心語意是「多少」（**how** many）；**quot**a 核心語意是「多大一份」（**how** large a part）。

詞搭 in quantity / quantities 大量；a large quantity of... = a large amount of... 大量的……

01 ___ The officer told the soldiers that they have to _____ their beliefs and follow every order in order to become a great soldier.

(A) abandon (B) symbolize
(C) accelerate (D) bombard

02 ___ The general _____ more back-up soldiers, due to the overwhelming enemy attacks. However, the headquarters had no units to spare for the general.

(A) mistook (B) comforted
(C) confused (D) requested

03 ___ The thief took everything _____ away from the house and left nothing behind. The owner of the house lost everything he owned overnight.

(A) liberal (B) distinct
(C) competent (D) valuable

04 ___ Soldiers who return home from the battlefield often suffer from severe _____ issues. More often than not, they will spend most of their time visiting a hospital in order to stabilize their symptoms.

(A) literary (B) threatening
(C) mental (D) gradual

05 ___ A lot of people spend their whole life _____ fame and wealth, and end up losing everything they have, such as their beloved friends or family members.

(A) surrounding (B) pursuing
(C) performing (D) persuading

06 ___ The _____ of the domestic violence sought aid from the authorities. However, no one gave her the help she needed, and thus resulted in the tragedy.

(A) shareholder (B) citizen
(C) victim (D) enemy

07 ___ One of the greatest _____ writers is William Shakespeare. In the Shakespearean tragedy, the hero must be the most tragic personality in the play, and the story is essentially a tale of suffering and disaster leading to death.

(A) remedy   (B) comedy
(C) dynasty   (D) tragedy

08 ___ The _____ human rights include the right to life and liberty, freedom from slavery and torture, freedom of opinion and expression, the right to work and education, and many more.

(A) fundamental   (B) facial
(C) industrial   (D) artificial

09 ___ The Mona Lisa, a portrait painting by the Italian artist Leonardo da Vinci, will be _____ in the local art museum for a duration of two weeks.

(A) flocked   (B) lengthened
(C) displayed   (D) clicked

10 ___ Joanna Gaines has created a design empire in just six years. With the help of her husband, she is now one of the most famous _____ designers in the world.

(A) inferior   (B) striking
(C) interior   (D) pessimistic

11 ___ The famous influencer got shot by a pistol last week. Luckily, his muscles _____ some of the damage from the bullets. Thus, he was discharged from the hospital a month later.

(A) alerted   (B) absorbed
(C) shoplifted   (D) excluded

12 ___ With the suspect sentenced to jail for life, justice was served. Everyone in the court agreed that the suspect _____ to be punished.

(A) preserved   (B) conserved
(C) observed   (D) deserved

13 ___ Although the government had surrendered, some local _____ forces still refused to give up and kept on fighting until the last man standing.

(A) resistance   (B) importance

(C) allowance   (D) sustenance

14 ___ The old man was stubborn. He refused to move out from his house even though the typhoon was coming. No one could _____ him to leave.

(A) misguide   (B) coincide

(C) persuade   (D) provide

15 ___ The tour package is an all-inclusive package. Everything you need is included in it. If you have further questions, please _____ our travel agents.

(A) include   (B) accuse

(C) receive   (D) consult

解答

1.(A) 2.(D) 3.(D) 4.(C) 5.(B) 6.(C) 7.(D) 8.(A) 9.(C) 10(C) 11.(B) 12.(D) 13.(A) 14.(C) 15.(D)

Level 2

Unit 21 – Unit 40 中階單字

因各家手機系統不同，若無法直接掃描，
仍可以至以下電腦雲端連結下載收聽。
（https://reurl.cc/kL2bd9）

impose

[ɪmˋpoz]

v. 強制執行；強加

The government imposed a general ban on using that particular app.
政府未明確說明而禁止使用該特定應用程式。

普 100
警特 109

> 秒殺解字 im(in)+pos(put)+e →「放」「裡面」，表示「強加」稅務、處罰、信仰、價值觀到人身上。

詞搭　impose + sth. + on + sb. 將某事強加於某人

---

imposing

[ɪmˋpozɪŋ]

adj. 壯觀的；印象深刻的

The Grand Canyon offers one of the most distinctive views in the US; it's really magnificent and imposing.
大峽谷是美國最著名的景觀之一，雄偉而壯觀。

普 108

同義字　impressive

---

corrective

[kəˋrɛktɪv]

adj. 矯正的；修正的

The company should take corrective measures to deal with its serious sales decline.
公司應採取修正措施來應對其嚴重的銷售下滑。

普 103

> 秒殺解字 cor(intensive prefix)+rec(straight)+t+ive → 本義拉「直」，引申為「矯正的」。

詞搭　corrective surgery 矯正手術

---

efficiency

[ɪˋfɪʃənsɪ]

n. 效率

There are some management skills to help improve employee efficiency and productivity.
有一些管理技巧是可以幫助提高員工的效率和生產力。

警特 108

> 秒殺解字 ef(=ex=out)+fic(do, make)+i+ency →「做」「出來」，表示「有成效」，引申為「效率」。

---

efficient

[ɪˋfɪʃənt]

adj. 有效率的

With better sustainable building materials, a new home buyer is getting a more energy efficient home with lower energy bills.
有了更好的可持續性建築材料，新購屋者能買到節能的房屋並且支付更低的能源帳單。

普 101
警特 105

字辨　effective [ɪˋfɛktɪv] adj. 有效的

inefficient [ɪnəˋfɪʃənt] **adj.** 無效率的	The new president will be faced with problems due to the inefficient management. 新總統將面臨管理效率低落的問題。	普 108

formal [ˋfɔrml] **adj.** 正式的	These two countries have achieved a formal agreement on the implementation of a peace plan. 兩國已就履行和平計劃達成正式協議。	普 **105** 警特 109

秒殺解字 form(form)+al → 講究「形式」，表示「正式的」。

詞搭	formal dress 禮服；on formal occasions 在正式場合
同義字	official
反義字	informal, casual

gesture [ˋdʒɛstʃɚ] **n.** 手勢；招手 **v.** 招手	Jesse made a confusing hand gesture to me, so I shouted at him to ask what it was. Jesse 對我做了一個令人困惑的手勢，所以我向他大喊，問那是什麼意思。	普 101

秒殺解字 gest(carry) +ure → 用「手勢」「帶」出想法。相關同源字有 sug**gest**（v. 建議；暗示）、con**gest**ed（adj. 道路擁擠的）、di**gest**（v. 消化；理解）。

同義字	signal

prison [ˋprɪzn] **n.** 監獄、監牢	Ken was sent to prison for attacking a man with a knife, while protecting his pregnant wife. Ken 因保護自己懷孕的妻子時用刀襲擊男子而被判入獄。	普 101

秒殺解字 pris(seize, take)+on → 「抓」人後關進「監獄」。

詞搭	put + sb. + in prison 把某人關進牢裡；be put in prison / jail；prison camp 戰俘集中營
衍生字	prisoner [ˋprɪznɚ] n. 囚犯；imprison [ɪmˋprɪzn] v. 將……監禁；imprisonment [ɪmˋprɪznmənt] n. 監禁
同義字	jail

profit
[`prɑfɪt]
n. 利潤
v. 對……有利；獲利

The company <u>made</u> a huge <u>profit</u> from dealing with all the recyclable waste.
這家公司在處理所有可回收廢棄物方面獲得了可觀的利潤。

🖋 秒殺解字 pro(forward)+fit(do, make) → 可順利地「往前」「做」，就會帶來「利潤」。

詞搭 make a profit 獲利；profit and loss 損益；net profit 淨利；gross profit 毛利；profit <u>from / by</u>... 從中獲利

衍生字 profitable [`prɑfɪtəbl] adj. 有利的；non-profit [ˌnɑn`prɑfɪt] adj. 非營利的

🔲 100
102
104

---

universe
[`junəˌvɝs]
n. 宇宙

Until now, humans have not yet discovered everything <u>in the universe</u>.
直到現在，人類還沒有發現宇宙中的一切。

🖋 秒殺解字 uni(one)+vers(turn)+e → 「宇宙」原意是沿著某「一」特定的方向「轉」，可用萬物「合」「一」來幫助記憶。

🔲 107

---

universally
[ˌjunə`vɝslɪ]
adv. 普遍地；一般地

The recently reopened park features universally accessible playground and more parking spaces.
最近重新開放的公園設有更容易讓大家使用的遊樂場和更多停車位。

🔲 103
110
🔲 107

---

anticipate
[æn`tɪsəˌpet]
v. 期待；預期

An experienced teacher can anticipate a student's needs and parents' expectations.
經驗豐富的老師可以預期學生的需求和父母的期望。

🖋 秒殺解字 anti(=ante=before)+cip(take)+ate → 在事「前」「拿」，表示「預期」、「期望」。

詞搭 anticipate + <u>N / Ving</u> 期待……

同義字 expect

🔲 100

---

anticipation
[ænˌtɪsə`peʃən]
n. 期待；預期

Kids are looking forward to the coming Christmas holiday with eager anticipation.
孩子們殷切期待著即將到來的聖誕節假期。

詞搭 in <u>anticipation / expectation</u> of... 期待……

同義字 expectation

🔲 100

prevalent

[`prɛvələnt]

adj. 盛行的；普遍的

Dropping out of school remains one of the most prevalent problems among teenagers.
輟學仍然是青少年中最普遍的問題之一。

> **秒殺解字** pre(before)+val(strong)+ent → 力量「強大」能往「前」推進，引申為「盛行的」、「普遍的」。可用表示「價值」的 value 當神隊友，**母音通轉**，來記憶 val、vail，表示「強的」、「值得的」。相關同源字有 **value** (n. 價值 v. 重視)、**valu**able (adj. 有價值的)、**valu**eless (adj. 不值錢的)、e**valu**ate (v. 評估；評價)、equi**val**en (adj. 等值的)、**val**id (adj. 有效的)、in**val**id (adj. 失效的 n. 病人)、a**vail**able (adj. 可用的、可得或買到的；有空的)、pre**vail** (v. 盛行；獲勝)、pre**vail**ing (adj. 盛行的、現有的)。

詞搭 be prevalent <u>in / among</u>... 盛行於……

同義字 common

prevalence

[`prɛvələns]

n. 盛行；普遍

Schools should put more emphasis on the issue of the prevalence of smoking among teenagers. 🔊 99
學校應更加重視青少年吸煙普遍的問題。

constantly

[`kɑnstəntlı]

adv. 持續地、不斷地

Ida constantly perfects her recipes in order to make 🔊 100
her dishes more appealing.
Ida 為了使她的菜餚更具吸引力不斷地讓自己的食譜更加完美。

> **秒殺解字** con(together)+st(stand)+ant+ly → 所有事件都「站」在「一起」，表示「不斷地」、「經常地」。

詞搭 be constantly changing 不斷地改變

同義字 continuously, all the time

render

[ˋrɛndɚ]

v. 使成為;提供;翻譯

It is unlikely that Keith will render a decision before tomorrow about whether to quit his job or not.

Keith 不太可能在明天之前就是否辭職做出決定。

> **秒殺解字** ren(back)+der(give) → 等同 give back,把東西「歸還給」,引申出「使成為」、「提供」的意思。相關同源字有 rent (n. 租金 v. 出租)、surrender (v./n. 投降)、donate (v. 捐贈)、donor (n. 捐贈者)、pardon (v./n. 原諒)、dose (n. 劑量 v. 配藥)、dosage (n. 劑量;服法;配藥)、overdose (v./n. 服藥過量)、edit (v. 編輯)、tradition (n. 傳統)、extradition (n. 引渡)、data (n. 資料;數據)、date (n. 日期;約會)、add (v. 增加;補充)、antidote (n. 解毒藥)、vend (v. 販賣)、vendor (n. 小販)。

詞搭 render + sb. / sth. + Adj 使某人/某物變得⋯⋯;render A into B = translate A into B 將 A 翻譯成 B

---

welfare

[ˋwɛlˌfɛr]

n. 福利;幸福;福祉

普 100
110

Lyle stopped getting welfare benefits when he finally found a minimum-wage job.

Lyle 終於找到了最低薪資工作然後停止請領救助金。

> **秒殺解字** 本義是「順利進行」(fare well),其中 fare 的意思是 go,well 的意思是「安好」,用在道別時,表示「一切順利地去旅行」,後衍生出「幸福」、「福祉」等意思。

詞搭 social / public welfare 社會/公共福利;welfare benefits 福利金

---

appreciate

[əˋpriʃɪˌet]

v. 欣賞;體會;感激;升值

普 102
警特 106
109

We really appreciate the council's diligence on traffic rules, and hope there will be fewer accidents happening.

我們非常感謝理事會對交通規則所做的努力,並希望事故的發生會減少。

> **秒殺解字** ap(=ad=to)+prec(price)+i+ate →「價格」往上跑,後來語意轉變,注重一個人的「價值」,因此產生「欣賞」、「感激」等衍生意思。可用 price 當神隊友,**s/ʃ 轉音**,母音**通轉**,來記憶 prec,皆表示「**價格**」。相關同源字有 price (n. 價格)、prize (n. 獎;獎賞)、praise (v./n. 讚揚)、precious (adj. 珍貴的)、appraise (v. 鑒定、估價)、depreciate (v. 貶值;輕視、貶低)。

同義字 realize

反義字 depreciate

appreciation

[ə͵priʃɪˋeʃən]

n. 感激；欣賞；升值

反義字 | depreciation

In appreciation of Mr. Lin's years of service, our department presented him with a gold medal.

為了感謝林先生的多年服務，我們部門向他頒發了金牌。

普 104
105
警特 107

---

overall

[ˋovɚ͵ɔl]

adj. 包括一切的

adv. 總的來說；包括一切地

The overall height of this new skyscraper, called Kingdom Tower, is 1,000 meters.

這座名為 "Kingdom Tower" 的新摩天大樓的總高度為 1,000 公尺。

秒殺解字 over+all → 「完全覆蓋」「一切」。

警特 109

---

revenue

[ˋrɛvənju]

n. 稅收；收入

The country's estimated tax revenue totalled $2 trillion last year.

這個國家去年的稅收總額估計為 2 萬億美元。

秒殺解字 re(back)+ven(come)+ue → 本義「回」「來」，類似 income，錢跑回來，表示「稅收」、「收入」。

詞搭 | revenue accounts 收益帳戶

普 106

---

violent

[ˋvaɪələnt]

adj. 暴力的；粗暴的

A YouTuber was shot in the violent incident last night, which shocked the whole country.

昨晚在一次暴力事件中有一名 YouTuber 被槍射中，這震驚了整個國家。

秒殺解字 源自拉丁文過去分詞 violare，表示「憑力量處理」(to treat with violence)。

詞搭 | a violent earthquake / attack / explosion 猛烈的地震／攻擊／爆炸
同義字 | aggressive, brutal, rough, savage
同義字 | nonviolent

普 101
警特 105

---

violence

[ˋvaɪələns]

n. 暴力；猛烈

Parents and some experts complain that sex and violence on TV may put kids in danger.

父母和一些專家投訴電視上的性與暴力可能會讓孩子面臨危險。

詞搭 | do violence to... 對⋯⋯施暴；domestic violence 家暴；resort to violence 訴諸暴力、動武

intense
[ɪn`tɛns]

adj. 強烈的;激烈的

警特 105

It would give me intense pleasure to see my favorite tennis player beat his competitor.
看到我最喜歡的網球運動員擊敗他的競爭對手,我會感到非常高興。

秒殺解字 in(toward)+tens(thin, stretch)+e → 心思「往……」「延展」,即「強烈的」。

詞搭 intense anger / heat 激怒/酷暑

同義字 strong, powerful

---

consumer
[kən`sumɚ]

n. 消費者

警 104
警特 107

The new rules will influence all consumers, as well as companies.
新規則將影響所有消費者以及公司。

秒殺解字 con(intensive prefix)+sum(take)+er → consume 本義「拿取」,後引申為「消耗」、「消費」,consumer 表示「消費者」。相關同源字有 assume (v. 認為;假定)、assumption (n. 認為;假定)、presume (v. 認為;假定)、presumption (n. 認為;假定)、resume (v. 再繼續;重新開始;再取得)。

詞搭 consumer rights 消費者權益;consumer confidence 消費者信心

---

consumption
[kən`sʌmpʃən]

n. 消耗 (量);攝取;消費

New technology in electric cars will lead to declining consumption of oil.
電動汽車的新技術導致石油消耗的減少。

---

membership
[`mɛmbɚˌʃɪp]

n. 會員身份

警 100

Dylan forgot to renew his membership with the retail store and, therefore, was not allowed to go inside.
Dylan 忘記了續簽這家零售商的會員資格,因此被禁止進入。

秒殺解字 member+ship → 有「會員資格」的「成員」。字尾 **ship** 本指「特性」、「狀態」,源自古英文,和表示船的 ship 不同源。**ship** 語意可再細分為四大類:第一,表示「職業」、「行業」,如 governor**ship**;第二,表示「擁有狀態」,如:owner**ship**;第三,表示「(特殊)技能」,如:workman**ship**;第四,表示「特定群體的所有成員」,如:reader**ship**。

詞搭 a membership card / fee 會員卡/費

 **Unit 22**

urban
[`ɝbən]

adj. 都市的

The country's urban unemployment rate reached a six-week high due to the global economic downturn.
由於全球經濟下滑，這個國家的都市失業率觸及六周新高。

普 108

秒殺解字 urb(city)+an → 「都市」的。相關同源字有 sub**urb**（n. 郊區）、sub**urb**an（adj. 郊區的；平淡乏味的）。

詞搭 urban problems / areas 都市問題／地區

反義字 rural

expense
[ɪk`spɛns]

n. 花費；費用；代價

Novia just went on holiday with her mother in Hualien at her expense.
Novia 剛與她的母親去花蓮度假，一切費用由她支付。

警特 107
108

秒殺解字 ex(out)+pens(weigh, pay)+e → 等同 weigh out、pay out，在商家「秤」「出」某物的重量後，買家把錢「付」「出去」，表示「花費」。相關同源字有 de**pend**（v 依靠）、ex**pend**（v. 花費）、sus**pend**（v. 停止；懸掛）、sus**pens**e（n. 懸念）、dis**pens**e（v. 分配）。

詞搭 at + sb's expense 花某人的錢；at the expense of... 以……為代價；school / traveling expenses 學／旅費

衍生字 expensive [ɪk`spɛnsɪv] a. 昂貴的

territory
[`tɛrə͵tɔrɪ]

n. 領土；地盤

Many animals depend on smells to mark their territories, such as spraying urine or leaving droppings.
許多動物都依靠氣味來標記自己的地盤，例如噴尿或留下糞便。

普 105
106
警特 107

秒殺解字 terr(dry, earth, land)+it+ory(place) → 「土地」的「場所」，表示「領土」。可用 **thirst** 當神隊友，**t/θ 轉音**，母音通轉，來記憶 **terr**，表示「乾燥」，相對於海洋或湖泊容納大量的水，較乾燥的區域，則是人類賴以居住的「土地」，因此 **terr** 又有「泥土」、「土地」等衍生意思。相關同源字有 **thirst**（n./v. 渴；渴望）、**thirst**y（adj. 口渴的）、Medi**terr**anean（n. /adj. 地中海）、sub**terr**anean（adj. 地下的）、extra**terr**estrial（n. 外星生物 adj. 地球外的）。

字辨 turf [tɝf] n. 流氓的地盤

201

territorial

[ˌtɛrəˈtɔrɪəl]

adj. 領土的

The committee finally solved the territorial disputes in the area which have lasted for 10 years.

委員會終於解決了這個地區已經持續了十年的土地糾紛。

<audio>105</audio>

詞搭 territorial <u>air / waters</u> 領空／領海；a territorial dispute 領土糾紛

---

invest

[ɪnˈvɛst]

v. 投資

Ellis made a fortune by investing in the US stock market.

Ellis 在美國股市投資發了大財。

秒殺解字 in(in, into)+vest(wear) → 原意是「穿」衣服，後來才有「把錢投入」（put money into）的意思，「投資」如同給某企業「穿上」資金。divest 是 invest 的反義字，字面上是「脫掉衣服」，除了表示「賣掉」、「出售」，還可以表示「脫去」，vest 還保留「穿」的意思。可用 **wear** 當神隊友，**v/w** 對應，**r/s 轉音**，母音通轉，來記憶 **vest**，皆和「穿」有關。vest 原意是「**穿**」，後來語意和詞性改變，用以表示「**背心**」。

詞搭 invest money in... 將錢投資於……；invest in... 投資於……

---

investment

[ɪnˈvɛstmənt]

n. 投資

Education requires a huge investment of money, time and energy and sometimes the results may not be obvious.

教育需要大量的金錢，時間和精力投資，有時效果可能並不明顯。

<audio>106</audio>

詞搭 make an investment in... 投資於……

---

investor

[ɪnˈvɛstɚ]

n. 投資者

Small investors are encouraged by our financial advisors to believe that the markets will improve.

我們的財務顧問鼓勵小投資者相信市場會有所改善。

---

terrible

[ˈtɛrəbl]

adj. 可怕的；極糟的

It's terrible manners to spread diseases to other people and you don't want to bring home an infectious illness, either.

將疾病傳播給其他人是一種糟糕的習慣，而你也不想帶傳染性疾病回家。

秒殺解字 terr(frighten)+ible →「可」「怕」的。相關同源字有 **terr**ibly（adv. 很、非常；嚴重地）、**terr**ific（adj. 非常好的）、**terr**ify（v. 使害怕）、**terr**ifying（adj. 使人害怕的）、**terr**ified（adj. 感到害怕）、**terr**or（n. 恐怖）、**terr**orist（n. 恐怖分子）、**terr**orism（n. 恐怖主義）、de**ter**（v. 制止、威懾）。

反義字 horrible, awful

undergo

[ˌʌndəˈgo]

v. 經歷；接受（治療、訓練）

The franchise has undergone massive changes recently, and many have quit holding its stock.

這個經銷權最近發生了巨大變化，許多人已放棄持有該股份。

圖 108

> （秒殺解字）under(under)+go → 從「下面」「走過」，表示「經歷」、「接受」。

時態　undergo, underwent, undergone

詞搭　undergo a change / transformation 經歷改變；undergo treatment / surgery / an operation 接受治療／手術／手術

massively

[ˈmæsɪvlɪ]

adv. 大量地；大大地；沉重地

More and more people are concerned about the news that the population of bees has been declining massively in Europe and the United States lately.

越來越多的人擔心最近歐洲和美國蜂群大量消失的消息。

> （秒殺解字）很多含有母音 a 的單字都表示「大」，主要是因為發 /a/ 或 /æ/ 時，口腔開口大，很容易讓人聯想到「大」。相關單字有 large（adj. 大的）、fat（adj. 肥胖的）、macro（adj. 巨大的）、major（adj. 大部分的）、vast（adj. 大量的）、grave（adj. 重大的）。

詞搭　massively popular 廣受歡迎

artery

[ˈɑrtərɪ]

n. 動脈

Eating too much fatty food may increase the risks of clogged arteries.

吃過多的高脂肪食物可能會增加動脈阻塞的風險。

> （秒殺解字）arter(artery)+y → 源自希臘文，表示「氣管」，後來才表示「動脈」，和 air（n. 空氣）、aerial（adj. 空氣的）同源。

詞搭　the main artery 大動脈

衍生字　arterial [ɑrˈtɪrɪəl] adj. 動脈的；（交通）幹道的

regulate

[ˈrɛgjəˌlet]

v. 規定；調節

Our government is in place to regulate the proper use of chemicals in food and ensures the safety of all consumers and living things.

我們的政府已經準備到位負責規範食品中化學物質的使用，並確保所有消費者和生物的安全。

普 100
警特 106

> （秒殺解字）reg(straight, rule)+ule+ate → 和 regular 同源，核心語意是「直的」、「統治」、「規則」等意，表示「規定」、「調節」。

regulation
[ˌrɛgjəˈleʃən]
n. 規定；法規

This car company was caught cheating on emissions, which violated the environmental protection regulations.
這家汽車公司因排放檢測作假而被捕，這違反了環境保護法規。

詞搭 comply with / conform to a regulation 遵守規定；contravene / breach a regulation 違反規定；under the new regulations 在新規定底下

---

inevitable
[ɪnˈɛvətəbl̩]
adj. 不可避免的；必然的

If the population continues to decline, school closures are inevitable.
如果人口繼續下降，就不可避免地要關閉學校。

曾 100

(秒殺解字) in(not)+e(=ex=out)+vit(shun)+able → 「閃」「不」開的，表示「不可避免的」等意思。

詞搭 an inevitable consequence / result 不可避免的結果；It is inevitable + that + S + V ... 是不可避免的

衍生字 inevitability [ɪnˌɛvətəˈbɪlətɪ] n. 不可避免之事

同義字 unavoidable

---

inevitably
[ɪnˈɛvətəblɪ]
adv. 不可避免地

Taking drugs might make you high for a while but it inevitably pushes you down into depression and anxiety.
吸毒可能會讓你情緒高昂興奮一陣子，但無可避免地會使你陷入抑鬱和焦慮狀態。

同義字 unavoidably

---

dominate
[ˈdɑməˌnet]
v. 統治；支配

Research shows that more high-educated people dominate the choice of using private hospital wards, because they appreciate the value of investing in health.
一項研究表明，受過高等教育的人在選擇私人醫院病房的使用上占有優勢，因為他們非常重視投資健康的價值。

曾 99

(秒殺解字) dom(rule, govern)+in+ate → 表示「統治」、「主宰」。可用表示「馴服」的 **tame** 當神隊友，**d/t 轉音**，母音通轉，來記憶 **dom**，表示「房子」。動物進到室內或家裡，要經「馴服」，**dom**in 因此衍生出「統治」（rule, govern）的意思。相關同源字有 **tame**（adj. 馴服的 v. 馴服）、**dom**e（n. 圓頂；半球形）、**dom**estic（adj. 國內的；家庭的、家事的）、**dom**ain（n. 領土；領域）。

domination

[ˌdɑməˈneʃən]

n. 支配；跋扈

The novel describes how a girl has been under the cruel domination of her uncle after her parents' death.
小說描述了一個女孩在父母去世後如何受到叔叔的殘酷控制。

高 108

---

dominant

[ˈdɑmənənt]

adj. 支配的；重要的

Most of my colleagues don't like the dominant and aggressive behavior of our boss and choose to quit their jobs.
我的大多數同事都不喜歡我們老闆統治性和挑釁的行為，而選擇辭職。

高 100
105
106
110

| 同義字 | domineering |

---

dominance

[ˈdɑmənəns]

n. 優勢；支配

If you can create your own niche and develop your own product, you are likely to achieve market dominance.
如果你可以創建自己的利基市場並開發自己的產品，則很可能會取得市場主導地位。

普 105

| 詞搭 | dominance over + sb. / sth. 對某人／某事物的支配；political / military dominance 政治／軍事優勢 |

---

struggle

[ˈstrʌgl̩]

n. 努力；難事
v. 努力；掙扎

Chester struggled desperately to finish the marathon race.
Chester 拼命地完成了馬拉松比賽。

普 106
學特 105

🖋 秒殺解字 字源不詳，但 le 通常表示「重覆動作」。相關單字有 wrest**le**（v. 摔角）、tramp**le**（v. 踐踏）、drag**gle**（v. 拖曳）、twin**kle**（v. 閃耀）。

| 詞搭 | struggle + to V 努力……；struggle for / against... 努力爭取／對抗……；a power struggle 權力鬥爭 |

---

relatively

[ˈrɛlətɪvlɪ]

adv. 相對地

Compared to the last edition, this one is relatively friendly for users.
與上一版相比，此版對用戶相對友好。

普 108

🖋 秒殺解字 relative+ly →「相對」「地」。

| 詞搭 | relatively speaking 相較而言 |

permanent

[`pɝ·mənənt]

adj. 永久的、永恆的

In order to cut costs, only six of the store's employees are permanent.
為了削減成本，這家商店只有 6 名固定員工。

普 99
110
警特 109

秒殺解字 per(through)+man(stay)+ent →「從頭到尾」都「待著」，引申為「永久的」。可用 re**main** 當神隊友，**母音通轉**，來記憶 **man**，皆表示「停留」。相關同源字有 re**main**（v. 維持；停留）、**man**sion（n. 大廈）。

詞搭 permanent resident 永久居留

同義字 lasting, long-lasting, perpetual

反義字 temporary, impermanent

---

permanently

[`pɝ·mənəntlɪ]

adv. 永久地

The accident permanently damaged Molly's legs, so she has to use the assistive device all the time.
那件意外事故造成 Molly 腿部永久傷害，因此她必須一直使用輔助設備。

普 107

詞搭 permanently disabled 終身殘障

反義字 temporarily, momentarily, briefly

---

contrary

[`kɑntrɛrɪ]

n. 相反

adj. 相反的；對立的

Davis insists he doesn't watch much TV; <u>on the contrary</u>, he does it every day.
Davis 堅持認為他不會看太多電視。相反地，他每天都看。

警特 105

詞搭 be contrary to... 與……相反；<u>on / quite</u> the contrary 相反地、正相反；contrary to all expectations 出乎意料地

---

influence

[`ɪnflʊəns]

n. 影響；作用

v. 影響

Researchers are doing a survey on how mobile games influence children's behavior.
研究人員正在調查手機遊戲如何影響兒童的行為。

普 106
高 108

秒殺解字 in(in)+flu(flow)+ence →「流」「入」，表示「影響」。相關同源字有 **flu**id（n. 液體）、**flu**sh（v. 沖洗；臉紅）fluency（n. 流暢）、**flu**ent（adj. 流暢的）、in**flu**enza（n. 流行性感冒）、af**flu**ent（adj. 富裕的）。

詞搭 have an <u>influence / effect / impact</u> on... 對……有影響；under the influence of… 受…的影響

同義字 effect, impact

反義字 affect, impact

influential

[ˌɪnfluˋɛnʃəl]

adj. 有影響力的

Mr. Green works in a highly influential magazine publishing company.

Green 先生在一家很有影響力的雜誌出版公司工作。

📖 100
108

詞搭 be influential in 在……很有影響力；an influential politician 有勢力的政治人物

---

decline

[dɪˋklaɪn]

n. 下降；下跌；衰退

v. 婉拒；下跌；衰退

Biologists are worried that the number of adult salmon in this river continues to decline.

生物學家擔心，這條河中成年鮭魚的數量持續下降。

🖋 **秒殺解字** de(from)+clin(lean, turn, bend)+e → 「從」某處開始「傾斜」，滑到較低的位置，表示「衰退」，衍生出「婉拒」幫忙或邀請的意思，而 turn down 也表示「拒絕」，語意和 refuse、reject 有些差異。可用表示「傾斜」、「倚」的 **lean** 當神隊友，**母音通轉**，來記憶表示「斜面」的 **clim**，和表示「傾斜」、「倚」的 **clin**，雖然 **lean** 的 c 脫落，但仍和兩個字根同源。相關同源字有 **lean**（v. 傾斜、倚）、**lad**der（n. 梯子）、**clim**ate（n. 氣候）、**clim**ax（n. 高潮 v. 達到高潮）、**clin**ic（n. 診所）、**clin**ical（adj. 診所的；臨床的）、**clien**t（n. 委託人、客戶）、in**clin**e（v. 傾向、易於；傾斜 n. 斜坡）。

詞搭 be in decline = be falling 衰退中；go / fall into decline 逐漸衰弱；decline + sb's invitation 婉拒某人的邀請

同義字 decrease

---

burst

[bɝst]

n. 噴；爆發

v. （使）爆破；（使）爆炸

adj. 破裂的

The gas pipes had burst and the building was on fire instantly.

瓦斯管線破裂，因而建築物立即發生火災。

🖋 **秒殺解字** 發 b 的音時，突然放開緊閉的雙唇，讓氣流迸發而出，因此有「爆破」的意思。相關單字有 **b**omb（n. 炸彈）、**b**elch（v. 打嗝）等。

時態 burst, burst, burst

詞搭 burst out 突然出現；burst out crying = burst into tears 突然大哭；burst out laughing = burst into laughter 突然大笑

negative

[ˋnɛgətɪv]

adj. 否定的；負面的

Experts find that there is a close relationship between increased negative thoughts and a woman's period.

專家發現，負面消極想法的增加與女性的經期兩者之間有著密切的關係。

普 102
警特 106

🖋 秒殺解字 neg(no, not, deny)+ate+ive →「沒有」、「不」、「否認」，表示「負面的」、「否定的」。

反義字 | positive, affirmative

---

reserve

[rɪˋzɝv]

n. 儲備；保護區
v. 預訂；保留

Some parking spaces are reserved for the elderly or families with kids under six years old.

一些停車位是為老年人或有 6 歲以下孩子的家庭保留的。

警特 108

🖋 秒殺解字 re(back)+serv(keep, protect)+e → keep back，本義「保留」到「後面」才使用，「保護」預定者的使用權。相關同源字有 con**serv**e（v. 保存；節約）、ob**serv**e（v. 觀察；注意到；遵守）、pre**serv**e（v. 維護；維持；保存）。

詞搭 | reserve a <u>ticket / a room</u> 訂票／訂房；keep + sth.+ in reserve 儲備某物；foreign exchange reserves 外匯存底；money in reserve 預備金

---

reservation

[ˌrɛzɚˋveʃən]

n. 預訂；保留

Owing to the heavy rain, Gavin cancelled our dinner reservations and ordered pizza delivery instead.

由於大雨，Gavin 取消了我們的晚餐預訂，然後預定披薩外送。

詞搭 | make a reservation for... 預訂……；without reservation 毫不保留

01 ___ During WWII, the Nazi Germans _____ a series of inhumane laws against the Jewish people. In the end, millions of Jews were murdered or forced to leave their family.

(A) disguised   (B) aroused
(C) merchandised   (D) imposed

02 ___ The manager asked his team to boost up the _____ of work. He did so by giving bonuses to those who perform well, which turned out to be a good move.

(A) efficiency   (B) supremacy
(C) emergency   (D) privacy

03 ___ It is considered appropriate for a man to wear suit and tie in a(n) _____ occasion, such as weddings or funerals.

(A) fundamental   (B) facial
(C) formal   (D) artificial

04 ___ This country needs to figure out a way to control the crime rate. Recently, the rate has gone through the roof and all of the _____ in the country are full.

(A) poisons   (B) colonies
(C) prisons   (D) enterprises

05 ___ Up until today, scientists are still debating whether_____ has an end or not. Most of them believe that it is still expanding.

(A) document   (B) universe
(C) harmony   (D) funeral

06 ___ If you come to the circus, you can _____ a wide range of performances, ranging from elephant show to stunt performances.

(A) anticipate   (B) arrest
(C) approach   (D) attain

07 ___ Our government takes great care of the poor by giving them all kinds of public _____. If people get paid below the minimum wage, the government will try its best to help them out.

(A) welfare   (B) luxuries
(C) strategies   (D) evaluations

08 ___ He barely made it out of the accident alive, which made him _____ his life even more. Now, he is doing volunteer work to contribute back to the society.

(A) stimulate   (B) compensate
(C) defeat   (D) appreciate

09 ___ As the birth rate gets lower, people tend to relocate to _____ areas in search of better opportunities. This phenomenon will make the gap between cities and countryside become even greater.

(A) messy   (B) authentic
(C) urban   (D) arbitrary

10 ___ Wild animals usually do not attack people aggressively. Instead, when they attack people, they are usually defending their _____.

(A) catalog   (B) obstacle
(C) territory   (D) exhibition

11 ___ The up-and-coming industry attracts thousands of people to _____ in it. With the huge amount of money, the future of the industry is looking even brighter.

(A) depict   (B) invest
(C) inspire   (D) terminate

12 ___ After the terrorist attack, the government decided to secretly form a special forces team whose members needed to _____ special training in order to deal with extreme situations.

(A) undergo   (B) deprive
(C) scrape   (D) patronize

13 ___ Despite the _____ loss, the losing team still fought until the last minute, which won them a big round of applause from the audience.

(A) mature
(B) portable
(C) evolutionary
(D) inevitable

14 ___ The kingdom has been _____ by the Louis family for hundreds of years. The infinite power of the royalty resulted in the corruption of the kingdom.

(A) dominated
(B) archived
(C) ascended
(D) invaded

15 ___ The birth rate of Taiwan keeps _____. The government is using every method they can to stop the trend.

(A) thrilling
(B) squeezing
(C) declining
(D) scattering

解答
1.(D) 2.(A) 3.(C) 4.(C) 5.(B) 6.(A) 7.(A) 8.(D) 9.(C) 10.(C) 11.(B) 12.(A) 13.(D) 14.(A) 15.(C)

merit

[`mɛrɪt]

n. 優點；功績

We need to consider the merits of both projects before making our final decision.
在做出最終決定之前，我們需要考慮兩個提案的優點。

警特 105

✒️ 秒殺解字 mer(share, part)+it → 本義是「一部分」，有績效可以獲得一部分獎賞，引申為「功績」、「優點」。

詞搭 on merit 依績效；the merits and demerits of + sth. 某事的優缺點

反義字 demerit

---

review

[rɪ`vju]

n. 評論

v. 評論；複習（功課）；回顧

Experts suggest that people review their budget every month and assess the overall annual budget to achieve financial goals.
專家建議人們每月檢查自己的預算並評估年度整體預算以實現財務目標。

✒️ 秒殺解字 re(again)+view(see) →「再」「看」一次。

詞搭 under review 檢討中

---

reviewer

[rɪ`vjuɚ]

n. 評論員、評論家

A reviewer made bad remarks about Harlan's new book, and the writer felt quite upset about it.
一位評論家對 Harlan 的新書給予不好的評價，他對此感到很沮喪。

同義字 critic

---

environment

[ɪn`vaɪrənmənt]

n. 環境

Our first task is to take the novices to become familiar with the physical environment of our company.
我們的首要任務是讓新手了解我們公司的環境。

普 100
101
高 108
警特 105

✒️ 秒殺解字 en(in)+viron(circle)+ment →「環繞」「其中」，引申為「環境」。

詞搭 protect the environment 保護環境

---

environmental

[ɪn͵vaɪrən`mɛntl]

adj. 環境的

Yedda joined an environmental group working to make our neighborhood a sustainable community by recycling and reducing its carbon footprint.
Yedda 加入了一個環保小組，致力於透過回收利用和減少碳足跡使我們的社區成為可永續發展的社區。

普 100
107
108
110
高 110
警特 106
109

詞搭 environmental destruction 環境的破壞；environmental assessment 環境影響評估

environment- ally

[ɛn͵vaɪrən`mɛntl̩ɪ]

adv. 有關環境方面

Riding a bike is always environmentally friendly and ~~beneficial to your health.~~ 【警特】108
騎自行車永遠是環保的，而且對你的健康也有益處。

| 詞搭 | environmentally friendly = eco-friendly 環保的 |

---

resume / résumé

[͵rɛzʊ`me]

n. 履歷表；摘要

[rɪ`zum]

v. 重新開始；重返；恢復

The YouTuber will resume live broadcasting as soon as his injury gets better. 【警特】105 106
等傷勢好轉後，YouTuber 直播主將會恢復直播。

秒殺解字 re(again)+sum(take)+e → 本義「再次」「拿取」，後引申為「（停止後）再繼續」。相關同源字有 assume（v. 認為；假定）、assumption（n. 認為；假定）、consume（v. 消耗；消費）、consumption（n. 消耗；消費）。

| 詞搭 | resume + Ving 重新開始……；resume one's seat 重新回到位子上 |

---

alternative

[ɔl`tɝnətɪv]

n. 選擇；替代方案
adj. 替代的

There is no alternative way to go to that remote island, except by airplane.
除了搭乘飛機，沒有其他方法可以去那個偏遠的島嶼。

秒殺解字 alter(other)+n+ate+ive → 有「其他」「選擇」。可用 other 當神隊友，l/ð 轉音，母音通轉，來記憶 alter，表示「另外的」、「其他的」、「不同的」。相關同源字有 alter（v. 改變）、alteration（n. 改變）、alternate（adj. 交替、輪流的；可供替代的）、alternation（n. 交替、輪流；間隔）、alien（n. 外國人；外星人）、alienate（v. 使疏遠）、alienation（n. 疏遠）、allergy（n. 過敏症；反感）。

| 詞搭 | have no alternative / option / choice but + to V 除……外別無選擇；an alternative route / method / approach 替代路線／方法／辦法；alternative energy 替代性能源 |

---

alternating

[`ɔltɚ͵netɪŋ]

adj. 交替的；交流的

My brother and I take care of our parents on alternating weeks. 【普】106
我的弟弟和我隔周輪流照顧父母。

differ

[`dɪfɚ]

v. 不同、差異

A lot of painkillers work basically the same, but sometimes the effects differ from one person to another. 〔普〕108

許多止痛藥作用基本上相同，但有時效果因人而異。

🪶**秒殺解字** dif(=dis=away)+fer(bear) →「帶」「走」，產生「差異」。可用 **bear** 當神隊友，**b/f 轉音，母音通轉**，來記憶 **fer**，表示「攜帶」、「生育」、「承受」。相關同源字有 in**fer**（v. 推論）、pre**fer**（v. 寧願）、suf**fer**（v. 受苦）、re**fer**（v. 提到）、trans**fer**（v. 轉移）、con**fer**ence（n. 正式會議）。

詞搭 : differ from... 與……不同；A differs from B in... = A is different from B in... A 與 B 在……方面不同

同義字 : vary

differentiate

[ˌdɪfəˈrɛnʃɪˌet]

v. 使有差異

If you want to build a great brand, you can differentiate it by creating an original story. 〔高〕108

如果你想建立一個偉大的品牌，可以透過運用原創故事來讓它與眾不同。

詞搭 : differentiate / distinguish / tell between A and B = differentiate / distinguish / tell A from B 區別 A 與 B 的不同

differential

[dɪfəˈrɛnʃəl]

adj. 差異的

Some employers have a differential salary structure based on employees' experience and education.

一些雇主根據員工的經驗和教育程度而採用不同的薪資結構。

injury

[`ɪndʒərɪ]

n. 傷害

The rescuer sustained only minor injuries to his legs and arms, but still had to stay in hospital for a few days. 〔普〕99

救援人員的腿和手臂僅受到輕傷，但仍得住院幾天。

🪶**秒殺解字** in(not)+jur(law, right)+y → 本義「不」「合法」，引申為「不公平」、「不正義」，更衍生出「傷害」的意思，因為「傷害」是「不」被「法律」所允許的。

詞搭 : suffer / sustain an injury 遭受傷害；a fatal injury 致命傷

sponsor
[ˋspɑnsɚ]
n. 贊助人、贊助商
v. 贊助

The international sports event was sponsored by some big corporations.
這個國際體育賽事是由一些大公司贊助的。

秒殺解字 spons(promise)+or → 「答應」、「保證」贊助你的人。相關同源字有 re**spond**（v. 反應；回答）、re**spons**e（n. 反應；回答）、re**spons**ible（adj. 負責的）、corre**spond**（v. 對應；一致；通信）、**spous**e（n. 配偶）。

衍生字 sponsorship [ˋspɑnsɚˏʃɪp] n. 贊助金

高 110
醫特 106

merchant
[ˋmɝtʃənt]
n. 商人

A local merchant had trouble with gangsters breaking into his store and stealing many of his possessions.
一名當地商人遇到歹徒闖入他的商店並偷走許多財物的麻煩。

秒殺解字 merch(market, trade)+ant → 從事「交易」的是「商人」。可用 **market** 當神隊友，**母音通轉**，來記憶 **merc**, **merch**，表示「市場」、「買賣」、「交易」；「市場」是「買賣」、「交易」的場所。相關同源字有 **market**（n. 市場 v. 銷售；行銷）、**market**ing（n. 行銷；交易）、**merch**andise（n. 商品；貨物 v. 行銷）、com**merc**e（n. 商業；貿易）、com**merc**ial（adj. 商業的 n. 商業廣告）、info**merc**ial（n. 置入式行銷節目）。

同義字 dealer, trader

merchandise
[ˋmɝtʃənˏdaɪz]
n. 商品
v. 行銷

This company inspects the merchandise carefully, particularly regarding children's safety.
這家公司仔細檢查商品，特別是與兒童安全方面有關的。

名詞同義字 goods

動詞同義字 market

醫 104

enterprise
[ˋɛntɚˏpraɪz]
n. 企業；進取心；重大計畫

Our education program helps students develop skills with enterprise development and employability.
我們的教育計劃可幫助學生發展具有冒險精神和就業能力的技能。

秒殺解字 enter(=inter=between)+pris(take, seize)+e → 把事業「抓」在手中。相關同源字有 **pris**on（n. 監獄）、im**pris**on（v. 監禁；限制）、sur**pris**e（v. 使驚訝）。

詞搭 a public / private enterprise 公營／私營企業；enterprise culture 企業文化

衍生字 entrepreneur [ˏɑntrəprəˋnɝ] n. 企業家

普 107
醫特 105

215

technology

[tɛkˋnɑlədʒɪ]

n. 科技

Modern technology has brought many advantages for all humans, but people should also consider its disadvantages.
現代技術為全人類帶來了很多好處，但是人們也應該考量它的缺點。

普 100
104
106
警特 105
108

> **秒殺解字** techn(art, skill)+o+logy(study of) → 研究「技藝」的「學問」。相關同源字有 **techn**ological (adj. 科技的、技術的)、**techn**ologist (n. 技術專家、工藝師)、**techn**ique (n. 技巧；技術)、**techn**ical (adj. 技術的；專門性的)、**techn**ician (n. 技工、技術人員)、**techn**ophobe (n. 科技恐懼者)、**techn**ophobia (n. 科技恐懼)、**techn**ophile (n. 科技迷)、**techn**o-savvy (n. 科技通)。

| 詞搭 | technology transfer 技術轉移；technology-intensive products 科技密集產品 |

---

civilization

[ˏsɪvələˋzeʃən]

n. 文明

Ancient Egypt was home to a significant civilization around the Mediterranean Sea for almost three thousand years.
古埃及是地中海附近近三千年的重要文明。

普 103

> **秒殺解字** civ(city)+il+ize+ate+ion → 使「都市」化，表示「使……變文明」。都市常代表文明，例如：urban 是「城市的」、「都市的」，而 urbane 表示「文雅的」、「有教養的」。

---

potential

[pəˋtɛnʃəl]

n. 潛力；潛能
adj. 潛在的；可能的

Miranda is young but she shows a lot of potential in medicine.
Miranda 雖年輕，但在醫學上顯示出很大的潛力。

普 107
高 108
警特 106
108

> **秒殺解字** pot(powerful)+ent+i+al →「有力量的」，表示「潛力」、「潛在的」。可用表示「權力」、「力量」的 **power** 當神隊友，**t/r/z/s 轉音，母音通轉**，來記憶 **poss**、**pot**，表示「有權力的」、「有力量的」。相關同源字有 **power** (n. 權力；力量 v. 驅動)、**power**ful (adj. 有力量的；強大的)、em**power** (v. 授權)、**pot**ency (n. 力量；影響力)、im**pot**ent (adj. 無能的；無力的)、omni**pot**ent (adj. 全能的)、**poss**ible (adj. 可能的)、**poss**ibly (adv. 可能地)、**poss**ibility (n. 可能性；機會 v. 授權)、**poss**ess (v. 擁有)。

| 詞搭 | a potential market / customer 潛在市場／客戶；achieve / fulfill / realize / reach + sb's full potential 完全發揮……的潛力 |

| 同義字 | possible |

potentially

[pə`tɛnʃəlɪ]

adv. 潛在地

The flu can be a potentially fatal disease, so people shouldn't neglect it.
流感是一種可能致命的疾病，因此人們不應忽視它。

---

potent

[`potn̩t]

adj. 強而有力的；有效的

This is a very potent drug but most people can't stand the side effects.
這是一種非常有效的藥物，但大多數人無法忍受副作用。

🔲 108

詞搭 a potent drug 強效藥品

同義字 effective, powerful

反義字 impotent

---

disturbing

[dɪs`tɝbɪŋ]

adj. 令人不安的

Mr. Mallon said the new statistics also revealed a disturbing truth about the growing population of homeless people.
Mallon 先生説，新的統計數字還揭示了一個令人不安的事實，即無家可歸的人口不斷增長。

秒殺解字 dis(completely)+turb(confuse)+ing → 「完全」「混亂」的，表示「令人不安的」。可用 **trouble** 當神隊友，**母音通轉**，來記憶 **turb**，表示「使混亂」。相關同源字有 **trouble** (v. 使煩惱；打擾 n. 麻煩)、**troubl**ed (adj. 焦慮的；有困難的)、**troub**ling (adj. 令人焦慮的)、**trouble**some (adj. 令人討厭的)、dis**turb** (v. 打擾；使困擾)、dis**turb**ance (n. 打擾；騷動)、dis**turb**ed (adj. 心理失常的；感到焦慮的)。

同義字 worrying, upsetting, troubling

---

predict

[prɪ`dɪkt]

v. 預測

Even with the latest technologies, people still can't predict when and where an earthquake will occur.
即使採用最新技術，人們仍然無法預測地震發生的時間和地點。

🔲 104
110

秒殺解字 pre(before)+dic(say)+t → 「先」「説」就是「預測」。相關同源字有 **dic**tionary (n. 字典)、ad**dic**t (n. 成癮者)、de**dic**ate (v. 奉獻)、contra**dic**t (v. 反駁；與……矛盾)、in**dic**ate (v. 指出；表明)、con**dic**tion (n. 情況)。

衍生字 prediction [prɪ`dɪkʃən] n. 預測

同義字 forecast, prophesy, foretell

unpredictable

[ˌʌnprɪˈdɪktəbl]

adj. 不可預測的

There are many factors, such as temperature, air pressure, and precipitation, that make weather so unpredictable.

有很多因素，例如溫度，氣壓和降水，使天氣變得不可預測。

 秒殺解字 un(not)+predict+able →「不」「可」「預測」的。

反義字 | predictable

---

melt

[mɛlt]

v. 融化

Human activities are the cause of the phenomenon that many glaciers are melting rapidly.

人類活動是許多冰川迅速融化的原因。

秒殺解字 melt(mild, soft) → mild（adj. 溫暖的；溫和的）、melt [mɛlt]（v. 融化）同源，**d/t 轉音，母音通轉**，核心語意是「柔軟的」（**soft**），衍生出「融化」的語意，而 **melt** 或 **melt away** 更衍生出「逐漸消失」、「消散」的語意。

詞搭 | melt away 逐漸消失；melt down 使（金屬）熔解

---

preconception

[ˌprikənˈsɛpʃən]

n. 偏見；成見

People tend to hold certain preconceptions about how African people live their lives.

人們傾向於對非洲人民的生活有某些成見。

秒殺解字 pre(before)+ conception →「事先」構成的「説」「想法」。

詞搭 | a preconception about / of + sb. / sth. 對某人／某事物的成見

---

humorless

[ˈhjumɚlɪs]

adj. 缺少幽默感的

Darnell is so humorless and stubborn that no girls would like to date him.

Darnell 是如此無趣且固執己見，所以沒有女孩願意和他約會。

秒殺解字 humor+less(without, lack, not) →「缺少」「幽默感」的。

反義字 | humorous

restriction

[rɪ`strɪkʃən]

n. 限制；約束

There are restrictions on how many people can go to the island, which is a way of protecting the natural environment.
為了保護自然環境，島上有人數的限制。

🖊 **秒殺解字** re(back)+stric(draw tight)+t+ion → 從「後面」「拉」「回來」，引申為「限制」。

詞搭 speed restrictions 速限；impose / place restrictions on + sth. 對……實行限制；lift / remove restrictions on + sth. 取消對……的限制

同義字 limit

enforce

[ɪn`fɔrs]

v. 實施、執行

Sometimes it's difficult to enforce discipline among kindergarten kids.
有時很難在幼兒園的孩子中加強紀律。

🖊 **秒殺解字** en(make)+forc(strong)+e → 「使」「力量」得以發揮，表示「實施」、「執行」。相關同源字有 **force**（v. 強迫 n. 力量）、rein**forc**e（v. 強化；加強）、**fort**（n. 要塞、堡壘）、**fort**ify（v. 加強）、com**fort**（v./n. 安慰）、ef**fort**（n. 努力）。

詞搭 enforce a law / ban 執行法律／禁令；enforce + sth. + on + sb. 迫使某人接受某事物

衍生字 enforcement [ɪn`fɔrsmənt] n. 實施、執行；reinforce [ˌriɪn`fɔrs] v. 強化、加強；reinforcement [ˌriɪn`fɔrsmənt] n. 強化、加強

同義字 carry out, implement

tourism
[`tʊrɪzəm]

n. 觀光業；觀光

Tourism is an important part of Thailand's economy; therefore, lockdowns did great harm to it.
旅遊業是泰國經濟的重要組成部分；因此，封城對它造成了極大的傷害。

普 104

秒殺解字 tour(turn)+ism →「旅行」的事業，表示「觀光業」。「旅行」是到處繞繞、逛逛、「轉轉」。可用 **turn** 當神隊友，**母音通轉**，來記憶 **tour**，皆表示「**轉動**」。相關同源字有 **turn**（v./n. 轉動；轉變）、re**turn**（v./n. 返回；歸還）、down**turn**（n. 經濟衰退）、**tour**（n./v. 旅行；巡迴演出）、**tour**nament（n. 錦標賽）、**tour**ney（n. 錦標賽）。

tourist
[`tʊrɪst]

n. 觀光客、遊客
adj. 觀光的

The Eiffel Tower is a major <u>tourist attraction</u> in Paris, and has become one of the most prominent scenic spots in the world.
埃菲爾鐵塔是巴黎的主要旅遊景點，並且已成為世界上最著名的景點之一。

普 107
高 110
警特 107

|詞搭| tourist agency 旅行社；tourist industry 觀光業

|同義字| traveler

touristy
[`tʊrəstɪ]

adj. 觀光客的

This place used to be very touristy, but now it's become boring with nothing attractive.
這個地方曾經是非常吸引旅客，但現在它變得乏味且沒什麼吸引力了。

普 107

worship
[`wɝˌʃɪp]

v. **n.** 崇拜，禮拜

Ancient people worshipped a variety of gods among different religions.
古代人們在不同的宗教信仰中崇拜各種神靈。

秒殺解字 wor(worth=value)+ship → 看到神的「價值」，做禮拜表示對神的敬意與愛慕。

|時態| worship, worship(p)ed, worship(p)ed

|詞搭| **worship the ground someone walks on** 拜倒在某人腳下；<u>hero / idol</u> worship 英雄／偶像崇拜

|字辨| warship [`wɔrˌʃɪp] n. 戰艦，軍艦

|同義字| adore

illusion
[ɪˋluʒən]
n. 錯覺、假象

Sabrina was under the illusion that her husband was still alive.
Sabrina 幻想她丈夫還活著。

🖋 (秒殺解字) il(=in=at, upon)+lus(play)+ion → 「玩弄」視線所見表象，引申為「錯覺」、「假象」。

詞搭 be under the illusion + that + S+ V 誤以為……；have no illusions about + sth. 很清楚某事；an optical illusion 錯視

disillusion
[ˌdɪsɪˋluʒən]
v. 使醒悟

Your experiences dating Peter disillusioned you about what it would be like being married to him.
你和 Peter 約會的經歷讓你對嫁給他的感覺幻滅了。

詞搭 become / grow disillusioned by / with... 看破……、對……不再抱有希望

nervous
[ˋnɝˑvəs]
adj. 神經的；緊張的

Sally always gets nervous whenever she has to take a plane, because she has fears of flying.
Sally 每次搭乘飛機時總是很緊張，因為她害怕飛行。

普 105
警特 107

🖋 (秒殺解字) nerv(nerve)+ous → 「神經的」，引申為「緊張的」。

詞搭 nervous breakdown 精神崩潰；nervous tension 神經緊張

同義字 tense

convention
[kənˋvɛnʃən]
n. 慣例；習俗；大型會議

It is a matter of convention that the newlyweds should toast everyone at their wedding banquet.
按照慣例，新婚夫婦將在婚禮上向所有人敬酒。

普 105

🖋 (秒殺解字) con(together)+ven(come)+t+ion → 「一起」到「來」，表示「慣例」、「習俗」，「大型會議」。相關同源字有 adventure (n. 冒險)、invent (v. 發明)、prevent (v. 阻止)、event (n. 事件)、eventual (adj. 最後的)、convenient (adj. 便利的)、convene (v. 集會)、conventional (adj. 傳統的)、avenue (n. 大街)、revenue (n. 國家稅收)。

詞搭 by convention / tradition 按傳統按慣例；social / international / constitutional convention 社會／國際／憲法慣例

衍生字 conventional [kənˋvɛnʃən!] adj. 傳統的、慣例的

同義字 custom, tradition, meeting, conference

blame
[blem]
n. **v.** 責備、歸咎

Joyce still <u>blamed</u> herself <u>for</u> not taking good care of her mother when she was ill in bed.
Joyce 仍然責備自己無法照顧好臥病在床的母親。

🔖 100

> **秒殺解字** 源自拉丁文的 blaspheme，表示「說不恭敬的話的」(evil-speaking)。

詞搭 blame + sb. + for + sth. = blame + sth.+ on + sb. 因某事責備某人；be to blame for + sth. 應對某事負責；<u>take / bear</u> the blame 承擔過錯／責任；put the blame on... 歸咎於……

---

complicate
[`kamplə͵ket]
v. 使複雜

Otto's misunderstanding greatly complicated the problem and caused conflicts between him and his parents.
Otto 的誤解使問題變得更加複雜，並導致他與父母之間發生衝突。

🔖 108

> **秒殺解字** com(together)+plic(fold)+ate → 「摺」在「一起」，糾結，就很「複雜」。可用 **fold** 當神隊友，**p/f轉音**，母音通轉，來記憶 **plic**，皆表示「對摺」。

衍生字 complication [͵kamplə`keʃən] n. 複雜
反義字 simplify

---

complicated
[`kamplə͵ketɪd]
adj. 複雜的

America has a complicated voting system and most foreigners have difficulty understanding it.
美國的投票系統很複雜，大多數外國人很難理解它。

🔖 103

同義字 complex

---

pendulum
[`pɛndʒələm]
n. 擺錘；鐘擺

The tennis match went back and forth, like a pendulum, with each player winning and losing sets, so it was hard to predict the outcome.
網球比賽就像鐘擺一樣來回擺動，每個球員都有輸贏，所以很難預測結果。

> **秒殺解字** pend(weigh, hang)+ule+um → 「掛」起來的「擺錘」、「鐘擺」。

詞搭 a pendulum clock 擺鐘

stormy

[`stɔrmɪ]

adj. 暴風雨的；激烈的

The road to the National Park closed yesterday afternoon and will remain closed today because of stormy weather conditions.

通往國家公園的道路於昨天下午關閉，由於天氣惡劣，今天將持續關閉。

🪶 秒殺解字 storm+y → 「暴風雨」「的」。

詞搭 | stormy weather 暴風雨天氣；stormy sea 波濤洶湧的海面

---

commerce

[`kamɝs]

n. 商業

Julie showed her genuine talent for commerce and soon found a job in an international bank.

曾 110
高 108

Julie 展現了她真正的商業才華，並很快在一家國際銀行找到了工作。

🪶 秒殺解字 com(together)+merc(market, trade)+e → 「一起」在「市場」所從事的「交易」。可用 **market** 當神隊友，母音通轉，來記憶 **merc, merch**，表示「市場」、「買賣」、「交易」；「市場」是「買賣」、「交易」的場所。相關同源字有 **market**（n. 市場 v. 銷售；行銷）、**market**ing（n. 行銷；交易）、**merch**ant（n. 商人）、**merch**andise（n. 商品；貨物 v. 行銷）、info**merc**ial（n. 置入式行銷節目）。

同義字 | trade

---

e-commerce

[ɪ`kamɝs]

n. 電子商務

An e-commerce website offers potential customers a new shopping experience that is available 24 hours a day.

警特 106

電子商務網站為潛在客戶提供了一種可以持續 24 小時不間斷購物的新方式。

---

commercial

[kə`mɝʃəl]

n. （電視、電台）廣告

adj. 商業的

Our company's top priorities must be commercial growth and employee welfare.

我們公司的首要任務必須是業績成長以及重視員工福利。

詞搭 | a commercial bank / building 商業銀行／大樓

colony

[`kɑlənɪ]

n. 殖民地;一群同類且有組織的動物

The researchers are collecting information about the loss of bees in the honeybee colony .
研究人員正在收集有關蜂群中蜜蜂數量減少的資訊。

警特 107

秒殺解字 col(cultivate, inhabit)+on+y → 在另外一地植入新體制,培養新「文化」,並移入新人口「居住於」該處。**cult、col** 同源,**母音通轉**,核心語意是「**耕種**」或「**居住**」。文化發軔大多和「耕種」有關,有文化的地方才有人「居住」。**cul**tivate (v. 耕種;栽培)、**cul**tivated (adj. 有教養的;耕種的;栽培的)、**cul**ture (n. 文化)、**cul**tural (adj. 文化的)、sub**cul**ture (n. 次文化)、agri**cul**ture (n. 農業)、agri**cul**tural (adj. 農業的)。

衍生字 colonial [kə`lonɪəl] adj. 殖民的;colonize [`kɑlə͵naɪz] v. 將……開拓為殖民地;colonist [`kɑlənɪst] n. 殖民者

sequence

[`sikwəns]

n. 順序;一連串

Experienced teachers should ask questions in a logical sequence for students to follow.
有經驗的老師應按邏輯順序提出問題,讓學生遵循。

秒殺解字 sequ(follow)+ence → 本義「跟著」走,表示「尾隨」,有先後「順序」的意思。可用 **second** 當神隊友,**母音通轉**,來記憶 **sequ, secut**,表示「跟隨」。**seco**nd 是「跟隨」在第一名後面、所以是「第二的」,而 **seco**nd 當動詞時,有「**贊成**」、「**附議**」的意思,意味著「跟隨」別人的意見。相關同源字有 **sequ**el (n. 續集;隨之而來的事)、con**sequ**ent (adj. 隨之而來的、由此引起的)、con**sequ**ently (adv. 因此)、con**sequ**ence (n. 結果)、con**secu**tive (adj. 連續的)、ex**ecu**te (v. 執行;處死)、sub**sequ**ent (adj. 隨後的)。

詞搭 in a / an... sequence 按照……的順序;in sequence 依次,逐一;out of sequence 不照順序;a sequence of... 一連串的……

同義字 order

ambition

[æm`bɪʃən]

n. 野心、抱負

Last year, Paul achieved his ambition of competing in the national speech contest and won the contest.
去年,Paul 實現了參加全國演講比賽的雄心壯志,並獲得了第一名。

警 104

秒殺解字 amb(=ambi=around)+it(go)+ion → 原指「四處」「去」拜票,後演變為「抱負」。

achieve / fulfill / realize an ambition 實現抱負

temporary
[ˋtɛmpəˏrɛrɪ]
adj. 暫時的

Most people would feel the blues or temporary depression some time in their lives due to challenges or changes.
由於挑戰或變化，大多數人會在生活中的某些時候感到憂鬱或暫時的沮喪。

105
107
108
109

 秒殺解字 tempor(time)+ary → 表示暫「時」的。**tempo**、**tempor** 表示「時間」。相關同源字有 **tempo**（n. 速度；拍子；步調）con**tempor**ary（adj. 當代的、同時代的 n. 同時代的人）。

詞搭 on a temporary basis = temporarily 暫時地；temporary suspension 暫停

同義字 impermanent

反義字 permanent

temporarily
[ˋtɛmpəˏrɛrəlɪ]
adv. 暫時地

The city library has temporarily reduced its opening hours because a new air conditioning system is being installed for the coming summer.
市立圖書館暫時減少了開放時間，因為正在為即將到來的夏季安裝了新的空調系統。

behave
[bɪˋhev]
v. 使守規矩；表現；行為舉止

It takes great patience for parents to teach their children to behave reasonably.
父母要非常有耐心地教導孩子適當的行為舉止。

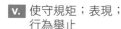 be(intensive prefix)+have(have) → be 是「加強語氣」，behave 是一個人所「擁有」的特殊表現方式。

詞搭 behave oneself 守規矩；behave well / properly 舉止得體 / 行為正當

反義字 misbehave

behavior
[bɪˋhevjɚ]
n. 行為

Studies show that drinking alcohol obviously has a great influence on human brains and behavior.
研究表明，飲酒顯然對人的大腦和行為有很大影響。

101
103
108

詞搭 abnormal / aggressive behavior 異常／攻擊行為

equivalent

[ɪˋkwɪvələnt]

n. 相等物
adj. 相等的

There is no equivalent to London's Albert Hall here in Taiwan. 普 106

台灣這裡沒有像倫敦的阿爾伯特音樂廳一樣的建築。

秒殺解字 equi(equal)+val(worth)+ent → 「相等的」「價值」。可用表示「價值」的 **value** 當神隊友，**母音通轉**，來記憶 **val**、**vail**，表示「強的」、「值得的」。相關同源字有 **value**（n. 價值 v. 重視）、**valu**able（adj. 有價值的）、**valu**eless（adj. 不值錢的）、e**valu**ate（v. 評估；評價）、**val**id（adj. 有效的）、in**val**id（adj. 失效的 n. 病人）、a**vail**able（adj. 可用的、可得或買到的；有空的）、pre**vail**（v. 盛行；獲勝）、pre**vail**ing（adj. 盛行的、現有的）、pre**val**ent（adj. 盛行的、普遍的）、pre**val**ence（n. 盛行、普遍）。

詞搭 be equivalent to... 相當於……；equivalent value 等

---

guilty

[ˋgɪltɪ]

adj. 有罪的

A 18-year-old man was found guilty of murdering his mother and abandoning her dead body.

一名 18 歲男子因為被發現謀殺母親並遺棄她的屍體，被判有罪。

秒殺解字 guilt+y → 有「罪」「的」。

詞搭 be guilty of... 有……的罪；be found guilty 被認定有罪；feel guilty about... 對……感到愧疚

反義字 innocent

---

insecticide

[ɪnˋsɛktə‚saɪd]

n. 殺蟲劑

Many insects began to develop resistance to the insecticide, and therefore, using insecticide is not a sustainable way of killing insects. 高 108

許多昆蟲開始對殺蟲劑產生抗藥性。因此，使用殺蟲劑不是殺死昆蟲的永續性方法。

秒殺解字 insect+i+cid(kill)+e → 「殺」「昆蟲」的化學藥劑。相關同源字有 de**cid**e（v. 決定）、sui**cid**e（n. 自殺）、pesti**cid**e（n. 殺蟲劑）。

psychology
[saɪˋkɑlədʒɪ]

n. 心理學

Observing shoppers in the marketplace gave Kristin direct data about crowd psychology.
觀察市場中的購物者可以直接讓 Kristin 獲得有關人群心理的資料。

曾 108
警特 105

秒殺解字 psych(mind, mental)+o+logy(study of) → 研究「心理」的「學問」。**psych** 表示「靈魂」、「精神」、「心智」、「心理的」。相關同源字有 **psych**e (n. 心靈；靈魂)、**psych**ic (adj. 靈魂的；精神的；通靈的 n. 通靈者)、**psych**iatry (n. 精神病學)、**psych**iatric (adj. 精神病的)、**psych**iatrist (n. 精神科醫師)。

psychological
[͵saɪkəˋlɑdʒəkḷ]

adj. 心理的；心理學的

More than half of the patients with sleep disorders have psychological problems.
一半以上的睡眠障礙患者有心理的問題。

詞搭 psychological warfare 心理戰

psychologist
[saɪˋkɑlədʒɪst]

n. 心理學家

A child psychologist is assessing and treating Kimberley to cope with her parents' divorce.
一名兒童心理學家正在評估和治療 Kimberley 以面對她父母的離婚。

警特 109

詞搭 clinical psychologist 臨床心理學家

virtually
[ˋvɝtʃʊəlɪ]

adv. 幾乎地；實際上

During the zoo's closure, visitors can view the webcams and explore the websites to enjoy the animals virtually.
在動物園關閉期間，訪客可以觀看網路攝影機並瀏覽網站以虛擬方式觀賞動物。

曾 107

秒殺解字 virtue(male, man)+u+al+ly → virtue 源自拉丁文，原意為「男子氣」(manliness)，引申為「有勇氣」、「有力氣」等，所衍生出來的意思，更是表示「實質的」。然而 1950 年代末期時，在電腦用語使用上，產生「模擬的」、「虛擬的」等幾乎相反的語意。

衍生字 virtual [ˋvɝtʃʊəl] adj. 幾乎的、虛擬的

同義字 practically, almost, nearly

01 ___ In order to keep the company from having any controversy, all the social media managers should _____ all the articles twice before they publish them online.

(A) avoid
(B) destroy
(C) review
(D) supply

02 ___ Psychologists have already proven that a person's personality is greatly influened by the ongoing interaction of character and _____.

(A) monument
(B) environment
(C) investment
(D) entertainment

03 ___ After a few years of rest, Stephanie, a famous singer, has decided to _____ her job in the next year.

(A) resume
(B) indicate
(C) receive
(D) worship

04 ___ If we don't find a(n) _____ way to make up for the loss, it will affect our profit significantly.

(A) negative
(B) alternative
(C) comparative
(D) informative

05 ___ Ashley is trying to get more funding for the project, so she is contacting other companies in order to reach out to potiential _____.

(A) backpackers
(B) captains
(C) managers
(D) sponsors

06 ___ We need to _____ the products in a variety of colors so that they will be more attractive to customers.

(A) associate
(B) generate
(C) investigate
(D) differentiate

07 ___ The machine operator got a hand _____ last week, and there's no
one to fill in his place right now.
(A) trend   (B) injury
(C) threat   (D) emotion

08 ___ The company created some sustainable cosmetic _____ and
earned huge profits from it.
(A) merchandise   (B) cattle
(C) liberty   (D) faculty

09 ___ She put a lot of effort into her score in order to work in a famous
_____. Finally, she was accepted and her dream came true.
(A) suspect   (B) substance
(C) enterprise   (D) prospect

10 ___ Although the product used the state-of-the-art _____ and featured
a gorgeous metal body, it didn't attract customers' attention because of
its high price.
(A) allowance   (B) technology
(C) inspiration   (D) psychology

11 ___ There are some paintings of ancient _____ hanging on the wall in
the museum, and it appeals to many historians to come to see it.
(A) liquidation   (B) civilization
(C) inspection   (D) transportation

12 ___ Despite everything going well, there were still some _____ risks
that could make us lose money with this project.
(A) potential   (B) artistic
(C) secondary   (D) sophisticated

13 ___ It is _____ that the head of this terrorist attack is still hiding in the
city and no one knows where he is.
(A) pioneering   (B) threatening
(C) challenging   (D) disturbing

14 ___ It is hard to _____ that the whole department would be laid off due to this pandemic. Around one hundred people lost their job because of it.

(A) dissolve
(C) enact

(B) predict
(D) disclose

15 ___ He is unpopular in his department because he always judges people with his _____ of race.

(A) affection
(C) preconception

(B) discrimination
(D) evaluation

passenger
[`pæsṇdʒɚ]
n. 乘客

Hundreds of passengers were stranded yesterday because of the railway strike.
昨天由於鐵路罷工，數百名乘客被困。

普 101
警特 108

（秒殺解字）pass(pass)+eng(age)+er → 搭車「經過」的人。

詞搭 a passenger plane 客機；transit passenger 過境旅客

---

funeral
[`fjunərəl]
n. 葬禮

The late President's funeral will be held next Wednesday.
已故總統的葬禮將於下週三舉行。

普 102

（秒殺解字）fun(dead, burial rites)+er+al → 源自拉丁文，表示「死」「埋葬」的意思

詞搭 attend a funeral 參加葬禮

---

fate
[fet]
n. 命運

My mother always thinks fate has been very unfair to her.
我母親總是認為命運對她非常不公平。

（秒殺解字）fa(speak)+t+e → 神「說」的話，表示「宿命」。

---

fatal
[`fetḷ]
adj. 致命的；無可挽回的

Henry was seriously wounded in the accident and suffered a fatal injury to the brain.
Henry 在意外事故中受了重傷，並且對大腦造成致命傷害。

高 108

詞搭 a fatal accident / illness / injury 致命的事故／疾病／傷害；a fatal mistake /error 致命的錯誤；deal + sb. + a fatal blow 給某人致命的一擊

衍生字 fatally [`fetḷɪ] adv. 致命地；fatality [fə`tælətɪ] n. 死亡者、致命性

同義字 deadly, lethal

attain
[ə`ten]

v. 達到；獲得

He finally attained his goal, but he did it at the expense of others.

他終於實現了自己的目標，但他人卻為此付出了犧牲代價。

曾 103

(秒殺解字) at(=ad=to)+tain(=tag=touch) →「去」「碰觸」，表示經過努力而「達成」。坊間書籍和網路常犯一個錯誤，把 attain 和 contain、maintain、obtain 歸類在一起，而事實上它們並不同源。

衍生字 attainment [ə`tenmənt] n. 獲得；成就；實現

同義字 achieve, accomplish, reach

---

arouse
[ə`rauz]

v. 引發、激起

The student's strange behavior has aroused the teacher's attention.

這名學生的奇怪行為已經引起了老師的注意。

曾 105

(秒殺解字) a(on)+rouse(rouse) →「處於」「喚起……」的「狀態」。

詞搭 arouse tremendous controversy 引起很大的爭議；
arouse widespread sympathy 激起廣泛的同情

字辨 arise [ə`raiz] v. 產生、形成

同義字 excite

---

comment
[`kamɛnt]

n. 評論
v. 做評論

Do you have any comment on what I proposed today?

您對我今天的建議有何評論？

曾 100

(秒殺解字) com(intensive prefix)+men(mind, think)+t → 是出自內「心」、大腦的想法。可用 **mind** 當神隊友，**d/t 轉音，母音通轉**，來記憶 **ment**，表示「心（智）」、「思考」。相關同源字有 **min**d（n. 心智；想法 v. 在意）、re**min**d（v. 提醒、使想起）、**men**tal（adj. 心理的、精神的）、**men**tality（n. 心態）、**men**tion（v./n. 提到）、**men**tor（n. 導師、指導者）、absent-**min**ded（adj. 心不在焉的）、**man**ia（n. 瘋狂）、**man**iac（n. 瘋子）、**man**darin（n. 華語）、auto**mat**ic（adj. 自動的）。

詞搭 make a comment on... = comment on... 對……評論；
no comment 不予置評、無可奉告

衍生字 commentary [`kamən͵tɛri] n. 評論、講評；commentator [`kamən͵tetə] n. 時事評論家、評論員；commentate [kamən͵tet] v. 實況報導

同義字 remark

inspire

[ɪn`spaɪr]

v. 鼓舞、激勵；使有靈感

My father hoped that the success of one of my cousins would inspire me to make greater efforts.
我父親希望我其中一位堂哥的成功能夠激勵我做出更大的努力。

警特 105 107

秒殺解字 in(in)+spir(breathe)+e → 往「內」「吹氣」，表示「使有靈感」。如果工作時精神萎靡，頭腦不靈光，出去吸幾口新鮮口氣，往往靈感就來了。相關同源字有 **spir**it (n. 精神；靈魂)、a**spir**e (v. 渴望)、con**spir**e (v. 同謀、密謀)、ex**pir**e (v. 期滿、屆期；終止)、per**spir**e (v. 流汗)、re**spir**e (v. 呼吸)。

詞搭 inspire + sb. + to V 激發某人從事……；inspire confidence 鼓舞信心

同義字 encourage, motivate, stimulate

inspiring

[ɪn`spaɪrɪŋ]

adj. 激勵人心的；啟發靈感的

The candidate's speech was inspiring and had touched many voters.
這位候選人的演講令人鼓舞，並感動了許多選民。

反義字 uninspiring

inspiration

[ˌɪnspə`reʃən]

n. 靈感；啟示

Hanna's always diligent and she's been a source of inspiration for me.
Hanna 一直都很勤奮而且是激勵我的源動力之一。

警特 108

詞搭 draw / derive inspiration from... 從……獲得靈感

allowance

[ə`laʊəns]

n. 津貼；零用錢

The manager says sales staff will get a generous mileage allowance if they drive their own cars for work.
經理說，如果銷售人員開自己的車上班，他們將獲得豐厚的里程津貼。

警 104

秒殺解字 allow+ance →「允許」使用的錢，引申為「津貼」、「零用錢」等。

同義字 pocket money

vein

[ven]

n. 靜脈

Whenever he gets angry, the veins in his forehead will stand out.
每當他生氣時，額頭上的靜脈就會突出。

秒殺解字 源自古英文，本表示「靜脈」、「動脈」及「脈搏」，後來特指「靜脈」，及「礦脈」、「葉脈」等。

字辨 a blood vessel 血管

harmony

[`hɑrmənɪ]

n. 和諧

My grandparents always say that family harmony is far more important than wealth.

我的祖父母總是説，家庭和睦遠比財富重要。

秒殺解字 harmon(a fitting)+y → 源自希臘文，表示「音樂上的一致」，引申為「和諧」。

詞搭 in harmony 和諧地

衍生字 harmonious [hɑr`monɪəs] adj. 和諧的

unfortunately

[ʌn`fɔrtʃənɪtlɪ]

adv. 不幸地

He hoped to arrive earlier, but unfortunately, he's stuck in a traffic jam now.

他希望能早點到達，但不幸的是，他現在塞在車陣中。

秒殺解字 un(not)+fortunate+ly →「不」「幸運」「地」。

反義字 fortunately, luckily

fortunate

[`fɔrtʃənɪt]

adj. 幸運的

It was fortunate that they had set out earlier than usual because the traffic's quite terrible now.

幸運的是，他們比往常更早出發，因為現在的交通狀況非常糟糕。

曾 108

同義字 lucky

misfortune

[mɪs`fɔrtʃən]

n. 不幸；災禍

She suffered a lot of misfortune over the past few years, but now she's happy she has gotten through it.

在過去的幾年中，她遭受了很多不幸，但現在她很高興度過了難關。

曾 102

秒殺解字 mis(bad, wrong)+ fortune →「壞」「運」。

詞搭 have the misfortune + to V / of Ving 不幸遭遇⋯⋯

同義字 bad luck

scatter

[`skætɚ]

v. 撒；分散

Mom will get crazy if you scatter things around.

如果你東西亂丟在四周，媽媽會發瘋。

警特 107 108

秒殺解字 scatter [`skætɚ] ( v. 撒；使分散 )、shatter [`ʃætɚ] (v. 粉碎；破壞) 同源，核心語意是「撒」、「散落」(strewn)，東西「粉碎」(shatter) 通常會「散落」、「分散」(scatter) 一地。

詞搭 scatter seeds 播種；scatter about 散播；scatter around 四散

normally

[`nɔrml̩ɪ]

adv. 正常地；平常

My motorcycle was functioning normally until yesterday. I think I'll have it fixed tomorrow.
我的摩托車在昨天開始故障了。我想明天將它修理一下。

高 108
警特 105

秒殺解字 norm(rule, norm)+al+ly → 按照「規則」、「標準」地，表示「通常」、「正常地」。

| 同義字 | usually, generally |
| 反義字 | abnormally |

---

sustain

[sə`sten]

v. 維持；支撐；承受

The remaining years of her life were sustained by a religious hope.
她的餘生全靠宗教的希望來維持。

警特 109

秒殺解字 sus(=sub=up from under)+tain(hold) → 本義是握著東西，由「由下往上」提起，引申為「支撐」、「維持」。相關同字有 contain（v. 容納）、content（n. 內容；滿足 adj. 滿意的）、obtain（v. 得到）、entertain（v. 使歡樂）、maintain（v. 維持）、maintenance（n. 維持、維修、保養）、sustenance（n. 食物；維持）、detain（v. 留下；使耽擱）、detention（n. 留下；使耽擱）、retain（v. 保留）、tenable（adj. 站得住腳的）、tenet（n. 信條；宗旨；原則）、tenant（n. 房客）、continue（v. 繼續、持續）、continual（adj. 連續、頻頻的）、continuous（adj. 連續不斷的）、continent（n. 大陸；洲）。

| 詞搭 | sustain great losses 蒙受重大損失 |
| 同義字 | maintain, support, suffer |

---

sustainability

[sə͵stenə`bɪlɪtɪ]

n. 永續性

The company's commitment to environmental sustainability has won the public's respect.
這家公司對環境永續發展的奉獻贏得了大眾的尊重。

---

sustainable

[sə`stenəb!]

adj. 可持續的

Cycling is a totally sustainable form of transport and should be greatly encouraged.
騎自行車是一種完全地永續性的運輸方式，應大力鼓勵。

警 107

sustainable growth / development 永續成長／發展

---

sustenance

[`sʌstənəns]

n. 食物；營養(品)；維持

The girl was quite feeble because of a long-term lack of sustenance.
由於長期缺乏營養，這個女孩相當虛弱。

exclude

[ɪk`sklud]

v. 排除在外、不包括

I must remind you that the price we offer excludes breakfast.

我必須提醒您，我們提供的價格不包括早餐。

書 99 108

秒殺解字 ex(out)+clud(close)+e → 把某對象「關」在「外」，表示「排除在外」。可用 **close** 當神隊友，**d/z/s/ʒ 轉音**，母音通轉，來記憶 **clud**、**clus**，皆表示「關閉」。相關同源字有 in**clud**e（v. 包括）、in**clud**ing（prep. 包括）、in**clud**ed（adj. 包括的）、in**clus**ive（adj. 包括的）、ex**clud**ing（prep. 除……之外）、ex**clus**ive（adj. 排外的）、con**clud**e（v. 下結論）、con**clus**ion（n. 結論）。

詞搭 exclude A from B 從 B 中排除 A；exclude + sb. + from + N / Ving 在某活動中排擠某人

衍生字 excluding [ɪk`skludɪŋ] prep. 不包括……在內

反義字 include

exclusive

[ɪk`sklusɪv]

n. 獨家新聞

adj. 除外的；獨家的

The quote for the trip is exclusive of the entrance fees of amusement parks.

這次旅行的報價不包括遊樂園的入園門票。

詞搭 exclusive of... = excluding... 不包括……；be exclusive to... 給……專用；exclusive distribution 總經銷；exclusive access / rights 獨家使用權；an exclusive report / interview / coverage 獨家報導／訪談／新聞報導

反義字 inclusive

realistic

[rɪə`lɪstɪk]

adj. 現實的；切合實際的

Be realistic—we just cannot afford such a big house!

面對現實吧！我們就是買不起這麼大的房子！

書 102

秒殺解字 realist+ic → 「務實的人」總是能「切合實際的」。

be realistic about... 對……講求實際

unrealistic

[ˌʌnrɪə`lɪstɪk]

adj. 不切實際的

In my opinion, your suggestions are unattainable and unrealistic.

我認為，你的建議是無法實現而且不切實際的。

physical

[`fɪzɪkl̩]

n. 健康檢查

adj. 身體的；生理的；物理的

Your physical strength will diminish rapidly if you do not exercise regularly.

如果不規律運動，你的體力會迅速下降。

秒殺解字 physic(nature)+al → 「自然」「的」，身體或物理都和「自然」相關。

習 105
醫特 108

| 詞搭 | physical education 體育；physical fitness / strength / examination 體適能／體力／體檢 |

| 反義字 | mental, psychological |

physically

[`fɪzɪkl̩ɪ]

adv. 身體上；生理上

The work is physically demanding and I don't think you can cope with it.

這項工作對體力要求很高，我認為你無法應付。

習 106

stay physically and mentally healthy 保持身心健康

mentally, psychologically

physician

[fə`zɪʃən]

n. 醫師

Before you take these pills, you'd better consult your physician and make sure they won't affect your sleep.

在服用這些藥之前，最好先諮詢醫生，並確保它們不會影響睡眠。

| 字辨 | surgeon [`sɝdʒən] n. 外科醫師 |

physics

[`fɪzɪks]

n. 物理學

Brandon is now studying physics at a college in London.

Brandon 現在在倫敦的一所大學讀物理學系。

| 衍生字 | physicist [`fɪzɪsɪst] n. 物理學家 |

insurance

[ɪn`ʃʊrəns]

n. 保險

Theodore has insurance of NT$3 million and his wife can make a claim on it if he dies first.

Theodore 有新台幣 300 萬元的保險，如果他先去世，他的妻子可以獲得理賠。

習 100

秒殺解字 in(en=make)+sure(sure)+ance → insure 即 make sure，也就是「確定」，「保險」功能在「確保」遭遇損失時可獲得賠償。相關同源字有 **sure**（adj. 確定的）、as**sure**（v. 使放心；保證）、reas**sure**（v. 使放心；使消除疑慮）、en**sure**（v. 擔保、確定）、in**sure**（v. 買保險；確定）。

| 詞搭 | life insurance 人壽保險；health insurance 健康保險；insurance agent 保險經紀人；insurance policy 保單 |

debate

[dɪ`bet]

n. 辯論（賽）
v. 辯論

Bilingual education will soon become a focus of public debate if no clear policy is further shaped and developed.

如果雙語教育沒有更進一步明確的政策與發展，它將很快成為公眾辯論的焦點。

> **(秒殺解字)** de(down)+bat(beat)+e →「辯論」就是要「打」「倒」對方。可用 **beat** 當神隊友，**母音通轉**，來記憶 **bat**，皆表示「打」。相關同源字有 **beat**（v. 打敗；打 n. 心跳、敲擊）、**bat**（n. 球棒 v. 打擊）、**bat**ter（v. 連續猛擊 n. 棒球打擊者）、**bat**tery（n. 電池；砲臺）、**bat**tle（v./n. 戰鬥）、com**bat**（v./n. 對抗）、**abat**e（v. 減輕、減弱）。

詞搭 the issue under debate 爭辯中的議題

衍生字 debatable [dɪ`betəbl] adj. 可爭論的、未定論的

outstanding

[ˌaʊt`stændɪŋ]

adj. 傑出的；重要的

The man who just won the scholarship was a quite outstanding college student.

剛獲得獎學金的那個人是一位非常傑出的大學生。

普 103
警特 108

> **(秒殺解字)** out(out)+stand(stand)+ing → outstand 表示能「站」在「外」，相當於 stand out、outstanding 指能在同儕中出類拔萃的，表示「傑出的」。

同義字 excellent, brilliant, superb, amazing

visual
[ˋvɪʒʊəl]
adj. 視力的；視覺的

Near-sightedness is a visual defect rather than a disease.
近視是視覺缺陷而不是疾病。

🖊 秒殺解字 vis(see)+u+al →「視」力的、「視」覺的。

詞搭　visual effect 視覺效果

衍生字　visualize [ˋvɪʒʊəˌlaɪz] v. 想像

---

visibility
[ˌvɪzəˋbɪlətɪ]
n. 能見度

The captain of the rescue team said that the search for survivors could be abandoned because of poor visibility.
搜救隊的隊長說，由於能見度不佳，搜尋倖存者的工作可能會被迫放棄。

🖊 秒殺解字 vis(see)+ibility →「可以」「看」到，表示「能見」度。

詞搭　high / low visibility 高／低能見度

---

graduate
[ˋgrædʒʊɪt]
n. 大學畢業生
adj. 研究所／生的

[ˋgrædʒʊˌet]
v. 畢業

Eileen is a graduate of history and now works for a private museum.　警特 106 109
Eileen 是歷史系畢業生，現在在一家私人博物館工作。

🖊 秒殺解字 grad(walk, go, step) +u+ate → 本義「走」，一步一步走終會「畢業」。相關同源字有 **grade**（n. 成績；年級；等級 v. 評分）、**grad**ual（adj. 逐漸的）、**grad**ually（adv. 逐漸地）、**grad**uation（n. 畢業）、under**grad**uate（n. 大學生）、Centi**grad**e（n./adj. 攝氏）、de**grad**e（v. 貶低；侮辱……的人格）、up**grad**e（v. 提高等級、升級 n. 升級品）、de**gree**（n. 程度；等級；學位；度數）、pro**gress**（n./v. 進步）、ag**gress**ion（n. 攻擊）、con**gress**（n. 國會）、in**gred**ient（n. 原料；構成要素）。

詞搭　graduate from... 從……畢業；a graduate school / student 研究所／生；graduate with honors 以優異成績畢業

衍生字　graduation [ˌgrædʒʊˋeʃən] n. 畢業；undergraduate [ˌʌndəˋgrædʒʊɪt] n. 大學生

extraordinary

[ɪk`strɔrdn̩ˌɛrɪ]

adj. 非凡的

I believe he'll get it done soon, because he's a man with extraordinary strength and willpower.

我相信他會很快完成這項任務,因為他是一個擁有非凡力量和意志力的人。

曾 104　警特 108

（秒殺解字） extra(out of, outside)+ord(order)+in+ary → 「超出」一般「順序」,表示「異常的」。相關同源字有 **order** (n. 順序、次序)、**ord**inary (adj. 普通的)、co**ord**inate (v. 協調)、sub**ord**inate (adj. 下級的 n. 下屬)。

同義字 | unusual, incredible

---

suspend

[sə`spɛnd]

v. 停止;勒令停學、停職;懸掛

Colbert was suspended from school last week for his problematic behavior.

Colbert 上週因行為問題被勒令停學。

警特 108
109

（秒殺解字） sus(=sub=up from under)+pend(hang) → 「由下往上」「懸掛」,等同 hang up,表示「懸掛」。相關同源字有 de**pend** (v 依靠)、ex**pend** (v. 花費)、ex**pens**e (n. 費用)、dis**pens**e (v. 分配)。

詞搭 | suspend payment 停止支付

衍生字 | suspense [sə`spɛns] n. 懸疑;suspension [sə`spɛnʃən] n. 停止、勒令停學/停職/禁賽

同義字 | hang

---

volunteer

[ˌvɑlən`tɪr]

n. 自願者;義工

v. 自告奮勇;自動提供

They don't get paid for rescuing people. They are all volunteers.

他們沒有因為救人而得到報酬。他們都是志工。

曾 107

The teacher's question was such a tough one that no one knew what to do with it. Felix then stood up and volunteered to answer it.

老師的問題如此艱難,以至於沒人知道如何回答。接著 Felix 站起來,自願回答。

（秒殺解字） vol(will)+unt+eer → 可用 **will** 當神隊友,**v/w 對應**,**母音通轉**,來記憶 **vol**,表示「意志」、「意願」。相關同源字有 **will** (aux. 將;願 v. 用意志力;立遺囑 n. 意志;遺囑)、**will**ing (adj. 願意的)、**wel**come (v. 歡迎;欣然接受)、un**will**ing (adj. 不願意的)、**vol**untary (adj. 志願、自發的)、bene**vol**ent (adj. 仁慈的)。

opponent

[ə`ponənt]

n. 對手;反對者

Our team struggled with all our might and finally beat our opponents.

我們的團隊竭盡全力,最終擊敗了對手。

警特 107

🖋️ **秒殺解字** op(=ob=before, against)+pos(put)+ent → 「放」在「前面」「反對」。

a political opponent 政敵;an opponent of abortion 反對墮胎者

|同義字| rival, competitor

|反義字| proponent, supporter

---

constitution

[ˌkɑnstə`tjuʃən]

n. 憲法

Britain's unwritten constitution allows for flexibility when the change of some circumstances takes place.

當某些情況發生變化時,英國不成文的憲法即可彈性調整。

🖋️ **秒殺解字** con(together)+stitut(stand)+e → 「站」在「一起」,引申為「組成」、「體質」、「憲法」。

---

controversy

[`kɑntrəˌvɝsɪ]

n. 爭議

There is always a great controversy over selling e-cigarettes in many countries.

銷售電子菸在許多國家一直存在著很大的爭議。

曾 104

🖋️ **秒殺解字** contr(=against)+o+vers(turn)+y → 「轉」過來「反對」而導致「爭議」。

|詞搭| without controversy 無庸置辯的;cause / provoke / arouse controversy over / about + sth. 引起關於某事的爭議

|衍生字| controversial [ˌkɑntrə`vɝʃəl] adj. 有爭議的

|同義字| argument

entertain

[ˌɛntə˙ten]

v. 娛樂

To celebrate Children's Day, the kindergarten hired a magician to entertain all these kids.
為了慶祝兒童節，幼兒園請來了魔術師娛樂所有孩子。

警特 105

(秒殺解字) enter(=inter=among)+tain(hold) →「娛樂」是掌「握」「內」心的悸動，賦予快樂。相關同源字有 con**tain**（ v. 容納）、con**ten**t（ n. 內容；滿足 adj. 滿意的）、ob**tain**（ v. 得到）、main**tain**（ v. 維持）、main**ten**ance（ n. 維持、維修、保養）、sus**tain**（ v. 維持）、sus**ten**ance（ n. 食物；維持）、de**tain**（ v. 留下；使耽擱）、de**ten**tion（ n. 留下；使耽擱）、re**tain**（ v. 保留）、**ten**able（ adj. 站得住腳的）、**ten**et（ n. 信條；宗旨；原則）、**ten**ant（ n. 房客）、con**tin**ue（ v. 繼續、持續）、con**tin**ual（ adj. 連續、頻頻的）、con**tin**uous（ adj. 連續不斷的）、con**tin**ent（ n. 大陸；洲）。

[詞搭] entertain + sb. + with + sth. 用某物娛樂／招待某人

[同義字] amuse

entertaining

[ˌɛntə˙tenɪŋ]

adj. 有娛樂性；令人愉快的

A clown is the most entertaining person at a circus.
小丑是馬戲團中最有趣的人。

警 106

[同義字] amusing, interesting

entertainment

[ˌɛntə˙tenmənt]

n. 消遣；娛樂節目

What do you usually do for entertainment when you stay home on weekends?
週末在家時你通常會做什麼娛樂活動？

striking

[˙straɪkɪŋ]

adj. 明顯的；給人深刻印象的

The police found there were striking similarities between these two murder cases.
警方發現這兩個謀殺案之間有驚人的相似之處。

高 108

(秒殺解字)「打擊」的力道強烈，給人留下深刻的印象，衍生語意有「明顯的」、「醒目的」。

[同義字] noticeable, conspicuous

delicate

[ˋdɛləkət]

adj. 脆弱的；纖細的；
精緻的

The vase is made of delicate ceramic material and should be handled with care.

這個花瓶是易碎的陶瓷材料製成的，應小心輕放。

🖋（秒殺解字）de(away)+lic(entice)+ate → 本義是「引誘」，衍生意思有「脆弱的」、「精緻的」等。

曾 103

| 同義字 | fragile, breakable, weak |
| 反義字 | strong |

squeeze

[skwiz]

v. 擠；壓榨；緊握

My mother squeezed some lemon juice onto the fish to make it taste better.

我媽媽在魚上擠了一些檸檬汁，使它的味道更好。

🖋（秒殺解字）squ 子音群常有「壓縮」、「擠壓」的意思。相關字有 squash（v. 壓碎）、squelch（v. 壓碎）。

曾 101

| 詞搭 | squeeze into... 擠進，擠入；squeeze + sth. + out 將某物擠出來；squeeze the trigger 扳動扳機 |
| 同義字 | squash |

arrival

[əˋraɪvl]

n. 到達、抵達

We are looking forward to your arrival next Monday.

我們期待您下週一的到來。

🖋（秒殺解字）ar(=ad=to)+riv(shore)+al → arrive 本指「到達」「河岸」邊，也就是「上陸」，後來語意改變，不限於河運，藉由各種交通工具抵達某地，皆可使用 arrive、arrival 是名詞。arrive、river（n. 河）同源，**母音通轉**，核心語意是「河岸」（**shore**）。

曾 105
警特 106

詞搭	upon / on arrival 在到達時
同義字	coming, advent
反義字	departure

specialist

[ˋspɛʃəlɪst]

n. 專家、專業人士

I think we might need a specialist to accomplish such a difficult mission.

我認為我們可能需要一位專家來完成如此艱鉅的任務。

🖋（秒殺解字）spec(look)+ial+ist → 「特別的」東西我們會多「看」，而在某方面很「特別」厲害的「人」是「專家」。

曾 107

| 詞搭 | specialist knowledge 專門知識； an eye specialist 眼科醫師 |
| 同義字 | expert |

specialize

[ˋspɛʃəlˌaɪz]

v. 專攻

specialize in... 專攻／專門從事……

The chef <u>specializes in</u> Japanese cuisine and the restaurant he runs is always full of gourmets.

這位主廚擅長日本料理，而他經營的餐廳總是充滿饕客。

---

specific

[spɪˋsɪfɪk]

adj. 特定的；特有的；明確的

be specific to 獨有的；be specific about... 明確說明……

general

My mother reminded me that the money deposited in the account could only be used for some specific purposes.

我的母親提醒我，存入帳戶的錢只能用於某些特定用途。

普 101
警特 105
109

---

specification

[ˌspɛsəfəˋkeʃən]

n. 詳述；規格；明細單

All the products will meet the strict specifications demanded by our customers.

所有產品都將符合客戶所制定的精確規格。

---

anxiety

[æŋˋzaɪətɪ]

n. 焦慮；渴望

The mother was filled with anxiety about her missing daughter.

這位母親對她失蹤的女兒感到焦慮不安。

> **（秒殺解字）** anx(painful, uneasy)+i+e+ty → 使人「痛苦的」、「擔心的」的事。可用 **anger** 和 **angry** 當神隊友，**g/k** 轉音，來記憶 **anxious**，核心語意皆是「痛苦的」、「擔心的」。**anger** 源自古北歐語，表示讓人感到極大悲「痛」（**painful**），14 世紀後產生「使……發怒」的語意 **anx**iety 是名詞。

anxious [ˋæŋkʃəs] adj. 焦慮的、渴望的； anxiously [ˋæŋkʃəslɪ] adv. 焦急地

concern, worry, apprehension

---

excess

[ɪkˋsɛs]

n. 過量；超過

adj. 超過的

An excess of enthusiasm is not always welcomed by all people.

過度熱情未必會受到所有人的歡迎。

> **（秒殺解字）** ex(out)+cess(go) →「走」到「外面」來，跨越界線，引申為「超過」。

in excess of... 超過……；an excess of... 過量的……；excess <u>baggage / luggage</u> 超重行李

excessive
[ɪk`sɛsɪv]
adj. 過量的；過度的

The doctor emphasizes that excessive drinking and liver cancer are closely related.
醫生強調，過量飲酒與肝癌有密切關係。

protester
[pro`tɛstɚ]
n. 抗議者；反對者

A parliamentarian came to the police department to make sure that those protesters arrested earlier were taken good care of.
一名議員來到警察局以確認稍早被捕的那些抗議者是否得到妥善照顧。

秒殺解字 pro(before)+test(testify, witness)+er → 本義在「前方」「作證」者，後來語意轉變，有了「作證是因為不認同」的語意，引申為「抗議者」。相關同源字有 **test**ify (v. 證明、作證)、**test**imony (n. 證詞)、con**test** (v./n. 競爭、比賽)、con**test**ant (n. 參加競賽者)、pro**test** (v/n. 抗議)。

automate
[`ɔtə‚met]
v. （使）自動化

Most of the production lines in this factory have been totally automated.
這家工廠的大多數生產線已完全自動化。

秒殺解字 auto(self)+mat(mind, think)+e → 「自己」會「思考」，就是「自動化」。

詞搭 a fully automated factory 完全自動化的工廠

衍生字 automatic [‚ɔtə`mætɪk] adj. 自動的；automated [`ɔto‚metɪd] adj. 自動化的

automatically
[‚ɔtə`mætɪkḷɪ]
adv. 自動地

The device will automatically send out alarm signals to the security guard once the office is broken into.
一旦辦公室遭闖入後，這項設備將會向警衛發出警報信號。

transportation
[‚trænspɚ`teʃən]
n. 交通運輸

Subways are a very important means of public transportation for a big city.　　　　警特 108
地鐵是大城市公共交通的重要工具。

秒殺解字 trans(across)+port(carry)+ation → 從一方「帶」到另一方，表示「運輸」。相關同源字有 im**port** (v./n. 進口)、ex**port** (v./n. 出口)、sup**port** (v./n. 支持)、re**port** (v./n. 報告；報導)、trans**port** (v. 運輸)。

incorporate

[ɪn`kɔrpəˌret]

v. 使結合；合併

Many novel functions will <u>be incorporated into</u> the new smartphones to be released next month.

許多新穎的功能將被整合到下個月即將發佈的新智慧型手機中。

🪶 **秒殺解字** in(in)+corp(body)+or+ate → 納入「體」「內」。**corp** 表示「**身體**」、「**形體**」。相關同源字有 **corp**s（n. 軍團）、**corp**se（n. 屍體）、**corp**orate（adj. 公司的；團體的；全體的）、**corp**oration（n. 公司）、in**corp**oration（n. 合併）。

詞搭 be incorporated into... 被結合成……；incorporate one firm with another 將一家公司與另一家合併

衍生字 incorporation [ɪnˌkɔrpə`reʃən] n. 合併

01 ___ All the _____ on board passed away because of the accident. However, the pilot was miraculously unharmed and was rescued an hour after the accident happened.

(A) operators   (B) volunteers
(C) passengers   (D) veterans

02 ___ Due to the non-disclosure agreement between the cast and the production company, no one in the cast knew about who died in the film when they were filming the _____ scene.

(A) industry   (B) surface
(C) scandal   (D) funeral

03 ___ The detective went to the crime scene and examined the body of the victim. After an hour of examination, he concluded that the victim died from a _____ blow in the head.

(A) fatal   (B) cynical
(C) pharmaceutical   (D) unparalleled

04 ___ After the final battle, Thanos finally _____ his goal of wiping out half of the lives in the world. Nonetheless, he did it at the expense of everything he had.

(A) sprained   (B) attained
(C) ejected   (D) refuted

05 ___ NBA superstar D'angelo Russell's personal slogan,"ice in the _____", shows his cold-blooded and calm personality when playing on the court.

(A) source   (B) endeavor
(C) veins   (D) salutation

06 ___ The invasion of German soldiers broke the _____ of the small village. The troops raided the town and captured all the men who were able to work.

(A) harmony (B) bureaucracy
(C) diversity (D) mortality

07 ___ Tesla, an energy company focusing on _____and reusable energy, recently released their lasted electric car model.

(A) sustainable (B) considerable
(C) unexplainable (D) interchangeable

08 ___ We want to create a level playing field for the players. As a result, those who fail the drug test will be _____ from the game.

(A) vibrated (B) subsidized
(C) excluded (D) refrained

09 ___ The plot of the movie is lackluster and tedious. The only good thing about the movie is its _____ effects. It seems that they spent all their budget on it.

(A) confidential (B) rhetorical
(C) superficial (D) visual

10 ___ The soldier was awarded with the presidential award due to his _____ performance on the battlefield. His bravery saved the lives of numerous comrades.

(A) customary (B) extraordinary
(C) ordinary (D) military

11 ___ Harry and Ron got _____ from Hogwarts because they broke the school rule of driving a flying car under the age of 18.

(A) suspended (B) defended
(C) permitted (D) devastated

12 ___ Although we are the lesser team, we can still win the game. As long as we stand together as one, we can beat our _____.

(A) angler   (B) militiaman
(C) opponent   (D) dissident

13 ___ The right to own a firearm is written in the _____ of America. The second amendment allows people to own a gun in order to overthrow a tyrant if needed.

(A) prevention   (B) contamination
(C) addiction   (D) constitution

14 ___ The _____ of the American Under Secretary of State aroused a lot of interest. People couldn't stop talking about it

(A) arrival   (B) original
(C) individual   (D) breakthrough

15 ___ At first, the _____ for animal rights were calm and peaceful. However, the aggressive act of the police caused a chaotic scenario to unfold.

(A) warriors   (B) protesters
(C) disciples   (D) adherents

解答
1.(C) 2.(D) 3.(A) 4.(B) 5.(C) 6.(A) 7.(A) 8.(C) 9.(B) 10.(D) 11.(A) 12.(C) 13.(D) 14.(A) 15.(B)

 **Unit 27**

---

tobacco
[tə`bæko]
n. 菸草

Many people doubt that the population of smokers will decline if the government increases the tax on tobacco.
許多人懷疑當政府增加菸草稅時吸菸人口是否會減少。

秒殺解字 源自西印度群島語，表示「菸斗」的意思。

詞搭 tobacco company / industry 菸草公司／行業

---

recover
[rɪ`kʌvɚ]
v. 恢復；找回

It took him three months to recover from the trauma surgery. 警特 107
他花了三個月的時間從創傷手術中康復。

秒殺解字 re(back)+cover(=cuperate=cap=take) → 把健康「取」「回」。

詞搭 recover / recuperate from... = get over... 從……恢復過來；
recover losses 彌補損失

同義字 get better / over / well, recuperate, regain, retrieve, get back

---

recovery
[rɪ`kʌvərɪ]
n. 復元、痊癒；找回

The doctor said that Belinda would make a quick recovery from the operation. 普 100
醫生說，Belinda 手術後將迅速復元。

---

intelligent
[ɪn`tɛlədʒənt]
adj. 聰明的、有才智的

With Artificial Intelligence, modern robots are really smart, but in fact, humans are still far more intelligent than the cleverest robot in the world.
有了人工智能，現代機器人確實很聰明，但是實際上，人類比世界上最聰明的機器人還是聰明得多。

秒殺解字 intel(=inter=between)+lig(choose)+ent →「從中」「挑選」事物所需的區辨能力，表示「聰明的」。相關同源字有 collect (v. 收集；聚集)、elect (v. 選舉)、select (v. 選擇)、neglect (v. 忽視、疏忽)、recollect (v. 回憶)、intellect (n. 智力)、intelligence (n. 聰明才智；情報)、lecture (n./v. 講課；演講)、legend (n. 傳說；傳奇人物)、elegant (adj. 優雅的)、college (n. 大學；學院)、colleague (n. 同事)、diligent (adj. 勤勉的)、diligence (n. 勤勉)。

衍生字 intelligence [ɪn`tɛlədʒəns] n. 聰明才智、情報

同義字 clever, smart, bright, brilliant, gifted

inspection
[ɪn`spɛkʃən]
n. 視察；檢查

Elevators are convenient, but do you know it costs a lot to undergo regular safety inspections?
電梯很方便，但是你知道定期進行安全檢查會花費很多嗎？

普 102
醫特 108

秒殺解字 in(into)+spec(look)+t+ion → 「檢查」需要往「內」「看」。相關同源字有 **spec**tator (n. 看比賽觀眾)、a**spec**t (n. 方面)、in**spec**t (v. 檢查)、re**spec**t (v./n. 尊敬)、su**spec**t (v. 懷疑)、per**spec**tive (n. 觀點)、pro**spec**t (n. 展望)。

詞搭 on inspection 經考察；make / carry out an inspection 檢查

同義字 examination, check

campus
[`kæmpəs]
n. （大學）校園

Motorcycles are not allowed on the campus of this university.
這所大學的校園內禁止摩托車通行。

秒殺解字 camp(filed)+us → 核心意思是「原野」、「戰場」。相關同源字有 **camp** (n. 營 v. 紮營)、**camp**aign (n./v. 運動)、**champ**ion (n. 冠軍)、**champ**ionship (n. 冠軍的地位；錦標賽)、**champ**agne (n. 香檳酒)。

詞搭 on campus 在校園內；off campus 在校園外

document
[`dɑkjəmənt]
n. 文件
v. 紀錄

These documents are confidential and should be kept with care.
這些文件是機密的，應小心保管。

圖 110

秒殺解字 doc(teach)+u+ment → 源自拉丁文「正式文件」的意思，政府的正式文件中含有「教」（teach）人正確做事的方法。相關同源字有 **doc**tor (n. 醫生；博士)、**doc**torate (n. 博士學位)、**doc**umentary (n. 記錄片 adj. 記錄的)、**doc**ile (adj. 易教的)、**doc**trine (n. 教義、教條)、**dec**orate (v. 裝飾、修飾)、**dec**ent (adj. 體面的、像樣的)、**dig**nify (v. 使有尊嚴、使高貴)、**dig**nity (n. 尊嚴)。

衍生字 documentary [ˌdɑkjə`mɛntərɪ] adj. 紀錄的 n. 紀錄片

同義字 record

widespread
[`waɪd͵sprɛd]
adj. 廣泛的、普遍的

The labor union's call for reducing working hours has received widespread support.
工會要求減少工作時間的呼籲得到了廣泛的支持。

秒殺解字 wide+spread → 「廣泛」「擴散」的，表示「廣泛的」、「遍佈的」。

詞搭 widespread support 廣泛的支持；widespread acceptance 大眾的接受

terrorism

[ˋtɛrəˌrɪzəm]

n. 恐怖主義

The police are considering taking more appropriate 曾 107 measures against terrorism.

警方正在考慮採取更適當的反恐措施。

🖋️（秒殺解字）terr(frighten)+or+ism →「恐怖主義」「使」人感到「害怕」。相關同源字有 **terr**ible（adj. 可怕、恐怖的；糟的）、**terr**ibly（adv. 很、非常；嚴重地）、**terr**ific（adj. 非常好的）、**terr**ify（v. 使害怕）、**terr**ifying（adj. 使人害怕的）、**terr**ified（adj. 感到害怕）、**terr**or（n. 恐怖）、de**ter**（v. 制止、威懾）。

詞搭 | international / cyber terrorism 國際／網路恐怖主義

---

terrorist

[ˋtɛrərɪst]

n. 恐怖份子

The three terrorists hijacking the jet were finally shot dead by the counter terrorism officer.

劫持飛機的三名恐怖分子最終被反恐部隊擊斃。

詞搭 | terrorist attack / offense / activity 恐怖攻擊／攻擊／活動

---

exceed

[ɪkˋsid]

v. 超過

Taking these vitamin pills will be helpful to your 曾 99
警特 106 recovery, but never exceed the recommended dose.

服用這些維他命藥丸將有助於你的康復，但絕不要超過推薦的劑量。

🖋️（秒殺解字）ex(out)+ceed(go) →「走」到「外面」來，跨越界線，引申為「超過」。

衍生字 | excess [ɪkˋsɛs] n. 過量 excessive [ɪkˋsɛsɪv] adj. 過量的、過度的、極度的

---

exceedingly

[ɪkˋsidɪŋlɪ]

adv. 極度地

That is an exceedingly difficult problem, so I don't 曾 99 think I can help you out this time.

這是一個非常困難的問題，所以我認為這次我無法幫助你。

同義字 | extremely, exceptionally, outstandingly

---

liquid

[ˋlɪkwɪd]

n. 液體
adj. 液體的

How much liquid do you think this jar contains? 曾 102

你認為這個罐子裡裝了多少液體？

🖋️（秒殺解字）liqu(fluid)+id → 會流動的東西，引申為「液體」。

同義字 | fluid

liquidation

[ˌlɪkwɪˋdeʃən]

n. （債務）清償；（公司）清算

詞搭 | go into liquidation 倒閉

Affected by the recession, many companies are now facing possible liquidation.
受經濟衰退影響，許多公司現在面臨清算的可能。

---

shoplift

[ˋʃɑpˌlɪft]

v. （在商家）偷竊、順手牽羊

衍生字 | shoplifter [ˋʃɑpˌlɪftɚ] n. 竊取商店東西的小偷

The man was caught shoplifting by a plainclothes guard. 🎧 106
該男子被一個便衣警衛抓到入店行竊。

秒殺解字 shot+lift → 在「商店」「拿起」商品，順手牽羊。**lift** (v. 舉起；撤銷 n. 電梯；搭便車) 和 **loft** (n. 閣樓、頂樓) 同源，**母音通轉**，核心語意是「舉高」（**raise**）。

---

sophisticated

[səˋfɪstəˌketɪd]

adj. 世故的；（機器、系統）精密的

詞搭 | sophisticated technology / equipment 精良工藝／尖端裝置

You don't have to act as if you are sophisticated. Just be yourself.
你不必表現得像是很老練一般。做你自己吧！

秒殺解字 soph(wise, wisdom)+ist+ic+ate+ed → 本義是「聰明的」，引申為「世故的」。相關同源字有 **sophi**sticate (n. 老練世故的人)、**soph**istication (n. 世故、老練；精密、複雜)、**soph**omore (n. 大二生、高二生)、philo**soph**y (n. 哲學；人生觀)。

---

damage

[ˋdæmɪdʒ]

v. **n.** 破壞、傷害

詞搭 | do / cause damage to + sb. / sth. 對某人或某物造成傷害

衍生字 | damaging [ˋdæmɪdʒɪŋ] adj. 有害

同義字 | harm

Most of the churches, schools, and temples in this city were seriously damaged during the civil war. 🖼 110
內戰期間，這座城市的大多數教堂、學校和廟宇都遭到嚴重破壞。

秒殺解字 dam(damage, harm)+age →「傷害」。**damn**, **demn** 同源，母音通轉，皆表示「**傷害**」。相關同源字有 **dam**ages (n. 賠償金)、**damn** (v. 咒罵；罵……該死)、con**demn** (v. 責難、譴責)。

secondary

[`sɛkən͵dɛrɪ]

adj. 次要的；中等教育的；第二的

I think your health should be your primary concern and how much you will have to spend on medical treatment is of secondary importance.

我認為你的健康應該是你主要關心的事，而需要花費多少醫療費用是次要的。

✎（秒殺解字）second+ary →「第二」的。

詞搭　be secondary to... 次於……；secondary education 中等／中學教育

---

reputation

[͵rɛpjə`teʃən]

n. 名譽、名聲、名氣

曾 100
警特 106

Most people in Taiwan think that many products made in Japan have long enjoyed a good reputation for their quality.

台灣大多數人認為，日本製造的許多產品長期以來一直以品質著稱。

✎（秒殺解字）re(again)+put(think)+ation → 讓人「再次」「思考」，表示有「聲譽」。相關同源字有 compute (v. 計算)、computer (n. 電腦)、dispute (v./n. 爭論)、disputable (adj. 有爭議的)、depute (v. 委託代理)、deputy (n. 代理人 adj. 代理的；副的)、deputation (n. 代表團)、repute (n. 名譽、聲望)、reputable (adj. 名聲好的)。

詞搭　by reputation 由於知名度；have a reputation for... 有……的好名聲

---

myth

[mɪθ]

n. 神話；迷思、錯誤的想法

曾 102

These stories for children are adapted from ancient myths.

這些兒童故事是根據古代神話改編而成的。

✎（秒殺解字）myth(speech, thought, word) → 源自希臘文「言語」、「想法」、「話」的意思，衍生意思有「神話」、「迷思」等。

衍生字　mythology [mɪ`θɑlədʒɪ] n. 神話；mythological [͵mɪθə`lɑdʒɪkl] adj. 神話的

同義字　fallacy

colleague
[`kɑlig]
n. 同事

Herbert is getting along very well with all of his colleagues.
Herbert 與所有同事相處得很好。

> **秒殺解字** col(together)+leag (=leg=choose)+ue → 被「選」來「一起」做事。相關同源字有 col**lec**t（v. 收集；聚集）、e**lec**t（v. 選舉）、se**lec**t（v. 選擇）、neg**lec**t（v. 忽視、疏忽）、recol**lec**t（v. 回憶）、intel**lec**t（n. 智力）、intel**lig**ent（adj. 聰明的）、intel**lig**ence（n. 聰明才智；情報）、**lec**ture（n./v. 講課；演講）、**leg**end（n. 傳說；傳奇人物）、e**leg**ant（adj. 優雅的）、col**leg**e（n. 大學；學院）、di**lig**ent（adj. 勤勉的）、di**lig**ence（n. 勤勉）。

| 同義字 | co-worker, associate |

monument
[`mɑnjəmənt]
n. 紀念碑

The monument was set up in memory of those who sacrificed themselves for the country during World War II.
這個紀念碑的建立是為了紀念那些在第二次世界大戰中為國家犧牲的人。

> **秒殺解字** mon(remind, warn)+u+ment → 讓人的「心」裡回憶起一些過往的建築，用以「警告」、「提醒」世人。

| 衍生字 | monumental [ˌmɑnjə`mɛntl] adj. 重大的 |
| 同義字 | memorial |

arrest
[ə`rɛst]
n. **v.** 逮捕

Marshall was arrested last night for drunk-driving.
Marshall 昨晚因酒後駕車被捕。

> **秒殺解字** ar(=ad=to)+re(back)+st(stand) →「站」在「後面」準備「逮捕」人。

詞搭	be under arrest 被逮捕；be under house arrest 被軟禁；<u>cardiac / respiratory</u> arrest 心跳／呼吸停止
名詞同義字	apprehension
動詞同義字	catch, apprehend

profoundly

[prə`faʊndlɪ]

adv. 深深地；極度地

I'm profoundly grateful to you for what you've done for my family.

圖 108

對於您為我的家人所做的一切，我深表謝意。

秒殺解字 pro(forward)+found(bottom)+ly → 到「底」了，還繼續「向前」推進，表示「深不見底」地。可用 **bottom** 當神隊友，**b/f 轉音**，**d/t 轉音**，**母音通轉**，來記憶 **fund**, **found**，皆表示「底部」、「基礎」。**bottom**（n. 底部 adj. 底部的）、**fund**（n. 基金 v. 提供資金）、**fund**amental（adj. 基本的；重要必須的）、**found**（v. 建立；創辦）、**found**er（n. 創立者、創辦人）、**found**ation（n. 地基；基礎；創辦；基金會）、pro**found**（adj. 深遠的；深奧的）、un**found**ed（adj. 無根據的）、well-**found**ed（adj. 有事實根據的）。

artistic [ɑr`tɪstɪk] **adj.** 藝術的；美妙的	These paintings have a very high artistic value. 這些畫有很高的藝術價值。 **秒殺解字** artist+ic → 「藝術家」的，表示「藝術的」。	普 108

alert [ə`lɝt] **n.** 警戒 **v.** 提醒 **adj.** 警戒的、警覺的	Facing a possible terrorist attack at the airport, the armed police remained alert and cautious. 面對可能在機場發生的恐怖襲擊，武裝警察保持警戒和謹慎。 **秒殺解字** 源自義大利語，表示「監視著」（à l'erte）。	普 102
詞搭	be on the alert for... 隨時提防／注意……；be on high alert 保持高度警覺；be alert to... 對……警覺／機敏；alert + sb. + to + sth. 提醒某人警覺某事	

romantic [ro`mæntɪk] **n.** 浪漫主義者 **adj.** 浪漫的；不切實際的	Paris is known as one of the most romantic cities in the world. 巴黎被譽為世界上最浪漫的城市之一。 **秒殺解字** romant(romance)+ic → 源自法語，表示有關於「浪漫故事」的。	普 107 高 108
詞搭	be romantic about... 對……充滿幻想；romantic ideas 不切實際的想法	
反義字	realistic	

challenge [`tʃælɪndʒ] **n.** 挑戰；質疑 **v.** 向……挑戰	The job is going to be tough and will pose many challenges, but I think I'd like to take them on. 這項工作將會很艱鉅，並且會帶來很多挑戰，但我想我要接受這些挑戰。 **秒殺解字** 源自拉丁文「中傷」（alumny）的意思，和 **call** 是同源字。call（v./n 叫喊）、**chall**enge（v./n. 挑戰），k/tʃ 轉音，母音通轉，核心語意都和「叫」（call）有關，可用對人「叫囂」來聯想「挑戰」。	普 107 警特 105
詞搭	face / take on / accept a challenge 面對挑戰；meet / rise to a challenge 迎接挑戰；challenge + sb. + to V = give / offer a challenge to + sb. 挑戰某人……；the physically challenged = the disabled / handicapped 行動不便人士	

challenging
[ˋtʃælɪndʒɪŋ]
adj. 有挑戰性的

James has decided to resign from the current job in order to take a more challenging one.
James 已決定辭職，以接受更具挑戰性的工作。

普 99

---

passion
[ˋpæʃən]
n. 熱情、熱愛

You'd better quit the job if you don't have any passion for it.
如果你對這項工作沒有熱情，最好辭職。

警特 107

秒殺解字 pass(suffer)+ion → 本表示「受苦」，後指內心的強烈情感，表示「熱情」。**pass**、**pat** 同源，t/s/ʃ 轉音，母音通轉，表示「受苦」。相關同源字有 **pass**ive (adj. 消極的、被動的)、**pat**ient (adj. 有耐心的 n. 病人)、**pat**ience (n. 耐心)、com**pass**ion (n. 同情)、com**pass**ionate (adj. 同情的)、com**pat**ible (adj. 相容的；能共處)。

詞搭 have a passion for... 熱愛……、對……很有熱忱；a man of passion 熱情的人；fly into a passion 動怒

---

passionate
[ˋpæʃənɪt]
adj. 熱情的、熱愛的；激昂的

We hope to have more passionate people to join us for the campaign.
我們希望有更多熱情的人加入我們的活動。

普 104

詞搭 be passionate about... 對……熱愛

---

dispute
[dɪˋspjut]
n. v. 爭執；質疑

I think it's time for you to settle the dispute with him.
我認為該是你解決跟他之間糾紛的時候了。

警特 105

秒殺解字 dis(apart)+put(count, consider, think)+e → 想法不一致，彼此的「想法」「離」得很遠。相關同源字有 com**put**e (v. 計算)、com**put**er (n. 電腦)、dis**put**able (adj. 有爭議的)、de**put**e (v. 委託代理)、de**put**y (n. 代理人 adj. 代理的；副的)、de**put**ation (n. 代表團)、re**put**e (n. 名譽、聲望)、re**put**ation (n. 名譽、聲望)、re**put**able (adj. 名聲好的)。

詞搭 be in dispute with + sb. 與某人起衝突；It is beyond dispute that... ……是毫無爭議的；without dispute 無疑地

名詞同義字 argument, disagreement

動詞同義字 argue, disagree

transform

[træns`fɔrm]

v. 變化；改變

It usually takes two months for a tadpole to transform into a frog.
蝌蚪通常要花兩個月才能變成青蛙。

> **秒殺解字** trans(across)+form(form) →「跨越」原本的「形體」，「變成」另一「形體」。相關同源字有 uni**form**（n. 制服）、re**form**（n./v. 改革）、con**form**（v. 遵守）。

詞搭 transform A into B 把 A 轉換成 B

曾 99
103
警特 109

transformation

[͵trænsfɚ`meʃən]

n. 轉型；變形；轉變

I've never seen Juliet in skirt—it's quite a transformation.
我從未見過 Juliet 穿裙子－這真是一種轉變。

詞搭 undergo a transformation 經歷轉變；transformation from A to / into B 從 A 轉型成 B

同義字 change

climate

[`klaɪmɪt]

n. 氣候

After retirement, my parents plan to move to a country with a warmer climate.
退休後，我的父母計劃搬到氣候溫暖的國家。

> **秒殺解字** clim(lean)+ate → 本指「傾斜面」，是受太陽照射地球的「傾斜」角度所影響。可用表示「傾斜」、「倚」的 **lean** 當神隊友，母音通轉，來記憶表示「斜面」的 **clim**，和表示「傾斜」、「倚」的 **clin**，雖然 **lean** 的 **c** 脫落，但仍和兩個字根同源。相關同源字有 **lean**（v. 傾斜、倚）、**lad**der（n. 梯子）、**clim**ax（n. 高潮 v. 達到高潮）、**clin**ic（n. 診所）、**clin**ical（adj. 診所的；臨床的）、**clien**t（n. 委託人、客戶）、de**clin**e（v. 衰退；婉拒；惡化 n. 衰退）、in**clin**e（v. 傾向、易於；傾斜 n. 斜坡）。

詞搭 a tropical climate 熱帶氣候；in the current / present political climate 在目前的政治氛圍

曾 110
警特 105
106
108

climatic

[klaɪ`mætɪk]

adj. 氣候的；風土的

Climatic changes are not always easy to predict.
氣候變化並非總是容易預測的。

高 108

259

maturity

[mə`tjʊrətɪ]

n. 成熟

My son asked me how long it would take for chicks to grow to maturity and I don't know the answer.

我兒子問我，小雞成熟長大需要多久的時間，這真的是考倒我了。

🖋️ 秒殺解字 matur(ripe)+ity → 成熟。

詞搭 reach / come to / go to maturity 達到成熟期

反義字 immaturity

mature

[mə`tjʊr]

v. 成熟
adj. 成熟的

A mature man will never do such silly things.

一個成熟的男人永遠不會做這種愚蠢的事情。

衍生字 premature [ˌprimə`tjʊr] adj. 早熟的、早產的

immature

[ˌɪmə`tjʊr]

adj. 不成熟的；幼稚的

It was really immature of Susan to do that.   曾 107

Susan 這樣做真的是不夠成熟。

詞搭 immature behavior 不成熟的行為

同義字 childish

neglect

[nɪg`lɛkt]

n. **v.** 忽視、忽略

No matter how busy you are, never neglect your own health condition.   曾 106

無論你有多忙，都不要忽視自己的健康狀況。

🖋️ 秒殺解字 neg(no, not)+lec(choose)+t → 「沒有」「選擇」，表示「忽視」。相關同源字有 collect（ v. 收集；聚集）、elect（ v. 選舉）、select（ v. 選擇）、recollect（ v. 回憶）、intellect（n. 智力）、intelligent（ adj. 聰明的）、intelligence（ n. 聰明才智；情報）、lecture（ n./v. 講課；演講）、legend（ n. 傳說；傳奇人物）、elegant（ adj. 優雅的）、college（ n. 大學；學院）、colleague（ n. 同事）、diligent（ adj. 勤勉的）、diligence（ n. 勤勉）。

衍生字 neglectful [nɪg`lɛktfəl] adj. 疏忽的；negligent [`nɛglɪdʒənt] adj. 疏忽的

同義字 ignore, omit, overlook

occur

[ə`kɝ]

v. 發生；突然想到

The school is now investigating how such an accident could have occurred on campus.
學校現在正在調查為何在校園內會發生這樣的意外事件。

🈵104

> **秒殺解字** oc(=ob=toward, against)+cur(run) → 「朝著」、「對著」「跑」過來，表示「發生」。

時態 occur, occurred, occurred

詞搭 it occurs/occurred to + sb. + to V 某人想到……

衍生字 occurrence [ə`kɝrəns] n. 發生；事件

ceremony

[`sɛrə‚monɪ]

n. 典禮

Our graduation ceremony will be held next Sunday.
我們的畢業典禮將於下週日舉行。

🈵105

> **秒殺解字** cere(rite)+mon+y → ceremony 源自羅馬近郊 Caere 鎮的舉辦的「古老儀式」，cere 即 Caere 的變體，ceremony 以前多指宗境慶典，後來當「典禮」使用。

詞搭 a wedding / marriage ceremony 婚禮；an opening / religious / coronation ceremony 開幕／宗教／加冕儀式；a graduation ceremony 畢業典禮；have / hold / perform a ceremony 舉行典禮；stand on / upon ceremony 拘謹，拘泥

衍生字 ceremonial [‚sɛrə`monɪəl] adj. 典禮的，儀式的；ceremonious [‚sɛrə`monɪəs] adj. 如典禮般的，極隆重的；拘於禮節的

detect

[dɪ`tɛkt]

v. 發現；查出

I can detect anger in her voice, so you'd better leave her alone now.
我可以從她的聲音中察覺到她的憤怒，所以你最好現在離她遠一點。

🈵99
106

> **秒殺解字** de(off)+tect(cover) → 「拿掉」「覆蓋物」，就是「查出」、「發現」。相關同源字有 protect (v. 保護)。

衍生字 detective [dɪ`tɛktɪv] n. 偵探、刑警 adj. 偵測的；detection [dɪ`tɛkʃən] n. 偵查；detector [dɪ`tɛktə] n. 探測器

demonstration

[‚dɛmən`streʃən]

n. 示範；示威活動

Let me give you a demonstration of how the washing machine works.
讓我給你示範一下如何操作洗衣機。

🈵99

> **秒殺解字** de(completely)+monstr(show)+ate+tion → 本義「顯示」。

humanity

[hju`mænətɪ]

n. 人類；人性；仁愛

The development of the new drugs for the coronavirus will contribute a lot to all humanity.
冠狀病毒新藥的開發將為全人類做出很大貢獻。

秒殺解字 human+ity →「人類」、「人性」。

反義字 | inhumanity

---

dedicate

[`dɛdə͵ket]

v. 奉獻

The Father has dedicated all his life to the welfare of these orphans.
這位神父畢生為這些孤兒的福利奉獻。

普 107
警特 105
106

秒殺解字 de(away)+dic(say)+ate →「說」「開」，指推辭其他事情，將時間和心思「奉獻」在某工作上。相關同源字有 **dic**tionary (n. 字典)、pre**dic**t (v. 預測)、ad**dic**t (n. 成癮者)、contra**dic**t (v. 反駁；與……矛盾)、in**dic**ate (v. 指出；表明)、con**di**tion (n. 情況)。

詞搭 | dedicate / devote oneself to + N / Ving = be dedicated / devoted to + N / Ving 某人奉獻／致力於……；dedicate + sth. + to + sb. 將某物獻給某人

衍生字 | dedication [͵dɛdə`keʃən] n. 奉獻

同義字 | devote

---

depressed

[dɪ`prɛst]

adj. 感到沮喪的

Norma became deeply depressed when she got to know her only son died in the war.
Norma 得知唯一的兒子在戰爭中去世時，她情緒非常低落。

高 108

秒殺解字 de(down)+press(press)+ed →「往下」「壓」，表示「感到沮喪的」。相關同源字有 **press** (v. 壓 n. 新聞界；新聞輿論)、**press**ure (n. 壓力 v. 對……施加壓力)、im**press** (v. 使印象深刻)、ex**press** (v. 表達 adj. 快速的 n. 快車;快遞)、op**press** (v. 壓迫)、re**press** (v. 壓抑;鎮壓)、sup**press** (v. 鎮壓;壓抑)。

詞搭 | be depressed about... 對……感到沮喪

同義字 | unhappy, sad, down, low, blue

depression
[dɪ`prɛʃən]

n. 沮喪；憂鬱症；（經濟）蕭條

I think a holiday will help relieve your <u>depression</u>.
我認為假期將有助於減輕你的沮喪情緒。

🔲 102
104
105
🔲 108

| 詞搭 | economic depression 經濟蕭條 |

| 同義字 | recession |

---

elaborate
[ɪ`læbəˌret]

v. 詳細說明

[ɪ`læbərɪt]

adj. 精緻的；精心製作的

Some of these arguments will be <u>elaborated</u> in the next chapter.
這些論證中的某些部分將在下一章中闡述。

🔲 105
106

Lisa has made <u>elaborate</u> preparations for her birthday party, but unfortunately, few went to attend it.
Lisa 為她的生日派對做了精心的準備，但不幸的是，很少人到場參加。

 （秒殺解字）e(=ex=out)+labor(work)+ate → 本義靠勞力「做」「出來」，後指「精心製作的」。相關同源字有 **labor**（n. 勞力的工作；勞工 v. 辛苦工作）、**labor**atory（n. 實驗室）、col**labor**ate（v. 合作）。

| 詞搭 | elaborate plans 用心良苦的計畫；elaborate <u>on / upon</u>... 詳細說明…… |

---

march
[mɑrtʃ]

n. 行軍；行進；步伐
v. 前進；行進

A few hundred students are planning a <u>march</u> on campus in protest over the school's high tuition policy.
數百名學生正計劃在校園遊行，以抗議學校的高學費政策。

（秒殺解字）源自法語，表示「大步走」(stride)。

| 詞搭 | be on the march 行軍 |

---

plastic
[`plæstɪk]

n. 塑膠
adj. 塑膠的

These flowers are made of <u>plastic</u>, but they look like real and fresh ones.
這些花是用塑膠製成的，但看起來像是新鮮的花朵。

🔲 102
🔲 106

（秒殺解字）plas(form, mold)+t+ic → 源自拉丁文，表示「可造形的」，後當「塑膠」解釋。

| 詞搭 | a plastic bag 塑膠袋；plastic money 信用卡；plastic surgery 美容整型手術；plastic surgeon 整型外科醫生 |

01 ___ After being shot three times in the limbs, the police officer finally _____ from the wounds and got back to work.

(A) assigned   (B) complicated
(C) entertained   (D) recovered

02 ___ Before the routine _____, the factory workers tried everything they could to hide the evidence of pollution they caused in the nearby river.

(A) generation   (B) adoption
(C) inspection   (D) conviction

03 ___ Inside these_____ are the proof that this government official received bribery before the election. With the firm evidence, he is definitely going to jail.

(A) documents   (B) statements
(C) apartments   (D) comments

04 ___ At the early stage of the _____ disease, panicked people stocked up on medical face masks and toilet paper.

(A) democratic   (B) essential
(C) widespread   (D) remarkable

05 ___ The United States Navy Seals successfully executed the leader, Osama bin Laden, of the infamous _____ group, al-Qaeda, on May 2, 2011.

(A) nobleman   (B) colleague
(C) suspect   (D) terrorist

06 ___ The total number of tourists _____ 10,000 during the day. As a result, the zoo had to launch an emergency plan to deal with the overcrowded situation.

(A) produced   (B) exceeded
(C) bred   (D) succeeded

07 ___ The man was caught red-handed _____ inside the mall by the security guard. Instead of surrendering and waiting for the police, the man tried to run away from the guard but failed and eventually led to an even greater punishment.

(A) educating　　　　　　　　(B) applying

(C) shoplifting　　　　　　　　(D) reproducing

08 ___ Due to the poor _____ of the company, no bank wants to give a loan to the company. Without any help, the company has to declare bankruptcy.

(A) reputation　　　　　　　　(B) operation

(C) organization　　　　　　　(D) recognition

09 ___ The fire alarm _____ the residents of the building to run away from the fire. However, after they ran out of the building, they found out that it was just a false alarm.

(A) represented　　　　　　　(B) alerted

(C) removed　　　　　　　　　(D) charged

10 ___ The old man gave a (n) _____ to the young prince with 3 difficult tests, one is to test his wisdom, another is to train his endurance, and the other is to develop his sympathy.

(A) challenge　　　　　　　　(B) language

(C) image　　　　　　　　　　(D) charge

11 ___ After a heated debate, the _____ was finally over. The two men shook hands with each other and there were no hard feelings between them.

(A) treatment　　　　　　　　(B) instance

(C) dispute　　　　　　　　　(D) observation

12 ___ After a huge noise, the sports car suddenly_____ into a giant robot. The robot started to speak with the little boy. At this time, the little boy realized that his car was actually an alien.

(A) transformed　　　　　　　(B) included

(C) performed　　　　　　　　(D) formulated

13 ___ Even if scientists continue to put out more evidence about global warming, there are still people who refuse to believe that _____ change is real and it is destroying our planet.

(A) climate (B) culture
(C) emotion (D) pleasure

14 ___ Jackman is a hard-working actor. He devotes most of his time into acting and often _____ his health. Recently, he was diagnosed with skin cancer and needs to take a long break from acting.

(A) infects (B) rejects
(C) neglects (D) suspects

15 ___ The AI _____ someone suspicious moving close to the front door, and it automatically issues a warning to the suspicious man and calls the police at the same time.

(A) protects (B) respects
(C) detects (D) expects

解答
1.(D) 2.(C) 3.(A) 4.(C) 5.(D) 6.(B) 7.(C) 8.(A) 9.(B) 10.(A) 11.(C) 12.(A) 13.(A) 14.(C) 15.(C)

nobleman
[`nobḷmən]
n. 貴族

The magnificent villa house was once the home of a nobleman.
這棟宏偉的別墅過去曾經是貴族的住所。

圖 103

秒殺解字 noble+man → 出身「貴族的」的人。

---

nobility
[no`bɪlətɪ]
n. 貴族;高貴

All members of the nobility will attend the king's funeral next week.
所有貴族成員將在下週參加國王的葬禮。

圖 103

詞搭 the nobility = the aristocracy 皇家貴族

---

polar
[`polɚ]
adj. 北 / 南極的

I hope we can appreciate the aurora in the lands of the polar region.
我希望我們可以在極地的高地上觀察到極光。

秒殺解字 pol(axis)+ar → 字面上是「地軸」的,引申為「北 (南) 極」,此說法源自「地軸」是穿過北極和南極的假想線。

詞搭 a polar bear 北極熊;the polar circles / lights 極圈／光

---

inquire
[ɪn`kwaɪr]
v. 詢問

She called the automobile technician and inquired when her car would be ready.
她打電話給車輛保養技術員,並詢問她的汽車何時會好。

秒殺解字 in(into)+quir(ask, seek)+e → 追根究柢「探問」。相關同源字有 **ques**t (n. 探索;尋求)、**ques**tion (n. 問題 v. 詢問)、**ques**tionnaire (n. 問卷)、**quer**y (n./v. 疑問)、con**quer** (v. 征服)、con**ques**t (n. 征服)、ac**quir**e (v. 獲得)、ac**quis**ition (n. 獲得;學到;收購)、in**quir**y (n. 詢問)、in**quis**itive (adj. 好奇的、好問的)、re**quir**e (v. 需要;要求)、re**ques**t (v./n. 要求、請求)、ex**quis**ite (adj. 精美的;高雅的)。

詞搭 inquire about... 詢問……;inquire into... 調查……;inquire after + sb. 問候某人 (健康狀況)

衍生字 inquiry [ɪn`kwaɪrɪ] n. 詢問、調查;inquisitive [ɪn`kwɪzətɪv] adj. 愛打聽的、好奇心重的

casual
[ˋkæʒʊəl]

adj. 非正式的；偶然的；無心的

Kent didn't know his casual behavior was totally inappropriate for such a formal occasion.

Kent 不知道在這樣的正式場合他的隨意行為是完全不合適的。

🖋️(秒殺解字) cas(fall)+u+al → 突然「落下」來，彷彿從天而降，突然發生，表示「偶然的」。

[詞搭] casual wear 便服；a casual encounter 邂逅

[衍生字] casually [ˋkæʒʊəlɪ] adv. 悠閒地、隨便地

[同義字] informal, occasional

[反義字] formal

doubtful
[ˋdaʊtfəl]

adj. 可疑的、懷疑的

We are doubtful of the quality and safety of these toys.

我們對這些玩具的品質和安全表示懷疑。

🖋️(秒殺解字) doubt+ful → 「懷疑」「的」。

[詞搭] be doubtful about... 對……起疑

[同義字] dubious

fraction
[ˋfrækʃən]

n. 小部分；微量；分數

It needed only a fraction of a second to solve the problem and I don't know why you didn't want to give it a try.

解決這個問題只需要一瞬間，我不知道你為什麼不想嘗試一下。

🖋️(秒殺解字) frac(break)+t+ion → 「破裂」的部分。可用 **break** 當神隊友，**b/f**，**g/k/dʒ** 轉音，母音通轉，來記憶 **frac**t、**frag**，皆表示「**破裂**」、「**破碎**」。相關同源字有 **frac**ture（v. 使斷裂 n. 骨折）、**frag**ile（adj. 易碎的；虛弱的）、**frag**ment（n. 碎片 v. 使成碎片）。

[詞搭] a fraction of... 一小部分的……；a fraction of a second 在一霎那

submarine

[`sʌbməˌrin]

n. 潛水艇
adj. 海底的

The submarine dived deep, just in time to avoid the 舊 106
enemy attack.
潛艇及時潛入深處，以避免受到敵人攻擊。

> **秒殺解字** sub(under)+mar(sea)+ine →「潛水艇」能夠在
> 「海」「下面」運行。**marine** [mə`rin]（adj. 海的；海運的）、
> **mari**time [`mærəˌtaɪm]（adj. 海運的；沿海的）、**mer**maid
> [`mɜˌmed]（n. 美人魚）同源，母音通轉，核心語意是「海」
> （sea）

詞搭 a submarine cable / plant / tunnel 海底電纜／植物／隧道；
nuclear submarine 核潛艇

landscape

[`lændskep]

n. 景色、風景

The maple trees and the mountains make the
landscape far more beautiful than you can imagine.
楓樹和山脈使風景變得比你想像的要美麗得多。

> **秒殺解字** land(land)+scape(condition) → 本指「土地」上的
> 「情況」，後指「風景」、「景色」。

詞搭 urban / rural landscape 都市／鄉村的景色；landscape painter /
artist / photographer 風景畫家／藝術家／攝影家；landscape
architecture 庭園設計

同義字 scenery

bare

[bɛr]

adj. 赤裸的；空的

My mother told me not to walk around in the living 舊 101
room in my bare feet.
媽媽告訴我不要赤腳在客廳走動。

> **秒殺解字** 源自古英語，表示「赤裸的」。

詞搭 bare to the waist 裸露上身；with + sb's bare hands 空手；
with + sb's head bare 光著頭未戴帽

衍生字 barehanded [`bɛrˌhændɪd] adj. 徒手的；barefoot [`bɛrˌfʊt] adj. 赤
腳的 (barefooted)；barely [`bɛrlɪ] adv. 僅僅、幾乎、幾乎不

同義字 naked, nude

designation

[ˌdɛzɪg`neʃən]

n. 命名

What was your official designation after you were 舊 105
promoted?
升遷後你的正式職稱是什麼？

> **秒殺解字** de(out)+sign(mark)+ation → 本義把「記號」畫「出
> 來」，引申為「命名」、「指派」。相關同源字有 **sign**（n.
> 記號）、**sign**ature（n. 簽名）、**sign**al（n. 信號）、**sign**ify（v.
> 表示）、de**sign**（v. 設計）、as**sign**（v. 分配）、re**sign**（v. 辭
> 去）。

straighten
[`stretn̩]

v. 弄直、（使）變直

Mary's hair is naturally curly and looks quite pretty. I just don't know why she always tries to straighten it.

瑪麗的頭髮自然捲曲，看上去很漂亮。我只是不知道為什麼她總是試圖要把它弄直。

107

秒殺解字 straight+en(make, become) →「使」「變直」或「變直」。

詞搭 straighten... out 將……弄直、改正……；straighten up 變直、打理

---

substitute
[`sʌbstəˌtjut]

n. 代替品
v. 代替

The chef strongly suggested that we substitute olive oil for butter in this recipe.

這位廚師強烈建議我們在此食譜中用橄欖油代替奶油。

秒殺解字 sub(under)+stitut(stand)+e →「立」於「下方」待命，準備「代替」、「替補」。

詞搭 A substitute for B = A take the place of B = A take B's place = A replace B　A 代替 B；substitute A for B = replace B with A 用 A 代替 B；substitute teacher 代課老師

衍生字 substitution [ˌsʌbstəˈtjuʃən] n. 代替品

同義字 replacement, sub

---

pioneer
[ˌpaɪəˈnɪr]

n. 開拓者、先鋒
v. 率先發明／使用／倡導

Dr. Brown's a pioneer in cardiac surgery.
Brown 博士是心臟外科手術的先驅。

106
警特106

It was the Wright Brothers who pioneered in early aviation.
Wright 兄弟是早期航空業的先驅。

秒殺解字 pion(foot)+eer → 源自古英語，本為「步兵」(foot-soldier) 的意思。古羅馬時期，特指步兵當中先行修橋鋪路以便部隊能迅速前進的兵工部隊，後來語意演變，變成「開拓者」、「先鋒」等意思。

同義字 forerunner [`forˌrʌnɚ] n. 前鋒；initiate [ɪˈnɪʃɪˌet] v. 開始實施；settler [`sɛtlɚ] n. 墾荒者、開拓者、移民、殖民者；colonizer [`kɑləˌnaɪzɚ] n. 殖民地開拓者

pioneering

[paɪə`nɪərɪŋ]

adj. 開創的、先驅的

Pioneering research shows that the fond experiences of childhood help children shape their minds and stabilize their emotions.

先驅性的研究表示，童年的美好經歷幫助孩子們塑造了自己的思想並穩定了他們的情緒。

詞搭 | pioneering work 先驅工作

---

access

[`æksɛs]

n. （對人、地、物的）接近；進入；存取（的權利，門路或方法）

v. 接觸到

警特 105

The only access to the village is by boat and there are no other choices.

到村莊的唯一方法是乘船，你別無選擇。

秒殺解字 ac(=ad=to)+cess(go) → 本義「向前走」，因此有「進入」、「入口」等衍生意思。

詞搭 | have access to... 接觸到……、使用……的機會或權利；random access 隨機存取

衍生字 | accessible [æk`sɛsəbl] adj. 可到達的、可進入的、易取得的；accessibility [æk͵sɛsə`bɪlətɪ] n. 易接近

---

fulfill

[fʊl`fɪl]

v. 實現；履行；滿足

The whole family thought Mr. Green did not fulfill his duties as a father.

全家人都認為 Green 先生並沒有履行父親的職責。

秒殺解字 ful(full)+fill →「填滿」，表示「實現」。

詞搭 | fulfill oneself 實現自我；fulfill + sb's duties / obligations 盡責；fulfill + sb's promise / expectations 履行承諾／如願

衍生字 | fulfillment [fʊl`fɪlmənt] n. 實現、成就

同義字 | achieve, realize, keep, satisfy

rebel

[`rɛbl]/[rɪ`bɛl]

n. 反叛者；叛軍
v. 造反、反叛
adj. 反叛的

Most of the people in this poor country were united to rebel against their president, who's incompetent and brutal.

這個貧窮國家的大多數人民團結起來反抗他們無能並且殘酷的總統。

(秒殺解字) re(again, opposite, against)+bel(war) → 「再次」發動「戰爭」「對抗」的人。**Bellona** 是羅馬神話中的女戰神，代表「戰爭」，英語中的字根 **bell**，和「戰爭」有關。相關同源字有 **bell**icose (adj. 好戰的、好鬥的)、**bell**igerent (adj. 好戰的、好鬥的)。

詞搭 | rebel against 反抗

衍生字 | rebellion [rɪ`bɛljən] n. 反叛；rebellious [rɪ`bɛljəs] adj. 造反的

同義字 | revolt

compulsive

[kəm`pʌlsɪv]

adj. 強迫的；強制的

Don't expect such a compulsive gambler like him to get a normal job and support his family.

不要指望像他這樣的嗜賭成性的人能正常工作並養家糊口。

(秒殺解字) com(together)+pul(push, drive)+s+ive → 「一起」「推」，表示「強迫的」。相關同源字有 **pul**se (n. 脈搏)、ap**peal** (v. 呼籲、懇求；上訴；吸引)、com**pel** (v. 強迫)、com**pul**sory (adj. 義務的)、dis**pel** (v. 驅散、消除)、ex**pel** (v. 逐出；開除)、ex**pul**sion (n. 逐出；開除)、im**pel** (v. 驅使、迫使)、im**pul**se (n. 衝動)、im**pul**sive (adj. 易衝動的)、pro**pel** (v. 推進；驅使)。

詞搭 | compulsive disorder 強迫症；compulsive hoarding 強迫囤積症

evaluate

[ɪ`væljʊˌet]

v. 評估

The doctor says the side-effects of this new drug are quite difficult to evaluate, so the patients need to decide whether they'll take it or not.

警特 108

醫生說，這種新藥的副作用很難評估，因此需要決定是否服藥的人是患者。

(秒殺解字) e(=ex=out)+valu(worth)+ate → 找「出」「價值」。

同義字 | assess, appraise

evaluation
[ɪˌvæljʊˋeʃən]
n. 評估、衡量

We'll employ different user fees to fund the evaluation of feasibility of building a gymnasium on the hill.
我們將採取不同的用戶費用來評估在山上修建體育館的可行性。

警特 109

| 同義字 | assessment |

perceive
[pɚˋsiv]
v. 察覺；認為

How will you perceive your new role in the new company?
你如何看待自己在新公司中的新角色？

警 104

🔖 **秒殺解字** per(thoroughly)+ceiv(take)+e → 本義「徹底」「拿到」，後語意轉抽象，指徹底抓住某個概念，引申為「察覺」。

| 詞搭 | perceive A as B 把 A 認為是 B |

| 衍生字 | perception [pɚˋsɛpʃən] n. 察覺能力、觀點 |

perceptibility
[pɚˌsɛptəˋbɪlətɪ]
n. 可感知力；察覺力

Brain injuries may gradually or immediately diminish one's perceptibility, and affect one's ability to think, act, or feel.
腦部受傷可能會逐漸或立即使人的感知力下降，並影響其思考，行動或感覺的能力。

unperceptive
[ˌʌnpɚˋsɛptɪv]
adj. 無知覺的

Some people are just so unperceptive in their surroundings, especially when they are addicted to mobile games.
有些人對周遭環境毫無察覺，特別是當他們沉迷於手機遊戲時。

| 反義字 | perceptive [pɚˋsɛptɪv] adj. 知覺敏銳的 |

attribute
[ˋætrəˌbjut]/
[əˋtrɪbjʊt]
n. 特質
v. 將……歸因於

I think Jack's most outstanding attribute is his perseverance.
我認為 Jack 最突出的特質是他的毅力。

警 101

🔖 **秒殺解字** at(=ad=to)+tribu(give)+t+e → 把發生原因歸「給」某事，責任歸「給」某人，或把某種特質歸「給」於某人或某事。相關同源字有 **tribu**te (n. 貢物；敬意)、con**tribu**te (v. 貢獻；造成；投稿)、dis**tribu**te (v. 分發、分配)

| 詞搭 | attribute / ascribe A to B 將 A 歸因於 B；physical attribute 身體素質 |

mysterious [mɪs`tɪrɪəs] **adj.** 神祕的	She is quite easy-going, and there is nothing mysterious about her character. 她很隨和，她的性格裡沒有什麼神祕的地方。 🖋 秒殺解字 mystery+ous →「神祕」「的」。	高 108 警特 107
同義字	enigmatic, secretive	

strategy [`strætədʒɪ] **n.** 策略；戰略	The manager says that we need a new strategy to improve our market share. 經理說，我們需要一種新的策略來提高我們的市占率。 🖋 秒殺解字 strat(army, organization)+eg(=ag=lead, drive)+y → 源自希臘文，表示「(領軍的)將軍」。若進一步拆解這個字，字面上的意思是「領導」「軍隊」，引申為「戰略」。	
詞搭	economic strategy 經濟政策	
衍生字	strategic [strə`tidʒɪk] adj. 戰略的	

luxury [`lʌkʃərɪ] **n.** 奢侈、豪華；奢侈品	I'm not accustomed to such luxury. It's really a waste of money. 我不習慣了這種奢侈。這真是浪費錢。 🖋 秒殺解字 lux(excess)+ure+y →源自拉丁文，表示「過度」，引申為「奢侈」。	警特 107
	live in luxury 生活奢侈；lead / live a life of luxury 過奢侈的生活；a luxury hotel / flat / liner 豪華旅館／公寓／郵輪	

luxurious [lʌg`ʒʊrɪəs] **adj.** 豪華的、奢侈的	I don't think I need such a big and luxurious house like this. 我認為我不需要這麼大又奢華的房子。	普 107

affection [ə`fɛkʃən] **n.** 愛好；情愛	The mother's affections were all centered on the youngest son. 這位母親的感情全部集中在最小的兒子上。 🖋 秒殺解字 af(=ad=to)+fec(do, make)+t+ion →「去」「做」，出自「愛好」、「情愛」。	普 102
詞搭	have (an) affection for... 深愛著……	
同義字	fondness	

affective
[əˈfɛktɪv]
adj. 感情的

Living alone and abroad since childhood, Peter always thinks he has no affective tie to his family.
Peter 從小就獨自生活在國外，他始終認為自己與家人之間沒有情感聯繫。

普 104

詞搭 seasonal affective disorder 季節性情緒失調

disaster
[dɪˈzæstə]
n. 災難；大失敗

If you go on hanging out with him, I think you're heading for disaster.
如果你繼續和他一起出去混，我想你將要走向災難。

普 100
警特 109

秒殺解字 dis(ill, bad)+aster(star) → 古代人認為「凶」「星」會帶來「厄運」及「災難」。相關同源字有 **astr**onaut (n. 太空人)、**astr**onomy (n. 天文學；星學)、**astr**onomer (n. 天文學家)、**astr**onomical (adj. 天文學的)、**astr**ology (n. 占星學)、**astr**ological (adj. 占星學的)、**astr**ologer (n. 占星學家)。

詞搭 a natural disaster 天然災害；be a complete / total disaster 徹底的失敗

衍生字 disastrous [dɪˈzæstrəs] adj. 災難的、造成災害的

同義字 catastrophe, tragedy

defeat
[dɪˈfit]
n. 失敗；戰敗
v. 擊敗

I must tell you that it's impossible to defeat a person like me.
我必須告訴你，打敗像我這樣的人是不可能的。

秒殺解字 de(=dis=not)+feat(do, make) → 「不」「做」了，表示「失敗」。

詞搭 defeat + sb. + by... 以……之差擊敗某人；admit / accept / concede defeat 承認失敗

同義字 beat

bombard
[bɑmˈbɑrd]
v. 轟炸、砲轟；向……連續提出問題

The enemy bombarded the town last night, killing and injuring hundreds of residents.
敵人昨晚轟炸了該鎮，造成數百名居民傷亡。

秒殺解字 bomb+ard → 如「炸彈」般「轟炸」。**bomb** [bɑm] (n. 炸彈)、**bombard**、**boom** [bum] (v. 發出隆隆聲；繁榮)同源，**b/m 轉音**，母音通轉，核心語意是「炸彈」。「發出隆隆聲」（**boom**）可聯想成是「炸彈」的爆炸聲響。

詞搭 bombard + sb. + with + sth. 不斷向某人提出問題或批評

routine
[ru`tin]

n. 慣例；例行公事
adj. 例行公事的；常規的

I think I like my current job because there's no routine at work and every day is different and a new challenge to me.

我想我喜歡我目前的工作，因為這裡沒有一成不變的工作，每一天都不一樣，這對我來說是新的挑戰。

普100 106

秒殺解字 route(=rupt=break) → rout e 源自拉丁文的 rupta（via），原意是強行開通、「破壞」樹林、草地所開拓出來的道路，後來衍生為「路線」、「途徑」，也用於美國城市間幹線公路編號，如 Route 54。rout ine 源自 rout e，每天要走的「路」，表示「例行公事」、「慣例」。相關同源字有 rob（v. 搶劫）、bank rupt（adj. 破產的）、inter rupt（v. 打斷）、cor rupt（adj. 貪污的）、dis rupt（v. 使中斷）、e rupt（v. 爆發）、ab rupt（adj. 突然的、意外的）。

詞搭 a daily routine 每天例行的事；establish a routine 建立慣例；routine tests / maintenance 例行檢查／定期保養；routine procedure 例行手續

同義字 ritual, regular

---

shell
[ʃɛl]

n. 貝殼；彈殼

The seashore is beautiful and covered with white sand and a variety of shells.

這裡的海邊很美，而且到處是白沙和各式各樣的貝殼。

普102
警特108

秒殺解字 shel ter [`ʃɛltə]（n. 避難所）、shell、shel f [ʃɛlf]（n. 架子）、shiel d [ʃild]（n. 盾）同源，母音通轉，核心語意都是「保護」（protect）。

詞搭 bring + sb. + out of + sb's shell 使……不再害羞

---

guard
[gɑrd]

n. 警衛；警戒
v. 守護

The prisoner bribed his way past the guards and escaped.

囚犯賄賂了警衛而後脫逃了。

警特109

William got a new job as a security guard.
William 換了一個擔任保全警衛的新工作。

秒殺解字 源自古法語 garder，表示「看守人」（keeper），從古法語借進英語時，為了清楚標示 g 的發音為 /g/ 而非 /dʒ/，會在 g 和母音中插入一個不發音的 u 提醒。

詞搭 be on guard = stand / keep guard 守衛；guard against... 防著……；keep guard on / over ... 警戒……；a security guard 保全人員

guardian

[ˈɡɑrdɪən]

n. 守護者；捍衛者；監護人

The child's parents or legal guardians should give their consent before the operation is performed.
手術前，需徵得孩子的父母或法定監護人的同意。

詞搭 a legal guardian 法定監護人

---

classify

[ˈklæsəˌfaɪ]

v. 將……分類、歸類

People working in libraries have to spend a lot of time every day classifying books.
在圖書館工作的人們每天必須花費大量時間對書籍進行分類。

圖 103 107

秒殺解字 class(class)+i+fy(make, do) →「做」「分類」。

詞搭 classify A as / under B 把 A 歸類於 B；a classified ad 分類廣告

衍生字 classification [ˌklæsəfəˈkeʃən] n. 分類

同義字 sort, categorize

---

crawl

[krɔl]

v. 爬

With the help of one of his comrades, the injured crawled slowly to a safer place.
在一位夥伴的幫助下，受傷者慢慢地爬到了更安全的地方。

秒殺解字 cr 可用來表示「爬行」或「蜷伏」。相關單字有 crawl (v. 爬行)、creep (v. 爬行)、crouch (v. 蜷縮)。

---

forgive

[fɚˈɡɪv]

v. 原諒

With tears in her eyes, Martha implored her husband to forgive her.
Martha 含著淚，懇求丈夫原諒她。

秒殺解字 for(completely)+give →「完全」「給」出去，表示放下一切，引申為「放棄」。

時態 時態：forgive, forgave, forgiven

詞搭 forgive + sb. + for N / Ving 原諒某人的某種行為

同義字 excuse, pardon

desperate

[ˋdɛspərɪt]

adj. 絕望的；危急的；
極渴望的

The situation is now quite desperate for the army, as they have no food and ammunition, little water, and limited medical supplies.
現在的局勢對軍隊來說是非常絕望的，他們沒有食物和彈藥，幾乎沒有水，而且醫療物資有限。

指 108

秒殺解字 de(without)+sper(hope)+ate → 「缺乏」「希望」，表示「絕望的」。相關同源字有 **speed**（n 速度）、**speed**ing（n. 超速）、de**spair**（n./v. 絕望）、de**spair**ing（adj. 絕望的）、de**sper**ately（adv. 不顧一切地、拼命地）、de**sper**ation（n. 絕望）、de**sper**ado（n. 亡命之徒）、pro**sper**（v. 繁榮、成功）、pro**sper**ity（n. 繁榮、成功）、pro**sper**ous（adj. 繁榮的）。

詞搭 be desperate + to V 極度渴望想要……；be desperate for + N 渴望得到……； a desperate shortage / illness / situation 奇缺／重病／危局

衍生字 desperately [ˋdɛspərɪtlɪ] adv. 不顧一切地、拼命地

同義字 hopeless, gloomy

ethical

[ˋɛθɪkl]

adj. 道德的、倫理的

Teachers are generally asked to have higher ethical and moral standards.
教師通常是被要求須具有較高的倫理和道德標準。

秒殺解字 eth(custom)+ic+al → 「倫理」、「道德」多半來自「傳統」。

字辨 ethnic [ˋɛθnɪk] adj. 種族的

同義字 moral

反義字 unethical

vividly

[ˋvɪvɪdlɪ]

adv. 生動地

The report is vividly written and quite touching.
這份報告寫得生動活潑，令人感動。

指 104

秒殺解字 viv(live)+id+ly → 栩栩如「生」地，表示「生動地」。相關同源字有 **viv**id（adj. 清楚的；鮮明的）、sur**viv**e（v. 倖存；生還；殘留）、re**viv**e（v. 使復甦、復活）、**vit**al（adj. 極重要、不可缺的）、**vit**amin（n. 維他命）、**vi**able（adj. 可實施的）。

accelerate
[æk`sɛlə͵ret]

v. 加速

What do you think we can do to accelerate the process for dealing with air pollution?
你認為我們可以採取什麼措施來加快處理空氣污染的進程？

🖊 **秒殺解字** ac(to)+celer(swift)+ate → 加「速」。

🔊 105

詞搭	accelerating the rate of economic growth 加速經濟成長速率
衍生字	acceleration [æk͵sɛlə`reʃən] n. 加速
反義字	decelerate

ambassador
[æm`bæsədɚ]

n. 大使

Mr. Taylor's a former ambassador to the United Kingdom.
Taylor 先生曾任駐英國大使。

🖊 **秒殺解字** amb(=ambi=around, both)+ass(=ag=drive, move)+ador → 代表政府在國外「到處」「走動」的人。**emb**assy（n. 大使館）和 **amb**assador 同源，母音通轉。

| 衍生字 | embassy [`ɛmbəsɪ] n. 大使館 |

🔊 104

appealing
[ə`pilɪŋ]

adj. 動人的、吸引人的、迷人的

Being a secretary to the general manager, Susan always wears a smile on her face and has an appealing personality.
Susan 身為總經理的祕書，總是面帶微笑，並具有吸引人的個性。

🖊 **秒殺解字** ap(=ad=to)+peal(=pel=push, drive)+ing →「朝……」「推」進，表示「吸引人的」。相關同源字有 **pul**se（n. 脈搏）、ap**peal**（v. 呼籲、懇求；上訴；吸引）、com**pel**（v. 強迫）、com**pul**sory（adj. 義務的）com**pul**sive（adj. 強迫的；強制的）、dis**pel**（v. 驅散、消除）、ex**pel**（v. 逐出；開除）、ex**pul**sion（n. 逐出；開除）、im**pel**（v. 驅使、迫使）、im**pul**se（n. 衝動）、im**pul**sive（adj. 易衝動的）、pro**pel**（v. 推進；驅使）。

🔊 99

| 同義字 | attractive, charming |
| 反義字 | unappealing |

moderate
[`mɑdərɪt]

v. 節制；和緩
adj. 適度的

The doctor says that moderate exercise is necessary for my mother, who just had surgery two days ago.
醫生說，我的母親兩天前剛剛做過手術，所以必須進行適度的運動。

🖊 **秒殺解字** mod(measure)+er+ate →被「模式」限制住，表示「適度的」、「溫和的」。

🔊 108

| 反義字 | extreme, immoderate |

01 ___ Inside the magnificent mansion lives a wealthy _____, whose grandfather made a fortune by discovering a gold mine.

(A) provider   (B) companion
(C) nobleman   (D) mammal

02 ___ Now, this will be the end of our museum tour. If you still have further questions regarding the history of the museum, please feel free to_____ out staff.

(A) require   (B) pursue
(C) inquire   (D) burden

03 ___ The police are _____ that the man is the only suspect of the crime. They think that there are more people behind the scene.

(A) doubtful   (B) successful
(C) deceitful   (D) thoughtful

04 ___ James Cameron, the director of the famous sci-fi film "Avatar", got on to a specially-made _____ and dived into the bottom of the Mariana Trench.

(A) method   (B) submarine
(C) office   (D) program

05 ___ Some people love to climb onto the peak of the mountain to enjoy the breathtaking _____. The brief moment will be carved deeply into their hearts and they will forever remember the view.

(A) policies   (B) materials
(C) communities   (D) landscapes

06 ___ Because of the sacrifices of the _____, we now are able to live freely on this land. We need to be grateful for their commitment and dedication.

(A) pioneers   (B) applicants
(C) defendants   (D) candidates

07 ___ The government sent out an army to deal with the local _____.
Without proper equipment and training, they would be wiped out quite
easily.

(A) militiamen   (B) supporters
(C) experts   (D) rebels

08 ___ We need to _____ the situation again because of the sudden
change. Since there is no one else to turn to, we are the only group
available to perform the task.

(A) estimate   (B) exceed
(C) evaluate   (D) eliminate

09 ___ The best _____ for us right now is to wait and try to maintain the
current situation. We have no power and force to turn the tide, and
keeping things as they are is the best and only option.

(A) psychology   (B) strategy
(C) technology   (D) energy

10 ___ Poor training, a lack of equipment, and a bad attitude are the recipe
for _____. The team really needs to be transformed in order to
perform well.

(A) disaster   (B) proposal
(C) trend   (D) formula

11 ___ Recently, the news has been _____ by the scandal of the newly-
elected mayor. It is reported that he bribed his way to victory in the
election and is now under investigation.

(A) bombarded   (B) inspired
(C) aroused   (D) misguided

12 ___ In this school, students are _____ into three different levels. The
first level consists of the best and smartest students. However, this
policy draws much criticism for the school.

(A) identified   (B) satisfied
(C) qualified   (D) classified

13 ___ According to science, if one _____ to the speed of light, one could live forever because time would be stopped when traveling at the speed of light.

(A) separated   (B) illustrated
(C) accelerated   (D) operated

14 ___ The murder of the _____caused an unfixable gap between the two nations. The two countries are now at the edge of war.

(A) expert   (B) president
(C) ambassador   (D) pilot

15 ___ After my investigation, the problem I found was not a huge issue. Thus, with only a _____ tuning, I think I can get the job done.

(A) moderate   (B) elaborate
(C) desperate   (D) illiterate

解答
1.(C) 2.(C) 3.(A) 4.(B) 5.(D) 6.(A) 7.(D) 8.(C) 9.(B) 10.(A) 11.(A) 12.(D) 13.(C) 14.(C) 15.(A)

contest
[`kantɛst]
n. 比賽;競爭

It is estimated that some 200 people will take part in the singing contest scheduled to be held next month.
估計將會有大約 200 人參加在下個月舉辦的歌唱比賽。

秒殺解字 con(together)+test(testify, witness) →本義是在大家「一起」「比賽」之前,請證人來作「證明」,後來語意改變,表示參加「比賽」。相關同源字有 con**test**ant (n. 競爭者)、pro**test** (v./n. 抗議)、**test**ify (v. 證明、作證)、**test**imony (n. 證詞)。

片語 a speech contest 演講比賽;a chess contest 西洋棋比賽

package
[`pækɪdʒ]
n. 組;包裹;一套
v. 包裝

A package without sender's name and address placed on my desk really puzzled me a lot. 曾 110
有一件放在我桌上並沒有註明寄件人姓名地址的包裹真的讓我很疑惑。

秒殺解字 pack(bundle)+age(condition) → 「捆」的「狀態」。相關同源字有 bever**age** (n. 飲料)、bagg**age** (n. 行李)、lugg**age** (n. 行李)、block**age** (n. 阻礙)、lever**age** (n. 槓桿作用)、short**age** (n.缺少)、orphan**age** (n. 孤兒院)、percent**age** (n. 百分比)。

同義字 parcel, packet

historic
[hɪs`tɔrɪk]
adj. 有歷史性的;歷史上著名的

The price of oil has recently reached historic levels and is expected to go down to a lower point next week. 曾 102
油價最近已達歷年低點,而且下周可望降到更低價位。

秒殺解字 histor(history)+ic(of) → 「歷史」「的」。

consistent
[kən`sɪstənt]
adj. 前後一致的;經常不變的

The final result of the experiment is consistent with their earlier supposition.
這項實驗最後結果與他們先前假設符合。

inconsistent

[ˌɪnkən`sɪstənt]

adj. 不一致的

The principal regrets that Mr. Clark's conduct <u>is inconsistent with</u> what is expected of a teacher.
校長對於 Clark 先生的行為不符合大家對老師的期望感到遺憾。

秒殺解字 con(together)+sist(stand)+ent → 「站」在「一起」，表示「前後一致的」。相關同源字有 con**sist**（ v. 包含）、con**sist**ency（ n. 一致）、as**sist**（ v. 幫助）、ex**sist**（ v. 存在）、in**sist**（ v. 堅持）、per**sist**（ v 堅持；持續）、re**sist**（ v. 抗拒）。

---

stumble

[`stʌmbl]

v. 絆倒；跟蹌；結巴

Jogging along the sidewalk, Joanne <u>stumbled on</u> a brick and was seriously wounded.
Joanne 沿著人行道慢跑時不小心被磚塊絆倒，傷勢嚴重。

秒殺解字 st 可表示「停止」，stumble 表示走路時因絆倒而「停止」前進，或者說話結巴，說說「停停」。相關字有 **st**op（ v./n. 停止）、**st**and（ v. 站住）、**st**ay（ v./n. 停留）、**st**ill（ adj. 靜止的）、**st**are（ v./n. 凝視）、**st**uff（ v. 使塞滿）、**st**ammer（ v./n. 結巴）、**st**artle（ v. 使嚇一跳）、**st**umble（ v. 絆倒）。

片語 stumble over + sth. 被某物絆倒

同義字 trip

---

pleading

[`plidɪŋ]

adj. 訴願的；懇求的

Running into difficulties, the orphanage sent pleading e-mails to the 10 major businesses and enterprises for financial support.
由於陷入困頓中，這家孤兒院發出懇求信函給十家主要企業，希望他們能夠給予財務上的協助。

普 102
高 108

秒殺解字 plead(please)+ing → 在法庭上律師提出「取悅」原告、說服法官的證據來辯護，表示「訴願的」、「懇求的」。

---

discriminate

[dɪ`skrɪməˌnet]

v. 區別；歧視（與 against 並用）

The supermarket manager was fired because he often <u>discriminated against</u> senior customers.
這家超市的經理被革職，因為他經常歧視年長顧客。

普 100
警特 109

秒殺解字 dis(away)+crim(separate)+in+ate → 把特定人事物「分開」，有「歧視」的味道。

片語 discriminate A from B 區別 A 與 B = discriminate between A and B

同義字 differentiate

discrimination

[dɪˌskrɪməˈneʃən]

n. 歧視;區別;辨識力

種族歧視在美國仍然是一個嚴重的問題。

Racial discrimination is still a serious problem in the United States.

譜 100
102
106

片語 | racial /sex / religious discrimination 種族／性別／宗教歧視

---

complaint

[kəmˈplent]

n. 抱怨、投訴

As more and more complaints about the quality of food and service arise, the restaurant's business is getting slower and slower.

由於愈來愈多人抱怨食物及服務的品質低落,這家餐廳的生意也就愈來愈差。

譜 100
學特 108

秒殺解字 com(intensive prefix)+plain(strike, beat the breast)+t(action) → 本義「搥胸」,以示「哀悼」,引申為「抱怨」。t 表示「行為」、「特質」、「狀態」名詞字尾。

片語 | make complaints about... = complain about... 抱怨……
同義字 | grievance

---

telescope

[ˈtɛləˌskop]

n. (單筒)望遠鏡

You won't be able to see the details of the moon's surface, as it can only be seen through a telescope.

你只能藉著望遠鏡來觀看,否則你將無法看到月球表面的細節。

秒殺解字 tele(far)+scop(look)+e → 用「望遠鏡」可以「看」到「遠方」的人事物。相關同源字有 **scop**e (n. 範圍)、micro**scop**e (n. 顯微鏡)、horo**scop**e (n. 占星術)。

字辨 | binoculars [baɪˈnɑkjələz] n. 雙筒望遠鏡 (恆用複數)

---

heritage

[ˈhɛrətɪdʒ]

n. 繼承物;遺產

The new museum is set up to preserve the cultural heritage of the indigenous/aboriginal people of Taiwan.

這座新的博物館設立目的是要保存台灣原住民文化遺產。

譜 107
108
110
高 110

秒殺解字 her(heir, left behind)+it+age → heritage 指「遺留」下來的傳統價值觀、信仰、文物、或建築物,heritable 表示「可繼承的」。可用表示「繼承人」的 **heir** 當神隊友,**母音通轉**,來記憶 **her**,皆和「繼承」、「遺留」有關。

同義字 | inheritance

heritable
[`hɛrətəbl]
adj. 會遺傳的；可繼承的

It may be improper to say that autism is a disease, but in fact, it is a <u>heritable</u> neurological disorder.
説自閉症是一種疾病或許不恰當，但事實上，那是一種會遺傳的神經失調症。

曾 99

---

sensation
[sɛn`seʃən]
n. 感覺；轟動

I always have <u>a sensation of</u> happiness while eating sweets.
享用甜食時，我總是會有一種幸福的感覺。

曾 102
106

秒殺解字 sens(feel)+ation → 表示「感覺」或「引起轟動的人或物」。

片語 cause a sensation 引起轟動

---

sentiment
[`sɛntəmənt]
n. 情緒；意見；觀點

Though John made no comments, I know he did not agree with my <u>sentiments</u>.
雖然 John 沒有發表評論，但我知道他並不同意我的觀點。

曾 108

秒殺解字 sent(feel)+i+ment → 表示「情緒」。可用 **sense** 當神隊友，**t/s 轉音**，母音通轉，來記憶 **sent**，皆表示「感覺」。相關同源字有 as**sent**（v. 同意）、con**sent**（v. 同意）、dis**sent**（v. 不同意）、re**sent**（v. 憤慨）。

片語 public sentiment 公眾意見

同義字 opinion

---

sensitive
[`sɛnsətɪv]
adj. 敏感的

Generally, women <u>are</u> more <u>sensitive about</u> age than men.
一般説來，關於年齡問題，女人比男人更敏感。

曾 99

片語 be sensitive <u>to / about</u> + sth. 對某事物很敏感

---

insensitive
[ɪn`sɛnsətɪv]
adj. 遲鈍的

The mayor was often criticized for <u>being</u> <u>insensitive to</u> the complaints from the general public.
市長因為對民眾怨言漠不關心常常遭受批評。

mortgage
[`mɔrgɪdʒ]

n. **v.** 典當；抵押

Even if you think your income is enough to let you afford the new house, the bank loan and mortgage are not easy to pay off.

即使你認為你的收入足以購入這棟新房，但銀行貸款及抵押等債務其實還是不容易清償的。

Without much cash available, Jennifer had to mortgage her house to start her flower shop business.

由於沒有很多現金，Jennifer 必須將她的房子辦理抵押貸款而後才能開始她的花店事業。

秒殺解字 mort(dead)+gage(pledge, promise) → mortgage 字面上的意思是「死」「誓」，「死」代表結束，「誓」表示用抵押品貸款，mortgage 本義是「清償貸款」，後指「抵押」、「典當」。相關同源字有 **mort**al (adj. 不免一死的)、**mort**ality (n. 死亡率)。

同義字 | loan

disclose
[dɪs`kloz]

v. 揭露

The new plan is just between Julia and me, so I'm sorry I can't <u>disclose</u> any of it <u>to</u> you.

這個新計劃只有 Julia 和我知道，所以很抱歉任何有關計畫內容我都無法向你透露。

秒殺解字 dis(opposite)+close(close) →「關」的「相反」動作，表示將不為人知的事「公諸於世」。

同義字 | reveal

普 106

barrier
[`bærɪr]

n. 障礙（物）

The elimination of the non-tariff barrier is believed to be of great help to international trade promotion.

排除非關稅障礙相信對促進國際貿易是有相當大的助益的。

普 105
107
110

秒殺解字 bar(bar, barrier)+r+ier → 表示「棒」、「條」、「障礙」。r 重複的理由和 preferred 重複 r 一樣，和 runner 重複 n 的理由一樣，這叫 consonant doubling。相關同源字有 **bar** (v. 阻礙)、em**bar**rass (v. 使尷尬)。

片語 | be a barrier to... 對……是個障礙（物）

同義字 | obstacle, hindrance

miracle
[ˈmɪrəkl̩]
n. 奇蹟

It's really a miracle that the real estate agent sold 5 houses in this community within a week.
這位房屋仲介能在一周內賣掉這個社區 5 間房子,這真是一個奇蹟。

🔊 102

> **秒殺解字** mir(wonderful, wonder)+acle → 「驚奇的」、「驚奇」的事物,表示「奇蹟」。相關同源字有 **mir**ror (n. 鏡子)、**mir**age (n. 海市蜃樓)、ad**mir**e (v. 欽佩)。

片語 work / perform miracles 產生奇蹟、有效、很靈

同義字 wonder

enact
[ɪnˈækt]
v. 制定(法律)

Under the Tobacco Hazards Prevention Law, all schools should enact smoke-free policies on campus.
在菸害防制條例管制下,所有學校在校園均應執行禁菸政策。

🔊 108

> **秒殺解字** en(make)+act(do) → 「使」人要去「做」的事,所以「制定法律」。

同義字 legislate

fantastic
[fænˈtæstɪk]
adj. 極好的;幻想的

The hotel is very popular because it provides a fantastic environment for tourists.
這家旅館頗受歡迎,因為它為觀光客提供超優環境。

🔊 99

> **秒殺解字** fan(appear, imagine)+tastic → 只「出現」在「想像」中的,表示為「極好的」、「幻想的」。相關同源字有 **fan**cy (v. 想要)、**fan**tasy (n. 空想)。

同義字 wonderful, excellent, superb, perfect, terrific, brilliant, attractive, amazing, incredible, unbelievable, marvelous, outstanding

invent
[ɪnˈvɛnt]
v. 發明;捏造

The technician is so smart that he can invent many useful tools that are helpful for his job.
這位技師如此聰明以至於他有能力發明許多有助於他自己工作的工具。

🔊 103
104

inventive
[ɪnˈvɛntɪv]
adj. 發明的

Decorated by the most inventive and creative baker of this store, the Doraemon birthday cakes have recently gained great popularity. 📘 101

這種多啦 A 夢生日蛋糕經過這家店的麵包師傅巧思創意裝飾之後，已經受到廣大歡迎。

🖊 **秒殺解字** in(in)+ven(come)+t+ive → 本義「來」到「內部」被「發現」，引申為「發明」。相關同源字有 ad**ven**ture（n. 冒險）、pre**ven**t（v. 阻止）、e**ven**t（n. 事件）、e**ven**tual（adj. 最後的）、con**ven**ient（adj. 便利的）、con**ven**e（v. 集會）、con**ven**tion（n. 大型會議；習俗）、con**ven**tional（adj. 傳統的）。

---

symbolize
[ˈsɪmblˌaɪz]
v. 象徵；代表

While the lion symbolizes strength or power, the lamb symbolizes gentleness or tenderness. 📘 104 📕 108

獅子象徵權勢或力量，而羔羊則是象徵溫和或柔弱。

🖊 **秒殺解字** sym(=syn=together)+bol(throw)+ize → 把東西「丟」「一起」是為了「比較」，隱含「類比」，甚至「代表」的意思，衍生出「象徵」的意思。

同義字 | represent

---

symbolic
[sɪmˈbɑlɪk]
adj. 象徵性的

Today's protest is symbolic of the factory workers' deep dissatisfaction with their working conditions. 📘 102

今天的抗爭象徵著工廠的工人對於他們的工作環境是相當不滿的。

---

abrupt
[əˈbrʌpt]
adj. 突然的、唐突的

The bus came to an abrupt halt because the five cars ahead of it piled up unexpectedly. 📘 104 110

由於前面五台轎車無預警地連環碰撞再一起，巴士突然煞停。

🖊 **秒殺解字** ab(away, off)+rupt(break) →「破裂」「開來」，因為破裂通常是「突然」發生。可用 **rob** 當神隊友，**b/p 轉音**，**母音通轉**，來記憶 **rupt**，表示「打斷」、「打破」、「破裂」。相關同源字有 **rob**（v. 搶劫）、bank**rupt**（adj. 破產的）、inter**rupt**（v. 打斷）、cor**rupt**（adj. 貪污的）、dis**rupt**（v. 使中斷）、e**rupt**（v. 爆發）。

同義字 | sudden, unexpected

dissolve

[dɪ`zɑlv]

v. 溶解；終止；消失

Put the sugar cube into warm water and it will dissolve soon.
把方糖放入溫水，它很快就會溶解。

📚 99

🪶 **秒殺解字** dis(apart)+solv(loosen)+e → 本義「鬆」「開」，後指「溶解」。相關同源字有 dis**solu**tion（n. 溶解；解散）、**solv**e（v. 解決）、**solu**tion（n. 解決方法）、re**solv**e（v. 決定；解決）、re**solu**tion（n. 決心；決議）、ab**solu**te（adj. 完全的；絕對的）。

詞搭 dissolve A in B 使 A 溶解於 B 之中；dissolve in + sth. 溶解於某物；dissolve in / into tears 淚眼汪汪

---

patch

[pætʃ]

n. 一小塊（土地、汙漬等）；補釘

v. 修補

A patch with a Hello Kitty logo was sewn on the skirt to cover the rip.
一張上面有 Hello Kitty 圖案的貼布被縫在裙子上，用來遮蓋裙子破損的部位。

I don't think I can help and I hope you'll soon patch things up with him.
我想我不了忙，我也希望你和他快點和解。

🪶 **秒殺解字** patch 是用來修補其他織物的一塊布料，和 piece（一塊）同源。

詞搭 a patch of... 一塊……

---

abuse

[ə`bjus]/ [ə`bjuz]

n. **v.** 虐待；辱罵；濫用

Recently, there has been an increase in number of child abuse cases in this community.
近來在這社區裏虐待小孩的案例有增加的趨勢。

🪶 **秒殺解字** ab(away, off)+use(use) → 偏「離」正當「用途」，衍生出「濫用」、「虐待」等意思。

詞搭 abuse one's position 濫用某人職位；abuse of power / privileges 濫用權力／特權；alcohol / drug abuse 酒精／藥物的濫用

induce
[ɪnˋdjus]

v. 唆使；勸誘；人工分娩

I believe nothing can <u>induce</u> her <u>to</u> marry that man.
我相信沒有任何事情可以誘使她跟那位男人結婚。

🪶 秒殺解字 in(in)+duc(lead)+e →「引導」到「內部」，表示「唆使」、「誘發」。相關同源字有 **educ**ate (v. 教育)、pro**duc**e (v. 生產)、pro**duc**tion (n. 生產)、re**duc**e (v. 減少)、re**duc**tion (n. 減少)、intro**duc**e (v. 介紹；引進)、intro**duc**tion (n. 介紹；引進)。

| 同義字 | persuade |

pretend
[prɪˋtɛnd]

v. 假裝

It's not right for us to <u>pretend to know</u> everything when we do not know anything of it.   🔊 99
當我們對一件事情完全不清楚，卻又假裝什麼都知道時，這樣是不對的。

🪶 秒殺解字 pre(before)+tend(thin, stretch) → 本義「延展」到「前方」，「假裝」的意思要到 1865 年才出現。

| 詞搭 | pretend ignorance 假裝不知情 |

pretentiously
[prɪˋtɛnʃlɪ]

adj. 自命不凡地；矯飾地、做作地

The title "senior marketing manager" on his business card sounded pretentiously important, but actually he's only a salesman.
他在名片上的頭銜「資深行銷經理」聽起來像是挺重要的人物，但實際上他只是一位銷售員而已。

reinforce
[ˌriɪnˋfɔrs]

v. 加強；補強（建築物）；增援

Gestures are useful in reinforcing what one wants to express in a conversation.
在對話中，用手勢來增強一個人想要表達的事情是很有用的。

🪶 秒殺解字 re(again)+in(=en=make)+force(strong) →「再」「使」「力量」得以發揮，表示「加強」、「增援」。

| 同義字 | strengthen, fortify |

agriculture
[ˋægrɪˌkʌltʃɚ]

n. 農業

People of this country depend on agriculture and tourism for most of their income.
這個國家的人民大部分收入是依賴農業及觀光業。

🪶 秒殺解字 agri(=agr=field)+cul(cultivate)+t+ure →「耕種」「田地」，表示「農業」。

| 同義字 | farming |

coincide
[ˌkoɪnˋsaɪd]

v. 同時發生；巧合

Next Saturday's concert is arranged to <u>coincide</u> <u>with</u> the art festival of the city.
下周六音樂會的演出是配合本市藝術季活動而安排的。

🪶 秒殺解字 co(together)+in(on)+cid(fall)+e → 「一起」「降落」在「上」，表示「同時發生」。相關同源字有 ac**cid**ent (n. 意外)、in**cid**ent (n. 事件)。

---

worthy
[ˋwɝðɪ]

adj. 值得的

The head of the police department said the case <u>was worthy of</u> further investigation.
警察局的主管說這個案件值得進一步的調查。

🪶 秒殺解字 worth(value)+y → 有「價值」的，表示「值得的」。

詞搭 | be worthy of + <u>N / Ving</u> = be worth + <u>N / Ving</u> 值得……

---

embarrassing
[ɪmˋbærəsɪŋ]

adj. 令人尷尬的

It's always embarrassing when we remind others that his or her fly is down.
當我們提醒他人拉鍊沒拉上時，這總是會讓人感到尷尬的。

🪶 秒殺解字 em(=en=into)+bar(bar)+r+ass → 處於被「阻擋」的狀態之「中」。r 重複的理由和 preferred 重複 r 一樣，和 runner 重複 n 的理由一樣，這叫 consonant doubling。相關同源字有 **bar** (v. 阻礙)、**bar**rier. (n. 障礙)。

同義字 | awkward

---

innocence
[ˋɪnəsn̩s]

n. 無罪、清白；純真

📷 101

Peter had a long talk with his lawyer, discussing ways to prove his innocence to the judge in the court.
Peter 跟他的律師談了好久，討論如何在法庭向法官證明他是無辜的。

🪶 秒殺解字 in(not)+noc(harm)+ence → 「沒有」「傷害」，引申出「無罪」、「純真」等意思。

反義字 | guilt

innocent
[`ɪnəsṇt]

adj. 無罪的、清白的

Some of the prisoners were finally proved innocent and were released.
這些囚犯當中，有些最後被證實無罪然後釋放了。

詞搭 be innocent of... 無……之罪；innocent of a crime 無罪的；
an innocent victim 無辜的受害者

同義字 naïve

反義字 guilty

innocently
[`ɪnəsəntlɪ]

adv. 無罪地；純潔地

Though he emphasized that he ran through the red light innocently, the policeman still gave him a ticket.
雖然他強調他闖紅燈是無辜地，警察還是開了他一張罰單。

siege
[sidʒ]

n. 圍攻

The town was under siege for months and finally had to surrender because of a shortage of food and ammunition.
這座城鎮被包圍了數月，由於食物及彈藥軍火短缺，最後必須投降。

普 101

秒殺解字 本義是「座位」（seat），西元 14 世紀，在軍事用法上，產生軍隊在堡壘前安頓「坐」下來的意思，亦即軍隊在堡壘前紮營，準備「圍攻」。

詞搭 lay siege to 圍攻、包圍；end / raise / lift the siege of…停止圍攻……、解……的圍

species
[`spiʃɪz]

n. 物種

Koalas are a protected species in Australia.
無尾熊在澳洲是受到保護的物種。

普 107
警特 106
107
109

秒殺解字 spec(look)+i+es → 藉著所「看」外表呈現的不同樣貌，來區分差異，表示「種類」。

meaningfully
[`minɪŋfʊlɪ]

adv. 意味深長地；有意義地

To reduce oil dependency meaningfully, we should try every possible way to improve the efficiency of our vehicles.
為了能夠真正（有意義地）減少對石油的依賴，我們應該嘗試每一種可能的方式來改善我們交通工具的效率。

秒殺解字 mean+ing+ful+ly → 饒富「意義」地，引申出「意味深長地」的意思。

同義字 significantly

legislator

[ˈlɛdʒɪsˌletə]

n. 立法委員

All legislators of the ruling party hoped to rush through the relief funds bill today.
執政黨的所有立法委員都希望能夠在今天通過紓困基金的法案。

| 同義字 | lawmaker |

legitimate

[lɪˈdʒɪtəmɪt]

adj. 合法的

曾 103
高 110

John said to the judge he's the only man that has a legitimate claim to the inheritance.
John 對法官說他是唯一可以合法要求繼承的人。

秒殺解字 leg(law)+is+lat(=fer=bear)+or → 「帶」來「法律」的「人」，表示「立法委員」。

amendment

[əˈmɛndmənt]

n. 修正；修正案

The opposition party decided to propose some necessary amendments to the bill.
反對黨決定提出對這個法案的一些必要的修正意見。

秒殺解字 a(=ex=out)+mend(fault)+ment → 讓「錯誤」「出去」，表示「修正」。

| 詞搭 | a constitutional amendment 憲法修正案 |
| 同義字 | modification |

slavery

[ˈslevərɪ]

n. 奴隸制度

高 108

It is Abraham Lincoln that abolished slavery in the United States.
美國的奴隸制度是由亞伯拉罕‧林肯廢除的。

秒殺解字 slave+ery → 奴役的「狀態」，引申為「奴隸制度」。

| 詞搭 | be a slave to... 被……所奴役 |

swell

[swɛl]

v. 腫大；膨脹

曾 101

I found my finger quickly swelled up when it was stung by a bee this morning.
我發現我的手指今早被蜜蜂螫過之後馬上就腫起來了。

swell, swelled [swɛld], swollen [ˈswolən] / swelled

swollen

[ˈswolən]

adj. 膨脹的；浮腫的；（河水）漲起的

Staying up too late last night, I now have swollen eyes.
由於昨晚熬夜太晚，現在我的眼睛腫起來了。

秒殺解字 sw- 開頭的單字大多有「搖擺」、「起伏」的意思，相關單字有：**sw**im、**sw**eep、**sw**ift 等。**sw**ell 是「腫脹」，身體部位腫脹如山脈起伏、波浪起伏，突出一塊，特別明顯。

adaptable

[ə`dæptəbl]

adj. 能適應的；可更改的

The soil of this area is quite <u>adaptable</u> to the growth of pineapples.

這個地區的土壤非常適合鳳梨的生長。

> (秒殺解字) ad(to)+apt(fit)+able → 「能」寫成最「合適」的版本，表示「能適應的」、「可更改的」。

同義字	flexible
反義字	inflexible

correspond

[ˌkɔrə`spɑnd]

v. 通信；符合

For the past few months, I've been <u>corresponding with</u> many other professors and experts to discuss this issue.   圖 108

過去幾個月以來，我一直都跟許多教授與專家通信聯絡來討論這個議題。

> (秒殺解字) cor(together)+re(back)+spond(promise) → 本義「答覆彼此」，引申出「一致」的意思，1640 年左右才衍生出「藉由書信溝通」、「通信」的意思。相關同源字有 re**spond** (v. 反應；回答)、re**spons**e (n. 反應；回答)。

詞搭　correspond with + sb. 與某人通信、符合……；correspond to... 相當於……

01 ___ The world's largest math _____ for high school students, International Mathematical Olympiad, will be held in Romania in 2018.

(A) contest   (B) content
(C) condition   (D) conjunction

02 ___ The company's performance has always been _____ since its foundation. However, recently, their sales performance has dropped significantly.

(A) intent   (B) content
(C) consistent   (D) competent

03 ___ We are all equal. There is no tolerance for _____ in this camp. Therefore, you should apologize to him right now.

(A) alienation   (B) delegation
(C) restoration   (D) discrimination

04 ___ Lately, I have received a couple of _____ regarding your attitude against the customers. Everyone needs to pay more respect to our customers and I don't want to get any more complaints like this in the future.

(A) companies   (B) complaints
(C) compliments   (D) comedies

05 ___ The Nobel Prize winner recalled that when he was a child, his father gave him a _____ as his birthday gift. 30 years later, the gift is already gone but his passion for the universe and star is not.

(A) summary   (B) telescope
(C) extract   (D) program

06 ___ The hundred-year-old temple is now protected by the government and labeled as an official cultural _____ site. If anyone tries to damage the temple, they will be punished.

(A) advantage   (B) package
(C) heritage   (D) tragedy

07 ___ After Peter got bitten by a spider, he became extremely _____ to any kinds of danger. Whenever there is an emergency, he will notice it before anyone else does.

(A) receptive
(B) positive
(C) cognitive
(D) sensitive

08 ___ Edward Snowden, an American from the National Security Agency, _____ that the U.S. government has been working with aliens for a long time.

(A) disclosed
(B) refrained
(C) subsidized
(D) devastated

09 ___ It is said that the newly-invented AI will dismiss all kinds of language _____ and help people communicate with foreigners more easily.

(A) barriers
(B) fridges
(C) porcelains
(D) closets

10 ___ Despite their differences, our colleagues still enjoyed a nice holiday together. It was truly a (n) _____!

(A) miracle
(B) obstacle
(C) muscle
(D) inmate

11 ___ This father is charged with _____ his wife and children for two years. They have lived a painful life.

(A) refusing
(B) confusing
(C) abusing
(D) accusing

12 ___ He was a stubborn man. Even up until he was about to pass away, he still _____ that he didn't care about his children. In fact, he loved his children so much that he refused to let them see him cry.

(A) received
(B) extended
(C) succeeded
(D) pretended

13 ___ His quick-witted response to the aggressive question saved him from the _____ situation. After the press conference, he immediately got a promotion from his boss.

(A) frightening   (B) embarrassing
(C) imposing   (D) threatening

14 ___ At the beginning, the suspect claimed that he was _____ and he was framed by the police. However, with the prosecutor bringing more and more evidence out, he finally pleaded guilty.

(A) innocent   (B) inconsistent
(C) incompetent   (D) inefficient

15 ___ The man woke up in the morning and found out that one of his eyes _____ up. He later realized that he was drunk last night and hit a street lamp on his way back home.

(A) declined   (B) swelled
(C) struggled   (D) invested

compensate
[`kampən,set]

v. 補償、彌補

The company will <u>compensate</u> us <u>for</u> the extra effort we made to increase sales.

我們為增進銷售業績格外努力，公司方面為此將給予我們補償。

 秒殺解字 com(together)+pens(weigh, hang, pay)+ate → 「一起」「掛」起來「秤重」，使兩端平衡，表示透過「付錢」讓失去的獲得「補償」，也有「彌補」的意思。相關同源字有 de**pend** (v 依靠)、ex**pend** (v. 花費)、ex**pens**e (n. 費用)、sus**pend** (v. 停止；懸掛)、sus**pens**e. (n. 懸念)、dis**pens**e (v. 分配)。

詞搭 compensate + sb. + for + sth. 補償某人某物；compensate for... 彌補……

compensation
[ˌkampən`seʃən]

n. 補償（不可數）

Yesterday Charlie just received one million dollars <u>in compensation</u> for the car accident injury.　　📖 100

Charlie 昨天剛收到車子意外事故傷害一百萬元金額的補償。

詞搭 in compensation 作補償；<u>claim / demand / seek</u> compensation for + sth. 要求補償某物

同義字 damages

divorce
[də`vɔrs]

n. v. 離婚

Their unhappy marriage tortured them both a lot and finally ended in divorce last month.　　📖 108
　　📖 109

他們不幸福的婚姻已經相當折磨雙方，上個月終於以離婚收場。

The couple next to our house were separated for five years and they both finally agreed to divorce last month.

我們家隔壁的那對夫妻已經分居 5 年，上個月他們雙方終於同意離婚。

 秒殺解字 di(=dis=aside)+vorc(=vert=turn)+e → **vorc** 為 **vert** 變形，**t/s 轉音**，母音通轉；divorce 字面上意思是「轉」身「離開」，最早表示「離開丈夫」，後衍生為「離婚」。

retirement

[rɪ`taɪrmənt]

n. 退休

The normal retirement age in Taiwan is 65.
在台灣一般正常退休年齡是 65 歲。

（秒殺解字）re(back)+tire(drag, draw)+ment → 「拉」「回去」，表示「退休」

---

embrace

[ɪm`bres]

n. 擁抱

v. 擁抱；欣然接受；包含

Though it is a job that involves heavy business travel, he thinks he would like to embrace it.
雖然這是一個需要經常奔波差旅的工作，他認為他會欣然接受。

（秒殺解字）em(=en=in)+brace(arms) → 將人圈在「手臂」「內」。相關同源字有 **brace**（n. 支柱）、**brace**let（n. 手鐲）。

詞搭 in a tender embrace 一個溫柔的擁抱；embrace democratic reforms 接受民主改革

---

reward

[rɪ`wɔrd]

n. 報酬

v. 報答；獎賞

The police offered a large reward for any valuable or critical clues about the murder case.
警方提出巨額懸賞，希望能夠找出有關這個謀殺案件有價值或是重要的線索。

（秒殺解字）re(intensive prefix)+ward(watch) → 仔細「看」過、評估才給「獎賞」。相關同源字有 **ward**（n. 病房）、a**ward**（n. 獎；獎品）。

詞搭 in reward for…作為……的獎賞；give + sb. + sth. + as a reward 給某人某物做報酬；reward + sb. + with + sth. 以某物獎勵某人

---

gaze

[gez]

v. 凝視

I felt quite embarrassed when I found the man sitting opposite me was gazing at me.
當我發現坐在我對面那個男的正在盯著我看時，我感到非常尷尬。

普 104
警特 105

（秒殺解字）可能源自斯堪地那維亞語，和 gawk（v. 呆頭呆腦地看）同源。

同義字 stare

300

relevant
[`rɛləvənt]
adj. 有關的

The teacher emphasized that our discussion should be relevant to the topic he laid down earlier.
老師強調我們的討論應該跟他先前規定的主題相關。

曾 106 108

秒殺解字 re(intensive prefix)+lev(lift, light)+ant → 「提起」重物使負擔變「輕」，本義是「減輕」，引申為「有幫助的」，再衍生出「依賴」的意思，最後才產生出「有關的」的意思。相關同源字有 **lev**er（ n. 槓桿 ）、al**lev**iate（ v. 緩和 ）、e**lev**ate（ v. 提升 ）、re**liev**e（ v. 減輕 ）、re**lief**（ n. 慰藉 ）。

同義字 pertinent

---

irrelevant
[ɪ`rɛləvənt]
adj. 無關的

He made lots of suggestions, but all of them seem irrelevant to the problem we're trying to solve.
他提出了許多意見，但是所有意見跟我們試著想解決的問題似乎毫無關聯。

秒殺解字 ir(=in=not)+relevant → 「無」「關的」。

---

patrol
[pə`trol]
n. **v.** 巡邏

Two security guards and a military working dog will patrol this high-tech factory site during the night.
兩位保全警衛以及一隻軍犬在夜晚時將會巡邏這家高科技廠區。

高 108

秒殺解字 源自法語，本義是「濺泥而行」（paddle about in mud），可能源自 pate（腳），巡邏要用「腳」。

時態 patrol, patrolled, patrolled

詞搭 be on patrol 巡邏中；a patrol <u>car / boat / craft</u> 巡邏車／艇／快艇

---

affirmative
[ə`fɝmətɪv]
n. 肯定詞；肯定語
adj. 肯定的；表示贊成的

You can take my proposal into consideration, but I do hope you give me an affirmative answer next week.
你可以考慮一下我的提議，但是我真的希望下周你給我一個肯定的答案。

曾 106

秒殺解字 af(=ad=to)+firm(firm)+at+ive → 本義「使」「穩固」，引申為「肯定的」、「表示贊成的」。相關同源字有 **firm**（ adj. 堅實的 ）、con**firm**（ v. 確認；證實 ）。

詞搭 answer in the affirmative 肯定的回答

同義字 negative

horror
[ˋhɔrɚ]

n. 恐怖；恐懼

Today the whole world still has to face the threat of famine and the horror of starvation.
時至今日，全世界仍須面對飢荒的威脅以及飢餓的恐懼。

 秒殺解字 horr(tremble, shake)+or → 本義「發抖」，引申為「恐怖」、「恐懼」。可用 **hair** 當神隊友，**母音通轉**，來記憶 **horror**。當人覺得「恐怖」（**horror**）時，常會「毛髮」（**hair**）直豎。

詞搭 | To one's horror,... 嚇壞某人的是……；a horror <u>film / story</u> 恐怖片／故事

同義字 | fear, terror, panic

---

oblige
[əˋblaɪdʒ]

v. 迫使；使負義務；施加恩惠

In Taiwan, the health insurance law obliges employers to pay 60% of premiums for their employees.
在台灣，健保法規規定／責成雇主必須為其員工支付 60% 的健保保費。

圖 108

Though they were divorced, they were obliged to care for their two kids.
雖然離婚了，他們還是有扶養照顧他們兩個小孩的義務。

 秒殺解字 ob(to)+lig(tie, bind)+e → 把人「綁」起來，表示法律或道義上「迫使」你去做。相關同源字有 **leag**ue（n. 聯盟）、re**lig**ion（n. 宗教）。

詞搭 | oblige + sb. + to V 迫使某人……、使某人有義務……；be obliged to + sb. + for + sth. 因某事而感激某人

---

delightfully
[dɪˋlaɪtfəlɪ]

adv. 愉快地；令人喜悅地

This magnificent hotel is delightfully situated overlooking the banks of the River Danube.
這家宏偉的酒店位置宜人，可俯瞰多瑙河河岸。

曾 106

秒殺解字 delight 和 delicious 同源，皆跟「引誘」（entice）有關，美食誘人，美景也同等誘人，「使人愉快」（delight）。

同義字 | pleasantly

delighted

[dɪ`laɪtɪd]

adj. 感到高興的

Of course, I'm quite <u>delighted by / at</u> the good news you bring us.
當然，你帶來的好消息讓我感覺非常欣喜。

Lucy was quite <u>delighted with</u> her new house and her neighbors.
Lucy 對於她的新房以及鄰居感到非常滿意。

---

racist

[`resɪst]

n. 種族主義者
adj. 種族主義的

His racist remarks are theoretically right but practically improper.
他的有關種族主義的言論在理論上是對的，但在實際上卻是不恰當的。

秒殺解字 race+ist →「種族」「主義者」。

詞搭 a racist society 種族主義社會；racist policies 種族歧視的政策

---

intervention

[ˌɪntɚ`vɛnʃən]

n. 干預

Had it not been for the prompt intervention and action of the police, the 3-year-old child might have been kidnapped.
要不是警方迅速介入以及立即行動，這個三歲小孩可能早就被綁架了。

高 108
警特 109

詞搭 <u>military / government</u> intervention 軍事／政府干預

---

intervene

[ˌɪntɚ`vin]

v. 介入、干預（與介詞 in 並用）

I do hope to help you, but it seems that he doesn't want me to intervene in the dispute between you both.
我真的希望能夠幫助你們，但他似乎不想要我介入干涉你們之間的紛爭。

秒殺解字 inter(between)+ven(come)+e →「來」到「中間」，表示「介入」、「干預」。相關同源字有 ad**ven**t (n. 出現)、ad**ven**ture (n. 冒險)、in**ven**t (v. 發明)、pre**ven**t (v. 預防；阻止)、e**ven**t (n. 事件)、con**ven**e (v. 集會)、con**ven**tion (n. 大型會議；習俗)、a**ven**ue (n. 大街)、re**ven**ue (n. 國家稅收)。

---

stimulate

[`stɪmjəˌlet]

v. 刺激；激勵

The President has drawn up a plan to efficiently stimulate the country's economic growth.
總統已經擬定一項可以有效刺激國家經濟成長的計畫。

曾 104

詞搭 stimulate + sb. + to V 激勵某人去從事……

stimulation

[ˌstɪmjəˈleʃən]

n. 刺激

Nowadays, most housewives often complain about a lack of intellectual stimulation when they are at home taking care of their children.

現今許多的家庭主婦常抱怨在家照顧小孩會使她們缺乏智能上的刺激。

普 100

> **秒殺解字** stimul(prick)+ation → stimul 是「刺」，stimulation 表示「刺激」。

---

collapse

[kəˈlæps]

n. **v.** 崩塌

Some old buildings in this area collapsed in last week's earthquake. Fortunately, no deaths were reported.

這個地區有些老舊建築在上週的地震中震垮了，所幸並無死亡事件報導。

普特 107

> **秒殺解字** col(together)+lapse(fall) →「一起」「滑落」。

同義字 fall down

---

strive

[straɪv]

v. 力爭、奮鬥、努力

Though our new products have gained great popularity, the R&D department is still striving to improve their quality.

雖然我們的新產品已經廣受歡迎，研發部門仍然非常努力在改善產品品質。

> **秒殺解字** 本義是「爭吵」(quarrel)，和 strife 同源，14 世紀，才衍生出「努力」的意思。

時態 strive, strove [strov] , striven [ˈstrɪvn̩]

用法 strive + to V 努力要……；strive for + sth. 努力爭取某物

---

presume

[prɪˈzum]

v. 推測；冒昧；佔便宜

I presumed that they wouldn't come to our party, but eventually they did appear.

我原先認定他們不會參加我們的宴會，但他們最後真的出現了。

> **秒殺解字** pre(before)+sum(take)+e → 本義是「事先」「拿」定想法，因此有「假定」的意思。相關同源字有 as**sum**e (v. 認為；假定)、as**sum**ption (n. 認為；假定)、con**sum**e (v. 消耗；消費)、con**sum**ption (n. 消耗；消費)。

同義字 assume

presumably
[prɪ`zuməblɪ]

adv. 據推測；大概；想必

He will presumably go to work by motorcycle before 🔊 108
he can afford a car.
在有能力買車之前，他大概會先騎機車上班吧。

---

interruption
[ˌɪntə`rʌpʃən]

n. 中斷；干擾

To meet the deadline, I spent a whole weekend
working on the project nearly without any
interruption.
為了趕上截止期限，我花了一整個週末時間，幾乎在不受
任何干擾情況下執行了這個計畫。

(秒殺解字) inter(between)+rupt(break)+ion → 介入「其中」，
「打斷」說話或活動程序。可用 **rob** 當神隊友，**b/p 轉音**，
母音通轉，來記憶 **rupt**，表示「打斷」、「打破」、「破
裂」。相關同源字有 **rob**（v. 搶劫）、bank**rupt**（adj. 破產的）、
inter**rupt**（v. 打斷）、cor**rupt**（adj. 貪污的）、dis**rupt**（v.
使中斷）、e**rupt**（v. 爆發）、ab**rupt**（adj. 突然的、意外的）。

---

ritual
[`rɪtʃʊəl]

n. 儀式；例行公事

Having a cup of coffee and a glance of newspaper 🔊 105
headlines are an important part of my morning
ritual.
喝杯咖啡以及瀏覽報紙標題是我每天早上重要例行公事。

(秒殺解字) rit(ritus=reason)+u+al → 源自拉丁語 **ritus**，表示
「宗教儀式」或「習俗」，極可能和 **reason** 同源，**t/z 轉音**，
母音通轉。

詞搭 religious rituals 宗教儀式

同義字 rite

Unit 34

realm

[rɛlm]

n. 領土；（知識、興趣的）範圍

Since high school, Jonathan has shown a great interest <u>in the realm of</u> astronomy.
從中學時代開始，Jonathan 就已經對天文學領域展現高度興趣。

（秒殺解字）realm 源自古法語，表示「統治」的領土範圍，和 regime（n. 政權）、regular（adj. 規律的）、regulation（n. 條例、法規）同源，皆跟「統治」（rule）有關。

詞搭　in the <u>realm /area / field of</u>... 在……的範圍／地區／領域之內

---

quarrel

[`kwɔrəl]

n. **v.** 爭吵

The quarrel between the two of them last night seemed quite fierce, but fortunately, they patched it up this morning.　警特 105
昨晚他們倆個似乎爭吵得蠻厲害的，所幸今天早上已經言歸於好了。

The couple often <u>quarreled over</u> trivia and recently they finally decided to divorce.
這對夫婦經常為小事情爭吵，最近他們終於決定離婚了。

（秒殺解字）quar(complain)+r+el → 喜歡「抱怨」，表示「爭吵」。

同義字　argument

---

genius

[`dʒinjəs]

n. 天份；天才

Mary has shown signs of <u>genius for</u> classical music since elementary school.
Mary 從小學時期開始就顯露出有古典音樂的天分。

（秒殺解字）gen(birth)+i+us → 「天才」是「天生」的。

同義字　talent

複數型　geniuses [`dʒinjəsɪz]

---

gravely

[`grevlɪ]

adv. 嚴肅地；嚴重地

The doctor called Roger and said very gravely to him that he was pessimistic about his mother's health condition.　警 105
醫師打電話給 Roger 並且很嚴肅沉重地告訴 Roger 說他對他母親的健康狀態不表樂觀。

（秒殺解字）grav(heavy)+e+ly → 「重」「地」，表示「嚴肅地」、「嚴重地」。

gravity

[`grævətɪ]

n. 地心引力；嚴重性；正經的樣子

Susan was informed of the gravity of her father's lung cancer by the hospital.
Susan 被醫院通知其父親肺癌的嚴重程度。

高 108
警特 107

gravitation

[ˌgrævə`teʃən]

n. 引力

Newton developed the theory of universal gravitation in 1687.
牛頓在 1687 年發展了萬有引力的定律。

authentic

[ɔ`θɛntɪk]

adj. 真正的

This café is quite famous for serving authentic Italian coffee and pasta.
這家咖啡廳因供應正宗的義大利咖啡及義大利麵而相當著名。

秒殺解字 aut(=auto=self)+hentic(doer, being) → 「自己」「做事的人」，按自己的意願去做事，所以是「真實的」、「真正的」。

同義字 genuine

反義字 fake

prescription

[prɪ`skrɪpʃən]

n. 處方

The doctor said I had to have his prescription filled at the nearest drugstore, or I wouldn't be able to get these drugs.
醫師說我必須將他開立的處方箋拿去最近的一家藥局配藥，否則的話，我是無法買到這些藥的。

普 107

秒殺解字 pre(before)+scrip(write)+t+ion → 醫生會「事先」「寫」下「藥方」。相關同源字有 prescribe（v. 開藥方）describe（v. 描寫）、description（n. 描寫）。

詞搭 write a prescription 開處方；fill a prescription 依處方配藥

clinical

[`klɪnɪkl]

adj. 臨床的

This new drug needs to undergo many clinical trials before being released to the market.
這項新藥在釋出市場開始銷售前，必須經過多次臨床試驗。

高 108

秒殺解字 clin(lean)+ic+al → clinic 本指讓病人「倚靠」的「病床」，病人可躺在病床等待醫生看診，後指「診所」。clinical 是形容詞。

詞搭 clinical trial / training 臨床試驗／訓練

postpone
[pos`pon]
v. 延期；延緩

The baseball game was postponed because of the typhoon.
這場棒球賽因為颱風而被延期。

🖋 秒殺解字 post(after)+pon(put)+e →「放」到「後面」，表示「延期」。

詞搭 postpone + N / Ving = put off + N / Ving 延期……；暫緩……

同義字 delay, put off

---

convenient
[kən`vinjənt]
adj. 方便的

You'll soon find that buses and subways are the most convenient ways of getting around in this city.
你很快就會發現在這個城市各地走動最便利的方式就是搭乘公車以及地鐵。

🖋 秒殺解字 con(together)+ven(come)+i+ent →「一起」到「來」，本義表示「可容納的」、「和諧的」，「便利的」是衍生語意。相關同源字有 advent（n. 出現）、adventure（n. 冒險）、invent（v. 發明）、prevent（v. 預防；阻止）event（n. 事件）、convene（v. 集會）、convention（n. 大型會議；習俗）、avenue（n. 大街）、revenue（n. 國家稅收）。

詞搭 be convenient for + sb. 對某人方便

反義字 inconvenient

普 99
警特 109

---

arbitrary
[`ɑrbə‚trɛrɪ]
adj. 隨心所欲的；武斷的

Did you take it into consideration seriously or was it only an arbitrary decision?
你是認真考慮過了，還是那只是個隨意的決定？

🖋 秒殺解字 arbiter(judge)+ary → 靠自己的觀察來「判斷」，常常過於主觀和「武斷」，arbitrary 有「武斷的」的意思，後來語義產生改變，產生「隨心所欲的」的意思。

詞搭 an arbitrary decision 武斷的決定；in arbitrary order 依任意的順序

高 108

---

condemn
[kən`dɛm]
v. 譴責

The plot of the movie is impressive, but it might be condemned for its sexism and racism.
這部電影情節令人印象深刻，但它可能會因為性別及種族歧視而遭到譴責。

🖋 秒殺解字 con(intensiveprefix)+demn(damage, harm) →「譴責」易造成「傷害」。相關同源字有 damage（n./v. 損害；傷害）、damn（v. 咒罵）。

詞搭 condemn + sb. + for + sth. 譴責某人某事；condemn A as B 譴責 A 為 B

普 100
101
高 110

conductor

[kənˋdʌktɚ]

n. （樂團的）指揮者；
列車長；導體

The conductor raised her baton and all members of the orchestra started to play.
指揮舉起了她的指揮棒，於是所有樂團團員開始演奏。

Today our science teacher told us that metal is a good conductor of heat.
今天我們的科學課程老師告訴我們說金屬是一種非常好的導熱物體。

秒殺解字 con(together)+duc(lead)+t+or →「引導」所有人「一起」做的「人」，表示「指揮者」。相關同源字有 **educ**ate（v. 教育）、pro**duc**e（v. 生產）、pro**duc**tion（n. 生產）、re**duc**e（v. 減少）、re**duc**tion（n. 減少）、intro**duc**e（v. 介紹；引進）、intro**duc**tion（n. 介紹；引進）、in**duc**e（v. 唆使）。

詞搭 bus conductor 公共汽車售票員；a semi-conductor 半導體

symptom

[ˋsɪmptəm]

n. 症狀

I think you have all the symptoms of the flu, so won't you go to see a doctor?
我覺得你有流行性感冒所有徵兆，所以你不去看醫生嗎？

會101
102
104

秒殺解字 sym(=syn=together)+ptom(fall) →「落」在「一起」，語意淡化後，表示「掉落」，後引申為天降疾病，所有疾病皆有其「症狀」。

詞搭 symptom complex 症候群

同義字 indication, sign

punish

[ˋpʌnɪʃ]

v. 懲罰

Anyone smoking on school premises will be punished, and even teachers are no exception.
任何人在學校場域抽菸的話都會受到處罰，即使是教師也不例外。

會103

秒殺解字 pun(punish)+ish → 可用表示「痛」的 **pain** 當神隊友，**母音通轉**，來記憶 **pun**，表示「處罰」。「處罰」通常會給人帶來身體或心理上的「**疼痛**」。相關同源字有 **pen**alty（n. 處罰）。

詞搭 punish + sb. + for... 因……處罰某人

radically

[`rædɪk!ɪ]

adv. 根本地；完全地；激進地

Our new smart phone design is radically different from all our competitors.

我們的新型智慧手機設計與我們所有競爭對手是完全不同的。

🖋️ **秒殺解字** rad(root)+ic+al+ly → 「根」本地，可用 **root** 當神隊友，**d/t 轉音**，母音通轉，來記憶 **rad**，皆表示「根」。

詞搭 a radically different approach 一種完全不同的方法

同義字 fundamentally

---

tornado

[tɔr`nedo]

n. 龍捲風

A tornado hit the small town last night and resulted in some 30 deaths.

昨晚一場龍捲風肆虐這座小城，結果造成大約 30 人死亡。

🖋️ **秒殺解字** tornado 和 thunder (v. 打雷) 同源，**torn**ado 本指夾著強風的大「雷」雨，後語義轉變，指「龍捲風」。

字辨 以下 3 個字均指『颱風』，只是因地而異名。typhoon [taɪ`fun] n. 颱風（發生於西太平洋沿岸的風暴）；hurricane [`hɝɪˌken] n. 颶風（發生於東太平洋或大西洋沿岸的風暴）；cyclone [`saɪklon] n. 氣旋（發生於南太平洋沿岸的風暴）。

同義字 twister

---

negotiation

[nɪˌgoʃɪ`eʃən]

n. 協商

The final details of the contract are still under secret negotiation.

合約最後細節目前仍在祕密協商洽談中。

The negotiation about pay may come to a halt because of the disharmony between the employer and their employees.

由於雇主與其員工的關係不和諧，薪資協商談判可能會終止。

🖋️ **秒殺解字** neg(not)+oti(ease)+ate+ion → 「協商」「不」「輕鬆」。相關同源字有 **ne**cessary（adj. 必要的）、**neg**ative（adj. 負面的）、**neg**lect（v. 忽視）。

同義字 talks, discussion

exploitation

[ˌɛksplɔɪˋteʃən]

n. 剝削行為；開發

Fair trade will help to stop the exploitation of those poor farmers in developing countries.
公平交易將可以協助停止對開發中國家農民的剝削壓榨。

(秒殺解字) ex(out)+ploit(plic=fold)+ate+ion → 由內往「外」「摺」，表示「開發」、「剝削行為」。

詞搭 exploitation right 採礦權；mine exploitation 礦產開發；exploitation of real estate 房地產開發

---

suicide

[ˋsuəˌsaɪd]

n. 自殺

She tried to <u>commit</u> suicide by slashing her wrist, but luckily, we found her just in time and prevented it.
她試圖割腕自殺，但還好我們及時發現她，阻止這件不幸事件發生。

高 108

(秒殺解字) sui(self)+cid(cut, kill)+e → 「殺」「自己」。相關同源字有 de**cid**e (v. 決定)、pesti**cid**e (n. 殺蟲劑)、insecti**cid**e (n. 殺蟲劑)。

詞搭 suicide rate 自殺率；suicide bomber 人體炸彈；suicide attack 自殺式攻擊

---

pitch

[pɪtʃ]

n. 程度；球場；瀝青；音調

v. 投 (球)；紮 (營)；扔擲

The disagreement between them seems to have reached such a high pitch that there will be no hope for a compromise between both sides.
他們的歧見似乎已經大到雙方之間將無妥協希望。

普 110
警特 109

All the factory workers worked at a feverish pitch today because their boss just announced a 20% pay raise.
工廠所有的工人今天工作特別勤奮努力，因為他們的老闆剛剛才宣布加薪百分之二十。

(秒殺解字) pitch 來自兩個不同的字源，一個和「猛推」(thrust)、「丟」(throw) 有關，另一個和「松脂」、「瀝青」有關。

詞搭 perfect pitch 絕對音感；a high-pitched voice 高音

01 ___   After 10 months of investigation, the supreme court finally affirmed that the accident that happened last year was caused by human error. All victims will receive all kinds of _____ from the city government.

(A) gravitations   (B) stimulations

(C) sensations   (D) compensation

02 ___   He was born and raised in Southern California by a singal mother. When he was just 2 years old, his parents _____ and his father left him and his mom.

(A) reduced   (B) produced

(C) divorced   (D) experienced

03 ___   The retired officers all came out on the street to protest against the government, who tried to cut their pension and ruin their _____ plans.

(A) retirement   (B) implement

(C) impairment   (D) supplement

04 ___   The young boy _____ at the bottomless hole and screamed his partner's name. However, no one responded to him except for the howling wind.

(A) organized   (B) gazed

(C) memorized   (D) recognized

05 ___   The police locked down the area and asked every _____ personnel to leave the site immediately because a murder case just happened.

(A) equivalent   (B) irrelevant

(C) dominant   (D) potent

06 ___   The robot was _____ the border when he got attacked by the unknown animal. Judging by the bite marks, it was probably assaulted by a pack of wolves.

(A) neglecting   (B) disputing

(C) patrolling   (D) challenging

07 ___ At first, I thought the tragic news was just a joke. However, after I heard the _____ sound in his voice, I knew he was serious.

(A) affirmative (B) comparative
(C) imaginative (D) innovative

08 ___ During the 60s, a lot of white people in the southern USA were _____. There were even laws against the welfare of black people.

(A) guards (B) pioneers
(C) diplomats (D) racists

09 ___ On the third month of the Arab-Israeli War, the United Nations finally decided to _____ and helped both sides to negotiate the terms of truce.

(A) intervene (B) dread
(C) interpret (D) endanger

10 ___ The professional video gamer illegally injected himself a variety of drugs to_____ his senses and increase his reaction speed.

(A) generate (B) investigate
(C) stimulate (D) motivate

11 ___ The simple verbal _____ between the two neighbors ended up in a standoff with the two men pointing guns at each other. Luckily, no one got hurt that day but they both had to spend a night in the police station.

(A) tenant (B) quarrel
(C) archive (D) revenge

12 ___ In some states of America, medical marijuana is legal as long as you have a _____ from doctor. You can take the prescription to a legal drug store and get the medicine you need.

(A) prescription (B) democratization
(C) combination (D) equation

13 ___ I just got the news that Tony had a car accident on his way to the office. As a result, we have to _____ the meeting until he recovers.

(A) detain (B) allocate
(C) postpone (D) thrill

14 ___ It is extremely_____ and rude of you to just punch the man without even knowing what was happening in the first place.

(A) contrary (B) literary
(C) temporary (D) arbitrary

15 ___ In ancient China, everyone needed to kneel in front of the emperor. If one refused to follow the order, he or she would be_____ because it was considered rude and arrogant to not kneel in front of the king.

(A) pitched (B) banished
(C) deported (D) punished

解答
1.(D) 2.(C) 3.(A) 4.(B) 5.(B) 6.(C) 7.(A) 8.(D) 9.(A) 10.(C) 11.(B) 12.(A) 13.(C) 14.(D) 15.(D)

penalty

[`pɛnḷtɪ]

n. 懲罰；不利；害處

Are you for or against the <u>death</u> <u>penalty</u>?
你是贊成還是反對死刑？

🖊️ 秒殺解字 pen(punish)+al+ty → 可用表示「痛」的 **pain** 當神隊友，**母音通轉**，來記憶 pen，表示「**處罰**」。「處罰」通常會給人帶來身體或心理上的「疼痛」。相關同源字有 **pun**ish（v. 處罰）。

pay the penalty 受到（……的）報應；<u>heavy / severe / stiff penalty</u> 嚴厲處罰

同義字 punishment

🏫 100
101

---

indispensable

[ˌɪndɪ`spɛnsəbḷ]

adj. 不可或缺的

Smart phones seem to have become indispensable devices for modern people.
對現代人而言，智慧手機似乎已成不可或缺的裝置。

🖊️ 秒殺解字 in(not)+dis(out)+pens(hang, weigh, pay)+able → 「不」「能」「掛」「出去」「秤重」。dispensable 表示藉秤重來「分配」的，引申為「可以分配出去的」，表示「非必要的」。indispensable 表示「不」「可以分配出去的」，引申為「必需的」。

詞搭 be indispensable to + <u>sb. / sth.</u> = be essential for + <u>sb. / sth.</u> 對某人／某物是不可或缺的

同義字 essential, necessary

反義字 dispensable, unnecessary

🏫 101

---

reliable

[rɪ`laɪəbḷ]

adj. 可信賴的

My parents hope that I marry a reliable man rather than a handsome guy.
我的父母希望我嫁的是一位可靠的男人而非只是一個帥哥而已。

🖊️ 秒殺解字 re(intensive prefix)+li(=ly=lig=tie)+able → 「可」把大家緊密「綁」在一起，表示「可信賴的」。

詞搭 a reliable source 可靠的來源

同義字 dependable

🏫 100
110
警特 106

messy

[ˋmɛsɪ]

adj. 雜亂的

My boss always says that an organized man won't have a messy office desk.

我的老闆總是說有條有理的人辦公桌是不會亂七八糟的。

> **秒殺解字** mess(=miss, mit=send)+y → 本義是「送」，語意幾經轉變，表示「放置」在桌上一道道的菜餚。後來 mess 又從一道菜餚演變為混在一起的菜餚，字源學家推測「混亂」的意思是從此衍生而來的，而 messy 是形容詞。

同義字	untidy
反義字	tidy, neat

loop

[lup]

n. 圓圈；環

The path that makes a wide loop around the lake is a nice place for walking or jogging.

環湖一大圈的小徑是散步或慢跑的好地方。

> **秒殺解字** 字源不詳，可用 o 的字形來聯想記憶，o 的形狀是「圓」的，含有 o 的單字也大多都跟「圓」有關。相關單字有 round (n. 圓形物)、dome (n. 圓屋頂)、dot (n. 小圓點)、hole (n. 孔、洞)、globe (n. 球體)。

詞搭	be in / out of the loop 在決策圈內／外

loophole

[luphol]

n. 漏洞；換氣孔；射彈孔

If such a loophole in taxation is not found and closed, the local government will lose billions of dollars of revenue each year.

如果如此一個稅務上的漏洞沒被發現以及關閉，地方政府每年將損失十億稅收。

詞搭	a loophole in the law = a legal loophole 法律漏洞；close / plug a tax loophole 堵塞稅收漏洞

exhibition

[ˏɛksəˋbɪʃən]

n. 展覽會

The local museum is staging an exhibition of modern fine rattan furniture.

當地博物館正在策畫一場現代精緻的藤製家具展覽。

> **秒殺解字** ex(out)+hibit(hold)+ion → 把東西「拿」到「外面」「展示」。相關同源字有 prohibit (v. 禁止)、prohibition (n. 禁止)。

詞搭	be on exhibition = be on display 展出中
同義字	display, show

obstacle
[`ɑbstəkl]
n. 障礙

Lack of working experience in the related field may be the biggest challenge and obstacle for me in applying for a new job.
缺乏相關領域工作經驗可能是我在找新工作時最大挑戰以及障礙。

 100
110
警特 105

秒殺解字 ob(before, against)+st(stand)+acle → 「站」在「前面」「反對」。

詞搭 be an <u>obstacle / barrier / hindrance</u> to... 是……的絆腳石、對……是個障礙（物）

同義字 barrier, hindrance, hurdle

flexible
[`flɛksəbl]
adj. 有彈性的

My schedule is flexible, and I think we can meet any time.
我的時間安排很靈活／有彈性，所以我想我們任何時間都可會面。

秒殺解字 flex(bend)+ible(able) → 「可」「彎曲的」，表示「有彈性的」。

同義字 adaptable

反義字 inflexible

comprehensive
[ˌkɑmprɪ`hɛnsɪv]
adj. 廣泛的；詳盡的；全面的

Ten minutes ago, the manager called to make sure if the data set I provided was comprehensive.
十分鐘前，經理打電話來確認我所提供資料是否完整無缺。

秒殺解字 com(together)+prehend(seize, take) → 學習時完全「抓」「一起」，表示「了解」。可用 **get** 當神隊友，**g/h 轉音**，來記憶 prehend 的 **hend**，兩者都和「抓」有關。

詞搭 a comprehensive <u>review / guide / study / survey</u> 綜合評論／指南／研究／調查；comprehensive insurance 保險全險

同義字 thorough, complete

comprehend
[ˌkɑmprɪ`hɛnd]
v. 了解

Mary's parents couldn't comprehend why she would want to divorce.
Mary 的父母無法理解為何她會想要離婚。

同義字 understand, grasp

contemplate

[ˋkɑntəmˏplet]

v. 考慮、仔細思考

Feeling a lack of motivation and bored with my current job, I'm contemplating applying for a one-year Australian working holiday visa.
由於感到目前工作很沉悶也沒有甚麼動力，所以我打算申請澳洲打工度假一年的簽證。

> **秒殺解字** com(intensive prefix)+templ(temple)+ate → contemplate 跟「廟宇」(temple) 有關，廟宇是供人們「靜坐冥想」和占卜之所，後來 contemplate 宗教色彩淡化，表示「考慮」、「仔細思考」。

詞搭 contemplate + N / Ving

同義字 consider

panic

[ˋpænɪk]

n. **v.** 驚恐
adj. 恐慌的

Juliana was in a panic about this afternoon's interview.
Juliana 對於今天下午的面試感到害怕。

The gunshot at midnight panicked the whole village.
半夜槍響聲使得整個村莊驚慌不已。

> **秒殺解字** panic 源自希臘神話中的牧羊神「潘恩」(Pan)。Pan 常常躲在隱蔽處，常突然跳出，用醜陋的面目將旅行者嚇得魂不附體。他還會發出神秘怪異的叫聲，引起牧群、人群恐慌，這種恐慌具有傳染力、毫無來由，這種恐懼感稱為「潘神之懼」（ Panic fear ）。

時態 panic, panicked [ˋpænɪkt], panicked (動名詞及現在分詞為 panicking [ˋpænɪkɪŋ])

詞搭 get into a panic 陷於驚惶中；panic reaction 異常的反應；a panic run on a bank 向銀行恐慌的擠兌；panic buying / selling 狂買／狂賣

同義字 fear, terror, horror

318

chemistry

[ˋkɛmɪstrɪ]

n. 化學

My sister majored in chemistry at college and became a high school teacher soon after graduation.

我姊姊大學主修化學，畢業後馬上就當上中學老師。

圖 108

秒殺解字 chemist+ry → chemistry 是由「化學家」和表「狀態」的 ry 字尾所組成的。

詞搭 applied chemistry 應用化學；organic / inorganic chemistry 有機／無機化學

---

denounce

[dɪˋnauns]

v. 公然譴責；告發

All the parents denounced the kindergarten publicly for abusing their children.

所有的家長公開譴責這家幼兒園虐待他們的小孩。

會 103

秒殺解字 de(down)+nounc(shout)+e → 對著「下方」「喊叫」，引申為「公然譴責」。相關同源字有 announce（v. 宣布）、pronounce（v. 發音；宣稱）、pronunciation（n. 發音）。

片語 denounce A as B 譴責 A 為 B；denounce A to B 向 B 告發 A

同義字 condemn

---

venture

[ˋvɛntʃɚ]

n. 投機事業；冒險
v. （使）冒險

After the general election, more international companies decided to increase investment in Taiwan and form joint ventures.

大選之後愈來愈多的國際企業決定增加對台灣的投資以建立合資事業。

警特 108

All the villagers admired William because yesterday, he ventured out of the village to start his life in the big city.

村民們都很羨慕 William，因為昨天他冒險走出村子，在大城市開始了自己的生活。

秒殺解字 ven(come)+t+ure → venture 是「到來」，表示「冒險」。venture 源自 adventure，通常指商業上的冒險、投資。相關同源字有 advent（n. 出現）、adventure（n. 冒險）、invent（v. 發明）、prevent（v. 預防；阻止）、event（n. 事件）、convene（v. 集會）、convention（n. 大型會議；習俗）、avenue（n. 大街）、revenue（n. 國家稅收）。

詞搭 a joint venture 合資事業；business / commercial venture 商業風險投資

enlarge
[ɪn`lardʒ]
v. 放大；詳述

The dormitory should be enlarged to accommodate more new students.
宿舍必須擴大以容納更多新生。

> **秒殺解字** en(make)+large → 「使」變「大」。

詞搭 enlarge on / upon... 詳述……；enlarge vocabulary 增加單詞量

同義字 blow up

---

stamp
[stæmp]
n. 郵票；印章
v. 蓋章；貼郵票；跺（腳）

The immigration officer will stamp your passport on your departure and arrival.
出入境時，移民局官員會在你的護照上蓋上戳印。

Quarreling with her mother, Mary stamped her foot and rushed back to her own room.
Mary 跟她媽媽吵架之後，她腳一跺就衝回自己房間了。

> **秒殺解字** 古義表示「在臼中擊打」，14 世紀時衍生出「用腳重踩」，因此有「跺腳」的意思，後來甚至衍生出「蓋章」的意思，因為蓋章需要大力壓。

詞搭 stamp the floor 踏響地板；stamp a letter 在信件上貼郵票；collect stamps 收集郵票

---

sovereignty
[`savrɪntɪ]
n. 君權；統治權；主權

All the three neighboring countries claimed sovereignty over that very small island.
三個鄰近國家都宣稱他們對那座非常小的島嶼擁有主權。

> **秒殺解字** sove(=sover=super)+reign+ty → sovereignty 源自古法語，sover 是 super，「超過」(over) 的意思；reign 的拼字是受「民俗詞源」(folk etymology) 影響而導致的錯誤拼法，reign 是「統治」的意思；ty 是名詞字尾。

---

prioritize
[praɪ`ɔrəˌtaɪz]
v. 按優先順序處理；給予……優先權

I know you're quite annoyed because you have a lot of work to do, but I think you should prioritize it.
我知道你今天因為有好多工作要做而感到很煩，但我認為你應該先確定事情的輕重緩急。

> **秒殺解字** priority+ize → pri 是「在……之前」，priority 擺在前面要先做的事情，指「優先事項」，而 prioritize 是「按優先順序處理」。

spontaneous

[spɑn`tenɪəs]

adj. 自發的；不由自主的；即席的

Juan's speech seemed spontaneous, but he had actually been preparing for it for a couple of days.
Juan 的演講看起來好像很即興自然，但實際上他早就已經準備好幾天了。

> **（秒殺解字）** spontaneous 源自拉丁文，表示「出自於自己的原因」（of one's own accord），因此有「自發的」、「不由自主的」等意思。

詞搭 a spontaneous action 自發的行動

spontaneously

[spɑn`tenɪəslɪ]

adv. 自然地；自發地

Early in the morning I found many neighbors working together spontaneously to shovel the snow on the road.
一大早我就發現許多鄰居自動自發地同心協力把路上積雪剷除。

sole

[sol]

adj. 單獨的、唯一的

His company was appointed the sole agent in Taiwan for the world's most famous lubricant.
他的公司被指派成為全世界最有名的機油在台灣的獨家代理商。

> **（秒殺解字）** sole 表示「單獨的」，衍生出一系列的同源字，如：**sol**itary（adj. 孤獨的）、**sol**itude（n. 孤獨）、**sol**o（n. 獨唱）、de**sol**ate（adj. 荒涼的）。

詞搭 the sole survivor / heir 唯一倖存者／繼承者

同義字 only

optimism
[`ɑptə͵mɪzəm]
n. 樂觀主義

They have cautious optimism for substantial growth in next year's sales performance. 高 108
他們對明年銷售表現即將有實質成長表示審慎樂觀。

秒殺解字 optim(best)+ism → 「最佳的」「主義」，表示「樂觀主義」。

詞搭 optimism about + N 對…的樂觀；cautious optimism 審慎樂觀；grounds / cause / reason for optimism 樂觀的理由

反義字 pessimism

optimistic
[͵ɑptə`mɪstɪk]
adj. 樂觀的

She's quite optimistic about her chances of winning the job offer, though there were many competitors. 普 102
雖然競爭對手真的很多，但她對於能夠贏得這個工作的機會相當樂觀。

詞搭 an optimistic estimate 樂觀的估計

反義字 pessimistic

reluctant
[rɪ`lʌktənt]
adj. 勉強的

All the kids had such a good time at Sea World that they were reluctant to leave. 警特 105
所有小孩在海洋世界都玩得如此開心以至於他們都心不甘情不願離場。

秒殺解字 re(against)+luct(struggle)+ant → 「奮力」「反抗」的。

詞搭 be reluctant + to V = be unwilling + to V 不願意從事……

同義字 unwilling

反義字 willing

illuminate
[ɪ`lumə͵net]
v. 照亮；闡明；啟發

Christmas is coming and all the streets in the neighborhood are decorated and illuminated with brilliant colored lights. 普 100 / 警特 109
聖誕節馬上到來，因此附近所有的街道都被鮮豔彩燈裝飾照亮著。

秒殺解字 il(in)+lumin(light)+ate → 在「裡面」「照光」，表示「照亮」、「闡明」、「啟發」。

詞搭 illuminate the / one's mind 啟發心智

同義字 light up

deliberate

[dɪˋlɪbəret]

v. 仔細考慮

[dɪˋlɪbərɪt]

adj. 謹慎的;故意的

It took us a whole day to <u>deliberate (on)</u> this important issue.
這個重要議題化了我們一整天時間審慎考慮。

🖋 秒殺解字 de(completely)+liber(=libra=level, balance)+ate → 「仔細考慮」各種可能情況,在各個層面「完全」取得「平衡」。

詞搭 deliberate <u>on / upon / about / over</u> + sth. 深思熟慮某事;take deliberate action 採取審慎的行動;a deliberate <u>lie / insult / attempt</u> 故意的謊言/侮辱/企圖;deliberate murder 蓄意謀殺

同義字 intentional

反義字 unintentional

ambiguously

[æmˋbɪgjʊəslɪ]

adv. 含糊不清地模稜兩可地

Your questions should be addressed more clearly. If you make them ambiguously, you won't get satisfactory answers.   🔊108
你的問題應該更清楚地陳述。如果你模稜兩可含糊不清,你將不會得到滿意答案。

🖋 秒殺解字 amb(=ambi=around, both)+ig(=ag=drive)+u+ous+ly → 整天「到處」「開車」「浪流連」(**wander**, **go about**, **go around**),就像一個浪子永遠不知道要回頭,不知道人生目的是什麼,引申為「含糊不清地」、「模稜兩可地」。

同義字 vaguely, unclearly

反義字 unambiguously, clearly

syndrome

[ˋsɪn͵drom]

n. 症候群

The irritable bowel syndrome vexes Alan so much that he has to visit the toliet very often each day.   🔊105
腸躁症候群讓 Alan 很苦惱,因此他每天都要一直跑廁所。

🖋 秒殺解字 syn(together)+drome(run) → 字面的意思是「一起」「跑」,曾經指「道路匯集之處」,1540 年代才有「併發症」、「症候群」的衍生語意。

詞搭 Acquired Immune Deficiency Syndrome 愛滋病

naive

[naˋiv]

adj. 天真的

Juliet was very naive and stupid to believe Peter would stay with her forever.
Juliet 非常天真,也非常笨,她居然相信 Peter 會跟她天長地久在一起。

🖋 秒殺解字 na(=nat=birth, born)+ive → 與「誕生」有關的,人「出生」的時候,本性都是「天真無邪的」。native 與 naive 是「雙飾詞」(**doublet**),都是源自拉丁語,再經由法語於 1654 年借入英語。

詞搭 it is naive to <u>think / suppose / assume</u> that + S + V... 天真認為……

同義字 innocent

peasant

[`pɛzn̩t]

n. 佃農

All the produce found in the castle was grown by local peasants.
城堡裡發現的所有農產品都是由本地農民所栽種的。

🪶(秒殺解字) peas(country)+ant(ing) → 本義是「住在鄉村地區的」，後指住在鄉下從事農事工作的「佃農」。

字辨 | farmer [`fɑrmɚ] n. (有自己田地，較為有錢的) 農夫

---

misery

[`mɪzərɪ]

n. 悲慘、不幸；痛苦；窮困

醫 102

Their final decision to get a divorce was a wise one because ten years of marriage was just a torture and misery for the couple.
他們最後決定要離婚是明智的，因為十年的婚姻對他們兩者來說只是一場折磨跟悲淒而已。

🪶(秒殺解字) miser(wretched)+y → 悲慘。

詞搭 | the miseries of life / war 人生／戰爭的苦難；put...out of its / one's misery 使⋯⋯解脫苦難；abject misery 極度痛苦

同義字 | grief

---

conceal

[kən`sil]

v. 隱藏

醫 99
　　100
警特 108
　　109

I'm not sure who did it, but I know someone concealed the crucial evidence about the case.
我不確定是誰幹的，但我知道有人隱瞞這個案件的關鍵證據。

🪶(秒殺解字) con(intensive prefix)+ceal(cover, hide) → 把事實或感覺「隱蔽」起來。

詞搭 | conceal + sth. + from + sb. 不讓某人知道某事；a concealed weapon 藏匿的武器

同義字 | hide

反義字 | reveal , disclose, spill the beans

---

tempt

[tɛmpt]

v. 引誘

It is said that credit cards often tempt people into buying things that are not really necessary.
聽說信用卡常常會誘惑人去買一些實際上並不是真正需要的東西。

🪶(秒殺解字) tempt(try) →「嘗試」，人們較願意嘗試誘人的事物，因此衍生出「誘惑」的意思。相關同源字有 attempt (v./n. 企圖)。

詞搭 | tempt + sb. + to V = tempt + sb. + into + Ving 引誘某人做某事

同義字 | seduce

temptation

[ˌtɛmpˋteʃən]

n. 誘惑

To all the students, their smartphones, which were locked in the teacher's drawer, were a strong temptation.

對所有的學生而言，鎖在老師抽屜裡的手機是種強烈的誘惑，不時在與他們的良心交戰。

曾 100

| 詞搭 | give away to temptation 屈服於誘惑 |

---

supplement

[ˋsʌpləmənt] /

[ˋsʌpləˌmɛnt]

n. 補充物；增刊

v. 補充

The doctor advised the pregnant woman that she should take vitamin supplements every day.

醫師建議那位孕婦應該每天服用維他命補充營養。

Cathy supplements her daughter's diet with eggs and fruit every day after her surgery due to the serious car accident.

Cathy 在她女兒嚴重車禍的手術後，每天以雞蛋和水果來補充她的飲食。

秒殺解字 sup(=sub=up from under)+ple(fill)+ment → 從「下」往上「填滿」，表示「補充」。

| 詞搭 | dietary / nutritional supplement 膳食補充劑／營養保健品 |

---

adaptation

[ˌædæpˋteʃən]

n. 適應；改編

Corrine came to the company for just one week, but she made a quick adaptation to the new working environment.

Corrine 來到這家公司才一個禮拜，但她很快就適應了新的工作環境。

曾 100

秒殺解字 ad(to)+apt(fit)+ation → 寫成最「合適」的版本，表示「適應」、「改編」。

---

suspicious

[səˋspɪʃəs]

adj. 可疑的；多疑的、猜疑的

I must say that I'm highly suspicious of his motivation.

我必須說我對他的動機表示高度懷疑。

曾 105
110

秒殺解字 sus(=sub=upfrom under)+spic(look)+i+ous → 從「下」往上偷偷「看」別人，引申為「猜疑的」。

| 詞搭 | be suspicious of / about... 懷疑…… |
| 同義字 | shady, wary |

suspiciousness
[sə`spɪʃəsnɪs]
n. 懷疑；可疑

The current situation will inevitably provoke suspiciousness among these cooperative institutions.
目前的局勢無可避免地將招致這些合作機構之間的猜忌。

普 102

---

posture
[`pɑstʃɚ]
n. 姿勢；立場態度
v. 擺姿勢

Samantha attended a beauty contest before and it is no wonder she has good posture.
Samantha 從前參加過選美比賽，所以難怪她儀態優雅。

普 101
104
警特 105

秒殺解字 pos(put)+ture → 將動作「放」在某一點，即「擺姿勢」。

詞搭 adopt a ... posture towards... 對⋯⋯採取⋯⋯立場

---

cooperate
[ko`ɑpəˌret]
v. 合作

When the two companies signed the contract, they both agreed that this was the best chance to cooperate with each other.
這兩家公司在簽約時，他們雙方都同意此時為合作最佳契機。

普 101

秒殺解字 co(together)+oper(work)+ate → 「一起」「工作」，引申為「合作」。

詞搭 cooperate with / in / on... 和 / 在⋯⋯合作

同義字 collaborate, work together

---

catalog
[`kætḷˌɔg]
n. 型錄 (= catalogue)

The newest catalog(ue) is available and will be mailed free upon request.
最新型錄業已發行，如蒙索閱，將免費寄送。

秒殺解字 cata(down, completely)+log(speak) → 一路「完整地」「說」「下來」，意指「清單」、「目錄」。相關同源字有 dia**log**（n. 對話）、**log**o（n. 標識）、ana**log**y（n. 類推）。

詞搭 catalogue of mistakes / crimes / cruelty 接二連三的錯誤／犯罪／暴行

字辨 the table of contents 書中的目錄

terminate

[ˈtɝməˌnet]

v. 終止、終結

They say they'll terminate my employment contract next month. I think I'll soon have to find a new job.

他們說將在下個月終止我的工作契約。我想我該馬上去找新工作了。

🔑 **秒殺解字** termin(end)+ate → 表示「終止」。相關同源字有 de**termin**e（v. 決定）、ex**termin**ate（v. 滅絕）。

詞搭 terminate a <u>contract / pregnancy / the cooperation</u> 終止合約／懷孕／合作

同義字 end

soberly

[ˈsobɚlɪ]

adv. 嚴肅地；冷靜地

During the funeral, all the widow's relatives and friends nodded at her soberly without saying anything.

在喪禮中，寡婦的所有親戚跟朋友都嚴肅地向她點頭致意，甚麼話都沒說。

🔑 **秒殺解字** so(=se=without)+ober(drunk)+ly → 「沒有」「酒醉的」，表示「嚴肅地」、「冷靜地」。

同義字 seriously

astronomical

[ˌæstrəˈnɑmɪkl]

adj. 天文學（上）的；龐大的

The company will have to pay an astronomical price for terminating the contract.

這家公司將必須對終止契約付出天價。

🔑 **秒殺解字** astro(star)+nom(law)+ic+al → 探究「星星」運行「定律」的學問有關，表示「天文學（上）的」，天上繁星數量繁多，令人目不暇給，引申為「龐大的」。

詞搭 an astronomical observatory 天文觀測台

01 ___ This year's debate revolves around the hot topic of the death _____. Both sides will focus on their own perspectives to try to convince the judges whether the death penalty should exist or not.

(A) society   (B) community
(C) penalty   (D) majority

02 ___ Water is _____ to all lives on earth. According to science, there is no life that can exist without water.

(A) memorable   (B) respectable
(C) indispensable   (D) available

03 ___ According to _____ sources, NBA star Rudy Gobert was diagnosed with coronavirus and the NBA is going to postpone the season.

(A) reliable   (B) adaptable
(C) remarkable   (D) comparable

04 ___ The best way to surmount any kinds of _____ is to trust yourself. If you truly believe that you can achieve something, your body and mind will coordinate together to help you reach the goal.

(A) rewards   (B) obstacles
(C) rituals   (D) miracles

05 ___ One of the best benefits of our company is that you can choose which day and what time you want to clock in to work. We give our employees a (n)_____ working schedule as long as they can get things done.

(A) vulnerable   (B) flexible
(C) indispensable   (D) flexible

06 ___ Many people were in a (n) _____ when they first learned about the horrible news. The police department had to work overtime to keep everyone under control.

(A) deposit   (B) asset
(C) panic   (D) remedy

07 ___ The _____ in the team is better than ever after they defeated the enemy team in the semi-final game. Now, the team is ready to take on another challenge and win it all this time.

(A) chemistry   (B) ministry
(C) ancestry   (D) industry

08 ___ If anything bad happens, the search and rescue team will _____ saving the women and children. Men are usually more physically superior to women and children, so they will have to wait longer to be rescued.

(A) sympathize   (B) revolutionize
(C) localize   (D) prioritize

09 ___ The _____ survivor of the accident lost his right arm, but he was grateful that he got out of the accident alive. The rest of his teammates all passed away in the terrifying car crash.

(A) cultural   (B) sole
(C) practical   (D) gradual

10 ___ The YouTuber is famous for his _____ mindset. No matter what happens, he will always face it with a positive attitude.

(A) optimistic   (B) artistic
(C) romantic   (D) specific

11 ___ Some students in the class were _____ to do their homework and were punished by their teacher. Still, they refused to cooperate with the teacher after being punished.

(A) reluctant   (B) unpleasant
(C) ignorant   (D) significant

12 ___ The local guide lighted several torches to_____ the road ahead. With the cave getting brighter, the expedition team finally witnessed the magnificent view of the million-year-old cave.

(A) illustrate   (B) estimate
(C) associate   (D) illuminate

13 ___ One of the deadliest diseases, AIDS (Acquired Immune Deficiency
_____), kills almost 1 million of people around the world each year.

(A) Statement
(B) Society
(C) Syndrome
(D) System

14 ___ The hunter calmly aimed his bow at the deer and precisely shot the
deer to immobilize it. Then, he went up to the prey and ended its
_____ with a clean stab to the heart.

(A) discovery
(B) military
(C) industry
(D) misery

15 ___ In some States of America, citizens are allowed to carry _____
firearms with them when they are out in the public, but they will have
to acquire some licenses before doing so.

(A) concealed
(B) connected
(C) revealed
(D) affected

depict
[dɪ`pɪkt]
v. 描述、描繪

The novel <u>depicts</u> the emperor <u>as</u> a rather cruel and merciless ruler.
這部小說把這個皇帝描寫成相當冷酷無情的統治者。

秒殺解字 de(down)+pic(paint)+t → 「畫」「下來」是「描繪」。相關同源字有 **pic**ture (n. 圖畫)、**paint** (v. 繪畫)。

詞搭 | depict A as B = describe A as B = portray A as B 將 A 描述為 B

同義字 | describe, portray

continental
[ˌkɑntə`nɛntl̩]
adj. 洲的；大陸的

The company is trying to expand its business into continental Europe.
這家公司正式的將事業版圖拓展到歐洲大陸。

秒殺解字 con(together)+tin(hold)+ent+al → 本義「握」住放在「一起」，使之「連續」不斷。continent 可用 continue 來輔助記憶，表示「連綿」不絕的土地，continental 是形容詞。

seemingly
[`simɪŋlɪ]
adv. 表面上

He remains vigorous and seemingly untroubled by the recent rumor about his affairs. 曾 103
他依然充滿活力，似乎不受最近的誹聞謠言所困擾。

秒殺解字 seeming+ly → 「表面上」「地」。

詞搭 | two seemingly unrelated events 兩個表面上無關的事件

同義字 | apparently

pregnancy
[`prɛgnənsɪ]
n. 懷孕

I remember my wife didn't have a good appetite during her first month of pregnancy. 曾 102
我記得我太太在懷孕第一個月食慾很不好。

秒殺解字 pre(before)+gn(birth)+ancy → 「誕生」「前」，表示「懷孕」。**gn** 視為零級字（zero grade），**gen** 是 e 級字（e grade），**gon**orrhea 是 o 級字（o gade），這是拉丁文中母音變化的典型例子。

詞搭 | a pregnancy test 驗孕、妊娠化驗；teenage pregnancies 少女懷孕

rage

[redʒ]

n. 憤怒;狂熱

v. 發怒;肆虐

Knowing her son cut class this morning, Mrs. Wang is now on the way to the school in a steaming rage.

得知兒子早上翹課,王太太怒氣沖沖,現在正在前往學校途中。

曾 103 104

🖋 **秒殺解字** 學者發現發 r 的音時,需牽動 18 條肌肉,舌微捲,費力較大。因此含有 r 的單字,通常表示「發出濁重隆隆聲的動作」,相關單字有 **rail**(v. 怒斥、譴責)、**roar**(v. 怒吼、咆哮)、**rumble**(v. 發出隆隆聲)、**rate**(v. 怒斥)等。

詞搭 be all the rage 大為流行;fly into a rage 勃然大怒;
rage <u>at / against</u>... 怒斥,對……大發雷霆

同義字 anger, fury

---

vulnerable

[`vʌlnərəbl]

adj. 脆弱的、(生理或心理)易受傷的;有弱點的

The Achilles tendon is the most vulnerable part in the heel.

阿基里斯腱是腳跟最脆弱的部分。

🖋 **秒殺解字** vulner(wound)+able → 易「受傷」的。

詞搭 be vulnerable to + sth. 易受某事物的攻擊或傷害;
a vulnerable <u>point / position</u> 易受攻擊的地點/位置

同義字 defenseless

---

conspiracy

[kən`spɪrəsɪ]

n. 陰謀

I was quite surprised the policeman <u>was charged with</u> conspiracy to commit murder.

我很驚訝這位警察被指控策畫謀殺。

🖋 **秒殺解字** con(together)+spir(breathe)+acy →「同」一鼻孔出「氣」,表示「同謀」,去做非法、不好的事。相關同源字有 **spir**it(n. 精神)、in**spir**e(v. 激勵)、a**spir**e(v. 渴望)、per**spir**e(v. 流汗)、re**spir**e(v. 呼吸)。

詞搭 a conspiracy of silence 緘默協定

offer

[`ɔfɚ]

n. 提議

v. 提供；主動提議

It's really a very nice job offer and I won't turn it down.

這真是一個非常好的工作機會，所以我不會錯過的。

The boss is kind enough to <u>offer</u> free lunch <u>to</u> all his clerks.

這位老闆還相當仁慈，他為他所有職員提供免費午餐。

秒殺解字 of(=ob=to)+fer(bear) →「帶」「往」，引申為「提供」。可用 **bear** 當神隊友，**b/f 轉音**，**母音通轉**，來記憶 **fer**，表示「攜帶」、「生育」、「承受」。相關同源字有 dif**fer**（v. 不同）、in**fer**（v. 推論）、pre**fer**（v. 寧願）、suf**fer**（v. 受苦）、re**fer**（v. 提到）、trans**fer**（v. 轉移）、con**fer**ence（n. 正式會議）。

詞搭 offer + sb. + sth. = offer + sth. + to + sb.　提供某人某物

同義字 provide, supply

extract

[`ɛkstrækt] /

[ɪk`strækt]

n. 萃取物；精華

v. 提煉；摘錄；獲取（情報、錢）

The oil <u>extracted from</u> olives is excellent for pasta cuisine.　📷 101

這種由橄欖萃取壓榨的油非常適合烹調義大利麵食。

秒殺解字 ex(out)+trac(drag, draw) +t →「拉」「出去」，表示「提煉」、「摘錄」。可用 **drag** 當神隊友，**d/t**，**g/k 轉音**，**母音通轉**，來記憶 **trac**。相關同源字有 at**trac**t（v. 吸引）、dis**trac**t（v. 使分心）、abs**trac**t（adj. 抽象的）、con**trac**t（n. 契約）、re**trac**t（v. 撤回）、sub**trac**t（v. 減去）、sub**trac**t（v. 減去）。

詞搭 extract A from B 從 B 提煉／摘錄 A

bulk

[bʌlk]

n. 大部分；大量

Things will become much cheaper if you buy them <u>in bulk</u>.

如果你成批大量購買東西就會變得便宜很多。

秒殺解字 發 b 的音時，雙唇緊閉，將氣流阻塞於口中，雙頰微微鼓起，因此有些含有 b 這個音的單字，會有「鼓脹」的意思，相關單字有 **b**all（n. 球）、**b**alloon（n. 氣球）、**b**ulge（v. 鼓脹）、**b**ulk（v. 使膨脹）等。

詞搭 bulk order 大宗訂單；bulk purchase 大批採購

patronage
[ˋpætrənɪdʒ]

n. 光顧、惠顧；贊助、資助

We welcome your patronage and will try our best to provide the best service.
歡迎光臨惠顧，我們也將竭盡所能提供最佳服務。

秒殺解字 patr(out)+on+age → patorn 本像指「父親」般的「保護者」，給予支持、資助。而 patronage 是指「顧客的光顧」給予店家支持。可用 **father** 當神隊友，**p/f**，**t/ð 轉音**，母音**通轉**，來記憶 **patr**，表示「父親」。

詞搭 thanks for patronage 銘謝惠顧； under the patronage of… 在……的贊助下

patronize
[ˋpetrəˌnaɪz]

v. 瞧不起；光顧；資助（patronise [英]）

The restaurant, formerly the mayor's mansion, is patronized by tourists from around the world.
這家餐廳先前是市長官邸，現在經常有來自全世界的觀光客前來光顧。

furious
[ˋfjʊrɪəs]

adj. 憤怒的、怒不可抑的

警特 107

Cathy's boyfriend was a little late for the date and she <u>was</u> quite <u>furious</u> <u>about</u> it.
Cathy 的男朋友約會稍微遲到一點，她為了這件事大發脾氣。

秒殺解字 發 f 的音時，是上排牙齒咬住下面嘴唇所發出的摩擦音，摩擦會生熱，因此含有 f 的單字，多跟「熱」有關。相關單字有 fire（n. 火）、fiery（adj. 火的）、fervor（n. 熱心）、fever（n. 發燒）、fervent（adj. 熱心的）。

詞搭 be <u>furious / angry</u> <u>about /at</u>... 對…感到極為憤怒；furious <u>debate / argument</u> 激烈的爭論

同義字 angry

fury
[ˋfjʊrɪ]

n. 震怒、暴怒

Christine flew into a fury when she found out that her boyfriend dated another girl.
當 Christine 得知男朋友跟另外一個女生約會時她勃然大怒。

片語 To one's fury,... 令某人憤怒的是，…；in a fury 盛怒之下

同義字 anger , rage

global
[`globḷ]
adj. 全球的、全世界的

If nothing is done about global warming, catastrophes of many kinds will soon arise.
如果我們對全球暖化的問題沒有任何作為的話，各種災難即將發生。

🪶 **秒殺解字** globe+al → 全「球」的。

詞搭 | global economy / politics 全球經濟／政治

104
105
106
107

diplomacy
[dɪ`ploməsɪ]
n. 外交；交際手腕

I don't think diplomacy will be able to settle the dispute between the two nations.
我不認為外交手段可以解決這兩個國家之間的紛爭。

🪶 **秒殺解字** di(two)+ple(fold)+o+ma+cy → diploma 本義是「對摺」成「兩半」的信件，後指「文憑」、「公文」，拉丁中的 diplomaticus 一字出現在國際條約「公文」標題上，diplomacy 的「外交」語意是從此處衍生出來的。

詞搭 | international diplomacy 國際外交

diplomat
[`dɪpləmæt]
n. 外交官

The Foreign Ministry says that more outstanding diplomats are needed to help deal with international relations and affairs.
外交部説需要更多頂尖外交官來協助處理國際關係事務。

詞搭 | career diplomat 職業外交官

diplomatic
[ˌdɪplə`mætɪk]
adj. 外交的；説話圓滑的

Christopher joined the diplomatic service soon after his graduation from college.
Christopher 大學畢業沒多久就進入外交部門服務了。

詞搭 | establish / break off diplomatic relations/ties 建立／斷絕外交關係

marketing
[`mɑrkɪtɪŋ]
n. 銷售；經銷

The manager asked me to devise a more effective marketing strategy for our new products.
經理要求我為我們新的產品制定一個更有效的行銷策略。

🪶 **秒殺解字** market+ing → market 名詞意思是「市場」，動詞是「推銷」，marketing 是行銷的「名詞」。

詞搭 | marketing network / management 行銷網絡／管理； a career in sales and marketing 市場營銷工作

marketable

[`mɑrkɪtəbl]

adj. 可賣的、適合在市場出售的

I believe our newly-designed tablet will soon become a highly <u>marketable product</u>.

我相信我們新設計的平板電腦即將成為非常暢銷的產品。

---

criminal

[`krɪmənl]

n. 罪犯

adj. 犯法的；刑法方面的

The police arrived and arrested the criminal, telling him that he had the right to remain silent.

警察抵達並逮捕罪犯，同時告訴他有權力保持緘默。

曾 99 107
警特 105 106

A criminal investigation is being conducted in order to find out as soon as possible who the murderer was.

刑事調查正在進行當中，希望能盡快水落石出，找出謀殺兇手。

(秒殺解字) crimin(crime)+al → criminal 是「罪犯」或「犯法的」。

詞搭 a criminal <u>case / court / offense / lawyer</u> 刑事案件／法庭／犯／律師

同義字 illegal

---

summary

[`sʌmərɪ]

n. 概述、概要

adj. 總括的；立即的

At the end of the meeting, the chairman gave a summary of today's discussion.

在會議結束時，主席針對今天的討論做摘要報告。

(秒殺解字) summ(=sum=amount, highest,top)+ary → summ 是字首 super、sur 的變形，本義是「在上的」（over, above）、「超出的」（beyond），表示「數量」、「最高的」、「頂端」。

詞搭 In summary,... = In sum,... = To sum up,... 總之，……概括來說，……；a summary execution 立即處決

---

sheer

[ʃɪr]

adj. 完全的；純然的

What he said was <u>sheer nonsense</u>, so just forget about it.

他所說的根本是胡說八道，所以呢，你就別把它當一回事。

曾 100

(秒殺解字) sheer 的源自印歐詞根 *sker，表示「切」(cut)，切掉不要的部分，留下來的東西比較「純」(pure)，「完全」沒有混到其他雜質，衍生出「完全的」的意思。

詞搭 sheer <u>luck / happiness / stupidity</u> 十足的運氣／快樂／愚蠢

同義字 pure, complete

反義字 incomplete

conjunction

[kənˈdʒʌŋkʃən]

n. 連接詞；結合、聯合

Do you know the two clauses should be joined together by a conjunction? 🔊 110

你知道這兩個子句必須用一個連接詞來連結起來嗎？

🐾(秒殺解字) con(together)+junc(join)+t+ion →「連結」在「一起」，可當「連接詞」解釋。可用 **join** 當神隊友，**母音通轉**，來記憶 **junc**，皆表示「連結」。

詞搭 in conjunction with... 連同、共同……，與……協力

recruit

[rɪˈkrut]

n. 新成員；新兵

v. 招募（員工、新兵）

The school is planning to recruit some college students to be voluntary teaching assistants during the summer vacation.

學校正打算在暑假期間招募一些大學學生擔任義務性的教學助理。

🐾(秒殺解字) re(again)+crui(grow)+t →「招募」是為了「再」「增加」「新成員」。相關同源字有 **crew**（n. 整組人員）、in**crea**se（v./n. 增加）、de**crea**se（v./n. 減少）。

詞搭 be recruited into the army 被徵召入伍

 **Unit 38**

---

prosperous

[`prɑspərəs]

adj. 興隆的、繁榮的；富裕的；順遂的

Beggars can be seen in every part of the world, and those prosperous countries are no exception.
世界各個角落都看得到乞丐，即使是繁榮國家也不例外。

普 107
警特 108

> （秒殺解字）pro(for)+sper(hope)+ous → 本義是符合一個人的「期望」，做事「開心」、「成功」，因此有「繁榮的」衍生意思。相關同源字有 de**spair**（n./v. 絕望）、de**sper**ate（adj. 絕望的）。

詞搭 a prosperous <u>businessman / town / country</u> 生意興隆的商人／繁榮的城鎮／國家；a prosperous landowner 富裕的地主

同義字 thriving

---

scrape

[skrep]

n. 輕微擦傷
v. 刮；擦傷

My mom always demands that I (should) <u>scrape</u> the mud <u>off</u> my shoes before I come into the house.
我媽媽總是規定我進入屋內之前一定要把鞋子的泥土清除乾淨。

普 100

> （秒殺解字）包含 scr 的單字，常具有「亂刮」、「亂抓」、「亂塗」等意思，做這些動作時常常會產生「尖銳」刺耳、令人感到不舒服的聲音。相關單字有 **scr**ape（v. 刮）、**scr**atch（v. 抓）、**scr**abble（v. 塗鴉）、**scr**eam（v. 尖叫）、**scr**eak（v. 刺耳的尖叫）等。

詞搭 scrape by = make ends meet 勉強餬口；scrape through 勉強通過、剛好及格

---

simplicity

[sɪm`plɪsətɪ]

n. 簡單；簡樸

Among the many car choices, I prefer the one that has the advantages of simplicity and low price.
在這麼多車子選項當中，我比較偏好具有簡樸及價廉等優點的那部。

> （秒殺解字）sim(one)+plic(fold)+ity → 只有「一」「摺」，表示「簡單」、「簡樸」。

---

simplify

[`sɪmplə͵faɪ]

v. 簡化、使簡單

What we expect you to do for us is help us simplify, rather than complicate, the existing problems.
我們期待你能幫我們的是簡化現存問題，而非把它們複雜化。

詞搭 simplify a problem 使問題變得簡單；simplify the tax system 簡化稅制

infant

[`ɪnfənt]

n. 嬰兒
adj. 嬰兒的;初期的

When John was just an infant, his mother died and since then he was raised by his grandmother. 🔊 104

當 John 還只是在小嬰兒強褓時期,媽媽就死了,而從那時開始,他就由祖母扶養長大。

Infant mortality has been drastically reduced because of the rapid progress achieved in modern medicine.

由於現代醫學快速成就的發展,嬰兒死亡率已經大幅降低了。

🐛 秒殺解字 in(not)+fa(speak)+n+t →「嬰兒」「不會」「說話」。

詞搭 an infant company 剛成立公司

vocabulary

[və`kæbjəˌlɛrɪ]

n. 字彙

Reading a wide range of books will help increase your vocabulary rapidly and efficiently.

博覽群書將快速有效增進你的字彙能力。

🐛 秒殺解字 voc(voice)+abul+ary → 每個字彙都能唸出「聲音」。相關同源字有 **voc**al (adj. 聲音的)、**voc**ation (n. 職業)、ad**voc**ate (n. 擁護者)、con**vok**e (v. 召集開會)、e**vok**e (v. 喚起)、pro**vok**e (v. 煽動)、pro**voc**ation (n. 激怒)、re**vok**e (v. 撤銷)、re**voc**ation (n. 撤銷)。

詞搭 active / passive vocabulary 表達／理解字彙

evolve

[ɪ`vɑlv]

v. 進化;發展為

Over the past few years, this local company has successfully evolved into a large-scale international enterprise. 🔊 107

過去幾年以來,這家當地小公司已經逐漸成功地發展成為一家大型國際企業。

🐛 秒殺解字 e(=ex=out)+volv(roll)+e →「轉」「出來」。**volv**、**volu** 同源,**u/v** 對應,皆表示「旋轉」、「滾動」。volv、volu 普遍存在動詞和名詞間的對應,例如:**evolv**e／**evolu**tion。

詞搭 evolve from / out of... 由……進化而來;
evolve into ……逐漸發展成為……

evolution

[ˌɛvə`luʃən]

n. 演化、進化；發展

In the course of evolution, many types of birds have apparently lost their capacity of flight.

在生物演化過程當中，許多鳥類很明顯地已經失去他們原本具有的飛行能力。

曾 100 103

| 詞搭 | the theory of evolution 進化論 |

| 同義字 | progression, development |

---

evolutionary

[ˌɛvə`luʃənˌɛrɪ]

adj. 進化（論）的；漸進的

Any method that is applied to speed up the evolutionary process of species is against nature.

任何被運用來加速物種進化過程的方法都是違反自然的。

曾 106

| 詞搭 | an evolutionary biologist / theorist 進化論生物學家／理論家 |

---

prompt

[prɑmpt]

v. 促使；提示；提詞
adj. 立刻的

I do hope to find out what on earth prompted you to do such a stupid thing.

我真的很希望能夠了解到底是甚麼原因讓你做出這麼一件愚蠢的事。

警特 109

Please try to be prompt, because we are running out of time.

請你快點，因為我們時間很有限。

秒殺解字 pro(forward)+empt(=take) → 「拿」到「前面」，表示「促使」、「提詞」。拼字時須注意，兩母音相碰，為了好發音，需刪除一個母音，通常是刪除前面的母音，但因 pro 在這裡要重讀，所以不刪除 o，轉而刪除後面的 e 字母。

| 詞搭 | a prompt reply / decision 立即的答覆／決定；a prompt note 即期支票；prompt cash 現款 |

---

deprive

[dɪ`praɪv]

v. 剝奪

For the past few months, sickness has deprived me of the chance to meet you.

過去幾個月以來，因為生病的關係讓我沒有機會跟你見面。

警特 105

秒殺解字 de(completly)+priv(release from)+e → 「完全」「解除」，引申為「剝奪」。相關同源字有 **priv**ate (adj. 私人的)、**priv**ilege (n. 特權)。

herder
[`hɝdæ]
n. 放牧人

My old friend Ben said he used to be a sheep herder when he was young.
我的老朋友 Ben 說他年輕時曾經是羊群放牧人。

(秒殺解字) herd+er → 驅使「牧群」的人，即「牧羊人」。

同義字 | shepherd

---

disapproval
[ˌdɪsə`pruvl]
n. 反對

There seems to be a look of disapproval on the teacher's face, though he said nothing about my plan.
雖然老師對於我的計畫甚麼話都沒說，但他臉上似乎有一種看得出來是不同意的表情。

醫 104

(秒殺解字) dis(not)+ap(=ad=to)+prov(prove, test)+al → approval 是通過「試驗」，「證明」是好的事物，就同意放行，表示「贊同」。dis 表示「不」、「沒有」。

詞搭 | with / in disapproval 反對；show / express disapproval 表示反對

反義字 | approval, agreement

---

foreigner
[`fɔrɪnæ]
n. 外國人

The taxi driver can tell from my accent that I'm a foreigner.
計程車司機從我的口音可以得知我是外國人。

(秒殺解字) foreign+er → foreign 本指「門外」，後來語義變寬，指「國外」，foreigner 是「外國人」。

---

soothe
[suð]
v. 使鎮定；減輕（疼痛）

To soothe my aching muscles, I think now I need a hot bath and good sleep.
為了舒緩我肌肉疼痛，我想現在我需要的是洗個熱水澡還有好好睡一覺。

(秒殺解字) soothe 本義是「存在」(to be)，存在代表「真實」(true)，後來衍生出「減輕 (疼痛)」等語義。

同義字 | calm, relieve

brand
[brænd]
n. 商標、牌子

This is a brand that consumers always associate with good quality.
這是一個消費者總是會將它與高級品質關聯的品牌。

🖋 **秒殺解字** brand 的本義是「火」(fire)、「火焰」(flame)，用火將鐵加熱，可在盒子上烙印出商品的「標籤」(mark)，brand 因此有「商標」、「牌子」的意思。

詞搭 own / store brand 自有品牌；a brand name 廠牌；a designer brand 名牌；brand loyalty 品牌忠誠度；brand leader / leading brand 主打品牌

indulge
[ɪn`dʌldʒ]
v. （使）沉迷；縱容

Kent indulged himself in gambling for a long time, so his wife decided to divorce him.
Kent 長期沉溺於賭博，因此他的太太決定跟他離婚。

🖋 **秒殺解字** in+dulg(engage oneself)+e → 使自己「沉溺」於……之中。

詞搭 indulge (oneself) in... 沉迷於……

subscriber
[səb`skraɪbə]
n. 訂閱者；電話用戶

I've been a subscriber to this art magazine for more than ten years.
我訂閱這家藝術雜誌已經超過十年了。

🖋 **秒殺解字** sub(under)+scrib(write)+er →「寫」在「下面」，讀完條款在下方簽名，表示願意「訂購」「者」。相關同源字有 describe (v. 描寫)、description (n. 描寫)、prescribe (v. 開處方)、prescription (n. 處方)。

詞搭 telephone subscribers 電話用戶；cable television subscribers 有線電視用戶

accumulate
[ə`kjumjə͵let]
v. 累積

These years Mr. Robinson has been accumulating enormous wealth through global e-commerce.
Robinson 先生這幾年以來從全球電子商務交易中累積了鉅額財富。

🖋 **秒殺解字** ac(=ad=to)+cumul(heap)+ate →「堆疊」起來，表示「累積」。相關同源字有 cumulus (n. 積雲) 等。

警特 105

同義字 pile up, amass, build up

distress
[dɪˋstrɛs]

n. 痛苦；危難
v. 使極痛苦、悲傷

The mother <u>was in</u> great <u>distress</u> when the doctor told her about her baby's death.

當醫師告知嬰兒的死訊時，這位母親感到非常悲痛。

普 100
高 110
警特 109

These complicated problems have been distressing him for a long time, and now they are still annoying him.

這些複雜的問題已經讓他操煩許久，直到現在還是困擾著他。

秒殺解字 dis(apart)+stress(draw tight) → 內心被「撕扯」或「拉」「開」，產生「痛苦」的感覺。

詞搭 distress signal (船、飛機) 遇難信號

hastily
[ˋhestɪlɪ]

adv. 倉促地、匆忙地

Such an important decision should not be made so hastily. I hope you think about it more carefully.

這麼重要的一個決定不應該如此倉促做出。我希望你更加小心考慮清楚。

秒殺解字 hasty+ly →「倉促地」、「輕率地」。

同義字 hurriedly, in haste, in a hurry, in a rush

notably
[ˋnotəblɪ]

adv. 明顯地；特別地

I notice that the skill level of our school basketball players has gone down notably.

我有注意到我們學校籃球隊員的球技水準已經顯著降低了。

高 108

秒殺解字 note(mark)+able+ly → 來自拉丁語 nota，原意是「標示」、「記號」；notably 表示特別做「記號」，引申為「明顯地」、「特別地」。

詞搭 notably successful 格外成功

反義字 especially, in particular

disrupt
[dɪsˋrʌpt]

v. 使中斷；使分裂；使混亂

The torrential rain this morning disrupted the travel between the two districts of the city.

今天早上的暴雨中斷了這個城市兩個區域之間的正常交通。

普 100
高 108
警特 107

秒殺解字 dis(apart)+rup(break)+t →「破碎」「分開」，表示去「干擾」或「中斷」某一事件、組織、或活動的正常運作。可用 **rob** 當神隊友，**b/p 轉音，母音通轉**，來記憶 **rup**，表示「打斷」、「打破」、「破裂」。相關同源字有 **rob** (v. 搶劫)、bank**rup**t (adj. 破產的)、inter**rup**t (v. 打斷)、cor**rup**t (adj. 貪污的)、e**rup**t (v. 爆發)、ab**rup**t (adj. 突然的、意外的)。

同義字 disturb

01 ___ The police revealed a sketch _____ the suspect based on the information that the witness gave. In the afternoon, they will post the sketch on their website.

(A) respecting   (B) depicting
(C) neglecting   (D) expecting

02 ___ The _____ harmless little bug is actually an extremely poisonous species. One small bite will paralyze an adult and may even lead to death.

(A) previously   (B) essentially
(C) seemingly   (D) frequently

03 ___ Nowadays, there is a new kind of syndrome called "road _____."
People who suffer this kind of syndrome will easily get angry when driving on the road.

(A) package   (B) stage
(C) percentage   (D) rage

04 ___ Thinking of her child made her extremely _____ . As soon as she heard a weeping voice of a little kid, she immediately transferred 20,000 dollars to the kidnapper. Later, she realized that her kid was actually studying in school and she was scammed.

(A) reasonable   (B) comparable
(C) considerable   (D) vulnerable

05 ___ There seems to be a _____ within the U.S. government. There are even people speculating that the government has been working with aliens for a long time.

(A) conspiracy   (B) pregnancy
(C) accountancy   (D) privacy

06 ___ The soldier is badly hurt in the battlefield, and he needs to be _____ from the field immediately. If he doesn't get medical treatment right now, he is going to die.

(A) elevated (B) disguised
(C) extracted (D) recruited

07 ___ Our manager specifically told me that I had to pay extra attention to this client because he just agreed to a _____ order.

(A) mercury (B) bulk
(C) casino (D) virus

08 ___ My brother called me and told me that our father was _____ right now because he knows about what I did in school. I'm now in serious trouble.

(A) furious (B) spontaneous
(C) luxurious (D) continuous

09 ___ Michael Jordan is probably the most famous name in the realm of basketball. His outstanding performances pushed the NBA into the _____ market.

(A) global (B) valuable
(C) comfortable (D) tribal

10 ___ She was assigned directly by the President to be the new _____ of United States. She has strong analytical, organizational and leadership skills. Moreover, she is able to communicate effectively, both in writing and orally.

(A) investor (B) consumer
(C) diplomat (D) sponsor

11 ___ The little _____ was abandoned by his mother on a cold winter day. Luckily, a kind-hearted old couple found the little baby and took care of him as if he had been their own child.

(A) tourist (B) merchant
(C) victim (D) infant

12 ___ Before Darwin discovered the theory of _____, most people had believed that all species were created by God at the same time.

(A) inspiration (B) ambition
(C) convention (D) evolution

13 ___ For the past few weeks, the noise of the construction site has _____ me of my sleep. Whenever I wanted to take a nap, I would be disturbed by the noisy sound of the heavy machinery.

(A) deprived (B) strived
(C) thrived (D) derived

14 ___ Recently, there has been a popularization of cellphone games, with more and more teenagers having _____ themselves in those games. It has become a serious problem that needs to be dealt with.

(A) disengaged (B) indulged
(C) managed (D) revenged

15 ___ During the live broadcast, the signal was constantly _____ because of the incoming typhoon. Half an hour later, we completely lost the signal and the show was ended.

(A) disclosed (B) dissolved
(C) disrupted (D) discriminated

解答
1.(B) 2.(C) 3.(D) 4.(D) 5.(A) 6.(C) 7.(B) 8.(A) 9.(A) 10.(C) 11.(D) 12.(D) 13.(A) 14.(B) 15.(C)

denotation

[ˌdinoˈteʃən]

n. 指示;原意

When talking about the definition of this word, we should notice both its denotation and connotation.
在談論有關這個字的定義時,我們應該注意其本義以及其涵意。

(秒殺解字) de(completely)+note(mark)+ation →本義是「完整地」「標示」出來,進一步來說,是藉由號誌或名稱「指示」某事,17 世紀初,衍生出「詞語的意思」,即「原意」。

曾 105

反義字 | connotation

rebound

[rɪˈbaʊnd]

n. **v.** 反彈、彈回

Recently oil prices have rebounded because of the elimination of the crisis in the Middle East.
最近油價因為中東戰爭危機解除已經呈現反彈現象。

(秒殺解字) re(back)+bound(bound, leap) →「跳」「回」,表示「反彈」、「彈回」。

高 108

詞搭 | rebound in prices 價格回升;on the rebound 在彈回之際

capitalism

[ˈkæpətḷˌɪzəm]

n. 資本主義

Capitalism is based on an open and fair marketplace, but there is also keen and cruel competition.
資本主義的前提是自由、公平的市場但也是激烈、無情的競爭。

曾 100

capitalist

[ˈkæpətḷˌɪst]

n. 資本主義者;資本家

adj. 資本主義的

Capitalist economy is free and open, but it is also highly competitive.
資本主義制度下的經濟是自由開放,但競爭也是相當激烈的。

曾 100

capitalistic

[ˌkæpɪtəˈlɪstɪk]

adj. 資本主義的;資本家的

The professor said my report was too simplified to account for the discrepancy between capitalistic and social systems.
我的教授說我的報告過於簡化,所以無法說明資本主義及社會主義制度兩者之間的差異。

(秒殺解字) capit(head)+al+ism → 古代人沒有衍生性金融商品,就以 **cattle** 的數量,也就是用牲口有幾「頭」來決定資產的多寡,同源字 **capit**al 表示「資本」,**capit**alism 表示「資本主義」。

曾 100

immigrant

[`ɪməgrənt]

n. 移民者（由外移入）；僑民

The US government emphasizes that illegal immigrants will be sent back across the border immediately after they are caught.

美國政府強調非法移民被捕之後會即刻經由邊境遣返。

秒殺解字 im(in)+migr(move)+ant → 往「內」「移動」的「移民者」，表示從他國移入境內的「移民者」。

衍生字 immigrate [`ɪmə,gret] v. 由外移民國內；
immigration [,ɪmə`greʃən] n. 移民（由外移入）

反義字 emigrant

---

architecture

[`ɑrkə,tɛktʃə]

n. 建築物

The Notre-Dame de Paris is the most impressive example of architecture I've seen on this trip to France.

巴黎聖母院是我這趟法國旅遊行程中最讓我感到印象深刻難以忘懷的建築物。

秒殺解字 archi(chief)+tect(builder)+ure → architect 本義是「主要的」「建築者」，是建築物的統籌、設計、主要規劃者，引申為「建築師」；architecture 是建築師所設計出來的「建築物」。

---

disguise

[dɪs`gaɪz]

n. **v.** 假扮、喬裝

I tried to hide my feelings, but in fact I just couldn't disguise my sadness.

我試著要隱藏我的情緒，但事實上我根本無法掩飾我的悲傷。

秒殺解字 dis(away)+guise(appearance) →「離開」原本的「外表」，表示「喬裝」、「假扮」，也可以表示「掩飾」感受等。

詞搭 disguise oneself as... 喬裝成……；a blessing in disguise 因禍得福

---

elevate

[`ɛlə,vet]

v. 上升；提升

Hoping to earn more money and elevate his living standards, Peter chooses to work extra hours every day.

希望能夠多賺點錢並且提高生活水準，Peter 選擇每天加班。

秒殺解字 e(=ex=out)+lev(lift)+ate →「提起」某物，使之往上動，「離開」較低的位置。相關同源字有 **lev**er（n. 槓桿）、al**lev**iate（v. 緩和）、re**liev**e（v. 減輕）、re**lief**（n. 慰藉）、re**lev**ant（adj. 相關的）。

consciously
[`kɑnʃəslɪ]

adv. 有意識地；自覺地

She might not consciously know what she did to you because she's a patient with mental disorders.
她也許並不清楚她對你做了些甚麼事，因為她是精神障礙的病患。

🖊 **秒殺解字** con(completely)+sci(know)+ous+ly → 「徹底」「知道」「地」，引申為「有意識地」。相關同源字有 **sci**ence（n. 科學）、con**sci**ence（n. 良心）。

📖 108

反義字 unconsciously

unanimity
[junə`nɪmɪtɪ]

n. 一致同意、全體一致

So far there's no unanimity of opinions as to the best location for the new parking lot.
目前為止，關於新設停車場的地點，大家的意見尚未一致。

🖊 **秒殺解字** un(=uni=one)+anim(mind, spirit)+ity → 「一」種「心思」，表示「一致同意」。

同義字 agreement, accord

abstraction
[æb`strækʃən]

n. 抽象

All the figures in this report have too much abstraction and won't help the readers understand the truth.
這份報告裡的數字有太多的抽象概念，所以無助於讀者理解實際情況。

🖊 **秒殺解字** abs(away, off)+trac(drag, draw)+t+ion → 「拉」「離」現實是「抽象」。可用 **drag** 當神隊友，**d/t**，**g/k** 轉音，母音通轉，來記憶 **trac**。相關同源字有 at**trac**t（v. 吸引）、dis**trac**t（v. 使分心）、ab**strac**t（adj. 抽象的）、con**trac**t（n. 契約）、re**trac**t（v. 撤回）、sub**trac**t（v. 減去）、ex**trac**t（v. 提煉）。

fasten
[`fæsn̩]

v. 繫緊

The cabin crew broadcast will remind you to keep your seat belt fastened at all times.
飛機上機艙人員廣播會提醒你隨時繫緊安全帶。

🖊 **秒殺解字** fast(firm)+en(make) → 「使」「牢固」。

同義字 do up

反義字 unfasten, undo, loosen

prejudice

[`prɛdʒədɪs]

n. 偏見

v. 使有偏見

I just couldn't understand the <u>racial prejudice</u> you hold.

我就是無法理解你所持有的種族偏見。

 秒殺解字 pre(before)+jud(judge)+ice → 未審「先」「判」，懷有「偏見」。

詞搭 have a prejudice against... = be prejudiced against... 對⋯⋯有偏見

gambler

[`gæmblɚ]

n. 賭博者、賭徒

Never think he's an entrepreneur, as he's only a gambler that never wins.

千萬別把他認為是甚麼企業家的，因為他只是穩輸不贏的賭徒而已。

 秒殺解字 gamble+er → gamble 和 game 同源，「賭博」（gamble）是利用有價之物來競爭輸贏的「遊戲」（game），是人類的一種娛樂方式；gambler 是「賭博者」。

gambling

[`gæmblɪŋ]

n. 賭博

Gambling is a very bad habit that will absolutely ruin your life.

賭博是一個絕對會毀掉你一生非常不好的習慣。

feasibility

[ˌfizə`bɪlətɪ]

n. 可行性

The latest study shows the feasibility of building a new bus transfer station in the downtown area.

最近一項研究報告顯示，在市中心區域建立一座新的巴士轉運站的可行性。

秒殺解字 feas(=fair=do, make)+ibility → 「可以」「做」。

詞搭 feasibility <u>study / analysis / report</u> 可行性研究／分析／報告

shiver

[`ʃɪvɚ]

n. **v.** （寒冷、害怕地）發抖

圖 108

Jack is wearing only a thin T-shirt and now he's <u>shivering</u> with cold.

Jack 身上只穿了一件薄薄的 T 恤衫，所以他現在正冷得發抖。

 秒殺解字 字源不詳，但有字源學家推測 shiver 是源自古英語，表示「下巴」（jaw），因寒冷或害怕發抖時牙齒打顫，會動到「下巴」。

詞搭 send shivers <u>up / down</u> + sb's spine 令某人不寒而慄

同義字 tremble, shudder

portable

[`pɔrtəbḷ]

adj. 可攜帶的、手提的

Nowadays portable computers are indispensable to insurance salespersons.

如今隨身攜帶型電腦對保險銷售人員而言是不可或缺的。

🖊 **秒殺解字** port(carry)＋able ，「可」「攜帶」的。相關同源字有im**port**（v./n. 進口）、ex**port**（v./n. 出口）、sup**port**（v./n. 支持）、re**port**（v./n. 報告；報導）、trans**port**（v. 運輸）。

字辨 potable [`potəbḷ] adj. 可飲用的

曾 101
警特 109

---

ministry

[`mɪnɪstrɪ]

n. （政府）部；牧師職務

The Ministry of Agriculture is starting to carry out its subsidy policy to cover farmers' losses to typhoons.

農業部門開始要實施補貼政策來彌補農民因為颱風來襲所造成的損失。

🖊 **秒殺解字** min(small)+is+ter+y → 從 minister 而來，原指「較小的」人、「地位較低的」的人，指做卑微事情的人。16 世紀初，指服務於教會的「僕人」，即「牧師」；到了 17 世紀衍生出「國王的僕人」，即「大臣」；現指「部長」、「大臣」，是「地位較低的」公「僕」。必須留意的是，字尾 **ter** 是比較級，坊間書籍或網路把此字的 ster 拆解出來，並解釋為「人」，並不正確。

詞搭 the Ministry of Internal Affairs 內政部；the Ministry of Education 教育部；the Ministry of National Defense 國防部；the Ministry of Foreign Affairs 外交部

曾 104

---

discount

[`dɪskaʊnt]

n. 折扣

[dɪs`kaʊnt]

v. 打折

This supermarket will give a 10% discount for cash payments.

這家超市會給付現顧客百分之十的折扣。

This is a one-price store and it does not discount at all.

這是一家不二價商店，所以是不會打折的。

🖊 **秒殺解字** dis(away)+count(count, compute) →「算」錢時扣除部分金額，拿「開」這些錢，引申為「折扣」

詞搭 give + sb. + a <u>10% / 25%</u> discount on + sth. 就某物給某人打 9／75 折

---

compatible

[kəm`pætəbl]

adj. （電腦）相容
的、可共存的

In some cases, the two operating systems may not be <u>compatible</u> <u>with</u> each other.
在某些情況之下這兩個作業系統可能會互不相容。

🖋 秒殺解字 com(together)+pat(suffer)+ible →「能」同甘「共」「苦」、表示「相容的」、「可共存的」。

警特 107

---

ankle

[`æŋkl]

n. 腳踝

Yesterday, I sprained my ankle while I was jogging.
昨天我做慢跑運動時扭到腳踝。

🖋 秒殺解字 ankle 和 angle 同源，**g/k 轉音**及**母音通轉**，本義是「彎曲」(bend)，「角度」(angle) 是衍生語意，可用腳踝可彎曲產生「角度」來聯想記憶。

普 101
103

詞搭 <u>break / twist / sprain</u> one's ankle 扭傷腳踝

hardship
[`hardʃɪp]
n. 艱苦、困苦

Our days of hardship finally came to an end and we all should have an optimistic attitude toward the future.

我們艱辛的日子總算結束了，所以大家都應持著樂觀態度迎向未來。

📝 102

🖋 秒殺解字 hard+ship → 表示「艱苦」的「狀態」。

| 詞搭 | bear hardship 忍受苦難 |
| 同義字 | suffering |

stable
[`stebḷ]
adj. 穩定的

If the foundations of the building are not stable enough, it'll collapse easily when an earthquake occurs.

如果這棟建築的基礎不夠穩固，發生地震時它就容易倒塌。

高 108

🖋 秒殺解字 sta(stand)+ble →「站」，衍生出「穩定的」之語意。

詞搭	be in stable condition 處於穩定的狀況
同義字	steady
反義字	unstable

dialect
[`daɪə‚lɛkt]
n. 方言

Cantonese is a regional dialect spoken in places such as Hong Kong, Macau, and the Canton Province of China.

廣東話是通行於香港、澳門以及中國廣東省等地的區域性方言。

📝 103

🖋 秒殺解字 dia(across,between)+lec(speak)+t →「跨越兩者之間」的「交談」，後語義限縮，指的是在某一群人中交談使用的「方言」。

| 詞搭 | a local dialect 當地方言 |

ominous
[`ɑmɪnəs]

adj. 預兆的；不吉利的

When an explosion was heard outside, she immediately felt something ominous was going to happen soon.

當外頭聽到一聲爆炸聲響時，她馬上感覺有甚麼不幸的事即將發生。

秒殺解字 omin(=omen)+ous →「預兆」的。

詞搭 an ominous silence 不祥的寂靜

反義字 auspicious

---

static
[`stætɪk]

adj. 停滯不動的；靜電的

Oil prices have remained considerably static for the past few months, meaning that current economic growth was rather stable.

過去數月以來油價保持相當持平，沒有變化，這意味著目前經濟成長也相當穩定。

秒殺解字 sta(stand)+t+ic → 本義「站」著不動的，引申為「停滯不動的」，另一個衍生意思是「靜電的」，靜電會使毛髮「站」起來。

詞搭 static electricity 靜電

反義字 dynamic

---

invade
[ɪn`ved]

v. 侵入、侵略

The guerrillas that invaded the border area were all wiped out by the government troops.

入侵邊界地區的游擊隊全部被政府軍消滅。

普 105
高 110

秒殺解字 in(in)+vad(go, walk)+e →「走」「進來」，表示「入侵」、「侵犯」。可用表示「涉水而行」的 **wade** 當神隊友，**v/w** 對應，**d/s/ʒ** 轉音，來記憶 **vad**、**vas**，表示「走」。

詞搭 invade + sb's privacy 侵犯某人的隱私

同義字 attack

---

chirp
[tʃɝp]

v. （鳥）發出啾啾叫聲

I think spring is coming because some birds are beginning to chirp among in the trees.

我認為春天快要來臨了，因為有些鳥兒已經開始在樹林間吱吱喳喳的叫著了。

秒殺解字 chirp 是擬聲字，如同中文裡的鳥叫「啾啾」、「吱吱喳喳」等，使用ㄐ或ㄓ來模擬鳥叫聲，而英文使用 ch 的音來模擬鳥的叫聲。

同義字 tweet, twitter

suckle

['sʌkl]

v. 給……哺乳；吮吸；養育

v. 吃奶

Taking kids to observe how cows suckle their calves is a good way to help them realize how parents take good care of their children.

帶小孩觀察乳牛如何給小牛餵奶是幫助小孩體會父母如何愛護照顧他們小孩一個很好的方式。

秒殺解字 suck 和 suckle 同源，suckle 是「吸」(suck) 的反覆動作。

---

aggression

[ə`grɛʃən]

n. 侵略

Do you ever find that your dog always shows aggression towards people in rags?

曾 107

你有發現到你的狗總是對衣衫襤褸的人表現出攻擊的意圖嗎？

秒殺解字 ag(=ad=to)+gress(go, step)+ion → 「朝」某方向「走」，入侵他人地盤。相關同源字有 pro**gress** (n./v. 進步)、con**gress** (n. 國會)。

詞搭 an unprovoked act of aggression against… 對……無端的侵犯

---

integral

[`ɪntəgrəl]

adj. 不可或缺的

Water, air, and food are integral parts of human life.

水、空氣以及食物等是構成人類生命整體不可或缺的一部分。

秒殺解字 in(not)+teg(=tag=touch)+er+al → 字面上的意思是「沒有」「接觸」過的，表示沒被汙染，表示「完整的」、「不可或缺的」。

詞搭 be integral to... 對……是不可或缺的

同義字 necessary, essential, indispensable

---

biological

[ˌbaɪə`lɑdʒɪkl]

adj. 生物的；生物學的

From the biological point of view, cloning is a significant breakthrough in medical science, though it is controversial.

警特 106

從生物學的觀點來看，生物複製是一個重大醫學突破，雖然它也充滿爭議性。

秒殺解字 bio(life)+logy(study of)+ic+al → 關於「生命」「研究」「的」。

詞搭 biological clock 生理時鐘；biological weapons / warfare / attack 生化武器／戰／攻擊

distort
[dɪsˋtɔrt]
v. 扭曲

Some domestic media tend to distort a certain politician's remarks.
有些國內媒體往往會去扭曲一些政治人物的言談。

曾 107

> 秒殺解字 dis(completely)+tort(twist) → 「完全」「扭曲」，表示「曲解」真相。相關同源字有 **tort**ure（n./v. 拷問）、re**tort**（v. 反駁）、con**tort**（v. 扭曲）。

詞搭 distorted <u>views / limbs</u> 偏見／扭曲的四肢

同義字 twist

tribal
[ˋtraɪbl̩]
adj. 部落的

A lot of tribal families in the mountains still cannot afford their children's school tuition and accommodation expenses.
山上許多部落家庭仍然無力支付他們小孩在校學費以及食宿費用。

> 秒殺解字 tribe+al → 「部落」「的」。tribe 原指羅馬原始「三大部落」，而「貢物」（tribute）是較弱的部落獻給強大部落的「禮物」。可用 **three** 當神隊友，**t/θ 轉音**，**母音通轉**，來記憶 **tri**，皆表示「三」。

remedy
[ˋrɛmədɪ]
n. 治療法；藥物；補救
v. 治療

My sister often says the best <u>remedy for</u> coping with grief is hard work or eating to my heart's content.
我姐姐常說排解憂傷最佳良方就是拚命努力工作或者是盡情吃喝一頓。

圖 108

> 秒殺解字 re(intensive prefix)+med(heal)+y → 本義「治療」。相關同源字有 **med**ical（adj. 醫學的）、**med**icine（n. 藥）。

詞搭 <u>cold / cough</u> remedy 感冒／咳嗽藥

同義字 cure, solution

deposit

[dɪ`pazɪt]

n. 存款；訂金
v. 存放（銀行）

My father told me that he <u>made a deposit</u> of ten thousand dollars <u>into</u> my bank account earlier this morning.
我父親告訴我說今天早上稍早時他在我的銀行帳戶存入一萬元。

餐104
警特108

🪶 **秒殺解字** de(away)+pos(put)+it → 把錢「放」在「一旁」，put away 即表示「存款」。

詞搭 deposit <u>in / into</u>…存放；deposit money <u>in / into</u> a bank (account) 將錢存放在銀行（戶頭）內；a deposit account 存款帳戶

反義字 withdraw

uniform

[`junə,fɔrm]

n. 制服
adj. 一致的

Some parents or scholars think that wearing school uniforms may depersonalize children.
一些家長或學者認為穿學校制服有可能使孩子去個性。

餐103

🪶 **秒殺解字** uni(one)+form(form) →「同一」「形式」的。

詞搭 in uniform 穿著制服

inflict

[ɪn`flɪkt]

v. 施加（傷害、打擊）

Your selfish behavior has inflicted suffering on others.
你的自私行為已經使別人遭受痛苦。

🪶 **秒殺解字** in(in)+flic(strike)+t →「打」「入」，表示「施加」。相關同源字有conflict（n./v. 衝突）。

詞搭 inflict + sth.+ on / upon + sb. 將（不好的）某事加諸於某人

innovation

[,ɪnə`veʃən]

n. 創新

The most important goal of our company is to achieve innovation.
我們公司現在想要達成的最重要目標就是創新。

餐106

🪶 **秒殺解字** in(in)+nov(new)+ate+ion → 引「進」「新的」想法、方法、發明，表示「創新」。可用new當神隊友，**v/w** 對應，**母音通轉**，來記憶nov，皆表示「新」。相關同源字有novel（n. 小說）、novice（n. 新手）、renovate（v. 更新）。

詞搭 technological innovation 技術創新

innovative

[ˋɪnəˌvetɪv]

adj. 創新的

Being imaginative, innovative, and energetic, Michael was appointed as the new director of the design department.

Michael 富有想像力及創意，同時也具有活力，因此被指派擔任設計部門的主管。

普 104
106
108
警特 106

詞搭 | an innovative approach to language teaching 創新的語言教學法

同義字 | creative

---

innovatively

[ˋɪnəˌvetɪvlɪ]

adv. 創新地

The manager encourages us to work hard and innovatively to meet our customers' expectations.

經理鼓勵我們努力工作並維持創新以符合顧客的期望。

普 106
警特 106

---

thoughtful

[ˋθɔtfəl]

adj. 體貼的；有思想的

It's very thoughtful of you to give me a ride to the airport.

你載我去機場實在是太體貼了。

普 107

秒殺解字 thought+ful → 會替人家「思考的」，引申為「體貼的」。

詞搭 | be thoughtful of others = be considerate of others 體貼某人

同義字 | considerate

---

sceptic

[ˋskɛptɪk]

n. 懷疑者（= skeptic [美]）

She is a sceptic about Chinese herbal medicine.

她是對中醫保持懷疑態度的人。

高 108

秒殺解字 scep(to look at)+t+ic → scept 即 spect（看），p 和 c 易位，兩者同源。sceptic 為古希臘一個懷疑真實知識可能性的學派成員，他們透過觀察來探究真相，後語意擴增，表示「懷疑者」。

01 ___ The new President signed a bill to make immigration more strict. A lot of _____ were affected by the policy and locked out of the country.

(A) journalists   (B) tenants

(C) agents   (D) immigrants

02 ___ The thief _____ himself as a security guard and ran past a series of security checkpoints. In the end, he stole an essential file from the company's database.

(A) confused   (B) refused

(C) disguised   (D) abused

03 ___ The general won many major battles in this war. After the war was ended, his status suddenly_____ through the roof because he was the reason that they won the war.

(A) anticipated   (B) concentrated

(C) elevated   (D) substantiated

04 ___ The association had _____ in regards to voting for the season's Most Valuable Player. Stephen Curry won the unanimous MVP Award for 2015-16 NBA Season, and became the first NBA player to ever earn such an achievement.

(A) unanimity   (B) facility

(C) quality   (D) majority

05 ___ The lady was pulled over because the police thought she didn't _____ her seatbelt. In reality, she did fasten her seatbelt the whole time and her dashboard camera proved her innocence.

(A) enforce   (B) fasten

(C) straighten   (D) threaten

06 ___ The meeting is not going to continue since you keep showing your racial _____ against the African-American woman.

(A) device   (B) justice

(C) prejudice   (D) office

07 ___ The _____ lost everything he had in the casino and even borrowed money from the local mob to try to win his money back. Now, he has no choice but to run away from his home and hide.

(A) predecessor (B) racist
(C) specialist (D) gambler

08 ___ The plane crashed into a snowy mountain. 25 people were on board but only 15 survived first impact. The survivors were all _____ with the sub-zero temperature and they had to find a way to keep warm.

(A) shivering (B) recovering
(C) delivering (D) discovering

09 ___ The game is _____ with any kinds of operating system. In other words, no matter if you are using a MacBook or a Windows product, you will be able to run the game on either system.

(A) capable (B) irresistible
(C) compatible (D) memorable

10 ___ The entrepreneur agreed to donate millions of dollars to help the community get through the_____ that the virus brought.

(A) tourism (B) hardship
(C) optimism (D) membership

11 ___ When you are taking a picture with a camera, it is suggested that you use both of your hands to make the camera _____. In this case, you can take a steady shot of the objects without blurring the picture.

(A) stable (B) sustainable
(C) inevitable (D) vulnerable

12 ___ Hundreds of years ago, the Vikings _____ the coasts of England and they made a fortune out of doing so. They were so strong that whenever people heard their horns or screams, they immediately ran away.

(A) invaded (B) concluded
(C) persuaded (D) waved

13 ___ The Artificial Intelligence technology will soon become a(n) _____ part of our society. Everything we use will be connected to the AI and it will help us manage all kinds of things.

(A) gradual (B) typical
(C) cultural (D) integral

14 ___ Even until today, people are still debating on whether teenage students should wear a _____to school or not. Both sides have great arguments, so it will continue to be a never-ending fight.

(A) sample (B) burden
(C) uniform (D) necessity

15 ___ Tony Stark is not only rich but also _____. He can think of things that no one else can. His creative mindset makes him one of the greatest inventors that ever exist.

(A) productive (B) effective
(C) corrective (D) innovative

解答
1.(D) 2.(C) 3.(C) 4.(A) 5.(B) 6.(C) 7.(D) 8.(A) 9.(C) 10.(B) 11.(A) 12.(A) 13.(D) 14.(C) 15.(D)

Level 3

Unit 41 – Unit 60 進階單字

因各家手機系統不同，若無法直接掃描，
仍可以至以下電腦雲端連結下載收聽。
（https://reurl.cc/px2bml）

breed
[brid]

n. 品種
v. 繁殖;產生 (惡果)

My father makes a living by breeding cattle.
我父親以養牛維生。

> 秒殺解字 br 有「破裂」、「分岔」的意思,相關單字有 **br**eak (v. 破碎)、**br**eech (n. 裂口)、**br**anch (n. 分支)、**br**onchitis (n. 支氣管炎)、**br**ook (n. 小溪流),而分岔開來就會產生「開枝散葉」、「繁衍」的意思,如:**br**other (n. 兄弟)、**br**eed (v. 繁殖)、**br**ood (n. 一窩雛鳥)。

普 110
警特 107

時態　breed, bred [brɛd], bred

同義字　procreate, reproduce

breeder
[ˋbridɚ]

n. 飼養培育動植物的人

Louisa's father is one of the top cow breeders in this county.
Louisa 的父親是本縣最頂尖乳牛飼養戶之一。

surrender
[sɚˋrɛndɚ]

n. **v.** 投降

All the soldiers said that they would rather die than surrender to their enemies.
所有士兵都說他們寧願死也不願意向他們的敵人投降。

普 102
高 108

Without a good supply of ammunition, the troops will be at the point of surrender.
由於沒有足夠的彈藥補給,軍隊很快就要投降了。

> 秒殺解字 sur(=super=over)+render(give back) → 把東西「歸還給」「上」頭,引申出「投降」、「屈服」的意思。

詞搭　surrender to... = yield to... = concede to... = give in to... 屈服於……; surrender oneself to the police 自首、投案

content
[kən`tɛnt]

n. 滿足
v. 使滿足
adj. 滿足的

Though he earns a small salary, he's fairly content with his life in the countryside. ⚠特 106
雖然領著微薄薪水，他對鄉間生活感到相當滿足。

🪶 **秒殺解字** con(together)+ten(hold)+t → 把東西「握」在「一起」，表示「滿足的」。

詞搭 be content with... = be contented with... = be satisfied with... = be pleased with... 對……感到滿意； to one's heart's content 心滿意足地，盡情地

同義字 satisfied

反義字 discontent, dissatisfied

content
[`kɑntɛnt]

n. 內容

The film is quite propular among young people, but in fact, it lacks content. 高 108
這部電影頗受年輕人歡迎，但事實上它缺乏內容。

popcorn
[`pɑp‚kɔrn]

n. 爆米花

A lot of people cannot do without popcorn and drinks when they go to a movie.
許多人去看電影是不能沒有爆米花跟飲料的。

🪶 **秒殺解字** pop 是爆炸聲，為擬聲字，corn 是玉米，popcorn 是爆米花。

asset
[`æsɛt]

n. 資產；有用的人／物／特質

Being hit by recession, the company decides to hold more liquid assets and cut down on real estate investments.
受到不景氣影響，這家公司決定加碼持有流動資產並減少不動產投資。

Mastering more than two foreign languages will be a great asset for people who want to go into international trade.
對有意從事國際貿易的人而言，精通兩種以上外國語言的能力將會是一大資產。

🪶 **秒殺解字** as(=ad=to)+set(enough) → 本指「使……足夠」，表示金錢足夠，可以清除債務，後引申為「資產」。

詞搭 personal / real assets 動／不動產

compile
[kəm`paɪl]
v. 彙編

Planning to compile a Who's Who of Teachers in Taiwan, we are now collecting necessary data.
我們計畫編纂台灣教師名人錄，所以現在正蒐集必要的資料中。

(秒殺解字) com(together)+pil(compress, ram down) +e → 把文件「堆疊」在「一起」，表示「彙編」。

詞搭	compile a(n) dictionary / list/index 彙編字典／名單／索引

journalism
[`dʒɝn!͵ɪzəm]
n. 新聞學

Thomas is deciding to go into journalism after graduation from college.
Thomas 決定畢業後從事新聞事業。

(秒殺解字) journal+ism → **journ** 表示「日」，源自法文。journal 表示「日記」、「雜誌」。相關同源字有 **journ**ey (n. 旅行)。

詞搭	the Department of Journalism 新聞系；take up journalism 從事新聞業
衍生字	journal [`dʒɝn!] n. 期刊；日記

journalist
[`dʒɝnəlɪst]
n. 新聞從業人員

In the press conference, a local journalist raised a tough question to query about the adequacy of the new policy.
在記者會當中，一位本地記者提出一個尖銳問題質疑新政策的正當性。

警特 108

字義	此字涵義廣泛，包含 reporter [rɪ`pɔrtə] n. 記者、editor [`ɛdɪtə] n. 編輯、newscaster [`njuz͵kæstə] n. 新聞廣播員、anchorman [`æŋkə͵mæn] n. 主播

unexpectedly

[ˌʌnɪkˋspɛktɪdlɪ]

adv. 意外地

On my way home from work, I met an old friend unexpectedly, and then we went to chat over coffee.
下班回家途中，與一位老友不期而遇，於是我們就去喝咖啡聊天。

His new novel received unexpectedly high popularity.
他的小說受到歡迎程度出乎預料的高。

 秒殺解字 un(not)+ex(out)+spec(look)+t+ed+ly → 「無法」「期待」「地」。expect 字面是往「外」「看」表示「期待」，可用喜出「望」「外」記憶。因為 ex 已經包含 /ks/ 兩個子音，因此省略後面字根 spect 開頭 s。

同義字 surprisingly, suddenly, abruptly, out of the blue

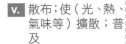 99
105

analyst

[ˋænḷɪst]

n. 分析師

As an advanced real estate analyst, Joan predicted a considerable drop in domestic house prices for next year.
身為一位資深的不動產分析師，Joan 預測明年國內房價跌幅頗深。

 秒殺解字 ana(back)+lys(loose)+t(one who) → 將東西從「後面」「鬆開」的「人」，引申為「分析師」。

詞搭 a political / military analyst 政治／軍事分析家

diffuse

[dɪˋfjuz]

v. 散布；使（光、熱、氣味等）擴散；普及

These pollutants, if not properly controlled, will diffuse into the soil easily and quickly.
若沒有得到適當管控，這些汙染物將很容易並且迅速擴散滲透到土壤中。

普 108

 秒殺解字 dif(=dis=apart)+fus(pour)+e → 往「四面八方」「倒」，表示「擴散」、「散布」。相關同源字有 confuse (v. 使困惑)、refuse (v. 拒絕)、transfusion (n. 輸血)。

disappointed

[ˌdɪsəˋpɔɪntɪd]

adj. 感到失望的

All the fans were quite disappointed at / about the result of the baseball game.
所有球迷都對棒球賽結果非常失望。

普 100

 秒殺解字 dis(opposite)+ap(=ad=to)+point(point)+ed → 「任命」（appoint）的「相反」動作，表示「罷黜」、「解職」，衍生出「感到失望的」的語意。

詞搭 be disappointed in + sb. 對某人失望；be disappointed with / about / at + sth. 對某事失望

367

transmit

[træns`mɪt]

v. 傳送;傳播

Some insects or animals can possibly transmit diseases of many kinds to human beings.

有些昆蟲或動物有可能把各種疾病傳染給人類。

秒殺解字 trans(across)+mit(send) → 「送」「過去」,表示「傳送」、「傳播」。相關同源字有 promise (v./n. 答應)、admit (v. 承認)、admission (n. 准許)、permit (v. 允許)、permission (n. 允許)、submit (v. 呈遞)、submission (n. 呈遞)、omit (v. 遺漏)、omission (n. 遺漏)。

時態 transmit, transmitted [træns`mɪtɪd], transmitted

詞搭 transmit a tradition from one generation to another 將一項傳統代代相傳

transmission

[træns`mɪʃən]

n. 傳送;傳播

Data transmission is expected to be faster under the 5G telecommunication framework.

在 5G 的電信通訊架構下,資料的傳輸可望更快。

intent

[ɪn`tɛnt]

n. 意圖

adj. 專注的

It was not her intent to hurt anybody; she shot the gun only to defend herself and protect her daughter.

她並沒有意圖要傷害到任何人;她開槍只是自我防衛同時也是要保護她女兒。

Mary had an intent look on her face when she was listening to the speaker at the podium.

當 Mary 在聆聽講台上演講者説話時,她的臉部表情非常專注。

秒殺解字 in(toward)+tent(thin, stretch) → 心思「往⋯⋯」「延展」,即「意圖」。

詞搭 be intent on + N / Ving = be determined + to V 專心致志於⋯

同義字 intention

telegraphy

[tə`lɛgrəfɪ]

n. 電信術(學);電報(學);電報系統

Though smartphones are the most convenient devices, telegraphy is still employed when secured communication is required.

雖然智慧手機是最方便的裝置,但為確保通信安全時,電報還是會被運用的。

秒殺解字 tele(far)+graph(write)+y → 透過電線將「遠方」傳來的文字符號透過靜電膽「寫」出來。

同義字 telegram

misleading

[mɪs`lidɪŋ]

adj. 誤導人的

Nowadays, cyberspace is flooded with fake news and misleading information, so we should think and check the source before we share.

現今網路世界充斥著假新聞跟誤導資訊，所以我們在分享之前，務必三思確認來源。

(秒殺解字) mis(badly, wrongly)+lead+ing → 「誤」「導」的。

同義字 | false

---

photograph

[`fotə͵græf]

n. 照片

v. 照相

聽背 107

An old, faded photograph reminded them of the hardships they experienced when they were young.

一張褪色泛黃老照片讓他們想起年輕時期所經歷過的艱辛。

(秒殺解字) photo(light)+graph(write) → 用「光」「寫」下的紀錄，表示「照片」。相關同源字有 **graph**（n. 圖表）、auto**graph**（n./v. 親筆簽名）、bio**graph**y（n. 傳記）、autobio**graph**y（n. 自傳）、calli**graph**y（n. 書法）、para**graph**（n. 段落）。

詞搭 | take a photograph 拍照；have / get one's photograph taken 請人拍照

同義字 | picture

---

photographer

[fə`tɑgrəfɚ]

n. 攝影師；攝影記者

This morning a photographer came to the campus to take graduation photos for us.

今天早上一位攝影師來到校園為我們拍畢業照。

字辨 | cameraman [`kæmərə͵mæn] n. 電影拍攝員／電視攝影記者

---

trivially

[`trɪvɪəlɪ]

adv. 瑣細地；平凡地

The task I assigned to you was trivially easy, and I don't know why you said it's too tough.

我指派給你的任務相當簡單，但我不明白為何你說它太棘手。

(秒殺解字) tri(three)+via(way)+al+ly → trivia 是瑣事，古代資訊封閉，街坊鄰居在「三」岔「路」口碰面時，會聊些八卦「瑣事」（trivial matter）；trivially 是瑣細地。

wealthy

[`wɛlθɪ]

adj. 富有的

I wish I were super rich and the wealthiest man in the world, but in fact, I'm now worrying about next month's rent.

我好希望自己是全世界超級富翁，但事實上我現在正在煩惱下個月的房租。

曾 103

> **秒殺解字** weal(well)+th+y → weal 和 well 同源，表示「好」，wealth 是模仿 health 所造出來的單字，表示「擁有大量財富」和「幸福美好」，wealthy 為「富有的」。

同義字 ｜ rich, affluent

---

advocate

[`ædvəkɪt]

n. 支持者、擁護者

[`ædvəˌket]

v. 提倡

With the increasing murder rate in recent years, many people are advocating the restoration of the death penalty.

由於近年來謀殺事件比例一直增高，有許多人正主張恢復死刑。

曾 101

> **秒殺解字** ad(to)+voc(call)+ate → 公開「發聲」支持某議題或某人。相關同源字有 **voc**abulary (n. 字彙)、**voc**al (adj. 聲音的)、**voc**ation (n. 職業)、con**vok**e (v. 召集開會)、e**vok**e (v. 喚起)、pro**vok**e(v. 煽動)、pro**voc**ation (n. 激怒)、re**vok**e (v. 撤銷)、re**voc**ation (n. 撤銷)。

詞搭 ｜ an advocate of + sth. 某事的支持者

---

restoration

[ˌrɛstəˈreʃən]

n. 修復；恢復

The Notre-Dame de Paris caught fire in 2019, and the restoration of it is indeed a huge challenge.

巴黎聖母院於 2019 年發生火災，而其重建復原工作的確是一大挑戰。

曾 107

> **秒殺解字** re(back, again)+st(set up)+or+ation → 本義是「重新」「設立」，衍生出「修復」、「恢復」等意思。

同義字 ｜ renovation, return

delegation
[ˌdɛləˈgeʃən]

n. 代表團；委任

The trade delegation is composed of three ministers and two entrepreneurs. 普105

這個貿易代表團由三位部長以及兩位企業家組成。

秒殺解字 de(away)+leg(law)+ate+ion → 依「法」被選出來「離開」本地到另一地的「代表團」，代表全體發言、投票、或決策。相關同源字有 **leg**al (adj. 合法的)、**leg**islate (v. 立法)、privi**leg**e (n. 特權)。

同義字 deputation

applaud
[əˈplɔd]

v. 鼓掌

The entire audience stood up and warmly applauded the young violinist for a full five minutes. 普106

所有的聽眾／觀眾都起立為這位年輕小提琴家熱烈鼓掌整整有五分鐘之久。

秒殺解字 ap(=ad=to)+plaud(clap) → 本義「鼓掌」。

詞搭 applaud + sb. + for... 因……而為某人鼓掌

同義字 clap, give + sb. + a big hand

anecdote
[ˈænɪkˌdot]

n. 軼事；趣聞

Last night, I chatted with my grandfather and, the whole night, he fetched up a lot of anecdotes about the old days. 普104

昨晚我跟爺爺聊天抬槓，整個晚上他都在回憶舊時許多軼事。

秒殺解字 an(not)+ec(=ex=out)+dot(give)+e →「不能」「給」「出去」，不能公開的秘密故事，即「軼事」。這個字源自於西元六世紀拜占庭史學家 Procopius 曾寫的一部未出版作品 Anekdota，書名意思是「未公開的事」。

同義字 story

unaware
[ˌʌnəˈwɛr]
adj. 未察覺到的

I <u>was</u> completely <u>unaware of</u> the malfunction of the brakes when I tried to stop my car.
當我試著要停住我的車時，我完全沒意識到剎車已經失去作用了。

🖋 **秒殺解字** un(not)+aware → 「未」「察覺的」。

詞搭 be unaware of... 知道……、察覺到……；be unaware that + S + V... 知道……

同義字 unconscious

反義字 aware, conscious

patriot
[ˈpetrɪət]
n. 愛國者

As an ardent patriot, the soldier said he would fight to death before he surrendered.  101
身為一位熱血愛國志士，這位軍人說他寧願戰死也絕不投降。

🖋 **秒殺解字** patr(father)+i+ot(person) → 愛「父親」之國的「人」。可用 **father** 當神隊友，**p/f**，**t/ð** 轉音，母音通轉，來記憶 **patr**，表示「父親」。

alienation
[ˌeljəˈneʃən]
n. 疏離

The psychiatrist reminded us that depressed people might often feel <u>a sense of</u> alienation from those around them.
心理醫師提醒我們，要注意鬱悶的人常常會與身邊的人有疏離感覺。

🖋 **秒殺解字** ali(another, other, different)+en+ation → 「另外的」、「其他的」、「不同的」。

詞搭 a sense of alienation 疏離感

interact
[ˌɪntəˈækt]
v. 互動

Kent has lived a life of solitude for many years and seldom <u>interacts with</u> others.
Kent 已經獨居數年，也鮮少與人互動。

🖋 **秒殺解字** inter(between)+act(do) → 「兩（多）者間」的「動作」交流。相關同源字有 ex**act**（adj. 精確的）、re**act**（v. 反應）、trans**act**（v. 交易）、en**act**（v. 制定）。

moisture
[ˈmɔɪstʃə]
n. 溼氣；水分

Being exposed to moisture, the pills seem to have lost their potency. 🖼 101
由於受潮，這些藥丸似乎已經失去藥效了。

🖋 **秒殺解字** moist+ure → 「潮濕」的「狀態」。

dissatisfaction
[dɪˌsætɪsˈfækʃən]
n. 不滿、不平

In yesterday's protest strike, the leader of the labor union voiced all workers' dissatisfaction about wages. 警特 106
在昨天的抗議罷工行動中，工會領袖發聲表達所有工人對薪資的不滿。

🖋️ **秒殺解字** dis(not)+satis(enough)+fac(make)+t+ion →「使」「不」「滿足」。

詞搭 express dissatisfaction at / with... 表達對……的不滿意

反義字 satisfaction

---

disorder
[dɪsˈɔrdə]
n. 無秩序、雜亂

Someone broke into the office last night and now it's in a state of disorder. 普 105 / 警特 106
昨晚有人闖入辦公室，而現在辦公室凌亂不堪。

🖋️ **秒殺解字** dis(not)+order →「無」「秩序」。

詞搭 be in disorder 陷入雜亂的狀況； a mental / psychiatric disorder 精神病

反義字 order

---

isolation
[ˌaɪsḷˈeʃən]
n. 孤立、隔絕

Don't consider this problem in isolation, as you should take all factors into consideration. 普 103
不要只單獨考慮這個問題；你應該把所有因素列入考量。

🖋️ **秒殺解字** isol(=insul=island)+ation → 像海上孤「島」與世「隔絕」。

詞搭 live in isolation 過著與世隔絕的生活；be in isolation from + sb. 脫離某人

---

isolationism
[ˌaɪsḷˈeʃənɪzm]
n. 孤立主義

Economic isolationism won't help solve current problems and I believe trade cooperation is the only key to our future prosperity.
經濟孤立主義將無助於解決問題，我也相信貿易合作才是促使我們未來繁榮的唯一方法。

---

stereotype
[ˈstɛrɪəˌtaɪp]
n. 刻板印象

We often see gender stereotypes in advertisements.
我們常常在廣告看到性別刻板印象的情況。

🖋️ **秒殺解字** stereo(firm, solid, three-dimensional)+type → 本指立體的印刷版。用同一版子印刷，所印製出來的樣式一模一樣，語意幾經轉變，衍生出「刻板印象」的意思。

詞搭 racial / sexual / cultural stereotype 種族／性別／文化上的刻版印象；fit the stereotype 符合刻板印象

circulate

[ˈsɝkjəˌlet]

v. 循環；流傳；散發；
分發

The blood in my body began to circulate quickly after the doctor gave me a shot, and then I felt like a new person.
醫師給我打一針後，我的血液馬上就開始循環，於是我覺得自己簡直是另外一個人了。

秒殺解字 circle(round)+ate → 形成一個「圓圈」，引申為「循環」、「流傳」。circle 在加接母音開頭的字尾時，如 -ate，先刪除字尾 e，並在 cl 和之間插入 u 字母，以維持最佳音節結構。cl、gl、bl 在加接母音開頭字尾時，插入 u 的相關例子有 particle / particulate、angle / angular、spectacle / spectacular、miracle / miraculous、fable / fabulous 等。

詞搭 Rumors began circulating that... ……的謠言開始散播

警特 109

---

impairment

[ɪmˈpɛrmənt]

n. 損傷

The organization is now offering free hearing aids for people with hearing impairment.
這個組織正提供免費助聽器給聽障人士。

秒殺解字 im(=in, into)+pair(worse)+ment → 使變「糟」，引申為「損傷」。有字源學家推測 pair 和 ped 同源，皆表示「腳」，pair 作「腳絆倒」解釋，絆倒造成「損傷」。

詞搭 hearing / mental / physical / visual / cognitive impairment 聽力受損／智力低下／身體損傷／視力損傷／認知損傷

---

discard

[dɪsˈkɑrd]

v. 丟棄

If you hope to make your room clean and tidy, you should first discard those old clothes.
如果你希望房間弄得乾淨整齊，首先你應先把那些舊衣服扔掉。

秒殺解字 dis(away)+card(card) →「丟掉」手上的「牌」，引申為「拋棄」。

詞搭 discard A for B 捨 A 取 B

同義字 throw away, get rid of

警 105

---

warrant

[ˈwɔrənt]

n. 正當理由；授權令
v. 保證；證明

He won't achieve anything. I'll warrant you.
他不會有甚麼成就，我敢保證。

詞搭 a search warrant 搜索狀；a warrant of arrest 逮捕令

warranty
[`wɔrəntɪ]
n. 保證（書）

The company doesn't provide a warranty for accidental damages, so Mary may have to pay for the repair of her cellphone.
這家公司並不提供意外損壞的保修服務，所以 Mary 可能必須自行付費修埋她的手機了。

秒殺解字 warrant+y → warranty 和 guarantee 同源，核心語意皆是「保證」。

詞搭 be under warranty = be under guarantee 在保固期內

同義字 guarantee

nominate
[`nɑmə‚net]
v. 提名

Last week, he was nominated by the Prime Minister as the Ambassador to Cuba and he'll be inaugurated next month.
上週他已被首相任命為駐古巴大使，而且即將在下個月就職到任。

曾 100
101

nomination
[‚nɑmə`neʃən]
n. 提名

Who do you think will get the Republican Presidential nomination next week?
你認為下週誰會獲得共和黨總統參選提名？

曾 101

秒殺解字 nom(name)+in+ate+ion → 提「名」。

詞搭 win the nomination as... 贏得……的提名

treasure
[`trɛʒɚ]
n. 寶藏；財寶
v. 珍惜；珍愛

During the war, a lot of treasures in the museum were looted by the enemy troops.
在戰爭期間，許多博物館裡的珍藏寶物被敵軍掠奪了。

曾 105
警特 107

秒殺解字 treas(put, store)+ure →「放置」、「儲存」寶藏的地方。

詞搭 buried treasure 埋藏的寶藏

treasury
[`trɛʒərɪ]
n. 寶庫；金庫

Next year's treasury budget of the company was just passed in the shareholders' meeting.
這家公司下一年度財務預算剛剛在股東會議中通過。

magnify
[`mæɡnə‚faɪ]
v. 放大、擴大

Reading glasses can magnify the words in newspapers and they can make reading more comfortable for old people.
老花眼鏡能夠放大報紙上的文字，如此一來可讓老人家閱讀更輕鬆。

秒殺解字 magn(great)+i+fy(make, do) →「使」變「大」。

同義字 exaggerate, enlarge

summon
[`sʌmən]

v. 召集；召喚；鼓起

Even though Alex <u>summoned up his courage</u> and invited Mary to a movie, she couldn't help but refuse his invitation eventually.
即使 Alex 鼓起勇氣邀請 Mary 去看電影，她最終還是忍不住拒絕了他的邀請。

> (秒殺解字) sum(=sub=under)+mon(warn) → 本義是「私下」「警告」，之後語意產生改變，12 世紀才有類似「召喚」、「召集」的意思。

| 詞搭 | summon + sb. + to V 召喚某人從事…；summon a conference 召開會議 |

---

summons
[`sʌmənz] [C]

n. 傳票；召喚；召集（會）

v. 傳喚；傳……到法院

Clive was given a summons to appear in court as a witness last week.   圖 108
Clive 上週被傳喚出庭作證。

Because Jack was a witness of the murder, he was summonsed to attend court yesterday afternoon.
由於傑克是謀殺案的證人，昨天下午他被傳喚出庭。

01 ___ After 2 months of siege, the baron of the castle finally decided to
_____. The baron walked out of the gate and negotiated the terms
of surrender with the enemy general.

(A) shiver   (B) recover
(C) surrender   (D) discover

02 ___ He threw all his _____ on the table and demanded a rematch
against the champion. Everyone else thought he lost his mind, but the
champion saw the determination in his eyes and agreed the deal.

(A) deposits   (B) assets
(C) panic   (D) remedies

03 ___ Peter disguises himself as a _____ at the Daily Bugle newspaper.
In reality, he is a superhero who fights evil in disguise.

(A) tenant   (B) journalist
(C) agent   (D) immigrant

04 ___ The guerilla fighters ambushed the convoy _____ and gained
massive advantage. However, the formal military was so much better
equipped than the fighters and eventually fought off the guerillas.

(A) unexpectedly   (B) traditionally
(C) dependably   (D) steeply

05 ___ If you want to become a(n) _____, you need to be curious and
research at all times. This helps you to ensure that your ideas are
practical, rather than just clever.

(A) analyst   (B) racist
(C) specialist   (D) capitalist

06 ___ My mom was _____ at me because I didn't perform well in the last
exam. I promised her that I would get a better score next time, and I
fulfilled my promise on this test.

(A) destined   (B) enlightened
(C) disappointed   (D) detailed

07 ___ The President keeps telling everyone that the mainstream media is full of _____ information and everyone should boycott those media outlets.

(A) alternating   (B) developing
(C) remaining   (D) misleading

08 ___ This little boy showed us maturity and courage. He called the 911 emergency workers to get help for his fainted mother, and this action saved his mother's life. We should _____ him for his behavior.

(A) applaud   (B) adjust
(C) detain   (D) betray

09 ___ The master thief was so quiet and agile that everyone in the house was _____ of his presence. In the end, he stole various items that are worth over 20,000 dollars.

(A) liberal   (B) unaware
(C) critical   (D) distinct

10 ___ The _____ said that he would rather die on the battlefield for glory than surrender and live like a rat. This is the kind of spirit that everyone should look up to.

(A) traitor   (B) legislator
(C) pioneer   (D) patriot

11 ___ The players can _____ with the AI characters to get various kinds of missions. The missions include "puzzle solving," "hostage rescue," and the fan-favorite, "the last man standing."

(A) extract   (B) contract
(C) interact   (D) attract

12 ___ To end the _____ of the country, the leader of the government ordered a curfew and announced that the country has entered a state of emergency.

(A) murder   (B) disaster
(C) barrier   (D) disorder

13 ___ Those who contracted the virus need to enter _____ as soon as possible to avoid spreading the virus to even more people.

(A) isolation   (B) contamination

(C) addiction   (D) prevention

14 ___ The deadly gas _____through the air ventilation to the whole company. In the end, the chemical leak resulted in 50 deaths and over one hundred people sickened.

(A) circulated   (B) contemplated

(C) formulated   (D) accelerated

15 ___ The judge issued a search _____ against the suspect. As a result, the police could finally enter his house and search for more evidence.

(A) sample   (B) assembly

(C) warrant   (D) foundation

解答
1.(C) 2.(B) 3.(B) 4.(A) 5.(A) 6.(C) 7.(D) 8.(A) 9.(B) 10.(D) 11.(C) 12.(D) 13.(A) 14.(A) 15.(C)

Unit 43

---

ethnic
[`ɛθnɪk]
adj. 族群的

With more and more immigrants and foreign laborers coming to Taiwan, now we have many ethnic restaurants available here.

隨著愈來愈多移民及外籍勞工來到台灣，現在我們這裡具有民族風味的食物及餐館變得普及了。

🖋 **秒殺解字** eth(custom)+n+ic → 擁有共同「習俗」的人，引申為同一「族群」的人。

詞搭 an ethnic group 族群；ethnic clothes / music 民族服裝／音樂；ethnic minority 少數民族

字辨 ethic [`ɛθɪk] n. 倫理

同義字 racial

---

disadvantage
[͵dɪsəd`væntɪdʒ]
n. 缺點；不利的條件

If you decide to work and live in big cities, you'd better consider whether the disadvantages will outweigh the advantages.

如果你決定要在大都市工作及生活你最好衡量一下其缺點是否大於優點。

🖋 **秒殺解字** dis(not)+adv(av=ab=from)+ant(=ante=before)+age → advantage 字面上是「從……」「前面」出來，表示佔有先機、「優勢」。dis 表示「不」（not）、「相反」（opposite）。

同義字 drawback, handicap

反義字 advantage

---

densely
[`dɛnslɪ]
adv. 稠密地

Tokyo is one of the most densely populated cities in the world.

東京是世界世上人口密度最高的城市之一。

🖋 **秒殺解字** dense+ly →「密集」地。

反義字 sparsely

transparent
[træns`pɛrənt]
adj. 透明的

To stimulate investment and ensure profits, the government should make its policies more transparent and stable.
為了刺激投資以及保證獲利，政府應該將其政策變得更透明穩定。

秒殺解字 trans(across, through)+par(appear, visible)+ent → 「穿透」某物「出現」，表示「透明的」。相關同源字有 ap**pear**（v. 出現）、ap**pear**ance（n. 出現；外表）、ap**par**ent（adj. 明顯的）、disap**pear**（v. 消失）、disap**pear**ance（n. 失蹤）。

詞搭 a transparent lie 易看穿的謊言

同義字 clear

反義字 opaque, translucent

---

seam
[sim] [C]
n. 縫；縫合處

The hand-made bag is much more expensive, but it has very strong seams and will last longer.
這個手工製作的袋子是貴了一點，但它的縫線處很牢固所以也會更耐用。

詞搭 come / break / fall apart at the seams 在接縫處裂開；a rich seam of + sth. 某物很豐富

---

seamless
[`simlɪs]
adj. 無縫的

The mending on the coat is almost seamless.
外套上幾乎看不到修補的隙縫痕跡。

秒殺解字 seam+less → 「無」「縫」的。

---

advertisement
[͵ædvɚ`taɪzmənt]
n. 廣告（常縮寫成 ad [æd]）

The agent decided to place their new car advertisements in some major automobile magazines.
這家代理商決定將他們新車廣告刊登在幾家汽車雜誌上。

秒殺解字 ad(to)+vert(turn)+ise+ment → 「廣告」是使人「轉」「向」，誘發購買動機。

---

advertising
[`ædvɚ͵taɪzɪŋ]
n. 廣告（業）
adj. 廣告的

Sophia's job in advertising is well-paid, but it is also a high-pressure one.
Sophia 在廣告業的工作薪水是很高，但壓力也很大。

詞搭 an advertising agency / agent / slogan 廣告公司／業者／標語

alarming

[əˋlɑrmɪŋ]

adj. 驚人的；令人擔憂的

The rise of the inflation rate has been quite alarming for the past few months.

過去幾個月以來通貨膨脹上升的比例令人感到驚恐擔憂。

秒殺解字 al(=ad=to)+arm(weapons)+ing → alarm 源自義大利語，在戰時警覺到危險，士兵會説 to arms，意思是拿起武器備戰，因此 alarm 有「警報器」、「驚慌」等意思，alarming 是形容詞。

高考 108

---

predecessor

[ˋprɛdɪˌsɛsɚ]

n. 前輩；前任者

I think you'll learn a lot from the mistakes your predecessors have made.

我想你可以從你的前輩曾經犯過的錯誤中得到不少經驗。

秒殺解字 pre(before)+de(away)+cess(go)+or →「先」「走」「開」的人。

普 108

反義字 successor

---

messenger

[ˋmɛsṇdʒɚ]

n. 信差；使者

The manager said these confidential documents should be delivered by a special messenger.

經理説這些機密文件必須由一位特派信差來遞送。

秒殺解字 messeng(message)+er →「發送」「訊息」的人。mess 等同 miss、mit，表示「送」(send)。

---

vocal

[ˋvokl̩]

adj. 歌唱的；口頭的；敢言的

She just had a vocal cord operation two days ago and it's a little difficult for her to talk now.

她兩天前才動過聲帶手術，所以現在要説話有點困難。

秒殺解字 voc(voice)+al →「聲音」「的」。相關同源字有 **voc**abulary (n. 字彙)、**voc**ation (n. 職業)、ad**voc**ate (n. 擁護者)、con**vok**e (v. 召集開會)、e**vok**e (v. 喚起)、pro**vok**e (v. 煽動)、pro**voc**ation (n. 激怒)、re**vok**e (v. 撤銷)、re**voc**ation (n. 撤銷)。

turmoil

[`tɝmɔɪl]

n. 騷動;混亂

The domestic stock exchange was in turmoil today because of the rumor that a major enterprise declared bankruptcy last night.
因為謠傳一家主要企業昨晚宣佈破產,國內證券市場今天一場混亂。

> **秒殺解字** 字源不明,但字源學家 Eric Partridge 推測 turmoil 和表「震動」的字根 **trem** 同源,可能是因為震動易引起「騷動」。相關同源字有 **trem**or (n. 顫抖;小地震)、**trem**ble (v. 顫抖)、**trem**endous (adj. 巨大的) 等。

詞搭 throw...into turmoil / chaos 使……陷入混亂;emotional / mental / political turmoil 情緒／精神／政治的混亂

同義字 chaos

cautious

[`kɔʃəs]

adj. 小心的、謹慎的

To deal with such a tough problem, you'd better take a more cautious approach.
為了能夠處理這個難纏的問題,你最好採取一種比較謹慎的方法。

> 曾 110
> 警特 108

> **秒殺解字** cau(see)+t+i+ous → 小心謹慎的人會謹慎察「看」。同義字 circumspect 也包含「看」的字根 spec,可見謹慎小心的人往往環顧四周,瞻前顧後。

詞搭 be cautious about... = be careful about... 謹慎處理……

同義字 careful

cautiously

[`kɔʃəslɪ]

adv. 小心地、謹慎地

I'm not familiar with the new machine, so I think I have to operate it more cautiously.
我對這部新的機器不熟悉,所以我認為在操作時我必須更加小心謹慎。

同義字 carefully, with caution

therapy

[`θɛrəpɪ]

n. 療法

Did you ever seek any therapy for your chronic depression?
您是否曾為長期抑鬱症尋求任何治療方法?

> 曾 104

> **秒殺解字** therap(healing)+y → 「療」法。

同義字 treatment

hymn
[hɪm]
n. 讚美詩；聖歌

At the end of the sacrifice ceremony, all the participants joined hands and sang a hymn.
在祭祀典禮結束時，所有參與人員手牽手高唱讚美詩歌。

 （秒殺解字）hymn 指「聖歌」，字源學家推測可能跟希臘神話中的婚姻之神 Hymen 有關，這個字衍生出「結婚歌曲」的意思。

詞搭 a hymn to + sth. 歌頌某事物；hymn book 聖歌集

---

resign
[rɪˋzaɪn]
v. 辭職；順從

Hermosa decided to resign from the company because of the constant humiliation in the workplace.
由於經常在職場上受到羞辱，Hermosa 決定辭職離開這家公司。

普 108
警特 108

 （秒殺解字）re(opposite)+sign(mark) → 畫個「相反」的「記號」表示取消，引申為「辭職」。相關同源字有 **sign**（n. 記號）、**sign**ature（n. 簽名）、**sign**al（n. 信號）、**sign**ify（v. 表示）、de**sign**（v. 設計）、as**sign**（v. 分配）。

---

ruling
[ˋrulɪŋ]
n. 統治；支配；規定
adj. 統治的；支配的

The media should always take responsibility as an independent watchdog over the ruling party and the government.
媒體始終應扮演承擔監督執政黨以及政府的獨立角色。

 （秒殺解字）rule+ing → 「統治」。

---

thrive
[θraɪv]
v. 繁榮、興隆；繁茂地生長

His organic produce business has immensely thrived well over these recent years.
他的有機農產品事業最近幾年成長非常茁壯。

（秒殺解字）thrive 和 thrifty 同源，核心語意皆表示「繁榮」、「興旺」。

同義字 prosper, boom

---

charitable
[ˋtʃærətəbl̩]
adj. 仁慈的、慈善的

A charitable foundation / organization is going to hold a charity concert next Saturday.
一個慈善基金會／組織即將在下週六舉辦一場慈善音樂會。

普 100
警特 105

反義字 uncharitable

charity

[`tʃærətɪ]

n. 慈善；博愛；施捨；慈善機構／事業

The high school students walked around the island, raising money for charity.

這些高中生徒步環島為慈善事業募集資金。

> 秒殺解字 char(like, deire)+i+ty → 「慈善」是愛人、「喜歡」人的事業。caress [kə`rɛs] ( n./v. 愛撫 )、charity、cherish [`tʃɛrɪʃ] (v. 珍愛) 同源，k/tʃ 轉音，母音通轉，核心語意都是「喜歡」(like) 或「渴望」(desire)。「愛撫」(caress) 表現出「喜歡」的行為。

---

solidarity

[ˌsɑlə`dærətɪ]

n. 團結

The strike lasted four hours in torrential rain, fully demonstrating the solidarity among the union members.

抗議活動在暴雨中持續四小時，充分展現工會成員之間的團結意志。

> 秒殺解字 solid(firm)+ar+i+ty → 穩固的狀態，引申為「團結」。

詞搭 show / express / demonstrate one's solidarity with + sb. 展現與某人團結一致的意志

---

accord

[ə`kɔrd]

n. 協定

v. 一致

The peace talks lasted for 5 days and finally the two leaders signed / reached an accord.

和談持續五天，兩國領袖終於簽署／達成協議。

🔊 101

> 秒殺解字 ac(=ad=to)+cord(heart) → 讓兩「心」趨於「一致」，因此有「和諧」、「協定」等衍生意思。可用 heart 當神隊友，k/h，d/t 轉音，母音通轉，來記憶 cord，皆表示「心」。相關同源字有 concord (n. 一致、和諧)、discord (n. 不和)、record (n./v. 紀錄)。

詞搭 be in accord with... = accord with... 與⋯⋯一致；
with one accord 全體一致地

refugee

[ˌrɛfjʊˋdʒi]

n. 難民

CARE International found that the refugees in the camp were in bad shape for food and even worse off for clothes.

國際關懷組織發現在難民營的難民需要食物供應，更需要衣物的救援。

秒殺解字 re(back)+fug(flee, run away)+ee → refugee 字面上是「逃」「回來」，尋求庇護、保護的「人」。

普 108
高 110

| 詞搭 | political refugees 政治難民；refugee camps 難民營 |

decay

[dɪˋke]

n. 腐爛；蛀牙；衰敗
v. 腐爛；侵蝕

If you stay in the habit of brushing your teeth immediately after eating, dental decay can be substantially avoided.

如果你能夠保持吃過東西之後隨即刷牙的習慣，基本上蛀牙的情況是可以避免的。

高 108

The meat will decay easily if not kept in the refrigerator.

肉要是沒有存放在冰箱裡的話就容易腐敗。

秒殺解字 de(off)+cay(fall) → 本義指「從……掉落」，源自法文。

| 詞搭 | a / two decayed tooth/teeth 一 / 兩顆蛀牙；dental / tooth decay 齲齒 |

centimeter

[ˋsɛntəˌmitə]

n. 公分、釐米（長度單位）

We have two rulers here. One has a scale in centimeters, and the other in inches.

我們有兩種尺規。一種是以公分為刻度的，另外一種則英吋的。

秒殺解字 cent(one hundredth)+i+meter →「百分之一」「公尺」，meter 表示「公尺」。1 cm = 0.01 公尺。

gossip

[ˋgɑsəp]

n. 八卦、閒言閒語
v. 聊八卦

Can you stop all such nonsense and gossip and be more serious?
你（們）可以停止這種無聊八卦然後正經一點嗎？

Can you just stop gossiping and focus on your work？
你（們）可以停止說三道四然後專注於你（們）的工作嗎？

(秒殺解字) gos(god)+sip(relative) → gossip 是由 God 和 sibb 所組成，意思是「和神有關係的人」，在古英文時期，表示「替選舉者洗禮或確保其成功的組織或人物」或「教父（母）」，中世紀時，轉為表示「熟識的人」，後來引申為「（熟識的人之間的）八卦、閒聊」。

詞搭 ｜ gossip about... 閒聊有關……的八卦；juicy / hot gossip 有趣的傳聞

boost

[bust]

n. 推動；促進
v. 提昇；增加

All of us are glad to see a tremendous boost in last quarter's sales.
我們所有的人都很高興看到上一季銷售業績遽增。

增 107
警特 107

Your encouragement will boost my confidence.
你的鼓勵將會增強我的信心。

(秒殺解字) 發 b 聲音時要先將雙唇緊閉，接著張嘴讓氣流從口中噴出，從氣流噴出引申出「推動」的意思。相關單字有 boom (v. 迅速成長或發展)。

詞搭 ｜ boost prices / sales 抬高物價／增加銷路；give + sb. + a boost 讓某人信心大增；a boost in pay 加薪

lyrical

[ˋlɪrɪkḷ]

adj. 抒情詩般的；感情豐富的

This novel is full of lyrical descriptions of the writer's childhood.
這本小說裡充滿了作家對其童年抒情性的敘述。

(秒殺解字) lyric(a lyric poem)+al → 「抒情詩」的。

詞搭 ｜ lyrical music 抒情音樂

dairy
['dɛrɪ]
n. 乳酪業

The consumption of dairy products is sometimes viewed as an index for standard of living.
乳製品的消費量有時被視為衡量生活水準高低的指標。

> 秒殺解字 dai(dairymaid)+ry(=ery=place) → 「擠奶女工」工作的「場所」，表示「乳品店」，引申為「乳酪業」。

詞搭 dairy products 乳酪產品；dairy farming 酪農業；dairy cow / cattle 乳牛

字辨 diary ['daɪərɪ] n. 日記

---

contact
['kɑntækt]
n. 聯繫；接觸
v. 聯繫

警特 107

Moving to this small remote mountain village after graduation, I almost lost contact with my college friends.
畢業之後移居此一遙遠山中小村，我幾乎已跟大學朋友失去聯絡了。

Many housewives are always busy at home every day and have hardly had any contact with the outside world.
許多家庭主婦每天總是忙於家事，跟外面的世界幾乎沒有甚麼聯繫。

> 秒殺解字 con(together)+tac(touch)+t → 「一起」「接觸」是「聯繫」、「接觸」。

用法 eye contact 目光接觸；business / personal contacts 商場上的人脈／私交

---

contagious
[kən'tedʒəs]
adj. 有傳染性的、感染的

Such diseases are highly contagious, so the doctor says isolation of patients is absolutely necessary.
這類疾病傳染性極高，所以醫師說病患的隔離是絕對必要的。

> 秒殺解字 con(together)+tag(touch)+i+ous → 「一起」「接觸」，「接觸」會帶來「傳染病」。

詞搭 a contagious disease 傳染病

同義字 infectious

subordinate

[sə`bɔrdṇɪt]

n. 部屬
v. 使居次要地位
adj. 次要的

He is a nice manager and is always kind to his subordinates. 📖 105

他是一位很好的經理，而且對待部屬總是很仁慈。

Our boss often emphasizes that individual's welfare is always <u>subordinate</u> to the collective goal.

我們老闆常常強調集體目標至上，個人福祉次之。

秒殺解字 sub(under)+ord(order)+in+ate →「順序」排在他人之「下」的。相關同源字有 **order**（n. 順序、次序）、**ord**inary（adj. 普通的）、extra**ord**inary（adj. 異常的）、co**ord**inate（v. 協調）、sub**ord**inate（adj. 下級的 n. 下屬）。

詞搭 a subordinate position 隸屬的職位；subordinate A to B 將 A 的優先次序置於 B 下

appetite

[`æpə͵taɪt]

n. 胃口；嗜好

I won't have any sweets before meals, because they'll spoil my appetite. 📖 102

吃飯前我是不吃甜食的，因為它們會破壞我的食慾。

秒殺解字 ap(=ad=to)+pet(go, seek)+ite →「去」「尋求」喜愛的食物。相關同源字有 **pet**ition（v./n. 請願）、com**pet**e（v. 競爭）、re**peat**（v./n. 重複）。

詞搭 have an <u>appetite / liking / passion</u> for + sth. 嗜好某物；<u>spoil / ruin</u> one's appetite 破壞胃口；loss of appetite 食慾不振

premium

[`primɪəm]

n. 保險費；溢價
adj. 高級的

Health-oriented people are usually more likely to pay a premium for organic food.

重視健康的人通常比較有可能願意付較高價錢購買有機食物。

Will you pay more for the so-called premium drinking water?

你願意多付點錢購買這種所謂頂級的飲用水嗎？

秒殺解字 pre(before)+em(buy, take)+i+um →「保險費」是「事先」「買」保障用以防範未然的。保費是多出來的一項保障，後來另產生「溢價」、「額外費用」的意思。em 本義是「拿」，這裡當「買」解釋，um 是名詞字尾。

詞搭 insurance premiums 保險費；<u>put / place</u> a premium on + sth. 給……很高的評價；premium <u>price / rate</u> 高價

torture

['tɔrtʃɚ]

n. 折磨

v. 折磨；拷問

Every day the rush-hour traffic was torture to Dorothy, so she finally decided to move to an apartment near her office.
每天交通尖峰時刻塞車對 Dorothy 而言簡直是折磨，所以她最後決定搬到公司附近的一棟公寓住。

102

The soldier was caught by the enemy and was cruelly tortured.
這位士兵被敵軍抓走並且受到嚴峻折磨。

秒殺解字 tort(twist)+ure → 遭到「拷問」，身體受到「折磨」，「扭曲」變形而吐露真相。相關同源字有 re**tort**（v. 反駁）、dis**tort**（v. 扭曲）、con**tort**（v. 扭曲）。

詞搭 be tortured into / with / by... 受到拷問而……、受到……折磨；be in torture 受苦

collide

[kə'laɪd]

v. 碰撞；衝突

The two cars collided at the crossroads and the two drivers as well as three passengers were all severely injured.
這兩部車碰撞在一起，兩位駕駛以及其它三位乘客都嚴重受傷。

107

秒殺解字 col(together)+lid(striking)+e →「碰撞」在「一起」。

詞搭 collide with + sth. 與某物碰撞；collide head-on 迎頭正面對撞

同義字 hit

depreciation

[dɪ,priʃɪ'eʃən]

n. 貶值；跌價折舊；輕視

Some domestic enterprises believe that recent currency depreciation will make it easier for them to compete with foreign firms.
有些國內企業相信最近貨幣貶值將有助於他們更容易與國外公司競爭。

秒殺解字 de(down)+prec(price)+i+ate+ion →「價格」往「下」跌，表示「貶值」或「輕視」。相關同源字有 ap**prec**iate（v. 感激；欣賞；增值）、**prec**ious（adj. 珍貴的）。

反義字 appreciation

infamous
[ˋɪnfəməs]
adj. 聲名狼藉的

The man who is going to jail is infamous for many murder cases. 📖 101

這位即將入獄的人因為犯下多起謀殺案件而惡名昭彰。

🖋 秒殺解字 in(not)+fam(speak)+ous → 「說」你的「不」好，表示「聲名狼藉的」。

詞搭 an infamous city / killer / crime 聲名狼藉的城市／殺手／罪行

同義字 notorious

---

buffet
[buˋfe]
n. 自助餐

[ˋbʌfɪt]
v. 打擊

Would you prefer a set meal or the buffet tonight?

今晚你想要吃套餐還是吃到飽自助餐？

Buffeted by misfortunes continuously, Susan became even stronger.

雖然一再受到厄運打擊，Susan 變得更加堅強。

🖋 秒殺解字 buffet 有兩個字源。第一個字源，本義是「一種櫥或櫃，通常用來貯藏食物、陶器和器皿的擱板」，後來語意改變，衍生出「自助餐」的意思。第二語意是「打擊」。發 b 聲音時要先將雙唇緊閉，彷彿上下嘴唇拍打，引申為「打擊」。相關單字有 **b**atter (v. 連續猛擊)、**b**ump (v. 猛擊)、**b**ang (v. 重擊作響)。

---

jealous
[ˋdʒɛləs]
adj. 嫉妒的、吃醋的

Constance is always jealous of her younger sister's fair complexion. 📖 102

Constance 總是嫉妒她妹妹擁有的姣好面貌。

🖋 秒殺解字 jeal+ous → 「忌妒」的。

---

jealousy
[ˋdʒɛləsɪ]
n. 嫉妒

Beatrice and Cynthia have been good friends for years but now they are divided by mutual suspicion and jealousy. 📖 102

Beatrice 與 Cynthia 原本是多年好友，但現在因為相互猜忌與嫉妒已經不合了。

詞搭 a pang / stab / twinge of jealousy 一陣嫉妒

apologize

[ə`pɑlə͵dʒaɪz]

v. 道歉、賠罪

Clara wrote a letter to her English teacher to <u>apologize</u> for her rudeness in class.

對於在課堂上的粗魯行為，Clara 寫了一封信給她的英文老師表達致歉。

🖋 (秒殺解字) apo(off, away)+log(speech)+ize → 把「話」說「開」「認錯」。

詞搭｜apologize to + sb. + for + sth. 因某事向某人道歉

---

naughty

[`nɔtɪ]

adj. 頑皮的

Really, I have never seen such a naughty boy in my 📖 101 life.

真的，我一生從未看過如此頑皮的男孩。

🖋 (秒殺解字) naught(nothing)+y → 視規矩如「無物」的，引申為「頑皮的」。

同義字｜mischievous

反義字｜good

01 ___ No one is perfect. Everyone has their own _____. If a person seems perfect on the surface, it just means that he or she knows how to hide their flaws.

(A) packages (B) disadvantages
(C) percentages (D) rages

02 ___ People are asking for a _____ trial for the suspect. Although he is charged with two murder cases, everyone is innocent until proven guilty.

(A) current (B) transparent
(C) coherent (D) apparent

03 ___ The doctor is famous for his surgery skills. Most of his patients said that the scars caused by the operations were almost _____.

(A) thoughtful (B) deceitful
(C) defenseless (D) seamless

04 ___ During the Super Bowl commercial break, a one-minute-long _____ can sometimes cost a company millions of dollars, if they wish to promote their products.

(A) monument (B) environment
(C) investment (D) advertisement

05 ___ The water level of the reservoir has decreased to an _____ level. Local government has no choice but to order a water rationing.

(A) alarming (B) challenging
(C) perplexing (D) ruling

06 ___ Traditional sports, the _____ of e-sports, is noticing the rise of e-sports and is starting to see it as a threat because e-sports generates millions of dollars of revenue each year and is gradually taking over traditional sports.

(A) guard (B) predecessor
(C) diplomat (D) racist

07 ___ The old man told the boy to be _____ about the road ahead. Many people mysteriously disappear in the forest, and no one knows why or what caused them to vanish.

(A) mysterious   (B) cautious
(C) luxurious   (D) contagious

08 ___ The news that the Prime Minister of Japan _____ from the government shocked a lot of people, including some of the Cabinet members.

(A) assigned   (B) issued
(C) resigned   (D) desired

09 ___ With the outbreak of the civil war, neighboring countries have to deal with the _____ problems, which can lead to a major social issue, if not handle correctly.

(A) investor   (B) consumer
(C) diplomat   (D) refugee

10 ___ Our manager offers us a bonus to _____ our morale and efficiency. If we reach a certain goal he set, we can get a variety of benefits, including paid days off or bonus money.

(A) boost   (B) distinguish
(C) protect   (D) promise

11 ___ The Center for Disease Control is tracking every person who had _____ with the patient. By doing so, they hope to minimize the spreading of the disease.

(A) contact   (B) recognition
(C) surface   (D) impact

12 ___ In the movie, viruses that can turn people into zombies are always _____ and deadly. However, in reality, viruses like that barely cause any real damage.

(A) furious   (B) suspicious
(C) contagious   (D) cautious

13 ___ Girls usually have a(n) _____ for sweet food. Even if they are already full because of the main dish, they can still enjoy desserts.

(A) rage   (B) catalog

(C) posture   (D) appetite

14 ___ The president's sudden resignation has caused great _____ to the country. Suddenly, everything was thrown into chaos.

(A) operation   (B) surface

(C) volume   (D) turmoil

15 ___ Because of his _____ and helpful character, Robin is respected by all of his friends.

(A) vulnerable   (B) portable

(C) marketable   (D) charitable

解答
1.(B) 2.(B) 3.(D) 4.(D) 5.(A) 6.(B) 7.(B) 8.(C) 9.(D) 10(A) 11.(A) 12.(C) 13.(D) 14.(D) 15.(D)

Unit 45

TRACK 045

---

poison
[ˈpɔɪzn̩]
n. 毒、毒藥
v. 使中毒、下毒於

One man's meat is another man's poison.
你喜歡的，別人不見得會喜歡。（青菜蘿蔔各有所好。）

Without proper control, industrial wastes will seriously pollute and even poison these rivers.
若無適當管制，工業廢棄物將會汙染甚至毒害這些河川。

---

poisonous
[ˈpɔɪznəs]
adj. 有毒的

The factory guarantees that it won't have any poisonous substances or gases as waste.
這家工廠保證不會排放任何有毒物質或氣體。

普 101

🪶（秒殺解字）poison+ous → 有「毒」的。

詞搭┊ a deadly poison 劇毒；food poisoning 食物中毒；rat poison 毒鼠藥；poison + sb. + with + sth. 用某物毒死某人

---

astounding
[əˈstaundɪŋ]
adj. 令人震驚的

It is quite astounding that she asked for a divorce a week after her wedding.
在婚禮一週之後她請求離婚，這件事情著實令人感到震驚。

🪶（秒殺解字）as(=ex=out)+tound(thunder)+ing →「打雷」會讓人感到「驚嚇」。astound 和 astonish 都源自古法文 estoner。可用 **thunder** 當神隊友，**t/θ 轉音**，母音通轉，來記憶 **tound** 和 **ton**，核心語意是「打雷」（**thunder**），「打雷」常會讓人感到「驚嚇」。

同義字┊ astonishing, surprising, amazing, startling

---

annoyed
[əˈnɔɪd]
adj. 感到惱怒的

We <u>were</u> quite <u>annoyed with</u> that Turkish buyer because he canceled their orders without prior notice.
我們對那位土耳其的買主非常生氣，因為他沒事先通知就把他們的訂單取消了。

高 108

🪶（秒殺解字）an(=ad=to)+noy(hate)+ed →「感到」「厭惡」的。

詞搭┊ be annoyed <u>by / about</u> + sth. 對某事感到氣惱；be annoyed <u>with / at</u> + sb. 對某人感到氣惱

同義字┊ irritated, angry

396

spill
[spɪl]

n. 灑出物
v. 灑出；洩密

The waitress apologized to me for accidentally spilling water on me. I didn't blame her and said it was OK.

這位女服務員不小心把水濺灑在我身上，她為此向我道歉。我沒有責備她並且對她說沒關係。

 秒殺解字 spl 子音組合有「潑濺開來」的意思。相關單字有 **spl**ash（v. 潑濺）、**spl**atter（v. 飛濺）等。

時態 | spill, spilled / spilt, spilled / spilt

---

shrinkage
[`ʃrɪŋkɪdʒ]

n. 收縮；減低

It is said that a high dose of vitamin B may help slow the rate of brain shrinkage in older people.

據說高劑量維他命 B 群也許有助減緩老人家腦部萎縮的速度。

高 108

 秒殺解字 shr 的子音組合有「變小」的意思。相關單字有 **shr**ivel（v. 枯萎）、**shr**ed（v. 撕碎）等。

---

summit
[`sʌmɪt]

n. 頂峰、頂點

I believe I'll have to work hard for more than 20 years before <u>reaching the summit of my career</u>.

我相信在達到事業的顛峰之前，我必須努力打拼超過 20 年。

普 99
警特 105

秒殺解字 sum(amount, highest, top)+mit → sum 是字首 super, sur 的變形，本義是「在上的」（over, above）、「超出的」（beyond），表示「數量」、「最高的」、「頂端」。相關同源字有 **sum**（n. 總數 v. 總結）、**sum**mary（n. 總結）、**sum**marize（v. 總結）。

詞搭 | a summit <u>conference / meeting</u> 高峰會議

同義字 | peak

---

cart
[kɑrt]

n. 手推車；貨運車

A shopping cart at a mall may save your energy but will never save your money.

購物中心的推車也許可以幫你省點力氣，但永遠不會幫你省錢。

秒殺解字 cart(basket) → 坊間書籍、網路常將 cart 列為 car 的同源字，其實不然。cart 在現代美式英語中特指超市裡面裝載商品的「手推車」，手推車上會有的大籃子，cart 的本義是「籃子」，和表示「搖籃」的 cradle 同源。

詞搭 | golf cart 高爾夫球車；put the cart before the horse 本末倒置

inferior
[ɪnˈfɪrɪɚ]

n. 下屬
adj. 較差的

The general manager is always kind and friendly to his inferiors.
總經理總是對他的部屬始終是很仁慈和善。

I believe I'm inferior to him in English, but as far as Japanese is concerned, I'm sure I'm superior.
我相信我英文是比他差，但是談到日文的話，我確信我是比他強的。

秒殺解字 infer(=infra=below)+ior → 較「下面」的，等同 lower，表示「較差的」、「下級的」；ior 是「比較級字尾」，源自拉丁文，相當於英文比較級字尾 er，如 junior、senior、inferior、superior、prior 不和 than 搭配，只可與介係詞 to 並用。

詞搭 be inferior to... 比……差 ≠ be superior to...；inferior quality / leather / goods 劣等品質／皮革／商品

反義字 superior

whistle
[ˈ(h)wɪsl̩]

n. 口哨；哨子
v. 吹口哨；吹哨子

A whistle was heard when the match came to an end.
哨聲響起比賽就結束了。

Jack seems to enjoy his work very much, because he always whistles while working.
Jack 似乎蠻喜歡他的工作，因為他在工作時總是會吹著口哨。

秒殺解字 現代英語中 wh 為首的單字在古英文都以 hw 為首，發音時像「呼呼聲」，衍生出「吹氣的聲音」。相關單字有 **wh**isper (v. 耳語；n. 低語)、**wh**imper (v. 啜泣)。

詞搭 blow a whistle 吹哨子；whistle at + sb. 對某人吹口哨

offend
[əˈfɛnd]

v. 觸怒；冒犯

I'm sorry if I have offended you, but I didn't mean it.
如果我有冒犯到你，那我說聲抱歉，但我是無心的。

曾 105
警特 105

秒殺解字 of(=ob=before, against)+fend(strike) → 原意是「在前面」「攻擊」、「對抗」他人。fence 是用來阻擋「攻擊」的「柵欄」，可用 **fence** 當神隊友，**d/s 轉音**，來記憶 **fend**、**fens**，表示「打」、「攻擊」。

詞搭 offend against the law 犯法；be offended by / at + sth. 被……冒犯

同義字 upset

offender

[əˋfɛndə]

n. 罪犯；冒犯者

Maybe some offenders are now still at large, but I'm sure they will end up in prison eventually.

也許有些罪犯現在仍逍遙法外，但我相信最後他們都會被繩之以法抓去坐牢。

詞搭 a first / repeated / persistent offender 初／累／慣犯

---

fertile

[ˋfɝtl]

adj. 肥沃的；能生育的、易受孕的

The land in this region is fertile enough for three crops a year to be possible.

這個區域土地肥沃，所以農作物一年三種是有可能的。

秒殺解字 fer(bear)+tile →「帶」來豐厚果實或小孩。infertile 是反義字，表示「不能生育的」、「土地貧瘠的」；in 表示「不」（not）、「相反」（opposite）。可用 **bear** 當神隊友，**b/f 轉音，母音通轉**，來記憶 **fer**，表示「攜帶」、「生育」、「承受」。相關同源字有 di**ffer**（v. 不同）、in**fer**（v. 推論）、pre**fer**（v. 寧願）、su**ffer**（v. 受苦）、re**fer**（v. 提到）、trans**fer**（v. 轉移）、con**fer**ence（n. 正式會議）、**fer**tility（n. 肥沃；繁殖力）。

詞搭 fertile fields / soil 肥沃的田地／土壤；a fertile imagination / mind / brain 富有創造力的想像力／心靈／頭腦

反義字 infertile, barren, sterile

---

pessimistic

[ˌpɛsəˋmɪstɪk]

adj. 悲觀的

The doctor said he was pessimistic about the chance of my father's recovery.

醫師說他對我父親康復的機會表示悲觀。

秒殺解字 pessim(worst)+ist+ic →表示「最壞的」，是「悲觀的」。

反義字 optimistic

曾 99
警特 108
109

---

code

[kod]

n. 代碼；密碼
v. 編碼；加密碼

The area code for Taipei is 02.

台北的區域號碼是 02。

秒殺解字 本指「系統編排和廣泛收集的法律彙編」，後來衍生出「密碼」的意思。

詞搭 area code 電話的區域號碼；zip code 郵遞區號；break the code 破解密碼；the dress code 服裝規定

曾 105

artificial

[ˌɑrtəˋfɪʃəl]

adj. 人工的；虛偽的；人造的、不自然的

The bakery emphasizes that the bread and cookies they make are 100% free from artificial preservatives.

這家麵包店強調他們所焙製的麵包以及餅乾是百分百完全沒有使用人造防腐劑。

（秒殺解字） art(art)+i+fic(do, make)+ial →「做」出來的藝術、技藝都屬「人工的」、「非天然的」。

詞搭 artificial <u>rain / respiration</u> 人造雨／人工呼吸；an artificial satellite 人造衛星；artificial flowers 假花；artificial intelligence 人工智慧

同義字 false, unnatural, man-made

反義字 natural, genuine, sincere

普 105

---

native

[ˋnetɪv]

n. 本地人；土著
adj. 祖國的、本地的、土生的

As a native of Peru, Spanish is Juan's mother tongue, but he also speaks English, French, Portuguese, and Italian.

Juan 是土生土長的秘魯人,所以西班牙語是他的母語,但他也(會)說英語、法語、葡萄牙語以及義大利語。

My wife and I have different <u>native languages</u>, but we share a common language for daily communication.

雖然我太太跟我母語不同,但日常溝通我們是使用一種共通語言。

（秒殺解字） nat(birth, born)+ive → 與「誕生」有關的,表示「出生」國、「出生」地的、「原產的」、「土生土長的」。naive 也和「誕生」有關,人「出生」的時候,本性都是「天真無邪的」。native 與 naive 是「雙飾詞」(**doublet**),都是源自拉丁語,再經由法語於 1654 年借入英語。

詞搭 native <u>language / tongue</u> = mother tongue = first language 母語；a native speaker of English 以英語為母語的人

同義字 indigenous

普 100
102
103
警特 105
109

medal

[`mɛdl]

n. 獎章

Annabelle beat her rival and finally won <u>the gold</u> <u>medal</u>. 🎧 102

Annabelle 擊敗她的對手，終於贏得金牌。

🪶 **秒殺解字** **metal**、**medal** 同源，**d/t** 轉音，核心語意是「金屬」。「獎牌」多由「金屬」製成。

詞搭 a <u>gold / silver / bronze</u> medal 金牌／銀牌／銅牌；be awarded medals 獲頒勳章

字辨 metal [`mɛtl] n. 金屬

---

click

[klɪk]

n. 喀喀的響聲

v. 按滑；發出喀喀聲

If you want to run the software, just <u>click</u> twice <u>on</u> the icon and it will do many things for you. 🎧 108

如果你想執行這個軟體，只要在其圖像上按兩下滑鼠，然後它就會幫你做很多事情。

🪶 **秒殺解字** 子音群 cl 接母音時，會產生如兩物撞擊的聲音，因此有些含 [kl] 音的單字與撞擊有關，或叮噹、喀嚓聲或相關動作，相關字有 **cl**ap（v/n. 拍手）、**cl**ash（v/n. 碰撞）、**cl**ock（n. 時鐘）、**cl**ip（v/n. 剪）、**cl**umsy（adj. 笨拙的）、**cl**ink（v/n. 叮噹聲）、**cl**ank（v. 叮噹）。

詞搭 click on + sth. 用電腦滑鼠點擊；click one's heels 喀的一聲將腳跟併攏

---

grocery

[`grosərɪ]

n. 食品雜貨

Shall we stop by the grocery store and pick up some toilet paper, soap and toothpaste? 🎧特 105

我們要不要在雜貨店停一下買些衛生紙、肥皂以及牙膏？

Cynthia got out of her car, carrying a bag of groceries, which she just bought at a supermarket.

Cynthia 從車子出來，隨身拎著一包剛剛在超市買的東西。

🪶 **秒殺解字** grocer+y →「批發商」所賣的「商品」，衍生出「食品雜貨」及「雜貨店」的意思。

lengthen

[ˋlɛŋθənd]

v. 加長

Apparently, you look much prettier wearing the lengthened skirt.

很明顯地，你穿上這條修改放長過後的裙子看起來漂亮多了。

(秒殺解字) leng(long)+th+en(make) →「使」「變長」。th 表示「行為」、「特質」、「狀態」，是源自古英文的名詞字尾。

反義字 | shorten

obedient

[əˋbidɪənt]

adj. 服從的、遵守的

Most dogs <u>are</u> faithful and <u>obedient</u> <u>to</u> people who raise them.

普 101
警特 106

大部分的狗對飼主都是忠實順從的。

(秒殺解字) ob(to)+ed(audio=hear)+i+ent →「聽」從命令或法律規則，就是「遵守的」。

詞搭 | obedient <u>children / pupil</u> 乖巧恭順的孩子／學生

反義字 | disobedient, rebellious

courteous
[`kɝtɪəs]
adj. 有禮貌的

All the clerks of the hotel are courteous and helpful. 普 101 警特 106
這家旅館的所有職員都謙恭有禮、服務殷勤。

秒殺解字 court(court)+e+ous → court 源自 cohort，原指「圍起來的花園」、「祕密的花園」，阻隔外人，只有獲得許可的人才能進入，後來衍生為「宮廷」，宮廷有諸多禮儀，因此 courteous 表示「有禮貌的」，discourteous 表示「不禮貌的」，dis 表示「相反」（opposite）。

同義字 polite

反義字 discourteous, rude, impolite, bad-mannered

---

courtesy
[`kɝtəsɪ]
n. 禮貌

I think I should write them a letter <u>out of</u> courtesy. 警特 107
基於禮貌，我想我應該給他們寫一封信。

詞搭 (by) courtesy of + 某機構　由某機構免費提供；a courtesy <u>bus / taxi / car</u> 免費接駁車；a courtesy <u>call / visit</u> 禮貌性拜訪

同義字 politeness

反義字 discourtesy, rudeness

---

errand
[`ɛrənd]
n. 差事、出差

Today I'm free and I can run an errand for you. 高 108
今天我沒事，可以幫你跑腿辦事。

秒殺解字 errand 在中世紀時表示「消息」、「訊息」，17 世紀時有「短途旅行」、「簡單任務」的衍生意思，後來當「差事」解釋。

詞搭 <u>do / run / go on</u> errands for + sb.　幫某人跑腿

flock

[flɑk]

n. （羊）群；群眾

v. 聚集

When Albert was taking a picture of me, a flock of wild geese just flew overhead.

正當 Albert 為我照相時，有一群野雁正好從上空飛過。

During peak season, hundreds of thousands of tourists will flock to the small island, annoying the local residents very much.

在旅遊旺季時，成千上萬的遊客將會湧入這座小島，這件事讓當地居民相當苦惱。

秒殺解字 源自古英語，本表示「一群人」，後語意延伸，表示「一群動物」。

詞搭 a flock of sheep / goats / people 一群綿羊／山羊／人

同義字 crowd

glimpse

[glɪmps]

n. v. 瞥見

Douglas was very happy because he finally had the chance to catch a glimpse of the artist's masterpieces in the museum.

Douglas 非常高興，因為他終於有機會在博物館一睹這位藝術家的傑作。

Clement took a glimpse of the new cellphone I just got and said it was a really nice gadget.

Clement 對我新買的手機瞄了一眼，然後說這玩意還真是不錯！

秒殺解字 含 gl 的單字有「高興」、「照耀或發光」、「看見」的意思。相關單字有 glad（adj. 高興地）、glee（n. 歡喜）、glow（v. 發光）、glisten（v. 閃耀）、gleam（v. 發微光）、glint（v. 閃閃發光）、glitter（v. 閃爍）、gloss（n. 表面的光澤）、glance（n. 瞥一眼）、glare（v. 怒視）、glimpse（n. 看一眼）、gloat（v. 沾沾自喜或幸災樂禍地看）。

同義字 catch sight of

comedy

[`kɑmədɪ]

n. 喜劇

I like the actress in the TV comedy.

我喜歡這個電視喜劇的女演員。

圖 108

秒殺解字 com(=comos=having fun)+ed(sing)+y → 本義「唱歌」「享樂」，後指故事有個歡樂的結局，引申為「喜劇」。comic 和 comedy 同源，但從拼字上已看不出字根 ode 的拼字樣貌。

comedian
[kə`mɪdɪən]

n. 喜劇演員

As a stand-up comedian, Jeremy did a good job on last night's show and won the respect and applause the entire audience.

作為一位獨角喜劇演員，Jeremy 昨晚演出表現傑出，獲得所有觀眾敬重及喝采。

| 同義字 | humor |
| 反義字 | tragedy |

irrational
[ɪ`ræʃənl]

adj. 無理的、無理性的；不合理的

You might think this is quite irrational, but I must say that's the way it goes.

你也許會覺得這件事相當不合理，但我必須說事情發展結果就是如此。

(秒殺解字) ir(not)+rat(reason)+ion+al → 「不」合「理」的。可用 **reason** 當神隊友，**t/z/ʃ 轉音**，母音通轉，來記憶 **rat**，皆表示「理由」、「推理判斷」。

| 同義字 | unreasonable |
| 反義字 | rational, reasonable |

rationale
[ˌræʃə`næl]

n. 基本理由；原理的闡述

The rationale for applying Grimm's Law to vocabulary teaching is to enhance students' confidence in vocabulary expansion.　圖 108

在字彙教學上運用格林法則的基本理由是要提升學生字彙擴增能力。

| 詞搭 | the rationale <u>behind / for / of</u>... ……的理由、依據 |

altitude
[`æltə͵tjud]

n. 高度、海拔

The captain says we are currently flying <u>at an altitude of</u> 10,000 meters.

機長說目前我們正在 10,000 米的高度上飛行。

(秒殺解字) alt(high)+i+tude → 「高」度。

| 詞搭 | <u>high / low</u> altitudes 高／低海拔 |
| 字辨 | attitude [`ætət͵jud] n. 態度 |

compliment
[`kampləmənt]
n. 讚美;恭維

[`kamplə‚mɛnt]
v. 讚美

詞搭 compliment + sb. + on + sth. 讚美某人某事;pay + sb. + a compliment 對某人表示讚美;return the compliment 回表敬意

同義字 praise

Phoebe is always fishing for compliments about her looks.
Phoebe 總是期待別人讚美她的外貌。

秒殺解字 com(intensive prefix)+pli(fill)+ment → 本義「滿」足人的虛榮心。

---

complimentary
[‚kamplə`mɛntərɪ]
adj. 讚美的;免費的

詞搭 a complimentary ticket / copy / address 招待券╱贈本╱祝詞

Many of the guests made some highly complimentary remarks about the food and service we offered.
許多客人對於我們所提供的食物以及服務讚譽有加。

---

digest
[`daɪdʒɛst]
n. 摘要

[daɪ`dʒɛst]
v. 消化;領悟

A digest of their investigation was put on your desk for your reference. 📖 108
他們調查報告的摘要已放在您桌上供您參考。

I prefer to eat more vegetables for supper because I find I don't digest meat easily.
晚餐我會選擇吃較多的蔬菜,因為我發現自己不容易消化肉類。

秒殺解字 di(=dis=apart)+gest(carry) → 本義「帶」「開」,因此有「消化」的意思。相關同源字有 **gest**ure (n./v. 手勢)、sug**gest** (v. 建議;暗示)、con**gest**ed (adj. 道路擁擠的)。

---

overhead
[`ovɚ‚hɛd]
adj. 頭頂上的
adv. 在高空中

Besides a desk lamp, the study room needs overhead lighting.
除了書桌檯燈以外,這個書房還要頂燈照明。

A flock of swallows are circling overhead.
一群燕子正在頭頂上空盤旋。

秒殺解字 over(over)+head → 在「頭」「上」的。

surgery
[ˋsɝˋdʒərɪ]
n. 外科手術

The patient is now having brain surgery.
這位病人正在接受腦部（外科）手術。

普 102

（秒殺解字）s(hand)+urg(=erg=work)+ery → 本義是從事「外科手術」的「工作」。可用 **work** 當神隊友，**k/dʒ** 轉音，母音通轉，來憶 **urg**，皆表示「作用」、「工作」。

詞搭 perform surgery / an operation on... 對……動手術；plastic surgery 整形外科手術；cosmetic surgery 美容整形外科手術；emergency surgery 緊急手術

同義字 operation

infect
[ɪnˋfɛkt]
v. 使感染

This ward is now full of patients badly infected with pneumonia.
這個病房裡住滿了嚴重感染肺炎的病人。

警特 105 108

（秒殺解字）in(in)+fec(do, make)+t → 細菌或病毒在人體「內」「做」工。相關同源字有 af**fec**t（v. 影響）、ef**fec**t（n. 影響）、de**fec**t（n. 缺點）、per**fec**t（adj. 完美的）。

ensure
[ɪnˋʃʊr]
v. 確保

These security cameras were installed to ensure that customers did not steal the merchandise.
安裝這些監控攝影機是為了確保消費者不會偷商品。

（秒殺解字）en(make)+sure(sure) → make sure 就是「確定」。

同義字 make sure, make certain, insure

microscope
[ˋmaɪkrəˌskop]
n. 顯微鏡

These germs can only be clearly seen with the aid of a microscope.
這些細菌必須借助顯微鏡才能夠清楚看見。

（秒殺解字）micro(small)+scope(look) → 讓「微小的」東西能被「看見」。相關同源字有 **scope**（n. 範圍）、tele**scope**（n. 望遠鏡）、horo**scope**（n. 占星術）。

詞搭 under / through a microscope 在顯微鏡下

字辨 a magnifying glass 放大鏡；telescope [ˋtɛləˌskop] n. 單筒望遠鏡；binoculars [baɪˋnɑkjələ˞z] n. 雙筒望遠鏡

boycott

[ˈbɔɪˌkɑt]

n. **v.** 杯葛

In 1980, the United States led a boycott of the Summer Olympic Games in Moscow to protest the Soviet invasion of Afghanistan.

1980 年，美國發動杯葛莫斯科奧運會，以抗議蘇聯侵略阿富汗。

101

(秒殺解字) 源自 19 世紀愛爾蘭的英國官員 Charles Boycott 的名字，因為他拒絕降低賦稅，而遭受地方人士抵制。後來 boycott 常指拒絕購買某物、使用某物，或拒絕參加某活動，需要注意的事，中文的杯葛由於被誤用，語意已經擴大。

---

ascend

[əˈsɛnd]

v. 上升；登上、攀登

In another ten minutes, the sun will be ascending above the horizon.

再過十分鐘，太陽馬上就要從地平線升起。

(秒殺解字) a(=ad=to)+scend(climb) → 「爬」上去，表示「登高」、「上升」等意思。

詞搭 ascend the throne 登上王位；in ascending order 按升序排列

同義字 climb up, go up

反義字 descend

---

monitor

[ˈmɑnətɚ]

n. 監視器

v. 監視、監控

The computer will be sold with a monitor display.

這部電腦將會連同一台顯示器一起銷售。

99

The intelligence and security department is starting to monitor his phone calls.

情治安全部門正開始對他的電話進行監聽。

(秒殺解字) mon(remind, warn)+it+or → 有「警告」功能的設備，引申為「監視器」。

---

nutrient

[ˈnjutrɪənt]

n. 養分

adj. 營養的

All the information about the nutrients of the vitamin pills should be displayed explicitly on the label.

所有有關維他命丸的營養資訊均應在標籤上明確揭露。

(秒殺解字) nutr(feed, nourish)+i+ent → 為生命和成長所需，而提供的食物或其它「養分」。

dynamic

[daɪˋnæmɪk]

adj. 充滿活力的;力
學的;動態的

Founded in 2018, this is a very young and dynamic enterprise.
成立於 2018 年,這是一家年輕又充滿活力的企業。

秒殺解字 dynam(force, power)+ic → 「力」學的。

同義字 active, energetic

反義字 static

digital

[ˋdɪdʒɪtl]

adj. 數位的

The company engages in the production of digital cameras.
這家公司從事數位相機的生產製造。

秒殺解字 digit(finger, nubmer)+al → 本義是「手指的」,因為每個人的手指有十隻,因此也指十位數以下的,但後來語意轉變,表示「數位的」。

詞搭 a digital watch / clock / TV 數位式手錶／時鐘／電視

01 ___ The man was bitten by a _____ snake and needed to be extracted from the mountains to the nearest hospital as soon as possible. Otherwise, he would die because of the venom.

(A) poisonous   (B) fabulous

(C) suspicious   (D) contagious

02 ___ He felt really _____ that his mother kept nagging on him and asking him to get a job. Thus, he left the house and rented a small apartment to live in.

(A) experienced   (B) annoyed

(C) unprecedented   (D) unparalleled

03 ___ The captain asks his crew not to _____ any secrets to the enemy. Even if they are captured, they should sacrifice themselves to protect their country at all cost.

(A) spill   (B) locate

(C) determine   (D) involve

04 ___ After winning the recent election, the politician reached the _____ of his career. Instead of being a good governor, he started to treat people rudely and break every promise he made before the election.

(A) summary   (B) commitment

(C) summit   (D) unanimity

05 ___ The guy was so happy about quitting his miserable job, that he _____ cheerfully while walking home.

(A) established   (B) settled

(C) sprinkled   (D) whistled

06 ___ The king was so arrogant that he destroyed all the temples and statues of Gods because he thought he was better than Gods. This _____ Hades, the God of the underworld. Hades showed up and cursed the king for his ignorance.

(A) pretended   (B) comprehended

(C) ascended   (D) offended

07 ___　The plain of Mesopotamia was once a _____ land and was said to
have been the place of birth for the first human civilization.

(A) fragile　　　　　　　　　　(B) native
(C) fertile　　　　　　　　　　(D) bleak

08 ___　The _____ mindset of the leader dragged the entire team down. At
first, they were positive and confident. However, after a small defeat,
they couldn't get back on their feet.

(A) optimistic　　　　　　　　(B) pessimistic
(C) romantic　　　　　　　　　(D) specific

09 ___　Alan Mathison Turing, the father of modern computer, is most famous
for his Turing Machine, which helped the Allies cracked the encrypted
_____ that the Germans used in World War II.

(A) codes　　　　　　　　　　(B) pendulums
(C) illusions　　　　　　　　　(D) enterprises

10 ___　The job mostly focuses on running _____ for the general manager.
Applicants must have at least one year of experience in related fields.

(A) funerals　　　　　　　　　(B) errands
(C) behaviors　　　　　　　　(D) colonies

11 ___　During your service time, you will encounter lots of _____ and
unreasonable commands, but you have to learn to endure them and
follow the orders.

(A) gradual　　　　　　　　　(B) irrational
(C) cultural　　　　　　　　　(D) integral

12 ___　We had a blast in the restaurant yesterday. The food was excellent
and the service was also top-notch. Moreover, the owner also provided
us with _____ dishes, and it made the night even better.

(A) military　　　　　　　　　(B) ordinary
(C) ridiculous　　　　　　　　(D) complimentary

13 ___ Some netizen started a protest against the idol group because they felt that the idols disrespected their country. However, not many people agreed with the _____.

(A) panic   (B) punishment
(C) boycott   (D) confinement

14 ___ Usually, this kind of wound is far from fatal. However, without proper medical treatment, it got _____ and eventually led to the death of the patient.

(A) neglected   (B) expected
(C) affected   (D) infected

15 ___ There were many criminal activities in this region. As a result, the detective set up numerous security cameras to _____ the area.

(A) monitor   (B) include
(C) distort   (D) invest

feedback
[`fid͵bæk]

n. 反應、回饋；批評
指教

The mayor said he welcomed feedback and comments of any kind about his public bicycle rental policy.
市長說他歡迎大家針對公共腳踏車租賃政策的任何回饋及評論。

高 108

🪶 秒殺解字 feed+back → 本指電子學中的「回授技術」，後語意擴增，指一般的「反應」、「回饋」。

同義字 reply, response

---

implement
[`ɪmplə͵mɛnt]

n. 工具、器具
v. 實施、執行

The store supplies agricultural implements at a reasonable price.
這家商店以合理價格供應農用工具。

高 108
警特 106

The project is perfect, but it needs a large budget to implement it.
這項計畫完美無瑕，但是它需要龐大預算來執行。

🪶 秒殺解字 im(in)+ple(fill)+ment → 將「內部」填「滿」，衍生出「執行」。

詞搭 implement a new plan / decision / policy 實施新計劃／決定／政策

同義字 carry out

---

dynasty
[`daɪnəstɪ]

n. 朝代、王朝

In history, the Tang Dynasty is considered the golden age of classical Chinese poetry.
在歷史上，唐朝被認為是中國古詩的黃金全盛時期。

普 107

🪶 秒殺解字 dyn(power, force)+ast+y → 擁有「權力」的統治者所建立的「王朝」。

dread
[drɛd]
n. **v.** 懼怕

Sabrina has a dread of cockroaches.
Sabrina 怕蟑螂。

高 108

I think most people dread going to the dentist.
我想大部分的人都害怕看牙醫。

秒殺解字 dread 是由 and-(against) 和 rǣdan (advise) 兩個元素所構成，中世紀時單字縮減，拼作 dreden，表示「建議不要做」、「警告」，後來表示「（因警告而給人所帶來的）恐懼」。

詞搭 dread + sb. + doing + sth. 害怕某人做某事；have a dread of… 害怕…；with dread 害怕地

---

hijack
[ˋhaɪ͵dʒæk]
n. **v.** 劫持（飛機）

The recent hijack of the airliner was supposedly plotted by a group that opposed the government.
最近一次劫機事件被認為是由反對政府的一群人密謀策劃的。

普 103
警特 108

One man and one woman hijacked an airplane bound for London and demanded the change of course to land in Baghdad, the capital of Iraq.
一男一女劫持了一架預計飛往倫敦的飛機，他們要求改變飛航路線並且降落在伊拉克首都巴格達。

秒殺解字 字源不明，其中有一說法是，持手槍的強盜常說：「Stick'em (them = arms) up high, Jack. （喂，把手舉起來。）」這句話，用以威脅對方，而 Jack 常用以呼喚不認識的人，如：「Hey, Jack! （喂，你！）」

revenge

[rɪˋvɛndʒ]

n. 報復
v. 為……報仇

Deborah took / got revenge on Andrew for betraying her by burning his motorcycle.

Andrew 對 Deborah 不忠，所以她就燒毀他的摩托車來報復。

I told Melissa that if she wanted to live a happier life, she should let go of all her thoughts of revenge.

我告訴 Melissa，如果她想過更快樂的日子，她就應該拋棄她所有想報復的怨念。

 秒殺解字 re(intensive prefix)+venge(avenge) → 本義是「展現」（show）力量，源自古法文。revenge 和 avenge 都有因受到冒犯或傷害，而做某事去懲罰他人的意思，但 revenge 大多是出自於仇恨而復仇，avenge 比較偏向為了公理正義而復仇，漫威改編的電影 The Avengers（復仇者聯盟），裡面的英雄都是為了人類公平、正義、安全而戰。

詞搭 give + sb. + his revenge 給某人雪恥的機會；
in revenge for + sth. 以報復……

endanger

[ɪnˋdendʒɚ]

v. 使有危險、危及

The air pollution produced by this factory will badly endanger the health of the local residents.

這家工廠所造成的空氣污染將嚴重危害本地居民的健康。

普 107
110
警特 105

 秒殺解字 en(make, in)+danger → 等同 put + sb. / sth.+ in danger 或 put + sb. / sth.+ at risk，表示「使處於危險之中」、「危及」。

詞搭 endanger + sb's life 危及……的性命；endangered species 瀕臨絕種的物種

cargo

[ˋkɑrgo]

n. 貨物

This cargo vessel can carry up to 150,000 tons of crude oil.

這艘貨船可載運多達 150,000 噸的原油。

 秒殺解字 car(load, charge)+go → 貨物需要「運送」。

同義字 freight

extinct
[ɪk`stɪŋkt]

adj. 絕種的、滅絕的

If not properly protected and preserved, a lot of animals will soon be endangered and <u>become extinct</u>.

如果沒有受到妥善保育養護，許多動物的生存很快就會受到危及並且瀕臨絕種。

秒殺解字 ex(out)+stinc(stick, prick)+t → 本義是用「刺」把東西給「分開」，若把某一物種給分離，即「滅絕」。相關同源字有 ex**tingu**ish（v. 熄滅）、di**stingu**ish（v. 辨別）、di**stinc**t（adj. 截然不同的）、in**stinc**t（n. 本能）。

詞搭 an extinct book 絕版書；an extinct species 滅絕的物種；an extinct volcano 死火山

反義字 active

---

extinction
[ɪk`stɪŋkʃən]

n. 絕種

The extinction of many rarely used languages in the world is only a matter of time.

世界上有許多鮮少使用語言即將瀕臨滅絕消失，這是遲早的事情。

📖 103 110

詞搭 on the <u>verge / edge / brink</u> of extinction 瀕臨絕種；in danger of extinction 有絕種的危險；<u>face / be threatened with</u> extinction 面臨滅絕

---

fluent
[`fluənt]

adj. 流利的

Though Florence has never studied or stayed in France, it's quite amazing that she is very fluent in French.

雖然 Florence 從來沒在法國念書或待過，她的法語卻是非常流利，這真是令人驚訝。

📖 100 108

秒殺解字 flu(flow)+ent →「流」利的。相關同源字有 **flu**id（n. 液體）、**flu**sh（v. 沖洗；臉紅）、in**flu**ence（v./n. 影響）、in**flu**enza（n. 流行性感冒）、af**flu**ent（adj. 富裕的）。

詞搭 be fluent in German = speak (in) fluent German = speak German fluently 說德語很流利

---

tenant
[`tɛnənt]

n. 房客

The policeman came to find out if the victim of the fire owned the house or if he's a tenant.

警察前來確認火災罹難者是屋主還是租屋房客。

📖 101 104

秒殺解字 ten(hold)+ant → 以任何名義「擁有」土地、住房的人。

詞搭 a tenant farmer 佃農

反義字 landlord

divine

[dəˋvaɪn]

adj. 神聖的；天堂般的

I don't think those players are really that fabulous. 📖 99

In fact, they are regarded as divine beings by some of their fans.

我不認為那些球員表現真的有那麼好。事實上他們只是被一些球迷神化而已。

🪶 **秒殺解字** div(god)+ine → 「神」的，引申為「神聖的」。

同義字 | sacred, holy

souvenir

[ˏsuvəˋnɪr]

n. 紀念品、紀念物

Before boarding, I quickly picked up some souvenirs at the airport duty-free shops for my wife and two daughters.

登機之前，我在機場免稅商店迅速挑了一些紀念品準備要送給太太以及兩個女兒。

🪶 **秒殺解字** sou(=sub=up from under)+ven(come)+ir → 由「下」上「來」到了心上，當「紀念品」解釋。相關同源字有adventure（n. 冒險）、invent（v. 發明）、prevent（v. 阻止）、event（n. 事件）、eventual（adj. 最後的）、convenient（adj. 便利的）、convene（v. 集會）、convention（n. 大型會議；習俗）、conventional（adj. 傳統的）、avenue（n. 大街）、revenue（n. 國家稅收）。

詞搭 | a souvenir shop 紀念品專賣店；as a souvenir of 當作……的紀念品

同義字 | memento, keepsake

destination

[ˏdɛstəˋneʃən]

n. 目的地

After 6 hours of trekking, all of us finally arrived at our destination hungry and exhausted.

經過 6 個小時的健行，我們終於又餓又累地抵達我們的目的地。

📖 99
100
📖特 105
106
108
109

🪶 **秒殺解字** de(completely)+st(stand)+in+ation → 「完全」「立」著不動的標的，引申為「目的地」。

a holiday / tourist destination 旅遊勝地；destination wedding 海外結婚、旅行結婚

destined

[ˋdɛstɪnd]

adj. 注定的

Fear it or not, death, itself, is what we are all destined to face and experience.

不管害怕與否，死亡本身就是我們注定要面對及經歷的事。

📖 106

fragrance

[`fregrəns]

n. 香味

I was fully intoxicated by the delicate fragrance of roses when I visited the garden.
參觀花園時，我被玫瑰微幽幽芳香所吸引。

秒殺解字 frag(sweet-smelling)+ance 香味。

同義字 scent, perfume

增 106

---

archive

[`ɑrkaɪv]

n. 文件、檔案、卷宗
v. 把……存檔／歸檔

Be sure to keep all the documents in the archives for future use.
務必將所有文件存檔以備日後運用。

This software is free and it can help users archive and retrieve files and documents more efficiently and safely.
這個軟體雖然免費的，但它能夠協助使用者更有效安全地儲存及檢索檔案文件。

秒殺解字 arch(first)+ive → 本表示「首要」之處，後表示許多文件、檔案保留的「首」選之處。

詞搭 electronic archiving systems 電子存檔系統

---

heightened

[`haɪtṇd]

adj. 增高的；加強的

A heightened level of anxiety often makes me feel extremely uncomfortable in the stomach.
高度焦慮經常會讓我胃部感到非常不舒服。

秒殺解字 height+en(make, become)+ed →「使變」「高」的。

---

descendant

[dɪ`sɛndənt]

n. 子孫、後代、後裔

The residents in this area are mainly the descendants of those refugees from the Vietnam war.
這個地區的居民主要是那些越戰難民的後裔。

秒殺解字 de(down)+scend(climb) → 往「下」「爬」上去，意味著「下來」、「下降」等意思。

反義字 ancestor, forefather, forebear, antecedent

transaction

[træn`zækʃən]

n. 交易、買賣；業務

So far there are no business transactions between these two companies.
目前這兩家公司沒有生意往來。

🖋 **秒殺解字** trans(across, through)+act(do) → 「交易」、「買賣」是「跨越」買賣兩方的「行為」。相關同源字有 ex**act**（adj. 精確的）、re**act**（v. 反應）、inter**act**（v. 互動）、en**act**（v. 制定）。

詞搭 cash transaction 現金交易；financial transactions 金融業務

---

thrill

[θrɪl]

n. 興奮
v. 刺激、使興奮

It really gave me a thrill to know that I won a scholarship to Harvard.
當我得知我已獲得就讀哈佛大學的獎學金時，真是讓我雀躍不已。

The students in the auditorium were thrilled by the sudden appearance of the celebrity on stage.
禮堂裡的學生都因這位名人突然現身在舞台上而感到熱血沸騰。

🖋 **秒殺解字** thrill 和 through(貫穿)同源，thrill 表示「刺激」情緒。

詞搭 a thrill of fear / pride / excitement 一陣恐懼／自豪／興奮；
the thrill of the chase / hunt 追求（某人）過程中的刺激感

同義字 excitement, excite

Unit 48

---

validity
[vəˋlɪdətɪ]
n. 有效性；確實性

The professor said there were reasons that he doubted the validity of those figures in the report.
教授說他合理懷疑報告裡的那些數據資料。

🏆 107

(秒殺解字) val(strong)+id+ty →「強大」，引申為「有效性」。

---

invalid
[ˋɪnvəlɪd]
n. 病弱的人；殘疾人

[ɪnˋvælɪd]
adj. 無效的

反義字 valid

The invalid in bed is Christopher's mother.
這位臥病在床的人是 Christopher 的母親。

(秒殺解字) in(not)+val(strong)+id →「沒有」「力量」的，引申為「失效的」。

---

disciplinary
[ˋdɪsəplɪnˌɛrɪ]
adj. 懲戒的；關於紀律的

It is reported that five players will have to face disciplinary action after a fight broke out during last week's basketball match.
根據報導，有五位球員在上週一場棒球比賽爆發打鬥事件後，將面臨懲罰的行動。

🏆 103

(秒殺解字) dis(apart)+cip(take)+le+ine+ary → discipline 和 disciple 同源。disciple 指一部分一部分地「拿」「走」，當人「學徒」，最終是拿走、學走師傅的一身本領和知識。disicpline 指管理學生和學徒的「紀律」。

詞搭 a disciplinary committee 懲戒委員會；disciplinary action 懲戒處分

---

chronic
[ˋkrɑnɪk]
adj. 慢性（病）的、長期的；慣常的

My mother is 75 and suffers from chronic pain in her knees.
我母親 75 歲，膝蓋罹患慢性疼痛症狀。

🏆 108

(秒殺解字) chron(time)+ic →「時間」的，表示「慢性的」、「長期的」。

詞搭 a chronic disease 慢性病；a chronic invalid 慢性病患者；a chronic liar 習慣說謊的人

反義字 acute

agenda

[ə`dʒɛndə]

n. 議程；工作事項

The secretary called me to make sure that I received a copy of the agenda for next week's conference.

祕書打電話跟我確認我是否已經收到一份下週即將召開會議的議程資料。

 秒殺解字 ag(do)+enda → 要「做」的事，表示「議程」。可用 **act** 當神隊友，**k/dʒ 轉音，母音通轉**，來記憶 **ag**，皆表示「做」、「行動」。相關同源字有 **ag**ent (n. 代理商；仲介)、**ag**ency (n. 代辦處；仲介)。

詞搭 be the next <u>item / subject</u> on the agenda 排入議程／工作事項的下個項目；be <u>high on / top of</u> the agenda 是最重要的待辦事項

agony

[`ægənɪ]

n. 痛苦

Martha lay on the operating table screaming <u>in agony</u> when the doctors came in.

當醫師進來時，Martha 躺在手術台上痛苦萬分大聲尖叫。

圖 108

秒殺解字 agon(struggle)+y → 本義是「掙扎」，引申為「痛苦」，可能源自於「因痛苦而掙扎」這意象。

詞搭 the death agony 臨死的掙扎

同義字 pain, suffering

allocate

[`ælə,ket]

v. 撥出、分配

As leader of this team, you'll have to take responsibility for allocating jobs to all of your members fairly and efficiently.

身為這個團隊的領導者，你有責任公平且有效率地分配工作給你團隊所有成員。

 秒殺解字 al(=ad=to)+loc(place)+ate → 將物品「置」於某「地方」。

詞搭 allocate + sth. + to + sb. 將某物分配給某人；allocate + sth. + for + sth. 撥出……用於……

allocative

[`ælə,ketɪv]

adj. 分配的、撥出的

Allocative efficiency refers to a state of economy in which marginal cost is as close as possible to the marginal benefits.

所謂分配效率所指的是一種經濟的狀態，在此狀態下邊際成本（追加付出的成本）是要盡可能接近邊際的利益（額外得到的好處）。

bleak

[blik]

adj. 陰冷的、黯淡的

The critic says that the outlook for the next quarter's economy growth is bleak.

這位評論家說下一季的經濟成長的前景將會是黯淡無光。

秒殺解字 blank(white) → **bleak** 原意是「蒼白的」，指大自然，因為呈現一片「蒼白的」景色，是表示「荒涼的」，指天氣是表示「陰冷的」，指人的臉色是表示「蒼白的」、「缺乏熱情的」，指將來、前景等是表示「無希望的」。

詞搭 a bleak future / prospect 黯淡的未來／前途； a bleak face 陰鬱的臉孔

同義字 gloomy, hopeless

bonus

[`bonəs]

n. 獎金、紅利

I promise you'll get a fat bonus from this transaction.

我保證你將從這筆交易中得到一大筆紅利。

秒殺解字 bon(good)+us → 當你表現「好」，給你額外的「好」處。

captive

[`kæptɪv]

n. 俘虜

adj. 被俘虜的、被關在籠內的

When our troops captured the town, we finally found two of our comrades had been captives for two weeks.

當我們軍隊攻入這座城鎮時，我們終於發現我們兩位已被俘兩週的同袍。

The two soldiers were held captive for crossing the border by mistake.

兩位士兵因為誤闖邊境所以被囚禁了。

秒殺解字 capt(grasp, take, have)+ive → 被「抓」走的。

詞搭 be taken / held captive 被俘虜；a captive audience 被迫收聽／收視的聽／觀眾

同義字 hostage

反義字 captor

bankruptcy
[ˋbæŋkrʌptsɪ]
n. 破產

Due to long-term problems with administration, this local bank finally had to declare bankruptcy.
由於長期管理不善，這家地方性銀行最後必須宣告破產。

🪶**秒殺解字** bank(bench)+rupt(break)+cy → 1553 年源自義大利語 banca rotta，字面意思是「打破」「長凳」。如果銀行家未在約定時間內，將其所保管的錢歸還給原持有人，市場上的長凳或桌子就會被人破壞。可用 **rob** 當神隊友，**b/p 轉音**，**母音通轉**，來記憶 **rupt**，表示「打斷」、「打破」、「破裂」。相關同源字有 **rob**（v. 搶劫）、inter**rupt**（v. 打斷）、cor**rupt**（adj. 貪污的）、dis**rupt**（v. 使中斷）、e**rupt**（v. 爆發）。

同義字 | insolvency

betray
[bɪˋtre]
v. 背叛、出賣；流露情感

I think Roger is the last person who would betray us. 📖101
我認為 Roger 是最不可能背叛我們的人。

🪶**秒殺解字** be(upon)+tray(deceive, hand over) → 把東西「給」敵方。

詞搭 | betray + sb. + to + sb. 將某人出賣給某人；betray oneself 露出本性；betray a confidence 洩漏祕密

fragile
[ˋfrædʒəl]
adj. 易碎的；脆弱的

My mother said I should be very careful with the crystal tray because it's fragile. 📖102
我媽媽說我應該小心拿好這個水晶盤，因為它很脆弱。

🪶**秒殺解字** frag(break)+ile →容易「破碎的」。可用 **break** 當神隊友，**b/f**，**g/k/dʒ 轉音**，**母音通轉**，來記憶 **frac**、**frag**，皆表示「破裂」、「破碎」。相關同源字有 **frac**tion（n. 極小的部分）、**frac**ture（v. 使斷裂 n. 骨折）、**frag**ment（n. 碎片 v. 使成碎片）。

詞搭 | fragile glass 易碎的玻璃；fragile health 虛弱的健康狀況

同義字 | delicate, breakable

反義字 | strong

detain

[dɪ`ten]

v. 監禁、拘留；使耽擱

The police detained the drunk driver to make further inquiries.
這位酒駕者被警方扣押居留做更進一步的審訊。

🪶 **秒殺解字** de(away)+tain(hold) → 本義本義是把人「握著」並「拉走」，引申出把人拉住，不讓人離開。相關同源字有con**tain**（v. 容納）、ob**tain**（v. 得到）、enter**tain**（v. 使歡樂）、main**tain**（v. 維持）、main**ten**ance（n. 維持、維修、保養）、sus**tain**（v. 維持）、sus**ten**ance（n. 食物，營養品；維持）、de**tain**（v. 留下；使耽擱）、de**ten**tion（n. 留下；使耽擱）、re**tain**（v. 保留）、**ten**able（adj. 站得住腳的）、**ten**et（n. 信條；宗旨；原則）、**ten**ant（n. 房客）、con**tin**ue（v. 繼續、持續）、con**tin**ual（adj. 連續、頻頻的）、con**tin**uous（adj. 連續不斷的）、con**tin**ent（n. 大陸；洲）。

曾 103

詞搭 detain + sb. + for questioning 拘留某人審問

同義字 delay

---

pneumonia

[nju`monjə]

n. 肺炎

Because he lacked proper medical care, the boy's cold and fever eventually led to pneumonia.
由於缺乏妥善醫療照護，這個男孩的感冒發燒症狀最後演變成為肺炎。

曾 102

🪶 **秒殺解字** pneumon(lung)+ia(disorder) →「肺部」的「疾病」，引申為「肺炎」。

---

eclipse

[ɪ`klɪps]

n. （日或月）蝕
v. 蝕；遮蔽

There will be an eclipse of the sun next week and all of us are anxious to witness such an amazing astronomical phenomenon.
下週將會有日蝕，而我們都非常渴望能夠見證如此令人讚嘆的天文現象。

曾 104
108

The weather bureau says that the moon will be totally eclipsed at 11:50 p.m. next Monday.
氣象局說下週一晚上 11 點 50 分將會出現月全蝕。

🪶 **秒殺解字** ec(=ex=out)+lip(leave)+s+e →「向外」移動「離開」，即一塊陰影，看起來好像是太陽或月亮的一部分或全部消失了。

詞搭 in eclipse （日月）虧蝕中的、失去光彩的；the <u>solar / lunar / total</u> eclipse 日／月／全蝕；a <u>partial / total</u> eclipse of the <u>sun / moon</u> 日／月全／偏蝕

eloquent

[`ɛləkwənt]

adj. 很有口才的、雄辯滔滔的

Marvin is such an eloquent speaker that he can easily move and inspire his audiences.

Marvin 很有口才，他可以輕易地感動並鼓舞聽眾。

秒殺解字 e(=ex=out)+loqu(speak)+ent →「說」「出來」，意指「辯才」無礙、滔滔不絕。相關同源字有 colloquial (adj. 口語的)。

同義字 articulate

eloquently

[`ɛləkwəntlɪ]

adv. 善辯地、滔滔不絕地

She argued her point eloquently at the hearing and then nobody raised objection to her proposal. 普 108

在聽證會上她滔滔不絕地為她的觀點辯護，於是就沒人對她的提議表示反對意見。

narration

[næ`reʃən]

n. 敘述

Next Saturday's soccer game will be aired live on Channel 5 with English narration.

下週六的足球比賽將在第 5 頻道以英語解說現場直播。

秒殺解字 narr(tell, explain)+ation →本義「解釋」，引申為「敘述」。

smuggle

[`smʌgl]

v. 走私

The gang was arrested and accused because they tried to smuggle drugs into our country. 普 106

這個犯罪集團被逮捕起訴，因為他們試圖走私毒品入境我國。

秒殺解字 smuggle 本義是「偷偷摸摸走」(sneak)，引申為「走私」。

migrate

[`maɪgret]

v. （鳥類、動物）遷徙；移居

Because of the changing political situation, more people in this country plan to migrate abroad.

由於政治局勢不穩定，這個國家有愈來愈多的人計畫移居海外。

秒殺解字 migr(move)+ate →「移動」。

migration

[maɪ`greʃən]

n. 遷移；（候鳥）遷徙

These animal science students will stay in this village for a whole week to observe the migration of wild geese. 篙 108

這些動物科學系的學生將在此村莊停留一整個禮拜來觀察野雁的遷徙。

migrant

[`maɪɡrənt]

n. 隨季節遷徙的動物（候鳥）或為了找工作的移居者

Some developing countries are in urgent need of migrant workers from abroad.

有些開發中國家急需來自海外的移工。

普 108
高 110

詞搭 | migrant workers / laborers 季節性移動的工人；
economic migrants 經濟移民

衍生字 | emigrate [`ɛməɡ͵ret] v. 移居國外；emigration [͵ɛmə`ɡreʃən] n. 移民出境；emigrant [`ɛməɡrənt] n. ( 由內移出 ) 移民；immigrate [`ɪmə͵ɡret] v. 由外移民國內；immigration [͵ɪmə`ɡreʃən] n. 由外移民國內；immigrant [`ɪmə͵ɡrənt] n. (由外移入) 移民、僑民

---

enlightened

[ɪn`laɪtn̩d]

adj. 開明的

My parents are quite enlightened in their views on nurturing and educating children.

我父母對養育及教育孩子的觀點是相當開明的。

秒殺解字 en(in)+light+en(make)+ed →「使⋯⋯」處於「光明」的狀態「中」的。

詞搭 | enlightened attitude / approach 開明的態度／方法

01 ___ We hope you have a great time in our summer camp and feel free to give us any _____ to help us improve the quality of the camp.

(A) package   (B) feedback
(C) reception   (D) paycheck

02 ___ The policy requires enormous manpower and budget to _____ it. Right now, we don't really have the ability to carry it out.

(A) worship   (B) distort
(C) implement   (D) neglect

03 ___ The Mongol Empire, the strongest _____ in history, emerged from the unification of Mongol and Turkish tribes under Genghis Khan.

(A) warranty   (B) penalty
(C) community   (D) dynasty

04 ___ Out of _____ and respect, people tend to stay away from grave yards or abandoned houses at night.

(A) dread   (B) defense
(C) attitude   (D) industry

05 ___ Dan Cooper, also known as D.B. Cooper, is the pseudonym of an unidentified man who once_____ a Boeing 727 aircraft in United States airspace between Portland and Seattle on the afternoon of November 24, 1971.

(A) hijacked   (B) educated
(C) organized   (D) flocked

06 ___ The exiled prince has waited 10 years to get his _____ on his brother, who usurped his throne and took away his fiancée.

(A) challenge   (B) package
(C) heritage   (D) revenge

07 ___ When the chickens become part of the leopard cats' diet, pleas for sympathy for an _____ species fall on deaf ears and local poachers are called in to take care of the problem.

(A) represented   (B) reduced
(C) authorized   (D) endangered

08 ___ The Suez Canal is an artificial sea-level waterway in Egypt, connecting the Mediterranean Sea to the Red Sea through the Isthmus of Suez. Millions of tons of _____ pass through the canal every day.

(A) merits   (B) cargo
(C) reviews   (D) casinos

09 ___ Christoph Waltz, one of the most talented actors, can include trilingual talents to his resumé. He speaks _____ English, French and German.

(A) current   (B) apparent
(C) fluent   (D) transparent

10 ___ The _____ of the apartment are asking the landlord not to raise their rents because they can't afford another rent increase.

(A) tenants   (B) merchants
(C) immigrants   (D) infants

11 ___ Because my aunt has untreatable cancer, she has been dealing with _____ pain for several months.

(A) specific   (B) traumatic
(C) chronic   (D) eccentric

12 ___ Rather than let the injured dog suffer in _____, the vet decided to put it to sleep. Although it broke his heart, it was the right thing to do.

(A) determination   (B) involvement
(C) expectation   (D) agony

13 ___ Once the story broke that the head of the CIA had elected to _____ his country, pandemonium broke loose within the ranks of government.

(A) transform   (B) arrest
(C) damage   (D) betray

14 ___ Tunnels were dug so that movers could _____ immigrants into the city without being caught.

(A) exceed   (B) smuggle
(C) incorporate   (D) struggle

15 ___ Although I spent years writing in shorthand, it became worthless once our company decided to _____ to electronic recording.

(A) estimate   (B) illuminate
(C) migrate   (D) associate

解答
1.(B) 2.(C) 3.(D) 4.(A) 5.(A) 6.(D) 7.(D) 8.(B) 9.(C) 10.(A) 11.(C) 12.(D) 13.(D) 14.(B) 15.(C)

 **Unit 49**

---

adversity
[ədˋvɝ·sətɪ]
n. 逆境

A true friend will never desert us in time of adversity.
真正的好朋友永遠不會在逆境時把我們棄之不顧的。

晉 102

🖋 秒殺解字 ad(against)+vers(turn)+ity → 「轉」而「反對」，即「逆轉向」，引申為「逆境」。

詞搭 sb's courage in the face of adversity 某人面對逆境的勇氣

---

advert
[ˋædvɝt]
n. 廣告（英）

[ədˋvɝt]
v. 談到；觸及

At the conference, the chairman adverted to some controversial issues and reminded us to settle them as soon as possible.
在會議中主席提到一些爭議性的問題，然後提醒我們要盡速把它們解決。

To sell my car, I put an advert / advertisement on the website three days ago, but so far, I haven't had any takers.
為了要把我的車賣掉，三天前我在網站上登了一則廣告，但到目前為止還沒有人想買。

🖋 秒殺解字 ad(to)+vert(turn) → 「轉」「到」某人或某事物上，即是「談到」，而「廣告」也是使人「轉」「向」，誘發購買動機。

同義字 mention

---

recession
[rɪˋsɛʃən]
n. （經濟）衰退、蕭條

During the period of economic recession last year, many factories closed.
在去年經濟不景氣期間有許多工廠倒閉了。

晉 100

🖋 秒殺解字 re(back)+cess(go)+ion → 「往後」「走」，表示「衰退」。

詞搭 a deep / severe economic recession 嚴重的經濟衰退；
be in recession 經濟蕭條

同義字 depression

virus
[ˋvaɪrəs]
n. 病毒、濾過性病毒

Dr. Robinson was said to be the first to raise the alarm about the spread of the latest chickenpox virus.
Robinson 聽説是第一位針對最近水痘病蔓延提出警示的醫師。

普 105

 秒殺解字 vir(poison, virus)+us → 病毒。

詞搭 a computer virus 電腦病毒；a virus disease 濾過性病毒症；a virus infection 病毒感染；patients infected with the AIDS virus 感染愛滋病毒的病人

字辨 bacterium [bækˋtɪrɪəm] n. 細菌；germ [dʒɝm] n. 細菌、病菌

---

cosmetic
[kɑzˋmɛtɪk]
n. 化妝品
adj. 表面的

The grocery store is small, but it sells a wide range of cosmetics at a very reasonable prices.
這家雜貨店雖然規模小，但它販售各式各樣的化妝品，價格相當合理公道。

普 106

I think the changes they proposed were purely cosmetic and couldn't do anything to deal with the real problems.
我認為他們所建議的改變只是在表面做做樣子而已，在解決實際問題上面並不會產生甚麼效用。

 秒殺解字 cosm(universe, order)+et+ic →「宇宙」的運作有一定的「秩序」，有其規律美，而「化妝品」可提升外貌的美麗程度，是一種調和之美。相關同源字有 **cosmo**s (n. 宇宙)、**cosmo**politan (adj. 國際化的)、macro**cosm** (n. 宏觀世界、整體)、micro**cosm** (n. 微觀世界、縮影)。

詞搭 the cosmetic industry 化妝品業；cosmetic products 美容產品；cosmetic surgery 整容外科手術；cosmetic exercises 表面文章

同義字 superficial

---

distraction
[dɪˋstrækʃən]
n. 分散注意力的事物；娛樂、消遣

If you find the television a distraction, I can turn it off now.
如果你覺得電視會讓你分心，我現在可以把它關掉。

普 108

 秒殺解字 dis(away)+trac(drag, draw)+t+ion →「拉」「走」某人注意力。可用 **drag** 當神隊友，**d/t**，**g/k** 轉音，母音通轉，來記憶 **trac**。相關同源字有 at**trac**t (v. 吸引)、dis**trac**t (v. 使分心)、abs**trac**t (adj. 抽象的)、con**trac**t (n. 契約)、re**trac**t (v. 撤回)、sub**trac**t (v. 減去)、ex**trac**t (v. 提煉)。

詞搭 drive + sb. + to distraction 搞得……到要發狂的地步；a distraction from... 從……轉移注意力

malaria
[məˋlɛrɪə]
n. 瘧疾

Last year, he fell terribly ill with malaria on a trip to Africa.
他去年在去非洲一趟行程中感染瘧疾,病況非常嚴重。

(秒殺解字) mal(bad)+aria(air) →「壞的」「空氣」,源自義大利語「毒氣」的意思,以前醫學不發達,認為瘧疾是因沼澤汙濁的空氣所致。

mercury
[ˋmɝkjərɪ]
n. 水銀、汞

Mercury is widely used in batteries and thermometers, but it may have toxic effects on our nervous, digestive and immune systems.
水銀廣泛使用在電池以及溫度計上面,但是它卻有可能對我們的神經、消化以及免疫系統造成毒性作用。

(秒殺解字) 源自羅馬神話中的信使之神─墨利丘(Mercury),神使墨丘利健步如飛、非常靈活,因此活性非常大的金屬元素水銀,就用信使之神的名字來命名了。

parliamentarian
[ˏpɑrləmɛnˋtɛrɪən]
n. 議院法學家;議員
adj. 國會的;議會(派)的

Mr. Thompson's a parliamentarian and is very much respected for his expertise in jurisprudence and his devotion to public affairs.
Thompson 先生是一位議員,因為法律素養專業以及對公共事務的奉獻,深受敬重。

(秒殺解字) parli(parley=speak)+a+ment+ar+ian → 源自法語 parley(說),-ian 表示「人」,指在國會殿堂為民喉舌的人,引申為「議員」。相關同源字有 **parli**ament(n. 議會,國會)、**parli**amentary(adj. 國會的)。

picturesque
[ˏpɪktʃəˋrɛsk]
adj. 如畫的

This old town is famous for its picturesque narrow streets and ancient temples.
這座古鎮因其古色古香的狹窄街廓以及古剎而著名。

(秒殺解字) picture+esque(quality) → 具備「圖畫」的「特質」。

nationwide
[ˋneʃənˏwaɪd]
adj. 全國的
adv. 在全國

A nationwide referendum will be held next month to decide the issue of same-sex marriage.
下個月將舉辦一場全國性公投來決定同性婚姻的議題。

(秒殺解字) nation+wide(extending through the whole of) → wide 代表「範圍」的形容詞或副詞尾,相關同源字有 world**wide**、island**wide**、city**wide**、company**wide**。

hysterically

[hɪs`tɛrɪklɪ]

adv. 歇斯底里地、情緒失控地

The moment she heard the bad news about her son, she started to scream hysterically.

她一聽到有關她兒子的噩耗就開始歇斯底里地大叫。

普 108

秒殺解字 hyster(womb)+ic+al+ly → 古希臘人認為 hysteria（歇斯底里症）是一種「婦女病」，此病源自女性的「子宮」。

---

debris

[də`bri / `debri]

n. 廢墟、殘垣斷瓦

The village was badly damaged by enemy bombing, and a lot of debris and dead bodies were found everywhere.

這座村莊受到敵人轟炸後嚴重受損，而且到處瓦礫成堆、屍體橫陳。

高 108

秒殺解字 de(away, off)+bris(break) → 源自古法文，相當於 break in pieces，「砸成」「碎片」。

詞搭 flying debris 飛散的碎片；plant / garden / industrial debris 植物／花園／工業廢棄物

字辨 remains [rɪ`menz] n. 遺跡、遺體；ruin [`rʊɪn] n. 廢墟；relics [`rɛlɪks] n. 遺跡

---

deceased

[dɪ`sist]

n. 死者
adj. 已故的

The lady's testimony was believed to be very helpful in revealing the cause of the death of the deceased.

這位女士的證詞在釐清有關死者死因這件事情上面，相信是助益良多的。

普 102

秒殺解字 de(away)+ease(=ced=go, yield)+ed → 本義「走」「開」，引申為「死者」。

---

deceitful

[dɪ`sitfəl]

adj. 騙人的、虛假的

One of our partners strongly suggested that we immediately stop the cooperation with that deceitful businessman.

我們的其中一位合夥人強烈建議我們立刻終止與那位不誠實商人的合作關係。

普 107

秒殺解字 de(from)+ceit(take, catch)+ful → 設陷阱將人「從」外面「抓」進來，引申為「騙人的」。

同義字 dishonest, untruthful

反義字 trustworthy

earthly

[ˋɝθlɪ]

adj. 塵世的；全然的（否定）

I must tell you that you have no earthly hope of winning. So, stop wasting your time.
我必須告訴你，你是完全沒有獲勝的機會的，所以呢，你就停止浪費時間吧！

(秒殺解字) earth+ly → 屬於這個「世界」的。

enchant

[ɪnˋtʃænt]

v. 使著迷

I like these poems very much because they seem to be the wisdom that enchants my heart.
我非常喜歡這些詩，因為他們似乎是陶醉我心靈的智慧。

(秒殺解字) en(in)+chant(sing) →「唱歌」使人「入」迷。

詞搭 ｜ be enchanted with 著迷於……

enchantment

[ɪnˋtʃæntmənt]

n. 愉悅；著迷

Taroko Gorge has long been a scenic spot full of deep mystery and enchantment. 📻 103
太魯閣長久以來一直都是一個充滿神祕奇幻相當迷人的景點。

trigger

[ˋtrɪgɚ]

n. 扳機
v. 引發

My doctor advises that I avoid eating nuts because they will easily trigger allergies.
我的醫師建議我避免食用堅果類食物，因為他們很容易引發過敏症狀。

If the border incident last week was not carefully dealt with, it may have become a trigger for more conflicts between the two countries.
如果上週的邊界事件沒有妥善處理的話，它有可能引發兩國間更多的衝突。

(秒殺解字) trigger 表示「拉」(pull)，引申為「引發」、「扳機」。

詞搭 ｜ trigger off... 觸發……；be the trigger point for + sth. 某事的觸發點；pull / squeeze the trigger 扣扳機

casino

[kə`sino]

n. 賭場

It was reported that a billionaire from China was murdered last night in the most famous casino in Macau.

根據報導，一位來自中國的億萬富翁昨晚在澳門最有名的那家賭場裡被殺了。

 秒殺解字 源自拉丁文的 casa，表示「小房子」，1820 年在義大利文中始見「官方設立的賭場」之衍生意思。

insane

[ɪn`sen]

adj. 瘋狂的

The pauper screamed like an insane person after he learned that he won the 5 billion dollar lottery.

這個窮光蛋得知中了 50 億彩券獎金後隨即就像個瘋子似地驚聲尖叫。

 秒殺解字 in(not)+sane(well, healthy, sane) → 神志「不」「健康的」，表示「瘋狂的」。

詞搭 go insane 發瘋；drive + sb. + insane / mad 逼得某人發瘋；an insane hospital / asylum 瘋人病院／瘋人院

同義字 crazy, mad, mentally ill

反義字 sane

Unit 50

---

interchangeable
[ˌɪntɚˋtʃendʒəbl̩]
adj. 可互替的

The two cars are of different models, but they share some interchangeable parts.
這兩台車分屬不同款式，但他們有一些可互相替代的共用零件。

🔖 106

🖋️ **秒殺解字** inter(between)+change+able →「在彼此之間」「可」「改變的」，引申為「替代的」。

同義字 substitutable [ˌsʌbstɪˋtjutəbl̩] adj. 可相互替代的

---

embark
[ɪmˋbɑrk]
v. 登船；投（資）

Early in the morning, they <u>embarked at</u> Keelung for Yokohama.
一大早他們在基隆登船預計前往橫濱。

🔖 108

The club is <u>embarking on / upon</u> a campaign to recruit more volunteers to work for those school kids in the remote villages.
這個社團正展開一項活動來招聘更多義工為偏鄉村落學童服務。

🖋️ **秒殺解字** em(=en=in)+bark(ship) →「進入」「船」。

反義字 disembark

---

plague
[pleg]
n. 瘟疫
v. 使痛苦、使心煩

The city is now suffering a plague of rats, and so far, there have been 20 confirmed deaths.
這個城市正遭受鼠疫肆虐，而截至目前為止，已有 20 個確認的死亡病例。

🔖 108

My grandmother has <u>been plagued with</u> arthritis for years.
我祖母受關節炎折磨已經好幾年了。

🖋️ **秒殺解字** plague(strike) → 瘟疫「襲擊」（strike）

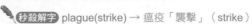

詞搭 the Black Plague 黑死病，鼠疫；avoid...like the plague 盡量避開……

字辨 plaque [plæk] n. 匾牌

immunity

[ɪˈmjunətɪ]

n. 免疫力

The doctor says this vaccine will give me <u>immunity against</u> the flu for up to 3 years.
醫師説接種這種疫苗可以讓我對流行性感冒有長達 3 年的免疫力。

(秒殺解字) im(not)+mun(service)+ity →「不」需提供「服務」，因此有「免除」（exempt）、「免責」的意思，1881 年產生「免疫力」的意思，因為「預防接種」讓人「免除」染上某些疾病的危機。相關同源字有 **mun**icipal (adj. 市的)。

詞搭 immunity to <u>measles / infection</u> 對麻疹／傳染病免疫；
immunity from taxation 免税

manipulate

[məˈnɪpjəˌlet]

v. 操縱；竄改

 106

The leader of the opposition party accused the prime minister of manipulating the media to suppress public opinions.
反對黨領袖控訴首相操控媒體試圖壓制大眾輿論。

(秒殺解字) man(hand)+i+pul(fill, full)+ate → 原意類似 handful，意圖把「手」「填滿」，即掌握一切在「手」中，常指以不正當手段來「操縱」他人或事物。

詞搭 manipulate <u>stocks / puppets</u> 操控股市／木偶；
manipulate <u>accounts / figures</u> 竄改帳目／數字

meek

[mik]

adj. 溫順的

 104

She looks very <u>meek and mild,</u> but in fact, she's quite fierce and vicious.
她看起來好像溫柔和善，但事實上她卻是相當兇猛邪惡的。

(秒殺解字) meek(soft) → 原意「軟的」。

詞搭 meek as a lamb 像小羊般地溫馴

dubious

[ˈdjubɪəs]

adj. 猶豫不決的；可疑的

 99

The result of the investigation is still dubious, so don't make any conclusions before it is clarified.
調查結果仍然未經證實，所以在沒有被澄清之前，切勿輕率下定論。

(秒殺解字) du(two)+b+ious → 心思在「二」端擺盪，懷疑東、懷疑西。

詞搭 be dubious about + <u>N / Ving</u> 猶豫是否該……

同義字 doubtful, suspicious

confidential
[ˌkɑnfəˋdɛnʃəl]
adj. 保密的、機密的

Your medical records are confidential and cannot be revealed without your permission.
你的醫療紀錄是機密的，所以未經你的允許是不可被揭露的。

 秒殺解字 con(intensive prefix)+fid(faith)+ent+ial → 有「信任」、「信心」，才能透露祕密或委託他人，表示「機密的」。可用 **faith** 當神隊友，**d/θ 轉音**，母音通轉，來記憶 **fid**，表示「信任」、「信心」。相關同源字有 con**fid**e (v. 透露)、con**fid**ent (adj. 自信的；有信心的)、con**fid**ence (n. 自信；信任)、dif**fid**ent (adj. 缺乏自信的)、dif**fid**ence (n. 缺乏自信)。

詞搭 confidential <u>information / documents</u> 機密資訊／文件；keep + sth. + confidential 保密某事；<u>highly / strictly</u> confidential 極機密的

---

confidentiality
[ˌkɑnfɪˌdɛnʃɪˋælɪtɪ]
n. 機密

We guarantee that all information you fill in / out will be treated with complete confidentiality.
我們保證您所填寫所有資料均會被視為絕對機密。

---

perplexing
[pəˋplɛksɪŋ]
adj. 令人困惑的

I admit the problems we are facing are quite perplexing and may be far beyond our abilities to solve.
我承認我們現在所面對的問題相當複雜棘手，而且也許會遠遠超過我們能力範圍之上。

 秒殺解字 per(through)+plex(fold) +ing → 「從頭到尾」都將東西「摺」在一起，因此隱含「糾結」的意思，引申為使人難懂的、「令人困惑的」。

同義字 confusing, puzzling

---

endeavor
[ɪnˋdɛvə]
n. v. 努力

All of our team members are now endeavoring to locate the source of such a tough problem.
我們所有團隊成員正竭盡全力希望能夠找出如此難纏問題的根源。

 秒殺解字 en(make, in)+deavor(duty) → 「使」成為自己應盡的「義務」，表示「努力地嘗試」；en**deavor** 和 **debt** 同源，**b/v 轉音**，母音通轉，核心語意是「欠債」。。

詞搭 endeavor + to V = make an <u>endeavor / attempt / effort</u> + to V 努力去從事……

438

salutation

[ˌsæljə`teʃən]

n. 致意；行禮；稱呼語

When the gentleman saw the lady sitting over there, he raised his hat in salutation. The lady then stood up and bowed in return.

當這位紳士看到坐在那邊的女士時，他就舉起他的帽子致意。女士於是起身回禮。

（秒殺解字）salu(=salv=greet)+t+ation →「打招呼」，引申為「致意」、「行禮」。

---

sarcastic

[sɑr`kæstɪk]

adj. 嘲諷的、挖苦的

I must tell you that I've been fed up with your sarcastic remarks.

我必須告訴你，你的冷嘲熱諷我受夠了。

高 108

（秒殺解字）sarc(tear the flesh)+as+tic → 本義是「撕肉」，後來語意延伸，表示「用言語去挖苦他人」，其痛苦可以和割肉相比擬。相關同源字有 **sarc**asm (n. 諷刺，挖苦的話)、**sarc**astically (adv. 諷刺地；挖苦地)。

---

liability

[ˌlaɪə`bɪlətɪ]

n. 責任；義務；不利；債務；傾向

Susan said she would assume liability for the car accident.

Susan 說她會承擔意外車禍事件的責任。

會 100

Heavy liabilities finally forced the company to go into bankruptcy.

沉重債務問題終使這家公司步入破產結局。

（秒殺解字）li(=lig=tie, bind)+able+ity → 緊密「綁」在一起，表示「責任」、「不利」、「傾向」等。

---

intonation

[ˌɪnto`neʃən]

n. 語調；吟詠

To master a language, it's important to pay attention to both pronunciation and intonation.

若要精通一種語言，很重要的是發音跟語調都必須留意。

（秒殺解字）in(in)+ton(tone)+ation →在「音調」的「裡面」，表示「語調」。相關同源字有 **ton**e (n. 語氣；音色)、**tun**e (n. 旋律；音調)、mono**ton**y (n. 單調、無聊)。

---

underlying

[ˌʌndɚ`laɪɪŋ]

adj. 隱含的，根本的

The underlying reason for the failure of this project is still unknown.

這項計畫失敗的根本因素仍然未知。

會 102
警特 107

（秒殺解字）under(under)+lie+ing →「位於」……「之下」的，表示「隱含的」、「根本的」。

詞搭 the underlying cause / motive 基本原因／潛在動機

accomplished

[ə`kɑmplɪʃt]

adj. 熟練某種才藝的、有造詣的

Patricia's mother is a highly accomplished pianist in Austria.

Patricia 的母親是在奧地利一位造詣頗深的鋼琴家。

秒殺解字 ac(=ad=to)+com(intensive prefix)+pli(fill)+ish+ed → 「去」填「滿」，能夠「完成」，就是「熟練的」。

同義字 skillful, proficient, adept

angler

[`æŋglə]

n. 垂釣者

The angler patiently waited by the river for two hours and could finally reel the fish in.

這位釣客耐心在河邊等待兩小時，現在終於可以收繞釣線把魚釣起了。

秒殺解字 angle(bend)+er → 垂釣需要「角度」，可用 **ankle** 當神隊友，**g/k 轉音**，來記憶 **angle**，表示「角度」；**angle** 本義是足踝「彎曲」，彎曲構成「角度」。

retrieve

[rɪ`triv]

v. 取回；恢復；補正

I believe the new computer I just bought will be able to store and retrieve information more efficiently.

我相信我剛買的電腦將能夠更有效率地儲存以及檢索資訊。

秒殺解字 re(back)+trieve(find) → 「找」「回去」，表示「取回」。

詞搭 retrieve a kid from the kidnaper 從綁匪取回孩子

同義字 recover, recuperate, regain, get back

dissident

[`dɪsədənt]

n. 異議份子
adj. 異議的

Those political dissidents complained about being harassed constantly by the police.

那些持不同政治觀點者抱怨經常受到警方騷擾。

秒殺解字 dis(apart)+sid(sit)+ent → 「分開」「坐」，不想坐一起，表示與政府「意見不同的」「異議人士」。可用 **sit** 當神隊友，**z/s，d/t 轉音**，**母音通轉**，來記憶 **sid**，皆表示「坐」。相關同源字有 pre**sid**ent (n. 總統；總裁)、re**sid**ent (n. 居民)。

詞搭 a dissident writer / newspaper 持異議的作家／報紙

同義字 dissenter

contaminate

[kən`tæmə͵net]

v. 污染

The manager of the restaurant said that those contaminated eggs wouldn't be used and would be properly disposed of.

餐廳經理說那些受到污染的蛋不會再被使用，而且他們會做妥善處理。

🖋 秒殺解字 con(together)+tamin(=tag=touch)+ate → 「一起」「接觸」，造成「污染」。

普 100
警特 109

同義字 pollute

---

contamination

[kən͵tæmə`neʃən]

n. 污染

The health department reminds all restaurants in this city to pay meticulous attention to food contamination during hot summer months.

衛生部門提醒本市餐廳業者在酷暑月份要特別注意食物污染問題。

高 108

同義字 pollution

01 ___ The recent virus epidemic caused an irreversible economic _____. Traditional stimulus methods were not effective.

(A) depression (B) obsession
(C) recession (D) aggression

02 ___ The Brain Boot Sector Virus, the first computer _____ in the world, began infecting disks in 1986. According to reports, it was the work of two brothers, Basit and Amjad Farooq Alvi, who ran a computer store in Pakistan.

(A) virus (B) major
(C) indicator (D) effect

03 ___ If you are a senior high school student, you should stay away from _____ like cellphone games or television.

(A) selections (B) distractions
(C) dysfunctions (D) productions

04 ___ _____, a chemical element with toxic effects on the nervous system, was often used in rich people's tombs to keep grave robbers away.

(A) Injury (B) Military
(C) Industry (D) Mercury

05 ___ After the autopsy, the police concluded that he survived the initial blast wave, but was killed by the flying _____ afterwards.

(A) debris (B) increase
(C) remains (D) results

06 ___ During Chinese Ghost Festival, people perform special ceremonies to avoid the wrath of the _____ such as putting the family's ancestral tablets on a table, burning incense, and preparing food three times that day.

(A) depressed (B) accomplished
(C) deceased (D) detailed

07 ____ At first, it was just a small quarrel between the players. However, one man in the audience threw a bottle at a player and _____ a massive fight between the players and the audience.

(A) worshiped   (B) melted

(C) differed   (D) triggered

08 ____ Las Vegas, one of the most prosperous cities in North America, earns most of its profits from _____ and hotels. Millions of tourists go there every day to try to win a fortune.

(A) casinos   (B) resumes

(C) reviews   (D) merits

09 ____ Everyone thinks he is _____ and unreasonable, but I see the determination in his eyes. As a result, I want to give him the opportunity.

(A) stormy   (B) complicated

(C) insane   (D) alternative

10 ____ I couldn't find the exact same component for the machine. However, these two parts are _____, so we can use this one to replace the old one.

(A) reasonable   (B) comparable

(C) interchangeable   (D) vulnerable

11 ____ The Black Death was the deadliest _____ recorded in human history. The Black Death resulted in the deaths of up to 200 million people in Europe and North Africa.

(A) vogue   (B) catalogue

(C) colleague   (D) plague

12 ____ Once you have contracted the virus and recovered from it, you will have the _____ of the same virus, which means that you will not get sick because of the same virus again.

(A) unanimity   (B) immunity

(C) facility   (D) community

13 ___ The authority is now investigating the candidate for attempts to
_____ the election.

(A) generate   (B) manipulate
(C) stimulate   (D) motivate

14 ___ The _____ documents can only be accessed by the president
himself. There is no way we can bypass the system without the
president's fingerprints.

(A) confidential   (B) potential
(C) influential   (D) spatial

15 ___ Chandler is most famous for his _____ nature and he is one of the
most beloved character in the TV series. He always mocks others.

(A) specific   (B) artistic
(C) romantic   (D) sarcastic

解答
1.(C) 2.(A) 3.(B) 4.(D) 5.(A) 6.(C) 7.(D) 8.(A) 9.(C) 10.(C) 11.(D) 12.(B) 13.(B) 14.(A) 15.(D)

traumatic

[trɔˋmætɪk]

adj. 外傷的；精神創傷的

Yes, that must be a traumatic experience, but anyway, it's in the past.

是的，那一定是一個痛苦難忘的經歷，但不管如何，這一切都過去了。

秒殺解字 trauma(wound)+t+ic →有「傷」的。

| 同義字 | upsetting |

---

ponder

[ˋpandə]

v. 仔細考慮

On her way home from work today, Mary <u>pondered (over)</u> one of her best friends' advice and then decided to quit next week.

在下班回家途中，Mary 仔細考量她其中一位好友的忠告建議，然後就決定下週辭職。

秒殺解字 pond(weigh, hang)+er →「掛」起來「秤重」，使兩端平衡，表示「仔細考慮」。相關同源字有 de**pend**（v 依靠）、ex**pend**（v. 花費）、ex**pens**e（n. 費用）、sus**pend**（v. 停止；懸掛）、sus**pens**e.（n. 懸念）、dis**pens**e（v. 分配）。

| 詞搭 | ponder <u>over / on / upon / about</u> + sth. 仔細考慮某事；ponder <u>how / what / whether</u> + S + V... 仔細考慮某事如何／什麼／是否…… |

| 同義字 | consider |

---

offspring

[ˋɔfˏsprɪŋ]

n. 後代、子孫

A mule is the offspring of a male donkey and a female horse.

曾 104

騾子是由公驢與母馬交配產生的後代。

秒殺解字 off(away)+spring(leap, burst forth) →「往外」「迸出」，產生「後代」。

| 同義字 | descendant |

| 反義字 | ancestor |

445

glitter

[ˋglɪtɚ]

n. 閃耀;光彩
v. 發光、閃爍

The glitter of the fireworks at night caught everyone's eyes.
晚上煙火的閃閃絢麗吸引著每個人的目光。

Look! Do you see the morning dew glittering in the sun?
瞧!你有看到晨露正在陽光下閃爍發亮嗎?

(秒殺解字) 含 gl 的單字有「高興」、「照耀或發光」、「看見」的意思。相關單字有 **gl**ad (adj. 高興地)、**gl**ee (n. 歡喜)、**gl**ass (n. 玻璃)、**gl**ow (v. 發光)、**gl**isten (v. 閃耀)、**gl**eam (v. 發微光)、**gl**immer (v. 發微光)、**gl**int (v. 閃閃發光)、**gl**oss (n. 表面的光澤)、**gl**ance (n. 瞥一眼)、**gl**are (v. 怒視)、**gl**impse (n. 看一眼)、**gl**oat (v. 沾沾自喜或幸災樂禍地看)。

---

warrior

[ˋwɔrɪɚ]

n. 戰士

A true warrior always values glory and honor above his own life.
一位真正的勇士始終是珍視榮耀勝過其生命。

(秒殺解字) war+r+i+or → 投入「戰爭」「者」。

---

decorative

[ˋdɛkərətɪv]

adj. 裝飾性的、裝潢用的

These plates actually serve no purpose; they are purely decorative.
這些碟盤實際上沒有甚麼用處,它們純粹是做擺飾用而已。

會 104

(秒殺解字) decor(beautiful)+ate+ive → 「使」「漂亮」「的」,引申為「裝飾性的」。

|詞搭| decorative art 裝飾藝術

---

genetic

[dʒəˋnɛtɪk]

adj. 基因的;遺傳(學)的

These years Dr. Sheffield has made a lot of significant contributions to the study of genetic engineering.
近幾年以來 Sheffield 博士對遺傳基因工程的研究已做出許多重大貢獻。

高 108

(秒殺解字) gen(birth, produce)+et+ic → 「生」下來是否「同類」是由「基因」所決定。

|詞搭| genetic modification / engineering = GM 基因改造工程;genetic defects / diseases / codes 遺傳基因缺陷/疾病/密碼

genetics
[dʒəˋnɛtɪks]

n. 基因學;遺傳學

This course will focus on the application of genetics to medical practice.
這個課程將著重遺傳學在醫學上的實際應用。

---

disciple
[dɪˋsaɪpḷ]

n. 門徒、跟隨者

A well-known religious leader was known to always surround himself with attractive female disciples in his temple.
眾所周知,一位著名的宗教領袖,在他的寺廟中總是圍繞著迷人的女弟子。

秒殺解字 dis(apart)+cip(take)+le → 指一部分一部分地「拿」「走」,當人「門徒」,最終是拿走、學走師傅的一身本領和知識。

詞搭 a disciple of Confucius / Tolstoy 孔夫子的門生／托爾斯泰的信徒

同義字 follower

---

scandal
[ˋskændḷ]

n. 醜聞

The candidate should first manage to cover up his scandal if he wants to win the election.
這位候選人如果想贏得這場選舉的話,他就必須先掩蓋他的醜聞。

秒殺解字 scand(=scan=climb)+al → 本義是「爬」,此處指須努力爬過去、跨過去的「障礙」、「絆腳石」。16世紀末時,scandal 專指對宗教不虔誠的行為而導致名聲敗壞,後來才有「醜聞」的語意產生。

詞搭 cause / create a financial scandal 引發／製造財經醜聞;
a political scandal 政治醜聞

---

arrogantly
[ˋærəgəntlɪ]

adv. 傲慢地、自大地

He didn't say yes or no to my proposal, but he just arrogantly said it was too boring to take an interest in.
他對我的提案不置可否,只是傲慢地說,太無聊了,沒興趣。

秒殺解字 ar(=ad=to)+rog(ask)+ant+ly → 「傲慢的」人,通常是認為自己比較重要,老是不斷「傲慢地」「要求」別人。相關同源字有 sur**rog**ate (adj. 代理的)、inter**rog**ate (v. 訊問、盤問)

同義字 proudly, conceitedly, haughtily

反義字 humbly, modestly

dual
[ˋdjuəl]

adj. 雙重的

Actually, it's not easy to fully understand her because she is a person with <u>dual</u> personalities.

說真的，要完全了解她實在不容易，因為她是具有雙重性格的人。

🖋 **(秒殺解字)** du(two)+al → 「雙重的」。可用 **two** 當神隊友，**d/t** 轉音，母音通轉，來記憶 **du**、**do**、**dou**、**di**，皆表示「雙」、「二」。相關同源字有 **du**el（v./n. 決鬥）、**du**plicate（v. 複製）、**do**zen（n. 一打）、**dou**ble（adj. 雙的；兩倍的）、**du**bious（adj. 可疑的；懷疑的）、**dou**bt（v./n. 懷疑）、**dou**btful（adj. 懷疑的；可疑的）、**di**ploma（n. 畢業文憑；證書）。

曾99

詞搭 dual <u>citizenship / nationality</u> 雙重國籍

---

lottery
[ˋlɑtərɪ]

n. 樂透、彩券

What would you like to do first if you won the lottery tomorrow?

如果你明天彩券中獎，你首先想做甚麼？

🖋 **(秒殺解字)** lot(chance)+t+ery → 憑「機會」中獎的「樂透」或「彩券」。

曾105

---

sandal
[ˋsændl̩]

n. 涼鞋

Sandals are quite popular during hot summer days, but they are in fact not suitable for formal occasions.

涼鞋在酷暑期間相當受到歡迎，但事實上並不適合正式場合。

🖋 **(秒殺解字)** 一種鞋子。字源不詳，有人推測源自波斯語。

曾104

詞搭 a pair of sandals 一雙涼鞋

---

retaliate
[rɪˋtælɪˏet]

v. 報復

If someone tries to be rude to me, I'll absolutely retaliate with equal rudeness.

如果有人試圖對我無禮，那麼我絕對會用同樣方式回敬。

🖋 **(秒殺解字)** re(back)+tali(suitable punishment)+ate → 他人怎麼對待你，你也要用相應的「懲罰」來「回報」惡行。

詞搭 retaliate against 向……報復

同義字 revenge, avenge, counter-attack, hit back, strike back

eccentric
[ɪk`sɛntrɪk]
adj. 古怪的

The old man has some eccentric habits that even his family cannot stand.
這位老人家有一些連他家人都無法忍受的古怪習慣。

 102

> **（秒殺解字）** ec(=ex=out)+centr(center)+ic → 「離開」「中心」，和大家不同，引申為「古怪反常的」。相關同源字有 **center**（n. 中心 v. 集中）、**centr**al（adj. 中心的）、con**centr**ate（v. 集中）。

同義字 strange, weird, odd, bizarre

---

addict
[`ædɪkt]
n. 成癮者

Karla's parents were very shocked to learn that their daughter was a drug addict.
Karla 的雙親得知女兒已是吸毒成癮的人時感到非常震驚。

曾 108
警特 109

> **（秒殺解字）** ad(to)+dic(say)+t → 隨時隨地都在「說」的人，表示「成癮者」。相關同源字有 **dic**tionary（n. 字典）、pre**dic**t（v. 預測）、de**dic**ate（v. 奉獻）、con**di**tion（n. 情況）。

詞搭 a drug / heroin / morphine addict 毒蟲；a TV / sports / cellphone addict 電視／運動／手機迷

---

addicted
[ə`dɪktɪd]
adj. 成癮的

Bennett has been addicted to drinking and smoking for more than 15 years, and now he's trying to quit these bad habits for health's sake.
Bennett 菸酒成癮至少 15 年，而為了健康的緣故，現在他試著要把它們戒掉。

---

addiction
[ə`dɪkʃən]
n. 上癮

Maggie was sent to a rehabilitation center where she would be helped to overcome her addiction.
Maggie 被遣送到一家戒毒康復之家，在那裡會有人協助她克服毒癮。

高 108

詞搭 addiction to alcohol 對酒精上癮；drug / heroin / morphine / alcohol addiction 毒癮／海洛因癮／嗎啡癮／酒癮

---

conceited
[kən`sitɪd]
adj. 自負的

Alison is very smart, but it seems that no one likes her because she's always so selfish and conceited.
Alison 非常聰明，但似乎沒人喜歡她，因為她總是那麼自私又自負。

警特 108

> **（秒殺解字）** con(intensive prefix)+ceit(=ceiv=take)+ed → conceit 為 self-conceit 的縮略形式，意思是把東西「拿進」自己的腦袋中，自我膨脹，表示「自負的」。

同義字 big-headed, arrogant, proud, cocky, haughty
反義字 humble, modest

seduce

[sɪˋdjus]

v. 勾引、挑逗、引誘

The coach wanted to seduce the cutest girl on the tennis team but she bravely rejected his advance.
這位教練想要勾引網球隊中那位最可愛的女孩，但她勇敢地拒絕他的追求。

My mother was finally seduced into buying this cellphone by the offer of a free flight to Hualien.
我媽媽最後受到一張免費飛往花蓮機票的誘惑，於是買了這支手機。

 秒殺解字 se(away)+duc(lead, tow)+e → 將人給「拉」「走」，表示「誘惑」他人做某事。

詞搭 seduce + sb. + into + Ving = lure + sb. + into + N / Ving = tempt + sb. + to V / into Ving 引誘某人做某事

同義字 tempt, lure, allure, entice

metric

[ˋmɛtrɪk]

adj. 公尺的

If you can offer us a 10% discount, we'll immediately place an order with you for 10,000 metric tons of apples and pears respectively.
如果你們可以給我們 10% 折扣的話，我們就會馬上向你們訂購蘋果與梨子各一萬公噸。

 秒殺解字 metr(=meter=measure)+ic →「公尺的」，「公尺」是「測量」的單位。此處的 metr 是從 meter 省略 e 而來的，大多數的 er / or 結尾的字根，加上母音為首的字尾時，e/o 會省略，相關單字有 entrance (= enter + ance)、central (= center + al)、actress(= actor + ess)、waiteress (= waiter + ess)、empress (= emperor + ess)。

詞搭 metric ton 公噸；metric system 十進位度量衡制度；go metric 採用十進制

legacy

[ˋlɛgəsɪ]

n. 遺產

The cultural legacy from the Qing Dynasty has become an attractive resource for this city's tourism.
從清朝流傳下來的文化遺產已經成為這個城市豐富的觀光資源。

秒殺解字 leg(law)+acy → 依「法」繼承「遺產」。相關同源字有 legal (adj. 合法的)、legislate (v. 立法)、privilege (n. 特權)、legitimate (adj. 合法的)、allege (v. 宣稱、指控)。

同義字 inheritance

Unit 52

meditate

[`mɛdə͵tet]

v. 深思熟慮；冥想；
打坐；計畫

Before making his final decision, Lyndon <u>meditated on</u> all the possible consequences that might arise.
在 Lyndon 做最後決定前，他思索著所有可能發生的後果。

> 秒殺解字 med(take appropriate measures)+it+ate → 本指因應時宜，採取合適「措施」(measure)，引申為「深思熟慮」、「計畫」等意思。相關同源字有 **med**ical (adj. 醫學的)、**med**icine (n. 藥)、re**med**y (n. 治療)。

詞搭 meditate <u>on / upon</u> + sth. 深思某事；meditate revenge 計畫著復仇

同義字 muse, ponder, consider, contemplate

---

harassment

[hə`ræsmənt]

n. 騷擾

The new law will be enacted to protect our employees from workplace harassment.
這項新的法律將會被執行以保護我們員工免於受到職場騷擾。

> 秒殺解字 har(set a dog on)+ass+ment 字源不詳，可能源自古法語，har 是獵人打獵時使喚狗的驚嘆詞，表示「嗾狗」(to set a dog on)，嗾狗追人會造成對方的困擾。

詞搭 <u>sexual / racial</u> harassment 性／種族騷擾

---

aptitude

[`æptə͵tjud]

n. 天資；才能

Wallis has shown a great <u>aptitude for</u> painting since her childhood.
Wallis 從小就展現出超高的繪畫天賦。

> 秒殺解字 apt(fit)+i+tude →「適合」做某事情之潛力。值得一提的是，**apt**itude 和 **att**itude 是「雙飾詞」(**doublet**)，簡言之就是同源字。attitude 本指畫像、雕像等藝術品的人物所擺出「合適的」動作或姿態，後指動作或姿態所呈現、反映出的「內心狀況」，引申為「態度」。

詞搭 have a natural aptitude for... 有……的天賦；an aptitude test 性向測驗

衍生字 apt [æpt] adj. 有……傾向的；be apt to V 傾向於……、易於……

同義字 同義字：ability, capability, gift, talent, genius

roam
[rom]

v. 漫步；遊蕩

My wife and I spent a whole day yesterday <u>roaming</u> <u>around</u> Rome, and we did have a good time.
我太太跟我昨天花了一整天在羅馬城閒逛，我們真的玩得很開心。

聽 107

The prepaid mobile phone service usually does not allow users to roam outside the service network.
採用預付機制的行動電話服務通常不會允許使用者在其服務網絡之外漫遊。

> (秒殺解字) 源自古英文，表示「閒逛」、「漫遊」。

詞搭 roam the <u>streets / countryside</u> 在街上遊蕩／在鄉間漫步

同義字 wander, rove, ramble

---

foul
[faʊl]

v. 弄髒
adj. 骯髒的；惡劣的

An oil tanker spilled several tons of oil along the coast, seriously fouling the surrounding waters.
一艘油輪在海岸邊溢出好幾噸的油，嚴重汙染了附近海域。

The food and service of the restaurant are not bad, but the toilets there are awful—they have a really foul smell .
這家餐廳的食物跟服務都不差，但那裡的廁所真是恐怖一味道太難聞了！

> (秒殺解字) 源自古英文，本義是「腐爛」、「發臭」，後來衍生出「骯髒的」、「惡劣的」。

詞搭 foul breath 口臭；a foul murder 兇殺；foul language 髒話 ；
in a foul <u>mood / temper</u> 心情差／壞脾氣；by fair means or foul =
by hook or by crook 不擇手段

同義字 disgusting

---

irritability
[ˌɪrətəˈbɪlətɪ]

n. 易怒；過敏

My doctor reminded me that constant feelings of sadness or irritability may denote a case of depression.
我的醫師提醒我說經常有悲傷以及煩躁不安的感覺有可能代表一種憂鬱症狀。

高 108

> (秒殺解字) irrit(excite, provoke)+able+ity → 容易被「激怒」。

uranium
[ju`renɪəm]

n. 鈾

Canada is the world's largest exporter of uranium.
加拿大是全世界最大的鈾礦輸出國。

秒殺解字 uran(Uranus)+ium → 放射性元素 uranium 是根據在它之前發現的天王星 Uranus 來命名的。

詞搭 enriched uranium 濃縮鈾

lament
[lə`mɛnt]

v. 悲嘆

The little girl kept lamenting over the misfortunes she suffered as a homeless child.
這位小女孩一直唉嘆著她無家可歸的不幸。

秒殺解字 lament(wail, weep) → lament，原意是「哭泣」，源自 lamentation，為逆向構詞，先有名詞才有動詞。

同義字 mourn, grieve

📺 103 107

disability
[͵dɪsə`bɪlətɪ]

n. 失能；障礙

Lisa is blind, but she never lets her disability prevent her from learning.
Lisa 雖然眼睛失明，但她從來不讓此一缺陷阻止她學習。

秒殺解字 dis(opposite)+ability →「有能力的」的「相反」，表示「失能」。

詞搭 learning / physical / mental disability 學習／身／心障礙；disability insurance 失能險

📺 99

rhetorical
[rɪ`tɔrɪkl̩]

adj. 修辭的

Metaphor and simile are two rhetorical forms of language application.
隱喻以及明喻是語言應用中的兩種修辭方法。

秒殺解字 rhetor(orator, teacher of rhetoric)+ic+al → 源自希臘文「談」的意思，字源亦跟重視「修辭」技巧的「演説者」有相關。

詞搭 rhetorical phrases 華麗詞藻

fabulous

[`fæbjələs]

adj. 極好的；鉅額的；寓言的；傳說的

Eileen was very excited when I told her she looked fabulous in her dress.
當我告訴 Eileen 說她穿這件洋裝漂亮極了時，她聽了非常興奮。

The dragon is a fabulous and mythical creature in Chinese culture.
龍是中國文化中傳說中的神祕動物。

秒殺解字 fable(speak)+ous → fable 在加接母音開頭的形容詞字尾 ous，先刪除字尾 e，並在 bl 和之間插入 u 字母，以維持最佳音節結構。cl、gl、bl 在加接母音開頭字尾時，插入 u 的相關例子有 circle / circulate、particle / particular、angle / angular、single / singular、spectacle / spectacular、miracle / miraculous 等。

詞搭 a fabulous creature / hero 傳說／寓言中的生物／英雄；fabulous wealth 巨額財富

同義字 wonderful, impressive, huge

allergic

[ə`lɝdʒɪk]

adj. 過敏的

If you want to cure your allergies, you should first get to know the kind of food that you're allergic to.
如果你想治療你的過敏症，首先你應了解你對甚麼食物過敏。

秒殺解字 all(=ali=other)+erg(work)+ic → 有「其他」異物，在身上「作用」，造成「過敏的」。

詞搭 be allergic to... 對……過敏；an allergic reaction to some medicines 對某些藥物的過敏反應

同義字 hypersensitive

superficial

[ˌsupɚ`fɪʃəl]

adj. 表面的；膚淺的

Some people think Derek is an interesting and easy-going guy, but I think he's very superficial.
有些人認為 Derek 風趣而且容易相處，但我卻認為他非常膚淺。

普 103
警特 106

秒殺解字 super(over)+fic(face)+ial →「面」之「上方」，是「表面的」、「膚淺的」。

詞搭 a superficial wound 皮肉傷；superficial examination / study 粗略的檢查／研究；superficial resemblance / similarity 表面的相似之處

同義字 shallow

反義字 deep, profound

lunatic

[`lunətɪk]

n. 瘋子

adj. 瘋狂的

Whenever he drives, he does it like a lunatic.
他每次開車都像瘋子一樣。

 秒殺解字 luna(moon)+ate+ic → Luna 是羅馬神話裏的月亮女神，lunatic 本義指受「月亮」影響，古人認為月亮會使人瘋狂，尤其是羅馬人，他們相信人受到月光照射精神會異常，所以不敢在有月亮的夜晚出門。

詞搭 ┊ a lunatic asylum 精神病院；the lunatic fringe 極端份子 [英]

同義字 ┊ nut, maniac, crazy, insane

tediously

[`tidɪəslɪ]

adv. 冗長無趣地

The farmer works in the fileds day in and day out, just as the sea waves beat the shore tediously.

📕 106

農夫日復一日地在地裡幹活，就像海浪拍打著海岸一樣乏味。

 秒殺解字 ted(weary)+i+ous+ly → 本義是「乏味的」。

詞搭 ┊ a tediously long lecture 一場冗長的演講

brink

[brɪŋk]

n. 邊緣

Warlike and incompetent, the autocratic president brought the country to the brink of war.

📕 103

這個專制獨裁的總統好戰又無能，把這個國家帶到戰爭邊緣。

 秒殺解字 brink 的意思是「邊緣」(edge)，源自斯堪地那亞語。

詞搭 ┊ on the brink of death / war / disaster 在死亡／戰爭／災難的邊緣

auction

[`ɔkʃən]

n. 拍賣（會）

v. 拍賣

Mr. Murray got a real good bargain at last week's furniture auction.
Murray 在上週的家具拍賣會中買到不少便宜貨。

A lot of fancy cars will be auctioned tomorrow.
有許多高檔汽車明天將要拍賣。

秒殺解字 auc(increase)+tion → 表示「拍賣」，喊價過程中，價格會「增加」。August、auction 同源，g/k 轉音。
August 是「八月」，是紀念奧古斯都（Augustus）的月份，「增加」奧古斯都的威望。相關同源字有 augment (v. 擴大、增加)。

詞搭 ┊ at auction 在拍賣時； put + sth. + up for auction 在拍賣時出售某物；auction house 拍賣行；auction off 拍賣

utensil

[ju`tɛnsl̩]

n. 器具、用具

This store sells a variety of <u>kitchen</u> <u>utensils</u>.

這家商店販售各式各樣的廚房器具。

秒殺解字 ut(use)+ensil → 廚房「使用」的器具。可用 **use** 當神隊友，來記憶 **ut**，**t/z/s** 轉音，皆表示「**使用**」。相關同源字有 **ut**ilize（v. 利用）、**ut**ility（n. 效用）、**ut**ilities（n. 水電）。

詞搭 <u>cooking / household</u> utensils 烹飪／家庭用具

圖 108

---

sloppy

[`slɑpɪ]

adj. 懶散的；邋遢的；草率的

While my daughter is very sloppy, my son is really neat.

我的女兒非常邋遢，但我的兒子卻真的很愛乾淨。

I like to wear sloppy pants / trousers because they are more comfortable.

在家時我喜歡穿寬鬆的褲子，因為它們比較舒適自在。

秒殺解字 slop(mud)+p+y → 本義是「泥濘的」（muddy），引申為「邋遢的」。

同義字 careless, untidy, slushy

---

virtuosity

[ˌvɝtʃʊ`ɑsətɪ]

n.（在藝術方面的）精湛技藝；對藝術品或古董等的愛好

All the audiences were stunned and overwhelmed by the virtuosity of the great pianist.

所有觀眾都被這位偉大鋼琴家的嫻熟琴藝震撼感動。

秒殺解字 virtuoso(showing extremely great skill)+ity → 源自義大利文「熟練的」(skilled) 的意思。

普 105

01 ___ The stalker's _____ of the victim took a dangerous turn when he started sneaking into her dorm room. In the end, the dorm security called the cops and arrested him.

(A) amendment   (B) entertainment
(C) harassment   (D) document

02 ___ In high school, she discovered her calling when she realized she had an _____ for learning foreign languages. She could learn a complete foreign language in just 2 months of time.

(A) attention   (B) attitude
(C) altitude   (D) aptitude

03 ___ With nowhere to really go and nothing to do, I decided to just _____ around town today and see if I could find anything interesting.

(A) stalk   (B) roam
(C) covet   (D) wade

04 ___ Because of his learning _____, the student had a difficult time solving multiplication problems in his mind.

(A) solidarity   (B) fertility
(C) disability   (D) adversity

05 ___ Albert Einstein possessed a truly _____ intellect, having discovered so many critical aspects of how our world functions.

(A) fabulous   (B) mysterious
(C) furious   (D) dubious

06 ___ He only has a _____ knowledge of American history so he is not a good choice to help you with your college research paper.

(A) superficial   (B) spatial
(C) industrial   (D) social

07 ___ All the students felt bored about the _____ long lecture. Some students even fell asleep half way through the speech.

(A) entirely   (B) generally
(C) especially   (D) tediously

08 ___ Psychologists found that people _____ to alcohol cannot go back to moderate drinking.

(A) addicted   (B) conflicted
(C) respected   (D) convicted

09 ___ The sudden death of the boy's father brought about the _____ effect on his life. He always feels guilty and helpless about it.

(A) unrealistic   (B) traumatic
(C) specific   (D) eccentric

10 ___ The speech of the speaker made me _____ for a while and I decided to make some changes to my living habits.

(A) consider   (B) render
(C) ponder   (D) murder

11 ___ As one of the best _____ in our country, Marcus is not afraid to face any situation in war.

(A) warriors   (B) survivors
(C) ambassadors   (D) traitors

12 ___ Because of Confucius's enthusiasm for education and his wise way of teaching, he had many _____ in his life, who learned a lot from him.

(A) disciples   (B) diplomats
(C) predecessors   (D) dissidents

13 ___ The robber tried to _____ the dog with a meat, but he failed. The dog was indifferent to it.

(A) produce   (B) induce
(C) seduce   (D) reproduce

14 ___ The _____ of the philosopher's thought and philosophy is so profound that many scholars still try to research his work to understand the deeper meanings.

(A) bankruptcy (B) literacy
(C) adjacency (D) legacy

15 ___ The customer just responded _____, as he thought he deserved great service just because he spent money.

(A) tediously (B) hysterically
(C) arrogantly (D) eloquently

解答
1.(C) 2.(D) 3.(B) 4.(C) 5.(A) 6.(A) 7.(D) 8.(A) 9.(B) 10.(C) 11.(A) 12.(A) 13.(C) 14.(D) 15.(C)

adherent [əd`hɪrənt] **n.** **adj.** 擁護者、追隨者	Orthodox Christianity has many adherents, especially throughout Eastern Europe.　普 102 東正教有許多信徒，尤其是在整個東歐。 秒殺解字 ad(to)+her(stick)+ent → 本義「黏著」，對群體或人物附著力強，表示堅持信奉的「擁護者」。

詞搭 | an adherent of Grimm's Law 格林法則的擁護者

同義字 | supporter, believer, follower, disciple

---

banish [`bænɪʃ] **v.** 放逐；驅除	The general seized power in a military coup and then banished the president-elect. 這位將軍在一場軍事政變中取得了權勢，然後就將總統當選人放逐。 秒殺解字 ban(outlaw, desert)+ish →「被剝奪法律權益」且「驅逐」出境。

詞搭 | banish + sb. / sth. + from / to + sth. 驅逐，流放……；banish the memory / thought / image 消除記憶／想法／意象

同義字 | exile

---

mortality [mɔr`tælətɪ] **n.** 死亡率；必死的命運	After my father's death, I suddenly realized that I also have to face my own mortality.　警特 105 父親過世之後，我突然意識到自己也必須面對終將一死的事實。 秒殺解字 mort(dead)+al+ity →「死」亡率或必「死」的命運。**mort** 表示「死亡」，**murd**er 亦是同源字，可和 **mort**al 一起記憶，**d/t** 轉音，母音通轉。相關同源字有 **mort**al（adj. 不免一死的；致命的）、im**mort**al（adj. 不死的；不朽的）、im**mort**ality（n. 不死；不朽）、**murd**er（v./n. 謀殺）、**murd**erer（n. 謀殺者）、**mort**gage（v./n. 抵押貸款）、night**mare**（n. 惡夢）、re**mors**e（n. 懊悔、自責）。

詞搭 | mortality rate 死亡率；infant mortality 嬰兒死亡率

反義字 | immortality

bureaucracy

[bjʊ`rɑkrəsɪ]

n. 官僚;繁文縟節

All the teachers believe that having a huge bureaucracy will severely limit the school's future development.

所有老師都相信龐大的官僚體系將嚴重限制學校未來發展。

🪶 秒殺解字 bureau(office)+cracy(rule) → 由「官僚機構」所「統治」。相關同源字有 auto**cracy**(n. 獨裁政治)、demo**cracy**(n. 民主政治)、 pluto**cracy**(n. 財閥政治)、aristo**cracy**(n. 上流社會)、geronto**cracy**(n. 老人政治)、theo**cracy**(n. 神權統治)、mobo**cracy**(n. 暴徒統治)、techno**cracy**(n. 技術統治論)、merito**cracy**(n. 菁英教育)。

詞搭 the reduction of unnecessary bureaucracy 去除不必要的官僚作法

衍生字 bureaucratic [ˌbjʊrə`krætɪk] adj. 官僚的

同義字 red tape

diversity

[daɪ`vɝsətɪ] / [dɪ`vɝsətɪ]

n. 多樣性、多元性

This state-run farm is set up to protect genetic diversity in plants. 警特 105

這座國營的農場設立的目的是要保護植物基因的多樣性。

🪶 秒殺解字 di(=dis=aside)+vers(turn)+ity → 「轉」到「旁邊」,因此有「多樣性」、「多元性」的意思。

詞搭 a wide diversity of... = a wide variety of... 各式各樣的……; cultural / ethnic / linguistic diversity 文化/種族/語言的多元化

同義字 variety

vibrate

[`vaɪbret]

v. 使震動、震動

Don't you see his voice is vibrating with anger? Just leave him alone.

你沒看到他現在非常憤怒聲音顫抖嗎?現在先別管他。

🪶 秒殺解字 vibr(vacillate)+ate → 本義是「搖擺」,引申為「震動」。

衍生字 vibrant [`vaɪbrənt] adj. 充滿活力的、(顏色)明亮的;vibration [vaɪ`breʃən] n. 震動、顫動

同義字 shake

visa
[`vizə]

n. 簽證

My visa to Thailand hasn't come through, so I cannot make my hotel booking yet.
我去泰國的簽證還沒簽發下來，所以我現在都不能先預訂旅館。

普 107
高 110

秒殺解字 從拉丁文 charta visa 借字，「認證的紙」，字面上的意思為被「看」過的紙。

詞搭 a(n) entry / exit / transit visa 入／出／過境簽證；a work / student / tourist / business / resident visa 工作／學生／觀光／商務／居留簽證

---

vogue
[vog]

n. 流行、時髦

The fashion icon says that short hair will once again be in vogue for women next spring.
這位時尚達人說短髮會在明年春天再度成為女士的流行風格。

普 103

秒殺解字 vog(go, come)+ue → 源自中古法語，表示「划船」，再往前推，源頭是表示「來去」，推測「流行」的語意可能和浪潮一陣一陣「來去」有關。

詞搭 be in / the vogue 正在流行中；come into vogue 開始風行

同義字 fashion

---

evacuate
[ɪ`vækjʊ͵et]

v. 撤離

If the dam does break, many towns will be flooded and hundreds of thousands of residents shall <u>be evacuated from</u> their homes.
如果水庫真的潰決了，那麼許多城鎮將會被淹沒，而數十萬的居民將會被撤離家園。

秒殺解字 e(=ex=out)+vac(empty)+u+ate → 「空」「出來」。

衍生字 evacuation [ɪ͵vækjʊ`eʃən] n. 撤離、避難

---

diagnose
[`daɪəgnoz]

v. 診斷

Lying in bed for a week, my grandmother <u>was</u> eventually <u>diagnosed with</u> lung cancer.
我祖母躺在病床一個禮拜，最後被診斷出患有肺癌。

普 110

秒殺解字 dia(between)+gnos(know)+e → 區別病症「之間」的差異，確切「知道」病因。k 在現代英語不發音，但仍可用 **know** 當神隊友，**g/k 轉音**，母音通轉，來記憶 **gnos**，皆表示「知道」。

詞搭 diagnose + sb. + <u>with / as</u> + 疾病 診斷某人罹患某病；diagnose + sth. + as + 疾病 將某物診斷為某種疾病

衍生字 diagnosis [͵daɪəg`nosɪs] n. 診斷

esteem

[ə`stim]

n. v. 尊敬

Because of her benevolence, the sister is held in high esteem by all the residents in this community.

由於她的仁慈，這位修女備受社區所有住民的敬重。

普 107

This kind teacher is highly esteemed by all of his students and colleagues.

這位仁慈的老師備受所有學生及同仁的推崇尊敬。

(秒殺解字) esteem(value) → 表示「尊敬」，**esteem** 和 **estim**ate 同源，母音通轉，核心語意是「重視」、「估價」、「價值」。

詞搭 hold + sb. + in high esteem / regard 很尊敬某人

衍生字 self-esteem [ˌsɛlfə`stim] n. 自尊

同義字 respect

---

devour

[dɪ`vaʊr]

v. 吞食、狼吞虎嚥

The hungry boy devoured his lunch in 5 minutes.

這位飢腸轆轆的男孩在 5 分鐘之內狼吞虎嚥吃完他的午餐。

(秒殺解字) de(down)+vour(swallow) → 整個「吞」「下」去。

詞搭 devour + sth. = gulp / wolf + sth. + down = gobble 狼吞虎嚥地吃

---

vacuum

[`vækjʊəm]

n. 真空；吸塵器

v. 吸塵

Dust, trash, and cookie crumbs are all over the carpet, so I think it's time to vacuum it.

地毯上到處都是灰塵、垃圾以及餅乾屑，所以我想該是用吸塵器清理（地毯）的時候了。

After knowing there's no hope for curing his cancer, Paul chose to live in a vacuum, trying to break off any connections with his friends.

在得知癌症已無治療希望後 Paul 選擇與世隔絕，試圖斷絕與所有朋友的往來。

(秒殺解字) vac(empty)+u+um → 真「空」。

詞搭 in a vacuum 處於真空狀態、與外界隔絕；a vacuum cleaner 真空吸塵器；a vacuum tube 真空管

toxic
[ˋtɑksɪk]
adj. 有毒的

The factory was accused of discharging toxic waste 108
into the river and will face fines up to two million
dollars.
這家工廠被指控將有毒廢棄物質排放至河中，因此即將面
臨高達兩百萬元的罰款。

秒殺解字 tox(poison)+ic → 含有「毒素」「的」。

同義字 poisonous

---

toxin
[ˋtɑksɪn]
n. 毒素

These vitamin pills will be helpful in eliminating the
toxins inside your body.
這些維他命將有助於排除你體內的毒素。

---

obsolete
[ˋɑbsəˏlit]
adj. 過時的；廢棄的

Cellphone apps will soon become obsolete when
other newer ones come out.
手機應用程式在其他新的程式問世之後很快就變過時的。

秒殺解字 ob(=away)+ol(accustomed)+et+e →「離開」「既
有習慣」，引申為「廢棄的」。

詞搭 obsolete weapons / battleships 淘汰的武器／戰艦；
make / render books obsolete 把書本淘汰

同義字 out-of-date, outdated, antiquated, old-fashioned

---

veteran
[ˋvɛtərən]
n. 退伍軍人；老手

Tom told me that his grandfather was a veteran of 曾 102
World War II.
Tom 告訴我說他的祖父是一位二次世界大戰退伍老兵。

秒殺解字 vet(old, aged)+er+an → 本義是「年長的」，引申
為「老手」。

詞搭 a veteran actor / leader / politician / journalist 資深／老練的演員／
領袖／政治人物／記者

字辨 veterinarian [ˏvɛtərəˋnɛrɪən] n. 獸醫

---

cozy
[ˋkozɪ]
adj. 舒適的

Last night we had a very cozy family gathering at a
fancy restaurant.
昨晚我們在一家豪華餐廳舉辦了一場溫馨愜意的家庭聚
會。

秒殺解字 可能源自斯堪地拿維亞語，意思是「舒適的」。

詞搭 warm and cozy 溫暖舒適；a cozy chat 溫馨閒談；be cozy with +
sb. 和某人關係密切

同義字 comfortable

outrageous

[aʊt`redʒəs]

adj. 令人震驚的

These days, the prices of new apartment buildings in this area are just outrageous, making it less affordable to the middle class.
近來此一地區新的公寓大樓價格高得嚇人，這使得中產階級更買不起了。

Frank's outrageous behavior makes him more and more unsociable.
Frank 的怪異行為使得他愈來愈孤僻了。

 秒殺解字 outer(=ultra=beyond)+age+ous → 源自拉丁文 ultraticum，表示「超過」，引申為「過分的」。

詞搭 an outrageous price / behavior / crime 駭人聽聞的價格／行為／罪行；an outrageous hairstyle 怪異的髮型；an outrageous attack on + sth. 對……的蠻橫攻擊

subconscious

[sʌb`kɑnʃəs]

n. 潛意識
adj. 潛意識的

Those unhappy memories of my childhood have long been buried deep within my subconscious.
我童年不快樂的回憶一直深深埋藏在我的潛意識裡。

I believe that a person's dream is indeed his subconscious reflection of himself.
我相信一個人的夢的確是他潛意識的反應。

秒殺解字 sub(under)+conscious → 在「意識」「下方」。

詞搭 a subconscious fear of failure 對失敗的潛意識恐懼

同義字 unconscious

pesticide

[`pɛstɪˌsaɪd]

n. 殺蟲劑

The pesticides can really kill pests, but they will also damage our health.
殺蟲劑的確可以殺死害蟲，但也將危害我們的健康

 警特 105

秒殺解字 pest(pest)+i+cid(kill)+e → 「殺」「害蟲」的化學藥劑。相關同源字有 de**cid**e（v. 決定）、sui**cid**e（n. 自殺）、insecti**cid**e（n. 殺蟲劑）。

unfamiliar
[ˌʌnfə`mɪljɚ]

adj. 不熟悉的

Could you please show me the way to the nearest post office? I'm new here and <u>unfamiliar with</u> the streets in this neighborhood.

能否請您指引我最近的一家郵局在哪兒？我是外地人，對這附近街道並不熟悉。

📖 105

🪶**秒殺解字** **famil**iar [fə`mɪljɚ]（adj. 熟悉的）、**famil**y [`fæməlɪ]（n. 家庭；家人）同源，**母音通轉**，核心語意是「**家庭**」、「**家人**」（**family**）。「**家庭**」、「**家人**」是我們所「**熟悉的**」。在 **famil**iar 的前方加上字首否定字首 un-，就形成 un**famil**iar，表示「**不熟悉的**」。

詞搭 be unfamiliar with... 不熟悉……

humiliate
[hju`mɪlɪˌet]

v. 使羞辱、使丟臉

I can't believe he should humiliate you in front of so many people you know.

我不敢相信他居然在這麼多你熟識的人面前公開羞辱你。

📖 103

🪶**秒殺解字** hum(human, earth, low)+ile+i+ate → **hum** 本義是「**泥土**」（**earth**），衍生出「**低下**」、「**卑微**」、「**人類**」的意思。

詞搭 humiliate oneself 丟臉，蒙羞

同義字 embarrass

humiliatingly
[hju`mɪlɪˌetɪŋlɪ]

adv. 羞辱地

The troops were finally humiliatingly defeated, due to a shortage of food and ammunition.

由於食物及彈藥短缺，軍隊最後飲恨屈辱，難堪敗北。

suffocate
[`sʌfəˌket]

v. 使窒息；窒息

The victims of the fire were reported to have suffocated in the fumes.

根據報導，這場火災的罹難者是被濃煙嗆死的。

🪶**秒殺解字** suf(=sub=under)+foc(throat)+ate →「**喉嚨**」「**下方**」卡住而無法呼吸，表示「（使）窒息而死」。**fauc**et [`fɔsɪt]（n. 水龍頭）、suf**foc**ate（v. 窒息而死）同源，**母音通轉**，核心語意是「**喉嚨**」（**throat**）。

同義字 choke

breakthrough

[`brek͵θru]

n. 突破

A major <u>breakthrough in</u> the peace talks was achieved after both sides demonstrated their sincerity.

在雙方展現誠意之後，和平談判就達成一項重大的突破。

曾 106

> 秒殺解字 break+through → 源自片語 break through，表示「突破」。

詞搭 <u>make / achieve</u> a breakthrough in... 在……上有所突破

---

barren

[`bærən]

adj. 荒蕪的；貧瘠的；不育的

This place used to be a stretch of barren land, but now apartments, office buildings, and shopping malls are everywhere.

這個地方過去曾是一片荒蕪不毛之地，但現在到處都是公寓建築、商業大樓以及購物中心。

> 秒殺解字 可能源自日耳曼語，通常指女子「不能生育後代的」。

詞搭 barren land 不毛之地

同義字 infertile

反義字 fertile

---

cynical

[`sınıkl]

adj. 懷疑的；挖苦的；憤世嫉俗的

After getting a divorce, Patty has a quite cynical view about men.

在離婚之後，Patty 對於男人的觀點就變偏激了。

Fifteen years of unhappy marriage finally ended with a divorce, but it also left her world-weary and cynical.

歷經 15 年不幸福的婚姻終於以離婚收場，但這也讓她變得悲觀厭世、憤世嫉俗。

> 秒殺解字 cyn(dog)+ic+al → 源自希臘文的 kunikos，表示「似狗」(dog-like)，這個詞常用來指犬儒學派哲學家，因犬儒學派的鼻祖綽號是 kuon，即「狗」。據說他曾當眾吼叫，在桌腿上小便，且在大街上手淫，一副玩世不恭。此外，犬儒學派的信眾喜歡指摘別人缺點，引此引申出「挖苦的」、「憤世嫉俗」等負面意涵。

詞搭 be cynical about... 對……嘲諷

衍生字 cynicism [`sını͵sızəm] n. 譏諷作風、犬儒主義

pharmaceutical
[ˌfɑrmə`sjutɪk!]

adj. 製藥的；配藥（學）的

The pharmaceutical industry has long been flourishing in Japan.
製藥業在日本向來是蓬勃發展。

> 秒殺解字 pharmac(drug)+eutic+al → 和藥相關的，引申為「製藥的」、「配藥的」。

詞搭 a pharmaceutical company 製藥公司

---

psychiatry
[saɪ`kaɪətrɪ]

n. 精神病學

曾 106

Psychiatry is the part of medical science that studies mental illness of human beings.
精神病學是醫學的一部分，專門研究人類心理疾病。

> 秒殺解字 psych(mind, mental)+iatr(cure)+y →「治療」「精神」疾病。**psych** 表示「靈魂」、「精神」、「心智」、「心理的」。相關同源字有 **psych**e (n. 心靈；靈魂)、**psych**ic (adj. 靈魂的；精神的；通靈的 n. 通靈者)、**psych**iatric (adj. 精神病的)、**psych**iatrist (n. 精神科醫師)、**psych**ology (n. 心理學)、**psych**ological (adj.心理學上的)、**psych**ologist (n. 心理學家)。

衍生字 psychiatrist [saɪ`kaɪətrɪst] n. 精神科醫師

---

deport
[dɪ`port]

v. 驅逐 出境

高 110

Those people are illegal immigrants and will soon be deported back to the countries they came from.
那些人都是非法移民，很快就會被遣返他們各自國家。

> 秒殺解字 de(off, away)+port(carry) →「帶」「離開」，表示「驅逐出境」。相關同源字有 im**port** (v./n. 進口)、ex**port** (v./n. 出口)、sup**port** (v./n. 支持)、re**port** (v./n. 報告；報導)、trans**port** (v. 運輸)。

---

devastate
[`dɛvəsˌtet]

v. 破壞、蹂躪

This automobile manufacturing factory was devastated during the civil war. Now it probably needs a long period of time to recover and rehabilitate it.
這家汽車製造廠在內戰期間遭受嚴重摧毀。現在它可能需要一段時間復原重建。

> 秒殺解字 de(completely)+vast(lay waste, destroy)+ate →「完全地」「破壞」。

衍生字 devastating [`dɛvəsˌtetɪŋ] adj. 毀滅性的

同義字 destroy, ravage

subsidize

[`sʌbsəˌdaɪz]

v. 給……津貼、補助

All private schools in Taiwan are partially subsidized by the government.
在台灣所有私立學校都受到政府補助。

🪶 **秒殺解字** sub(under)+sid(sit)+y → 讓人安穩「坐在」「下面」，引申為「補助」。可用 **sit** 當神隊友，**z/s**、**d/t 轉音，母音通轉**，來記憶 **sid**，皆表示「**坐**」。相關同源字有 pre**sid**ent (n. 總統；總裁)、dis**sid**ent (adj. 意見不同的)、re**sid**ent (n. 居民)。

---

refrain

[rɪ`fren]

n. 副歌；一再重複的話

v. 忍住；節制

Now we are entering a place where all people should refrain from smoking.
現在我們正進入一個所有人都不能吸菸的地方。

普 102
警特 107

The refrain of this song is not as I had imagined, so I need more time to practice it.
這首歌的副歌沒有想像中的那麼簡單，所以我需要更多時間練習。

🪶 **秒殺解字** re(back)+frain(bridle, break) → 動詞和名詞的來源不同，當動詞用時，表示用「馬勒」拉「回」，引申為「忍住」、「節制」；當名詞用時，表示「斷開」(break off)，引申為「終止」，「終止」後再重新開始，可引申為「重複」(repeat)，而現今的語意是「副歌」、一再重複的話」。

詞搭 refrain from + <u>N / Ving</u> 忍住不……

---

insider

[`ɪnˌsaɪdɚ]

n. 內部的人

According to the insider, the stock price of this company will drop drastically because its sales results have worsened for the past two quarters.
根據知情人士，這家公司因為銷售狀況在過去兩季以來持續惡化，所以股價將會急遽下跌。

🪶 **秒殺解字** inside+er →「內部的」「人」。

詞搭 insider <u>trading / dealing</u> 內線交易

反義字 outsider

instinctive

[ɪnˈstɪŋktɪv]

adj. 本能的、直覺的

When I saw that a tiger came near me, I was scared and my instinctive response was to make a run for it (= escape by running).

當我看到一隻老虎靠近我，我嚇壞了，於是我本能反應就是快跑溜之大吉呀。

 秒殺解字 in(in)+stinc(stick, prick)+t+ive → 內心像是被「刺」到，會有「本能」的反應。相關同源字有 ex**tingu**ish（v. 熄滅）、ex**tinc**t（adj. 絕種的）、di**stingu**ish（v. 辨別）、di**stinc**t（adj. 截然不同的）、in**stinc**t（n. 本能）。

詞搭 instinctive reaction 本能的反應

obsession

[əbˈsɛʃən]

n. 執著；著迷；無法擺脫的念頭

I don't know why she has had an obsession with death.

我不知道為何她老是有一種想死的念頭。

📕 107

 秒殺解字 ob(against)+sess(sit)+ion → 一直「坐」在「對面」，使人無法擺脫被「監看」的狀態，引申為「圍困」，現代更產生被念頭困住的衍生語意，表示「著迷」、「無法擺脫的念頭」。

同義字 preoccupation

oversee

[ˌovɚˈsi]

v. 監督；管理

As a sales manager, Mr. Miller's job is to oversee the sales promotion business.

身為銷售經理 Miller 先生的工作是負責監管銷售業務的推展。

 秒殺解字 over+see →「在上面」「看」，表示「監督」、「管理」。

同義字 supervise, superintend, be in charge of

dining

[ˈdaɪnɪŋ]

n. 進餐

Dining alone usually makes me feel more at ease and comfortable, and of course, I won't put much thought into my eating.

一個人吃飯通常會讓我感覺更自在舒適，當然，我不會在吃飯上花太多心思。

秒殺解字 dine(eat)+ing → 進餐。

詞搭 a dining car / table / room 餐車／桌／廳

closet
[`klɑzɪt]
n. 衣櫥
v. 封閉

Joanne's new house is equipped with many storage closets. 🔈 103
Joanne 的新房子配置有許多儲藏壁櫃。

To achieve better performance on the coming college entrance examination, I have decided, from now on, to <u>closet myself</u> in my room with my books.
為了能夠在即將到來的大學入學考試獲致更好表現，我已決定從現在開始閉關讀書。

🪶 秒殺解字 close(close)+t → closet 源自拉丁詞 clausum，意思是「關閉的空間」（**closed space**）。我們平常講的 **WC**，又作 **water closet**，意為「廁所」，正是一個「不能公開」、「祕密」的場所。**be in the closet** 表示「隱瞞自己是同性戀」，**come out of the closet** 表示「承認自己是同性戀」、「出櫃」。

詞搭 closet oneself 關……

unexplainable
[ˌʌnɪk`splenəbl]
adj. 無法解釋的

The doctor says my allergy to many different kinds of food is unexplainable. 🔈 105
醫師說我對許多不同種類食物過敏的原因無法解釋。

🪶 秒殺解字 un(not)+explain+able → 「不」「能」「解釋」的。

fridge
[frɪdʒ]
n. 電冰箱

I got two fridges in my house. One only keeps fruits and vegetables and the other is exclusively for fish and meat.
我家有兩台冰箱，一台只保存水果以及蔬菜，另一台則是專放魚跟肉類。

🪶 秒殺解字 fridge 為 refrigerator 的截短詞 (clipping)，re-(again)+friger(make cool)+a+e+or → 「再」「冷」，表示可使食物變冷、保存食物的「冰箱」。

同義字 refrigerator

01 ____ If you are _____ to the philosophy of Buddhism, you will not become attached to any material possessions.

(A) inconsistent   (B) potent
(C) incompetent   (D) adherent

02 ____ With a few words of encouragement, my husband managed to _____ my fears. If it hadn't been for him, I could have never finished the task.

(A) punish   (B) ban
(C) banish   (D) publish

03 ____ In the waiting room, we were given numerous documents to complete as part of the hospital's pretreatment _____.

(A) bureaucracy   (B) agency
(C) emergency   (D) bankruptcy

04 ____ Once the idea of using scarves as decorations took effect, it came into _____ for many teenage girls who cared about their appearance.

(A) plague   (B) vogue
(C) catalogue   (D) colleague

05 ____ Unfortunately, it wasn't possible to _____ the village completely before the rebels attacked, so the casualties were high.

(A) retaliate   (B) contaminate
(C) evacuate   (D) manipulate

06 ____ Two physicians failed to _____ the fatal cancer in him since he didn't have the usual signs and symptoms associated with the disease.

(A) refuse   (B) increase
(C) seduce   (D) diagnose

07 ___ She cautiously brought out the birthday cake, knowing the hungry children would grab and _____ the cake the minute she put it on the table.

(A) devour   (B) measure
(C) destroy   (D) avoid

08 ___ _____ employees feel it is unfair to pay new workers the same as those who have been at the company more than ten years.

(A) Fragile   (B) Bleak
(C) Veteran   (D) Chronic

09 ___ I don't know how to get along with _____ people because I am shy and afraid of talking to strangers.

(A) popular   (B) aware
(C) primary   (D) unfamiliar

10 ___ The student burst into tears when the teacher _____ him in front of the whole class of students.

(A) associated   (B) humiliated
(C) investigated   (D) separated

11 ___ I heard that your progress in the project is a(n) _____ for our company, and we should celebrate it today.

(A) destination   (B) breakthrough
(C) transaction   (D) agenda

12 ___ He is such a _____ person that he always arbitrarily criticizes others online before knowing the truth.

(A) local   (B) critical
(C) medical   (D) cynical

13 ___ Because of the serious epidemic, the employees of the _____ industry work overtime every day.

(A) physical   (B) practical
(C) pharmaceutical   (D) vocal

14 ___ The government is considering that foreign refugees can be _____ for one year after entering the country.

(A) subsidized   (B) authorized
(C) organized   (D) localized

15 ___ After the man heard that his son failed the big test, he thought it was _____ and scolded his son fiercely.

(A) outrageous   (B) obvious
(C) continuous   (D) subconscious

argumentation
[ˌɑrgjəmɛnˋteʃən]
n. 立論；辯論

The prime minister made a very clear argumentation in support of his new policy.
總理提出非常清楚的論點來支持自己的新政策。

曾 99

(秒殺解字) arg(make clear)+u+ment+ation → 辯論是讓真理越辯越「明」(make clear)。

詞搭 the faultless argumentation 正確的論證

---

delete
[dɪˋlit]
v. 刪除

You'd better back up all your files in case you delete them accidentally.
你最好將你所有檔案備份以防不小心把它們給刪除了。

(秒殺解字) del(wipe out)+ete → 本義「抹去」，引申為「刪除」。

詞搭 delete A from B 從 B 刪除 A

---

disengage
[ˌdɪsɪnˋgedʒ]
v. 解開；使脫離；脫出

I hope I can disengage myself from his influence.
我想擺脫他對我的影響。

曾 105

If you disengage the clutch but do not accelerate, the car may stall and stop abruptly.
如果你鬆開離合器然後又沒加油，車子就有可能會熄火突然停止。

(秒殺解字) dis(opposite)+engage →「銜接」、「齧合」的「相反動作」，表示「解開」、「鬆脫」。

詞搭 disengage from... 解放、擺脫 (約束、契約……)

反義字 engage

---

crutch
[krʌtʃ]
n. 拐杖

Elton had to walk on crutches because he broke his leg.
Elton 必須拄著拐杖走路，因為他摔斷了腿。

曾 101

(秒殺解字) cr 子音群可用來表示「撞擊」動作，如：crash (n. 相撞), crack (v. 重擊)。撞擊易造成破裂、分離、「捲曲」，crutch 是可以幫助身體「彎曲」、站不直的人，走路更順暢的「拐杖」。相關單字有 crook (v. 使彎曲成勾狀)、crouch (v. 蜷縮)。

詞搭 a pair of crutches 一對枴杖；be on crutches 拄著枴杖

unparalleled

[ʌn`pærə͵lɛld]

adj. 無比的；前所未有的

The newly published book has achieved <u>an unparalleled success</u> in getting readers interested in political science.
這本新出版的書在讓讀者對政治學感興趣方面取得了空前的成功。

 秒殺解字 un(not)+parallel+ed →「沒有」「相同的」，表示「無比的」。

---

endurance

[ɪn`djʊrəns]

n. 忍耐；持久力；耐力

Running a marathon can fully test an athlete's endurance and perseverance as well.
跑馬拉松可以完全考驗運動員的耐力以及毅力。

秒殺解字 en(make)+dur(hard)+ance →「使」變「強硬」，所以是「忍耐」。

詞搭 endurance <u>race / test</u> 耐力競賽／測試

---

homogeneous

[͵homə`dʒɪnɪəs]

adj. 由同類事物或人組成的

Many people think Japanese culture is homogeneous, but it is, in fact, heterogeneous, meaning one that is formed by multiple ethnic groups and diverse cultural traditions.
許多人認為日本文化是單一性的，事實上它是多元性的也就是由多種種族以及多樣不同文化傳統所構成的。

秒殺解字 homo(same)+gen(kind)+e+ous →「同」「種」的。

詞搭 homogeneous products 同質產品

---

submissive

[sʌb`mɪsɪv]

adj. 順從的

As a servant, Maria is always humble and submissive.
身為一位僕人，Maria 總是謙遜順從。

圖 110

秒殺解字 sub(under)+miss(send)+ive → 本義「送」到「下面」的，引申為「服從的」。相關同源字有 **miss**ion（n. 任務）、pro**mise**（v./n. 答應）、ad**mit**（v. 承認）、ad**miss**ion（n. 准許）、per**mit**（v. 允許）、per**miss**ion（n. 允許）、sub**mit**（v. 呈遞；順從）、sub**miss**ion（n. 呈遞；順從）、o**mit**（v. 遺漏）、o**miss**ion（n. 遺漏）。

詞搭 be submissive to + sb.　服從某人

同義字 obedient [ə`bidjənt] adj. 服從的

sprain
[spren]
n. 扭傷
v. 扭到

He sprained his ankle playing football and was then 普 101
sent to the hospital for medical treatment.
他在踢足球時雙腳腳踝扭傷,然後被送到醫院治療。

🖋 **秒殺解字** 字源不詳,但可用 spr 常見的核心語意來輔助記憶,
spr 有「向外或向前快速迸發的動作」,通常 sprain 是在快速
迸發的動作中發生。相關單字有 **spr**ay (v. 噴灑)、**spr**inkle (v.
撒)、**spr**ead (v. 擴散) 等。

詞搭 | sprain + sb's <u>ankle / wrist</u> 扭傷腳踝/手腕

同義字 | twist , wrench

alleviate
[ə`livɪ͵et]
v. 減輕、緩和

If you find the drug cannot alleviate your pain, be 普 105
sure to tell your doctor and ask if a new prescription 警特 108
is possible.
如果你發現這種藥並無法減輕你的痛苦,務必要告訴你的
醫師,並請教是否可能另開新的處方藥籤。

🖋 **秒殺解字** al(=ad=to)+lev(light)+i+ate → 減「輕」痛苦。相關
同源字有 **lev**er (n. 槓桿)、e**lev**ate (v. 提升)、re**liev**e (v.
減輕)、re**lie**f (n. 慰藉)、re**lev**ant (adj. 相關的)。

alleviation
[ə͵livɪ`eʃən]
n. 減輕、緩和;鎮痛物

This NGO is going to undertake and carry out
a <u>poverty alleviation</u> project for some African
countries.
這個非政府組織即將為一些非洲國家肩負並執行一項脫貧
計畫。

詞搭 | poverty alleviation 脫貧

adjacent
[ə`dʒesənt]
adj. 鄰近的、緊接的

Justin lives in an old apartment <u>adjacent to</u> a
railroad, but he doesn't seem to be annoyed by the
rumbling sound of the trains.
Justin 住在毗連鐵路的一棟老舊公寓,但他的生活似乎不
被轟隆轟隆火車聲響困擾。

🖋 **秒殺解字** ad(to)+jac(lie)+ent →「躺」「在附近」,引申為「鄰
近的」。

詞搭 | adjacent to... 靠近……的、與……鄰接的

adjacency

[ə`dʒesnsɪ]

n. 鄰接

The adjacency of the two countries makes it easier for the residents on the border to have some small business opportunities.

這兩個國家毗鄰的特性使得邊界上的居民更有機會做小生意。

---

coherent

[ko`hɪrənt]

adj. 連貫的;前後一致的

They seemed unable to reach a consensus, and they didn't have a coherent plan for next season's sales promotion.

他們似乎沒有達成共識,針對於下一季促銷活動,也沒有一個協調一致的計畫。

秒殺解字 co(together)+her(stick)+ent →「黏著」在「一起」,表示「連貫的」、「前後一致的」。相關同源字有 in**her**e (v. 本質上屬於)、ad**her**e (v. 黏著;堅持信奉)、co**her**e (adj. 連貫、有條理;結合為一體)、**hes**itate (v. 遲疑、猶豫)、**hes**itant (adj. 遲疑的、猶豫的)、**hes**itation (n. 遲疑、猶豫)。

詞搭 a coherent account / explanation / argument 連貫一致的陳述/解釋/論點

衍生字 coherence [ko`hɪrəns] n. 連貫性;incoherence [ˌɪnko`hɪrəns] n. 不連貫

反義字 incoherent

---

eject

[ɪ`dʒɛkt]

v. 逐出;噴出;彈射出

Those noisy customers were finally ejected from the restaurant for causing trouble. 齊 106

那些喧嘩吵鬧的顧客最後因為鬧事被餐廳趕出來。

秒殺解字 e(=ex=out)+jec(throw)+t →「丟」到「外面」,表示「逐出」、「噴出」。相關同源字有 re**jec**t (v. 拒絕)、sub**jec**t (v. 使臣服)、ob**jec**t (v. 反對)、in**jec**t (v. 注射)。

詞搭 eject + sb. + from office 免除某人的職

---

ejection

[ɪ`dʒɛkʃən]

n. 噴出;排斥;驅逐

Automatic ejection seats on a fighter plane can help save the lives of pilots when there is danger. 齊 103

戰鬥機上自動彈射座椅可以在飛機處於危急狀態時協助拯救飛行員生命。

refute
[rɪ`fjut]
v. 駁斥、否認

Though I couldn't refute his explanation, I was still not satisfied with him.
雖然我無法針對他的解釋加以反駁，但是我還是對他感到不滿。

🖊 秒殺解字 re(back)+fut(beat)+e → 「打」「回去」，表示「駁斥」、否認」。

詞搭　refute a(n) argument / proposal / statement 駁斥一個論點／提議／聲明

同義字　rebut, deny

porcelain
[`pɔrslɪn]
n. 瓷器

All the tableware used in this restaurant is made of fine porcelain.　103
這家餐廳所使用的餐具都是用精緻瓷器做成。

🖊 秒殺解字 源自義大利語的 **porc**ellana，表示「貝」(shell)，瓷器之所以和「貝」連結，是因為他們的外表皆有光澤，而 **porc**ellana 這個字追本溯源，也和「豬」有關，相關同源字有 **pork** (n. 豬肉) 和 **poc**ine (adj. 像豬的)。但為什麼瓷器會和豬有關呢？據說，因為瓷器上半部的表面和豬的背部所呈現的曲線相似，引此用豬來命名。

詞搭　a piece of porcelain 一件瓷器；pottery and porcelain 陶瓷；porcelain tile 瓷磚；porcelain ware 瓷器

household
[`haʊsˌhold]
n. 家庭；戶
adj. 家庭的；家事的；家喻戶曉的

My mother has to do all household chores after we have our breakfast and go to school.
在我們用完早餐上學後，我母親必須做所有的家務事。

I don't think my salary, alone, can cover all household expenses.
我不認為單就我一個人的薪水可以支付所有的家庭開銷。

🖊 秒殺解字 house+hold(possession, holding) → 本指家庭所擁有的人和物，包含僕人、家具等，後指「家庭」。

詞搭　a household name = a celebrity 家喻戶曉的人物；household chores 家事

名詞同義字　house

動詞同義字　domestic

guild

[gɪld]

n. 協會；同業公會

Do you know all the members of the guild?
你認識同業公會裡所有的成員嗎？

🖋 秒殺解字 源自古斯堪地那維亞語，表示「組織」
（brotherhood）和「報酬」（payment），可用加入「組織」來
互助分擔風險、犧牲付出獲得報酬來聯想。

---

inmate

[`ɪnmet]

n. （監獄，精神病院
等的）被收容者；
囚犯

The prison inmates are not allowed to smoke in jail.　🔲普 101
囚犯是不被允許在監獄裡抽菸的。

🖋 秒殺解字 in(inside)+mate(companion) → 本指共同住在裡面
的夥伴，引申為「（監獄，精神病院等的)被收容者」。

---

intermittently

[ɪntə`mɪtəntlɪ]

adv. 間歇地

It has been raining intermittently for four hours.　🔲普 106
雨已經斷斷續續地下了四個小時了。

🖋 秒殺解字 inter(between)+mit(send)+t+ent+ly → 「送」進「兩
者之間」，表示「打斷」，引申為「斷斷續續地」、「間歇地」。

---

outbreak

[`aʊt,brek]

n. 爆發；暴動

Some epidemiologists warned that the poor
sanitary conditions and crowded environments in
many underdeveloped countries would lead to an
outbreak of cholera and malaria.
一些流行病學家警告，許多未開發中國家不良衛生條件以
及擁擠的環境將導致霍亂以及瘧疾等疾病的爆發。

🔲普 105
🔲警特 105

🖋 秒殺解字 out+break → 源自片語 break out，表示「爆發」、
「突然發生」。

詞搭　the outbreak of the World War II 第二次世界大戰的爆發；
a slave outbreak 奴隸暴動

fabricate

[`fæbrɪˌket]

v. 捏造;製造

The reason Antonio gave for his absence was obviously fabricated. His father called me to confirm this.

Antonio 對於他缺席所給的理由明顯是捏造的。他的父親打電話來請我確認這件事。

🖋 秒殺解字 fabric(make, build)+ate →「捏造」、「製造」。

詞搭 fabricate a story 編造故事;fabricate a document 偽造文書;fabricated food 合成加工食品

同義字 invent, make up, manufacture

fabrication

[ˌfæbrɪ`keʃən]

n. 捏造;製造

The fabrication procedure of these optical lenses is rather time-consuming.

這些光學鏡片的製造流程是相當耗費時間的。

詞搭 a complete / total / pure fabrication 徹底的捏造

odor

[`odə]

n. (難聞的)氣味、風味

Frankly speaking, I don't like the odor of the perfume she's wearing.

坦白說,我不喜歡她擦的香水味道。

圖 106

🖋 秒殺解字 odor(smell) →「氣味」。ozone [`ozon] (n. 臭氧)、odor 同源,d/z 轉音,母音通轉,核心語意是「氣味」(odor)。

詞搭 body odor 體味;strong / unpleasant / pungent / offensive odor 刺激氣味

衍生字 odorous [`odərəs] adj. 芬芳的;deodorant [di`odərənt] n. 制汗劑、除臭劑

franchise

[`frænˌtʃaɪz]

n. 經銷權;選舉權

Mr. Evans has just acquired a franchise for the newest model of electric motorcycles.

Evans 先生剛剛取得最新款式電動摩托車的特許經銷權。

🖋 秒殺解字 franch(frank=free)+ise → 本義是「被免除的」,通常指免除奴役、負擔或其它限制,這個字也表示被賦予的權力,引申出「經銷權」、「選舉權」的意思。

詞搭 the franchise for a chain store 連鎖店的營業權;franchise rights 特許經營權;franchise chain 特許連鎖

animation
[ˌænəˋmeʃən]
n. 動畫；活力

My daughter likes these digital books very much because they contain many vivid and interesting animations.

我的女兒很喜歡這些數位書籍，因為它們包含許多生動有趣的動畫。

🖋 **秒殺解字** anim(breath, spirit, life)+ation → 本義是「呼吸」，動物會呼吸代表還活著、有「靈魂」（spirit）。聖經提到上帝按自己的形象，用塵土造人，在他的鼻孔吹了一口氣，人於是有了呼吸、有了靈，活了起來，所以 anim 又和「生命」有關，因為動物有了「呼吸」，就有了「生命」，就會「動」。

詞搭 with animation 活力十足、生動地；computer animation 電腦動畫；3-D animations 3D 立體動畫； comic and animation 動漫

animator
[ˋænəˌmetɚ]
n. 動畫師

The cartoon series now playing on TV is produced by the most famous animators in the world.

現在正在電視上演的系列卡通影片是由全世界最有名的動畫師們所繪製的。

unnecessary
[ʌnˋnɛsəˌsɛrɪ]
adj. 不必要的

Apparently, it's unnecessary to tell her about the truth.

顯然地，告訴她事實真相是沒必要的。

🖋 **秒殺解字** un(not)+necessary →「不」「必要的」。

詞搭 unnecessary expenses 不必要的開支

同義字 needless, dispensable

反義字 necessary, indispensable, essential

unprecedented
[ʌnˋprɛsəˌdɛntɪd]
adj. 史無前例的

The unemployment rate has now reached an unprecedented level.

失業率現在已達前所未有的地步。

🖋 **秒殺解字** un(not)+pre(before)+ced(go)+ent +ed →「無」「前」人「走」過的。

詞搭 unprecedented scale 史無前例的規模；unprecedented prosperity 空前的繁榮

forsake
[fə`sek]
v. 遺棄

When the two little boys knew their parents were going to divorce, they pleaded with their mother not to forsake them.
當這兩個小男孩得知其父母即將離婚時，他們就懇求母親別遺棄他們。

I think it's time to forsake a lot of your bad habits.
我認為現在該是你革除許多不良習慣的時候了。

（秒殺解字） for(completely)+sake(dispute, blame) → 源自古英文，表示「指責」、「爭論」，後來語意改變，表示「遺棄」。

時態 | forsake, forsook [fə`sʊk], forsaken [fə`sekən]

同義字 | abandon, give up, desert

referee
[ˌrɛfə`ri]
n. v. 裁判

I know you all are not satisfied with the result of the match, but I think you have to respect the referee's decision.
我知道你們對比賽結果不滿意，但我認為你必須尊重裁判的決定。

醫 103

（秒殺解字） re(back)+fer(bear)+ee → refer 指「往後」「帶」，引申為「提及」、「歸於」。referee 是裁判，其任務是判斷球或成功歸屬哪支隊伍。

詞搭 | chief referee 裁判長

speculation
[ˌspɛkjə`leʃən]
n. 推測；投機風險事業

Rumors that diesel cars wouldn't be allowed to enter the downtown area of this city was eventually dismissed as pure speculation.
謠傳柴油車將不被允許進入本市市區，最後被證實純粹只是猜測而已。

醫 100
警特 106

（秒殺解字） spec(look)+ule+ate+ion → 原意是「沉思」，彷彿「看見」某事物，後來衍生為「推測」、「投機」，兩者都必須先預「見」而做決策。相關同源字有 **spec**tator（ n. 看比賽觀眾）、a**spec**t（ n. 方面）、in**spec**t（ v. 檢查）、re**spec**t（ v./n. 尊敬）、su**spec**t（ v. 懷疑）、per**spec**tive（ n. 觀點）、pro**spec**t（ n. 展望）。

詞搭 | speculation about / on 關於……的猜測

同義字 | guess

compassion

[kəm`pæʃən]

n. 同情心、同情

I wonder why the doctor didn't show any <u>compassion for</u> his patients.
我不明白為何這位醫師對他的病患毫無側隱之心？

com(together)+pass(suffer)+ion → 能同甘「共」「苦」、能「共同」感受他人「遭遇」。相關同源字有 **pass**ion (n. 熱情；熱愛)、**pass**ionate (adj. 熱情的；熱愛的)、**pass**ive (adj. 消極的、被動的)、**pat**ient (adj. 有耐心的 n. 病人)、**pat**ience (n. 耐心)、com**pass**ionate (adj. 同情的)、com**pat**ible (adj. 相容的；能共處)。

詞搭 <u>feel / show / have</u> compassion for... 對……有同情心

衍生字 compassionate [kəm`pæʃənɪt] adj. 有同情心的

同義字 sympathy, pity

---

glisten

[`glɪsn̩]

n. v. 閃耀、發光

Diana's eyes soon <u>glistened with</u> tears when Luther went down on bended knee to ask her to marry him.
當 Luther 單腳跪地向 Diana 求婚時，她頓時眼裡閃爍晶瑩淚珠。

秒殺解字 含 **gl** 的單字有「高興」、「照耀或發光」、「看見」的意思。相關單字有 **gl**ad (adj. 高興地)、**gl**ee (n. 歡喜)、**gl**ass (n. 玻璃)、**gl**ow (v. 發光)、**gl**eam (v. 發微光)、**gl**immer (v. 發微光)、**gl**int (v. 閃閃發光)、**gl**itter (v. 閃爍)、**gl**oss (n. 表面的光澤)、**gl**ance (n. 瞥一眼)、**gl**are (v. 怒視)、**gl**impse (n. 看一眼)、**gl**oat (v. 沾沾自喜或幸災樂禍地看)。

詞搭 glisten with... 閃爍著……

---

cuisine

[kwɪ`zin]

n. 菜餚、料理；烹飪（法）

Lots of people know that this restaurant is the only place in town where you can taste real Chinese cuisine.
很多人都知道這家餐廳是城內唯一可以讓你嚐到道地中國菜的地方。

秒殺解字 cuis(cook)+ine →核心語意是「煮」（**cook**）。相關同源字還有 **cook** [kʊk] (v. 烹調 n. 廚師)、**kitch**en [`kɪtʃɪn] ( n. 廚房 )、bis**cuit** [`bɪskɪt] (n. 餅乾)。

詞搭 <u>French / Cantonese</u> cuisine 法國／廣東菜；fusion cuisine 無國界料理；haute cuisine 高級烹飪術、名菜

曾 105
107
警特 105

484

shun

[ʃʌn]

v. 躲開、避開

In conducting the investigation of the murder case, I was asked to shun subjectivity.

在做這項謀殺案件調查時，我被要求不可帶有主觀意思。

秒殺解字 字於不詳。可用「閃」的台語發音，來輔助記憶。

時態 | shun, shunned [ʃʌnd] , shunned [ʃʌnd]

圖 99

---

smother

[`smʌðɚ]

v. 悶死；悶熄；窒息

Be careful not to let kids play with plastic bags because they might smother or choke themselves with the bags.

小心不要讓小孩接觸或玩塑膠袋，因為它們有可能會讓小孩窒息悶死。

秒殺解字 本義是「濃煙」(dense、suffocating、smoke)，引申為「悶死」、「窒息」。

同義字 | strangle, suffocate

---

conserve

[kən`sɝv]

v. 節約使用；保存；保護

More and more eco-friendly construction problems are being encouraged in order to conserve electricity and protect our environments.

愈來愈多的綠建築被鼓勵，目的是希望能夠省電也能保護我們的環境。

秒殺解字 con(intensive prefix)+serv(protect, keep)+e → 本義「保護」、「保持」。相關同源字有ob**serv**e (v. 觀察；注意到；遵守)、pre**serv**e (v. 維護；維持；保存)、re**serv**e (v. 保留；預定)。

詞搭 | conserve water / electricity / energy 節約用水／用電／能源

衍生字 | conservation [ˌkɑnsɚ`veʃən] n. 保護、保存、節約；conservative [kən`sɝvətɪv] adj. 保守的 n. 保守派人士

同義字 | preserve

圖 100

---

covet

[`kʌvɪt]

v. 貪圖

The politician has long coveted power, but he was finally put in jail because he was taking bribes.

這個政客長期以來一直覬覦垂涎權勢，但最後還是因為收賄鋃鐺入獄。

秒殺解字 源自拉丁語 cupidus，表示「渴求的」，這個字也衍生出小愛神 Cuipd 一字。

graphic

[ˋgræfɪk]

adj. 生動的；繪畫的

We all gave the tour guide a big hand because he gave a graphic description of how the old castle was invaded.

我們大家都熱烈為這位導遊鼓掌，因為他把這座古老城堡如何被攻占做了非常生動的敘述。

曾 104

 秒殺解字 graph(write, draw)+ic → 和「寫」、「畫」有關的，引申為畫畫「栩栩如生的」或描述「生動的」。可用表示「雕刻」的 **carve** 當神隊友、**g/k**，**m/f/v 轉音**，**母音通轉**，來記憶 **graph**、**gram**，皆表示「寫」。古代用刻字來記錄，引申為「寫」（**write**）、「畫」（**draw**）、「描述」（**describe**）。相關同源字有 **graph**（n. 圖表）、auto**graph**（n./v. 親筆簽名）、bio**graph**y（n. 傳記）、autobio**graph**y（n. 自傳）、calli**graph**y（n. 書法）、para**graph**（n. 段落）、**gram**mar（n. 文法）、dia**gram**（n. 圖表）、pro**gram**（n. 計畫;節目;程式 v. 設計程式）。

詞搭 in graphic detail 栩實地、詳盡地

同義字 vivid

stalk

[stɔk]

n. 莖、枝節

v. 跟蹤

The stalks of these flowers were bent because of the strong wind.

因為強風的關係，這些花的花柄被折斷了。

The man was arrested for stalking a school girl for a whole week.

這個人因為一整個禮拜都在跟蹤騷擾一位女學生而被捕。

秒殺解字 名詞和動詞的來源不同，當名詞用時，表示「站立」(stand)，植物的「莖」大多是直「立」著；當動詞用時，本義是「偷偷走」，和 steal（偷）同源，兩者皆不是正大光明的動作。

lush

[lʌʃ]

adj. 綠意盎然的；奢
華的

The lush grassland along the stream attracts many campers every day.

這片沿著溪流翠綠鬱蔥的草地每天吸引許多露營愛好者到來。

 本義是「鬆的」(loose)，大約 17 世紀初才有「綠意盎然的」的意思產生。

---

wade

[wed]

v. 涉水而行

The troops <u>waded across</u> the river, trying to reach the border as soon as possible.

軍隊涉過河水，試圖能夠盡快抵達邊界。

 w 的本義表示「不穩定、搖擺的動作」，相關單字有 **w**ag (v. 搖尾巴)、**w**aggle (v. 搖擺)、**w**aver (v. 搖擺不定)。

詞搭　wade across a stream 涉水過河；wade in... 進入淺水中、插手、介入；wade through... 費力地讀完……、涉水 (泥濘等)；wade into... 精神飽滿地開始、猛烈攻擊

01 ___ There are finally some pieces of evidence that can prove that all the scandals about his romance were _____ by others.

(A) located (B) complicated
(C) fabricated (D) communicated

02 ___ The _____ did very well at the box office, and it reached over 10 million viewers since its release last week.

(A) ejection (B) alleviation
(C) animation (D) argumentation

03 ___ The TV series added a lot of _____ plots in it in order to extend the time of the program.

(A) traditional (B) unnecessary
(C) memorable (D) destructive

04 ___ During the 1st to 2nd Centuries, the Rome Empire reached _____ stability and prosperity in its history.

(A) unprecedented (B) conceited
(C) affected (D) devoted

05 ___ The _____ was accused of preferring the team from his country, so he was suspended temporarily.

(A) warrior (B) survivor
(C) agent (D) referee

06 ___ The _____ about the president being engaged in money laundering is fabricated by his political opponent.

(A) expectation (B) fabrication
(C) auction (D) speculation

07 ___ If the murderer had _____ and sympathy, he would not have killed so many people in such a cruel way.

(A) compassion (B) omission
(C) recession (D) expression

08 ___ The Japanese restaurant has many different types of delicious Japanese_____, and I usually come here every week.

(A) virus (B) mission
(C) cuisine (D) mercury

09 ___ He was sentenced to death because he _____ 5 people with hemp rope in the past two weeks.

(A) retrieved (B) embarked
(C) enchanted (D) smothered

10 ___ The teacher tried to _____ his students' pressure by reducing the amount of homework.

(A) accelerated (B) alleviated
(C) allocated (D) authorized

11 ___ Because of the _____ of COVID-19, people around the world are prohibited from traveling abroad.

(A) tension (B) outbreak
(C) campaign (D) extent

12 ___ Steve Jobs has a _____ story of success in the industry of technology.

(A) essential (B) remarkable
(C) household (D) democratic

13 ___ John's father always tried to _____ his ideas, which made him lose confidence.

(A) refute (B) refuse
(C) dispute (D) abuse

14 ___ The machine will _____ water in a steady stream if you press the button in front of it.

(A) reject   (B) reflect
(C) project   (D) eject

15 ___ The new department store is _____ to my home, so it is very convenient for me to go shopping.

(A) consistent   (B) coherent
(C) inherent   (D) adjacent

premise
['prɛmɪs]

n. 前提；假設

We all think the conclusions you've made so far are based on a false premise.

我們都認為你目前所做的結論都是基於錯誤的前提。

秒殺解字　pre(before)+mis(send)+e →「送」「前面」，表示「前提」。相關同源字有 **miss**ion（n. 任務）、pro**mis**e（v./ n. 答應）、ad**mit**（v. 承認）、ad**miss**ion（n. 准許）、per**mit**（v. 允許）、per**miss**ion（n. 允許）、sub**mit**（v. 呈遞；順從）、sub**miss**ion（n. 呈遞；順從）、o**mit**（v. 遺漏）、o**miss**ion（n. 遺漏）。

詞搭　on the premise 在⋯⋯前提下；major premise 大前提；off the premises 建築物外；be consumed on the premises（酒類）需在店內飲用

obituary
[ə'bɪtʃʊˌɛrɪ]

n. 報紙上的訃聞

This morning I happened to read <u>an obituary notice</u> of one of my high school teachers in the newspaper.

今天早上我碰巧在報紙上看到一則我一位中學老師訃聞通告。

秒殺解字　ob(toward)+it(go)+u+ary →「走」「向」死亡，是死亡的委婉語，引申為「訃聞」。相關同源字有 ex**it**（n. 出口 v. 出去）、amb**it**ion（n. 雄心、抱負）、amb**it**ious（adj. 有雄心的）、in**it**ial（adj. 最初的）、trans**it**（n. 運輸）、trans**it**ion（n. 轉變；過渡）、**it**inerary（n. 旅行計劃）。

proliferation
[prəˌlɪfə'reʃən]

n. 增殖；擴散

The proliferation of spam has long annoyed many people.

垃圾郵件的氾濫長久以來一直困擾著許多人。

秒殺解字　prol(offspring)+i+fer(bear)+ate+ion →「生育」「後代」，表示「增殖」、「擴散」。可用 **bear** 當神隊友，**b/f 轉音**，**母音通轉**，來記憶 **fer**，表示「攜帶」、「生育」、「承受」。相關同源字有 dif**fer**（v. 不同）、in**fer**（v. 推論）、pre**fer**（v. 寧願）、suf**fer**（v. 受苦）、re**fer**（v. 提到）、trans**fer**（v. 轉移）、con**fer**ence（n. 正式會議）。

詞搭　cell proliferation 細胞增殖；the proliferation of nuclear weapons 核武擴散

starkly

[`stɑrklɪ]

adv. 明顯地；完全地；嚴厲地

You don't have to worry about us because we are starkly aware of all the possible risks we may face. 圖 108
你不用為我們擔心，因為我們對於可能面臨的所有可能風險十分清楚明瞭。

🖊️ 秒殺解字 stark(severe)+ly → 「嚴厲」「地」。

---

afflict

[ə`flɪktɪŋ]

v. 使痛苦、折磨

Environmental pollution is now afflicting the whole world. 醫 99
環境汙染正危害著全世界。

🖊️ 秒殺解字 af(=ad=to)+flict(strike) → 「去」「打」，表示「使痛苦」。相關同源字有con**flict**（v./n. 衝突；牴觸）、in**flict**（v. 施加）。

---

genre

[`ʒɑnrə]

n. 型別；流派

Novels and short stories are of different genres.
小說跟短篇故事是屬於不同類型的。

🖊️ 秒殺解字 gen(kind)+re 源自法語，表示「類別」，後指「型別」、「流派」。

---

database

[`detə‚bes]

n. 資料庫

You won't be able to access the database without a password.
沒有密碼你是無法進入資料庫的。

🖊️ 秒殺解字 data+base → 「資料」庫。

詞搭 database server 資料庫伺服器；database access 資料庫存取

---

median

[`midɪən]

n. 中位數；中線；中點

adj. 中間的、中央的

A financial expert predicts that median household income will greatly fall this year because of the severe depression.
一位財經專家預測，由於嚴重的經濟蕭條，今年家庭平均收入將巨幅下降。

🖊️ 秒殺解字 med (middle)+i+an → 在「中間的」。可用 **mid**dle 當神隊友，母音通轉，來記憶 **med**，皆表示「中間」。相關同源字有 **mid**dle（adj. 中間的 n. 中間）、**mid**st（n. 中間）、a**mid**（prep. 在……之中）、a**mid**st（prep. 在……之中）、**med**ia（n. 媒體）、multi**med**ia（adj./n. 多媒體）、**med**iate（v. 調停解決、斡旋）、**med**ieval（adj. 中古時期的）、im**med**iate（adj. 立即的）、inter**med**iate（adj. 中間的）、**Med**iterranean（n./adj. 地中海）。

詞搭 the median family income 中等家庭的收入；median value 中位數

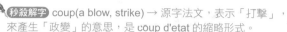

coup
[ku]

n. 意想不到的成就；
政變

It was really a tremendous coup for us to get such an important contract.
我們能夠拿下如此重要的合同，這真是相當令人意想不到的成就。

秒殺解字 coup(a blow, strike) → 源字法文，表示「打擊」，來產生「政變」的意思，是 coup d'etat 的縮短形式。

詞搭 a bloodless coup 不流血政變；a military coup 軍事政變；coup de grace 致命一擊

gravel
[`grævl]

n. 砂礫、碎石

The path around the park is paved with gravel.
環繞公園的小徑是用礫石鋪成的。

秒殺解字 源自古法語，和 grit (沙粒；沙礫) 同源。

詞搭 a gravel path 石子路

proximity
[prɑk`sɪmətɪ]

n. 接近；附近

Cameron's house is in close proximity to ours. 圖 110
Cameron 的房子離我們家很近。

秒殺解字 proxim(near)+i+ty → 「接近」、「附近」。

詞搭 close proximity 極為貼近；in close proximity to... 非常接近……；in the proximity of... 在……附近；proximity of blood 近親

衍生字 approximate [ə`prɑksəmɪt] / [ə`prɑksə‚met] adj. 大約的、近似的 v. 接近；approximately [ə`prɑksəmɪtlɪ] adv. 大約

culinary
[`kjulɪ‚nɛrɪ]

adj. 烹飪的；廚房的

Charlotte decides to take some culinary courses before getting married.
Charlotte 決定在結婚前上一些烹飪課程。

秒殺解字 culin(cook)+ary → 和「烹煮」有關的。相關同源字有 **cook** [kʊk] (v. 烹調 n. 廚師)、**kitch**en [`kɪtʃɪn] ( n. 廚房 )、**cook**er ( n. 爐具 )、**cuis**ine [kwɪ`zin] (n. 烹飪；菜餚)、bis**cuit** [`bɪskɪt] (n. 餅乾)。

詞搭 culinary workers 廚工；culinary skills / arts 烹調技術／廚藝；culinary delights 佳餚

predator
[`prɛdətɚ]

n. 掠食者

Local people, especially females, generally avoid going to that park at night because some sexual predators are said to prowl there.
當地人，尤其是女性，通常會避免在晚上到那座公園，因為據說有些會尾隨做案的色魔經常在那邊出沒。

秒殺解字 pred(prey)+at+or → 「掠食」者。

反義字 prey

anatomy

[ə`nætəmɪ]

n. 解剖學；解剖

The anatomy of human bodies is far more complex than you can imagine.

人體的解剖構造是遠比你所想像的還要複雜。

秒殺解字 ana(up)+tom(cut)+y → 「分解」「切割」，表示「解剖」。

字辨 autonomy [ɔ`tɑnəmɪ] n. 自治、自治權

---

affluent

[`æflʊənt]

adj. 富裕的

Born to an affluent family, Barnett always spends money lavishly.

Barnett 生於富裕家庭，所以他花錢總是揮霍無度。

秒殺解字 af(=ad=to)+flu(flow)+ent → 本義「流」「向」，1753 年才有錢財流入，表示「富裕」的意思，可用台灣錢「淹」腳目這句諺語來幫助記憶。相關同源字有 **flu**id (n. 液體)、**flu**sh (v. 沖洗；臉紅)、**flu**ency (n. 流暢)、**flu**ent (adj. 流暢的)、in**flu**ence (v./n. 影響)、in**flu**enza (n. 流行性感冒)。

詞搭 an affluent society 富裕的社會

同義字 wealthy, rich

---

obstruction

[əb`strʌkʃən]

n. 阻礙、妨礙；阻塞物

Many trains were delayed because some kind of obstruction was found on the railway tracks earlier.

許多班的火車延誤了，因為稍早在鐵軌上發現有些障礙物。

秒殺解字 ob(before, against)+struct(build)+ion → 在「前方」路上「建築」東西「反對」，引申成「阻塞」、「阻止」。相關同源字有 **struct**ure (n. 結構；建築物)、con**struct** (v. 建造、建設)、de**stroy** (v. 破壞)、in**struct** (v. 教導；命令)、in**stru**ment (n. 儀器；樂器)、ob**struct** (v. 阻塞；阻止)。

詞搭 obstruction of justice 妨礙司法；intestinal obstruction 腸阻塞

同義字 blockage

proprietary
[prə`praɪəˌtɛrɪ]

adj. 專有的；專利的；所有人的；業主的

Proprietary medicines are generally more expensive, but they are not necessarily more effective.
專利藥品通常是比較貴的，但是它們未必就比較有效。

(秒殺解字) propr(=proper=one's own)+i+et+ary →源自 property，屬於「自己的」。表示「專利的」、「所有人的」。**priv**, **propr**, **proper**，**p/v 轉音**，母音通轉，和字首 **pre**、**pro** 同源，核心語意皆表示「前」（**before**）。自己的事會擺在「前面」，因此衍生出「自己的」、「私人的」意思。相關同源字有 **priv**ate（adj. 私人的）、**priv**acy（n. 隱私）、**priv**ilege（n. 特權）、**proper**（adj. 適合的）、**proper**ty（n. 財產）、ap**propr**iate（adj. 適合的）。

詞搭 proprietary technology / product / medicines 專利技術／產品／藥品；proprietary rights 所有權

entrepreneurial
[ˌɑntrəprə`njʊrɪəl]

adj. 企業家的；創業者的

It is their entrepreneurial spirit that inspires us and earns our respect.
是他們的企業精神啟發激勵了我們並因此而獲得我們的尊敬。

(秒殺解字) entrepreneur+ial →「企業家」的。

rampant
[`ræmpənt]

adj. 蔓延的；猖獗的

With the development of Internet technology, I believe crimes on the Internet will become increasingly rampant.
隨著網際網路的進步發展，我認為網路犯罪也會越來越猖獗。

(秒殺解字) 源自古法語的 ramper，表示「爬」（climb），後來指「不受限制地成長」（growing without check），引申為「蔓延的」、「猖獗的」。

詞搭 rampant inflation 無法抑制的通膨

同義字 widespread

sibling
[`sɪblɪŋ]

n. 兄弟姊妹其中一個

I have three siblings: two brothers and one sister.
我有三個兄弟姊妹：兩個兄弟，一個姐妹。

普 99
警特 109

(秒殺解字) 源自古英文的 sibb，表示「男性親戚」（kinsman），後來語義擴增，表示「兄弟姊妹其中一個」。

replicate

[`rɛplɪ͵ket]

v. 複製

Our teacher warns us that many computer viruses will replicate themselves and even pass along from one user to another.
我們老師警告我們，許多電腦病毒會自我複製，甚至會從一個電腦用戶傳到另一個電腦用戶。

秒殺解字 re(back, again)+plic(fold)+ate →「再」「摺」一次，表示「複製」。可用 **fold** 當神隊友，**p/f 轉音**，母音通轉，來記憶 **plic**，皆表示「對摺」。

衍生字 replica [`rɛplɪkə] n. 複製品

influx

[`ɪnflʌks]

n. 湧入、流入、注入

It's possible that there will be an influx of several thousand refugees from across the border over the next few weeks.
在未來幾週內可能將會有數千名的難民從邊境湧入。

秒殺解字 in(in)+flu(flow)+x →「流」「入」。相關同源字有 **flu**id（n. 液體）、**flu**sh（v. 沖洗；臉紅）、**flu**ency（n. 流暢）、**flu**ent（adj. 流暢的）、in**flu**ence（v./n. 影響）、in**flu**enza（n. 流行性感冒）、af**flu**ent（adj. 富裕的）。

詞搭 an influx of customers / tourists 顧客／觀光客的蜂擁而來

pristine

[`prɪstin]

adj. 完好如新的、未受破壞的

Last night I got a smartphone. It's only one month old but is still in pristine condition.
昨晚我買了一支智慧型手機。只用了一個月，但卻是完好如新。

秒殺解字 prist(first, before)+ine → 可用 first 來記憶 prist，表示「前面」。pristine 表示保持最初狀態，「完好如新的」。

詞搭 a pristine copy 原始版本；the pristine Arctic sky 純淨的北極天空

gourmet
[`gʊrme]
n. 美食家
adj. 提供美食的；
（食品）優質的

Do you know if there is any café that offers gourmet coffee?
你知道已沒有哪家咖啡廳棍供頂級咖啡嗎？

The restaurant is run by a gourmet chef.
這家餐廳是由一位金牌主廚所經營。

✒ 秒殺解字 源自法語，表示「品嚐葡萄酒的人」，後語義擴增，表示「美食家」。

詞搭 a gourmet restaurant 美食餐廳；gourmet powder 味精、味素；gourmet coffee 頂級咖啡；gourmet food 美食；French gourmet cuisine 法國美食菜餚

---

holistic
[ho`lɪstɪk]
adj. 全面的；整體的

I think we need a holistic approach to our current problems.
我認為我們需要一個能夠解決我們目前所碰到問題全面性的方法。

🔖 104

✒ 秒殺解字 hol(whole)+ist+ic →「全面的」、「整體的」。

詞搭 a holistic approach 整體分析；holistic <u>health / education</u> 全人健康／教育

---

fraternity
[frə`tɝ·nətɪ]
n. 同行朋友；友誼；大學的兄弟會

Grover is the most distinguished member of the legal fraternity of this city.
Grover 是這個城市律師界中最優秀的一位成員。

🔖 103
🔖特 109

✒ 秒殺解字 frater(brother)+n+ity → 表示「兄弟」般的同行朋友、友誼、大學的兄弟會。可用 **brother** 當神隊友，**b/f**、**t/ð 轉音**，母音通轉，來記憶 **frater**，皆表示「兄弟」。相關同源字有 **brother** [`brʌðɚ]（n. 兄弟）、**brother**hood [`brʌðɚ͵hʊd]（n. 友誼）、**frater**nal [frə`tɝ·nl]（adj. 兄弟的；友好的）。

詞搭 sports fraternity 體壇；the medical fraternity 醫界同仁；an angling fraternity 一群釣友；liberty, equality, and fraternity 自由、平等、博愛

trickle

[ˈtrɪkl̩]

n. 細流
v. 滴；使淌

Eileen started to cry loudly when she found blood trickling out of her nose for unknown reasons.　圖 108
當 Eileen 發現不知道甚麼原因有血從她的鼻子滴下時，她開始嚎啕大哭。

秒殺解字 字源不詳。或許是源自 stricklen（流）。

詞搭 trickle down 向下滴流

---

homage

[ˈhɑmidʒ]

n. 敬意

Early in the morning, many students went to the funeral to <u>pay homage to</u> their beloved teacher.　醫 103
一大早許多學生就前往喪禮現場向他們所鍾愛的老師致敬。

秒殺解字 hom(=hom=man)+age → 本義是「人」，特指「僕人」，後來衍生出「臣服之禮」、「效忠的宣誓」，引申為「敬意」。相關同源字有 **hom**icide（n. 謀殺）。

詞搭 pay homage to... 向……表示敬意

---

salient

[ˈselɪənt]

adj. 顯著的、突出的

At the conference, Janice emphasized again and again the salient features of her new design.
在會議裡 Janice 一再強調她的設計中突出的特色。

秒殺解字 sal(jump, leap)+i+ent →「跳」出來，表示「顯著的」、「突出的」。相關同源字有 in**sul**t（v./n. 侮辱）、re**sul**t（v. 導致 n. 結果）、as**saul**t（v./n. 攻擊）、**sal**mon（n. 鮭魚）。

詞搭 a salient feature 顯著的特色；the salient points 要點

---

facade

[fəˈsɑd]

n.（建築物的）正面；假象

You seem to know little of Lilian. In fact, she's a quite pessimistic person behind her optimistic facade.
你似乎對 Lilian 了解不多。事實上，在樂觀外面的背後其實她是一個蠻悲觀的人。

秒殺解字 fac(face)+ade → 建物物的正「面」。

---

kinship

[ˈkɪnʃɪp]

n. 親屬關係

In different societies and cultures, there are different systems of kinship.　醫 101
在不同社會以及文化中會有不同的親屬關係稱呼體系。

秒殺解字 kin(family, kind)+ship →「親屬」「關係」。

詞搭 kinship with 和……的親屬關係；kinship between... 和……之間的親屬關係

nicotine

[ˋnɪkəˌtin]

n. 尼古丁

I think I'll never go to that café because it's always full of smoke and nicotine.

我想我不會再去那家咖啡餐館，因為那裡總是充滿著菸味以及尼古丁。

 秒殺解字 nicot(Jean Nicot)+ine → 駐葡萄牙的法國外大使 Jean Nicot 在 1560 年時，將菸草和種子寄回巴黎，「尼古丁」就是從他的名字而來。

詞搭 nicotine patch 尼古丁貼片 (貼於皮膚上以助戒菸)

字辨 tobacco [təˋbæko] n. 菸草

landfill

[ˋlændfɪl]

n. 垃圾掩埋 (場)

You might know little about this park. In fact, it was a landfill site 20 years ago.

你也許對這個公園不甚了解。事實上，它在 20 年前是一座垃圾掩埋場。

 秒殺解字 land+fill →「土地」「填滿」表示「垃圾掩埋」、「垃圾掩埋場」。

詞搭 a large-sized landfill site 大型垃圾掩埋場

arsenic

[ˋɑrsnɪk]

n. 砷；砒霜

The man was accused of killing his colleague with arsenic.

這個人被控訴以砒霜謀害他的同事。

 秒殺解字 源自希臘語的 arsenikon，表示「砒霜」。砒霜是一種毒，又名「三氧化二砷」。

burgeoning

[ˋbɝˋdʒənɪŋ]

adj. 急速發展的；新興的

It's a burgeoning market and you'll make more money if you get into it as early as possible.

這是一個新興市場，所以你若能盡早進入，你會賺得更多。

秒殺解字 burgeon(bud)+ing → burgeon 源自古法語，表示「枝芽」。burgeoning 表示「發芽的」，引申為「急速發展的」。

詞搭 burgeoning industries 新興產業

aroma

[ə`romə]

n. 香味、芬芳

We sniffed the aroma of coffee when we entered Pandora's house.

當我們一踏進 Pandora 的房子就聞到一陣咖啡香味撲鼻而來。

> 秒殺解字 aroma(sweet odor) →「香味」，常指咖啡香或食物的香味。

詞搭 the aroma of hot coffee / fresh fruit 熱咖啡／新鮮水果的香味

衍生字 aromatic [ˌærə`mætɪk] adj. 芬芳的

---

erratic

[ɪ`rætɪk]

adj. 不規律的；飄忽不定的；不穩定

I didn't know Rosemary's behavior was erratic until now. She might be nice to you now, but might turn out to be a cold fish tomorrow.

我到今天才知道 Rosemary 是一個難以捉摸的人。她很有可能現在對你很好，但也可能明天就變成冷冰冰的人。

> 秒殺解字 err(wander)+ate+ic →到處「遊蕩」表示「不規律的」、「飄忽不定的」。

詞搭 an erratic woman 反覆無常的女人；erratic behavior 古怪的行為

---

calculus

[`kælkjələs]

n. 微積分；結石

I flunked my calculus exam, and I think I'll have to take it again.

我微積分考試不及格，所以我想應該必須重考一次了。

> 秒殺解字 calc(pebble, reckon)+ ule+us → 源自拉丁文，表示「(計算用的)石頭」。可用表示「粉筆」的 **chalk** 當神隊友，**k/tʃ** 轉音，母音通轉，來記憶 **calc**，其核心語意是「小石頭」（**small stone**）或「石灰石」（**limestone**）。「粉筆」本是石灰加水，做成塊狀物體，用來在物品的表面做紀錄，而「計算」（**calculate**）的典故是相傳以前的人會用排石頭的方式來做計算，特別是「石灰石」（**limestone**）。相關同源字有 **chalk**（n. 石灰岩；粉筆）、**calc**ium（n. 鈣）、**calc**ulate（v. 計算）、**calc**ulation（n. 計算）、**calc**ulator（n. 計算機）。

詞搭 differential / integral calculus 微／積分學；urinary / renal calculus 尿／腎結石

衍生字 calculate [`kælkjəˌlet] v. 計算；miscalculate [mɪs`kælkjəˌlet] v. 算錯）；calculation [ˌkælkjə`leʃən] n. 計算；calculator [`kælkjəˌletɚ] n. 計算機

abduction

[æb`dʌkʃən]

n. 誘拐、綁架

The man looked quite friendly, but he was accused of abduction.
這個人看起來相當友善，但卻被指控綁架。

> (秒殺解字) ab(away, off)+duc(lead, tow)+tion → 把人「拉」「走」，表示「綁架」。相關同源字有 **educ**ate（v. 教育）、pro**duc**e（v. 生產）、pro**duc**tion（n. 生產）、re**duc**e（v. 減少）、re**duc**tion（n. 減少）、intro**duc**e（v. 介紹；引進）、intro**duc**tion（n. 介紹；引進）、in**duc**e（v. 唆使）。

詞搭 | cases of child abduction 誘拐兒童案件

同義字 | kidnapping

strife

[straɪf]

n. 衝突、不和

Sophia decided to leave her family because of the strife between her parents.
Sophia 因為父母不和決定離家。

> (秒殺解字) 源自古法語，意思是「爭吵」(quarrel)，和表示「努力」、「鬥爭」的 strive 同源。

詞搭 | internal strife 內鬥；the labor-management strife 勞資衝突

同義字 | conflict

01 ___ It is a country _____ by civil wars and racial discrimination.

(A) afflicted   (B) tempted
(C) concealed   (D) suspended

02 ___ After watching the drama, I was still confused about the _____ of it. Was it a comedy or a tragedy?

(A) rage   (B) genre
(C) catalog   (D) posture

03 ___ Because of the economic crisis, the _____ household income fell dramatically this year.

(A) reasonable   (B) furious
(C) median   (D) vulnerable

04 ___ No one knows how to overcome the _____ between these two groups. They are always fighting against each other.

(A) passion   (B) illusion
(C) strife   (D) custom

05 ___ _____ , such as lions and wolves, are good at hunting skills.

(A) Protesters   (B) Traitors
(C) Murders   (D) Predators

06 ___ When you come to this museum, you can always smell a kind of fruity _____.

(A) aroma   (B) sequence
(C) commerce   (D) convention

07 ___ This guy comes from a wealthy and _____ family. He doesn't have any money issues.

(A) affluent   (B) complicated
(C) stormy   (D) spontaneous

08 ___ There's some kind of _____ on the road. Just report to the authorities to remove it.

(A) dysfunction　　　　　　(B) production
(C) operation　　　　　　　(D) obstruction

09 ___ In this class, students are required to use their _____ skills to present a business plan.

(A) industrial　　　　　　　(B) entrepreneurial
(C) spatial　　　　　　　　(D) facial

10 ___ The epidemic is _____, especially in cities with huge populations.

(A) reluctant　　　　　　　(B) relevant
(C) rampant　　　　　　　　(D) ignorant

11 ___ This artwork is recognized as the most valuable work of this artist, and it is very hard to _____.

(A) allocate　　　　　　　　(B) suffocate
(C) replicate　　　　　　　　(D) accumulate

12 ___ Because of the deed of this brave soldier, everyone paid _____ to him.

(A) mortgage　　　　　　　(B) heritage
(C) shrinkage　　　　　　　(D) homage

13 ___ A _____ industry of electronic sports has greatly boosted the global economy.

(A) remaining　　　　　　　(B) frightening
(C) challenging　　　　　　(D) burgeoning

14 ___ In this tribe, they have a system of _____ which is totally different from others.

(A) illustration　　　　　　(B) contract
(C) hardship　　　　　　　(D) kinship

15 ___ Because a huge _____ is located around the site, few people want to live there.

(A) supplement　　　　　　(B) landfill
(C) syndrome　　　　　　　(D) venture

1.(A) 2.(B) 3.(C) 4.(C) 5.(D) 6.(A) 7.(A) 8.(D) 9.(B) 10.(C) 11.(C) 12.(D) 13.(D) 14.(D) 15.(B)

heartland
[`hɑrt͵lænd]
n. 心臟地區

Many people say this area will be reserved as the heartland for the automobile manufacturing industry.
許多人都説這個地區將保留作為汽車製造工業的重地。

秒殺解字 heart(center, core)+land → 「中心」「地區」，表示「心臟地帶」、「重地」。

詞搭 Germany's industrial heartland 德國的工業中心

---

camouflage
[`kæmə͵flɑʒ]
n. v. 偽裝、掩飾；
保護色

Many animals have a natural camouflage that helps them hide from their enemies.
許多動物擁有一種保護色可以協助他們避開敵人的攻擊。

秒殺解字 源自法語，表示「假裝」（disguise），引申為「掩飾」。

詞搭 a natural camouflage 天然的偽裝；camouflage clothing / color 迷彩服／色；radar camouflage 防雷達偽裝；camouflage A with B 以 B 掩飾 A

---

crave
[krev]
v. 渴望獲得

No matter how rich they are, many people still crave more wealth.
不管已經多麼富有，許多人仍然渴望冀求更多財富。

秒殺解字 源自古英文，表示「懇求」，引申為「渴望獲得」。

詞搭 crave for... 渴望……

同義字 covet

---

benevolent
[bə`nɛvələnt]
adj. 仁慈的、慈善的

My grandmother is so benevolent that she spends all of her free time working for charities.
我祖母非常仁慈，她把所有的空閒時間都花在慈善事業上。

秒殺解字 bene(good, well)+vol(will)+ent → 「好」「意願」。可用 **will** 當神隊友，**v/w** 對應，**母音通轉**，來記憶 vol, vol，表示「意志」、「意願」。相關同源字有 will（aux. 將；願 v. 用意志力；立遺囑 n. 意志；遺囑）、will**ing**（adj. 願意的）、**wel**come（v. 歡迎；欣然接受）、un**will**ing（adj. 不願意的）、**vol**untary（adj. 志願、自發的）、**vol**unteer（n. 義工 v. 自願做……）、male**vol**ent（adj. 惡意的）。

衍生字 benevolence [bə`nɛvələns] n. 仁慈

同義字 kind, generous

反義字 malevolent, evil

inscription

[ɪnˋskrɪpʃən]

n. 刻文、碑文；題詞

The author wrote some inscriptions on the inside front cover of the book and sent it to me.
作者在書的扉頁上題了一些字然後將書送給我。

（秒殺解字）in(in)+scrip(write)+tion → 字面意思是「寫在」「裡面」，以前紙張未發明時，習慣把字「刻」在物品上。相關同源字有 **scrib**ble（v./n. 胡寫；塗鴉）、**scrip**t（n. 腳本；手寫；筆跡）、de**scrib**e（v. 描寫）、de**scrip**tion（n. 描寫）、pre**scrib**e（v. 開藥方）、pre**scrip**tion（n. 藥方）、in**scrib**e（v. 刻、寫、印）、sub**scrib**e（v. 訂閱、訂購；認捐）、sub**scrip**tion（n. 訂閱費；認捐）、tran**scrib**e（v. 抄寫、謄寫；改編）、tran**scrip**t（n. 抄寫；文字本）、tran**scrip**tion（n. 抄寫；文字本）、manu**scrip**t（n. 原稿、手稿）、post**scrip**t（n. 信末簽名後的附筆）、a**scrib**e（v. 把……歸因於）、con**scrip**t（v. 招募）。

詞搭｜stone inscription 石刻；tablet inscription 碑文

gadget

[ˋgædʒɪt]

n. 小器具、小裝置

My mother likes to buy some useful kitchen gadgets whenever she goes to a kitchenware store.
每當我媽媽去一家廚具店時總喜歡買一些有用的廚房器具。

（秒殺解字）源自船員之間的行話，用來指稱船上缺少的任何小機械或小東西，後語義擴增，指「小器具」、「小裝置」。

同義字｜device

outweigh

[aʊtˋwe]

v. 比…重要

The advantages of the plan proposed by William outweigh its disadvantages, so we decided to adopt it.
William 所提議的計畫優點多於缺點，所以我們決定採用。

（秒殺解字）out+weight →「比……更重要」。相關同源字有。以 out 當字首，形成動詞，用以表示「超越」或「勝過」，如：outlive、outnumber、outgrow。

詞搭｜far outweigh 遠大於……

jeopardize

[ˋdʒɛpəˌdˌaɪz]

v. 危害；使瀕於危險

Don't you know that a wrong decision like this might jeopardize your career?
你不知道像這樣一個錯誤的決定有可能會危及／危害你未來生涯？

（秒殺解字）jeo(game)+pard(part)+ize → jeopardy 源自法語的 jeu parti，表示「勢均力敵的遊戲」，遊戲者處於危險之中；jeopardize 是其動詞形式，表示「危害」、「使瀕於危險」。

同義字｜put / place... in jeopardy, endanger, put...in danger / peril, put...at risk

505

insomnia
[ɪn`sɑmnɪə]
n. 失眠症

I often suffer from insomnia because I have a huge workload and my work is stressful. 🔲 108
我常常因為巨大工作量以及來自工作的壓力而失眠。

秒殺解字 in(not)+somn(sleep)+ia →「無法」「睡覺」的「症狀」。

詞搭 suffer from chronic insomnia 患長期失眠症；insomnia therapy 失眠治療

衍生字 insomniac [ɪn`sɑmnɪæk] n. 失眠症患者 adj. 失眠症的

---

dichotomy
[daɪ`kɑtəmɪ]
n. 分裂；二分法

I seldom trust any candidates, because there is often a <u>dichotomy between</u> what they say and what they do.
我幾乎不會相信那些候選人，因為通常他們的言行之間常有天壤之別的差距。

秒殺解字 dich(two)+o+tom(cut)+y →「切成」「兩份」。

---

venerable
[`vɛnərəb!]
adj. 可敬的；德高望重的；莊嚴的

Professor Ellis is a venerable scholar, so he really deserves our respect. 🔲 107
Ellis 是位可敬的學者。他真的值得我們尊敬。

秒殺解字 ven(beauty, love, desire)+er+able → 本義和「美麗」、「愛」、「渴望」有關，美麗的人常受到關愛，人們也大多渴望與之親近，但 venerable 後來衍生出新的語義，表示「可敬的」、「德高望重的」。有趣的是，司掌愛與美的女神 Venus 也是從 ven 這個字根來的。

同義字 honorable

---

meticulous
[mə`tɪkjələs]
adj. 精細的；嚴密的；一絲不苟的

Mr. Brown is regarded by all as the most meticulous teacher in our department. 🔲 106
Brown 先生被公認為是本系最嚴謹的教師。

秒殺解字 met(fear)+ic+ule+ous → 原意是「害怕」、「恐懼」，進到英文中，產生「嚴密的」、「一絲不苟的」等語義，推測會有這樣的語意產生，是因為「害怕更要小心行事」。

詞搭 be meticulous <u>in / about</u> + sth. 對某事一絲不苟；meticulous <u>design / construction</u> 精心設計／施工；a meticulous craftsman 細心的工匠

perpetuate
[pə`pɛtʃʊˏet]
v. 使持續；使永存

The rising high house prices will perpetuate existing class inequalities.
高房價只會使現存的階級不平等持續下去。

> （秒殺解字）per(through)+pet(go to, rush, fly)+u+ate → 從頭到尾「衝」、「飛」向某目標，引申為「使持續」、「使永存」。相關同源字有 ap**pet**ite (n. 胃口)、com**pet**ition (n. 競賽)。

---

maniac
[`menɪˏæk]
n. 瘋子

You drove like a maniac and now I feel dizzy and a little uncomfortable.
你開車開得像瘋子一樣。我現在感覺有點暈眩也很不舒服。

> （秒殺解字）mani(strong desire)+ac(one who) → 本指有「強烈慾望的人」，後指「瘋子」。

詞搭 | a fishing / homicidal / religious / sex maniac 釣魚迷 / 殺人魔 / 宗教狂熱者 / 色情狂

同義字 | lunatic, freak

---

commotion
[kə`moʃən]
n. 騷動

Don't you think you're just making a great commotion about nothing?
你不覺得你是在無理取鬧嗎？

> （秒殺解字）com(together)+mot(move)+e → 大家「一起」「動」，表示「騷動」。

詞搭 | cause a commotion 引發騷動

---

penchant
[`pɛntʃənt]
n. 偏好、傾向、嗜好

📀 105

Though Tom is severely allergic to seafood, he still has a penchant for it.
雖然 Tom 對海鮮會嚴重過敏，他仍然有這個偏好。

> （秒殺解字）pench(=pend=hang)+ant → 本義是往……「掛」，引申為「傾向」（incline），表示「偏好」。

詞搭 | a penchant for + sth. 酷愛某物

---

arid
[`ærɪd]
adj. 乾旱的；不毛的；枯燥的；無生氣的

The desert is so arid that almost nothing can grow there.
沙漠極其乾燥以至於幾乎沒有任何東西／植物可以在那生長存活。

> （秒殺解字）ar(dry)+id → 源自拉丁文的 arere，表示「乾燥的」。

詞搭 | arid climate 乾燥氣候；arid region 乾燥區

同義字 | dry

lucid

[`lusɪd]

adj. 易懂的；清晰的；頭腦清楚的

I'm quite puzzled by the current political situation, so please provide a lucid analysis of it.

我現在對當前政治情勢相當困惑不解，所以拜託針對它提供簡單明瞭的分析。

秒殺解字 luc(shine, light, clear) → 核心語意是「照耀」、「光」，表示「清晰的」。相關同源字有 **light**（n. 光、光線；燈 adj. 亮的 v. 點燃；照亮）、**light**en（v. 使變亮）、**Lucy** [`lusɪ]（n. 露西）、**luc**id [`lusɪd]（adj. 清晰的）、e**luc**idate（v. 闡明）、pe**lluc**id（adj. 清澄的）、trans**luc**ent（adj. 半透明的）、il**lustr**ate [`ɪləstret]（v. 舉例說明；插圖說明）、il**lustr**ation（n. 實例說明；圖解）、**luna**r [`lunɚ]（adj. 月亮的）同源，母音通轉，核心語意是「光」（**light**），可用 **light** 或 **Lucy** 當神隊友，來記憶這組單字。

詞搭 a lucid explanation 易懂的說明；a lucid stream 清澈小溪

同義字 clear

redeem

[rɪ`dim]

v. 彌補；贖回

Juliana has finally saved enough money to go to the pawn shop and redeem her diamond ring.

Juliana 終於已經存夠錢了，因此決定到當鋪贖回她的鑽戒。

秒殺解字 red(=re=back)+eem(=sum=take, buy) →「買」「回來」，表示「彌補」、「贖回」。red 是 re 的變體，常用以黏接母音為首的字根，如：redundant、redeem。

詞搭 redeem... from... 從……贖回

同義字 make up for

plethora

[`plɛθərə]

n. 過多、過剩；多血症

The orphanage is now overwhelmed by the sudden plethora of food and toys donated by thousands of kind people.

突然之間有好幾千位善心人士捐贈食物以及玩具，現在孤兒院正為了過剩的捐贈物品感到困擾煩惱。

秒殺解字 pleth(full)+ora →原意是「多血症」，表示「過多」、「過剩」。可用 **full** 當神隊友，**p/f 轉音**，母音通轉，來記憶 **pleth**，皆表示「充滿的」。

詞搭 a plethora of problems / advice 過多的問題／忠告

Unit 60

---

swath

[swɑθ]

n. 長條田地；（鐮刀或割草機）收割的寬度、帶狀地

A huge swath of land is now being cultivated to grow remunerative crops.

一大片的土地正在開墾準備種植高經濟價值農作物。

🖊️ 秒殺解字 swath(track, footstep) → 源自古英文，指「足跡」，後來指鐮刀割除稻麥、雜草後所形成的帶狀區域，之所以會有這樣的語意產生，推測是雜草或稻麥生長之處，不易「通行」，必須用鐮刀割除後才有辦法通過。

詞搭 cut a swath 出風頭；cut a swath through... 大肆破壞……

---

conjure

[`kʌndʒɚ]

v. 唸咒召喚；施魔法、變魔術

The magician conjured up a rabbit out of a hat in an instant and all the audience applauded loudly.

魔術師瞬間從一頂帽子裡變出一隻兔子，於是所有觀眾都熱烈鼓掌。

🖊️ 秒殺解字 con(together)+jur(swear)+e →「一起」「發誓」，如同透過念咒語的儀式，「召喚」，或者「施魔法」，使東西出現或消失。

詞搭 a name to conjure with 受尊敬而有影響力的名字；conjure up 唸咒召喚、喚起、瞬間做成； conjure + sth. + out of 從……裡變出……

---

paraphrase

[`pærəˌfrez]

n. v. 以更簡短、清晰的方式改述

The teacher tried to paraphrase the essay into two short paragraphs, hoping to make it easier for students to understand the context.

老師試著把這篇文章意譯成兩段短文，希望能夠加以簡化讓學生了解上下文意。

🖊️ 秒殺解字 para(alongside)+phrase(tell) →用語意「接近」的詞語來「述說」，引申為「以更簡短、清晰的方式改述」。

nuance

[nju`ɑns]

n. （色彩、音調、意義、情感、見解等的）細微差異

When drawing a portrait of the model, the painter successfully captured the nuance of her facial expression.

在為這個模特兒畫人像時，這位畫家成功地將她的面部表情刻劃得細緻入微。

秒殺解字 源自拉丁文，表示「雲」(cloud) 和「遮擋」(shade)，後來衍生出「模糊」的語意。看東西時模糊，視線自然會有差異，引申為「(色彩、音調、意義、情感、見解等的) 細微差異」。

詞搭 various nuances of meaning 意義的種種細微差異； diverse nuances 多樣化的細微差別

衍生字 nuanced [`nuɑnst] adj. 具有細微差別的、微妙的

treatise

[`tritɪs]

n. 論文；專著

Professor Bowell is going to publish a treatise on patent law.

Bowell 即將出版有關專利法的專書著作。

秒殺解字 treat(deal with)+ise → 寫作「處理」嚴肅議題，引申為「論文」、「專著」。

詞搭 a treatise on / upon COVID-19 / febrile disease / pestilence 有關新冠肺炎／傷寒／瘟疫的論文

grapple

[`græp!]

n. 扭打

v. 扭打；努力解決

曾 99

The two wrestlers have grappled each other for a long time because they were evenly matched.

兩位摔跤選手已經扭打成一團好久一段時間了，因為他們仍然勢均力敵，不分軒輊。

秒殺解字 含 gr 的單字多有「抓」的意思，grapple 指「抓」住彼此，扭打在一起。相關單字有 grab (v. 抓取)、grasp (v. 抓緊)、grip (n. 握緊)。

詞搭 grapple with the thief / problem 與小偷扭打／盡力解決問題

同義字 wrestle

unwittingly

[ˌʌn`wɪtɪŋlɪ]

adv. 不知情地；無意地

Tom had been working very hard every day for years, and he saved money until he unwittingly had enough money to buy a house.

多年來，湯姆每天都非常努力地工作，他存錢，一直到他不知不覺有了足夠的錢買房子。

秒殺解字 un(not)+witting+ly → 「不」「知道」地或「不」「了解」地。

同義字 unknowingly

grumpy
[ˋgrʌmpɪ]
adj. 脾氣暴躁的

Joyce is usually a little grumpy because she suffers 高 108
from insomnia and doesn't sleep well.
每當 Joyce 失眠時她的脾氣就會有點暴躁。

秒殺解字 含 gr 的字，常表示「咕噥」、「發牢騷」、「抱怨」
等意思。**gr**umpy 指「脾氣暴躁的」，脾氣暴躁的人多有上述
特質。相關單字有 **gr**udge（n. 怨恨）、**gr**ievance（n. 抱怨）、
dis**gr**untled（adj. 不滿的）。

同義字 grouchy, bad-tempered, ill-tempered, short-tempered, quick-
tempered, irritable, crabby, cantankerous, stroppy

tactile
[ˋtæk͵taɪl]
adj. 觸覺的

The tactile senses and a good sense of hearing are
especially important to the blind.
觸覺和良好的聽覺對盲人尤其重要。

秒殺解字 tac(touch)+t+ile →「觸」覺「的」。相關同源字有
con**tac**t（n./v. 接觸；聯絡）、con**tag**ion（n. 接觸傳染病）、
con**tag**ious（adj. 接觸傳染性的）、con**tam**inate（v. 污染）、
in**tac**t（adj. 原封不動的；完整無損的）、**tang**ible（adj. 明
確的；可觸知的）、in**tang**ible（adj. 難以捉摸的、無實體的）、
in**teg**er（n. 完整的事物）、in**teg**ral（adj. 完整的）、
in**teg**rate（v. 使成一體）、en**tire**（adj. 全部的）。

詞搭 tactile sensation 觸感

homophobia
[hɑməˋfobɪə]
n. 同性戀恐懼症

May 17 is the International Day Against
Homophobia, Transphobia, and Biphobia
(IDAHOTB).
五月十七日是國際不再恐同日。

秒殺解字 homo(homosexual)+phobia(fear) →「恐懼」「同
性戀」。相關同源字有 **phobia**（n. 恐懼）、**phobic**（adj.
恐懼的）、techno**phobia**（n. 科技恐懼症）、techno**phobic**
（adj. 恐懼科技的）、techno**phobe**（n. 科技恐懼者）、
biblio**phobia**（n. 書籍恐懼症）、zoo**phobia** [͵zoəˋfobɪə]
（n. 動物恐懼症）、claustro**phobia**（n. 幽閉恐懼症）、
photo**phobia**（n. 畏光症）、socio**phobia**（n. 社交恐懼
症）。

衍生字 homophobic [͵homəˋfobɪk] adj. 害怕同性戀的

vandalism

[ˋvændlɪzəm]

n. 故意破壞公物的行為

More than 20 juvenile offenders were arrested, with some of them on suspicion of vandalism.
昨晚超過 20 名青年罪犯被捕,其中有些人還有蓄意破壞的嫌疑。

（秒殺解字）vandal+ism → vandal 源自 Vandals(汪達爾人),屬於日耳曼民族,汪達爾人在西元 455 年開始攻擊羅馬帝國,掠奪土地,甚至建國。Henri Grégoire 用此字造出 vandalism 一字,原指在法國大革命時,村落、藝術品受到破壞的狀況,後泛指「故意破壞公物的行為」。

詞搭　environmental vandalism 環境破壞行為;wanton and mindless vandalism 無端且毫無顧忌的故意破壞

deforestation

[ˌdifɔrəsˋteʃən]

n. 砍伐森林

Deforestation is the most serious environmental problem in many countries.
在許多國家砍伐森林是一項最嚴重的環境問題。

圖 103

（秒殺解字）de(away)+forest+ation →「移除」「森林」,引申為「砍伐森林」。

vigilance

[ˋvɪdʒələns]

n. 警覺;警戒

Thanks to the vigilance of some of the residents in the community, the fire did not spread and was soon extinguished.
幸虧社區裡某些居民的機警,火災沒有蔓延,而且很快就被撲滅。

圖 106

（秒殺解字）vig(watch, wake, lively)+ile+ance →「醒著」、「警戒」。可用表示「醒來」、「叫醒」的 **wake** 當神隊友,**v/w** 對應,**g/k/dʒ** 轉音,母音通轉,來記憶 **vig**、**veg**,皆表示「醒來」、「醒著的」,醒來之後體力最好,就不是死氣沉沉,表示「有活力的」。相關同源字有 **wak**e(v. 醒來;叫醒)、**awak**e(adj. 醒著的 v. 醒來、叫醒)、**awak**en(v. 叫醒;使覺醒)、**watch**(v. 看;注意 n. 錶;看守;警戒)、**witch**(n. 女巫)、**wick**ed(adj. 壞的;邪惡的)、**vig**or(n. 精力)、**vig**orous(adj. 激烈的;精力充沛的)、**veg**etable(n. 蔬菜;植物人)、**veg**etarian(n. 素食主義者)。

pervert

[pə`vɝt]

v. 歪曲;使變壞

Research suggests that TV violence may seriously pervert the minds of young people

研究顯示,電視暴力可能會嚴重扭曲年輕人的心智思想。

秒殺解字 per(away)+vert(turn) → 字面上的意思是「轉」「開」,本指「偏離」「宗教教義」、「法律」、「事實」等,衍生出「歪曲」、「使變壞」等意思。

詞搭 pervert the course of justice 妨礙司法公正;pervert (the mind of) a child 把小孩 (的思想) 教壞

rodent

[`rodnt]

n. 囓齒動物

Rats and rabbits are rodents and they have long sharp front teeth that are good for gnawing.

老鼠以及兔子是囓齒動物,他們具有利於啃咬的長尖前齒。

秒殺解字 rod(gnaw)+ent →「咬」,表示「囓齒動物」,如老鼠或兔子等。可用表示「老鼠」的 **rat** 當神隊友,**d/t/s/ʒ 轉音,母音通轉**,來記憶 **rod**、**ros**,表示「咬」,因為老鼠是囓齒類動物,有愛咬東西的特性。相關同源字有 **rat** (n. 鼠)、cor**rod**e (v. 腐蝕;損害)、cor**ros**ive (adj. 腐蝕性的)、cor**ros**ion (n. 腐蝕)、e**rod**e (v. 侵蝕;使風化)、e**ros**ion (n. 侵蝕;風化)、**raz**or (n. 刮鬍刀)、e**ras**e (v. 消除;擦掉)。

unrelenting

[ˌʌnrɪ`lɛntɪŋ]

adj. 不鬆懈的;堅定的

The unrelenting pressures of your workplace will no doubt greatly affect your health.  102

持續無法鬆懈的職場工作壓力毫無疑問地會嚴重影響你的健康。

秒殺解字 un(not)+re(intensive)+len(gentle, soft, bend)+t+ing →「絕不」「軟化」「的」,引申為「不鬆懈的」。

詞搭 unrelenting efforts 不懈的努力;unrelenting pressure 持續的壓力;unrelenting assault / pursuit 無情的突襲/追擊

infiltrate

[ɪn`filtret]

v. (使)滲入;(使)滲透

Foreign rebel forces have been found to infiltrate into this country. 曾 106

外國反叛勢力已被發現滲透進入這個國家了。

秒殺解字 in(in)+filtr(=filte)+ate →「滲」「入」。

詞搭 infiltrate + sb. + into + sth. 暗中使某人進入;infiltrate spies into a neighboring country 派間諜進入鄰國

衍生字 infiltration [ˌɪnfɪl`treʃən] n. 滲透

minuscule

[mɪ`nʌskjul]

adj. 極小的

同義字 minute

The chances of his father's recovery are minuscule.
他父親康復得機會渺茫。

秒殺解字 min(little)+us+cule(small) → 表示「極的」。

---

valor

[`vælɚ]

n. 英勇

The leader's valor encouraged all the soldiers to fight bravely.
這位領導者的英勇鼓勵所有士兵勇敢作戰。

秒殺解字 val(worth, strong)+or → 「值得的」、「強大的」，引申為「英勇」，特別指戰場上。可用表示「價值」的 **value** 當神隊友，**母音通轉**，來記憶 **val**、**vail**，表示「強的」、「值得的」。相關同源字有 **valu**e (n. 價值 v. 重視)、**valu**able (adj. 有價值的)、**valu**eless (adj. 不值錢的)、e**valu**ate (v. 評估；評價)、equi**val**ent (adj. 等值的)、**val**id (adj. 有效的)、in**val**id (adj. 失效的 n. 病人)、a**vail**able (adj. 可用的、可得或買到的；有空的)、pre**vail** (v. 盛行；獲勝)、pre**vail**ing (adj. 盛行的、現有的)、pre**val**ent (adj. 盛行的、普遍的)、pre**val**ence (n. 盛行、普遍)。

同義字 courage, bravery

---

awash

[ə`wɑʃ]

adj. 被淹沒的；泛濫的

The toilet leaks badly, leaving the bathroom floor awash with smelly water.
廁所漏水嚴重使得浴室地板污水氾濫成災。

秒殺解字 a(on)+wash → 「上面」被水覆蓋、「沖刷」，引申為「被淹沒的」、「泛濫的」。

詞搭 be awash with... 充滿……

01 ___ Some soldiers use leaves or branches as a _____ to hide themselves.

(A) patronage   (B) package
(C) camouflage   (D) damage

02 ___ Many teenagers _____ attention from others because they lack love from parents.

(A) possess   (B) expose
(C) approve   (D) crave

03 ___ Her _____ acts of donating money helped many poor students to go to school.

(A) benevolent   (B) equivalent
(C) prevalent   (D) apparent

04 ___ The _____ on the gate is French. I don't understand the meaning of it.

(A) stimulation   (B) intervention
(C) inscription   (D) compensation

05 ___ The smartphones, iPads and other _____ sell very fast because of the high demand.

(A) debris   (B) cosmetics
(C) barriers   (D) gadgets

06 ___ The lecturer claims the advantages of using pesticides _____ the disadvantages of not using it.

(A) examine   (B) outweigh
(C) preserve   (D) recall

07 ___ The use of the chemicals has _____ the wild life in this area. Many animals died and even become endangered.

(A) authorized   (B) jeopardized
(C) memorized   (D) subsidized

08 ___ Since I was a child, I suffered from a serious _____. Therefore, I always feel sleepy in the morning.

(A) insomnia   (B) malaria
(C) distraction   (D) pneumonia

09 ___ The violence and strife has _____in this country for decades

(A) humiliated   (B) evaluated
(C) perpetuated   (D) educated

10 ___ Having a _____ dream means that when you dream, you know clearly that you are dreaming.

(A) innocent   (B) abrupt
(C) major   (D) lucid

11 ___ You can't just copy words from others' essays. Try to _____ it in your own words.

(A) paraphrase   (B) increase
(C) purchase   (D) release

12 ___ Many second language learners have difficulty understanding the _____ between prepositions, such as in, on, at.

(A) nuance   (B) allowance
(C) dominance   (D) resistance

13 ___ These _____ books are very popular. Actually, they are designed for the blind.

(A) fertile   (B) meek
(C) tactile   (D) earthly

14 ___ Global warming and _____ of woods are the main causes of the greenhouse effect.

(A) exploitation   (B) reputation
(C) deforestation   (D) transportation

15 ___ The country is _____ with money because many global companies have invested money in it.

(A) awash   (B) perplexing
(C) confidential   (D) dubious

解答
1.(C) 2.(D) 3.(A) 4.(C) 5.(D) 6.(B) 7.(B) 8.(A) 9.(C) 10.(D) 11.(A) 12.(A) 13.(C) 14.(C) 15.(A)

索引 Index

語研力 *E085*

（格林法則）秒殺解字單字記憶法：
六大名師陪練大考英單力，全民英檢、統測、學測、高考、普考等公職考試必備

作　　者	黃宏祿、魏延斌、楊智民、廖柏州、陳冠名、林麗英
顧　　問	曾文旭
出版總監	陳逸祺、耿文國
主　　編	陳蕙芳
執行編輯	翁芯俐
美術編輯	李依靜
法律顧問	北辰著作權事務所

印　　製	世和印製企業有限公司
初　　版	2023 年 09 月

（本書為《格林法則魔法學校二部曲：六大名師打造格林法則 公職英文單字魔法書 高考、普考、特考、銀行、國營事業滿分神之捷徑，一考就上》修訂版）

出　　版	凱信企業集團－凱信企業管理顧問有限公司
電　　話	（02）2773-6566
傳　　真	（02）2778-1033
地　　址	106 台北市大安區忠孝東路四段 218 之 4 號 12 樓
信　　箱	kaihsinbooks@gmail.com

定　　價	新台幣 599 元／港幣 200 元
產品內容	1 書

總 經 銷	采舍國際有限公司
地　　址	235 新北市中和區中山路二段 366 巷 10 號 3 樓
電　　話	（02）8245-8786
傳　　真	（02）8245-8718

國家圖書館出版品預行編目資料

（格林法則）秒殺解字單字記憶法：六大名師陪練大考英單力，全民英檢、統測、學測、高考、普考等公職考試必備／黃宏祿，魏廷斌，楊智民，廖柏州，陳冠名，林麗英合著 . － 初版 . － 臺北市：凱信企業集團凱信企業管理顧問有限公司，2023.09
　面；　公分
ISBN 978-626-7354-04-9(平裝)

1.CST: 英語 2.CST: 詞彙 3.CST: 試題

805.12　　　　　　　　　　112012739

凱信企管

用對的方法充實自己，
讓人生變得更美好！

凱信企管

用對的方法充實自己，
讓人生變得更美好！